感恩劉毅老師，感謝「一口氣英語」！

我們從幼兒園學英語，學到高中、大學，甚至博士畢業，會做很多試卷，可是一見到外國人，往往張口結舌，聽不懂，不會說，變成英語上的「聾啞人」！「聾啞英語」如同癌症，困擾了數代英語人！我們多希望有一種教材，有一種方法，有一種良丹妙藥，讓我們治癒「聾啞英語」頑症，同時又能兼顧考試。直到遇見台灣「英語天王」劉毅老師的「一口氣英語」。

劉毅老師頒發授權書
給趙艷花校長

趙老師學校主辦，劉毅老師親授「一口氣英語萬人講座」

「劉毅英文」稱雄台灣補教界近半個世紀，「一口氣英語」功不可沒！劉毅老師前無古人，後無來者的英語功底，成就了「一口氣英語」的靈魂。「一口氣英語」從詞彙學到文法，從演講到作文，從中英文成語到會話，各種題材、各種形式，包羅萬象。

康克教育感恩劉毅老師

　　感恩劉毅老師發明「一口氣英語」，2014年5月河南省鄭州市「康克教育」孫參軍老師，在接受「一口氣英語會話、演講」師訓後，經授權迅速在中原四省—河南省、河北省、安徽省、山西省，20多個城市、30多個分校開班授課，人數由5,000人倍速增長至12,000人次。

孫參軍校長與劉毅老師

　　2016年11、12月，受邀到「中國少林功夫弟子武僧院」，推廣「一口氣英語」教學，實現500人大班授課，全場武僧將少林功夫與「一口氣英語」完美詮釋，為打造未來功夫明星堅實的語言功底。

贏在學習・勝在改變

　　福建省福州市「沖聰教育」劉偉老師接受「一口氣英語演講」師訓後，讓同學從害怕、緊張、不敢，到充滿自信，並勇敢參加第十三屆「星星火炬英語風采大賽」，32位學生於福建省賽中，取得優異的成績。評委表示，學生演講的內容很有深度，驚訝不已！同年「沖聰教育」學生人數快速激增！

「一飛教育」陳佳明校長主持，
由劉毅老師親授「一口氣英語全國師資培訓」

劉毅獲頒「中國教育聯盟終身成就獎」

牛新哲主席代表「中國教育培訓聯盟」感謝「一口氣英語」創始人劉毅老師，終身致力於英語教育之卓越成就，給與全方位的獎勵，奠定角色模範，繼而鼓勵後輩，投入更多心力於英語教育領域，特別頒發「中國教育聯盟終生成就獎」，劉毅老師成為首位獲此殊榮的台灣之光。

劉毅老師於2017年2月6日在台北舉行「用會話背7000字」講座

爲什麼要改名爲「一口氣背會話」？

　　「一口氣英語」已經出版 12 册，爲了使讀者方便閱讀，改編成「一口氣背會話上集①～⑥」和「一口氣背會話下集⑦～⑫」。我們最新發現，背的時候，如果連中文一起背，更有效果。當我們學英文的時候，往往受到中文的干擾，中英文一起背，當你想說英文時，就立刻可以想到你所背過的句子。例如，你要請客，如果只背：Be my quest. I'm paying. I got it. 你雖然會講這些英文，但到時候你往往會想不起來，加上中文，你腦筋更清楚它的意思：Be my quest. 我請客。I'm paying. 我來付錢。I got it. 我買單。連中文一起背，變成直覺後，你想忘都忘不掉。

　　背了又忘記，是人類學習語言最大的障礙。我們經過長時間研究，終於發現，只要將背好的東西再加把勁，變成直覺，就永遠不會忘記。「一口氣背會話」的發明，歷經千辛萬苦，根據編者的實際背誦經驗，一次一句、三句、六句，雖然容易背，但也很容易忘，一次九句最適合記憶，而且要特殊設計。像 2361-6101，這個電話號碼很難記，如果改成 2-361-6101，容易一點，但是，如果改成 211-311-411，這九個數字，就更容易記憶了。「一口氣背會話」就是根據這個原理研發而成。

　　美國人平常說的話，和他們所寫下來的文章，太多地方不同，由於書寫英文和口語英文不同，大部分美國人都不敢將他們平日所說的話，付諸文字，他們非常害怕寫錯，很害怕寫的東西不合文法，所以，大部分美國的出版品，不管是文章、小說、語言教材，與他們平時所說的話，格格不入。我們使用那些外國人編的語言教材，當然不容易說出來。

我看到一位學生家長，總是神采奕奕，我問她如何保養身體，她告訴我，她每天唸佛經，本來是看著佛經唸，後來唸得比看得快，最後不用看也可以唸，一天不唸就難過。「一口氣背會話」每個單元九句，練習到 10 秒鐘唸完，每一冊 12 個單元共 108 句，剛好 2 分鐘唸完。建議讀者把「一口氣背會話」每天大聲唸，一個單元練到 10 秒鐘之內，再唸下一個單元，到最後，不管早晚，對著牆上的時鐘，目標是 2 分鐘之內背完 108 句的中英文。

　　我們每天不知浪費多少時間在胡思亂想，煩惱的事越想越煩，反而影響心情，也影響身體健康。「一口氣背會話」剛好解決了這個問題。編者自從每天自言自語背「一口氣背會話」以來，真是愉快。等人的時候背一背，不再無聊；跟別人意見不同的時候背一背，心平氣和。在台灣真好，每天自言自語說英文，路上碰到陌生人，都對你另眼相看，Speaking English well is a sign of success. 只要會說英文，就受到別人尊敬。

　　「一口氣背會話」的取材，經過再三研究，務必讓我們的讀者，背了之後，英語表達能力要勝過所有美國人，而且所背的英文也適合書寫。老師如果教學生，建議除了讓學生每個單元須在 10 秒鐘內背完之外，還可以要求他們默寫，這樣子同學又會說又會寫。英文會說、會寫以後，聽和讀還有什麼問題？！

劉　毅

BOOK 1 每天要說的話

▶1-1 早上到學校見到老師、同學，都可說：

> Great to see you.
> So good to see you.
> What's going on?

▶1-2 上完課後，和老師說：

> Great class.
> Thank you, teacher.
> You are the best.

▶1-3 再稱讚老師說：

> You're an excellent teacher.
> Your material is great.
> Your methods are useful.

▶1-4 老師可以鼓勵同學，同學也可以鼓勵同學：

> You're doing fine.
> You got it.
> Keep on going.

▶1-5 下課後，邀請同學一起走：

> Let's go.
> Let's jet.
> Let's get out of here.

▶1-6 回家路上，可邀請同學吃東西：

> Let's grab a bite.
> What do you like?
> What do you feel like eating?

► 1-7 走到麥當勞點餐：

I'll have a Big Mac.
I'll have a small fries.
And a large Coke, please.

► 1-8 稱讚食物好吃：

Mmmmm. Mmmmm.
This is delicious.
This tastes great!

► 1-9 吃飽飯後說：

I'm full.
I'm stuffed.
I can't eat another bite.

► 1-10 提議散步：

Let's go for a walk.
Let's get some exercise.
A walk would do us good.

► 1-11 走累了說：

I'm beat.
I'm bushed.
I'm exhausted.

► 1-12 回到家說：

I'm home.
Home, sweet home!
There's no place like home.

BOOK 1

1. Great to see you.

Great *to see you*.	很高興見到你。
So good *to see you*.	看見你眞好。
What's going on?	有什麼事發生？
What's up today?	今天有什麼計劃？
What are you doing?	你要做什麼？
Anything exciting?	有沒有什麼好玩的事？
You look great.	你看起來很棒。
You look high-spirited.	你看起來精力充沛。
You look like you're ready for anything.	你看起來已經準備好做任何事。

** ————————————

go on 發生；繼續

exciting〔ɪk'saɪtɪŋ〕*adj.* 刺激的；好玩的

high-spirited〔'haɪ͵spɪrɪtɪd〕*adj.* 精力充沛的

ready〔'rɛdɪ〕*adj.* 準備好的

【背景說明】

　　　無論在任何時候、任何地方，只要看見你喜歡的人，你都可以說這九句話。

1. ***Great to see you.***

Great to see you.

great〔gret〕*adj.* 很棒的

　　　這句話是個省略句，源自：It's great to see you. 字面的意思是「看到你很棒。」引申為「很高興見到你。」可以加強語氣說成：It's *really* great to see you.（真高興見到你。）也可以加長為：It's really great to see you here.（在這裡看到你真高興。）或 It's so great to see you today.（今天看到你真高興。）最熱情的說法是：***I can't tell you how great it is to see you.***（我說不出來，我看到你有多高興。）

　　　可將 ***Hey***，***My***，***Boy*** 放在 ***Great to see you.*** 或 It's great to see you. 的前面，成為：

　　　Hey, it's great to see you.
　　　　（嘿，很高興見到你。）
　　　My, it's great to see you.
　　　　（哎呀，很高興見到你。）
　　　Boy, it's great to see you.
　　　　（哇，很高興見到你。）

hey〔he〕*interj.* 嘿　　my〔maɪ〕*interj.* 哎呀
boy〔bɔɪ〕*interj.* 咦；哇

要常說 *Hey*，*My*，*Boy* 這類的感嘆詞，說起話來才像美國人，可參照 p.236, 237, 701, 706, 1260, 1261, 1275。

下面都是美國人常説的話，意思接近：

> ***Great to see you*.**【第一常用】
> = Good to see you.【第二常用】
> （高興見到你。）
> = Nice to see you.【第三常用】
> （見到你眞好。）

> = Wonderful to see you.【第八常用】
> （很高興見到你。）
> = Glad to see you.（很高興見到你。）【第七常用】
> = Pleased to see you.【第九常用】
> （見到你眞愉快。）
> 【pleased〔plizd〕*adj.* 感到愉快的】

> = It's great to see you.【第四常用】
> （非常高興見到你。）
> = It's good to see you.（高興見到你。）【第五常用】
> = It's nice to see you.（見到你眞好。）【第六常用】

> = It's wonderful to see you.【第十一常用】
> （很高興見到你。）
> = I'm glad to see you.【第十常用】
> （我很高興見到你。）
> = I'm pleased to see you.【第十二常用】
> （見到你我眞愉快。）

2. *So good to see you.*

　　這句話源自 It's so good to see you. 意思是「看見你真好。」so 加強 good 的語氣，等於 very，但是說 *Very good to see you.* 有點太正式，有做作的味道。

　　可加強語氣說成：It's really so good to see you.（看到你真好。）或 It's always so good to see see you.（總是看見你真好。）可加長為：Wow, it's so good to see you here.（哇啊，在這裡見到你真好。）可開玩笑地說：It's so good to see you. You always make me smile.（看到你真好。你總是讓我高興。）

> It's so good to see you.

3. *What's going on?*
go on 發生；繼續

　　這句話的意思是「發生什麼事？」中國人見了面，喜歡說「你吃飽了沒有？」或「你吃過了沒有？」可能因為中國人最早是農業社會，比較窮困，而美國人一向擔心發生什麼事，見了面會說：*What's going on?* 或 What's up?（發生什麼事？）或 What's happening?（發生什麼事？）

　　這些話並不一定真的在問發生什麼事，只是用來見面時打招呼，避免尷尬。通常都用 Nothing much.（沒什麼事。）來回答，就像中國人見了面打招呼說：「吃過飯了沒有？」通常都用「吃過了。」來回答。

BOOK 1

　　　What's going on? 也可以加長為：What's going on with you?（你發生什麼事？）也可以用完成進行式，說成：What's been going on lately?（你最近怎麼樣啊？）【lately〔ˈletlɪ〕*adv.* 最近】

4. ***What's up today?***

　　　這句話字面的意思是「今天發生什麼事？」引申為「今天有什麼計劃？」（= *What's your plan today?* ）

　　　　What's up today?
　　　= What's happening today?
　　　= What's going on today?
　　　　　（今天有什麼計劃？）【在此 today = for today】

What's up today?

I'm going out with some friends.

　　　【比較】 What's up? 和 ***What's up today?*** 意思不同。

　　　　What's up?（發生什麼事？）
　　　　常表示問候，沒什麼特別意思，就像中國人問「吃飽飯沒有？」

　　　　What's up today?（今天有什麼計劃？）
　　　　這句話也是問候語，但是在問「你今天有什麼計劃？」

5. *What are you doing?*

這句話的字面意思是「你正在做什麼？」可以引申為其他意思，要看當時的情況和語氣來決定。

What are you doing?

下面四種 *What are you doing?* 有不同的意思：

① *What are you doing?* 【字面意思，正常情況】
= What are you doing right now?
（你現在正在做什麼？）

② *What are you doing?* 【語氣不友善，表責備】
= What do you think you're doing?
（你到底在幹什麼？）

③ *What are you doing?* 【久未見面的老朋友，想問他做什麼工作】
= What kind of work are you doing?
（你現在在做什麼工作？）

④ *What are you doing?* 【打招呼用語，每天見到朋友都可說】
= What are you going to do?（你要做什麼？）

根據這個單元中的內容，可以推測，*What are you doing?* 在此是第 4 個意思，是 What are you going to do?

如果單獨使用，問別人今天有什麼計劃，就要加上 today，說成：What are you going to do today? 別人才知道你的意思。

下面兩句話含意不同：

What are you doing?

【根據語氣、情況，有上述四種意思】

What are you doing today?（你今天有什麼計劃？）

(= *What's your plan today?*)

　　所以，***What are you doing today?*** 和 ***What's up today?　What's happening today?*** 及 What's going on today? 意思相同，都表示「你今天有什麼計劃？」

6. *Anything exciting?*

exciting〔ɪk'saɪtɪŋ〕*adj.* 刺激的；好玩的

　　這句話的意思是「有沒有什麼好玩的事？」是一個省略句，源自：Is anything exciting? 可以加長為：Is anything exciting going on?（有沒有什麼好玩的事情發生？）或 Is there anything exciting going on?（有沒有什麼好玩的事情發生？）【*go on* 進行；發生】

下面都是美國人常說的話：

Anything exciting?

Anything exciting? 【第一常用】

Anything exciting going on?

（有沒有什麼好玩的事情發生？）【第二常用】

Anything exciting going on today? 【第五常用】

（今天有沒有什麼好玩的事情發生？）

Anything exciting happening? 【第三常用】

（有沒有什麼好玩的事情發生？）

Anything exciting happening today? 【第四常用】

（今天有沒有什麼好玩的事情發生？）

7. *You look great.*

這句話的意思是「你看起來很棒。」這是美國人見到朋友，喜歡説的話。可以加強語氣説成：You **really** look great.（你真的看起來很棒。）可加上感嘆詞：

My, you look great.（哎呀，你看起來很棒。）

Wow, you look great.（哇啊，你看起來很棒。）

最加強語氣的説法是：**Boy**, you really look great.（乖乖，你真的看起來很棒。）

下面各句都是美國人見面時常説的話，句意相近：

> *You look great.*【第一常用】
> = You look wonderful.
>   （你看起來很棒。）【第二常用】
> = You look terrific.【第三常用】
>   （你看起來很棒。）
>
>
> You look great.
>
> wonderful〔'wʌndəfəl〕*adj.* 很棒的
> terrific〔tə'rıfık〕*adj.* 很棒的
>
> = You look outstanding.【第六常用】
>   （你看起來很傑出。）
> = You look cool.（你看起來很酷。）【第十二常用】
> = You look marvelous.【第四常用】
>   （你看起來很出色。）

outstanding〔'aut'stændıŋ〕*adj.* 傑出的
cool〔kul〕*adj.* 很棒的；酷的
marvelous〔'mɑrvļəs〕*adj.* 出色的；很棒的

BOOK 1

= You look gorgeous. (你看起來很漂亮。)【第十常用】
= You look fabulous. (你看起來好極了。)【第七常用】
= You look fantastic. (你看起來好極了。)【第五常用】

gorgeous〔'gɔrdʒəs〕adj. 很漂亮的
fabulous〔'fæbjələs〕adj. 極好的
fantastic〔fæn'tæstɪk〕adj. 極好的

= You look super. (你看起來好極了。)【第八常用】
= You look excellent. (你看起來非常好。)【第九常用】
= You look phenomenal.【第十一常用】
　　(你看起來好極了。)

super〔'supɚ〕adj. 最好的
excellent〔'ɛkslənt〕adj. 優秀的
phenomenal〔fə'nɑmənḷ〕adj. 優秀的

= You look spiffy.【第十三常用】
　　(你看起來非常出色。)
= You look dapper.【第十五常用】
　　(你看起來很帥。)
= You look smart.【第十四常用】
　　(你看起來非常帥。)

spiffy〔'spɪfɪ〕adj. 出色的
dapper〔'dæpɚ〕adj. 漂亮整潔的
smart〔smɑrt〕adj. 帥的；漂亮的；聰明的

8. *You look high-spirited.*
　high-spirited〔'haɪ,spɪrɪtɪd〕adj. 精力充沛的

　　　這句話的意思是「你看起來精力充沛。」也就是
　「你看起來很有精神。」

可以加強語氣說成：

You really look high-spirited.
（你眞的看起來很有精神。）
You look so high-spirited.【so = very】
（你看起來非常有精神。）
My goodness! You look so high-spirited.
（天啊！你看起來眞有精神。）
【*My goodness!* 哎呀！；天啊！】

下面各句意思相同，都是美國人常說的話：

You look high-spirited.【第三常用】
You look in high spirits.【第六常用】
（你看起來很有精神。）
You look like you're in high spirits.【第十一常用】
（你看起來好像很有精神。）
【*in high spirits* 心情很好；興高采烈】

You look full of spirit.【第四常用】
（你看起來很有精神。）
You look like you're full of spirit.
（你看起來好像很有精神。）【第十常用】
【*be full of* 充滿】

You look full of life.（你看起來充滿活力。）【第一常用】
You look full of energy.【第二常用】
（你看起來精力充沛。）
You look full of pep.（你看起來充滿活力。）【第五常用】
life〔laɪf〕*n.* 活力　　energy〔ˈɛnədʒɪ〕*n.* 精力；活力
pep〔pɛp〕*n.* 活力

BOOK 1

You look peppy. (你看起來精力充沛。)【第八常用】
You look lively. (你看起來充滿活力。)【第七常用】

peppy〔ˈpɛpɪ〕 *adj.* 活潑的；精力充沛的
lively〔ˈlaɪvlɪ〕 *adj.* 活潑的；充滿活力的

You look chipper. (你看起來充滿活力。)【第九常用】
You look exuberant.【第十二常用】
(你看起來精力充沛。)

chipper〔ˈtʃɪpɚ〕 *adj.* 活潑的
exuberant〔ɪgˈz(j)ubərənt〕 *adj.* 精力充沛的

9. ***You look like you're ready for anything.***

ready〔ˈrɛdɪ〕 *adj.* 準備好的

　　這句話的字面意思是「你看起來像是你已經為任何事準備好了。」也就是「**你看起來已經準備好做任何事。**」這是美國人見面時喜歡講的話，和中國人的思想不同。這句話可簡化為：You look like you're ready. (你看起來已經準備好了。) 或 You look ready. (你看起來已經準備好了。) anything 可改成 any challenge，說成：You look like you're ready for any challenge. (你看起來像是已經準備好應付任何挑戰。)

You look like you're ready for anything.

　　你背了這一回的九句話，以後你見到外國人，就不會尷尬了，你就有很多話可說了。

【對話練習】

1. A : **Great to see you.**

   B : It's good to see you.
   I'm glad to see you.
   You're looking good.
   【glad〔glæd〕*adj.* 高興的】

A：很高興見到你。

B：見到你真好。
很高興見到你。
你看起來氣色很好。

2. A : **So good to see you.**

   B : It's good to see you, too.
   It's such a nice day.
   I'm glad I ran into you.
   【*run into* 偶然遇到】

A：看見你真好。

B：看見你真好。
今天真是美好的一天。
真高興遇到你。

3. A : **What's going on?**

   B : Not much.
   Same old thing.
   I'm keeping busy.

A：有什麼事發生？

B：沒什麼。
老樣子。
我一直都很忙。

4. A : **What's up today?**

   B : Nothing special.
   Just my regular schedule.
   Just the same routine.
   【regular〔'rɛgjələ〕*adj.* 通常的
   schedule〔'skɛdʒul〕*n.* 預定（表）；時間表
   routine〔ru'tin〕*n.* 例行公事】

A：今天有什麼計劃？

B：沒什麼特別的。
只是平常會做的事。
都是同樣的例行公事。

5. A: **What are you doing?**

　　B: I just finished a class.
　　　 I'm taking a coffee break.
　　　 I'm going to the teachers'
　　　 lounge. 【lounge〔laʊndʒ〕*n.* 休息室】

A: 你要做什麼？

B: 我剛上完課。
　　我要喝咖啡休息一下。
　　我正要去教師休息室。

6. A: **Anything exciting?**

　　B: Nothing that I know of.
　　　 Same old, same old.
　　　 I'm just doing what I normally
　　　 do. 【normally〔'nɔrmḷɪ〕*adv.* 通常】

A: 有沒有好玩的事？

B: 據我所知沒有。
　　老樣子，老樣子。
　　我只是做平常做的事。

7. A: **You look great.**

　　B: I was going to say the same thing.
　　　 You look great, too.
　　　 I really like your outfit.
　　　 【outfit〔'aʊt,fɪt〕*n.* 服裝】

A: 你看起來很棒。

B: 我正要說同樣的話。
　　你看起來也很棒。
　　我眞的很喜歡你穿的
　　衣服。

8. A: **You look high-spirited.**

　　B: You are so right.
　　　 I just met a girl.
　　　 I think I'm in love.

A: 你看起來精力充沛。

B: 你說得很對。
　　我剛認識一個女孩。
　　我想我戀愛了。

9. A: **You look like you're ready for
　　　 anything.**

　　B: My, what a compliment.
　　　 I do feel full of energy
　　　 today.
　　　 I wish I could feel this way
　　　 every day.
　　　 【compliment〔'kɑmpləmənt〕*n.* 稱讚】

A: 你看起來已經準備好
　　做任何事。

B: 噢，眞是很棒的讚美。
　　我今天的確覺得充滿
　　活力。
　　我希望我每天都能有
　　這樣的感覺。

2. Great class. (*I*)

Great class.	好棒的一課。
Thank you, teacher.	老師，謝謝你。
You are the best.	你最棒。
I like your class.	我喜歡上你的課。
I learn so much.	我學到好多東西。
You can really teach.	你真是會教。
You're interesting.	你真有趣。
You make it fun.	你上課很風趣。
You're a terrific teacher.	你教得很棒。

** ———————————————

great 〔 gret 〕 *adj.* 很棒的
interesting 〔'ɪntrɪstɪŋ 〕 *adj.* 有趣的
fun 〔 fʌn 〕 *adj.* 有趣的
terrific 〔 tə'rɪfɪk 〕 *adj.* 很棒的

【背景説明】

上英文課，是講英文最好的機會。老師敎得好，你下課後，就可説這九句話，來稱讚老師。中國人比較保守，不習慣當面稱讚老師，但美國人卻常説這些話。

1. ***Great class.***

great〔gret〕*adj.* 很棒的　　class〔klæs〕*n.* 課

這句話的意思是「好棒的一堂課。」源自：That was a great class.（那是一堂很棒的課。）因爲課上完了，所以用 That，不能説：*This was a great class.*（誤）這是中國人的思想。

Great class.

Great class. 可加長爲：Great class today.（今天這堂課眞棒。）也可説成：***Nice class. Good class.*** 或 ***Wonderful class.*** 都表示「好棒的一堂課。」

説完 ***Great class.*** 後，可再補上三句：

We like your class.
（我們喜歡上你的課。）
We really enjoy your class.
（我們眞的喜歡上你的課。）
Everyone thinks your class is the best.
（大家都認爲你的課最好。）

當談到 "*Great class.*" 的時候，是指整個一堂課 (*the whole class period*)。美國人所説的「一堂課」，叫做 a period 或 a class，第一節課，稱爲 first period 或 first class。在美國學校，小學、國中、高中，或大學，一天有六至八堂課 (*six to eight classes*)，但是 period 是書寫英文，美國人不説 *Great period.* (誤)

2. *Thank you, teacher.*

這句話的意思是「謝謝你，老師。」也可説成：Thanks, teacher. (謝謝，老師。) 可指名地説：Thank you, Miss Lee. (謝謝妳，李老師。)

Thank you, teacher.

美國小孩稱呼老師，和中國人不一樣，中國人稱「劉老師」，美國人不稱 *Teacher Liu* (誤)。

美國學生稱呼老師：

Teacher. (老師。)

Sir. (老師。)【對男老師的尊稱】

Ma'am. (老師。)【對女老師的尊稱】
〔 mæm 〕

Mr. Smith. (史密斯先生。)

Ms. Parker. (派克小姐。)

　　過去，對於已婚的女老師，通常稱為 Mrs. Stone.（史東太太。）因為以前的美國女性，結婚後，通常會把自己的姓去掉，冠夫姓，近年來，女權高漲，不管結不結婚，冠不冠夫姓，稱呼女老師，多稱作 Ms.〔mɪz〕，較少稱作 Mrs. 或 Miss，因為稱作 Ms. 比較安全，萬一這位婦女結婚後又離婚，你都不會說錯。

　　幼稚園的小孩子，習慣用名字稱呼老師，如 Miss Jennifer（珍妮佛小姐），或 Mr. Leo（里歐先生）。

　　到了大學以後，稱呼老師就常會加上頭銜，如 Dr. White（懷特博士），如果不是博士，像助教、講師，就稱為 Mr. White（懷特先生）。

3. *You are the best.*

　　這句話的意思是「你最棒。」最高級形容詞前面，通常要加 the。*You are the best.* 也可說成： You are the best teacher.

（你是最棒的老師。）可加強語氣說成：You are the very best.（你是非常棒的。）或 You are the best of the best.（你是超棒的。）

You are the best.

可加長為：

> You are the best teacher I have.
> （你是我最好的老師。）
> You are the best teacher I know.
> （你是我所認識最好的老師。）
> You are the best teacher in our school.
> （你是我們學校最好的老師。）

4. *I like your class.*

這句話的意思是「我喜歡上你的課。」可加長為：I like your class better than any other. （我最喜歡上你的課。）（ = *I like your class better than the others.* ）也可說成：I enjoy your class. （我喜歡上你的課。）或 I love your class. （我喜歡上你的課。）

> I like your class better than any other.

【enjoy〔ɪnˈdʒɔɪ〕v. 喜歡　love〔lʌv〕v. 喜歡；喜愛】

I like your class. 可以加強語氣說成：

> I like being in your class.
> （我喜歡上你的課。）
> I like your class the best.
> （我最喜歡上你的課。）
> I like your class the most.
> （我最喜歡上你的課。）

5. *I learn so much.*

這句話的意思是「我學到好多東西。」用現在式表示不變的事實。源自：I learn so much every time I attend your class. (我每次上你的課都學到很多東西。) 或 I always learn so much. (我總是學到很多。) 可加強語氣說成：I learn so much from you. (我從你那邊學到很多東西。)

【比較】下面兩句話含意不同：

I learn so much.【暗示每次都學很多】
I learned so much.【只表示這次學很多】
(我學了很多東西。)

下面都是美國人常說的話，我們按照使用頻率排列：

① *I learn so much.*
　　【第一常用】

I learn so much.

② I learn a lot.【第二常用】
　　(我學到很多。)
③ I learn a great deal.
　　(我學到很多。)【第三常用】
　　【*a lot* 很多　*a great deal* 很多】

④ I learn many things. (我學到很多東西。)
⑤ I learn lots of things. (我學到很多東西。)
　　【*lots of* 很多的】

6. *You can really teach.*

這句話的意思是「你真會教書。」可加長為：
Everyone thinks you can really teach. (大家都認
為你真會教書。) 或 You can really teach better
than anyone. (你真是教得比任何人好。)

You can really teach. 和中國人思想很接近：

中文： 你真會開車。
英文： *You can really drive.*

中文： 你真會跳舞。
英文： *You can really dance.*

中文： 你真會唱歌。
英文： *You can really sing.*

中文： 你真會做菜。
英文： *You can really cook.*

You can really teach.

7. *You're interesting.*

interesting (ˈɪntrɪstɪŋ) *adj.* 有趣的

這句話的意思是「你真有趣。」原則上，interest
這個字，人當主詞用過去分詞，像 I'm interested in
English. (我對英文有興趣。)「非人」做主詞，用現
在分詞，像：This place is interesting. (這個地方
很有趣。) 或 This movie is interesting. (這部電影
很有趣。)

在 ***You're interesting.*** 中，我們應該把 You
當作「非人」來處理，interesting 當作「令人覺
得有趣的」來解釋。這句話也可説成：You're an
interesting teacher.（你是個風趣的老師。）或
You're an interesting person.（你是個風趣的人。）
可加強語氣説成：You're always interesting.
（你總是那麼風趣。）

8. ***You make it fun.***

fun〔fʌn〕*adj.* 有趣的

You make it fun.

　　這句話字面的意思是「你
把它變得很有趣。」引申為
「你上課很風趣。」在此 it 是
指 learning，所以可説成：You make learning fun.
（你教得使我們學起來很有趣。）或 You make your
class fun.（你把課教得很有趣。）

　　You make it fun. 可加長為：You always make
it fun.（你總是教得很有趣。）或 You make it fun
to learn.（你教得使我們學起來很有趣。）

【比較】下面兩句話意思不同：

> You are fun.（和你在一起很有趣。）
> （= *You are fun to be with.*）
> ***You make it fun.***（你上課很風趣。）
> it 可指前面所説的話，或不明確的情況，只要
> 上下文清楚即可。

9. *You're a terrific teacher.*

terrific〔tə'rıfık〕*adj.* 很棒的

這句話字面的意思是「你是一個很棒的老師。」
引申為「你教得很棒。」可加強語氣說成：Everyone
says *you're a terrific teacher.*（大家都說你教得很
棒。）句中的 terrific 可用 good（好的）、excellent
（極佳的）、great（很棒的）、wonderful（很棒的）、
super（超棒的）等字來取代。

中國人表達思想的方式和美國人不同，中國人
不習慣說「你是一個很好的老師。」而說「你教得很
好。」但是美國人卻常說 You're a good teacher.
之類的話。

比較下列中英文的不同：

中文： 你教得很好。
英文： *You're a good teacher.*

中文： 你很會開車。
英文： *You're a good driver.*

中文： 你很會做菜。
英文： *You're a good cook.*

中文： 你管理得很好。
英文： *You're a good manager.*

中文： 你很會唱歌。
英文： *You're a good singer.*

You're a good teacher.

cook〔kʊk〕*n.* 廚師　manager〔'mænɪdʒɚ〕*n.* 經理
singer〔'sɪŋɚ〕*n.* 唱歌者；歌手

【對話練習】

1. A : **Great class.**

   B : I thought it was excellent, too.
   You students were wonderful.
   Your participation made it great.
   〖participation〔pɑr͵tɪsə'peʃən〕*n.* 參與〗

   A：好棒的一課。

   B：我也覺得很棒。
   你們這些學生真優秀。
   你們的參與讓這堂課
   變得很棒。

2. A : **Thank you, teacher.**

   B : You are very welcome.
   Teaching you is my pleasure.
   Teaching students like you
   is fun. 〖pleasure〔'plɛʒɚ〕*n.* 榮幸〗

   A：老師，謝謝你。

   B：不客氣。
   教你們是我的榮幸。
   能夠教到像你們這樣
   的學生真是有趣。

3. A : **You are the best.**

   B : Thanks for saying that.
   I know it's not true.
   Today's class was very special.

   A：你最棒。

   B：謝謝你這麼說。
   我知道這不是真的。
   今天的課很特別。

4. A : **I like your class.**

   B : I'm so glad you do.
   I'm glad it's interesting.
   That makes learning easier.

   A：我喜歡上你的課。

   B：很高興你喜歡。
   很高興這堂課很有趣。
   這樣學習就容易多了。

5. A : **I learn so much.**

   B : So do I.
   I learn more and more every day.
   That is the wonderful thing
   about teaching.

   A：我學到好多東西。

   B：我也是。
   我每天都學到愈來愈多
   的東西。
   這就是教書很棒的地方。

6. A：**You can really teach.**

B：I don't deserve such praise.
I just do my best every day.
Teaching is very important to
me. 〔deserve (dɪ'zɝv) n. 應得〕

A：你真會教書。

B：我不值得這樣的讚美。
我只是每天都盡力而為。
教書對我來說非常重要。

7. A：**You're interesting.**

B：I try to be.
I give it my all.
I want you to enjoy it.
〔***give it one's all*** 盡全力〕

A：你真有趣。

B：我盡力而為。
我盡全力。
我希望你們會喜歡。

8. A：**You make it fun.**

B：You students make it fun,
too.
You really do a great job in
class.
You guys and gals are the
best. 〔guy (gaɪ) n. (男)人
gal (gæl) n. 女孩子〕

A：你上課很風趣。

B：你們這些學生也使這堂
課變得很有趣。
你們在課堂上表現得
很好。
你們是最棒的。

9. A：**You're a terrific teacher.**

B：You are a terrific student, too.
You are one of the best.
Your future will be bright.
〔bright (braɪt) adj. 光明的；有希望的〕

A：你教得很棒。

B：你也是個很棒的學生。
你很優秀。
你未來的前途一片光明。

3. Great class. (II)

You're an excellent teacher.	你是個很棒的老師。
Your material is great.	你的教材真好。
Your methods are useful.	你的方法很有用。
You're never dull.	和你在一起絕不會無聊。
You're full of pep.	你充滿活力。
You keep us on our toes.	你讓我們專心上課。
I like your teaching.	我喜歡上你的課。
I like your style.	我喜歡你的方式。
You do a good job.	你教得真好。

** ————————————

excellent〔ˈɛkslənt〕*adj.* 優秀的

material〔məˈtɪrɪəl〕*n.* 資料；教材

method〔ˈmɛθəd〕*n.* 方法

dull〔dʌl〕*adj.* 乏味的；無聊的   *be full of* 充滿

pep〔pɛp〕*n.* 活力   *on one's toes* 警覺的

style〔staɪl〕*n.* 風格

BOOK 1

【背景說明】

　　稱讚別人是一種美德，利人利己，在日常生活當中，我們每天都有機會使用，所以，對老師的稱讚，我們有兩回，背好以後，可以連續說十八句。

1. *You're an excellent teacher.*
   excellent〔ˈɛkslənt〕adj. 極佳的；優秀的

　　　　這句話字面的意思是「你是一個很好的老師。」引申為「你教得很好。」(= *You teach so well.*)

2. *Your material is great.*
   material〔məˈtɪrɪəl〕n. 資料；教材
   great〔gret〕adj. 很棒的；極好的

　　　　這句話的意思是「你的教材真好。」源自：Your teaching material is great. (你的教材很棒。) 凡是老師所選的課本或發的講義，都叫作 material。也可說成：What you teach in class is great. (你在課堂上教的很棒。) 或 The material you use in class is great. (你在課堂上所用的教材很棒。)

Your material is great.

3. *Your methods are useful.*

method〔'mɛθəd〕*n.* 方法
useful〔'jusfəl〕*adj.* 有用的

這句話的意思是「你的
方法很有用。」可以加長為：

I think your methods are so useful.
（我認為你的方法很有用。）
Your teaching methods are really useful.
（你的教法真的很有用。）
I feel your teaching methods are very useful.
（我覺得你的教法非常有用。）

下面都是美國人常説的話：

Your methods are useful.【第一常用】
Your methods are helpful.【第二常用】
（你的方法很有幫助。）
【helpful〔'hɛlpfəl〕*adj.* 有幫助的；有用的】

Your methods are valuable.【第七常用】
（你的方法很珍貴。）
Your methods are effective.【第九常用】
（你的方法很有效。）
Your methods are beneficial.【第八常用】
（你的方法很有益。）

valuable〔'væljuəbḷ〕*adj.* 珍貴的
effective〔ə'fɛktɪv, ɪ'fɛktɪv〕*adj.* 有效的
beneficial〔͵bɛnə'fɪʃəl〕*adj.* 有益的

BOOK 1

Your methods help me a lot. 【第三常用】
（你的方法對我很有幫助。）
Your methods help me greatly. 【第四常用】
（你的方法對我幫助很大。）
【greatly〔ˈgretlɪ〕*adv.* 大大地】

The way you teach is so useful. 【第五常用】
（你的教法很有用。）
The way you teach is very helpful. 【第六常用】
（你的教法很有幫助。）

4. *You're never dull.*
   dull〔dʌl〕*adj.* 乏味的；無聊的

> 　　dull 這個字對中國人和美國人都很難唸，容易
> 和 doll 混淆（doll〔dɑl〕*n.* 洋娃娃），只要能夠區
> 別 /ʌ/ 和 /ɑ/ 的發音，就不會唸錯。

/ʌ/ 嘴巴半開，用喉　　　/ɑ/ 嘴巴張最大，與國
嚨發音。　　　　　　　　語注音「ㄚ」類似。

> 　　doll 的發音和 dollar〔ˈdɑlɚ〕前面發音相同，
> 發〔dɑl〕的時候，/ɑ/ 的發音，嘴巴張最大。dull
> 中 u 的發音讀成 /ʌ/，嘴巴不張大，用喉嚨發出來，
> 像 up 這個字一樣，u 讀 /ʌ/。

BOOK 1

美國老師常教小孩子唸：Do<u>lls</u> are never d<u>u</u>ll.
　　　　　　　　　　/ɑ/　　　　　/ʌ/
（洋娃娃絕不會無趣。）來區別 /ɑ/ 和 /ʌ/ 的發音。

　　You're never dull. 的意思是「你從不乏味」，引申為「和你在一起絕不會無聊。」這是美國人喜歡說的話，中國人不常說。

　　You're never dull.（和你在一起絕不會無聊。）
　= You're never boring.
　= You're interesting.
　【boring〔'borɪŋ〕*adj.* 無聊的】

5. ***You're full of pep***.
　be full of 充滿　　pep〔pɛp〕*n.* 精力；活力

　　　　這個字來自於 pepper〔'pɛpɚ〕*n.* 胡椒
　吃了胡椒，或聞了胡椒，都會刺
　激感官，就是「活力」的意思，
　full of pep 就是「充滿了活力」。

　　You're full of pep.
　（你精力充沛。）
　= You're full of energy.
　= You're full of power.
　= You're peppy.

pepper

　energy〔'ɛnɚdʒɪ〕*n.* 活力　　power〔'pauɚ〕*n.* 力量
　peppy〔'pɛpɪ〕*adj.* 精力充沛的

　　美國人習慣看到人很有精神，就會說：***You're full of pep***.

6. **You keep us on our toes.**

   on *one's* **toes** ①警覺的 (= *alert*)
      ②有活力的 (= *energetic*) ③準備好的 (= *ready*)

on *one's* **toes** 字面的意思是「踮著腳尖」，如：

   He stands **on his toes** to make himself look
      taller. (他踮了腳尖，讓自己看起來高一點。)

   on *one's* **toes** 可能源
自賽跑起跑時，踮著腳尖，
準備聽槍聲，那個時候一
定是「準備好了」、「有活力
的」、「有警覺的」。

   You keep us **on our toes.** 的意思是「你使我們
有警覺」，在此引申為「你讓我們上課專心聽講。」

【例】We must be **on our toes** for the test.
     = *We must be ready for the test.*
     (我們必須準備好考試。)

The strong competition keeps us **on
   our toes.**
= *The strong competition keeps us alert.*
(這個強的競爭者使我們保持警覺。)
alert〔ə'lɝt〕*adj.* 警覺的
competition〔͵kɑmpə'tɪʃən〕*n.* 競爭的對手

Exercising keeps us **on our toes.**
= *Exercising keeps us energetic.*
(運動使我們充滿活力。)
【energetic〔͵ɛnɚ'dʒɛtɪk〕*adj.* 充滿活力的】

7. *I like your teaching*.

　　這句話字面的意思是「我喜歡你教的東西。」引申爲「我喜歡上你的課。」美國人喜歡説 I like～。有些人每天説幾百句，看到了女生穿著漂亮的衣服，他們就會説：I like your clothes. (我喜歡妳的衣服。) 在餐桌上，看到好吃的菜，他們就會説：I like this dish. (我喜歡這道菜。)【dish〔dɪʃ〕*n.* 菜餚】

I like your clothes.

下面是美國人常説的話：

　　I like your teaching.【第一常用】
　　I like your teaching style.【第二常用】
　　　(我喜歡你的教法。)
　　I like your teaching method.【第五常用】
　　　(我喜歡你的教法。)

　　I like your teaching techniques.【第六常用】
　　　(我喜歡你的教法。)
　　I like the way you teach.【第四常用】
　　　(我喜歡你上課的方式。)
　　I like how you teach.【第三常用】
　　　(我喜歡你的教法。)
　　【technique〔tɛkˈnik〕*n.* 方法；技巧】

BOOK 1

8. *I like your style.*

style〔staɪl〕*n.* 風格

這句話字面的意思
是「我喜歡你的風格。」
在這裡的意思是「我喜
歡你的方式。」可以加
長為：I like your
style of teaching.（我
喜歡你教書的方式。）或加強語氣說成：I really like
your teaching style.（我真的喜歡你教書的方式。）
your style 的意思是 the way you do something，
所以，也可說成：I like the way you teach.（我喜
歡你教書的方式。）

9. *You do a good job.*

這句話在這裡的意思是「你教得很好。」*You do
a good job.* 可說成：You do good work. 意思相同，
但 work 前不可加冠詞，因為 work 是不可數名詞。
可以加強語氣說成：

You really do a good job.
（你真的教得很好。）
I really think *you do a good job*.
（我真的認為你教得很好。）
Everyone thinks *you do a good job*.
（大家都認為你教得很好。）

BOOK 1

【比較】

You do a good job. (你教得眞好。)

(語氣謙卑，可用於學生對老師説，也適合老師對學生説。)

You're doing a great job. (你表現得很好。)

這句話適合老師對學生説，學生對老師説，就不太禮貌
了。現在進行式總共有八種用法，可以表示現在的感情
和情緒，有加強語氣的作用，在這裡表示稱讚。(詳見
「文法寶典」p.342)

例： John is doing fine work at school.
　　　(約翰在學校裡表現很好。)【表稱讚】
　　　簡單地説，現在進行式的語氣，比現在式要
　　　強，在會話中，美國人常用現在進行式。

下面是美國人常説的話：

You do a good job.
You do a great job.
You do a perfect job.

You do an excellent job.
You do an awesome job.
You do an amazing job.

【對話練習】

1. A：**You're an excellent teacher**.
   　B：That's nice to hear.
   　　　Thanks for the compliment.
   　　　I'm glad you like the class.
   　　　【compliment〔ˈkɑmpləmənt〕
   　　　　n. 稱讚】

A：你教得很好。
B：聽到你這麼說我眞高興。
　　謝謝你的稱讚。
　　我很高興你喜歡這堂課。

2. A：**Your material is great**.
   　B：I'm glad you like it.
   　　　We try hard.
   　　　Material is very important.
   　　　【*try hard*　盡力而爲】

A：你的教材眞好。
B：我很高興你喜歡。
　　我們盡力而爲。
　　教材是很重要的。

3. A：**Your methods are useful**.
   　B：I like to hear that.
   　　　I do my best.
   　　　That's my goal.
   　　　【*do one's best*　盡力
   　　　　goal〔gol〕*n.* 目標】

A：你的方法很有用。
B：聽你這麼說，我很高興。
　　我盡我最大的努力。
　　那是我的目標。

4. A：**You're never dull**.
   　B：That's good to hear.
   　　　That's music to my ears.
   　　　You make my day.
   　　　【*be music to one's ears*　令某人感覺悅耳
   　　　　make one's day　使某人很高興】

A：和你在一起絕對不會無聊。
B：聽到你這麼說我眞高興。
　　很高興聽到你這麼說。
　　你讓我很高興。

5. A : **You're full of pep.**

    B : I like what I do.

       I try my best.

       I enjoy teaching very much.

A：你充滿活力。

B：我喜歡我的工作。

    我盡我最大的努力。

    我非常喜歡教書。

6. A : **You keep us on our toes.**

    B : That's my job.

       That's why I am here.

       I'm glad to hear that.

A：你讓我們專心上課。

B：那是我的工作。

    那就是我來這裡的原因。

    我很高興聽到你這麼說。

7. A : **I like your teaching.**

    B : I'm glad you like it.

       I appreciate hearing that.

       It's nice of you to say so.

     【appreciate〔ə'priʃɪ͵et〕*v.* 感激】

A：我喜歡上你的課。

B：我很高興你喜歡。

    我很感謝你這麼說。

    你這麼說真是體貼。

8. A : **I like your style.**

    B : Thanks so much.

       That means a lot.

       I'm happy to hear that.

A：我喜歡你的方式。

B：非常謝謝你。

    那對我非常重要。

    聽你這麼說我很高興。

9. A : **You do a good job.**

    B : I thank you for the praise.

       It's kind of you to say so.

       It's so nice to receive a

       compliment.

     【praise〔prez〕*n.* 稱讚

      kind〔kaɪnd〕*adj.* 體貼的   receive〔rɪ'siv〕*v.* 受到】

A：你教得真好。

B：謝謝你的讚美。

    你這麼說真是體貼。

    被讚美的感覺真好。

4. You're doing fine.

You're doing fine.	你表現得很好。
You got it.	你知道該怎麼做。
Keep on going.	繼續努力。
That's the way.	你的做法對。
That's how to do it.	就是這麼做。
Don't change a thing.	不要改變。
Keep working hard.	繼續努力。
Keep doing great.	繼續好好地做。
Keep on doing what you are doing.	繼續做你現在正在做的事情。

** ————————————

do〔du〕*v.* 進展;表現;做
fine〔faɪn〕*adj.* 很好的   way〔we〕*n.* 方式;做法
keep on 持續;繼續   great〔gret〕*adj.* 很好的;很棒的
change〔tʃendʒ〕*v.* 改變
keep〔kip〕*v.* 持續   ***work hard*** 努力

BOOK 1

【背景説明】

　　這九句話太有用了，老師可以用來鼓勵學生，
老板可以用來鼓勵員工。

1. **You're doing fine.**

You're doing fine.

　　do 在此當作不完全
不及物動詞，相當於 be
動詞，後面接形容詞做
主詞補語，這個時候 do
作「進展」、「表現」或「做」解。為了配合這個句型，
有些字典把常用的形容詞 fine，good，great 當作
副詞，則太勉強了。do 用現在進行式，表示「稱讚
或責備」，用法很多，美國人稱讚時，常說的話有：

You're doing fine.（你表現得很好。）【第一常用】
You're doing great.（你表現得很棒。）【第二常用】
You're doing excellent.【第四常用】
　（你表現得非常好。）

You're doing good.（你表現得很好。）【第三常用】
You're doing awesome.【第六常用】
　（你表現得非常棒。）
You're doing fantastic.【第五常用】
　（你表現得好極了。）

awesome〔ˋɔsəm〕 adj. 很棒的
fantastic〔fænˋtæstɪk〕 adj. 很棒的

美國人責備時，常說的話有：

> You're doing bad. (你表現得很糟。)【第一常用】
> You're doing lousy. (你表現得很差。)【第二常用】
> You're doing awful. (你表現得很糟糕。)【第三常用】
>
> 【lousy〔ˈlauzɪ〕*adj.* 差勁的　awful〔ˈɔful, ˈɔfḷ〕*adj.* 很糟的】

【比較】 do 可當不及物和及物動詞。

> You're doing great. (你表現得很好。)
> 　【do 是不完全不及物動詞，須接補語】
> = You're doing a great job. (你做得很好。)
> 　【do 是及物動詞，後接受詞】
> = You're doing well. (你做得很好。)
> 　【do 是完全不及物動詞，well 是副詞】

do 後面可接形容詞或副詞，意思往往相同。

2. *You got it.*

You got it.

You got it. 字面意思是「你拿到了。」可引申出很多意思，要看上下文而定。在這裡是指「你懂了；你知道該怎麼做。」等於 You know what you are doing. 或 You know what to do.

　　美國人在日常生活中，常說 "*You got it.*"，你要勇敢地說，不要怕說錯，自然會說，所有引申意思都圍繞著字面意思。*You got it.* 還有一個常用的意思是「我同意。」，等於 OK. 或 No problem.。

3. *Keep on going.*

   keep on 持續；繼續

Keep on going.

   　　這句話字面的意思是
「繼續走。」在此引申為
「再接再勵；繼續努力。」
也可說成：Continue.
（繼續。）或 Continue on.
（繼續不停。）或 Continue working.（繼續努力。）

在文法上 keep＋V-ing 表「繼續做某事，中間不停」，
　　　　keep on＋V-ing 表「繼續做某事，中間有停頓」

【比較】 Keep going.（繼續努力，不要停。）【中間不停】
　　　　 Keep on going.（繼續努力；再接再勵。）
　　　　【中間有停頓】

4. *That's the way.*

   way〔we〕*n.* 方法；方式

   　　這句話字面的意思是「那是方法。」引申為「你
的做法對。」源自：That's the right way to do it.
（那樣做是對的。）可加強語氣說成：That's the
way to do it every time.（每一次都應該那樣做。）
或 That's exactly the right way to do it.（那樣做
完全正確。）【exactly〔ɪg'zæktlɪ〕*adv.* 完全地】

   下面都是美國人常說的話：

   That's the way.【第一常用】
   That's the right way.（那樣做是對的。）【第四常用】
   That's the right way to do it.【第五常用】
   （那樣做是對的。）

That's the way to do it. 【第二常用】
（那樣做是對的。）
That's the way I like it. 【第九常用】
（我喜歡那種做法。）
That's the way it should be done. 【第三常用】
（應該那樣做才對。）

That's how to do it. （就是這麼做。）【第六常用】
You have the right way. 【第七常用】
（你的做法正確。）
You're doing it the right way. 【第八常用】
（你的做法正確。）

5. *That's how to do it.*

　　這句話源自：*That's the way how to do it.* 【文
法對，但美國人不用】

　　美國人習慣說：***That's the way to do it***. （就是這麼
做。）或 ***That's how to do it***. （就是這麼做。）

6. *Don't change a thing.*
change〔tʃendʒ〕v. 改變

Don't change a thing.

　　這句話字面的意思
是「不要改變任何一件
事。」引申為「不要改
變。」可以加強語氣說
成：Don't change a single thing. （一點都不要改變。）
【single〔'sɪŋl〕adj. 單一的】或 I don't want you to
change anything. （我不要你改變任何事。）

當稱讚別人時，一句話講完，可再説 ***Don't change a thing***. 來加強。

【例1】 You're doing great. ***Don't change a thing***. (你做得很好。不要改變。)

【例2】 This is perfect. ***Don't change a thing***.
(這很棒。不要改變。)
【 perfect〔ˈpɝfɪkt〕*adj.* 完美的 】

【例3】 You're doing the right thing. ***Don't change a thing***.
(你做得對。不要改變。)

7. ***Keep working hard***.
keep〔kip〕*v.* 持續　　***work hard*** 努力

這句話可加強語氣
説成：I want you to
keep working hard.
(我要你持續努力。)
老板可跟員工説：
Please keep working
hard at your job. (請

> *I want you to keep working hard.*

你持續努力工作。) 老師可跟同學説：Keep working
hard in class. (在課堂上要持續努力。)【 ***in class*** 在課
堂上 】或 Keep working hard in school. (在學校要持
續努力用功。)【 ***in school*** 在學校；在上課 (= *at school*) 】

【比較】 要注意 keep 和 keep on 的不同：

Keep working hard. 【正】

Keep on working hard. 【誤】

【叫別人持續努力，怎麼能夠中斷呢？working hard 是一種心理狀態，中間不可停頓。】

Keep working. (持續工作，不要停。)【正】

Keep on working. 【正】

(繼續工作。)【通常要停下來的人繼續工作】

8. ***Keep doing great.***

great 〔 gret 〕 *adj.* 很好的；很棒的

這句話的意思是「持續好好地做。」可以加長爲：Keep doing a great job. (持續表現良好。)(= *Keep doing great work.*) 或 I hope you can keep doing great. (我希望你能好好地做。) 也有美國人説：Keep doing an excellent job. (持續表現良好。) (= *Continue doing an excellent job.*)

9. ***Keep on doing what you are doing.***

這句話的意思是「繼續做你現在正在做的事。」可加強語氣説成：Please keep on doing exactly what you are doing right now. (請你繼續確實地做你現在正在做的事。)【exactly 〔 ɪgˈzæktlɪ 〕 *adv.* 精確地；確切地】

Keep working hard.
Keep doing great.
***Keep on doing what
you are doing.***

BOOK 1

【對話練習】

1. A：**You're doing fine**.

　B：Thank you for the
　　 compliment.
　　 That's nice to hear.
　　 I appreciate your saying that.
　　【compliment〔'kɑmpləmənt〕
　　　 n. 稱讚
　　　 appreciate〔ə'priʃɪ,et〕*v.* 感激】

　　　　　　A：你做得很好。

　　　　　　B：謝謝你的稱讚。

　　　　　　　　很高興聽你這麼說。
　　　　　　　　我很感激你這麼說。

2. A：**You got it**.

　B：I'm glad you think so.
　　 I'm trying as hard as I can.
　　 I'm trying to do it right.
　　【*as…as one can*　儘可能…
　　　 right〔raɪt〕*adv.* 正確地】

　　　　　　A：你懂了。

　　　　　　B：很高興你這麼認為。
　　　　　　　　我全力以赴。
　　　　　　　　我試著把它做好。

3. A：**Keep on going**.

　B：I will.
　　 I'll do my best.
　　 I'll keep going.
　　【*do one's best*　盡力】

　　　　　　A：再接再勵；繼續努力。

　　　　　　B：我會的。
　　　　　　　　我會盡力。
　　　　　　　　我會不停地努力。

4. A：**That's the way**.

　B：Are you sure it's OK?
　　 Am I really doing it right?
　　 I'll be so happy if I am.

　　　　　　A：你的做法對。

　　　　　　B：你確定這樣可以嗎？
　　　　　　　　我這樣做真的對嗎？
　　　　　　　　如果這樣真的是對的，
　　　　　　　　我會很開心。

5. A：**That's how to do it**.

　B：I was hoping this was right.
　　I thought it was correct.
　　Thanks for reassuring me.
　　【reassure〔‚riə'ʃur〕v. 使安心】

6. A：**Don't change a thing**.

　B：I promise I won't.
　　I'll keep everything the same.
　　I won't change a single thing.

7. A：**Keep working hard**.

　B：Of course!
　　I'll never let up.
　　I won't stop trying.

8. A：**Keep doing great**.

　B：Don't worry, I will.
　　I'll keep doing a great job.
　　I won't disappoint you.
　　【disappoint〔‚dɪsə'pɔɪnt〕v. 使失望】

9. A：**Keep on doing what you
　　are doing!**

　B：I will for sure.
　　You have my word on it.
　　I will continue doing well.

　　【*for sure* 一定　　word〔wɝd〕n. 約定；諾言】

A：你的做法對。

B：我希望這是對的。
　我想這樣是正確的。
　謝謝你讓我安心多了。

A：不要改變。

B：我保證我不會。
　我會讓一切繼續保持原樣。
　我不會改變任何事。

A：繼續努力。

B：當然！
　我從不會鬆懈。
　我不會停止努力。

A：繼續好好地做。

B：別擔心，我會的。
　我會繼續好好地做。
　我不會讓你失望的。

A：繼續做你現在正在做的
　事！

B：我一定會的。
　我向你保證。
　我會繼續好好地做。

5. Let's go.

Let's go.	我們走吧。
Let's jet.	我們走吧。
Let's get out of here.	我們離開這裡吧。
Where are you going?	你要去哪裡？
Are you heading home?	你要回家嗎？
Want to get a bite to eat?	要不要去吃點東西？
I'm hungry.	我餓了。
I could use a snack.	我有點想吃點心。
Let's go eat.	我們去吃吧。

** ————————————————

jet〔dʒɛt〕*v.* 噴射　　***get out*** 離開

head〔hɛd〕*v.* 向～走去

bite〔baɪt〕*n.* 一口（食物）

use〔juz〕*v.* 使用；吸（煙）；喝（飲料）；吃（點心）

snack〔snæk〕*n.* 點心

【背景說明】

　　　邀請朋友一起走的時候，就可以說這些話，一般人只會說 Let's go. 你可以連續說九句，什麼叫英文流利，就是連續不停地說。

1. **Let's jet.**
   jet〔dʒɛt〕v. 噴射

　　　jet 當名詞，主要意思是「噴射飛機」(＝*jet plane*)，當動詞講，主要意思是「噴射」，美國人說 **Let's jet.** 的意思是 Let's go.，但語氣比較強烈。

　　　Let's jet. 字面意思是「我們噴射吧。」引申為「我們走吧。」說這句話有幽默的語氣。

下面都是美國人常說的話：

> **Let's jet.**【第六常用】
> = Let's go.【第一常用】
> = Let's move.【第四常用】

> = Let's leave.【第二常用】
> = Let's roll.【第五常用】
> = Let's get moving.【第三常用】

Let's jet.

　　　也許美國人有些年紀稍大的，沒有聽別人說過 **Let's jet.**，但是現在美國很多年輕人很喜歡說 **Let's jet.** 你說 **Let's jet.** 美國人一定聽得懂。

2. **Let's get out of here.**

   get out 離開

   　　這句話的意思是「我們離開這裡吧。」要說成
   Let's get outta here. 才像是美國人說的話。outta
   　　　　〔′autə〕
   是美國口語的字，意思是 out of。

   　　美國人也常說成：Let's go now. (我們現在走
   吧。) 或 Let's leave now. (我們現在離開吧。)

3. **Are you heading home?**

   head 〔hɛd〕v. 向～走去

   Are you heading home?

   　　head 主要意思是
   「人的頭」，因為頭的
   主要部分是面孔，面
   向什麼地方，就朝向
   什麼地方去，所以
   head 當動詞用是「向～走去」，這句話的意思是
   「你要回家嗎？」等於 Are you going home?

   下了班、下了課，你可以跟朋友說這三句話：

   　　Where are you ***heading***?
   　　(你到哪裡去？)
   　　Are you ***heading*** my way?
   　　(你是不是跟我同路？)
   　　Let's go together. (我們一起走吧。)

BOOK 1

4. ***Want to get a bite to eat?*** (要不要去吃點東西？)
　　bite〔baɪt〕*n.* 一口（食物）

　　【比較】　Want to get a bite?【一般語氣】
　　　　　　Want to get a bite to eat?【加強語氣】
　　　　　　Do you want to get a bite to eat?【較正式】
　　　　　　【get a bite = grab a bite】

5. ***I could use a snack.***
　　snack〔snæk〕*n.* 點心【snake〔snek〕*n.* 蛇】
　　use〔juz〕*v.* 使用；吸（煙）；喝（飲料）；吃（點心）
　　美國人常用 could use 表示「有點想吃（喝等）」。

snack

　　　這句話字面的意思是「我可以使用
點心。」引申為「我有點想吃點心。」這
句話中國人不習慣說，但美國人常說，
源自：*If you feel like eating*, *I could
use* a snack.，小心，不要將 snack 唸
成 snake，唸 snack 時，嘴巴要裂開，
a 讀成 /æ/。

snake

　　　說這句話的語氣是非常客氣的建議，用假設法動
詞 could 表示說話者認為不一定非吃不可。

【例】　I *could use* a cup of coffee. (我有點想喝杯咖啡。)
　　　　I *could use* a cigarette. (我有點想抽根煙。)
　　　　I *could use* a piece of gum.
　　　　　(我有點想吃口香糖。)【gum〔gʌm〕*n.* 口香糖】

　　　　I *could use* a drink. (我有點想喝杯飲料。)
　　　　I *could use* a mint. (我有點想吃薄荷糖。)
　　　　I *could use* something sweet.
　　　　　(我有點想吃甜食。)【mint〔mɪnt〕*n.* 薄荷糖】

【比較】 下列的句子，語氣從弱到強：

> I ***could use*** a snack. (我有點想吃點心。)【語氣最弱】
> I would like a snack. (我想吃點心。)
> I'd like a snack. (我要吃點心。)
> I want a snack. (我要吃點心。)【一般語氣】
> I need a snack. (我需要吃點心。)
> I've got to have a snack.
> (我必須吃點心。)【***have got to*** 必須】
>
> 【語氣最強】

【比較】 ***I could use a snack*.【正】**
　　　　I could have a snack【正】
　　　　I could eat a snack.【正，美國人極少使用】

6. *Let's go eat.*

　　　這句話的意思是「我們去吃吧。」源自 Let's go to eat. 或 Let's go and eat.

Let's go eat.

但這兩句話，雖然文法上沒有錯，但是美國人絕對不會説。美國人最大的痛苦，就是説的跟寫的不一樣，有時想説的話卻不敢寫下來，怕文法錯。所以，大部分的美國人寫的文章和書，都不生動。

【比較】 ***Let's go eat*.【正】**
　　　　Let's go out and eat. 【正】
　　　　Let's go to eat. 【劣】(文法對，但美國人不説)
　　　　Let's go and eat. 【劣】(文法對，但美國人不説)

BOOK 1

【對話練習】

1. A：**Let's go.**

   B：OK.
      I'm ready.
      Let's get going.

2. A：**Let's jet.**

   B：Why the hurry?
      Why leave so soon?
      Let's stay longer.
      【hurry〔ˈhɝɪ〕n. 匆忙】

3. A：**Let's get out of here.**

   B：That's a good idea.
      I'm ready to go.
      I'll meet you at the door.

4. A：**Where are you going?**

   B：I'm going to the store.
      I need to buy some things.
      My refrigerator is almost
      empty.

   【refrigerator〔rɪˈfrɪdʒəˌretɚ〕n. 冰箱】

A：我們走吧。

B：好的。
   我準備好了。
   我們走吧。

A：我們走吧。

B：為什麼這麼急？
   為什麼要這麼早離開？
   我們待久一點吧。

A：我們離開這裡吧。

B：好主意。
   我準備好要走了。
   我在門口等你。

A：你要去哪裡？

B：我要去那家店。
   我必須去買一些東西。
   我的冰箱幾乎是空的。

5. A : **Are you heading home?**

   B : Yes, I am.

   I'm going home.

   I've got a lot to do.

A：你要回家嗎？

B：是的，我要。

我要回家

我有很多事情要做。

6. A : **Want to get a bite to eat?**

   B : Sure.

   That sounds great.

   I'm with you.

   【*be with sb.* 同意某人】

A：要不要去吃點東西？

B：好。

聽起來不錯。

我同意。

7. A : **I'm hungry.**

   B : I'm not so hungry.

   I could use a drink.

   I'll join you anyway.

A：我餓了。

B：我沒那麼餓。

我想喝杯飲料。

我還是會跟你一起吃。

8. A : **I could use a snack.**

   B : Me too.

   That sounds good.

   Let's get a snack.

   【get〔gɛt〕*v.* 吃】

A：我有點想吃點心。

B：我也是。

聽起來不錯。

我們去吃點心吧。

9. A : **Let's go eat.**

   B : How about a little later?

   I'm not that hungry right now.

   Let's go eat in about an

   hour.

A：我們去吃吧。

B：晚一點怎麼樣？

我現在沒有那麼餓。

我們大約一個小時後

再去吃吧。

6. *Let's grab a bite.*

Let's grab a bite.	我們去吃點東西吧。
What do you like?	你喜歡什麼？
What do you feel like eating?	你想要吃什麼？
You choose.	你選擇。
You decide.	你決定。
What do you recommend?	你推薦什麼？
How about McDonald's?	你覺得麥當勞怎麼樣？
It's fast and convenient.	它又快又方便。
What do you think?	你覺得如何？

＊＊ ───────────────

grab〔græb〕*v.* 抓　　bite〔baɪt〕*n.* 一口（食物）
choose〔tʃuz〕*v.* 選擇
recommend〔͵rɛkə'mɛnd〕*v.* 推薦
McDonald's〔mək'dɑnl̩dz〕*n.* 麥當勞（餐廳）
convenient〔kən'vinjənt〕*adj.* 方便的

【背景説明】

　　這九句話很有用，背完以後，你就可以用英文，邀請朋友一起去吃東西了。不要忘記，要背熟至 5 秒鐘之内。只要背到不須經過思考，就終生不會忘記。

1. ***Let's grab a bite.***
grab〔græb〕*v.* 抓
bite〔baɪt〕*n.* 一口（食物）

Let's grab a bite.

　　這句話字面的意思是「我們去抓一口食物吧。」引申爲「我們去吃點東西吧。」這種説法很多，如：

> ***Let's grab a bite.***【第一常用】
> = Let's grab something to eat.【第四常用】
> 　　（我們找點東西吃吧。）
> = Let's go get a bite.【第二常用】
> 　　（我們去吃點東西吧。）
>
> = Let's eat.（我們去吃東西吧。）【第六常用】
> = Let's go eat.（我們去吃東西吧。）【第三常用】
> = Let's get something to eat.【第五常用】
> 　　（我們找點東西吃吧。）

　　下面兩句話，句意不同：

【比較】***Let's grab a bite.***（我們去吃點東西吧。）
　　　　Let's take a bite.（我們嚐一口吧。）

BOOK 1

2. *What do you like?*

　　　這句話的意思是「你喜歡什麼？」可加長為：
What do you like to eat? (你喜歡吃什麼？) 或
What do you usually like to eat? (你通常喜歡
吃什麼？)

What do you like? 美國人也常說成：

What food do you like?
(你喜歡吃什麼食物？)
What kind of food do you like?
(你喜歡哪一種食物？)
What kind of food do you like to eat?
(你喜歡吃哪一種食物？)

3. *What do you feel like eating?*

feel like + V-ing 想要～【feel like 後常接動名詞，有時
也接名詞為受詞】

　　　這句話的意思是「你
想要吃什麼？」中國人說
英文，不太會用 "feel
like + V-ing"，美國人卻
常說。這句話也可以說
成：What do you *feel
like having*? 或 What do you *feel like*?

What do you
feel like eating?

【例】 What do you *feel like*?（你想要什麼？）

【疑問代名詞 What 在疑問句中做 feel like 的受詞。】

What do you *feel like eating*?

（你想要吃什麼？）

What do you *feel like doing*?

（你想要做什麼？）

What do you *feel like drinking*?

（你想要喝什麼？）

Where do you *feel like going*?

（你想要去哪裡？）

When do you *feel like leaving*?

（你想要什麼時候走？）

4. *You choose*.（你選擇。）

You decide.（你決定。）

What do you recommend?

（你推薦什麼？）

choose〔tʃuz〕*v.* 選擇

recommend〔͵rɛkə′mɛnd〕*v.* 推薦

　　這三句話非常體貼，你要常說，別人會喜歡你。

　　可以加強語氣說成：

I want you to choose.（我要你選擇。）

I want you to decide.（我要你決定。）

What do you recommend?（你推薦什麼？）

這三句話說膩了，可改成：

> I'll let you choose. (我會讓你選擇。)
> I'll let you decide. (我會讓你決定。)
> What do you suggest? (你建議什麼？)
> 【suggest〔səg'dʒɛst〕*v.* 建議】

5. *How about McDonald's?*

How about~? ~如何？

McDonald's〔mək'danḷdz〕*n.* 麥當勞（餐廳）

這句話的意思是「你覺得麥當勞怎麼樣？」

【比較】 ***How about McDonald's?*** 【正】

How do you feel about McDonald's? 【正】

How about going to McDonald's? 【劣】

【文法正確，但美國人不說，因為太累贅。】

如果說成：What about McDonald's? 就是指「你覺得麥當勞這家餐廳怎麼樣？」

【例】 A: ***What about*** McDonald's?

（你覺得麥當勞餐廳怎樣？）

B: I think it's a great place.

（我覺得它是個好地方。）

為什麼 McDonald's 有 's？因為是表示 *McDonald's restaurant* 的省略。

（詳見「文法寶典」p.96）

6. *It's fast and convenient.*

convenient〔kən'vinjənt〕*adj.* 方便的

這句話的意思是
「它又快又方便。」也可
說成：It's a fast and
convenient place.（它是
一個又快又方便的地方。）
美國人也常說成：It's
quick and easy.（它又快又簡單。）或 It's a quick
and easy place.（它是個又快又簡單的地方。）

【easy〔'izɪ〕*adj.* 簡單的；令人舒適的；給人方便的】

It's fast and convenient. 可加強語氣說成：
The service is fast and eating there is
convenient.（服務很快，在那邊吃東西很方便。）

7. *What do you think?*

　　當你跟朋友做過建議後，你就可以說：What
do you think? 意思是「你認為怎麼樣？」可加長
為：What do you think about that?（你覺得那樣
怎麼樣？）或 What do you think about my idea?
（你覺得我的點子如何？）idea 可改成 suggestion，
說成：What do you think about my suggestion?
（你覺得我的建議怎麼樣？）

　　中國人不習慣說：*What do you think?* 因為中
國人的思想中，認為「如何」，就是英文的 how。

【比較】 中文：你覺得怎麼樣？

英文： ***What do you think?*** 【正】

How do you think? 【誤】

How do you think? 的意思是「你如何思考？」應該
改成：How do you feel about that? 才對。

下面都是美國人常説的話，第一至第八常用，使用頻率非
常接近：

What do you think? （你覺得怎麼樣？）【第二常用】

What do you say? （你覺得怎麼樣？）【第一常用】

How do you feel about that? 【第三常用】
（你覺得那樣如何？）
【在此不可簡化爲：*How do you feel?*】

How do you feel about doing that? 【第十常用】
（你覺得那樣做怎麼樣？）

Do you agree? （你同意嗎？）【第七常用】

Does that sound OK to you? 【第八常用】
（你覺得那樣聽起來可以嗎？）

Would you like that?

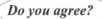
Do you agree?

（你喜歡那樣嗎？）【第六常用】

【sound〔saund〕*v.* 聽起來】

Is that OK? 【第四常用】
（那樣可以嗎？）

Is that a good idea?
（那是個好主意嗎？）【第五常用】

Is that something you want to do? 【第九常用】
（那是你想做的嗎？）

【對話練習】

1. A : **Let's grab a bite.**

   B : That's an excellent idea.
   I'm really hungry.
   I'm so hungry I could eat a
   horse!

   A：我們去吃點東西吧。

   B：好主意。

   我的確餓了。

   我餓得可以吃下一匹馬！

2. A : **What do you like?**

   B : I like everything.
   I'm not a picky eater.
   I'll let you decide.
   【picky 〔'pɪkɪ〕 *adj.* 挑剔的
   eater 〔'itɚ〕 *n.* 吃的人】

   A：你喜歡什麼？

   B：我什麼都喜歡。

   我不挑食。

   讓你決定吧。

3. A : **What do you feel like eating?**

   B : Anything is OK.
   Anything will satisfy me.
   I love all kinds of food.
   【satisfy 〔'sætɪs,faɪ〕 *v.* 使滿意】

   A：你想要吃什麼？

   B：什麼都可以。

   任何食物我都愛。

   所有的食物都能令我滿
   意。

4. A : **You choose.**

   B : OK, if you insist.
   Let's eat nearby.
   Let's have something simple.
   【insist 〔ɪn'sɪst〕 *v.* 堅持
   nearby 〔'nɪr'baɪ〕 *adv.* 在附近   have 〔hæv〕 *v.* 吃】

   A：你選擇。

   B：好，如果你堅持的話。

   我們到附近吃吧。

   我們吃點簡單的東西吧。

5. A：**You decide.**

B：I really don't know.
I need your help.
Why don't you decide?

6. A：**What do you recommend?**

B：I recommend the noodles.
They are fresh and delicious.
They are the best in town.
【noodle (ˈnudl) n. 麵
fresh (frɛʃ) adj. 新鮮的】

7. A：**How about McDonald's?**

B：That's a good choice.
I love to eat McDonald's food.
It was my favorite when I was little.
【favorite (ˈfevərɪt) n. 最喜愛的人或物】

8. A：**It's fast and convenient.**

B：It sure is.
It's reliable, too.
The quality is always the same.
【reliable (rɪˈlaɪəbl) adj. 可靠的】

9. A：**What do you think?**

B：You made an excellent choice.
I could not have done better.
I'm very happy with your
decision.【*be happy with*　對～很滿意】

A：你決定。

B：我真的不知道。
我需要你的幫助。
你為什麼不決定？

A：你推薦什麼？

B：我推薦吃麵。
那既新鮮又美味。
那是城裡最棒的。

A：你覺得麥當勞怎麼樣？

B：那是個好的選擇。
我愛吃麥當勞的食物。
那是我小時候的最愛。

A：這又快又方便。

B：的確是。
也很可靠。
它的品質永遠都一樣。

A：你認為怎麼樣？

B：你做了一個很好的選擇。
我無法選得比你好。
我很滿意你的決定。

7. *I'll have a Big Mac.*

I'll have a Big Mac.	我要一個麥香堡。
I'll have a small fries.	我要一份小薯條。
And a large Coke, please.	還要一杯大杯可口可樂。
I'd like a milk shake.	我要一杯奶昔。
Make it strawberry.	要草莓口味的。
That'll be for here.	要在這裡吃。
Can I have extra ketchup?	我可以多要一些蕃茄醬嗎？
Can I have more napkins?	我可以多要一些紙巾嗎？
Thank you.	謝謝你。

** ————————————————

have〔hæv〕*v.* 有；吃   *Big Mac* 麥香堡
fries〔fraɪz〕*n. pl.* 薯條（= *French fries*）
milk shake 奶昔   strawberry〔'strɔ,bɛrɪ〕*n.* 草莓
for here 內用（↔ *to go* 外帶）
extra〔'ɛkstrə〕*adj.* 額外的
ketchup〔'kɛtʃəp〕*n.* 蕃茄醬
napkin〔'næpkɪn〕*n.* 餐巾紙（= *paper napkin*）

【背景説明】

這九句話背熟以後，到麥當勞吃東西，你就
可以用英文點餐了，非常有趣，你試試看，因為
你説英文，會使麥當勞的櫃台人員很緊張。

1. ***I'll have a Big Mac.***
   have〔hæv〕*v.* 吃
   Big Mac〔'bɪg͵mæk〕*n.* 麥香堡

   have 的主要意思是「有」，在這裡作「吃」解。這
   句話字面的意思是「我會吃一個麥香堡。」(= *I want
   to eat a Big Mac.*) 在此引申為「我要一個麥香堡。」

   Big Mac 這個字是複合名詞，重音在 Big，是
   麥當勞自創的字。

   Mac 源自於 McDonald's (麥當勞餐廳)。***Mac***
   〔mək'danͺdz〕
   或 ***Mc***，是指 son of~ (~的兒子)，源自古時候，蘇
   格蘭人和愛爾蘭人，只有名字沒有姓 (family name)，
   他們就把 ***Mac*** 加在原有的名字前面，成為姓。
   如：麥帥的全名是：Douglas ***Mac***Arthur (道格拉
   〔'dʌgləs〕〔mək'arθɚ〕
   斯・麥克阿瑟)。

   所以，凡是 ***Mac*** 或 ***Mc*** 開頭的字，都是姓，而
   不是名字。很多麥當勞的產品，為了表示是麥家的東
   西，產品名稱前面，都加上 ***Mc***，像：***Mc***Chicken
   (麥香雞)、***Mc***Nugget (麥克雞塊)、Egg ***Mc***Muffin
   〔mək'nʌgɪt〕〔mək'mʌfɪn〕
   (滿福堡加蛋) 等。

BOOK 1

　　凡是某人的姓前面有 *Mac* 或 *Mc* 的時候，美國人都會簡稱 *Mac*。如：*Mac*Arthur 的好朋友，就可以稱他作 *Mac*，看到他的時候，就可以說："Hi, *Mac*." （嗨，老麥。）叫 "*Mac*"，表示很親切。

　　雖然 *Mc* 和 *Mac* 都可以加在名字的前面，成為姓，但是單獨存在時，一定要用 *Mac*，因為英文字的組成，需要母音字母 a，e，i，o，u，或半母音字母 y，如：an，by 等，都有母音字母或半母音字母。

　　Big Mac 字面的意思是「大老麥」，在麥當勞餐廳中，是最大的招牌漢堡。麥當勞餐廳把 *Mac* 翻成「麥香」，把 *Big Mac* 翻成「麥香堡」。

　　到餐廳吃飯點菜，不是去買東西，所以不能說成：*I want to buy a Big Mac.* 這句話並沒有錯，只是表示要外帶，不是在餐廳裡吃。你去 pizza 店裡買披薩，就可以說：I want to buy a pizza. 表示你買了要帶走。

I'll have a Big Mac.

　　在麥當勞點餐內用時，中國人的思想和外國人不同。

中國人思想是：我要買一個麥香堡。
　　　　　　　（ *I want to buy a Big Mac.* ）【不可說】
美國人思想是：我要吃一個麥香堡。
　　　　　　　（ *I'll have a Big Mac.* ）
　　　　　　　【道地的美國話】

I'll have a Big Mac. I'll have a small fries. And a large Coke, please. 這三句話如果付諸於文字，美國人就會認為第三句是錯的，因為 And 後面沒有主詞和動詞，所以寫的時候，就要改成：*And I'll have a large Coke, too.*【口語不說】

　　這三句話，如果你背得很快，自然就會合併成這樣一句，你試試看，這句話適合書寫，也適合說。
I'll have a Big Mac, small fries, and a large Coke.
（我要吃一個麥香堡，一份小薯條，和一杯大杯可口可樂。）
【這也是美國人在麥當勞點餐最常說的話，small fries 前面省略 a，避免重覆，但是，and 後面，就要加 a。】

I'll have～. 是最通俗的說法，還有其他說法：

　　I'll have a Big Mac. 【第一常用】
　　= I'll take a *Big Mac*. 【第四常用】
　　　（我要買一個麥香堡。）
　　= I'd like a *Big Mac*. 【第三常用】
　　　（我想要一個麥香堡。）

Big Mac

　　= I want a *Big Mac*, please. 【第二常用】
　　　（我想要一個麥香堡。）
　　= Give me a *Big Mac*, please. 【第六常用】
　　　（請給我一個麥香堡。）
　　= A *Big Mac*, please. 【第五常用】
　　　（請給我一個麥香堡。）

BOOK 1

2. *I'll have a small fries*.

fries 〔fraɪz〕 *n. pl.* 薯條

fries

　　這句話的意思是「我要一份小薯條。」美國人吃的油炸薯條 (fries)，源自法國的烹飪方式，所以又稱爲 French fries，或 French fried potatoes (法式油炸馬鈴薯)，不要和洋芋片 (potato chips) 搞混。

　　fries 永遠是複數形，因爲薯條不可能光炸一條。如果指定要大、中、或小份的薯條，就要加冠詞 a，像 a large fries (一份大薯條)，a medium fries (一份中薯條)，a small fries (一份小薯條)。如果是兩份小薯條，就說成 two small fries。如果單指薯條時，就不可加冠詞。

【例】I'd like some fries. Make it a large.
　　　(我要一些薯條。要一份大的。)
　　　【如不加 a，則句意不清楚，因爲未說明一份或兩份。】

3. *And a large Coke, please*.

Coke 〔kok〕 *n.* 可口可樂 (= Coca-Cola 〔'kokə'kolə〕)

　　這句話的意思是「還要一杯大杯可口可樂。」Coke 特別是指「可口可樂」，字首須大寫，如指一般可樂，則須說成 cola〔'kolə〕，如百事可樂，皇冠可樂等。

　　我們中國人所說的「汽水」，應該是 soda〔'sodə〕。小寫的 coke 是指「焦炭」，是一種燃料，或是「古柯鹼」(cocaine〔ko'ken〕) 的簡稱。

BOOK 1

4. *I'd like a milk shake.*

shake〔ʃek〕*n.* ①搖動

②（牛奶和冰淇淋打在一起的）混合飲料

這句話的意思是「我要一杯奶昔。」shake 的主要意思是「搖動」，milk shake 是牛奶和不同口味的冰淇淋打在一起的飲料的通稱，一般人稱爲「奶昔」，是按照英語發音來翻譯的。如果和草莓冰淇淋打在一起，就稱爲 strawberry milk shake（草莓奶昔），也可稱爲 strawberry shake。

strawberry shake

麥當勞有 strawberry（草莓）、chocolate（巧克力）和 vanilla（香草）口味的奶昔。很奇怪，美
〔vəˋnɪlə〕
國人在台灣喜歡喝木瓜牛奶，他們稱作 papaya milk shake。如果在美國賣木瓜牛奶，一定能賺大錢。

5. *Make it strawberry.*

strawberry〔ˋstrɔ,bɛrɪ〕*n.* 草莓

這句話的意思是「要草莓口味的。」源自：Make it a strawberry shake.（要草莓口味的奶昔。）

I'd like～.
Make it＋關鍵字.

【是美國人常用的口語句型】

【例1】 **I'd like** a Coke.

（我要一杯可口可樂。）

Make it medium.

（要中杯的。）

（= **Make it** a medium one.）

Coke

【例2】 **I'd like** a pie.

（我要一個派。）

Make it apple.

（要蘋果派。）

（= **Make it** an apple pie.）

apple pie

【例3】 **I'd like** a Big Mac.

（我要一個麥香堡。）

Make it quick.（快一點。）

在會話中，要常說 **make it~** 。

【例1】 A: I'm going to buy a cup of coffee.

（我要去買一杯咖啡。）

B: Can you **make it two**?

（可以買兩杯嗎？）

【例2】 Waiter: Can I take your order?

（我可以為您點餐嗎？）

A: I'll have the special of the day.

（我要吃今日特餐。）

B: **Make it two.**（要兩份。）

BOOK 1

BOOK 1

6. *That'll be for here.*

這句話的意思是「要在這裡吃。」

That'll 是 That will 的省略。但是，That'll 的
發音，該讀成〔ˈðæt!〕。

下面都是美國人常說的話：

That'll be for here.【第一常用】
= I'll have it *here*.【第四常用】
（我要在這裡吃。）
= I'll eat it *here*.（我要在這裡吃。）【第五常用】
= I want it *for here*.【第三常用】
（我要在這裡吃。）
= *For here*.（要在這裡吃。）【第二常用】

如果要外帶，就可說：

That'll be *to go*.（要外帶。）【第一常用】
= That's *to go*.（要外帶。）【第四常用】
= I want it *to go*.（我要外帶。）【第三常用】
= *To go*.（要外帶。）【第二常用】

7. *Can I have extra ketchup?*

extra〔ˈɛkstrə〕*adj.* 額外的
ketchup〔ˈkɛtʃəp〕*n.* 蕃茄醬
（= catsup〔ˈkætsəp〕= catchup〔ˈkætʃəp,ˈkɛtʃəp〕）

這句話的意思是「我可以多要一些蕃茄醬嗎？」
也可說成：Can I have more ketchup? 意思相同。

ketchup 是一種以蕃茄為主要原料，和其他添加物製成的調味品。而 tomato sauce 中文也稱作「蕃茄醬」，是將蕃茄煮成醬汁製成，兩個是完全不同的東西。

ketchup 是不可數名詞，原則上不加 s，但是，在麥當勞，蕃茄醬是小包小包地裝起來，所以也可以說成：Can I have extra packets of ketchup? (我可以多要幾包蕃茄醬嗎？)【packet (ˈpækɪt) *n.* 小包】

two packets of ketchup

如果你想要指定數量，就可以說：

Can I have two packets of ketchup?
或 Can I have two ketchups?
(我可不可以要兩包蕃茄醬？)
【在這裡 ketchup 可以數，是例外，像「兩杯咖啡」，可說成 two coffees 一樣。】

8. *Can I have more napkins?*
= Can I have extra napkins?
napkin (ˈnæpkɪn) *n.* 餐巾；餐巾紙

這句話的意思是「我可以多要一些紙巾嗎？」也可說成：Can I have extra napkins? 意思相同。

napkin 的主要意思是「餐巾」，現在 napkin 也可以用紙製造，稱作 paper napkin 或 napkin，即使是餐桌上的一個小方塊紙巾，都稱作 napkin。

【比較】

餐　巾	napkin
餐巾紙	napkin；paper napkin
面　紙	tissue
衛生紙	toilet paper

　　有很多中國人在餐廳裡，想跟別人要餐巾紙 (napkin)，卻說成 *tissue paper* (誤)，外國人聽了會覺得怪怪的，即使是「面紙」，美國人也說成 tissue 或 Kleenex〔ˈklinɛks〕*n.* 紙巾【原是「可麗舒」紙巾廠牌名字】

　　以前，麥當勞的紙巾都隨便顧客拿，現在為了省錢，一個人只給一兩張紙巾，你如果想多要，就可以說：

> Can I have *more napkins*?
> （我可以多要幾張紙巾嗎？）
> = Can you give me *more napkins*?
> = I'd like some *more napkins*.
> = *More napkins*, please.

　　以上的句子中，more 都可以用 extra 來代替，如果你要指定數量時，你就可以在 more 或 extra 前加上數目字。如：

> Can I have two more napkins?
> = Can I have two extra napkins?
> （我可以多要兩張紙巾嗎？）

BOOK 1

9. 麥當勞簡介

1955 年，有一個人叫做 Ray Kroc，他是推
〔 re 〕〔 krɑk 〕
銷員，推銷 milk shake 的機器。他看到有一家叫
做 McDonald's 的漢堡店，在加州洛杉磯的
San Bernardino 很有名，他就跑去要求和他們合
〔'sæn͵bɝnə'dino 〕
作，正好老闆也想退休，就讓 Ray Kroc 接下去
經營。

1968 年，麥香堡（Big Mac）正式誕生，由於
口味特別，轟動全國。此後麥當勞不斷研發新產品，
1973 年推出 Egg McMuffin（滿福堡加蛋），1979 年
推出 Happy Meal（快樂兒童餐）。由於不斷創新，
使得麥當勞至今仍然屹立不搖。

【對話練習】

1. A：**I'll have a Big Mac.**
   B：Is that all?
   Would you like something else?
   How about a drink with that?

   A：我要一個麥香堡。
   B：就這樣嗎？
   你還要別的東西嗎？

   要不要點個飲料一起吃？

2. A：**I'll have a small fries.**
   B：Would you like ketchup with that?
   Is that for here or to go?
   Please wait two minutes.

   A：我要一份小薯條。
   B：要不要蕃茄醬配著吃？

   是要在這裡吃還是外帶？
   請稍候兩分鐘。

3. A：**And a large Coke, please.**
   B：OK, coming right up.
   With or without ice?
   The straws are over there.
   【straw〔strɔ〕*n.* 吸管】

   A：還要一杯大杯可口可樂。
   B：好，馬上來。
   要不要加冰塊？
   吸管在那邊。

4. A：**I'd like a milk shake.**
   B：What size do you want?
   What flavor do you want?
   Would you like a large or a small?

   A：我要一杯奶昔。
   B：你要多大杯的？
   你要什麼口味的？
   你要大杯還是小杯的？

5. A：**Make it strawberry.**

   B：Sure thing.
   One strawberry shake
   coming right up.
   Do you need a tray?
   【tray〔tre〕*n.* 托盤】

A：要草莓口味的。

B：好。
   草莓奶昔馬上來。

   你需要托盤嗎？

6. A：**That'll be for here.**

   B：OK, I understand.
   I'll get your order.
   I'll be right back.
   【order〔ˈɔrdɚ〕*n.* 點菜】

A：要在這裡吃。

B：好，我知道了。
   我會來爲你點餐。
   我馬上回來。

7. A：**Can I have extra ketchup?**

   B：Of course you can.
   Would you like more than
   one?
   Have as many as you'd like.

A：我可以多要一些蕃茄醬嗎？

B：當然可以。
   你要不要再多一點呢？

   你要多少都可以。

8. A：**Can I have more napkins?**

   B：Sure, as many as you need.
   Help yourself.
   They're right on the counter.
   【counter〔ˈkaʊntɚ〕*n.* 櫃台】

A：我可以多要一些紙巾嗎？

B：當然可以，需要多少都可以。
   自己拿。
   就在櫃台上。

9. A：**Thank you.**

   B：You're very welcome.
   Have a nice day.
   Please come again.

A：謝謝你。

B：不客氣。
   祝你有個愉快的一天。
   請再度光臨。

BOOK 1

8. This is delicious.

Mmmmm. Mmmmm.	嗯！嗯！【注意語調】
This is delicious.	眞好吃。
This tastes great!	眞是可口！
I love it.	我太喜歡了。
The flavor is awesome.	味道眞棒。
It's out of this world.	太棒了。
It's mouth-watering.	眞是好吃。
I can't get enough.	我欲罷不能。
I could eat this all day.	太好吃了，我不會吃膩。

** ──────

delicious〔dɪ'lɪʃəs〕*adj.* 好吃的
taste〔test〕*v.* 嚐起來
flavor〔'flevɚ〕*n.* 味道
awesome〔'ɔsəm〕*adj.* 很棒的
mouth-watering〔'mauθ'watərɪŋ〕*adj.* 令人垂涎的

BOOK 1

【背景説明】

　　　和朋友吃東西的時候，沒有話説會很尷尬，
讚美食物是不錯的選擇。

1. 當美國人吃到好東西，就會
發出 "Mmmmm" 的聲音。
發音時只要嘴巴閉上，用鼻
子發音即可，這個字在字典

Mmmmm.
Mmmmm.

上沒有，Mmmmm. 至少要寫三個 m，這個字專門用
在吃到好吃的東西時，所發出的。須注意語調，第一
個 Mmmmm. (⤴)，第二個 Mmmmm. (⤵)。

2. ***This is delicious.***

delicious〔dɪˈlɪʃəs〕*adj.* 好吃的

　　　這句話字面的意思是「這個是好吃的。」也就
是「眞好吃。」可加強語氣説成：This is really
delicious.（這個眞好吃。）或 This is so delicious.
（這個非常好吃。）也可説成：This tastes delicious.
（這個嚐起來很好吃。）

3. ***This tastes great!***

taste〔test〕*v.* 嚐起來　　great〔gret〕*adj.* 很棒的

　　　這句話字面意思是「這個嚐起來很棒！」也就是
「眞好吃！」smell, feel, taste, sound 這四個感官動
詞，相當於 be 動詞，後須接形容詞，做主詞補語。

　　　　　This tastes great!（眞好吃！）
　　　　　= This tastes good!

4. ***I love it.***

　　這句話字面的意思是「我愛它。」在此引申爲
「我太喜歡了。」美國人碰到喜歡的東西，他會
說：***I love it.*** 或 I like it.

　　love 在英漢字典上，主要作「愛」解，所謂
「愛」，就是「很喜歡」，在這裡的 ***I love it.*** 就是「我
很喜歡這道菜。」在美國，***I love it.*** 的使用頻率非常
高，如到了一家他很喜歡的餐廳，美國人會說：***I
love this restaurant.***（我非常喜歡這家餐廳。）

　　看到很喜歡的遊戲，他
會說：***I love this game.***
（我愛死這個遊戲了。）當
你送美國人禮物，他也會
說：***I love it.***（我眞喜歡你
的禮物。）

　　用 like 來取代 love 也可以，但語氣較弱。

5. ***The flavor is awesome.***
flavor〔ˈflevɚ〕 *n.* 味道
awesome〔ˈɔsəm〕 *adj.* 很棒的

　　這句話的意思是「味道眞棒。」也可說成：This
flavor is awesome.（這個味道很棒。）可加長爲：
The flavor of this is awesome.（這個味道很棒。）

下面都是美國人常說的話，我們按照使用頻率排列，第一至五句，使用頻率很接近：

① ***The flavor is awesome.*** 【第一常用】
② The flavor is amazing. 【第二常用】
　（味道太令人驚訝了。）
　【amazing〔ə'mezɪŋ〕*adj.* 令人驚訝的】

③ The flavor is excellent. 【第三常用】
　（味道太好了。）
④ The flavor is great. （味道太棒了。）
⑤ The flavor is wonderful. （味道太棒了。）
　【excellent〔'ɛkslənt〕*adj.* 極好的】

⑥ The flavor is outstanding. （味道太好了。）
⑦ The flavor is fantastic. （味道太棒了。）
　outstanding〔'aʊt'stændɪŋ〕*adj.* 突出的；傑出的
　fantastic〔fæn'tæstɪk〕*adj.* 很棒的

⑧ The flavor is super.
　（味道太好了。）
⑨ The flavor is terrific.
　（味道太棒了。）
⑩ The flavor is incredible.
　（味道好到令人不敢相信。）

The flavor is super.

super〔'supɚ〕*adj.* 極好的
terrific〔tə'rɪfɪk〕*adj.* 很棒的
incredible〔ɪn'krɛdəbl̩〕*adj.* 令人無法相信的

BOOK 1

6. *It's out of this world.*

這句話字面意思是「這個在世界之外。」或「這個東西不屬於這個世界。」引申為「太棒了；好得不得了。」等於 It's terrific. 或 It's super.

特別注意：*out of this world* 不可說成 *out of the world*（誤，無此用法）。

當你覺得某個東西非常好的時候，你都可以說：

　　It's out of this world.

當你看到老師書教得很好，你可以跟老師說：

　　Your teaching is *out of this world.*
　　（你教得眞棒。）

She is out of this world.

當你看到一位美女，你可以說：

　　She is *out of this world.*
　　（她眞是美如天仙。）

吃東西的例子太多了，如：

　　This hamburger is *out of this world.*
　　（這漢堡眞是太好吃了。）

　　These beef noodles are *out of this world.*
　　（這牛肉麵太棒了。）【noodle〔'nudl〕*n.* 麵】

　　This fish is *out of this world.*
　　（這魚眞是好吃極了。）

　　This steak is *out of this world.*（這牛排太棒了。）

　　This cake is *out of this world.*
　　（這個蛋糕太好吃了。）

7. *It's mouth-watering.*

mouth-watering〔ˈmaʊθˈwɑtərɪŋ〕*adj.* 令人垂涎的

（＝*mouthwatering*）

當你聞到美味的佳
餚，口水自然分泌出來，
中國人說：「令人流口水。」
美國人也說：*It's mouth-
watering.* 這句話也可說

It's mouth-watering.

成：It makes my mouth water.

當你走進一家麵包店，聞到香味，你就可以說：

Mmmmm. *It's mouth-watering.*（嗯！眞香。）

＝Mmmmm. It makes my mouth water.

中國人只在餐前說「嗯，眞香！」美國人在餐
前、用餐時，都會說：*It's mouth-watering.*

mouth-watering 也可直接修飾名詞，例如：
It's a *mouth-watering* dish.（這是一道美味的菜。）

8. *I can't get enough.*

get 主要意思是「得到」，在這個句中作「吃」
解，字面意思是「我怎麼吃都不夠。」引申為「太
好吃了，我欲罷不能。」這句話也可說成：I can't
eat enough of this.

【比較】 ***I can't get enough.***

（太好吃了，我還可以再吃，欲罷不能。）

I don't get enough. （我得到的不夠多。）

（ = *I don't have enough.* ）

9. ***I could eat this all day.***

I could eat this all day.

這句話是假設法，是由 I wish I could eat this all day. 簡化而來。字面意思是「但願我能夠整天吃這個東西。」引申為「這個東西太好吃了，我不會吃膩。」

這句話美國人使用頻率很高，以後你碰到好吃的東西，你如果這樣說，美國人會嚇一跳，他會覺得你的英文怎麼這麼好。美國人還常説：

I could eat this every day.

（我每天吃這個東西也不會膩。）

I could eat this all the time.

（這個東西我永遠吃不膩。）

我們也可以舉一反三，當你喜歡做一件事時，你可以説：I could do this all day.

（我整天做這件事也不會煩。）

= I could do this every day.

（這件事我每天做都不會煩。）

= I could do this all the time.

（我可以一直做這件事。）

【對話練習】

1. A : **Mmmm. Mmmm.**

   B : I know what that means.
   I'm so glad you like it.
   I think it's excellent, too.

   A：嗯！嗯！

   B：我知道這代表什麼。
   我很高興你喜歡。
   我也覺得很棒。

2. A : **This is delicious.**

   B : I agree.
   It's tasty.
   It's very nice.
   【tasty〔'testɪ〕*adj.* 好吃的】

   A：真好吃。

   B：我同意。
   真好吃。
   非常好吃。

3. A : **This tastes great!**

   B : It's wonderful.
   It's marvelous.
   It smells so good.

   A：真是可口！

   B：很棒。
   很棒。
   聞起來很香。

4. A : **I love it.**

   B : I like it, too.
   It tastes great.
   The flavor is excellent.

   A：我太喜歡了。

   B：我也喜歡。
   真好吃。
   味道真棒。

5. A : **The flavor is awesome.**

   B : It sure is.
   It's outstanding.
   It's fantastic.
   【sure〔ʃur〕*adv.* 的確】

   A：味道真棒。

   B：的確是。
   太棒了。
   太棒了。

6. A：**It's out of this world**.

   B：You're right.
   It's very delicious.
   It's the best I've ever
   tasted.
   【taste〔test〕*v.* 品嚐】

    A：太棒了。

    B：你說得對。
   真好吃。
   這是我所嚐過最好吃的。

7. A：**It's mouth-watering**.

   B：It really is.
   It's just great.
   I like it a lot.
   【*a lot* 非常】

    A：真是好吃。

    B：的確是。
   真是太棒了。
   我非常喜歡。

8. A：**I can't get enough**.

   B：Me either.
   I just love it.
   I can't stop eating this.

    A：我欲罷不能。

    B：我也是。
   我太喜歡了。
   我真是欲罷不能。

9. A：**I could eat this all day**.

   B：Me too.
   It really tastes great.
   I could eat this every day.

    A：太好吃了，我不會吃膩。

    B：我也是。
   真是好吃。
   我每天吃這東西也不會膩。

9. I'm full.

I'm full.	我吃飽了。
I'm stuffed.	我吃得很飽。
I can't eat another bite.	我一口也吃不下了。
I ate too much.	我吃太多了。
I need a rest.	我需要休息一下。
I need to take it easy.	我需要輕鬆一下。
I'll gain weight.	我會增加體重。
I'll get fat.	我會變胖。
I need to walk it off.	我需要散散步把它消耗掉。

** ————————

full〔fʊl〕*adj.* 吃飽的
stuffed〔stʌft〕*adj.* 吃得很飽的
bite〔baɪt〕*n.* 一口（食物）　　rest〔rɛst〕*n.* 休息
take it easy 放輕鬆　　gain〔gen〕*v.* 增加
weight〔wet〕*n.* 體重
gain weight 增加體重；變胖
fat〔fæt〕*adj.* 胖的　　*walk off* 以散步消除

BOOK 1

【背景説明】

　　當你吃飽了，不想再吃，就可以説這九句話。

1. **I'm full.**
   full〔ful〕*adj.* 滿的；吃飽的

　　這句話的意思是「我吃飽了。」也可説成：I feel full. (我覺得飽了。) 可以加強語氣説成：I'm really full. (我真的很飽。) 或 I'm so full. (我非常飽。)【so = very】也有美國人説：I'm very full. (我非常飽。) 或 I'm too full. (我太飽了。) 最加強語氣的説法是：

I'm too full to eat any more.

(我太飽，吃不下了。)

I'm too full to eat any more.

【比較】　下面三句話意思相同：

I'm full.【第一常用】

My stomach is full.【第二常用】

(我肚子飽了。)

My belly is full.【第三常用】

(我肚子飽了。)

stomach〔'stʌmək〕*n.* 胃；腹部
belly〔'bɛlɪ〕*n* 肚子

BOOK 1

2. *I'm stuffed.*

　　stuff〔stʌf〕*v.* 填塞；使吃得很飽

　　　　這句話字面的意思是「我被填塞了。」引申為「我吃得很飽。」是由 I'm stuffed with food. 簡化而來。

　　　　也可加強語氣說成：
I'm stuffed to the gills.
字面的意思是「我已經被填塞到腮這麼高了」，引申為「我吃得太飽了。」

I'm stuffed to the gills.

　　【gills〔gɪlz〕*n. pl.*（人的）腮】

3. *I can't eat another bite.*

　　bite〔baɪt〕*n.* 一口（食物）

　　　　這句話字面的意思是「我不能吃下另外一口」也就是「我一口也吃不下了。」可以加強語氣說成：
I really can't eat another bite.（我真的一口也吃不下了。）也可說成：I can't eat another thing.（我沒辦法再吃任何東西。）或 I can't eat any more.
（我沒辦法再吃了。）

　　【比較】下面兩句話意思相同：

　　　　I can't eat another bite.【較常用】
　　　　= I can't take another bite.【常用】
　　　　【take〔tek〕*v.* 吃；喝】

4. *I ate too much.*

這句話的意思是「我吃
太多了。」可加強語氣說成：
Oh, my God, I ate too
much. (噢，天啊，我吃太
多了。) 或 I really ate
too much. (我真的吃了太多。)

Oh, my God,
I ate too much.

5. *I need a rest.*
rest〔rɛst〕*n., v.* 休息

這句話的意思是「我需要休息一下。」美國人也
常說成：I need a short rest. (我需要休息一會兒。)
或 I need a little rest. (我需要休息一下子。)

下面各句意思相同，都是美國人常說的話，前
三句使用頻率非常接近：

I need a rest.【第一常用】
= I need to take a rest.【第三常用】
(我需要休息一下。)

= I need to rest. (我需要休息一下。)【第二常用】
【*take a rest* 休息一下】

= I need a break. (我需要休息一下。)【第五常用】
= I need to take a break.【第六常用】
(我需要休息一下。)

= I need to relax. (我需要休息一下。)【第四常用】
break〔brek〕*n.* 休息時間　*take a break* 休息一下
relax〔rɪ'læks〕*v.* 放鬆；休息

6. *I need to take it easy.*

   take it easy 放輕鬆；休息

   這句話的意思是「我需要放輕鬆。」在吃飯的時候說這句話，表示「我需要休息一下。」含有「我需要吃慢一點。」或「我不要再吃了。」的意思。可以加長爲：I need to take it easy for a while. (我需要休息一會兒。)

   在這裡 *I need to take it easy.* 有兩個涵義：

   ① I need to slow down.
      (我需要放慢速度。)
   ② I need to stop eating.
      (我需要停止吃。)

7. *I'll gain weight.*

   gain〔gen〕*v.* 增加
   weight〔wet〕*n.* 體重   *gain weight* 增加體重；變胖

   這句話字面的意思是「我將增加體重。」也就是「我會變胖。」等於 I'll get fat. 也可説成：I'll add weight. (我會增加體重。)【add〔æd〕*v.* 增加】

   I'll gain weight. 可加強語氣説成：

   I'm afraid I'll gain too much weight.
   (我恐怕會增加太多體重。)
   I'll gain weight for sure.
   (我一定會增加體重。)
   I'll gain weight from this meal.
   (吃這一餐飯我會增加體重。)
   I'm afraid~ 恐怕   *for sure* 一定   meal〔mil〕*n.* 一餐

8. ***I'll get fat.***

fat〔fæt〕*adj.* 胖的

這句話的意思是「我會變胖。」(= *I'll become fat.*) 可加強語氣說成：I'm going to become fat.（我會變胖。）

下面都是美國人常說的話：

I'll get fat.【第一常用】
I'll get too fat.（我會變很胖。）【第二常用】

I'll get too fat from this.【第三常用】
（吃這個會讓我變很胖。）
I'll get fat from this meal.【第四常用】
（吃這餐飯我會變很胖。）

I'm afraid I'll get too fat.【第七常用】
（恐怕我會變得太胖。）
I'm worried I'll get too fat.【第八常用】
（我擔心我會變得太胖。）

I don't want to get fat.
（我不想變胖。）【第五常用】
I don't want to get too fat.
（我不想變得太胖。）
【第六常用】

I don't want to get fat.

9. *I need to walk it off.*

walk off　以散步消除（＝ *get rid of by walking* ）

這句話字面的意思
是「我需要散步消除它。」
在此引申爲「我需要散步
把它消耗掉。」可以加強
語氣說成：I need to walk
off all the food I just ate.

I need to walk it off.

（我需要散步來消耗我剛剛所吃的所有食物。）或
I need to walk off all the calories I've just
consumed.（我需要走路來消耗我剛剛吃下去的卡路
里。）〔calorie〔'kælərɪ〕*n.* 卡路里　　consume〔kən'sjum〕
v. 吃；喝；消耗〕*I need to walk it off.* 中的 it 在此指
「飽的感覺」（ feeling of fullness ）或「吃下去的食
物」（ the food I ate ）。

　　美國人吃太多、喝太多，就會覺得不舒服，下
面是他們常說的話：

I ate too much. *I need to walk it off.*
（我吃太多了。我需要散步把它消耗掉。）

I'm so stuffed. *I need to walk it off.*
（我吃得很飽。我需要散步把它消耗掉。）

I feel bloated, so *I need to walk it off.*
（我覺得很脹，所以我需要散步把它消耗掉。）
〔bloated〔'blotɪd〕*adj.* 膨脹的〕

【對話練習】

1. A：**I'm full.**

   B：I don't believe you.
   Keep eating.
   Try some more.
   【try〔traɪ〕*v.* 嚐試；試吃】

   A：我吃飽了。

   B：我不相信。
   再繼續吃。
   多吃點。

2. A：**I'm stuffed.**

   B：I'm stuffed, too.
   That was a big meal.
   That meal really filled me up.
   【meal〔mil〕*n.* 一餐
   fill up 裝滿；填滿】

   A：我吃得很飽。

   B：我也吃得很飽。
   真是豐盛的一餐。
   這一餐真的把我填得
   好飽。

3. A：**I can't eat another bite.**

   B：I don't want to hear that.
   I know you can eat more.
   Please don't be polite.

   A：我一口也吃不下了。

   B：我不想聽你這麼說。
   我知道你還吃得下。
   請不要客氣。

4. A：**I ate too much.**

   B：Take a rest.
   Have a drink.
   Wait a little while.

   A：我吃太多了。

   B：休息一下。
   喝杯飲料。
   等一下再吃。

BOOK 1

5. A : **I need a rest**.　　　　　　A：我需要休息一下。

B : That's a very good idea.　　B：那真是個好主意。

Let's rest for ten minutes.　　我們休息個十分鐘吧。

Let's have some water　　　我們喝些水聊一下。

and chat.【chat〔 tʃæt 〕*v.* 聊天】

6. A : **I need to take it easy**.　　A：我需要輕鬆一下。

B : I can't blame you.　　　　B：我不怪你。

I understand.　　　　　　我了解。

I totally agree.　　　　　我完全同意。

　　【blame〔 blem 〕*v.* 責備】

7. A : **I'll gain weight**.　　　　　A：我會變胖。

B : Don't worry about it.　　　B：別擔心。

You won't get fat.　　　　你不會變胖。

You don't do this every day.　你又不是每天都這樣。

8. A : **I'll get fat**.　　　　　　　A：我會變胖。

B : No, you won't get fat.　　　B：不，你不會變胖。

One meal won't harm you.　吃一餐不會怎麼樣。

Just do some exercise　　　等一下做一些運動就

later on.【harm〔 hɑrm 〕*v.* 傷害　好了。

later on 以後】

9. A : **I need to walk it off**.　　A：我需要散步把它消耗掉。

B : That's a good idea.　　　　B：好主意。

I'll join you.　　　　　　我和你一起去。

Let's take a walk.　　　　我們去散步吧。

　　【join〔 dʒɔɪn 〕*v.* 加入；跟…一起做同樣的事】

10. Let's go for a walk.

Let's go for a walk.	我們去散步吧。
Let's get some exercise.	我們去做些運動。
A walk would do us good.	散步對我們有好處。
Walking is great.	散步很棒。
Walking is healthy.	散步有益健康。
It's the best exercise there is.	散步是最好的運動。
Where shall we go?	你說我們去哪裡？
Any place in mind?	你有沒有想到任何地方？
I'll follow you anywhere.	我願意跟你去任何地方。

**────────────────

go for a walk 去散步

exercise〔'ɛksɚ‚saɪz〕 *n.* 運動

good〔gud〕 *n.* 好處　　*do sb. good* 對某人有好處

great〔gret〕 *adj.* 很棒的

healthy〔'hɛlθɪ〕 *adj.* 健康的　　follow〔'falo〕 *v.* 跟隨

【背景說明】

　　散步是最好的運動，全世界的人都喜歡散步，你每天都有機會用英文說這九句話，建議別人和你一起去散步。

1. ***Let's go for a walk.***
　go for a walk　去散步

　　　這句話的意思是「我們去散步吧。」可加強語氣說成：Let's you and I go for a walk.（我們兩個去散步吧。）

　　「去散步」的表達方式有很多：

　　┌　take a walk　去散步
　　└　= go for a walk

　　┌　= take a stroll
　　└　= go for a stroll
　　　= stretch *one's* legs

　　【stroll〔strol〕*n.* 散步　　stretch〔strɛtʃ〕*v.* 伸展】

　　　其中，美國人最常說的是：Let's take a walk. 和 ***Let's go for a walk***. 而 Let's stretch our legs. 也常用。

　　　美國老一輩的人喜歡說 Let's take a stroll. 或 Let's go for a stroll. 之類的話。有時年輕人故意講 Let's take a stroll.，有點故意做作，模仿老一輩的人的味道。

BOOK 1

2. ***Let's get some exercise.***
exercise (ˈɛksə͵saɪz) *n.* 運動

這句話的意思是「我們去做些運動吧。」可加強語氣說成：Let's go out and get some exercise.（我們出去做些運動吧。）

下面三句話意思相同，都是美國人常說的話：

> ***Let's get some exercise.***【第二常用】
> = Let's exercise.【第一常用】
> = Let's work out.【第三常用】【***work out*** 運動】

在字典上，「做運動」是 do / take / get exercise，但是美式英語不說 *take exercise*。

【比較】Let's exercise.【正】
Let's take exercise.【英式英語，美國人不說】
Let's do exercise.【正】
Let's get exercise.【正】

3. ***A walk would do us good.***
do sb. ***good***　對某人有好處

A walk would do us good.

這句話的意思是「散步對我們有好處。」也可說成：
A walk is good for us.
（散步對我們很好。）或

A walk is great for us.（散步對我們很棒。）也可加長為：I think going for a walk would do us good.（我認為去散步會對我們有好處。）

【比較】 A walk *would* do us good.【謙虛語氣】

【用假設法助動詞 would，表示「客氣」，說話
者謙虛地認為自己不該說的】

A walk *will* do us good.【一般語氣】

4. *Walking is great.*

walk〔wɔk〕v. 走路；散步
great〔gret〕adj. 很棒的

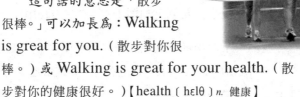

Walking is great.

這句話的意思是「散步
很棒。」可以加長為：Walking
is great for you. (散步對你很
棒。) 或 Walking is great for your health. (散
步對你的健康很好。)【health〔hɛlθ〕n. 健康】

5. *Walking is healthy.*

healthy〔'hɛlθɪ〕adj. 健康的；有益健康的

這句話的意思是「散步是有益健康的。」可加長
為：Walking is healthy for you. (散步有益你的健
康。) 或 Walking is healthy for everyone. (散步
有益大家的健康。)

可加強語氣說成：

Walking is so healthy. (散步是非常有益健康的。)
Walking is very healthy. (散步是很有益健康的。)
Walking is extremely healthy.
(散步是非常有益健康的。)

so〔so〕adv. 非常 (= *very*)
extremely〔ɪk'strimlɪ〕adv. 極度地；非常

很多人搞不清楚 healthy 和 healthful 的區別。很簡單，只要記住 healthy，而不要管 healthful。在字典上：

> *healthy*〔ˈhɛlθɪ〕*adj.* ①健康的
> ②有益健康的
> healthful〔ˈhɛlθfəl〕*adj.* 有益健康的

所以，healthy 包含 healthful。問了很多美國人，他們都說很少用到 healthful，只用 healthy。

我們從小所學的英文觀念是：healthy 是「健康的」，而 *healthful* 是「有益健康的」，考試中也常考。事實上，我們學錯了。美國人極少用 *healthful*，常使用 healthy，在梁實秋所編著的「英文大辭典」中，也有提到。

a healthy climate

【比較 1】

中文：　你很健康。

英文：　You're very healthy.【正】
　　　　You're very healthful.【誤】

雖然在 The American Heritage Dictionary p.809 中有提到，a healthy climate 和 a healthful climate 都可表「有益健康的天氣」，但是美國人在日常生活中，幾乎不用 healthful。所以，我們只要記住 healthy 就行了，因為 healthy 包含了 healthful。

BOOK 1

【比較 2】

Walking is healthy.

【正，美國人常説】

Walking is healthful.

【正，美國人極少説】

Walking is healthy.

6. ***It's the best exercise there is.***

　　這句話源自：It's the best exercise *that* there is. 當主詞的關係代名詞，在 there is 之前，可省略。

【詳見「文法寶典」p.647】

　　這句話字面的意思是「它是目前存在的最好的運動。」等於 It's the best exercise that exists. 在這裡引申爲「散步是最好的運動。」【exist〔ɪgˈzɪst〕*v.* 存在】

【比較】　Walking is the best exercise.【一般語氣】

　　　　Walking is the best exercise *there is*.

　　　　【加強語氣】

　　在任何最高級後面，都可加上 there is 來加強語氣，例如：

Häagen-Dazs is the best ice cream *there is*.

　〔ˈhagənˌdɑz〕

（Häagen-Dazs 是最好的冰淇淋。）

A Mercedes is the best car *there is*.

　〔məˈsedɪz〕

（賓士車是最好的車。）

Mercedes

7. *Where shall we go?*

shall 在疑問句中，用於第一、三人稱，表「徵求對方意見」，此時 shall 等於 do you want to...【詳見「文法寶典」p.310】。

> ***Where shall we go?***【最常用】
> （你說我們要去哪裡？）
> = Where do you want to go?【較常用】
> = Where would you like to go?【常用】

下面兩句，shall 和 will 語氣不同：

【比較】 Where ***shall*** we go?【客氣，徵求對方意見】
Where ***will*** we go?
【一般語氣，少用，有點像在旅行團問導遊：「我們要去哪裡？」】

8. *Any place in mind?*

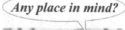

Any place in mind?

這句話的意思是「你有想到去任何地方嗎？」，源自：*Do you have* any place in mind? 美國人也常說：Any special place in mind?（你有沒有想到什麼特別的地方？）(= *Do you have any special place in mind?*)
【*have…in mind* 想到；考慮到；打算】

這句話不可說成：*Any place on your mind?*（誤）美國人常說的 What's on your mind? 意思是：① 你在想什麼？② 你有什麼心事？

下面都是美國人常說的話：

> ***Any place in mind?*** 【第一常用】
> Any place you feel like going? 【第三常用】
> （你有想要去任何地方嗎？）
> 【*feel like + V-ing*　想要～】
>
> Any place come to your mind? 【第五常用】
> （你有想到任何地方嗎？）
> （= *Does any place come to your mind?* ）
> Any place come to mind? 【第四常用】
> （你有想到任何地方嗎？）
> （= *Does any place come to mind?* ）
> Can you think of any place? 【第二常用】
> （你能想到任何地方嗎？）
> 【***come to*** *one's* ***mind***　出現在某人的腦海中】

9. ***I'll follow you anywhere.***
   follow 〔'falo 〕*v.* 跟隨

I'll follow you anywhere.

這句話的意思是「我願意跟你去任何地方。」
可加長爲：I'll follow you anywhere you want to go. （我願意跟你去任何你想要去的地方。）當你說：I'll always follow you. （我會永遠跟隨你。）就不能說：*I'll always follow you anywhere.*
【誤，句意重覆】

下面是美國人常說的話：

I'll follow you anywhere.【第一常用】

I'll go anywhere you go.【第三常用】

（ 我願意跟你去任何地方。 ）

I'll go wherever you go.

（ 我願意跟你去任何地方。 ）

【第二常用】

I'll follow you till
I'm old and gray.

Wherever you go, I'll go.

（ 無論你去哪裡，我都去。 ）

【第四常用】

Wherever you go, I'll go, too.【第五常用】

（ 無論你去哪裡，我也會去。 ）

Wherever you go, I'll follow you.【第六常用】

（ 無論你去哪裡，我都會跟你去。 ）

可以幽默地說：

I'll follow you anywhere in the world.

（ 我會跟你去世界上任何地方。 ）

I'll follow you for the rest of my life.

（ 我這一輩子都要跟著你。 ）

I'll follow you till I'm old and gray.

（ 我將一直跟隨你，直到我白髮蒼蒼。 ）

rest〔rɛst〕 *n.* 剩餘；殘餘

the rest of *one's* **life** 某人的餘生

gray〔gre〕 *adj.* （頭髮）斑白的；灰白的

old and gray 白髮蒼蒼（是美國人常說的慣用語）

【對話練習】

1. A：**Let's go for a walk.**
   B：Sounds great.
     Let's do it.
     I love to go for a walk.

   A：我們去散步吧。
   B：聽起來很棒。
     走吧。
     我愛散步。

2. A：**Let's get some exercise.**
   B：That's a great idea.
     I like that.
     That sounds good to me.

   A：我們去做些運動。
   B：好主意。
     我喜歡。
     聽起來不錯。

3. A：**A walk would do us good.**
   B：I agree.
     I'm with you.
     You're exactly right.
     【*be with sb.* 同意某人
       exactly〔ɪg'zæktlɪ〕*adv.* 完全地】

   A：散步對我們有好處。
   B：我同意。
     我同意你。
     你完全正確。

4. A：**Walking is great.**
   B：That's true.
     I totally agree.
     I can't agree with you more.
     【totally〔'totḷɪ〕*adv.* 完全地】

   A：散步很棒。
   B：沒錯。
     我完全同意。
     我非常同意。

5. A：**Walking is healthy.**
   B：You are right.
     It's a fact.
     It can't be denied.
     【deny〔dɪ'naɪ〕*v.* 否認】

   A：散步有益健康。
   B：你說的對。
     這是事實。
     這是不容否認的。

6. A : **Walking is the best exercise there is.**

   B : That's so true.
   I can't argue with that.
   You can say that again.
   【argue〔'ɑrgjʊ〕*v.* 爭論】

A：散步是最好的運動。

B：沒錯。
你說得對。
你說得真對。

7. A : **Where shall we go?**

   B : You choose.
   You decide.
   Any place is fine.

A：你說我們要去哪裡？

B：你選擇。
你決定。
任何地方都可以。

8. A : **Any place in mind?**

   B : Anywhere is fine.
   I'll go anywhere.
   Where would you like to go?

A：你有沒有想到任何地方？

B：任何地方都可以。
我任何地方都去。
你想去哪裡？

9. A : **I'll follow you anywhere.**

   B : You are so nice to say that.
   I feel the same way about you.
   I would follow you anywhere, too.

A：我願意跟你去任何地方。

B：你這麼說真體貼。
我對你也有同樣的感覺。

我也願意跟你去任何地方。

11.　I need to go home.

I'm beat.	我好累。
I'm bushed.	我很累。
I'm exhausted.	我累死了。
I need to go home.	我必須回家。
I need to get back.	我必須回去。
I can't stay.	我不能留下來。
I have things to do.	我有事情要做。
I have to go.	我必須走了。
Let's call it a day.	我們今天到此爲止。

** ————————————————

beat〔bit〕*adj.* 疲倦的
bushed〔buʃt〕*adj.* 疲倦的
exhausted〔ɪg'zɔstɪd〕*adj.* 筋疲力盡的
stay〔ste〕*v.* 停留
call it a day 今天到此爲止

【背景說明】

　　這九句話幾乎天天都用得到，你只要累了、
想回家，就可說這些話。

1. **I'm beat.**

beat〔bit〕*v.* 打敗　*adj.* 疲倦的；筋疲力盡的
　（*= exhausted*）

　　beat 的主要意思是
「打敗」，**I'm beat.** 字
面的意思是「我被打敗
了。」你看美國人多幽
默，他們說：「我被打
敗了。」意思就是「我

I'm beat.

好累。」現在 beat 已經變成純粹的形容詞。也可說
成：I'm feeling beat.（我覺得很累。）

I'm beat. 可加強語氣說成：

　　I'm really beat.（我真的好累。）【第一常用】
　　I'm so beat.（我很累。）【第二常用】
　　I'm very beat.（我非常累。）【第三常用】

　　I'm totally beat.（我非常累。）【第四常用】
　　I'm completely beat.（我非常累。）【第五常用】
　　【totally（完全地）和 completely（完全地），在此用
　　　來加強語氣，作「非常地」解。】

BOOK 1

2. *I'm bushed.*

 bush〔buʃ〕*v.* 使筋疲力盡（= *exhaust*）　　*n.* 灌木叢
 bushed〔buʃt〕*adj.* 筋疲力盡的；非常疲倦的
 （= *very tired*）

　　bush 的主要意思是「灌木叢」，當動詞時，可作

「使筋疲力盡」解，可能源
自古時候打仗，躲在灌木叢
裡太久，使人筋疲力盡。
I'm bushed. 意思是「我好
累。」bushed 已經變成純粹
的形容詞。

I'm bushed.

　【例】　After all that exercise, *I'm bushed.*
　　　　（做了那麼多運動後，我很累。）

3. *I'm exhausted.*

 exhaust〔ɪgˈzɔst〕*v.* 使筋疲力盡
 exhausted〔ɪgˈzɔstɪd〕*adj.* 筋疲力盡的

　　這句話字面的意思是「我筋疲力盡。」引申爲

「我累死了。」可用 really，so 或 very 來加強語
氣，像：I'm really exhausted.（我眞的累死了。）

下面都是美國人常説的話：

　　　I'm beat.（我好累。）【第三常用】
　　　I'm bushed.（我很累。）【第五常用】
　　　I'm exhausted.（我累死了。）【第四常用】

I'm tired. (我好累。)【第一常用】

I'm very tired. (我非常累。)【第二常用】

I'm extremely tired. (我累死了。)【第六常用】

tired〔 taɪrd 〕*adj.* 疲倦的

extremely〔 ɪk'strimlɪ 〕*adv.* 極度地;非常地

4. *I need to go home.*

這句話的意思是「我必須回家。」可加長為:

Excuse me. I need to go home. (對不起,我必須回家。) 或 I'm afraid

I need to go home.

(我恐怕必須回家。)

也可加上 now,説成:

I need to go home

now. (我現在必須回家。)

I need to
go home.

下面是美國人常説的話:

I need to go home.【第一常用】

I have to go home. (我必須回家。)【第二常用】

I must go home. (我必須回家。)【第四常用】

It's time for me to go home. 【第三常用】
(該是我回家的時候了。)

It's time for me to be going home.
(該是我回家的時候了。)【第五常用】

BOOK 1

5. *I need to get back.*

　　get back　回去（= *return to a place*）

　　　　這句話的意思是「我必須
回去。」在這裡可加長爲：

I need to get back.

I need to <u>get back</u> <u>home</u>.
　　　　動詞片語　　*adv.*

I need to <u>get back</u> <u>home</u> <u>now</u>.
　　　　動詞片語　　*adv.*　　*adv.*

6. *I can't stay.*

　　stay〔ste〕*v.* 停留

　　　　這句話的意思是「我不能留下來。」可加長爲：

　　I can't stay any longer.（我不能再待了。）

　　I can't stay any more.（我不能再待了。）

　　I can't stay here any longer.

　　（我不能再待在這裡了。）

　　【*not…any longer* 再也不…　　*not…any more* 不再…】

　　I can't stay. 可以加強語説成：

　　I have to go. *I can't stay.*

　　（我必須走了。我不能留下來。）

　　My time is up. *I can't stay.*

　　（我的時間到了。我不能再待了。）

　　【up〔ʌp〕*adv.* 終結】

7. *I have things to do*.

　　這句話的意思是「我有事情要做。」可加長為：
I have some things to do. (我有一些事要做。) 或
I have many things to do. (我有很多事要做。)

【比較】***I have things to do***. 【通俗，一般人喜歡說】
　　　　 I have stuff to do. 【年輕人喜歡用 stuff】
　　　　 (我有事情要做。)【stuff〔stʌf〕*n*. 東西；事物】

8. *I have to go*.

> *I have to go.*

　　這句話的意思是「我
必須走了。」可加強語氣
說成：I have to go now.
(我現在必須走了。) 或
I must go right now.
(我現在就必須走了。)【*right now* 現在；立刻】

【比較】　下面兩句話意思相同：
　　　　　I have to go. 【較常用，語氣輕鬆】
　　　　 = I must go. 【常用，語氣較強】

下面都是美國人常說的話：
　　I have to go. 【第一常用】
　　I have to run. (我必須趕快走了。)【第三常用】
　　I have to leave. (我必須離開了。)【第四常用】
　　【run〔rʌn〕*v.* 快速地移動】

I have to hit the road.【第五常用】
（我必須上路了。）
I have to be going.【第二常用】
（我必須走了。）
I have to say good-bye now.【第六常用】
（我現在必須說再見了。）
【*hit the road* 上路】

9. *Let's call it a day.*

 call it a day 今天到此為止（= *call it quits*）

這句話字面的意思是
「我們把它叫作一天。」
引申為「我們今天到此為
止。」可加上 OK？來緩
和語氣，說成：Let's call
it a day, OK?（我們今天
到此為止，好嗎？）

Let's call it a day.

【比較】下面三句話意思相同：

 Let's call it a day.【第一常用】
= Let's call it quits.【第二常用】
（我們今天到此為止。）
= Let's stop for today.【第三常用】
（我們今天到此為止。）
【quits〔kwɪts〕*adj.* 互不相欠的
 call it quits 是慣用語，表「停止」。】

【對話練習】

1. A：**I'm beat.**

   B：Take a break.
   Take a rest.
   Rest a while.
   【rest〔rɛst〕*n., v.* 休息
   take a break 休息一下】

A：我好累。

B：休息一下。
休息一下。
休息一下。

2. A：**I'm bushed.**

   B：I know how you feel.
   I'm tired, too.
   It's been a long day.

A：我好累。

B：我懂你的感覺。
我也累了。
今天真是漫長的一天。

3. A：**I'm exhausted.**

   B：Take it easy.
   Go get a drink.
   Take a little break.
   【***take it easy*** 放輕鬆
   drink〔drɪŋk〕*n.* 飲料】

A：我好累。

B：放輕鬆。
去喝杯飲料。
稍微休息一下。

4. A：**I need to go home.**

   B：I understand.
   It's getting late.
   You have lots of things to
   do.

A：我必須回家。

B：我了解。
時間不早了。
你有很多事情要做。

5. A： **I can't stay.**

   B： Sure you can.

   I need your help.

   Just 15 more minutes.

A： 我不能留下來。

B： 你當然可以。

我需要你的幫助。

再十五分鐘就好。

6. A： **I need to get back.**

   B： Please stay.

   Don't go.

   Keep me company.

   【*keep one's company* 和某人作伴】

A： 我必須回去。

B： 請留下來。

不要走。

和我作伴。

7. A： **I have things to do.**

   B： No problem.

   Do what you have to do.

   Take care of your business.

   【*take care of* 處理

   business (ˈbɪznɪs) *n.* 事情】

A： 我有事情要做。

B： 沒問題。

去做你必須做的事吧。

去做你的事吧。

8. A： **I have to go.**

   B： Are you sure?

   Can't you stay?

   Stay a while, please.

A： 我得走了。

B： 你確定嗎？

你不能留下來嗎？

請再多留一會兒。

9. A： **Let's call it a day.**

   B： Good idea.

   I agree.

   It's time to go.

A： 我們今天到此爲止。

B： 好主意。

我同意。

是該走的時候了。

BOOK 1

12. I'm home.

I'm *home*.	我回家了。
Home, sweet *home*!	家，甜蜜的家！
There's no place like *home*.	沒有一個地方比得上家。
I had a great day.	我今天過得很愉快。
Everything went right for me.	我每件事都很順利。
Today was really my day.	我今天運氣真好。
It's been a long day.	今天真是漫長的一天。
I did so much.	我做了很多事。
I learned a lot.	我學到了很多。

** ————————————

sweet〔swit〕*adj.* 甜蜜的；舒服的
great〔gret〕*adj.* 很棒的   right〔raɪt〕*adv.* 順利地
go right 順利；進行順利

【背景説明】

　　當你忙了一天回到家，説了這九句英文，家人聽到一定很高興。

1. *I'm home.*

　　這句話字面的意思是「我在家了。」引申爲「我回家了。」可以加強語氣説成：Thank God, I'm home. (謝天謝地，我回家了。) 或 I'm glad I'm home. (眞高興我回家了。)【glad〔glæd〕*adj.* 高興的】也有美國人説：I'm so happy to be home. (我眞高興回到家。)

2. *Home, sweet home!*

　　這句話源自："Home, home, sweet, sweet home!" (家！家！甜蜜，甜蜜的家！) 是「甜蜜的家庭」中的歌詞。這句話雖然沒有動詞，但已經表達了完整思想，可以看作是一個句子。

　　美國人常把 "Home, sweet home!" 裱框掛在牆上或繡在門口的腳踏墊或枕頭上。

3. *There's no place like home.*

這句話的意思是「沒有一個地方比得上家。」源自諺語：Be it ever so humble, there's no place like home. (家雖簡陋，但沒有一個地方比家更溫暖；在家千日好，出門事事難。) 可以加強語氣說成：There's no other place in the world like my home. (在世界上沒有其他地方像我家那麼好。)

There's no place like home.

下面都是美國人常說的話，我們按照使用頻率排列：

① *There's no place like home.* 【第一常用】

② No place is better than home. 【第二常用】
　　(沒有地方比家更好。)

③ No place is as good as home. 【第三常用】
　　(沒有地方像家一樣好。)

④ My home is the best.
　　(我的家是最好的。)

⑤ My home is the best place.
　　(我的家是最好的地方。)

⑥ My home is my favorite place.
　　(我家是我最喜愛的地方。)

【favorite (ˈfevərɪt) *adj.* 最喜愛的】

4. *I had a great day.*

great〔gret〕*adj.* 很棒的

這句話字面的意思是「我有很棒的一天。」引申爲「我今天過得很愉快。」可加長爲：I had a great day today. (我今天過得很愉快。) 或 Let me tell you, I had a great day. (我可以肯定地說，我今天過得很愉快。)【*Let me tell you* 是慣用語，可看成插入語，詳見「東華英漢大辭典」p.3583】

I had a great day. 也可説成：Today was a great day. (今天過得很愉快。) 或 It was a great day. (今天過得很愉快。)

下面都是美國人常說的話：

I had a great day.【第一常用】
I had a very good day.【第四常用】
(我今天過得非常愉快。)
【較少人説：I had a good day.】
I had a lucky day. (我今天很幸運。)【第八常用】

I had a wonderful day.【第二常用】
(我今天過得很愉快。)
I had a terrific day.【第五常用】
(我今天過得很愉快。)
I had a fantastic day.【第六常用】
(我今天過得很愉快。)
wonderful〔'wʌndəfəl〕*adj.* 很棒的
terrific〔tə'rɪfɪk〕*adj.* 很棒的
fantastic〔fæn'tæstɪk〕*adj.* 很棒的

I had a great day.

BOOK 1

I had an excellent day. 【第三常用】
（我今天過得很愉快。）
I had an awesome day. 【第七常用】
（我今天過得很愉快。）

excellent〔'ɛkslənt〕*adj.* 極好的
awesome〔'ɔsəm〕*adj.* 很棒的

5. *Everything went right for me.*
right〔raɪt〕*adv.* 順利地
go right 順利；進行順利

> *Everything went right for me.*

這句話字面的意思是
「我一切進行順利。」引申
為「我每件事都很順利。」可加長為：Everything
went right for me today.（今天我每件事都很順利。）
或 Everything that I did today went right for
me.（今天我做的每件事都很順利。）可簡化為：
Everything went right.（每件事都很順利。）相反的
是：Everything went wrong.（每件事都不順利。）
【*go wrong* 失敗；出毛病】

下面各句意思相同，都是美國人常說的話：

Everything went right for me. 【第一常用】
Everything went my way. 【第三常用】
（我一切都很順利。）
Everything went well. 【第二常用】
（一切都很順利。）

go one's way 順利（「不順利」則是 go wrong）
go well 順利

Everything was perfect for me. 【第六常用】
（我一切都很好。）
Everything I did turned out great. 【第四常用】
（我做的每件事結果都很好。）
Everything that happened was good.
（所發生的每一件事都很好。）【第五常用】
【perfect〔'pɝfɪkt〕*adj.* 完美的　*turn out* 結果（成爲）】

6. *Today was really my day.*

　　這句話字面的意思是「今
天眞的是我的日子。」引申爲：
① 我今天眞幸運。(= *Today*
was really my lucky day.)
② 我今天眞得意。(= *Today*
was really a good day for
me.) 可簡化爲：Today was
my day. (我今天很幸運。)

Today was really my day.

【比較】 下面兩句話意思相同，説話時間不同：

Today is my day. 【説話者覺得一天還沒過去】
Today was my day. 【説話者覺得一天已經結束了】

　　Today was my day. 的相反是：Today was
not my day. (我今天眞倒楣。)(= *Today was a bad*
day for me.)

7. *It's been a long day.*

這句話的意思是「今天眞是漫長的一天。」可能很愉快，也可能不愉快，要看上下文情況而定。如果是好的，你還可以說：It's been a good day. (今天運氣好。) 不好的，就可以說：It's been a bad day. (今天運氣不好。)

It's been a long day.

It's been a long day. 可加長爲：It has been a very long day. (今天眞是非常漫長的一天。) 或 It has been such a long day for me. (對我來說，今天眞是非常漫長的一天。)

這句話用現在完成式，表示「從過去到現在一直…」。

【比較】下面三句話，說話者的心理狀況不同：

It's a long day.

【講這句話，表示說話者認爲一天還沒過去。】

It was a long day.

【說這句話時，說話者認爲，今天已經結束了。】

It's been a long day.

【工作完成，想要停止的時候說。】

8. *I did so much.*

這句話的意思是「我做了很多事。」雖然 so 等於 very，但美國人不說：*I did very much.*【誤】單獨講這句話時，美國人常加上 today，像
I did so much today.
（我今天做了很多事。）

I did so much.

下面都是美國人常說的話，第一句和第二句使用頻率很接近：

① I did a lot.【第一常用】
② *I did so much.*【第二常用】
　　（我做了很多事。）
③ I did so many things.【第三常用】
　　（我做了很多事。）【*a lot* 很多】

④ I did a great deal.（我做了很多事。）
⑤ I did a lot of things.（我做了很多事。）
　　【*a great deal* 很多】

⑥ I accomplished a lot.
　　（我完成了很多事。）
⑦ I accomplished so much.
　　（我完成了很多事。）
　　【accomplish〔ə'kɑmplɪʃ〕*v.* 完成】

9. *I learned a lot*.

　　這句話的意思是「我學到了很多。」美國人常加上 today，說成：I learned a lot today.（我今天學到了很多。）可加長為：I feel satisfied because I learned a lot today.（我覺得很滿足，因為我今天學到了很多。）
【satisfied〔'sætɪs,faɪd〕*adj.* 滿足的】

下面都是美國人常說的話：

I learned a lot.

I learned a lot today.
【第一常用】
I learned a lot from today.
（我今天學了很多。）【第三常用】

I learned so much today.【第二常用】
（我今天學了很多。）
I learned so much from today.【第四常用】
（我今天學了很多。）

I learned some important things today.【第九常用】
（我今天學了一些重要的東西。）
I learned a lot of things today.【第八常用】
（我今天學了很多東西。）

Today was a learning day.【第五常用】
（今天是學習的一天。）
Today was a day in which I learned a lot.
（我今天學了很多。）【第十常用】

It was a learning day for me.【第六常用】
（對我而言，今天是學習的一天。）
It was a day full of learning.【第七常用】
（今天是充滿學習的一天。）【full〔fʊl〕*adj.* 充滿的】

BOOK 1

【對話練習】

1. A：**I'm home.**

   B：Welcome home.

   　　I'm glad you're back.

   　　It's good to see you.

2. A：**Home, sweet home!**

   B：It is a wonderful place.

   　　I love my home, too.

   　　Home is the very best place.

3. A：**There's no place like home.**

   B：You're so right.

   　　I totally agree.

   　　Home is the best.

   　　【totally〔'totlɪ〕*adv.* 完全地】

4. A：**I had a great day.**

   B：That's fantastic.

   　　I'm so happy for you.

   　　Do you want to give me

   　　any details?

5. A：**Everything went right for me.**

   B：Great.

   　　You deserve it.

   　　That's good to hear.

   　　【deserve〔dɪ'zɝv〕*v.* 應得】

A：我回來了。

B：歡迎回家。

　　我很高興你回來了。

　　很高興看到你。

A：家，甜蜜的家！

B：家是很棒的地方。

　　我也愛我的家。

　　家是最好的地方。

A：沒有一個地方比得上家。

B：你說得很對。

　　我完全同意。

　　家是最好的。

A：我今天過得很愉快。

B：太棒了。

　　我真為你高興。

　　你想不想告訴我一些

　　細節？

A：我每件事都很順利。

B：太棒了。

　　這是你應得的。

　　聽到你這麼說真高興。

BOOK 1

6. A：**Today was really my day**.   A：我今天運氣眞好。

    B：Good for you.   B：太好了。

      I'm glad to hear that.   聽你這麼說我很高興。

      Can you tell me about it?   你能告訴我事情的經過嗎？

7. A：**It's been a long day**.   A：今天眞是漫長的一天。

    B：You must be tired.   B：你一定很疲倦了。

      You must be beat.   你一定累壞了。

      You need a rest.   你需要休息一下。

      【rest〔rɛst〕*n.* 休息】

8. A：**I did so much**.   A：我做了很多事。

    B：Really?   B：眞的嗎？

      Tell me about it.   告訴我事情的經過。

      I'd like to hear what you   我想聽聽你做了些什麼。

      did.

9. A：**I learned a lot**.   A：我學到好多東西。

    B：I'm glad to hear that.   B：聽你這麼說眞高興。

      That's the most important   這是最重要的。

      thing.

      Learning is what life is all   人生的意義就是要學習。

      about.

      【*~is what…is all about* …的意義就是~】

「一口氣背會話」經 BOOK 1

唸英文要像唸經一樣，每天大聲唸，從起床到睡覺，唸得比看得快，最後不看也會唸，養成習慣後，你會全身舒爽，你試試看，奇妙無比。

1. Great *to see you.*
   So good *to see you.*
   What's going on?

   What's up today?
   What are you doing?
   Anything exciting?

   You look great.
   You look high-spirited.
   You look like you're ready for anything.

2. Great class.
   Thank you, teacher.
   You are the best.

   I like your class.
   I learn so much.
   You can really teach.

   You're interesting.
   You make it fun.
   You're a terrific teacher.

3. You're an excellent teacher.
   Your material is great.
   Your methods are useful.

   You're never dull.
   You're full of pep.
   You keep us on our toes.

   I like your teaching.
   I like your style.
   You do a good job.

4. *You're* doing fine.
   You got it.
   Keep on going.

   That's the way.
   That's how to do it.
   Don't change a thing.

   Keep working hard.
   Keep doing great.
   Keep on doing what you are doing.

5. *Let's* go.
   Let's jet.
   Let's get out of here.

   Where are you going?
   Are you heading home?
   Want to get a bite to eat?

   I'm hungry.
   I could use a snack.
   Let's go eat.

6. Let's grab a bite.
   What do you like?
   What do you feel like eating?

   You choose.
   You decide.
   What do you recommend?

   How about McDonald's?
   It's fast and convenient.
   What do you think?

7. *I'll have* a Big Mac.
I'll have a small fries.
And a large Coke, please.

I'd like a milk shake.
Make it strawberry.
That'll be for here.

Can I have extra ketchup?
Can I have more napkins?
Thank you.

8. Mmmmm. Mmmmm.
This is delicious.
This tastes great!

I love it.
The flavor is awesome.
It's out of this world.

It's mouth-watering.
I can't get enough.
I could eat this all day.

9. *I'm* full.
I'm stuffed.
I can't eat another bite.

I ate too much.
I need a rest.
I need to take it easy.

I'll gain weight.
I'll get fat.
I need to walk it off.

10. *Let's* go for a walk.
Let's get some exercise.
A walk would do us good.

Walking is great.
Walking is healthy.
It's the best exercise there is.

Where shall we go?
Any place in mind?
I'll follow you anywhere.

11. *I'm* beat.
I'm bushed.
I'm exhausted.

I need to go home.
I need to get back.
I can't stay.

I have things to do.
I have to go.
Let's call it a day.

12. I'm *home*.
Home, sweet *home!*
There's no place like *home*

I had a great day.
Everything went right for me.
Today was really my day.

It's been a long day.
I did so much.
I learned a lot.

BOOK 2 買禮物去派對

▶2-1 邀請同學、朋友參加
生日宴會時，可以說：

I'm having a party.
It's Friday night.
I want you to come.

▶2-2 為了買生日禮物，要去購物中心買東西，需要問路：

Excuse me, sir.
I'm looking for a mall.
Is there a mall around here?

▶2-3 到了購物中心買筆：

I'm looking for a pen.
I want a ballpoint pen.
Do you have any good ones?

▶2-4 和店員討價還價：

Can you lower the price?
Can you make it cheaper?
That's way too high.

▶2-5 買了筆以後，就去參加生日宴會：

Happy birthday!
Congratulations!
You must be feeling great!

▶2-6 送禮物的時候說：

Here's a little something.
I got this for you.
I hope you like it.

▶2-7 收到禮物時說：

> Thank you so much.
> It's wonderful.
> It's what I always wanted.
> ⋮

▶2-8 收到禮物後，繼續再說感謝的話：

> What can I say?
> I'm speechless.
> You shouldn't have.
> ⋮

▶2-9 稱讚別人送的禮物：

> This is topnotch.
> This is superb.
> I'm very impressed.
> ⋮

▶2-10 收到禮物的人，可以繼續說：

> I'm so lucky!
> I'm really blessed!
> I'm the luckiest person
>   in the world.
> ⋮

▶2-11 宴會結束，問別人要不要搭便車：

> Do you need a ride?
> Can I give you a lift?
> How are you getting home?
> ⋮

▶2-12 感謝別人開車載你：

> Thanks for the ride.
> You are a good driver.
> I owe you one.
> ⋮

1. I'm having a party.

I'm having a party.	我要舉辦宴會。
It's Friday night.	時間是星期五晚上。
I want you to come.	我希望你能來。
You're invited.	我邀請你來。
Are you free?	你有空嗎？
Can you make it?	你能來嗎？
You gotta be there.	你一定要來。
You gotta show up.	你一定要出現。
It won't be the same without you.	沒有你就不一樣了。

** ———————————

have a party 舉辦宴會

invite〔ɪnˋvaɪt〕*v.* 邀請　　free〔fri〕*adj.* 有空的

make it 能來；成功；辦到

gotta〔ˋgɑtə〕【口語英語】必須（= *got to*）

show up 出現　　same〔sem〕*adj.* 相同的；一樣的

【背景說明】

　　外國人和中國人一樣，喜歡邀請朋友到家裡吃飯，背了這九句話以後，你就可以用英文邀請朋友到家裡來吃飯了。

1. *I'm having a party.*（我要舉辦一個宴會。）

   have a party 舉辦宴會（*= give a party = throw a party*）

   party 有很多種：a dinner party（晚宴）、a birthday party（生日宴會）、a tea party（茶會）、a welcome party（迎新會）、a farewell party（送別會）等。

   I'm having a party.

   I'm having a party.

   【這句話最常用，現在進行式可表不久的未來】

   = I'll have a party.

   = I'm going to have a party.

   = I'm planning a party.

   【比較】I'm having a dinner party.

   　　　（我要舉辦一個晚宴。）【純粹吃晚餐】

   I'm having a party.

   　　　（我要舉辦一個宴會。）

   　　　沒有特別指定，對於年輕人也許是舞會，對於成年人，也許是吃飯、喝酒等，因為平常常在一起，只要說 *I'm having a party.* 大致就知道是什麼樣的 party。

在字典上，「舉辦宴會」的說法有：have a party，
throw a party，give a party，hold a party，但是
只有公司、政府機關才用 hold a party。像：The
Lion's Club is holding a party.（獅子會將舉辦宴會。）

> ***I'm having a party.***【最常用】
> = I'm throwing a party.【常用】
> = I'm giving a party.【常用】
> = *I'm holding a party.*【誤，個人不說 hold
>   a party 之類的話】

2. *It's Friday night.*（時間是星期五晚上。）

如果要指明確定時間，就可以在 It's Friday
night. 後面，再加上一句話，說明時間是幾點鐘。

> ***It's Friday night.***
> It's six o'clock.
> = It's at six.
> = It's at six o'clock.
> = It starts at six.

【比較1】 It's Friday night at six.【較常用，和中國人
習慣一樣，日期在前面，時間在後面。】
It's at six o'clock, Friday night.
【較正式，非一般口語】

【比較2】 ***It's Friday night.***【通俗，美國人常說】
It's on Friday night.【通俗，美國人常說】
It's Friday evening.【較少使用】
It's on Friday evening.【文法對，美國人較少使用】
It's this Friday night.【強調是這個星期五晚上】

BOOK 2

3. ***I want you to come.*** (我希望你來。)

want〔wɑnt〕*v.* 想要；希望

> want 在此作「希望」解。這句話不背，中國人
> 永遠不會說。有些美國人也說：I want you to be
> there. (我希望你來。) 或 I want to invite you.
> (我想要邀請你。) 對於比較不熟的朋友，才說：
> I hope you can come. (我希望你能來。) 或 I
> hope you can be there. (我希望你能來。)

4. ***You're invited.***

invite〔ɪn'vaɪt〕*v.* 邀請

> 這句話中國人不會說，因為是被動語態，不合乎
> 中國人的說話習慣，但美國人常說，表示「我邀請你。」

【比較】 ***You're invited.***【常用】
　　　　 I invite you.【較少用】
　　　　 I invite you to come. (我邀請你來。)【常用】
　　　　 I'm inviting you.【常用】
　　　　 (我要邀請你。)【「現在進行式」在這裡表「未來」】

5. ***Are you free?***

free〔fri〕*adj.* 自由的；有空的

> 邀請別人時，先問別人有沒有空，就不會被直接
> 拒絕了。

Are you free? (你有空嗎？)【第一常用】
= Are you available?【第三常用】
= Do you have time?【第二常用】
【available〔ə'veləbḷ〕*adj.* 有空的】

也可以說：

> Are you busy?（你忙不忙？）【第一常用】
> = Are you doing anything?【第二常用】
> （你有沒有什麼事要做？）
> = Are you tied up?（你忙嗎？）【第三常用】
> 【*be tied up*　忙碌】

Are you free? 在這一回中，為什麼不用 *Will you be free?*

英文有十二種時態，表示「未來」，就應該用「未來式」。但是，*Are you free?* Are you busy? Are you available? 是例外，就像「來去動詞」一樣，可用現在式，代替未來式。

【詳見「文法寶典」p.327】

【比較1】 ***Are you free?***【可指現在或未來，一般語氣】
　　　　 Will you be free?【指未來，加強語氣】
　　　　 （你會有空嗎？）

【比較2】 Are you free tomorrow?
　　　　 （你明天有空嗎？）【一般語氣，常用】
　　　　 Will you be free tomorrow?
　　　　 （你明天會有空嗎？）【加強語氣，較少用】

很多人學了文法，英文反而說不好，因為對文法沒有徹底了解，文法就會成為學英文的絆腳石。要把文法徹底了解，可不簡單，最簡單的方法，就是把「一口氣背會話」背好，從「背景說明」中，了解文法。

BOOK 2

6. *Can you make it?*

　　make it 成功；辦到；做好；能來

　　　　make it 有很多用法，美國人天天説，不管大小事情，
　　只要辦到了，他們都説，如：

　　　　I think you can *make it*. (我想你會成功。)
　　　　You *made it*. (你成功了；你辦到了。)

　　　　當你和朋友過馬路，
　　號誌燈快要變紅燈了，你
　　們及時穿越，你就可以
　　説：We made it. (我們
　　過來了。) 和朋友坐火車、
　　坐汽車，到了目的地，你

We made it.

　　也可以説：We made it. (我們到了。) 所以，make it
　　有無限多的翻法，要看實際情況，或上下文而定。

7. *You gotta be there.* (你一定要去。)
　　gotta〔ˈɡɑtə〕必須 (= *got to* = *have got to*)

　　　　You gotta be there.【最常説，不適合寫】
　　　　= *You got to be there*.【劣，表強調，正常情況下，不説也不寫】
　　　　= You've got to be there.【適合説，適合寫】
　　　　= You have to be there.【適合説，適合寫】

8. *You gotta show up*. (你一定要出現。)
　　show up 出現 (= *appear*)

　　　　經過再三研究，還是把 You gotta be there. 及 *You
　　gotta show up*. 放在「一口氣背會話」中，因爲美國人太
　　常説了。

最新的 The American Heritage Dictionary
中，已經有這個字。你一定要説 gotta，説話才像
美國人。

　　美國人常説 *You gotta show up.* 但這句話他
們寫出來的卻是：You have to show up. 而不是
You got to show up.【劣】，因爲太強調 got 了，
正常情況下，美國人都不説。

9. *It won't be the same without you.*（沒有你就不一樣了。）
same〔sem〕*adj.* 相同的；一樣的

　　這句話也可以説成：It won't be a party
without you.（沒有你就不算是宴會了。）

10. 補充説明

　　這一回是萬用會話句型，如果你想要請朋友吃
晚餐，只要把第一句改一改，變成：

> *I want to invite you to dinner.*
> （我想要請你吃晚餐。）
> It's Friday night.
> I want you to come.
>
> You're invited.
> Are you free?
> Can you make it?
>
> You gotta be there.
> You gotta show up.
> It won't be the same without you.

BOOK 2

【對話練習】

1. A：**I'm having a party.**　　　　　A：我要舉辦宴會。

　 B：Great.　　　　　　　　　　　B：太棒了。
　　　 Wonderful.　　　　　　　　　　太棒了。
　　　 When is it?　　　　　　　　　　是什麼時候？
　　　【great〔gret〕adj. 很棒的】

2. A：**It's Friday night.**　　　　　　A：是星期五晚上。

　 B：That's perfect.　　　　　　　　B：太完美了。
　　　 Friday night is fine.　　　　　　星期五晚上很好。
　　　 What time?　　　　　　　　　　什麼時間？
　　　【perfect〔'pɝfɪkt〕adj. 完美的】

3. A：**I want you to come.**　　　　　A：我希望你能來。

　 B：I wouldn't miss it.　　　　　　B：我不會錯過的。
　　　 I'll be there.　　　　　　　　　我會去。
　　　 What time should I come?　　　我應該幾點到？
　　　【miss〔mɪs〕v. 錯過】

4. A：**You're invited.**　　　　　　　A：我邀請你來。

　 B：Oh, that's great.　　　　　　　B：哦，太棒了。
　　　 Is it OK if I bring a couple　　　我可以帶幾個朋友去
　　　 of friends?　　　　　　　　　　嗎？
　　　 I know they'll enjoy it, too.　　我知道他們也會玩
　　　【*a couple of* 幾個】　　　　　得很愉快。

5. A : **Are you free?**

   B : When?
       For what?
       What do you want to do?

6. A : **Can you make it?**

   B : Can I make it?
       You must be kidding.
       I wouldn't miss it for the
       world.
     【*for the world* 絕（不）；無論如何】

7. A : **You gotta be there.**

   B : I'm there.
       Don't worry about it.
       I will definitely make it.

8. A : **You gotta show up.**

   B : Count me in.
       I will show up.
       I guarantee it.
     【*count in* 將…算在內；使…參加
       guarantee〔͵gærən'ti〕*v.* 保證】

9. A : **It won't be a party without you.**

   B : Thanks.
       You flatter me.
       I'll be there for sure.
     【flatter〔'flætɚ〕*v.* 奉承；恭維】

A：你有空嗎？

B：什麼時候？
    有什麼事嗎？
    你想做什麼？

A：你能來嗎？

B：我能去嗎？
    你一定是在開玩笑。
    我絕不會錯過的。

A：你一定要來。

B：我會去。
    不用擔心。
    我一定會到的。

A：你一定要出現。

B：我會參加。
    我會出現。
    我保證。

A：沒有你就不算是宴會。

B：謝謝。
    你使我受寵若驚。
    我一定會去的。

BOOK 2

2. *I'm looking for a mall.*

Excuse me, sir.	先生，打擾一下。
I'm looking for a mall.	我正在找購物中心。
Is there a mall around here?	這附近有購物中心嗎？
I'm new here.	我對這裡不熟。
I don't have a clue.	我對這裡一無所知。
Can you tell me where it is?	你能告訴我在哪裡嗎？
Do you live here?	你住在這裡嗎？
Do you know this area?	你對這個地區熟嗎？
Any shopping center will do.	任何購物中心都可以。

** ——————————————

look for 尋找   mall〔mɔl〕*n.* 購物中心

around〔ə'raʊnd〕*prep.* 在…附近

new〔nju〕*adj.* 不熟悉…的   clue〔klu〕*n.* 線索

do not have a clue 一無所知   area〔'ɛrɪə〕*n.* 地區

shopping center 購物中心

do〔du〕*v.* 可以；行得通

【背景説明】

到了國外，問路是練習説英文的方法之一。
背熟了這九句，你就可以常常找人問路了。

1. *Excuse me, sir.* (先生，打擾一下。)

美國人的習慣是，當拜託別人的時候，都先説：
"*Excuse me, sir.*" 如果對方是女士，就要説：
"*Excuse me, ma'am.*" (小姐，打擾一下。)
【ma'am〔mæm〕*n.* 太太；小姐】

ma'am 是對女性的尊稱，不管是小姐或是太太，
都可以用。如果對小姐，就可以説：Excuse me, miss.
(小姐，打擾一下。)【不可寫成：*Excuse me, Miss.*】

Excuse me, sir. 也可説成：Pardon me, sir.
(先生，對不起。)【pardon〔'pɑrdn̩〕*v.* 原諒】

2. *I'm looking for a mall.* (我正在找購物中心。)
mall〔mɔl〕*n.* 購物中心 (= *shopping center*)

> 這句話中外文化不同，中國人問路時永遠不
> 會説：「我正在找～。」但是美國人卻常説："*I'm*
> *looking for～.*"
>
> 【比較】 *I'm looking for a mall.* 【最常用】
> = I'm trying to find a mall. 【較常用】
>   (我想找購物中心。)
> = I'm searching for a mall. 【常用】
>   (我在找購物中心。)
>
> 【*try to V.* 試著～；想要～ *search for* 尋找】

3. *Is there a mall around here?* (這附近有購物中心嗎？)

around〔ə'raʊnd〕*prep.* 在…附近

這句話也可說成：Is there a mall nearby?
(這附近有購物中心嗎？) 美國人也常說：Does
this area have a mall? (這個地區有購物中心嗎？)

【nearby〔'nɪr'baɪ〕*adv.* 在附近】

4. *I'm new here.* (我對這裡不熟。)

new〔nju〕*adj.* 不熟悉的

這句話美國人也常說成：I'm new around here.
(我對這附近不熟。) 也有美國人說：I'm not
familiar with this area. (我對這個地區不熟。)

【familiar〔fə'mɪljɚ〕*adj.* 熟悉的】

5. *I don't have a clue.*

clue〔klu〕*n.* 線索   *do not have a clue* 一無所知

這句話字面的意思是「我連一個線索都沒有。」
引申為「我一無所知。」等於 I have no idea at all.
(我一點都不知道。)【*not…at all* 一點也不】

6. *Can you tell me where it is?* (你能告訴我在哪裡嗎？)

這句話美國人也常說成：Can you tell me
where? (你能告訴我在哪裡嗎？) 或 Where is the
mall? (購物中心在哪裡？) 或 Do you know where
there's a mall? (你知道哪裡有購物中心嗎？)

BOOK 2

7. *Do you live here?*

美國人問路的時候，常會問對方是否是當地人。

> ***Do you live here?*** (你住在這裡嗎？)【第二常用】
>
> = Are you a local? (你是不是本地人？)【第三常用】
>
> = Are you a resident? 【第四常用】
>
> (你是不是本地居民？)
>
> = Are you from here? 【第一常用】
>
> (你是不是這裡的人？)

local (ˈlokl̩) *n.* 本地人
resident (ˈrɛzədənt) *n.* 居民 (在此是指 local resident「本地居民」)

你英文說得很好，美國人會問你：Where are you from? (你是哪裡人？)

你可以回答：

> I live here. (我住這裡。)【最常用】
> I'm a local. (我是本地人。)【常用】
> I'm a resident. (我是本地居民。)【年輕人較少用】
> I'm from here. (我是這裡的人。)【最常用】

8. *Do you know this area?* (你對這個地區熟嗎？)
area (ˈɛrɪə) *n.* 地區

> 這句話也可以說成：Are you familiar with
> this area? (你對這個地區熟嗎？)
> 【*be familiar with*　對～熟悉】
>
> 可加強語氣說成：Do you know this area
> very well? (你是不是對這個地區很熟悉？)

9. ***Any shopping center will do.*** (任何購物中心都可以。)

shopping center 購物中心　　do〔du〕*v.* 可以；行

　　在這裡，do 是完全不及物動詞，表示「可以；行」。這句話也可以說成：Any shopping center is OK. (任何購物中心都可以。)

10. 介紹美國的 *mall*

　　中國人有夜市 (night market) 和百貨公司 (department store)。美國有購物中心 (mall)，在美國人的生活中，mall 佔有極重要的地位，與他們的生活息息相關。

　　除了買東西以外，他們還可以在那裡吃飯 (eat)、看電影 (go see a movie)、檢查眼睛 (see the eye doctor)、看牙齒 (see the dentist)。

　　在 mall 裡面，還有律師事務所 (law services)、稅務服務 (tax services)、商務中心 (business center) 等，甚至還有遊樂場 (amusement park)。

　　美國最大的購物中心是在明尼蘇達州的 The Mall of America (美國購物中心)，有五層樓高，大得不得了，你一天都逛不完。

圖片中的 The Mall 是專有名詞，這是台北市的「遠企購物中心」的英文名字，所以這兩個字的字首都大寫。

【對話練習】

1. A：**Excuse me, sir.**

   B：Yes, what can I do for you?
   How can I help?
   How may I be of service?

   A：先生，打擾一下。

   B：嗯，我能為你做什麼？
   需要我怎麼幫忙？
   有什麼能替你效勞的？

2. A：**I'm looking for a mall.**

   B：Oh, you want to find a mall?
   Let me see.
   I'm sorry. I can't help you.

   A：我正在找購物中心。

   B：哦，你想找購物中心嗎？
   我想想看。
   很抱歉，我幫不了你。

3. A：**Is there a mall around here?**

   B：Yes, there is.
   I know of a mall.
   It's about a mile from here.
   【*know of* 聽說 (= *hear of*)】

   A：這附近有購物中心嗎？

   B：是的，有。
   我聽說有一家購物中心。
   離這裡大約一英哩。

4. A：**I'm new here.**

   B：I could tell.
   You looked lost.
   You looked like you needed
   some help.
   【tell〔tɛl〕*v.* 知道；看出
   lost〔lɔst〕*adj.* 困惑的】

   A：我對這裡不熟。

   B：我看得出來。
   你顯得很困惑。
   你看起來像需要一些幫
   助。

5. A : **I don't have a clue.**

   B : Don't worry.
       I'll set you straight.
       I'll point you in the right
       direction.

       【*set sb. straight* 糾正某人的錯誤
          point〔pɔɪnt〕*v.* 指給（某人）】

A：我對這裡一無所知。

B：別擔心。
    我會糾正你的錯誤。
    我會替你指出正確的方向。

6. A : **Can you tell me where it is?**

   B : Sure. I can tell you.
       There is a mall about a
       minute from here.
       It's called The Mall of
       America.

A：你能告訴我它在哪裡嗎？

B：當然。我可以告訴你。
    離這裡大約一分鐘的路
    程，有個購物中心。
    它叫「美國購物中心」。

7. A : **Do you live here?**

   B : Yes, I do.
       I'm a local.
       I've lived here all my life.

A：你住在這裡嗎？

B：是的，我住這裡。
    我是本地人。
    我從小就住這裡。

8. A : **Do you know this area?**

   B : Yes, I know it pretty well.
       I'm familiar with this area.
       What do you want to know?

A：你對這個地區熟嗎？

B：是的，我對這個地區很熟。
    我很熟悉這個地區。
    你想知道些什麼？

9. A : **Any shopping center will do.**

   B : Like I said, you have a choice.
       I doubt you'll need to check
       out the other one.
       The one up the street has just
       about everything.

A：任何購物中心都可以。

B：就像我所說的，你可以選擇。
    不過我懷疑你還需要去另
    一家看看。
    街道那頭的那一家幾乎什麼
    都有。

3. I'm looking for a pen.

I'm looking for a pen.	我在找一支筆。
I want a ballpoint pen.	我要買一支原子筆。
Do you have any good ones?	你們有沒有什麼好的？
What's on sale?	有什麼特價品？
What's your best buy?	買什麼最划算？
Do you have any specials?	你們有沒有什麼特價品？
I like this!	我喜歡這個！
I'll take it!	我要買這個！
How much is it?	這個多少錢？

BOOK 2

** ——————————————

look for 尋找

ballpoint pen〔'bɔl͵pɔɪnt'pɛn〕*n.* 原子筆

on sale 特價　　*the best buy* 最划算的貨品

special〔'spɛʃəl〕*n.* 特價品

like〔laɪk〕*v.* 喜歡；想要　　take〔tek〕*v.* 拿；買

【背景説明】

這九句是要買東西時説的話。背了以後，
你去買東西的時候，就可以用英文説了。

1. *I'm looking for a pen.*

中國人去買東西，都直接説：「我要買…。」美
國人習慣先説：*I'm looking for ~*，作爲開場白。

I'm looking for a pen. 的意思是「我在找一支
筆。」這句話和中國人説話的習慣不同，我們一定
要背下來才會使用。

一般説來，當美國人説 I'm looking for a *pen*.
意思就是「我要買一支**原子筆**。」美國人説 pen，就
是指「原子筆」，中國人説「筆」，是指原子筆、鋼
筆或鉛筆等。美國人從前説 pen，是指 fountain
pen（鋼筆），現在説 pen，就是指 ballpoint pen
（原子筆），因爲鋼筆已經不流行，而鉛筆的英文
叫 pencil。

I'm looking for ~. 是美國人的口頭禪，凡
是他們想買東西，或問路時，都習慣先説：*I'm
looking for ~*，像他們去找加油站的時候，都
會説：*I'm looking for* a gas station.（我要找
加油站。）【*gas station* 加油站】

BOOK 2

2. *I want a ballpoint pen.*

ballpoint pen〔ˈbɔlˌpɔɪntˈpɛn〕*n.* 原子筆

　(= *ball-point pen*)

　　幾乎在所有的字典上，ballpoint pen 等於 *ball pen* 和 *ball-point*，但是美國人都不用，美國人說「原子筆」，一定說 pen 或 ballpoint pen。

　　在中國人說話的習慣中，要買一支原子筆，會說:「我要買一支原子筆。」美國人卻有不同的說法。

　中文: 我要買一支原子筆。

　英文: *I want a ballpoint pen.*【第二常用】

　　　　I want a pen.【第一常用】

　　　　I'd like a ballpoint pen.【第三常用】

　　　　I want to buy a ballpoint pen.【第四常用】

　　　　I'd like to buy a ballpoint pen.【第五常用】

　　　　【*I'd like*　我想要 (= *I want*)】

　　爲什麼 *I want a pen.* 最常用？因爲美國人的語言習慣，能簡化就簡化。

3. *Do you have any good ones?*

　　去買東西的會話公式是:

　　　　I'm looking for a pen. (我在找一支筆。)

　　　　I want a ballpoint pen. (我要買一支原子筆。)

　　　　Do you have any good ones?

　　　　(你們有沒有什麼好的？)

　　美國人買東西的習慣是，大多先說: *I'm looking for~.* 再說: *I want~.* 我們要背下來，說話才像美國人。

【例1】 *I'm looking for* a watch.

（我在找一隻錶；我想買一隻錶。）

I want a Rolex watch.

（我要買一隻勞力士的錶。）

Do you have any?（你們有沒有賣？）

【Rolex〔ˈrolɛks〕*n.* 勞力士】

【例2】 *I'm looking for* a shirt.

（我在找一件襯衫；我想買一件襯衫。）

I want a sports shirt.

（我要買一件運動衫。）【不可用 *sport shirt*】

Do you have any good ones?（你們有沒有好的？）

【sports〔sports〕*adj.* 運動的】

【例3】 *I'm looking for* sneakers.

（我在找運動鞋；我想買運動鞋。）

I want a pair of Nikes.

（我要買一雙耐吉運動鞋。）

Show me your newest style.

（把你們最新款式拿給我看看。）

sneakers〔ˈsnikɚz〕*n. pl.* 運動鞋　　*a pair of* 一雙
Nikes〔ˈnaɪkiz〕*n. pl.* 耐吉運動鞋　　show〔ʃo〕*v.* 給～看

這個會話公式背熟後，可以視情況改變，問別人有
沒有賣，就可以說："*Do you have any?*" 請店員把東
西拿給你看，就可以說："*Show me what you have.*"

---

4. *What's on sale?*（有什麼特價品？）

on sale 特價；拍賣

What's on sale? 也可說成：Anything on sale?
（有什麼特價品嗎？）on sale（特價）不要和 for sale
（出售）搞混。

【比較】 The books are **on sale**. (這些書特價出售。)
　　　　 The books are **for sale**. (這些書是要賣的。)

　　很奇怪,美國人的大東西,如房子、汽車、船等,
絕不會說 on sale。

【中文】 這棟房子廉價出售。
【英文】 *This house is on sale.* 【誤】
　　　　 This house is for sale at a reduced
　　　　 price. 【正】【reduced〔rɪ'dʒust〕*adj.* 減少的】

　　美國人習慣在聖誕節送禮物,從 11 月份開始,
百貨公司就開始促銷聖誕禮物,12 月 26 日開始,百
貨公司所有的商品,都開
始拋售,有的折扣甚至高
達 2.5 折 (75% off),在
百貨公司的櫥窗上會寫著:
"ON SALE" 或 "SALE"。

5. *What's your best buy?*
　　buy〔baɪ〕*n.* 買到的東西;便宜貨 (= *bargain*)
　　the best buy 　最划算的貨品 (= *the best deal*)

　　　　有些字典上把 the best buy 翻成「最便宜的貨
　　品」是錯誤的。the best buy 通常是高價的貨品,
　　打了最大的折扣 (the biggest discount)。*What's*
　　your best buy? 的字面意思是「什麼是你們折扣最多
　　的東西?」也就是「跟你們買什麼最划算?」也可說
　　成:What's the best buy? (買什麼最划算?) 或加
　　強語氣說成:What's the best thing I can buy for
　　a good price? (我買什麼東西價錢最划算?)

　　　　有時候在機場的免稅店，剛推出的名牌的商品，
會打折促銷。有一次，編者到機場，問 "What's the
best buy?" 就以五折的價
錢，買到最新款的 Gucci
的皮包。【Gucci〔'gutʃɪ〕*n.*
古奇】所以，以後不管到
哪裡買東西，都要先問：

Any new arrivals?（有沒有新貨？）
What's your best buy?（跟你們買什麼東西最划算？）
Any good deals?（有沒有便宜的東西？）
【arrivals〔ə'raɪvl̩z〕*n. pl.*（新）到貨　　deal〔dil〕*n.* 交易】

這三句話，將讓你買到又便宜、又好的東西。

6. ***Do you have any specials?***（你們有沒有什麼特價品？）
special〔'spɛʃəl〕*n.* 特價品

　　　　這句話可以簡化為：Any specials?（有特價品嗎？）
下面是美國人常説的話，我們按照使用頻率排列：

① ***Do you have any specials?***【第一常用】
② Do you have any bargains?【第二常用】
　　（你們有沒有什麼便宜的東西？）
③ Do you have any discounts?【第三常用】
　　（你們有沒有什麼折扣？）

④ Any specials?（有什麼特價品嗎？）
⑤ Any bargains?（有便宜的東西嗎？）
⑥ Any discounts?（有折扣嗎？）
【bargain〔'bɑrgɪn〕*n.* 便宜貨　　discount〔'dɪskaʊnt〕*n.* 折扣】

7. *I like this!*

like〔laɪk〕*v.* 喜歡；想要

　　like 的主要意思是「喜歡」，這句話字面的意思是「我喜歡這個！」可引申爲「我想要這個！」美國人買東西的時候，說 "*I like this!*" 意思就是「我想要這個！」等於 I want this!

8. *I'll take it!* (我要買這個！)

take〔tek〕*v.* 拿；買

　　take 的主要意思是「拿」，在此作「買」解，這句話美國人也常説成：I'm going to buy it! (我要買這個！) 或 I want to buy it! (我想要買這個！) 或 I want it! (我要買這個！)

9. *How much is it?* (多少錢？)

　　買東西問多少錢的説法很多，比較下列説法：

　　How much? (多少錢？)【第四常用】

= How much for this? (這個多少錢？)【第二常用】

= *How much is it?*【第一常用】【it 可用 this 代替】

= How much does it cost? (這個多少錢？)【第三常用】
　【it 可用 this 代替】

= What's the cost? (價錢是多少？)【第五常用】

= What's the price? (價錢是多少？)【第六常用】

= What does it sell for?【第九常用】【it 可用 this 代替】
　(這個要賣多少錢？)

= What's the price on this? (這個的價格是多少？)【第七常用】

= Please tell me the price. (請告訴我價錢。)【第八常用】

BOOK 2

【對話練習】

1. A：**I'm looking for a pen.**
   B：**We have so many kinds.**
   Are you looking for
   something special?
   Have anything in mind?

   A：我要找一支筆。
   B：我們有很多種。
   你要找什麼特別的筆嗎？
   你有想買哪一種嗎？

2. A：**I want a ballpoint pen.**
   B：**Here is what we have.**
   What brand do you like?
   What color are you looking
   for? 【brand〔 brænd 〕*n.* 牌子】

   A：我想買一支原子筆。
   B：我們有這些。
   你喜歡哪種品牌？
   你要找什麼顏色的？

3. A：**Do you have any good ones?**
   B：**Sure.**
   We have many nice pens.
   Take a look at these.
   【*take a look at* 看一看】

   A：你們有沒有什麼好的？
   B：當然有。
   我們有很多很好的筆。
   你看看這些筆。

4. A：**What's on sale?**
   B：**We have some really good**
   deals.
   What's your price range?
   How much do you want to
   spend? 【range〔 rendʒ 〕*n.* 範圍】

   A：有什麼特價品？
   B：我們有些超值商品。

   你的預算是多少？
   你打算花多少錢買？

5. A： **What's your best buy?**

   B： We have many good deals.
   Everything here is discounted.
   These things are all on sale.
   【discount〔dɪs'kaʊnt〕*v.* 打折】

A： 跟你們買什麼最划算？

B： 我們有很多划算的東西。
   這裡每樣東西都有打折。
   這些東西都有特價。

6. A： **Do you have any specials?**

   B： Sure.
   We have specials.
   Our prices can't be beat.
   【beat〔bit〕*v.* 打敗；勝過】

A： 你們有沒有什麼特價品？

B： 當然有。
   我們有特價品。
   我們的價錢是最低的。

7. A： **I like this!**

   B： That's a good choice.
   That's a popular brand.
   We sell a lot of those.

A： 我喜歡這個！

B： 你選得不錯。
   這個品牌很受歡迎。
   我們賣了很多。

8. A： **I'll take it!**

   B： Is it a gift?
   Do you want me to wrap it?
   Will that be cash or credit
   card?【wrap〔ræp〕*v.* 包裝
   cash〔kæʃ〕*n.* 現金】

A： 我要買這個！

B： 這是禮物嗎？
   需要我幫你包裝嗎？
   付現或刷卡？

9. A： **How much is it?**

   B： It's only a hundred dollars.
   How are you going to pay?
   Cash or credit card?
   【*credit card* 信用卡】

A： 這個多少錢？

B： 只要一百元。
   你要怎麼付錢？
   是付現還是刷卡？

4. Can you lower the price?

Can you lower the price?	你能不能降低價格？
Can you make it cheaper?	你能不能便宜一點？
That's way too high.	那個價格眞的是太高了。
That's too expensive.	太貴了。
I can't afford it.	我買不起。
Please help me out.	請你幫幫我的忙。
How about a deal?	要不要給我一個好的價錢？
How about 20% off?	打個八折如何？
I'd really appreciate it.	我會非常感激。

BOOK 2

** ———————————————

lower〔'loʊ〕v. 降低　　price〔praɪs〕n. 價格
cheaper〔'tʃipʊ〕adj. 較便宜的
way〔we〕adv. 非常　　afford〔ə'fɔrd〕v. 負擔得起
help sb. out 幫助某人擺脫困難；幫助某人解決問題；
　　幫某人的忙
deal〔dil〕n. 交易　　*20% off* 打八折
really〔'rɪəlɪ〕adv. 非常；十分
appreciate〔ə'priʃɪ,et〕v. 感激

【背景說明】

　　不管在美國，或全世界任何地方買東西，都要學會還價。買東西要勇敢地還價，還要有回頭的勇氣，才不會吃虧。

1. ***Can you lower the price?*** （你能不能降低價格？）
lower〔'loɚ〕*v.* 降低
price〔praɪs〕*n.* 價格

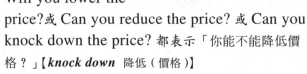

Can you lower the price?

　　lower 當形容詞時，是指「比較低的」，在這裡當動詞，作「降低」解。

　　這句話也可以說成：Will you lower the price? 或 Can you reduce the price? 或 Can you knock down the price? 都表示「你能不能降低價格？」【*knock down* 降低（價格）】

　　Can you lower the price? 也可簡化成：Please lower the price. （請降低價格。）或直接說：Lower the price. （降低價格。）

2. ***Can you make it cheaper?*** （你能不能便宜一點？）
cheaper〔'tʃipɚ〕*adj.* 較便宜的

　　這句話的句意是「你能不能使它變便宜一點？」，引申為「你能不能便宜一點？」也可以說成：Make it cheaper. （便宜一點。）可加強語氣說成：Can you make this price a little lower for me? （你能不能幫我把價錢降低一點？）

BOOK 2

3. **That's way too high.**（那個價格真的是太高了。）
   way〔we〕*adv.* 非常

> way 一般作「方法」解，在此是副詞，表「非常」。這句話也可說成：That's *way* too high for me.（那個價格對我而言太高了。）或只說：That's too high.（價格太高了。）也可加強語氣說：That's *way*, *way* too high.（那個價格真的是太高了。）（= *That's very, very expensive.*）

美國人很喜歡用 way 來加強語氣。

【例1】 A: Let's walk to the train station.
            （我們走到火車站吧。）
         B: That's *way* too far.（那太遠了。）

【例2】 A: Let's rent a limo.
            （我們租一部豪華轎車吧。）
         B: That's *way* too expensive.（太貴了。）
         【limo〔'lɪmo〕*n.* 豪華轎車（= limousine〔,lɪmə'zin〕）】

That's way too high. 中的 That 是指 The price。

【例】 The price is very high.（價格很高。）
       The price is very low.（價格很低。）

美國人和中國人一樣，價格用高（high）、低（low）來形容。

4. **That's too expensive.**（太貴了。）

> 本句中的 That 是指所要買的東西，而不是指價格，有些中國人說價格很貴，或很便宜，但美國人卻不這麼說，英文中的 price（價格），不能和 expensive 或 cheap 連用。

【比較1】 *The price is not so expensive.* 【誤】
　　　　The price is not so high. 【正】
　　　　（價格不是很高。）

【比較2】 *The price of this ring is very expensive.* 【誤】
　　　　The price of this ring is very high. 【正】
　　　　（這枚戒指的價格很高。）
　　　　This ring is very expensive.
　　　　（這枚戒指很貴。）【正】

5. *I can't afford it.*

afford〔ə'fɔrd〕*v.* 負擔得起

　　　凡是你買不起，或能力不足以做什麼事，就可
以說：*I can't afford it.* 意思是「我負擔不起。」
或加長為：I can't afford to buy it.（我買不起。）

【例1】 A: Let's go have a steak.（我們去吃牛排吧。）
　　　　B: *I can't afford it.*（我吃不起。）
　　　　【steak〔stek〕*n.* 牛排；have a steak 也可說
　　　　成 have steak。】

【例2】 A: Let's take a taxi to the mall.
　　　　　（我們坐計程車去購物中心。）
　　　　B: *I can't afford it.* Let's take a bus.
　　　　　（我負擔不起。我們坐公車吧。）
　　　　【mall〔mɔl〕*n.* 購物中心】

【例3】 A: Let's go to the park today.
　　　　　（我們今天去公園吧。）
　　　　B: Oh, *I can't afford it.* I'm too busy.
　　　　　（哦，我抽不出時間。我太忙了。）

BOOK 2

6. ***Please help me out.***

help sb. out 幫助某人擺脫困難；幫助某人解決問題；
　　　　　　幫某人的忙

> 很多人弄不清楚 help *sb.* out 和 help *sb.* 的區
> 別。help *sb.* out 字典上的解釋是「幫助某人擺脫困
> 難」，其實應該翻成「幫某人的忙」，或「協助某人」。
> help *sb.* out 比 help *sb.* 語氣較緩和。

【比較1】 Please help me. (請幫助我；請救救我。)
　　　　Please ***help me out***. (請你幫幫我的忙。)

再看下面 help *sb.* out 的例子：

【例1】 A: I'm short of cash. Please ***help me out***.
　　　　　(我缺乏現金。請幫幫我的忙。)
　　　　B: OK. How much do you need?
　　　　　(好。你需要多少？)
　　　　【***be short of*** 缺乏　　cash〔kæʃ〕*n.* 現金】

【例2】 A: I have a big test tomorrow. Please ***help
　　　　　me out***. (我明天有重要的考試。請幫幫我的忙。)
　　　　B: Sure. What can I do for you?
　　　　　(好。我能爲你做什麼？)【big〔bɪg〕*adj.* 重要的】

【例3】 A: I need a ride. Please ***help me out***.
　　　　　(我需要搭便車。請幫幫我的忙。)
　　　　B: No problem. (沒問題。)【ride〔raɪd〕*n.* 搭乘】

　　　　如果説：I need a ride. Please help me. 這裡
　　　的 Please help me. 就表示很緊急，可翻成「我需
　　　要搭便車。拜託你救救我。」

只要記住：**小事情用 *help out*，大事情用 *help*。**

7. *How about a deal?*

deal〔dil〕*n.* 交易

　　deal 的主要意思是「交易」，在這裡是指 good deal「好的交易」。這句話的字面意思是「一個好的交易如何？」引申為「要不要給我一個好的價錢？」(= *Can you give me a good price?*)

美國人說話喜歡省略，常說 a deal，代替 a good deal。

【比較1】　***How about a deal?*** 【通俗，美國人常說】
　　　　　How about a good deal? 【正，但美國人少說】

【比較2】　Can you give me a deal? 【通俗，美國人常說】
　　　　　（你能不能給我一個好價錢？）
　　　　　Can you give me a good deal?
　　　　　【正，美國人較少說】

8. *How about 20% off?*

　　這句話是 How do you feel about 20% off? 的省略。20% off 意思是「去掉 20%」，就是「打八折」，等於 a 20% discount。

<u>dis¦count</u>〔'dɪskaʊnt〕*n.* 折扣
不　　算

從字根上可以知道，20% discount，或 20% off，都表示「不算 20%」，即「折扣 20%」，也就是中國人所說的「打八折」。

How about 20% off? (打個八折如何？) 【第一常用】

= How about a 20% discount? 【第三常用】

= Can you give me 20% off? 【第二常用】

= Can you give me a 20% discount? 【第四常用】

BOOK 2

9. ***I'd really appreciate it.***

really〔'rɪəlɪ〕*adv.* 非常；十分
appreciate〔ə'priʃɪ,et〕*v.* 感激

【比較】 I really appreciate it. (我非常感激。)
I'd really appreciate it. (我會非常感激。)

I'd really appreciate it. 是省略了 if 子句，
在心中沒有說出來。源自：*If you helped me out*,
I would really appreciate it.

凡是拜託別人做事情，才能說：***I'd really
appreciate it.*** (我會非常感激。) 事後感激別人，
就只說：I really appreciate it. (我非常感激。)

比較下面兩組句子，你就清楚了：

I can't do it alone. (我沒辦法獨力做這件事。)
I need your help. (我需要你的幫忙。)
I'd really appreciate it. 【事前說】
 (我**會**非常感激。)【alone〔ə'lon〕*adv.* 獨自地】

Thanks for the favor. (謝謝你的幫忙。)
You're a big help. (你幫了很多忙。)
I really appreciate it.
 (我非常感激。)【事後說】
 【favor〔'fevɚ〕*n.* 好意；恩惠　help〔hɛlp〕*n.* 幫忙】

I'd really appreciate it. 可加長為：I'd really
appreciate it if you could help. (如果你能幫助我，
我會非常感激。)

【對話練習】

1. A：**Can you lower the price?**
　　B：I'm sorry, I can't.
　　　Our prices are fixed.
　　　That's our store policy.
　　　【fixed〔fɪkst〕*adj.* 固定的
　　　　policy〔'pɑləsɪ〕*n.* 政策】

　　A：你能不能降低價格？
　　B：很抱歉，沒辦法。
　　　我們的價格是固定的。
　　　這是我們商店的政策。

2. A：**Can you make it cheaper?**
　　B：Ah, let me see.
　　　I think we can.
　　　Let me ask my manager.
　　　【manager〔'mænɪdʒɚ〕*n.* 經理】

　　A：你能不能便宜一點？
　　B：啊，讓我想一想。
　　　我想應該可以。
　　　讓我問一下經理。

3. A：**That's way too high**.
　　B：I'm sorry you think so.
　　　That's the regular price.
　　　It's the cheapest price
　　　around.【*regular price* 定價
　　　around〔ə'raʊnd〕*adv.* 到處】

　　A：那個價格真的是太高了。
　　B：你認為如此，我覺得很遺憾。
　　　這是定價。
　　　這是最便宜的價錢了。

4. A：**That's too expensive**.
　　B：I'll lower the price just
　　　for you.
　　　I can give you a deal.
　　　I can take five dollars off.

　　A：太貴了。
　　B：我只為你降價。

　　　我可以給你一個好價錢。
　　　我可以少算五元。

5. A: **I can't afford it.**
   B: Maybe I can help.
   Let me see what I can do.
   I think we can lower the price.

A：我買不起。
B：我也許幫得上忙。
我想想看我能做些什麼。
我想我們可以降低價格。

6. A: **Please help me out.**
   B: I'd love to but the boss is out right now.
   I'm not really authorized to give a discount.
   However, if you pay cash, perhaps I can do something.
   【authorized (ˈɔθəˌraɪzd) *adj.* 經授權的】

A：請你幫幫我的忙。
B：我很樂意，不過老闆目前不在。
我沒有權力給你折扣。

不過如果你付現，也許我可以做些什麼。

7. A: **How about a deal?**
   B: That's difficult.
   That's not easy.
   I have to get permission.

A：要不要給我一個好的價錢？
B：那很難。
那不容易。
我必須得到許可。

8. A: **How about 20% off?**
   B: I can give you 10% off.
   That is the lowest I can go.
   That's the final price.
   【*final price* 最後底價】

A：打個八折如何？
B：我可以打你九折。
這是我所能給的最低價錢。
這是最後底價。

9. A: **I'd really appreciate it.**
   B: I know you would.
   I'll try my best.
   Let me see what I can do.
   【*try one's best* 盡力】

A：我會非常感激。
B：我知道你會。
我會盡力。
讓我看看我能做什麼。

BOOK 2

5. Happy birthday!

Happy birthday!	生日快樂！
Congratulations!	恭喜！恭喜！
You must be feeling great!	你一定覺得很棒！
It's a big day.	今天是你的大日子。
It's your special day.	今天是你特別的日子。
We should celebrate.	我們應該慶祝一下。
Enjoy yourself.	希望你玩得愉快。
Have a super day.	祝你有美好的一天。
I wish you all the best.	祝你萬事如意。

BOOK 2

** ——————————————————————

congratulations〔kənˌgrætʃəˈleʃənz〕*n. pl.* 恭喜
great〔gret〕*adj.* 很棒的   big〔bɪg〕*adj.* 重要的
special〔ˈspɛʃəl〕*adj.* 特別的
celebrate〔ˈsɛləˌbret〕*v.* 慶祝
enjoy oneself 玩得愉快   super〔ˈsupɚ〕*adj.* 極佳的
wish〔wɪʃ〕*v.* 祝（某人…）   *all the best* 萬事如意

【背景説明】

美國人和中國人一樣，過生日要祝福別人生日快樂，一般人只會說：Happy birthday! 而你會連續說九句，別人會認為你既會說英文，又熱情。

這一回的「一口氣背會話」，是一組萬用祝福句，***Happy birthday!*** 只是一個代表。

如果碰到朋友有任何喜事，你可以先說 Congratulations! 再加上 How do you feel?

> Congratulations!
> How do you feel?
> You must be feeling great.
> ⋮

碰到朋友結婚時，只要稍做修改，你可以說：

Congratulations!
What a beautiful wedding!
（多美好的婚禮啊！）
You must be feeling great!

It's a big day.
It's your special day.
May you always be so happy. （祝你們永遠幸福。）

Enjoy yourselves.
Have a super day.
I wish you all the best.
【wedding〔'wɛdɪŋ〕*n.* 婚禮】

1. *Happy birthday!*（生日快樂！）

　　這句話是美國人祝福別人生日時，最常說的話，源自：I wish you a happy birthday!（我祝你生日快樂！）*Happy birthday!* 雖然沒有動詞，但因為已經表達完整思想，就算是一個句子。這句話已經變成一個句型：

> *Happy birthday!*（生日快樂！）
> Happy New Year!（新年快樂！）
> Merry Christmas!（聖誕快樂！）
> 【merry〔ˈmɛrɪ〕*adj.* 快樂的；這是固定用法，不可說成 *Happy Christmas!*（誤）】

　　Happy birthday! 也可加強語氣說成：Happy birthday to you!（祝你生日快樂！），這句話來自生日快樂歌。

2. *Congratulations!*（恭喜！恭喜！）
congratulations〔kənˌɡrætʃəˈleʃənz〕*n. pl.* 恭喜

　　congratulation 這個字主要意思是「祝賀」，當「恭喜」解時，要用複數形，寫成 *Congratulations.* 或 *Congratulations!*，用句點或驚嘆號都可以。這一個字，就是一個完整的句子。

　　美國人和中國人一樣，碰到好事情，像結婚、生日、升官等，都會說 *Congratulations!* 中國人習慣說「恭喜！恭喜！」兩句話，美國人只說 "*Congratulations!*" 一個字。

3. ***You must be feeling great!***（你一定覺得很棒！）

great〔gret〕*adj.* 很棒的

　　這句話用現在進行式，表示加強語氣。現在進行式的用法，除了表示「現在正在～」，還有其他用法。現在進行式在會話中很常使用，強調**現在的感情和情緒**，如「同情」、「責備」、「讚賞」等。(詳見「文法寶典」p.342)

【比較 1】 Do you feel better?【一般語氣】
　　　　　（你感覺好點了嗎？）
　　　　　Are you feeling better?
　　　　　（你有沒有覺得好一點呢？）
　　　　　【加強語氣，充滿感情，表示同情】

【比較 2】 Why don't you study?【一般語氣】
　　　　　（你為什麼不讀書？）
　　　　　Why aren't you studying?【加強語氣，表責備】
　　　　　（你為什麼沒有在讀書？）

【比較 3】 You do a good job.【一般語氣】
　　　　　（你表現得很好。）
　　　　　You are doing a good job!
　　　　　（你表現得真好！）
　　　　　【加強語氣，充滿感情，表稱讚】

【比較 4】 You must feel great.
　　　　　（你一定覺得很棒。）
　　　　　【一般語氣】
　　　　　You must be feeling great!
　　　　　（你一定覺得很棒！）
　　　　　【加強語氣】

You must be feeling great!

4. *It's a big day.* (今天是你的大日子。)

　　big〔 bɪg 〕*adj.* 大的；重要的

　　　　it 可以代表時間或日期。(詳見「文法寶典」p.111)

　　　　【例】 A: What day is *it*? (今天星期幾？)
　　　　　　　　B: *It* is Sunday. (今天是星期天。)
　　　　　　　　　　(= *Today is Sunday.*)

> 　　*big day* 和中文的「大日子」一樣，但美國人比中國人更常使用，凡是重要的日子，美國人都稱做 *big day*，像生日、結婚當天、畢業日、面談日、入學考試當天，都可算是 big day。看到一對年輕人要結婚了，就可以問：*When is your big day?* (你們什麼時候結婚？)(= *When is your wedding day?*) When is your big day? 必須看上下文或當時情況而定，有很多意思。

5. *Enjoy yourself.*

　　enjoy oneself　玩得愉快

　　　　　　這句話源自：I hope you enjoy yourself. 字面的意思是「希望你享受你自己。」引申爲「好好玩吧。」或「希望你玩得愉快。」等於 Have fun. (玩得愉快。) 或 Have a good time. (玩得愉快。)

6. *Have a super day.* (祝你有美好的一天。)

　　super〔'supɚ 〕*adj.* 極佳的 (= *excellent* ; *fantastic* ; *wonderful*)

　　　　　　這句話源自：I hope you have a super day. (我希望你有美好的一天。) 這類的說法很多，可用來祝福別人，也可用在和人道別時說。

BOOK 2

下面都是美國人常說的話：

> ***Have a super day***. (祝你有美好的一天。)【第二常用】
> = Have a great day. 【第一常用】
>   【great 可用 good 代替，兩者最常用】
> = Have a wonderful day. 【第三常用】

> = Have a happy day. 【第六常用】
> = Have a terrific day. 【第四常用】
> = Have an awesome day. 【第五常用】

【terrific〔tə'rɪfɪk〕*adj.* 很棒的　awesome〔'ɔsəm〕*adj.* 很棒的】

7. ***I wish you all the best***. (祝你萬事如意。)
　　 間接受詞　　直接受詞

all the best　萬事如意

> 　　 wish 作「祝福」解，後面接兩個受詞，間接受
> 詞是 you，直接受詞是 all the best。
>
> 　　 all the best 意思是「萬事如意；一切順利」，源
> 自：*May **all the best** things happen to you.* (希望
> 所有的好事都發生在你身上。)
>
> 　　 ***I wish you all the best***. 也可說成：I wish
> you only the best. 【此時的 only 等於 nothing but。】
> I wish you all the best. 還有另外一個意思，是
> 「祝福大家都好。」
>
> 【比較1】 這句話，因爲停頓不同，就有兩個不同的意思。
> 　　　　 I wish you/*all the best*.
> 　　　　 (我祝你，萬事如意。)
> 　　　　 I wish you all/*the best*. 【you all = all of you 】
> 　　　　 (我祝福大家，都如意。)

【比較 2】　all the best 比 the best 語氣更強。

I wish you *the best*.【一般語氣】

（我祝你事事如意。）

I wish you *all the best*.

（我祝你萬事如意。）

【語氣較強，all 是副詞，加強 the best 的語氣】

8. 補充說明

　　我們在書中或在考題中，也曾看過：*"Many happy returns of the day."* 也是「祝你生日快樂」之意。

　　return 在此是名詞，the day 是指 your birthday，這句話源自 I hope that you have many happy returns *of your birthday*. 字面意思是「我希望你還有很多快樂的生日回來。」引申為「祝你萬壽無疆、長命百歲。」這是美國少數受過高等教育的人喜歡說的話、或寫在卡片上的生日祝賀辭，一般年輕人較少用。

┌─【劉毅老師的話】─────
│　　背「一口氣背會話」背一段時間後，
│　就可以開始背「一口氣背演講」。和朋友
│　交互地背，比較容易專心。
└─────────────

BOOK 2

【對話練習】

1. A: **Happy birthday!**　　　　A:生日快樂！

　B: Thank you.　　　　　　　B:謝謝你。
　　 You're so sweet.　　　　　　你眞是體貼。
　　 How did you know?　　　　　你怎麼知道的？
　　　【sweet〔swit〕*adj.* 親切的；體貼的】

2. A: **Congratulations!**　　　　A:恭喜！恭喜！

　B: Thanks a lot.　　　　　　　B:非常感謝你。
　　 You're very kind.　　　　　　你人眞好。
　　 I really appreciate it.　　　　我眞的很感激。

3. A: **You must be feeling great!**　A:你一定覺得很棒！

　B: You'd better believe it.　　　B:你最好相信這件事。
　　 I'm on cloud nine.　　　　　　我開心極了。
　　 I'm on top of the world.　　　我超快樂。
　　　【*on cloud nine* 極幸運的
　　　　on top of the world 非常高興的】

4. A: **It's a big day**.　　　　　A:今天是你的大日子。

　B: Hey, it only comes once a　　B:嘿，一年只有一次。
　　 year.
　　 I gotta celebrate in style.　　　我一定要大肆慶祝。
　　 I'm gonna live it up today.　　我今天要好好狂歡。
　　　【gotta〔'gɑtə〕*v.* 必須（ = *have to* ）
　　　　in style 擺排場；講氣派　　*live it up* 享受人生】

5. A : **It's your special day**.

   B : Not really.

   It's not that special.

   It's just another day.

   【another〔əˈnʌðə〕*adj.* 另一類似的】

A：今天是你特別的日子。

B：其實不算是。

沒那麼特別。

只是平常的日子而已。

6. A : **We should celebrate**.

   B : Good idea!

   We should!

   Yes, let's celebrate!

A：我們應該慶祝一下。

B：好主意！

我們的確應該！

好，我們去慶祝吧！

7. A : **Enjoy yourself**.

   B : OK. I will.

   I'll try.

   I'll do my best.

   【*do one's best* 盡力】

A：祝你玩得愉快。

B：好，我會的。

我會試試。

我會盡力。

8. A : **Have a super day**.

   B : Thanks.

   You too.

   You have one, too.

A：祝你有美好的一天。

B：謝謝。

你也是。

也祝你有美好的一天。

9. A : **I wish you all the best**.

   B : You too.

   I wish you well.

   Thank you very much.

   【*wish sb. well* 希望某人好運】

A：祝你萬事如意。

B：你也是。

我祝福你好運。

非常謝謝你。

BOOK 2

6. Here's a little something.

Here's a little something.	這是個小東西。
I got this for you.	這是我買來送給你的。
I hope you like it.	我希望你喜歡。
It's not much.	這不值多少錢。
You deserve more.	你應該得到更多。
You deserve the best.	你應該得到最好的。
You're one of a kind.	你非常特別。
You're so special.	你很特別。
You're really great.	你真的很棒。

**────────────────

little〔'lɪtḷ〕*adj.* 小的   get〔gɛt〕*v.* 買；帶來
deserve〔dɪ'zɜv〕*v.* 應得   *one of a kind* 特別的
special〔'spɛʃəl〕*adj.* 特別的
really〔'rɪəlɪ〕*adv.* 真地   great〔gret〕*adj.* 很棒的

【背景説明】

　　送禮物給別人，不是施捨，除了送禮外，更要有尊敬之心，才能表現出你的誠意及謙虛。

　　這一回太精彩了，句子太美了，你看第一句 *Here's a little something.*，説這句話多謙虛、多有教養。It's not much. You deserve more. You deserve the best. 多麼合乎中國人的文化。最後三句 *You're one of a kind.* You're so special. You're really great. 更是精彩，見到任何人，都可以用來稱讚他。

1. *Here's a little something.* (這是個小東西。)
   = Here's a little gift. (這是個小禮物。)
   = Here's a little present. (這是個小禮物。)
   【gift〔gɪft〕*n.* 禮物　　present〔'prɛznt〕*n.* 禮物】

> 　　這些句子後面都可以加上 "for you"，來加強語氣，如：*Here's a little something for you.* (這個小東西是要送給你的。)
>
> 　　也可以再加強語氣，説成：*Here's a little something special for you.* (這個特別的小東西是要送給你的。)
>
> 也有美國人説：
>
> 　　*I have a little something for you.*
> 　　(我有個小東西要送你。)
> = I have a little gift for you. (我有個小禮物要送你。)
> = I have a little present for you.
> 　　(我有個小禮物要送你。)

BOOK 2

> 當然，也可以再加強語氣說成：
> *I have a little something special for you.*
> （我有個特別的小東西要送你。）

2. *I got this for you.*（這是我買來送給你的。）

get 主要意思是「得到」，在此的 got 可指
①買（= *bought*）；②帶來（= *brought*）。

這句話可視情況說成：I bought this for you.
（我買了這個東西給你。）或 I brought this for you.
（我帶了這個東西給你。）

3. *It's not much.*（這不值多少錢。）

美國人和中國人一樣，很謙虛，即使送貴重的禮
物，也會說不值多少錢。

　　It's not much.
= It's not expensive.（這並不貴。）
= It didn't cost a lot.（這沒花多少錢。）
【cost〔kɔst〕*v.* 花費，因為已經買了，所以用過去式】

4. *You deserve more.*（你應該得到更多。）
deserve〔dɪ'zɝv〕*v.* 應得

這句話源自：*You deserve more* than this.（你
應該得到的比這個更多。）或 *You deserve more* than
I'm giving you.（你應該得到的，比我給你的多。）
在此 more 是代名詞，表示「更多」。

5. *You deserve the best.*（你應該得到最好的。）

這句話在這裡是 You deserve the best gift.（你應該得到最好的禮物。）的省略，也可加強語氣說成：You deserve only the best.（你應該到最好的。）【only 等於 nothing but】不管你送什麼禮物給別人，都可以說這句話，來表示謙虛。

6. *You're one of a kind.*（你非常特別。）

one of a kind 中的 a 等於 the same，這句話字面意思是「你是同類中唯一的一個。」引申為「你非常特別。」

【比較】

You're *one of a kind*.
（你很特別。）

You're one of a kind.

You're *two of a kind*.
（你們兩個屬於同一類。）

= You're alike.（你們兩個很像。）

【alike〔əˋlaɪk〕*adj.* 相像的】

美國人有個諺語，句中的 a 用法和 one of a kind 的 a 相同：

Two of a trade never agree.（【諺】同行相忌。）

【句中的 a 等於 the same】

【trade〔tred〕*n.* 行業   agree〔əˋgri〕*v.* 和諧相處】

You're one of a kind. 的類似說法還有：

You're very special.（你非常特別。）

You're unique.（你很獨特。）

There's no one like you.（沒有人像你一樣。）

【unique〔juˋnik〕*adj.* 獨特的】

one of a kind 在所有字典中，都找不到這個成語，但美國人常用。

【例1】 You're the best. *You're one of a kind.*
（你很棒。你非常特別。）

【例2】 No one can compare with you. *You're one of a kind.* （沒有人能比得上你。你非常特別。）
【compare〔kəm'pɛr〕v. 比較；匹敵】

【例3】 You have your own style. *You're one of a kind.*（你很有個人風格。你非常特別。）
【style〔staɪl〕n. 風格】

【例4】 There's nothing else like this. *It's one of a kind.*（沒有任何其他東西像這個東西，它非常特別。）

【例5】 This is a great place. *It's one of a kind.*
（這個地方很棒，非常特別。）

【例6】 One Breath English is a unique method. *It's one of a kind.* 〔'mɛθəd〕n. 方法
（「一口氣背會話」是一個獨特的方法，非常特別。）

7. *You're really great.*

You're great. （你很棒。）【一般語氣】
You're really great. （你真的很棒。）【語氣較強】
You're truly great. （你真是棒。）【語氣較強】
【truly〔'trulɪ〕adv. 真地】

You're more than great. （你非常棒。）【語氣很強】
You're the greatest. （你最棒。）【語氣最強】
You're greater than anybody.
（你比任何人都棒。）【語氣最強】【*more than* 不只…而已；非常】

【對話練習】

1. A：**Here's a little something.**
   B：Thank you.
   　　You're too kind.
   　　I don't deserve it.

　　A：這是個小東西。
　　B：謝謝。
　　　　你太客氣了。
　　　　我受之有愧。

2. A：**I got this for you.**
   B：You're so nice.
   　　What can I say?
   　　I'm overwhelmed.
   　　【overwhelmed (ˌovɚ'hwɛlmd) adj.
   　　深受感動的】

　　A：這是我買來送給你的。
　　B：你人真好。
　　　　我能說什麼呢？
　　　　我太感動了。

3. A：**I hope you like it.**
   B：I know I'll like it.
   　　It's just what I needed.
   　　It's just what I always wanted.

　　A：我希望你喜歡。
　　B：我知道我會喜歡的。
　　　　這正是我所需要的。
　　　　這正是我一直想要的。

4. A：**It's not much.**
   B：I like it.
   　　It's great.
   　　It's the thought that counts.
   　　【thought (θɔt) n. 想法
   　　　count (kaʊnt) v. 重要】

　　A：這不值多少錢。
　　B：我喜歡。
　　　　這太棒了。
　　　　心意最重要。

5. A：**You deserve more.**
   B：Not really.
   　　Don't say that.
   　　This is just fine.
   　　【just (dʒʌst) adv. 真地；的確】

　　A：你應該得到更多。
　　B：其實不是。
　　　　別這麼說。
　　　　這真的太好了。

BOOK 2

BOOK 2

6. A：**You deserve the best.**　　　A：你應該得到最好的。

　B：No, I don't.　　　　　　　　B：不，我不是。

　　You flatter me.　　　　　　　　我真是受寵若驚。

　　I'm speechless.　　　　　　　　我不知道該說什麼。

　　【flatter (ˈflætɚ) v. 奉承；恭維
　　　speechless (ˈspitʃlɪs) adj. 說不出
　　　話的】

7. A：**You're one of a kind.**　　　A：你非常特別。

　B：Thank you very much.　　　　B：非常感謝你。

　　What a nice compliment!　　　　多麼好的讚美啊！

　　I don't deserve such praise.　　　這樣的讚美我不敢當。

　　【compliment (ˈkɑmpləmənt) n.
　　　稱讚 (= praise)】

8. A：**You're so special.**　　　　A：你很特別。

　B：You're not so bad yourself.　　B：你也不賴。

　　That means a lot coming　　　　你的讚美對我意義重

　　from you.　　　　　　　　　　大。

　　Everyone knows how sincere　　每個人都知道你有多

　　you are.　　　　　　　　　　麼真誠。

9. A：**You're really great.**　　　　A：你真是太棒了。

　B：You too.　　　　　　　　　　B：你也是。

　　You're great, too.　　　　　　　你也很棒。

　　You're better than I am.　　　　你比我更優秀。

7. *Receiving a Gift* (I)

Thank you so much.	非常感謝你。
It's wonderful.	這東西眞棒。
It's what I always wanted.	這是我一直想要的。
It's perfect.	這個東西眞完美。
How did you know?	你怎麼知道？
It's just what I needed.	這正是我需要的。
You're so thoughtful.	你眞是體貼。
I'm really grateful.	我眞的很感激。
I can't thank you enough.	我感激不盡。

BOOK 2

** ──────────────

wonderful〔'wʌndɚfəl〕*adj.* 很棒的
perfect〔'pɝfɪkt〕*adj.* 完美的
thoughtful〔'θɔtfəl〕*adj.* 體貼的
grateful〔'gretfəl〕*adj.* 感激的

【背景説明】

別人送你禮物，你應該多説一些感謝的話，除
了當場説以外，過了一段時間以後，最好再次提起，
表示感謝，感謝的話説越多越好，但要出自誠心。

1. ***Thank you so much.*** (非常感謝你。)

這句話和 Thank you very much. 一樣。表示
Thank you. 的用法很多。(詳見「劉毅演講式英語①」
英語會話總整理①–1)

2. ***It's wonderful.*** (這東西眞棒。)
wonderful〔ˈwʌndɚfəl〕*adj.* 很棒的

看到好東西，就可以説 ***It's wonderful.*** 這類的
句子。我們按照特別的方式排列，你很容易就可以
背下來。

　　It's great. (這東西很好。)【第一常用】
= It's super.〔ˈsupɚ〕(這東西很棒。)【第四常用】
= It's perfect.〔ˈpɝfɪkt〕(這東西很完美。)【第二常用】

= ***It's wonderful.*** (這東西眞棒。)【第三常用】
= It's fantastic.〔fænˈtæstɪk〕(這東西眞好。)【第五常用】
= It's terrific.〔təˈrɪfɪk〕(這東西眞棒。)【第六常用】

= It's marvelous.〔ˈmɑrvləs〕(這東西好極了。)【第七常用】
= It's excellent.〔ˈɛkslənt〕(這東西非常棒。)【第八常用】
= It's outstanding.〔ˌaʊtˈstændɪŋ〕(這東西太好了。)
　　【第九常用】

看到你喜歡的人，你也可以用類似的說法來稱
讚他們。

> You're great. (你很好。)【第一常用】
> = You're super. (你很棒。)【第四常用】
> = You're perfect. (你很完美。)【第九常用】
>
> = You're wonderful. (你真棒。)【第二常用】
> = You're fantastic. (你真出色。)【第五常用】
> = You're terrific. (你真優秀。)【第六常用】
>
> = You're marvelous. (你非常出色。)【第三常用】
> = You're excellent. (你非常優秀。)【第七常用】
> = You're outstanding. (你非常傑出。)【第八常用】

BOOK 2

3. *It's what I always wanted.*

這句話意思是「這是我一直想要的。」但是
不可說成 *It's what I always needed.* (誤)，可以
說：It's just what I needed. (這正是我所需要
的。)【just 作「正是；就是」解】

有位英文老師問，為什麼這句話和 always 連
用，不用現在式呢？學生考了很多考題，都是
always 和現在式連用。

① always 可以和過去式連用，表示過去的習慣。

【例1】 She *always wore* red when she was a
teenager. 【teenager〔'tin,edʒɚ〕*n.* 青少年】
(她十幾歲的時候，總是穿紅色的衣服。)

【例2】 She *was always* a good student in high
school. (她在高中的時候，一直是個好學生。)

【例3】 I *always wanted* to learn Spanish
when I was a university student.
（當我唸大學的時候，我老是想學西班牙文。）
【Spanish〔'spænɪʃ〕*n.* 西班牙文】

② always 可和過去式連用，代替現在完成式。
（在「東華英漢大辭典」p.94 有說明。）

【例1】 *It's what I always wanted.*【常用】
= It's what I've always wanted.【常用】
（這是我一直想要的。）

【例2】 I always wanted to be a writer.
= I've always wanted to be a writer.
（我一直想要當作家。）

【例3】 I always wanted to visit Paris.
= I've always wanted to visit Paris.
（我一直想要去巴黎玩。）
【人在巴黎可說，人不在巴黎也可說。】

很多人學了文法，以為 always 一定和現在式連用，這個錯誤的觀念，會阻礙他們學英文。現在式動詞，表示現在如此，過去如此，未來也如此。例如：
He is always late. （他總是遲到。）

但是在這裡，always 不能和 want 的現在式連用。

中文： 我總是想要去巴黎玩。

英文： *I always want to visit Paris.*
【誤，因為不是不變的事實】
I always wanted to visit Paris.【正】
【always 和過去式連用，代替現在完成式】

I've always wanted to visit Paris.【正】

在這裡的「總是想」，是指「一直想」，英文該用現
在完成式。但為什麼 I always want you to tell
me the truth. 卻可以呢？因為這表示不變的事實。
所以，想要利用文法規則造句，真是太難了。

4. *How did you know?*

這句話的意思是「你怎麼知道的？」在這裡可
加長為：How did you know I like this?（你是
怎麼知道我喜歡這個的？）美國人和中國人一樣，
喜歡問「你怎麼知道的？」你也可以說 "Who told
you?"（誰告訴你的？）或 "How did you find
out?"（你怎麼發現的？）【*find out* 發現】

說英文的時候，可將「一口氣背會話」中的
句子變一變，今天說 How did you know?，明
天說 Who told you?，後天再說 How did you
find out?，這樣進步更快。

當別人問你："How did you know?"，你就
可以回答："*A little bird told me.*" 字面意思是
「一隻小鳥告訴我的。」a little bird 代表「某人」
（= *someone*），暗示
你不想告訴對方此人
是誰，可引申為「消息
靈通人士告訴我的。」
說這句話有幽默的語
氣。

How did you know?

A little bird told me.

你也可以回答：***I heard it through the grapevine.***

【grapevine〔'grep,vaɪn〕*n.* 葡萄藤　vine〔vaɪn〕*n.* 藤蔓】

這句話可能源自葡萄藤爬來爬去，形容消息一個接一個地傳過來，字面意思是「我聽到這個消息，從葡萄藤傳過來的。」表示「我有內幕消息。」由於這句話使用太普遍，字典上已經直接把 the grapevine 當成成語，翻成「內幕消息；謠傳」。

或是回答：***My spies told me.*** 這句話可直接翻成「我的間諜告訴我的。」【spy〔spaɪ〕*n.* 間諜】和 "A little bird told me." "I heard it through the grapevine." 同義，都表示不願意告訴對方，你的消息來源。

【比較1】 My spies told me.【正，spies 一定用複數形式】
My spy told me.【誤】

【比較2】 A little bird told me.
【較常用，女人及老一輩子的人喜歡說】
I heard it through the grapevine.【最常用】
My spies told me.【較不常用，幽默用語】

5. ***You're so thoughtful.***

You're so thoughtful.（你真是體貼。）
= You're so considerate.
= You're very thoughtful.〔'θɔtfəl〕*adj.* 體貼的
= You're very considerate.〔kən'sɪdərɪt〕*adj.* 體貼的

【比較】 ***You're so thoughtful.***【通俗，常用】
It's so thoughtful of you.【正確，較少用】

6. *I'm really grateful.*

grateful〔'gretfəl〕 *adj.* 感激的

　　grateful 這個字美國人常用，他們喜歡聽，你也要常說。

> 下面六句，語氣由弱到強排列：
>
> 弱　I'm *grateful*. (我很感激。)【一般語氣】
> 　　I'm so *grateful*. (我很感激。)
> 　　I'm very *grateful*. (我非常感激。)
>
> 　　I'm really *grateful*. (我真的很感激。)
> 　　I'm especially *grateful*. (我特別感激。)
> 強　I'm more than *grateful*.【語氣最強】
> 　　　(我感激得不得了。)【*more than* 作「不只～而已」解】

7. *I can't thank you enough.*

　　這句話字面意思是「我怎麼謝你都不夠。」和中文的「我感激不盡。」有異曲同工之妙。可加長為：

I can't thank you enough
for such a wonderful gift.
(你送我這麼好的禮物，我
感激不盡。)

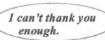

【比較】

> *I can't thank you enough*.【通俗，常用】
> *I can't thank you too much*.【劣】

在字典上或文法書中常見到，can't…enough 等於 can't…too much，當你說 *I can't thank you too much.* 美國人聽得懂，但覺得怪怪的，覺得像是外國人講的英文。

【對話練習】

1. A：**Thank you so much**.　　　　　A：非常感謝你。

   B：You're welcome.　　　　　　　B：不客氣。
   　　It's nothing.　　　　　　　　　沒什麼。
   　　Don't mention it.　　　　　　　不客氣。
   　　【mention (ˈmɛnʃən) *v.* 提到】

2. A：**It's wonderful**.　　　　　　　A：這東西眞棒。

   B：That's good.　　　　　　　　　B：太好了。
   　　You deserve it.　　　　　　　　這是你應得的。
   　　I'm glad you like it.　　　　　　我很高興你喜歡。
   　　【glad (glæd) *adj.* 高興的】

3. A：**It's what I always wanted**.　　A：這是我一直想要的。

   B：Really?　　　　　　　　　　　B：眞的嗎？
   　　That's great.　　　　　　　　　太好了。
   　　I was hoping you'd say that.　　　我就希望你會這麼說。

4. A：**It's perfect**.　　　　　　　　A：這個東西眞完美。

   B：Do you really think so?　　　　　B：你眞的這麼認爲嗎？
   　　You don't have to say that.　　　你用不著那樣說。
   　　Do you really mean it?　　　　　你是認眞的嗎？

5. A：**How did you know?**　　　　　A：你怎麼知道的？

   B：A little bird told me.　　　　　　B：消息靈通人士告訴我的。
   　　I heard it through the　　　　　　我有內幕消息。
   　　grapevine.
   　　My spies told me.　　　　　　　我的間諜告訴我的。

6. A : **It's just what I needed**.

   B : That's great.

      That's nice to hear.

      That's just what I wanted
to hear.

    A：這正是我需要的。

    B：太好了。

        聽到你這麼說真好。

        這正是我想聽到的。

7. A : **You're so thoughtful**.

   B : Not really.

      I just do my best.

      I'm glad you think so.

      【*try one's best* 盡力 】

    A：你真是體貼。

    B：沒有啦。

        我只是盡力而已。

        很高興你這麼認為。

8. A : **I'm really grateful**.

   B : Any time.

      No problem.

      Don't say that.

      【*Any time*. 不客氣。

        No problem. 不客氣。】

    A：我真的很感激。

    B：不客氣。

        不客氣。

        別那樣說。

9. A : **I can't thank you enough**.

   B : My pleasure.

      Don't say another word.

      It's the least I can do.

      【pleasure〔ˈplɛʒɚ〕*n.* 榮幸 】

    A：感激不盡。

    B：這是我的榮幸。

        別再說了。

        這是我最起碼能做的。

BOOK 2

8. Receiving a Gift (*II*)

What can I say?	我該說什麼呢？
I'm speechless.	我說不出話來了。
You shouldn't have.	你不該這麼做的。
I really don't deserve it.	我實在不敢當。
You're too good to me.	你對我太好了。
I really like this gift.	我真的很喜歡這個禮物。
It's very useful.	這個東西很實用。
I was going to buy one.	我本來要買一個。
You read my mind.	你真是了解我。

** ——————————————————

speechless〔'spitʃlɪs〕*adj.* 說不出話的
deserve〔dɪ'zɝv〕*v.* 應得　　gift〔gɪft〕*n.* 禮物
useful〔'jusfəl〕*adj.* 實用的
read *one's **mind*** 了解某人的想法

【背景說明】

這個單元緊接著上一個單元，主題相同，是別人贈送你禮物後的感謝話。感謝別人的話，說越多越好，不花費你一分錢，效果無窮。

1. *What can I say?* (我該說什麼呢 ？)

這句話太重要了，是萬用句，幾乎不管外國人說什麼，正面或負面，你都可以回答： *What can I say?*

【例1】 A: You did a great job. (你做得非常好。)【正面】
　　　　 B: *What can I say?* (我該說什麼呢 ？)

【例2】 A: You did a lousy job.
　　　　　　 (你做得真差勁。)【負面】
　　　　 B: *What can I say?* (我該說什麼呢 ？)
　　　　 【lousy〔ˈlauzɪ〕 *adj.* 差勁的 】

【例3】 A: Here's something for you.
　　　　　　 (這個東西送給你。)【正面】
　　　　 B: Wow! *What can I say?*
　　　　　　 (哇啊！我該說什麼呢 ？)
　　　　 【wow〔waʊ〕 *interj.* 哇啊 】

【例4】 A: Why did you run that red light?
　　　　　　 (你為什麼闖紅燈 ？)【負面】
　　　　 B: *What can I say?* I was in a hurry.
　　　　　　 (我該說什麼呢 ？我趕時間。)
　　　　 【run〔rʌn〕 *v.* 闖過　 *in a hurry* 匆忙 】

BOOK 2

【例5】 A: You are a kindhearted person.
（你的心腸眞好。）【正面】

B: ***What can I say?*** (我該說什麼呢？)

【kindhearted（'kaɪnd'hɑrtɪd）*adj.* 心腸好的】

【例6】 A: You are twenty minutes late.
（你遲到二十分鐘。）【負面】

B: ***What can I say?*** (我該說什麼呢？)

What can I say? 也可說成 I don't know what
to say. (我不知道該說什麼。)

2. ***I'm speechless.***

speechless（'spitʃlɪs）*adj.* 說不出話的

> ***I'm speechless.*** (我說不出話來了。)
> = Words fail me. (我說不出話來了。)【本句是慣用句】
> = What can I say? (我能說什麼呢？)

3. ***You shouldn't have.***

這句話是假設法的過去式，表示「與過去事實
相反」，源自 You shouldn't have *done that.*【正】
（你不該那麼做。）

比較下面兩個例子的不同：

【例1】 A: I got this for you. (我買這個東西要送給你。)
B: ***You shouldn't have.*** (你不該這麼做的。)

【例2】 A: I want to buy you a gift.
（我要買個禮物給你。）

B: ***You shouldn't.*** (你不應該買。)
Please don't. (請不要買。)

4. *I really don't deserve it.*
   deserve〔dɪ'zɜv〕v. 應得

   這句話字面的意思是「我眞的不應該得到它。」
   可引申爲「我眞的不敢當。」你可以只説 I don't
   deserve it. (我不敢當。) 或者説 I'm not worthy
   of it. (我不敢當。)【worthy〔'wɜðɪ〕adj. 值得的】

5. *You're too good to me.*

   在這裡 to me 的 to，是介系詞，不要和不定詞
   的 too~to「太~而不…」弄混。

   > 【比較】You're good to me.【一般語氣】
   > (你對我很好。)
   > You're so good to me.【語氣較強】
   > (你對我眞好。)
   > *You're too good to me.*【語氣最強】
   > (你對我太好了。)
   >
   > *You're too good to me.* 也可説成 You're too
   > kind to me. (你對我太好了。) 或 You're too nice
   > to me. (你對我太好了。)

6. *I really like this gift.*
   gift〔gɪft〕n. 禮物

   中國人比較保守，收到別人的禮物，通常不當
   場打開，等到回家才偷笑或嫌棄。美國人的風俗是，
   一面折禮物，一面要表現出很興奮的樣子，不管禮
   物好壞，他們從小都被教育，必須説感謝的話，
   I really like this gift. (我眞的很喜歡這個禮物。)
   是最典型的表達方法。

7. ***It's very useful.***

useful〔'jusfəl〕*adj.* 有用的;實用的

　　這句話字面的意思是「它很有用。」在這裡的
意思是「這個東西很實用。」說完 ***It's very useful.***
可再接著說:I can use it a lot. (我可以常常使用
它。)【a lot 在此作「常常」解】

8. ***I was going to buy one.***

　　這句話的意思是「我本來要買一個」,也可說成
I was going to get one. (我本來要買一個。) 或
I was planning to buy one. (我本來打算買一個。)
或 I was planning to get one. (我本來打算買一
個。)【get 在此作「買」解】

9. ***You read my mind.***

read〔rid〕*v.* 讀 (過去式和過去分詞要唸成〔rɛd〕)
read one's mind 知道某人在想什麼;看出某人的心思

　　read 在此是過去式,要唸成〔rɛd〕,這句話的
意思是「你知道我的想法。」(= *You knew what
I was thinking.*)

美國人常喜歡開玩笑,說:

　　　I can read you like a book.
　　= I know you very well. (我非常了解你。)

【比較】 I can read you like a book. 【正】
　　　　I can read your mind. 【正】
　　　　I can read your mind like a book. 【誤】

【對話練習】

1. A：**What can I say?**　　　　A：我該說什麼呢？
   B：Don't say anything.　　　　B：什麼都別說。
   　　Just accept it.　　　　　　　收下就是了。
   　　You deserve it.　　　　　　　這是你應得的。

2. A：**I'm speechless.**　　　　　A：我說不出話來了。
   B：That doesn't happen very often.　　B：這種情況不常發生。
   　　It's rare to see you at a loss　　　很少看到你會說不出
   　　for words.　　　　　　　　　話來。
   　　Wow, I know it must be good.　　哇，我就知道它一定很
   　　【*at a loss for words*　不知道說什　棒。
   　　　麼話才好】

3. A：**You shouldn't have.**　　　A：你不該這麼做的。
   B：I enjoyed it.　　　　　　　B：我喜歡這麼做。
   　　It was a pleasure.　　　　　　這是我的榮幸。
   　　It's the least I could do.　　　　這是我最起碼能做的。
   　　【pleasure (ˈplɛʒɚ) *n.* 榮幸】

4. A：**I really don't deserve it.**　A：我實在不敢當。
   B：Sure you do.　　　　　　　B：你當之無愧。
   　　Of course you do.　　　　　　你當然值得。
   　　No one deserves it more.　　　沒有人比你更應該得到。

5. A：**You are too good to me.**　A：你對我太好了。
   B：No, I'm not.　　　　　　　B：不，我沒有。
   　　Don't say that.　　　　　　　你別這麼說。
   　　I do what I like to do.　　　　我只做我喜歡做的。

BOOK 2

6. A：**I really like this gift**.

  B：That's great!
  I'm so relieved.
  I'm so happy.

  【great〔gret〕*adj.* 很棒的；
   極好的
   relieved〔rɪ'livd〕*adj.* 放心的】

  A：我真的很喜歡這個禮物。

  B：太好了！
   那我就放心了。
   我很高興。

7. A：**It's very useful**.

  B：I hope so.
  I was hoping you would
  say that.
  I hope it'll come in handy.

  【*come in handy* 可派上用場】

  A：這個東西很實用。

  B：我希望是。
   我原本就希望你會這麼說。

   我希望這個東西可以派上
   用場。

8. A：**I was going to buy one**.

  B：I knew you needed one.
  That's why I got it.
  I hope I saved you some
  trouble.

  【save〔sev〕*v.* 節省】

  A：我本來要買一個。

  B：我知道你需要。
   這就是我為什麼買它的原因。
   我希望能為你省掉一些
   麻煩。

9. A：**You read my mind**.

  B：You are a good friend.
  I know the way you think.
  I know everything about
  you.

  A：你真是了解我。

  B：你是我的好朋友。
   我知道你的想法。
   我知道你的一切。

9. This is topnotch.

This is topnotch.	這個東西眞高級。
This is superb.	這個東西太棒了。
I'm very impressed.	眞令我心動。
It's very nice.	這眞是好東西。
It's high quality.	品質非常好。
It must be worth a lot.	一定很值錢吧。
It's excellent.	這東西眞是好。
It's outstanding.	棒透了。
I like it so much.	我太喜歡了。

BOOK 2

**

topnotch〔'tɑp'nɑtʃ〕*adj.* 高級的；一流的 (= *top-notch*)
superb〔su'pɝb〕*adj.* 極佳的
impressed〔ɪm'prɛst〕*adj.* 印象深刻的
quality〔'kwɑlətɪ〕*n.* 品質　　worth〔wɝθ〕*adj.* 值…
excellent〔'ɛkslənt〕*adj.* 優秀的；極好的
outstanding〔'aut'stændɪŋ〕*adj.* 傑出的；很棒的
　(= *very good*)

BOOK 2

【背景説明】

　　當你看到一部高級汽車，或一只名貴的手錶，你都可以説這九句話。有教養的美國人很喜歡説讚美的話，人人都應該學會説讚美的話，稱讚別人，別人快樂，自己也快樂。

1. *This is topnotch.*

topnotch〔'tɑp'nɑtʃ〕adj. 高級的；一流的 (= *top-notch*)

　　　　topnotch 這個字，是 top 和 notch 兩個字的組合，notch 原義是「刻痕；切痕」，任何用刀子或斧頭砍下的痕跡，都叫 notch，源自美國印地安戰士，每戰勝一次，就在圖騰上留下一道刻痕 (notch)，刻痕累積越高，表示他越英勇，「最棒的戰士」即稱為 *topnotch* warrior。在這裡，notch 的意思是「水平；等級」，而 top 指「最高的；最佳的」，故 *topnotch* 即指「高級的；一流的」。

　　　This is topnotch. (這個東西眞高級。)【第一常用】
= This is top grade. (這個東西是最高級的。)【第六常用】
= This is top of the line. 【第四常用】
　　(這是同類中最好的。)

　　所有中外字典中，只有「東華英漢大辭典」，將 top grade 寫成 *top-grade*，所以 *top-grade* 這種寫法，尚不普遍。

top〔tɑp〕adj. 最高的　n. 最好的事物　　grade〔gred〕n. 等級
line〔laɪn〕adj. 種類　　*be top of the line* 是同類中最好的

> = This is first-class.【第二常用】
> （這個東西是第一流的。）
> = This is first-rate. （這個東西是第一流的。）【第三常用】
> = This is the best of the best.【第五常用】
> （這個東西是最棒的。）

first-class〔ˈfɝstˈklæs〕*adj.* 第一流的；最高級的
first-rate〔ˈfɝstˈret〕*adj.* 第一流的

　　無論是東西、事物或人，只要是「非常好、一流的」，都可以用 *topnotch* 來形容，例如：

The watch is *topnotch*. （這只錶眞高級。）
The present is *topnotch*. （這個禮物太棒了。）
This is a *topnotch* job. （你的工作表現非常出色。）
(= *You did a great job.*)

This is a *topnotch* performance.
（這個表演眞是無懈可擊。）
He is a *topnotch* lawyer. （他是一流的律師。）
The service here is *topnotch*.
（這裡的服務是一流的。）

performance〔pɚˈfɔrməns〕*n.* 表演
lawyer〔ˈlɔjɚ〕*n.* 律師

2. *This is superb.*

superb〔suˈpɝb〕*adj.* 很棒的

> ***This is superb.*** （這個東西眞棒。）
> = This is great. （這個東西眞棒。）
> = This is excellent. （這個東西太好了。）

> ⎰ = This is terrific. (這個東西眞棒。)
> ⎱ = This is fantastic. (這個東西眞棒。)
> ⎱ = This is marvelous. (這個東西眞棒。)

terrific〔tə'rıfık〕*adj.* 很棒的
fantastic〔fæn'tæstık〕*adj.* 很棒的
marvelous〔'mɑrvḷəs〕*adj.* 很棒的

當別人送禮物給你，一般美國人會說：This is great. 有兩個含意：① 這個禮物眞棒；② 感覺太棒了。但是，***This is superb.*** 只表示「**這個東西眞**〔su'pɝb〕**棒。**」；如果指「**感覺眞棒。**」，要用 This is super.〔'supɚ〕

> ⎰ ***This is super.*** (感覺太棒了。)
> ⎱   〔'supɚ〕
> ⎱ = This is great.
> ⎱ = This is excellent.

> ⎰ = This is terrific.
> ⎱ = This is fantastic.
> ⎱ = This is marvelous.

【比較】***This is superb.*** (這個東西眞棒。)
〔su'pɝb〕

This is super. (太棒了；感覺太好了。)
〔'supɚ〕

【例 I】 A: This is a present for you.
(這個禮物送給你。)

B: ***This is superb.*** (這個禮物太棒了。)
〔su'pɝb〕

【例 2】 A: This is a present for you.
（這個禮物送給你。）

B: This is super. (太棒了；感覺太好了。)
〔'supə〕

This is super.

3. *I'm very impressed.*

impressed 〔ɪm'prɛst〕 *adj.* 印象深刻的

這個字來自 impress，從字根上分析，是「印
在心裡」，*I'm very impressed.* 字面的意思是「我
被某件事情印在心裡。」引申為「我印象很深刻。」
在不同的句子、不同的上下文中，有不同的翻譯。

【例 1】 Your English is very good. *I'm very
impressed.* (你的英文很好，我很佩服。)

【例 2】 Your gift is wonderful. *I'm very impressed.*
(你的禮物太好了，我一輩子都記得。)

【例 3】 This is a great car. *I'm very impressed.*
(這部車真棒，我很心動。)

BOOK 2

【例4】 You did a great job. *I'm very impressed.*
（你做得很好，**我很感動。**）

【例5】 The view here is great. *I'm very impressed.*
（這裡的景色真美，**令我難以忘懷。**）

【例6】 This is a great speech. *I'm very impressed.*
（這個演講真棒，**我非常感動。**）

【view〔vju〕*n.* 風景　　speech〔spitʃ〕*n.* 演講】

【例7】 She is very beautiful. *I'm very impressed.*
（她非常漂亮，**我印象深刻。**）

【例8】 That was a nice meal. *I'm very impressed.*
（那餐飯真棒，**令我回味無窮。**）

【例9】 That was a wonderful date. *I'm very impressed.*
（那真是一次美好的約會，**我永生難忘。**）

【meal〔mil〕*n.* 一餐　　date〔det〕*n.* 約會】

　　凡是任何事情給你深刻、持續的感覺，你都可以說：
I'm very impressed.

4. ***It's high quality***.

quality〔′kwɑlətɪ〕*n.* 品質

學了文法，而文法又學不通的人，就不敢講這句話，這句話是由 It's of high quality. 省略而來。

（詳見「文法寶典」p. 546）

It's high quality. (這個東西品質很好。)
= It's of high quality.
= It's top quality.

【 top quality = top-quality，但在 be 動詞後，要寫成 top quality。】

美國人說話比較喜歡簡潔，他們常說 : ***It's high quality***. 較少說 It's of high quality. 說 It's of high quality. 有一點咬文嚼字的味道。

5. ***It must be worth a lot***. (一定很值錢吧。)

worth〔wɝθ〕*adj.* 值…

must 作「一定」解，worth 這個字是個特殊的形容詞，其後要接名詞或動名詞做受詞。

這句話也可以說成 :

It must be expensive. (這東西一定很貴吧。)
It must have cost a lot.

(這個東西一定需要花費很多錢。)

【 must have + p.p. 表「現在推測過去」，作「當時一定」解。cost〔kɔst〕*v.* 花費；值～】

當你看到別人戴著很名貴的手錶，你就可以說 :

Where did you get it? ***It must be worth a lot***.

(你在哪裡買的？一定很貴吧。)【 get〔gɛt〕*v.* 買】

BOOK 2

BOOK 2

【對話練習】

1. A：**This is topnotch.**
   B：I agree.
      You're right.
      It's excellent.

   A：這東西真高級。
   B：我同意。
      你說得對。
      這東西真棒。

2. A：**This is superb.**
   B：I totally agree.
      I think it's extraordinary.
      It's almost perfect.

   【totally（'totḷɪ）*adv.* 完全地
      extraordinary（ɪk'strɔrdn̩ˌɛrɪ）
      adj. 特別的】

   A：這個東西太棒了。
   B：我完全同意。
      我認為它很特別。
      它近乎完美。

3. A：**I'm very impressed.**
   B：So am I.
      Me too.
      It's very impressive.

   A：真令我心動。
   B：我也是。
      我也是。
      這個東西真是令人心動。

4. A：**It's very nice.**
   B：I'm glad you like it.
      Use it wisely.
      It should last a long time.

   【wisely（'waɪzlɪ）*adv.* 聰明地
      last（læst）*v.* 持久；耐久】

   A：這真是好東西。
   B：很高興你喜歡
      要聰明地使用它。
      應該可以用很久。

5. A：**It's high quality**.
   B：Do you really think so.
   I hope you are right.
   I really have no idea.
   【*have no idea* 不知道】

6. A：**It must be worth a lot**.
   B：I bet you're right.
   I'm sure it is.
   It looks expensive.
   【bet〔bɛt〕*v.* 確信；敢說】

7. A：**It's excellent**.
   B：It sure is!
   It's marvelous.
   That's my opinion, too.
   【sure〔ʃʊr〕*adv.* 的確
   opinion〔ə'pɪnjən〕*n.* 意見】

8. A：**It's outstanding**.
   B：I think so, too.
   It's truly remarkable.
   It must have cost a fortune.
   【remarkable〔rɪ'mɑrkəbl̩〕
   adj. 非凡的；卓越的
   fortune〔'fɔrtʃən〕*n.* 一大筆錢】

9. A：**I like it so much**.
   B：So do I.
   It's really nice.
   I like it, too.

A：品質非常好。
B：你真的這麼認為嗎？
　　我希望你說得對。
　　我真的不知道。

A：這一定很值錢吧。
B：你說得很對。
　　肯定是。
　　看起來很貴。

A：這東西真是好。
B：的確是！
　　真是太棒了。
　　我也這麼認為。

A：棒透了。
B：我也這麼認為。
　　真的是很棒。
　　它一定值不少錢吧。

A：我非常喜歡。
B：我也是。
　　這真是太棒了。
　　我也喜歡。

10. I'm so lucky!

I'm so lucky!	我真幸運！
I'm really blessed!	我真幸福！
I'm the luckiest person in the world.	我是全世界最幸運的人。
Everything is perfect.	一切都很完美。
Everything is going my way.	每件事都很順利。
You are the reason why!	就是因爲你的緣故！
Thanks a bunch.	非常感謝。
I owe you a lot.	我非常感謝你。
I'm a lucky dog.	我真幸運。

** ———————————————————

lucky (ˈlʌkɪ) *adj.* 幸運的
blessed (blɛst) *p.p.* 幸福的；幸運的
perfect (ˈpɝfɪkt) *adj.* 完美的
go one's way 對某人有利　　reason (ˈrizṇ) *n.* 理由
bunch (bʌntʃ) *n.* 一堆；一把　　owe (o) *v.* 欠

【背景說明】

這九句話太好用了，當你和你喜歡的人在一起的時候，你就可以說：I'm so lucky! I'm really blessed! 等。

1. *I'm really blessed!*
bless〔blɛs〕*v.* 祝福
blessed〔blɛst〕*p.p.* 幸福的【注意發音】

> bless 這個字很常用，像 God bless you.（願上帝保佑你。）*I'm really blessed!* 字面的意思是「我眞的受到上帝的祝福！」就像中文裡的「我眞的受到上帝的眷顧！」一樣，可引申爲「我眞的很幸福！」這句話也可說成：I feel blessed!（我覺得很幸福！）這兩句的 blessed 是過去分詞，要唸成〔blɛst〕。
>
> blessed 也可當純粹形容詞，唸作〔'blɛsɪd〕。
> blessed 這個字，有兩種發音：
> ① blessed〔blɛst〕【bless 的過去式和過去分詞】
> ② blessed〔'blɛsɪd〕*adj.* 幸福的；帶來愉快的

【比較 1】 I'm *blessed* with good health.
〔blɛst〕【blessed 是過去分詞】
（我幸而有健康的身體。）
* *be blessed with* 有幸得到
（= *be lucky enough to have*）

What a *blessed* family!
〔'blɛsɪd〕【blessed 是形容詞】
（多麼幸福的家庭！）

【比較2】 We are so *blessed*.
　　　　　　　〔blɛst〕
　　　　（我們真幸福。）【blessed 是過去分詞】
　　　　To give is more *blessed* than to receive.
　　　　　　　　　　　　　〔'blɛsɪd〕
　　　　（施比受有福。）【blessed 是形容詞】

【比較3】 We are *blessed* by your gift.
　　　　　　　〔blɛst〕
　　　　（你的禮物給我們帶來幸福。）【blessed 是過去分詞】
　　　　What a *blessed* gift!【blessed 是形容詞】
　　　　　　　　　　　〔'blɛsɪd〕
　　　　（= *This is a needed gift!*)
　　　　（這禮物正合我需要！）

2. *Everything is perfect.*（一切都很完美。）
   perfect〔'pɝfɪkt〕*adj.* 完美的

　　　　這句話也可說成：Things are perfect.（一切
都很完美。）美國人也常說：Everything is great.
或 Things are great. 都表示「一切都很好；一切都
順利。」

3. *Everything is going my way.*
   go one's way ①對某人有利 ②與某人同路

　　　　這句話的字面意思是「一切都與我同路。」引
申為「我一切順利。」也可以說成：Everything is
working out.（一切都很順利。）
   【*work out*（順利）進行；有好結果】

4. ***You are the reason why!***

　　reason〔'rizn̩〕*n.* 原因；理由

　　　　這句話在此源自：You are the reason why
　　everything is going my way!【正】（一切順利都
　　是因為你！）

　　　　You are the reason why!（就是因為你的緣故！）
　　　　= It's all because of you!（一切都是因為你！）
　　　　= It's all due to you!（一切都是由於你！）
　　　　【***due to*** 由於】

5. ***Thanks a bunch.***（多謝。）

　　thanks〔θæŋks〕*n. pl.* 感謝　　　bunch〔bʌntʃ〕*n.* 一堆

　　　　thanks 這個字是名詞，永遠要用複數形，前面
　　可加形容詞，像 Many thanks.（多謝。）
　　thanks 這個名詞很奇怪，後面可以加副詞片語，
　　如：Thanks a lot. Thanks so much. 感覺上，
　　thanks 像是動詞，但卻不是動詞。thanks 是名
　　詞，thank 才是動詞。

　　　　【比較】 Thanks.【輕鬆、通俗】
　　　　　　　 Thank you.【較正式】

　　　　Thanks a bunch. 這句話字面的意思是「感謝
　　一堆。」引申為「非常感謝。」等於 Thanks a lot.
　　說這句話，有一點幽默的味道。

　　　　【例1】 A: Here is what you asked for.
　　　　　　　　　（這是你所要的。）
　　　　　　　 B: ***Thanks a bunch.***（多謝。）

【例2】 A: I found what you needed.
 （我找到你需要的東西。）

 B: ***Thanks a bunch***. （多謝。）

在美國口語中，常用 ***a bunch*** 來取代 a lot。
其他例子還有：

I owe you ***a bunch***. （非常感謝你。）
（ = *I owe you a lot.* ）
【owe〔o〕v. 欠　　***owe sb. a lot*** 很感謝某人】

There is ***a bunch*** of food. （有好多食物。）
（ = *There is a lot of food.* ）

bunch 也可以表示「一群人」。

You're a nice ***bunch***. （你們是一群好人。）
（ = *You're a nice group of people.* ）

You're the best of the ***bunch***.
（你是這一群人中最好的。）
（ = *You're the best of the group.* ）

6. ***I owe you a lot.***
 owe〔o〕v. 欠

這句話字面的意思是「我欠你很多。」引申爲
「我非常感謝你。」

美國人很喜歡說 I owe you. 之類的話，表示
感謝，這些話，讓別人聽起來很舒服。

下面都是美國人常説的話：

I owe you. (我感謝你。)【第一常用】

I owe you one. (我欠你一次人情。)【第二常用】

I owe you a big one. (我欠你一個大人情。)【第四常用】

I owe you a favor. (我欠你一次人情。)【第三常用】

I owe you a big favor. (我欠你一個大人情。)【第五常用】

I owe you a huge favor. (我虧欠你太多了。)【第六常用】

I owe you a lot. (我欠你很多。)【第八常用】

I owe you an awful lot. (我虧欠你太多。)【第十常用】

I owe you a hell of a lot. (我虧欠你太多。)【第十一常用】

awful 〔'ɔful 〕 *adj.* 非常的；很大的 (= *very great*)

a hell of a lot 許多；大量 (= *a large amount*)

I owe you *big*. (我欠你很多人情。)【第十二常用】

【在 NTC's Dictionary 中有】

I owe you *big time*. (我欠你很多人情。)【第七常用】

I owe you so much. (我欠你很多。)【第九常用】

根據 The American Heritage Dictionary，big time 當形容
詞或副詞用時，須寫成 bigtime 或 big-time；當名詞用時，寫
成 big time。在 I owe you big time. 中，我們把 big time
當名詞用，是大多數美國人的共同看法，作「快樂的時光」解
【見「東華英漢大辭典」p.301】。*I owe you big time.* 中的 big time
引申爲「很多人情」。

I owe you everything. 【第十三用】

(我的一切都歸功於你。)【owe 〔o〕*v.* 將～歸功於】

I owe you my life. (我的一生都歸功於你。)【第十四常用】

I owe you *more than I can say*. 【第十五常用】

(我欠你的超過我所能說的。)

BOOK 2

7. *I'm a lucky dog.*

這句話字面的意思是「我是隻幸運的狗。」語氣
既謙卑又幽默，表示「我很幸運。」暗示「我不該如
此幸運。」

> *I'm a lucky dog.* (我很幸運。)
> = I'm a lucky man.
> = I'm a lucky person.
> = I'm a lucky guy.
> 【guy〔gaɪ〕 *n.* 傢伙；人】

在中文裡說「你真是好狗運。」美國人就常
說 "You lucky dog." (= *You're a lucky dog.*)
一模一樣的思想，暗示「你不該如此幸運。」
但是中國人不常說「我有好狗運。」美國人卻常
說：*I'm a lucky dog.* 來自我幽默一番。

【例】 You got the prettiest girl in school.
　　　 You're a lucky dog.
　　　 (你交到全校最漂亮的女孩。你真是好狗運。)
　　　 【pretty〔'prɪtɪ〕 *adj.* 漂亮的】
　　　 I got into the best university. *I'm a lucky*
　　　 dog. (我考進最好的大學。我運氣真好。)

　　　 You treat me so well. *I'm a lucky dog.*
　　　 (你對我真好。我很幸運。)【treat〔trit〕 *v.* 對待】
　　　 You're the best friend in the world.
　　　 I'm a lucky dog.
　　　 (你是全世界最好的朋友。我真幸運。)

【對話練習】

1. A：**I'm so lucky!**

　B：You deserve it.

　　You earned it.

　　It's not luck.

　　【earn〔ɝn〕*v.* 贏得；獲得

　　　luck〔lʌk〕*n.* 運氣】

　　　　　　　　　　　　A：我真幸運！

　　　　　　　　　　　　B：這是你應得的。

　　　　　　　　　　　　　　你努力得來的。

　　　　　　　　　　　　　　這並不是運氣。

2. A：**I'm really blessed!**

　B：I agree.

　　You are blessed.

　　You are very fortunate.

　　【fortunate〔'fɔrtʃənɪt〕*adj.* 幸運的】

　　　　　　　　　　　　A：我真幸福！

　　　　　　　　　　　　B：我同意。

　　　　　　　　　　　　　　你很幸福。

　　　　　　　　　　　　　　你非常幸運。

3. A：**I'm the luckiest person in the world.**

　B：You deserve it.

　　You're a good guy.

　　You are so considerate of others.【guy〔gaɪ〕*n.* 人

　　considerate〔kən'sɪdərɪt〕*adj.* 體貼的】

　　　　　　　　　　　　A：我是全世界最幸運的人。

　　　　　　　　　　　　B：這是你應得的。

　　　　　　　　　　　　　　你人很好。

　　　　　　　　　　　　　　你很體貼別人。

4. A：**Everything is perfect.**

　B：You're right.

　　Things are great.

　　Enjoy it while it lasts.

　　【last〔læst〕*v.* 持續】

　　　　　　　　　　　　A：一切都很完美。

　　　　　　　　　　　　B：你說得對。

　　　　　　　　　　　　　　一切都很好。

　　　　　　　　　　　　　　要及時行樂。

BOOK 2

BOOK 2

5. A : **Everything is going my way**.　　　A：每件事都很順利。

　　B : That's great.　　　　　　　　　　B：太棒了。
　　　　Lucky you.　　　　　　　　　　　你真幸運。
　　　　Good for you.　　　　　　　　　太好了。

6. A : **You are the reason why!**　　　　A：就是因為你的緣故！

　　B : Not really.　　　　　　　　　　　B：不完全是。
　　　　I disagree.　　　　　　　　　　　我不同意。
　　　　You did it.　　　　　　　　　　　是因為你。

7. A : **Thanks a bunch**.　　　　　　　　A：非常感謝。

　　B : Anytime. (= *Any time*.)　　　　B：隨時願意效勞。
　　　　You're welcome.　　　　　　　　　【可引申為「不客氣。」】
　　　　It's my pleasure.　　　　　　　　不客氣。
　　　　【pleasure (ˈplɛʒɚ) *n.* 榮幸】　　這是我的榮幸。

8. A : **I owe you a lot**.　　　　　　　　A：我非常感謝你。

　　B : Don't say that.　　　　　　　　　B：別這麼說。
　　　　That's not true.　　　　　　　　　那不是事實。
　　　　That's what friends are for.　　　朋友就是該互相幫忙。

9. A : **I'm a lucky dog**.　　　　　　　　A：我真是幸運。

　　B : You sure are.　　　　　　　　　　B：你的確是。
　　　　You can say that again.　　　　　你說得對。
　　　　Don't forget it.　　　　　　　　　不要忘了。
　　　　【sure (ʃur) *adv.* 的確；當然】

11. Do you need a ride?

Do you need a ride?	你要搭便車嗎？
Can I give you a lift?	我能送你嗎？
How are you getting home?	你要怎麼回家？
Let me take you.	讓我載你吧。
Let me drive you.	讓我開車載你。
It's no problem at all.	一點問題也沒有。
Ride with me.	和我一起坐車。
I enjoy your company.	我喜歡你陪我。
It'd be my pleasure.	這將是我的榮幸。

BOOK 2

** ————————————

ride〔raɪd〕*v., n.* 搭乘；乘車　　lift〔lɪft〕*n.* 搭便車
take〔tek〕*v.* 帶領　　drive〔draɪv〕*v.* 開車載
not…at all 一點也不　　enjoy〔ɪn'dʒɔɪ〕*v.* 喜歡
company〔'kʌmpənɪ〕*n.* 陪伴
pleasure〔'plɛʒɚ〕*n.* 快樂；榮幸

【背景説明】

邀請別人搭便車的機會很多,背了這九句話以後,你就可以用英文説了,聽了這些話,別人會認爲你是個熱情的好人。

1. ***Do you need a ride?***
ride〔raɪd〕*n.* 騎;搭車

這句話字面的意思是「你需不需要搭車?」引申爲「你要搭便車嗎?」***Do you need a ride?*** 可以簡化成: Need a ride? (要搭便車嗎?)

2. ***Can I give you a lift?***
lift〔lɪft〕*n.* 舉起;提升;搭便車

下面都是美國人邀請別人搭便車的説法,我們按照使用頻率排列:

① Do you need a ride? (你要搭便車嗎?) 【第一常用】

② Do you need a lift? (你要搭便車嗎?) 【第二常用】

③ Do you want a ride? (你要搭便車嗎?) 【第三常用】

④ Do you want a lift? (你要搭便車嗎?)

⑤ Can I give you a ride? (我能開車送你嗎?)

⑥ ***Can I give you a lift?*** (我能送你嗎?)

⑦ How about a ride? (要搭便車嗎?)

⑧ How about a lift? (要搭便車嗎?)

【***How about~?*** ~如何? 】

3. *How are you getting home?*

在會話中，美國人常用現在進行式，表示情感。

【比較】 How do you get home?（你怎麼回家？）

　　　　【一般語氣，用現在式表示不變的事實，過去
　　　　和現在都一樣。】

　　　　How are you getting home?（你要怎麼回家？）
　　　　【表示關心，及現在正在。】

【例 1 】 A: How do you get home?（你怎麼回家？）
　　　　 B: I usually take the bus.（我通常搭公車。）

【例 2 】 A: *How are you getting home?*
　　　　　　（你要怎麼回家？）
　　　　 B: I don't know. I don't have a ride.
　　　　　　（我不知道。我無車可搭。）

> *How are you getting home?* 中的 home，可改成
> 其他地點，要注意：除了 home、there 前無介系詞外，
> 其他的名詞前面，都需要有介系詞。如：
>
> How are you getting *there*?（你要怎麼去那裡？）
> How are you getting *to school*?（你要怎麼去上學？）
> How are you getting *to work*?（你要怎麼去上班？）
>
> How are you getting *to the mall*?
> 　（你要怎麼去購物中心？）【mall〔mɔl〕*n.* 購物中心】
> How are you getting *to the movies*?
> 　（你要怎麼去看電影？）
> 　【movies 為什麼用複數？詳見 p.494】
> How are you getting *to the party*?
> 　（你要怎麼去宴會？）

4. *Let me take you.*

take〔tek〕*v.* 拿；帶領

這句話字面的意思是「讓我帶領你。」等於
Let me lead you. 但是，在這裡的意思卻是「讓
我載你。」後面可以加上所要去的地點：

> ***Let me take you.***（讓我載你。）
> Let me take you ***home.***（讓我載你回家。）
> Let me take you ***there.***（讓我載你去那裡。）
>
> Let me take you ***to school.***（讓我載你去上學。）
> Let me take you ***to the train station.***
> （讓我載你去火車站。）
> Let me take you ***to the hospital.***
> （讓我載你去醫院。）

上面各句的 take，
不一定是指「開車載」，
也可以是指「帶領」。

Let me drive you.

5. *Let me drive you.*

drive〔draɪv〕*v.* 開車載

這句話的意思是「讓我開車載你。」後面可加地
點，像：

> Let me drive you ***home.***（讓我開車載你回家。）
> Let me drive you ***there.***（讓我開車載你去那裡。）
> Let me drive you ***to the station.***
> （讓我開車載你到車站。）

Let me drive you. 也可説成：Let me give you a
ride. 都表示「讓我開車載你。」

6. *It's no problem at all.*

　　not…at all 一點也不

　　　　這句話的意思是「一點問題也沒有。」是美國人常說的 No problem.（沒問題。）的加強語氣。

　　　　It's no problem at all.【第一常用】
　　　　（一點問題也沒有。）
　　　= It's no trouble at all.【第二常用】
　　　　（一點也不麻煩。）
　　　= It's no bother at all.（一點也不麻煩。）【第三常用】
　　　= It's no inconvenience at all.【第四常用】
　　　　（一點也不會不方便。）
　　　【trouble〔ˈtrʌbl̩〕*n.* 麻煩　　bother〔ˈbɑðɚ〕*n.* 麻煩】

　　　　上面的句子，在本單元的情況下，It's 不可省略，但 at all 可以省略。

7. *Ride with me.*

　　ride〔raɪd〕*v.* 搭乘；乘坐（交通工具）

　　　　ride 這個字，是及物和不及物兩用動詞，源自「騎馬」(ride a horse；
ride on a horse)，現在也
可以用在搭乘其他交通工
具，如：ride in a bus（搭
公車）、ride on a train（搭
火車）、ride on a bicycle
（騎腳踏車）。

> ***Ride with me.*** 的意思是「和我一起坐車。」可加長爲：You can ride with me.（你可以和我一起坐車。）或 Please ride with me.（請和我一起坐車。）比較禮貌的說法是：I invite you to ride with me.（我邀請你和我一起坐車。）

除了說 ***Ride with me.*** 以外，還可以說：Go with me.（和我一起走。）或 Leave with me.（和我一起離開。）

8. ***I enjoy your company.***
enjoy〔ɪn'dʒɔɪ〕*v.* 喜歡
company〔'kʌmpənɪ〕*n.* 公司；陪伴

company 的主要意思是「公司」，在此作「陪伴」解。這句話的意思是「我喜歡你陪我。」

9. ***It'd be my pleasure.***（這將是我的榮幸。）
pleasure〔'plɛʒɚ〕*n.* 快樂；榮幸

【比較1】 ***It'd be my pleasure.***【常用】
It would be my pleasure.
【少用，老一輩的人才說】

【比較2】 ***It'd be my pleasure.***（這將是我的榮幸。）
It's my pleasure.（這是我的榮幸。）

從 ***It'd be my pleasure.*** 中的 It'd 可知，是假設法，省略了 If 子句。這句話源自：*If you would ride with me*, it would be my pleasure.

凡是前面有了要求的內容，後面就可以用假設法的
It'd be my pleasure.

【例1】 How about dinner with me?
　　　 It'd be my pleasure.
　　　 （跟我吃晚飯好嗎？這將是我的榮幸。）
　　　 【How about dinner with me?
　　　 　 = How about having dinner with me?】

【例2】 Please accompany me.
　　　 It'd be my pleasure.
　　　 （請陪伴我。這將是我的榮幸。）
　　　 【accompany〔ə'kʌmpənɪ〕v. 陪伴】

【例3】 Can you give me a ride?
　　　 It'd be my pleasure.
　　　 （你能讓我搭便車嗎？這將是我的榮幸。）

It's my pleasure. 通常是在別人感謝你的回答話。

【例1】 A: Thank you for helping me.
　　　　 （謝謝你幫助我。）
　　　 B: ***It's my pleasure.*** （這是我的榮幸；不客氣。）

【例2】 A: What a thoughtful gift! Thank you.
　　　　 （真是體貼的禮物！謝謝你。）
　　　 B: ***It's my pleasure.***
　　　　 （這是我的榮幸；不客氣。）

【例3】 A: Thanks for treating me. （謝謝你請我。）
　　　　 【treat〔trit〕v. 款待；請客】
　　　 B: ***It's my pleasure.*** （這是我的榮幸；不客氣。）

【對話練習】

1. A：**Do you need a ride?**　　　　A：你要搭便車嗎？

　　B：Yes, I do.　　　　　　　　　B：是的，我要。

　　　　I could use one.　　　　　　我想搭便車。

　　　　Thanks for asking.　　　　　謝謝你問我。

　　　　【*could use* 想要】

2. A：**Can I give you a lift?**　　　A：我能送你嗎？

　　B：No, thank you.　　　　　　　B：不用，謝謝。

　　　　I already have a ride.　　　　我有便車可搭了。

　　　　I appreciate the offer.　　　　謝謝你的提議。

　　　　【appreciate〔əˈpriʃɪˌet〕*v.* 感激

　　　　offer〔ˈɔfɚ〕*n.* 提供；提議】

3. A：**How are you getting home?**　A：你怎麼回家？

　　B：I don't know.　　　　　　　B：我不知道。

　　　　I'm not sure yet.　　　　　　我還不確定。

　　　　I haven't decided.　　　　　我尚未決定。

　　　　【*not…yet* 尚未】

4. A：**Let me take you.**　　　　　A：讓我載你吧。

　　B：That would be great!　　　　B：太棒了！

　　　　When are you leaving?　　　你什麼時候要離開？

　　　　I'm ready whenever you　　　只要你準備好，我隨時

　　　　are.　　　　　　　　　　　都可以。

BOOK 2

5. A：**Let me drive you**.
   B：That sounds great.
   I need a ride.
   I'm ready anytime.

A：讓我開車載你。
B：聽起來很棒。
我需要搭便車。
我隨時都準備好了。

6. A：**It's no problem at all**.
   B：Are you sure it's not out of your way?
   It seems like I'm taking you way off your route.
   At least let me put some gas in your tank. 【route〔rut〕*n.* 路線
   gas〔gæs〕*n.* 汽油
   tank〔tæŋk〕*n.* 油箱】

A：一點問題也沒有。
B：你確定順路嗎？

我似乎會讓你遠離你的路線。
至少讓我出些油錢。

7. A：**Ride with me**.
   B：No, thanks.
   I drove here.
   I have my car.

A：和我一起坐車。
B：不了，謝謝。
我開車來的。
我自己有車。

8. A：**I enjoy your company**.
   B：Thanks.
   It's kind of you to say so.
   I enjoy your company, too.

A：我喜歡你陪我。
B：謝謝。
你這麼說人真好。
我也喜歡你陪我。

9. A：**It'd be my pleasure**.
   B：Are you sure?
   Do you mean it?
   I don't want to trouble you.
   【trouble〔'trʌbl〕*v.* 麻煩】

A：這將是我的榮幸。
B：你確定嗎？
你是認真的嗎？
我不想麻煩你。

BOOK 2

12. Thanks for the ride.

Thanks for the ride.	謝謝你開車載我。
You are a good driver.	你很會開車。
I owe you one.	我欠你一次人情。
I really appreciate it.	我真的很感激。
You've helped me a lot.	你幫我很多忙。
You've saved me a lot of trouble.	你幫我省掉很多麻煩。
Take care.	保重。
Drive safely.	開車要注意安全。
Catch you tomorrow.	明天見。

**

ride〔raɪd〕n. 搭乘　　owe〔o〕v. 欠
appreciate〔ə'priʃɪ͵et〕v. 為…表示感激
save〔sev〕v. 省去　　trouble〔'trʌbl̩〕n. 麻煩
take care 保重　　safely〔'seflɪ〕adv. 安全地
catch〔kætʃ〕v. 抓住

【背景説明】

別人開車載你到目的地後,感謝的話,説愈多愈好。背完這九句話以後,你就比美國人還會説了。

1. ***Thanks for the ride.***

   ride〔raɪd〕*n.* 搭乘

   這句話的意思是「謝謝你開車載我。」下面都是美國人常説的話:

   Thanks for the ride.【第一常用】

   Thanks for the lift. (謝謝你讓我搭便車。)【第二常用】

   Thanks for driving me. (謝謝你開車載我。)【第四常用】

   Thanks for taking me. (謝謝你載我。)【第五常用】

   I appreciate the ride. (感謝你開車載我。)【第三常用】

   【appreciate〔ə'priʃɪ,et〕*v.* 感激】

2. ***You are a good driver.***

   這句話的意思是「你很會開車。」中國人和外國人的思想不一樣。

   【比較】中文: 你很會開車。

   　　　英文: You are a good driver.【最常用】

   　　　　　　You drive well.【常用】

   　　　　　　You drove very well.

   　　　　　　【極少用,也許是老一輩的人用】

   　　　中文: 你很會管理。

   　　　英文: You are a good manager.【最常用】

   　　　　　　You manage very well.【極少用】

下面的句子，美國人也常說：

You are a wonderful driver. (你車開得很棒。)
You are an excellent driver. (你車開得很好。)
You are a skilled driver. (你開車技術很好。)

You are a safe driver. (你開車很安全。)
You are a careful driver. (你開車很小心。)
You are a cautious driver. (你開車很小心。)

excellent〔'ɛksḷənt〕adj. 極好的
skilled〔skɪld〕adj. 有技巧的；熟練的
cautious〔'kɔʃəs〕adj. 小心的

3. *I owe you one.*

owe〔o〕v. 欠

　　這句話的意思是「我欠你一次人情。」你也可以
只說：I owe you. (我感謝你。) 也可以加強語氣，
說成：I owe you a big one. (我欠你一次大人情。)
【詳見 p.10–7】

Thanks for the ride.
You are a good driver.
I owe you one.

4. *I really appreciate it*.

ap｜preci｜ate　從字根上分析，表示「估價」，引申爲
to　price　v.

「重視」，再引申爲「賞識」，所以受詞通常爲非人，
不可接人表示感激。

I really appreciate it. 在美國人的思想當中，是
「我非常重視這件事情。」如：

> I appreciate your kindness.
> （我很感激你的好意。）

爲什麼中國人不會用 appreciate 這個字呢？
因爲中國人的思想是感激某人，而美國人是「賞識」
某事。中文說「謝謝你的幫助。」英文要說成：

> I *appreciate* your help.
> = I *thank* you *for* your help.

要記住，appreciate 後接非人，thank 後面要先接人。

反正，要常說 I appreciate it. 或 I really appreciate it.
表示感謝。

中文：我感謝你。

英文：*I appreciate you.*【和中文意思不符】

　　　I appreciate it. 【正】

　　　I appreciate you. 的意思是「我很賞識你。」
　　　(= *I value you.*)

BOOK 2

5. *You've helped me a lot.* (你幫我很多忙。)
   You've saved me a lot of trouble.
   (你幫我省掉很多麻煩。)
   save〔sev〕v. 省去

   這兩句話美國人常說，用於表示感謝。

   【比較1】 *You've helped me a lot.*【通俗，常說】
   　　　　 You have helped me a lot.
   　　　　　【正，但美國人不說，只有書寫的時候才用】

   【比較2】 *You've saved me a lot of trouble.*
   　　　　　【通俗，常說】
   　　　　 You have saved me a lot of trouble.
   　　　　　【正，但美國人不說，只有書寫的時候才用】

6. *Take care.*

   　　Take care. 通常是指 Take care of yourself.
   當美國人和朋友、家人道別的時候，常說 Take
   care.

   　　【比較】 Take care. (保重。)【語氣輕鬆】
   　　　　　 Take care of yourself.
   　　　　　　(好好照顧自己。)【語氣較強】

   　　但是，在這裡，*Take care.* 的意思是「小心。」
   等於 Be careful. 在文法上，take care 後面可接動
   名詞或不定詞 (to + 原形動詞)，或 that 子句，事實
   上，美國人多用 Take care + V-ing。

【例1】 ***Take care*** driving home.
It's foggy out tonight.
（開車回家要小心。今天晚上外面有霧。）
【foggy〔'fɑgɪ〕 *adj.* 有霧的】

【例2】 ***Take care*** walking on the floor.
It's slippery.
（走在地板上要小心。很滑。）
【slippery〔'slɪpərɪ〕 *adj.* 滑的】

【例3】 ***Take care*** eating the soup.
It's very hot.
（小心喝湯。很燙。）
【soup〔sup〕 *n.* 湯】

【例4】 ***Take care.*** （小心。）
You need to wear more.
（你必須多穿點衣服。）
You are going to catch cold.
（你會感冒。）【***catch cold*** 感冒】

7. ***Drive safely.***

safely〔'seflɪ〕 *adv.* 安全地

【比較】 ***Drive safely.*** （開車注意安全。）【最常用】
Drive carefully. （小心開車。）【常用】
Be safe. （要注意安全。）
【年輕一代喜歡說的話】
Be careful going home. （回家要小心。）

8. *Catch you tomorrow.*

catch〔kætʃ〕v. 抓住

這句話字面的意思是「明天要抓你。」引申為「明天見。」是美國人的幽默用語。你也可以說：

Catch you later. (待會兒見。)
= I'll catch you later.

或是說：I'll try to catch you later. (我待會會儘量想辦法去見你。) **Catch you later.** 也許是待會兒見，也許是明天，或一年以後見面，講這句話的意思是，希望能夠很快見到你。

【比較】

Catch you tomorrow.
【輕鬆、幽默】
See you tomorrow.
【較正式】

Catch you tomorrow.

說話要幽默，要像美國人，就要常使用 catch。

【例1】 Slow down. (慢一點。)
I'm exhausted. (我很累。)
I need to catch my breath.
(我需要喘一口氣，休息一下。)

slow down 減速
exhausted〔ɪg'zɔstɪd〕adj. 筋疲力盡的
catch one's breath 喘一口氣

【例2】 Good job. (做得好。)
You did it. (你辦到了。)
Now you're catching on. (現在你懂了。)
【*catch on* 了解】

BOOK 2

【對話練習】

1. A：**Thanks for the ride.**

　　B：Any time.

　　　It's my pleasure.

　　　You're more than welcome.

　　　【*Any time.* 不客氣】

A：謝謝你開車載我。

B：不客氣。

　　這是我的榮幸。

　　眞的不客氣。

2. A：**You are a good driver.**

　　B：You think so?

　　　Thank you.

　　　You flatter me.

　　　【flatter〔'flætɚ〕*v.* 恭維；奉承】

A：你很會開車。

B：你這麼認爲嗎？

　　謝謝。

　　你使我受寵若驚。

3. A：**I owe you one.**

　　B：No, you don't.

　　　Don't say that.

　　　We're friends.

A：我欠你一次人情。

B：不，你沒有。

　　別那麼說。

　　我們是朋友。

4. A：**I really appreciate it.**

　　B：Think nothing of it.

　　　The pleasure was all mine.

　　　I know you'd do the same

　　　for me.

A：我眞的很感激。

B：別放在心上。

　　這是我的榮幸。

　　我知道換作是你也會爲

　　我這麼做。

BOOK 2

BOOK 2

5. A：**You've helped me a lot.**

　B：Don't mention it.
　　Don't be polite.
　　You don't need to say that.
　　【polite〔pə'laɪt〕*adj.* 有禮貌的；
　　　客氣的】

A：你幫我很多忙。

B：不客氣。
　　不客氣。
　　你不必這麼說。

6. A：**You've saved me a lot of
　　trouble.**

　B：It was nothing.
　　I'm glad I could help.
　　Anything for a friend.
　　【glad〔glæd〕*adj.* 高興的】

A：你幫我省掉很多麻煩。

B：沒什麼。
　　我很高興能幫上忙。
　　為了朋友，兩肋插刀，
　　在所不辭。

7. A：**Take care.**

　B：I will.
　　Don't worry.
　　I'll be careful.

A：保重。

B：我會的。
　　別擔心。
　　我會小心的。

8. A：**Drive safely.**

　B：I sure will.
　　I always do.
　　I'm very careful.

A：開車注意安全。

B：我一定會。
　　我總是如此。
　　我非常小心。

9. A：**Catch you tomorrow.**

　B：OK.
　　See you tomorrow.
　　Have a good one.

A：明天見。

B：好的。
　　明天見。
　　再見。

「一口氣背會話」經 BOOK 2

唸「一口氣英語」要像唸經一樣，每天大聲唸，從起床到睡覺，唸得比看得快，最後不看也會唸，養成習慣後，你會全身舒爽，你試試看，奇妙無比。速度只要快到一分鐘之內唸完，就終生不會忘記。

1. I'm having a party.
   It's Friday night.
   I want you to come.

   You're invited.
   Are you free?
   Can you make it?

   You gotta be there.
   You gotta show up.
   It won't be the same without you.

2. Excuse me, sir.
   I'm looking for a mall.
   Is there a mall around here?

   I'm new here.
   I don't have a clue.
   Can you tell me where it is?

   Do you live here?
   Do you know this area?
   Any shopping center will do.

3. *I'm* looking for a pen.
   I want a ballpoint pen.
   Do you have any good ones?

   What's on sale?
   What's your best buy?
   Do you have any specials?

   I like this!
   I'll take it!
   How much is it?

4. *Can you* lower the price?
   Can you make it cheaper?
   That's way too high.

   That's too expensive.
   I can't afford it.
   Please help me out.

   How about a deal?
   How about 20% off?
   I'd really appreciate it.

5. Happy birthday!
   Congratulations!
   You must be feeling great!

   It's a big day.
   It's your special day.
   We should celebrate.

   Enjoy yourself.
   Have a super day.
   I wish you all the best.

6. Here's a little something.
   I got this for you.
   I hope you like it.

   It's not much.
   You deserve more.
   You deserve the best.

   You're one of a kind.
   You're so special.
   You're really great.

7. Thank you so much.
   It's wonderful.
   It's what I always wanted.

   It's perfect.
   How did you know?
   It's just what I needed.

   You're so thoughtful.
   I'm really grateful.
   I can't thank you enough.

8. What can I say?
   I'm speechless.
   You shouldn't have.

   I really don't deserve it.
   You're too good to me.
   I really like this gift.

   It's very useful.
   I was going to buy one.
   You read my mind.

9. *This is* topnotch.
   This is superb.
   I'm very impressed.

   It's very nice.
   It's high quality.
   It must be worth a lot.

   It's excellent.
   It's outstanding.
   I like it so much.

10. *I'm* so lucky!
    I'm really blessed!
    I'm the luckiest person in the world.

    Everything is perfect.
    Everything is going my way.
    You are the reason why!

    Thanks a bunch.
    I owe you a lot.
    I'm a lucky dog.

11. Do you need a ride?
    Can I give you a lift?
    How are you getting home?

    Let me take you.
    Let me drive you.
    It's no problem at all.

    Ride with me.
    I enjoy your company.
    It'd be my pleasure.

12. Thanks for the ride.
    You are a good driver.
    I owe you one.

    I really appreciate it.
    You've helped me a lot.
    You've saved me a lot of trouble.

    Take care.
    Drive safely.
    Catch you tomorrow.

　　剛開始背「一口氣背會話」，也許困難一點。只要堅持下去，一旦學會背快的技巧，就能一本接一本地背下去。每一本108句中英文背到兩分鐘之內，就變成直覺，終生不會忘記，唯有不忘記，才能不斷地累積。

BOOK 3 搭計程車用餐

▶ 3-1 在大城市裡,招手叫計程車時,可以說:

Hey!
Taxi!
Over here!

▶ 3-2 剛到一個陌生的城市,可以問計程車司機,哪裡好玩:

I'm looking for fun.
Where is the action?
Where is a happening place?

▶ 3-3 想要再問計程車司機,哪裡有好的餐廳:

I need some help.
I'd like your advice.
Where's a good place to eat?

▶ 3-4 要下計程車時,可問司機車費多少:

What's the fare?
How much do I owe you?
How much should I pay?

▶ 3-5 到了目的地,你可以和同行的朋友說:

Here we are.
We are here.
We made it.

▶ 3-6 進到餐廳,看到接待員,就可說:

Table for two.
Nonsmoking section.
Can we sit by a window?

▶ 3-7 入座後，看完菜單，就可跟服務生說：

We're ready to order.
We know what we want.
Can you take our order now?

▶ 3-8 在餐桌上，可勸朋友多吃一點：

Eat up!
Eat some more!
Eat as much as you can.

▶ 3-9 當你喜歡一個地方的時候，就可說：

I like this place.
It's my kind of place.
It's just perfect for me.

▶ 3-10 在餐廳吃完飯後，要叫服務生來結帳，就可說：

We're ready.
We're done.
Check, please.

▶ 3-11 如果你想要去洗手間，可請你的朋友等一下：

Excuse me a moment.
I'll be right back.
Please wait for me.

▶ 3-12 約會結束，要和朋友說再見時，可說：

It's about that time.
It's time to say good-bye.
I have to get going.

1. *Calling a Taxi*

Hey!	嘿！
Taxi!	計程車！
Over here!	這裡！
How're you doing?	你好嗎？
Thanks for stopping.	謝謝你停下來。
Downtown, please.	請到市中心。
I just arrived.	我剛到。
I want to go downtown.	我要到市中心。
I want to see the sights.	我要看看值得看的東西。

BOOK 3

**

hey〔he〕*interj.* 嘿
downtown〔'daʊn'taʊn〕*n.* 市中心　　*adv.* 到市中心
sights〔saɪts〕*n. pl.* 風景；名勝；值得看的東西
see the sights 觀光；看值得看的東西

【背景說明】

在國外各大城市裡，你只要招手就可以叫到計程車，背好這九句話，你就可以用英文招計程車，而且可以和司機用英語交談。

1. *Hey!*

hey〔he〕*interj.* 嘿！喂！啊！

凡是想引起別人注意（attract attention），或表示驚奇（surprise），感謝（appreciation），懷疑（wonder），快樂（pleasure）等，都可以用 *Hey!*。

【例1】 *Hey!* Excuse me. I'm waiting in line.
Don't cut in line.
（嘿！對不起，我在排隊。請不要插隊。）
【想引起別人注意】

【例2】 *Hey!* What a surprise! Great to see you!
（嘿！真想不到！真高興見到你！）【表示驚奇】

【例3】 *Hey!* This is wonderful! Thank you
so much. （嘿！這東西真棒！非常謝謝你。）
【表示感激】

【例4】 *Hey!* Really? Let me think about it.
I'm not sure.
（嘿！真的嗎？讓我想想看，我不確定。）【表示懷疑】

【例5】 ***Hey!*** This is great!　I'm so lucky.

（嘿！這個真棒！我真幸運。）【表示快樂】

hey〔he〕主要用在引起別人注意，或打招呼。

hi〔haɪ〕主要用在打招呼。

中國人看到外國人，喜歡說 ***Hello***, ***hello!***（誤），其
　　　　　　　　　　　　　　〔hə'lo〕
實應該說：***Hey!*** Excuse me! 才對。走在路上看到
外國人，你可以說：***Hey!*** What's up?（嘿！怎麼樣
啊？）或 Hi! What's up?（嗨！怎麼樣啊？）

【比較】 ***Hey!*** Taxi!【正】

Hi! Taxi!【誤】

【Hey! 和 Hi! 都可做打招呼用語，但是 Hi! 不
用於引起別人注意。】

2. ***Taxi!***

taxi〔'tæksɪ〕*n.* 計程車

有些美國人也把 taxi 稱作 cab〔kæb〕*n.* 計程車，
或 taxicab〔'tæksɪ͵kæb〕*n.* 計程車，例如：

I need a taxi.（我需要一部計程車。）

= I need a cab.

= I need a taxicab.

但是，叫計程車的時候，只
說 "***Hey***, ***taxi!***"。

【比較】 ***Hey! Taxi!***【正】

Hey! Cab!【誤】

Hey! Taxicab!【誤】

3. *Over here!*

當你叫一個人過來，可以說：Come here. 或
Come over here. 或 Over here. 美國人的習慣，
叫計程車過來，他們通常喊 Over here! 或 Here!。

4. *How're you doing?*

do 在這句話中作「進行」解，整句話字面意思是
「你進行得如何？」引申為「你好嗎？」這是美國人見
面最常說的話，不管對認
識或不認識的人都可以
說。這句話說慢一點，是
How are you doing?，
說快一點，就將 are 省略，
成為 How you doing?

How're you doing?

【例1】 A: *How're you doing?*（你好嗎？）
B: OK. Not bad. How about you?
（很好，不錯。你呢？）

【例2】 A: *How are you doing?*（你好嗎？）
B: Pretty good. Doing OK.
（很好，一切順利。）

【例3】 A: *How you doing?*（你好嗎？）
B: Fine. Doing great.（很好，一切都好。）

【比較1】 How are you?【正式】
How are you doing?【常用】
How're you doing?【最常用】
How you doing?【常用】

【比較 2】 How are you doing?

（你好嗎？）【純粹問候語】

What are you doing?（你在做什麼？）

【有問候的意思，也有其他意思】

【例】 A: What are you doing?

（你在做什麼啊？）

B: Not much.（沒做什麼事。）

A 在和 B 打招呼，就像中國人問「吃飽飯了沒有？」，並不一定真的想問「吃飽了沒有？」
What are you doing? 有四個意思，詳見 p.8。

BOOK 3

5. *Thanks for stopping.*（謝謝你停下來。）

這句話只有在街上招計程車時才說，也可說成：Thanks for picking me up.（謝謝你載我。）或只說 Thanks.。如果是搭在飯店門口排隊的計程車，這句話就可以不必說，直接說下一句。

6. *Downtown, please.*

downtown〔'daʊn'taʊn〕*n.* 市中心

每個城市都有較繁華的地區，稱作 downtown，有些地方 downtown 範圍很大，你可以和司機說：
Please take me to the center of downtown.

（請載我到市中心最熱鬧的地方。）

7. *I just arrived.*

在計程車上，和司機聊天，想知道這個地區的情況，美國人常說：

I just arrived.（我剛到。）
I just got here.（我剛到這裡。）
I'm new in town.（我對這個城市不熟。）

I just flew in today.（我今天才坐飛機來的。）
I'm just visiting. I don't know where to go.
（我只是來玩的。不知道去哪裡。）
It's my first time here. This city is new
　　to me.（我第一次來這裡。這個城市我不熟。）

8. *I want to go downtown.*

downtown (ˈdaʊnˈtaʊn) *adv.* 到市中心

go downtown 的 downtown 是副詞，前面不要加 to，用法和 here, there, home 類似。

【比較】Let's go downtown.（我們到市中心去。）【正】
　　　　Let's go to downtown.【誤】
　　　　Let's go to the downtown.【誤】

這句話的意思是「我要到市中心。」I want to go~ 是美國人最常和計程車司機說的話，其他常用的還有：

Take me downtown.（載我到市中心。）
I need to get downtown.（我需要到市中心。）

9. *I want to see the sights.*

sights〔saɪts〕*n. pl.* 名勝；風景；值得看的東西
see the sights 觀光；看值得看的東西
（= *see sth. worth seeing*）

> sights 不一定只指「風景」，凡是「名勝；古蹟；任何值得看的東西」，都叫做 sights。這句話可以翻成「我要看看值得看的東西。」在美國，每個城市的市中心，都有比較有名的建築物、公園、廣場、街道、購物中心等，都叫做 sights。

I want to see the sights. 也可說成：I want
to do some sightseeing.（我想去觀光。）也有
人說：

I want to look around.（我要到處看看。）
I want to walk around.（我要到處走走。）
I want to see what's going on.
（我要看看有什麼好看的。）
I want to see what's up.
（我要看看有什麼事。）

───【劉毅老師的話】───
「一口氣背會話」中英文一起背，
可跟著 CD 唸，模仿美國人的發音，說
起來就像美國人。

【對話練習】

1. A：**Hey!**
   B：Yes, sir.
   　　I see you.
   　　I'll be right there.

A：嘿！
B：是的，先生。
　　我看見你了。
　　我馬上就到。

2. A：**Taxi!**
   B：One moment.
   　　I'm on my way.
   　　I'll be there in a sec.
   　　【sec〔sɛk〕*n.* 秒（= *second*）】

A：計程車！
B：等一下。
　　我就要過去了。
　　我馬上就到。

3. A：**Over here.**
   B：OK.
   　　I'm coming.
   　　Just let me turn around.

A：這裡。
B：好。
　　我來了。
　　讓我轉過來。

4. A：**How're you doing?**
   B：I'm doing great.
   　　I'm having a good day.
   　　Everything is fine.

A：你好嗎？
B：很好。
　　我今天很愉快。
　　一切順利。

5. A：**Thanks for stopping.**
   B：You're welcome.
   　　It's my job.
   　　In fact, it's my pleasure.

A：謝謝你停下來。
B：不客氣。
　　這是我的工作。
　　事實上，這是我的榮幸。

6. A：**Downtown, please.**

   B：OK.

   You got it.

   Whereabouts downtown?

   【whereabouts〔ˌhwɛrə'baʊts〕
       adv. 在何處】

7. A：**I just arrived.**

   B：Welcome.

   Glad to have you.

   Hope you enjoy your stay.

8. A：**I want to see the sights.**

   B：Sure thing.

   No problem.

   I can take you where you
   want to go.

9. A：**I want to go downtown.**

   B：At your service.

   I'll take you there.

   Any place in particular?

   【*in particular* 特別】

A：請到市中心。

B：好的。

   沒問題。

   市中心的哪裡？

A：我剛到。

B：歡迎。

   很高興載到你。

   希望你喜歡這裡。

A：我想要到處看看。

B：當然可以。

   沒問題。

   你想去哪裡我都可以載
   你去。

A：我要到市中心。

B：隨時聽候差遣。

   我會載你去。

   有特別想去哪個地方嗎？

BOOK 3

2. I'm looking for fun.

I'm looking for fun.	我在找好玩的地方。
Where is the action?	哪裡最好玩？
Where is a happening place?	哪裡最熱鬧？
I want some excitement.	我要找一些好玩的事。
Where should I go?	我該去哪裡？
Where do people go?	人們都去哪裡啊？
Please fill me in.	請告訴我詳情。
Please give me the lowdown.	請告訴我實際情況。
Can you introduce a good place?	你能不能介紹一個好地方？

**————————————————

fun〔fʌn〕*n.* 樂趣；有趣的人或物
action〔'ækʃən〕*n.* 行動；活動
happening〔'hæpənɪŋ〕*adj.* 熱門的
excitement〔ɪk'saɪtmənt〕*n.* 興奮；刺激；令人興奮
　的事；好玩的事　　*fill sb. in* 告訴某人詳情
lowdown〔'lo͵daʊn〕*n.* 內幕；真相；實情
introduce〔͵ɪntrə'djus〕*v.* 介紹

【背景説明】

　　　　到外國坐計程車，跟計程車司機聊天，不僅能練習英文，還可以得到很多資訊。

1. *I'm looking for fun.*（我在找好玩的地方。）
   fun〔fʌn〕*n.* 樂趣；有趣的事物或人

   > 　　美國人想問別人事情的時候，最常用的，就是
   > *I'm looking for~*. 在這裡的 fun 是指 a fun
   > place（有趣的地方）。
   > 　　　　　　　　　　　　　　　　　　fun〔fʌn〕*adj.* 有趣的
   >
   > 　　*I'm looking for fun.*
   > = I'm looking for a fun place.
   > = I'm looking for an exciting place.
   > 　　　　　　　　　〔ɪk'saɪtɪŋ〕*adj.* 令人興奮的；好玩的

2. *Where is the action?*（哪裡最好玩？）
   action〔'ækʃən〕*n.* 行動；活動

   　　action 的主要意思是「行動；活動」，這句話字面的意思是「活動在哪裡？」引申為「哪裡最熱鬧？；哪裡最好玩？」根據句意和情況，可以有各種不同的意思。美國人也常把這句話說成：Where is the action at?

   　　Where is the action? 也可用在句中，成為名詞子句，此時應用敘述句的型式。

【例1】 New York City's Times Square is *where the action is*.

    (= New York City's Times Square is the most exciting place.)

    （紐約市的時代廣場是最熱鬧的地方。）

Times Square

【例2】 For scientists, MIT is *where the action is*.

    (= For scientists, MIT is the most exciting place.)

    （對於科學家而言，麻省理工學院是他們最嚮往的地方。）

【例3】 A Chinese night market is *where the action is*.

    (= A Chinese night market is the most exciting place.)（中國的夜市是最熱鬧的地方。）

【比較1】 ***Where is the action?***

    【正，是慣用語，固定用法，不能更改】

    Where is an action?【誤，此句無任何意義】

【比較2】 從下面比較可知，***Where is the action?*** 或 ***where the action is*** 已成為固定用法，不可更改。

    A Chinese night market is ***where the action is***.【正】

    A Chinese night market is *the action*.【誤】

    A Chinese night market is *where a happening place*.【誤】

    A Chinese night market is ***a happening place***.【正】

3. *Where is a happening place?* (哪裡有熱鬧的地方？)

happening〔ˈhæpənɪŋ〕*adj.* 熱鬧的；熱門的

> happening 當形容詞的用法，在字典上很難找
> 到，但美國人常說。這句話的意思是「哪裡有熱鬧的
> 地方？」相反的說法是：Where is a dead place?
> (哪裡沒有人去？)

【例1】 Shanghai is *a happening place*.
(上海是個熱門的地方。)

【例2】 Las Vegas is *a happening place*. The
casinos are full of action; the hotels
have wonderful shows; the restaurants
have fantastic buffets.

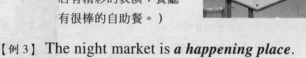

(拉斯維加斯是個熱門的
地方。賭場很熱鬧；飯
店有精彩的表演；餐廳
有很棒的自助餐。)

【例3】 The night market is *a happening place*.
It's noisy. It's exciting.
(夜市是一個熱鬧的地方。那裡很吵，很好玩。)

【比較1】 Where is *a* happening place?【較常說】
(哪裡有熱鬧的地方？)

Where is *the* happening place?【常說】
(= *Where is the most happening place?*)
(哪裡最熱鬧？)
【美國人說話喜歡簡短，省略了 most】

【比較2】 當你想知道好幾個地方，你就問：

Where is a happening place?

（哪裡有熱鬧的地方？）

當你想知道最熱鬧的地方在哪裡時，你就問：

Where is the happening place?

（哪裡最熱鬧？）

【例1】 A: Where is *a happening place*?

B: I know a few.　There is one near here.

I can take you there.

（我知道幾個。有一個在這附近。我可以帶你去。）

【例2】 A: Where is *the happening place*?

B: The best place is

The Hard Rock Café.

（最好的地方是硬石餐廳。）

Hard Rock Café

4. *I want some excitement.*

（我要找一些好玩的事。）

excitement〔ɪk'saɪtmənt〕*n.* 興奮；

刺激；令人興奮的事；好玩的事

這句話中國人不會說，要背下來才會使用。

【比較】

中文： 我要找一些好玩的事。

英文： *I want some excitement.*【常用】

I'm looking for some excitement.【常用】

I want to have some excitement.【正，不常用】

5. *Where do people go?*（人們都到哪裡去啊？）

　　美國人和中國人一樣，喜歡問別人：「人們都到哪裡去啊？」英文就是：

> **Where do people go?**
> = Where does the crowd go?
> 　　　　　〔kraʊd〕*n.* 人群
> = Where is the crowd?

6. *Please fill me in.*（請告訴我詳情。）

fill〔fɪl〕*v.* 填滿

fill sb. in　告訴某人最新消息；告訴某人詳情；告訴某人應該知道的事（*tell sb. what sb. should know*）

　　fill 的主要意思是「填滿」，fill me in 的字面意思是「把我填進去」，也就是「不要漏掉我」，引申為「告訴我詳情」或「告訴我應該知道的事」。

【例 1】 I missed school yesterday. ***Please fill me in*** on our homework.
　　　　（我昨天沒去上學。請告訴我家庭作業是什麼。）
　　　　【school 表「上學」，不可說成 *the school*。】

【例 2】 What did she say about me? ***Please fill me in***.
　　　　（她說了什麼關於我的事？拜託你詳細告訴我。）
　　　　【這裡的 Please fill me in. 等於 Please tell me all about it.】

BOOK 3

【例3】 How was your date? I heard it was
　　　 great. ***Please fill me in.***

　　　（你的約會如何？我聽說很棒。請告訴我詳情。）

【例4】 How was your weekend? What did
　　　 you do? ***Please fill me in.***

　　　（你週末過得如何？你做了什麼事？請告訴
　　　　我詳細情況。）

7. *Please give me the lowdown.*

lowdown〔'loˌdaʊn〕*n.* 內幕；真相；實情
(= *inside information*)

　　這句話的意思是「請告訴我實際情況；請告訴
我一些小道消息。」lowdown 這個字是由 low 和
down 所組成，low 是「低的」，down 是「下面」，
合在一起就表示「內幕；真相；實情」。

　　當公司來了一個新的員工，美國人就會問：
What's the lowdown on that guy?（那個傢伙是
什麼來歷？）

　　　在會話中，美國人常說 *lowdown*：

【例1】 His business went bankrupt. What's
　　　 the *lowdown*?

　　　（他的公司破產了。有什麼內幕消息？）

【例2】 They got a divorce. What's the *lowdown*?

　　　（他們離婚了。有什麼內幕消息？）

What's the lowdown? 也可說成 What's the scoop? 都表示「有什麼新的內幕消息；有什麼不為人知的事？」【scoop〔skup〕*n.* 獨家新聞】

【比較1】

Please give me the lowdown.【語氣普通】
（請告訴我內幕消息。）
Please give me the scoop.【語氣高尚，強調最新消息】
（請告訴我獨家消息。）

lowdown 當名詞解，並沒有不好的意思，是指「內幕消息」(inside information)，或「實情」(the whole truth)，當形容詞的時候，才有「卑賤的；下等的」意思。

【比較2】 lowdown〔'lo'daʊn〕*n.* 內幕；實情【無連字號】
low-down〔'lo'daʊn〕*adj.* 卑賤的；下等的
　　　　　【有連字號】

BOOK 3

如果一堆男生，坐計程車，跟司機說：*"Please give me the lowdown."* 司機也許會認為你是在暗示，哪裡有男人可以去的地方。但是，一般說來，不管男生或女生，都可以跟別人說：*Please give me the lowdown.* 並沒有負面的暗示。

美國人見面打招呼，也常說：What's the scoop? 表示問「情況怎麼樣？有什麼新的消息？」

scoop 的意思是「獨家新聞」，台灣有一家雜誌，叫「獨家報導」，它的英文名字就是 Scoop Weekly。

Scoop Weekly

8. *Can you introduce a good place?*

（你能不能介紹一個好地方？）

introduce〔͵ɪntrə'djus〕*v.* 介紹

中國人習慣說「介紹我一個好地方。」或「介紹一個好地方給我。」美國人卻習慣說："introduce a good place"，或 "introduce a good place to me"，不說 "introduce me a good place"（誤）。因為 introduce 不是授與動詞，而是及物動詞，後面只能有一個受詞。

【比較】 *Can you introduce a good place?*
　　　　【正，最常用，美國人說話喜歡說一半】

Can you introduce a good place to me?
【正，常用】

Can you introduce me a good place?
【誤，這是中國人的思想】

Can you introduce a good place?

【對話練習】

1. A : **I'm looking for fun.**
   B : Tell me what kind.
   Tell me what you like.
   I can help you out.

   A：我在找好玩的地方。
   B：告訴我是哪一種。
   　　告訴我你喜歡什麼。
   　　我可以幫你的忙。

2. A : **Where is the action?**
   B : The action is downtown.
   It's in the city.
   It's near the theater district.
   【theater (ˈθiətɚ) *n.* 戲院
   district (ˈdɪstrɪkt) *n.* 區域】

   A：哪裡最好玩？
   B：市中心最好玩。
   　　就在城市裡。
   　　就在戲院區附近。

3. A : **Where is a happening place?**
   B : I know a great place.
   It's pretty wild.
   It's always packed with
   people.
   【wild (waɪld) *adj.* 瘋狂的
   packed (pækt) *adj.* 擠滿的】

   A：哪裡有熱鬧的地方？
   B：我知道有個地方很棒。
   　　那裡可以玩得很瘋。
   　　那裡總是擠滿了人。

4. A : **I want some excitement.**
   B : Me too.
   I'll join you.
   Let's go have some fun.

   A：我要找一些好玩的事。
   B：我也是。
   　　我要加入你。
   　　我們去好好玩一玩吧。

BOOK 3

5. A：**Where should I go?**

   B：It depends on you.
   There are lots of places.
   You can go anywhere you like.

A：我該去哪裡？

B：看你自己。
   有很多地方可去。
   你想去哪裡都可以。

6. A：**Where do people go?**

   B：Most people walk around the
   shopping district.
   Some people go to the malls.
   Others like the club scene.
   【scene〔sin〕*n.* 活動領域】

A：人們都到哪裡去啊？

B：大部份的人都去逛購物
   區。
   有些人去購物中心。
   有些人喜歡俱樂部。

7. A：**Please fill me in.**

   B：No problem.
   You got it.
   I'll tell you all I know.

A：請告訴我詳情。

B：沒問題。
   沒問題。
   我會把我知道的都告訴你。

8. A：**Please give me the lowdown.**

   B：Here's what I know.
   That area is really hot.
   There is a lot of action there.

A：請告訴我實際情況。

B：以下就是我所知道的。
   那個地區真的很熱門。
   那裡很熱鬧。

9. A：**Can you introduce a good
   place?**

   B：You bet.
   I'll take you to my favorite
   spot.
   I'm sure you'll like it.
   【spot〔spat〕*n.* 地點】

A：你能不能介紹一個好地
   方？

B：當然可以。
   我會帶你去我最喜歡的
   地方。
   我確定你會喜歡。

3. *Where's a good place to eat?*

I need some help.	我需要幫忙。
I'd like your advice.	請給我一些建議。
Where's a good place to eat?	想吃東西，去哪裡比較好？
I want good food.	我想吃好的東西。
I want a great meal.	我想好好吃一頓。
I want the best food around.	我想要吃附近最好的食物。
Where do the locals go?	本地人都去哪裡吃東西？
Where's a popular place?	大家喜歡去哪裡？
I want to eat where the locals eat.	我要去本地人吃東西的地方。

BOOK 3

** ─────────────────

advice〔əd'vaɪs〕*n.* 勸告；建議
great〔gret〕*adj.* 很棒的   meal〔mil〕*n.* 一餐
around〔ə'raʊnd〕*adv.* 在附近   local〔'lokl̩〕*n.* 本地人
popular〔'pɑpjələ˞〕*adj.* 受歡迎的；討人喜歡的

【背景説明】

　　每個人到了外國，都想吃吃當地有名的館子，
這九句話背熟了以後，可以問計程車司機，可以問
店員，或任何你所見到的當地人。

1. *I need some help.*

　　這句話的意思是「我
需要一些幫助。」請求別
人幫忙的時候，可先說：
Excuse me, sir. 或 I
need some help.

I need some help.

【比較】　***I need some help.*** 【語氣輕鬆】
　　　　　（我需要一些幫助。）
　　　　　I need your help. 【語氣緊急】
　　　　　（我需要你救我。）

2. *I'd like your advice.*
advice〔əd'vaɪs〕*n.* 勸告；建議

　　當你想要請教別人的時候，美國人習慣說 *I'd
like your advice.* 這句話的字面意思是「我想要你
的建議。」引申為「請給我一些建議。」

這句話也可以説成：I need your advice.（我需要
你的建議。）

3. *I want good food.*（我想吃好的東西。）

這句話字面的意思是「我要好的食物。」這是美國人的想法，和中國人不一樣。中國人會說：「我想吃好的東西。」

【比較】***I want good food.***【最常用，美國人的思想】

I want some good food.【常用，美國人的思想】

I want to eat some good food.

【常用，這句話中國人和美國人思想相同】

4. *I want a great meal.*

great〔gret〕*adj.* 很棒的

meal〔mil〕*n.* 一餐

這句話字面的意思是「我要一頓好飯。」引申為「我想好好吃一頓。」

【比較】***I want a great meal.***【最常用】

I want to eat a great meal.【正】

I want a great meal *to eat.*【誤】

（由於 to eat 來修飾 meal 是多餘的）

5. *I want the best food around.*

around〔ə'raʊnd〕*adv.* 在附近

這句話字面的意思是「我要附近最好的食物。」引申為「我想要吃附近最好的食物。」

【比較】***I want the best food around.***【最常用】

I want to eat the best food around.【正】

6. *Where do the locals go?*

local〔ˈlokḷ〕*n.* 本地人

> Where do
> the locals go?

　　這句話字面的意思是「本地人去哪裡？」在這裡引申爲「本地人都去哪裡吃東西？」

這句話也可説成：

Where do the locals eat?

　= Where do the people around here eat?

　= Where do the people around here like to eat?
　= Where do the people around here go?

7. *Where's a popular place?*

popular〔ˈpɑpjələ〕*adj.* 受歡迎的；討人喜歡的

【比較 1】 *a popular place* 和 *the popular place* 不同：

Where's a popular place? (= *Where's a fun place? = Where's an exciting place?*)

　　這句話字面的意思是「哪裡是受歡迎的地方？」在這裡引申爲「哪裡有好玩的地方？」，或「大家喜歡去哪裡？」(= *Where's a place people like to go?*)，是在問幾個好玩的地方其中之一，不是在問最好玩的地方。

Where's the popular place?
(= *Where's the best place?*)

　　這句話字面的意思是「哪裡是最受歡迎的地方？」引申爲「哪裡最好玩？」，或「大家最喜歡去哪裡？」。

【比較 2】　Where's the popular place?
　　　　　【常用，因爲美國人喜歡簡略，省略了 most】
　　　　　Where's the most popular place?【少用】

8.　*I want to eat where the locals eat.*

　　　　　這句話的意思是「我要去本地人吃東西的地方。」
也可以説成：I want to go where the locals go.
（我要去本地人去的地方。）

　　　　　如果你要吃本地人吃的東西，你就可以説：
I want to eat what the locals eat.（我要吃本地
人吃的東西。）

想吃當地菜的其他説法還有：

　　　　I want to eat with the locals.【最常用】
　　　　　（我要和當地人一起吃東西。）
　　　　I want to try some local food.【最常用】
　　　　　（我要試試當地的食物。）
　　　　I want to eat local food.【最常用】
　　　　　（我要吃當地的食物。）

　　　　I want to try a local restaurant.【常用】
　　　　　（我要試試當地的餐廳。）
　　　　I want to check out the local food.【常用】
　　　　　（我要試試當地的食物。）
　　　　【*check out*　檢查；看一看；試一試】
　　　　I want to eat in a local place.【常用】
　　　　　（我要到當地吃東西。）

BOOK 3

【對話練習】

1. A：I need some help.

   B：Sure.
   What do you need?
   I hope I can help you.

   A：我需要幫忙。

   B：好的。
   你需要什麼建議？
   希望我能幫得上忙。

2. A：I'd like your advice.

   B：What about?
   I have plenty of advice.
   I just hope it's useful to you.

   A：請給我一些建議。

   B：關於哪一方面的？
   我有很多建議。
   我希望會對你有用。

3. A：Where's a good place to eat?

   B：It depends.
   What do you want?
   How much do you want to
   spend?

   A：想吃東西，去哪裡比較好？

   B：看情形。
   你想吃什麼？
   你的預算有多少？

4. A：I want good food.

   B：OK.
   I know a few places.
   Would you like me to take
   you to one?

   A：我想吃好的東西。

   B：好的。
   我知道一些地方。
   你要我帶你去其中一個
   嗎？

5. A：I want a great meal.

   B：I know a nice place.
   Their food is delicious.
   It's not far from here.

   A：我想好好吃一頓。

   B：我知道有個地方不錯。
   那裡的食物很好吃。
   離這裡不遠。

BOOK 3

6. A：I want the best food
　　　around.

　　B：There is only one place.
　　　It's really the best.
　　　Their food is very famous.

　　A：我想要吃附近最好的食
　　　物。

　　B：只有一個地方。
　　　眞的是最棒的。
　　　他們的食物很有名。

7. A：Where do the locals go?

　　B：There are several places.
　　　They are all popular.
　　　I'll show you the best
　　　one.

　　A：本地人都去哪裡吃東西？

　　B：有好幾個地方。
　　　它們都很受歡迎。
　　　我會告訴你最好的一家。

8. A：Where's a popular place?

　　B：I know a great place.
　　　It's called Ruth's Chris.
　　　You'll like it for sure.
　　　【Ruth's Chris (ˈruθsˌkrɪs)】

　　A：大家喜歡去哪裡？

　　B：我知道有個地方很棒。
　　　就叫「茹絲葵」。
　　　你一定會喜歡。
　　　【「茹絲葵」是美國有名的
　　　牛排餐館】

9. A：I want to eat where the
　　　locals eat.

　　B：Good idea.
　　　Smart choice.
　　　The locals know the best
　　　places.

　　A：我要去本地人吃東西的地
　　　方。

　　B：好主意。
　　　聰明的選擇。
　　　本地人知道哪裡最好。

BOOK 3

4. *What's the fare?*

What's the fare?	車費是多少錢？
How much do I owe you?	我該給你多少錢？
How much should I pay?	我該付多少錢？
Here you go.	拿去吧。
Here is one hundred.	這裡是一百元。
Just give me twenty back.	只要找我二十元就好。
Keep the rest.	其餘的你留著。
That's your tip.	算是你的小費。
Have a good one.	再見。

BOOK 3

**

fare〔fɛr〕*n.* 車資　　owe〔o〕*v.* 欠
pay〔pe〕*v.* 付錢　　*Here you go.* 拿去吧。
rest〔rɛst〕*n.* 其餘的事物　　tip〔tɪp〕*n.* 小費
Have a good one. 再見。

【背景說明】

　　出國旅遊，到全世界各大城市搭計程車，該怎麼付錢，該怎麼付小費，這一回都有詳細的說明。

1. *What's the fare?*
   fare〔fɛr〕*n.* 車費；票價

　　這句話的意思是「車費是什麼？」引申為「車費是多少錢？」在這裡的 *the fare*，是指 the taxi fare，凡是火車、公車、計程車、飛機的車費、票價，都稱作 *the fare*。

　　因為是在計程車裡面，所以只要說 the fare 就明白了。

【比較】***What's the fare?***【在計程車裡面說】
　　　　What's the taxi fare?【在計程車裡面不說】

在飯店裡面，你要出去玩的時候，你可以問櫃台：

What's *the taxi fare* to the airport?
（到機場的計程車費是多少錢？）
What's *the bus fare* to downtown?
（到市中心的公車票價是多少錢？）
What's *the airfare* to Hong Kong?
〔'ɛr͵fɛr〕*n.* 飛機票價
（到香港的機票是多少錢？）

fare 單獨使用時，一定要用定冠詞 the，不可用 a。

【比較】***What's the fare?***【正】
　　　　What's a fare?【誤】

What's the fare? 也可說成：

> What's the price? (價錢多少？)
>
> = What's the charge? (費用多少？)
>   〔 tʃɑrdʒ 〕*n.* 費用
>
> = What's the cost? (費用多少？)

2. ***How much do I owe you?***

owe 〔 o 〕*v.* 欠

這句話字面的意思是「我欠你多少錢？」引申爲「我該付你多少錢？」。

每一個城市或機場的計程車，都有不同的計費方式，有的要額外加上行李費，像舊金山機場到市區，就要額外加價，所以，即使你看到了計程車跳錶的金額，你還是要問一問：***How much do I owe you?*** 或 How much is it? 或 What's the cost?

3. ***Here you go.***

這句話是由 Here it is. (東西在這裡。) You can go. (你可以走了。) 演變而來。美國人常說 ***Here you go.*** 但是，所有的字典都沒有明確說明，連 The American Heritage Dictionary 都找不到，我們在此非徹底研究不可。

【例1】 ***Here you go.*** Here is what you wanted.
(給你。這是你想要的東西。)

【例2】 *Here you go*. Here is your receipt.
（給你。這是你的收據。）　〔rɪ'sit〕*n.* 收據

【例3】 I can lend you twenty. *Here you go*.
（我可以借你二十元。拿去。）

【例4】 *Here you go*. I got this for you.
（給你啊。我買了這個東西給你。）

【例5】 This is the pen you lent me. *Here you go*.
（這是你借我的筆。還給你。）

【例6】 *Here you go*. This is your room key.
（給你。這是你的房間鑰匙。）
【這句話通常是飯店櫃台人員說的話】

在商店裡面，店員幫你包好東西後，把東西給你時，通常會說：

Here you go. Have a nice day.
（好了。再見。）

Here you go. 和 Here you are. 及 Here it is.
意義相同。但是，Here it is. 有時強調
「找到了」的意味，此時作「東西就在
這裡。」解。

Here it is.

【比較】 I found it. *Here it is*.
（我找到了。東西就在這裡。）

Here you go.

I found it.
$\begin{cases} \textit{Here you go.} \\ \textit{Here you are.} \\ \textit{Here it is.} \end{cases}$

（我找到了。拿去。）

4. *Here is one hundred.* (這裡是一百元。)

　　這句話是 Here is one hundred dollars. 的省略。也有美國人説成 Here is a hundred. 或 Here is a hundred bucks.

〔 bʌks 〕 *n. pl.* 元

Here is one hundred. 在這裡也可以説成：***Here's one hundred.***

當給計程車司機大鈔的時候，最好先講清楚給的是一百元，避免他以爲你只給他五十元。

Here is one hundred.

5. *Just give me twenty back.* (只要找我二十元就好。)

　　編者在美國紐約、舊金山、英國倫敦等，太多地方坐計程車，給了錢，司機都不想找錢，講了這句話，他就非找不可。

　　以前在美國，計程車司機都是先找錢給你，你再給他小費。現在由於大城市的司機素質變差，往往會敲詐觀光客。

　　在美國，只有在餐廳，是給百分之十五的小費，住旅館，給個一兩元，坐計程車，給個零頭就可以。如果計程車費是十八元，你給他二十元，你就只要説：Keep the change. (不用找了。)如果計程車費是七十元，你給他一百元，你如果説 Keep the change. 你就太吃虧了。他又不想找錢，此時你就説：*Just give me twenty back.*

(只要找我二十元就好。)

如果你碰到計程車司機硬是不想找錢，你就可以說：

> *Excuse me*.（對不起。）
>
> *I'm waiting*.（我在等。）
>
> *You forgot my change*.（你忘了找錢給我。）
> 〔 tʃendʒ 〕*n.* 找錢；零錢

或說：

> Please give me the change.（請找我錢。）

如果計程車司機問："No tip?"（沒有小費啊？）
你就說：

> I want my change first.（我要你先找我錢。）
>
> Then I'll give you the tip.
>
> （然後我才會給你小費。）

　　坐計程車，沒有零錢給小費時，為了避免爭吵，最好的方法，就是說：*Just give me* 多少錢 *back*. 即使在台灣，這句話都可以用得到。如果你看到車子很新，司機服務很好，車費是七十元，你給他一百元，你就可以說：*Just give me twenty back*.（只要找我二十元就好。）這句話也可說成：Just give me twenty. 或 Just give me twenty dollars back.

6. *Have a good one.* (再見。)

> 這句話和 Have a good day. 及 Have a nice
> day. 意義相同，但是，*Have a good one.* 中的 one，
> 是指 day，morning，afternoon，evening 或
> night，所以在任何時間和別人道別的時候，都可
> 以說 *Have a good one.*

　　早上再見的時候，可以說：Have a good
morning. 下午再見的時候，可以說：Have a
good afternoon. 晚上
再見的時候，可以說：
Have a good evening.
或 Have a good night.
但是任何時候都可以說：
Have a good one.

Have a good one.

【例1】　Nice talking to you. (很高興和你談話。)
　　　　I have to go. (我必須走了。)
　　　　Have a good one. (再見。)

【例2】　Drive *safe*. (小心開車。)(= *Drive safely.*)
　　　　Take care. (保重。)
　　　　Have a good one. (再見。)
　　　　【safe 主要當形容詞，在此當副詞】

【例3】　We're done. (我們做完了。)
　　　　See you tomorrow. (明天見。)
　　　　Have a good one. (再見。)

【對話練習】

1. A：**What's the fare?**　　　　　　A：車費是多少錢？

　　B：Let me see.　　　　　　　　　B：我看看。
　　　 It's seventy-five.　　　　　　　　 七十五元。
　　　 It's a little high because　　　　　 因為交通狀況，所以有點
　　　 of the traffic.　　　　　　　　　　 貴。

2. A：**How much do I owe you?**　　A：我該給你多少錢？

　　B：The fare is seventy.　　　　　　B：車費是七十元。
　　　 Would you like a receipt?　　　　　 你要收據嗎？
　　　 It's no trouble at all.　　　　　　　 一點都不麻煩。
　　　 【receipt〔rɪ'sit〕*n.* 收據】

3. A：**How much should I pay?**　　A：我該付多少錢？

　　B：The meter says seventy.　　　　B：計費錶上顯示七十元。
　　　 The toll is forty.　　　　　　　　 高速公路通行費是四十元。
　　　 Your total is one hundred　　　　　 總共是一百一十元。
　　　 and ten. 【meter〔'mitɚ〕*n.* 計費表
　　　 toll〔tol〕*n.* 高速公路通行費
　　　 total〔'totḷ〕*n.* 總數】

4. A：**Here you go.**　　　　　　　　A：給你。

　　B：Thank you very much.　　　　　B：非常感謝你。
　　　 That's two hundred.　　　　　　　 你給的是 200 元。
　　　 So your change is ninety.　　　　　 所以要找你 90 元。
　　　 【change〔tʃendʒ〕*n.* 零錢；找零】

BOOK 3

5. A: **Here is one hundred.**　　　　A: 這裡是一百元。

　　B: Thank you.　　　　　　　　　B: 謝謝。
　　　 Let me get your change.　　　　 我找你錢。
　　　 It's coming right up.　　　　　 馬上就好。
　　　【right〔raɪt〕*adv.* 立刻；馬上】

6. A: **Just give me twenty back.**　　A: 只要找我二十元就好。

　　B: OK.　　　　　　　　　　　　B: 好的。
　　　 Thanks a lot.　　　　　　　　　 多謝。
　　　 Here is your change.　　　　　　 這是找你的錢。

7. A: **Keep the rest.**　　　　　　　A: 其餘的你留著。

　　B: Thanks.　　　　　　　　　　B: 謝謝。
　　　 Thanks a lot.　　　　　　　　　 多謝。
　　　 You are very kind.　　　　　　 你人眞好。

8. A: **That's your tip.**　　　　　　A: 那是給你的小費。

　　B: That's really not necessary.　　B: 眞的不需要。
　　　 But I appreciate it.　　　　　　 不過還是很感激你。
　　　 Have a great day.　　　　　　 祝你擁有美好的一天。
　　　【appreciate〔əˈpriʃɪˌet〕*v.* 感激】

9. A: **Have a good one.**　　　　　A: 再見。

　　B: You too.　　　　　　　　　　B: 再見。
　　　 Enjoy the day.　　　　　　　　 再見。
　　　 Hope to see you again.　　　　 希望能再見到你。

5. Here we are.

Here we are.	我們到了。
We are here.	我們到了。
We made it.	我們到了。
This is it.	就是這裡。
This is the place.	就是這個地方。
It looks good.	看起來不錯。
Let's go in.	我們進去吧。
Let's check it out.	我們進去看看。
Let's give it a try.	我們試一試吧。

BOOK 3

** ──────────────

make it 成功；辦到   *check sth. out* 調查；看看

give it a try 試一試

【背景説明】

和朋友一起到達目的地，像餐廳或飯店門口，一般人只會説"Here we are."，背完這一回，你就可以用英文和朋友連續説九句。

1. *Here we are.*（我們到了。）
   We are here.（我們到了。）

> 一般句子的重音，在倒數第一個主要字上，就是倒數第一個名詞、動詞、形容詞或副詞上，但是，這句話是例外。無論坐車、走路，在到達目的地時，美國人都習慣説 "***Here*** we are."，這句話是 We are *here*. 的倒裝句，因爲強調 here 而倒裝。
>
> 【比較】 Here we áre.【一般語氣】
> Hére we are.【語氣最強】
> We are hére.【語氣稍強】
> We're hére.【語氣輕鬆】

2. *We made it.*

> 這句話字面的意思是：「我們做好了它。」引申爲「我們做到了；我們辦到了；我們趕到了；我們成功了…等。」***We made it.*** 有無限多的意思，要看前後句意來判斷，在這裡的意思是「我們到了。」

3. *This is it*.

　　這句話的字面意思是「這個是它。」引申為「就是這裡。」it 是指你所要去的場所。

　　美國人很喜歡說 ***This is it***.，句中的 it 可指「地方」、「時間」、「東西」等。

【例1】 ***This is it***. This is the place I told you about.
（就是這裡，這就是我告訴過你的地方。）【it 指地方】

【例2】 ***This is it***. It's your big day.
（就是今天，今天是你的大日子。）
【it 指重要時間，在此指今天】

【例3】 Here it is. I found it. ***This is it***. 【it 指東西】
（就是這個，我找到了，這就是。）

4. *This is the place*.

　　這句話的意思是「就是這個地方。」This 指 Here，所以，也有人說 "Here is the place."
美國人到了目的地，習慣說：

　　　　Here we are. (我們到了。)
　　= We are here.
　　= We've arrived.

This is the place.

　　　　This is it. (就是這裡。)
　　= ***This is the place***.
　　= Here is the place.

5. *It looks good*.

　　這句話美國人最喜歡說，看到什麼好東西，他們都喜歡說：***It looks good***. 或 It looks nice.
在這裡是指「這個地方不錯。」(= *It's not bad*.)

6. *Let's go in.*

到了餐廳門口，請朋友一起進去，就說：

Let's go in.（我們進去吧。）
= Let's do it.
= Let's go for it.

【在此情況下，這三句話意義相同，go for it 的主要意思是「大膽試一試」。】

7. *Let's check it out.*

check〔tʃɛk〕*v.* 檢查；核對
check sth. out 檢查；調查；查看

check 的主要意思是「檢查」，在字典上很難找到 check *sth.* out 這個成語，但美國人常用。

【例1】 Go in. Take a look. **Check it out.**
（進去，看一看，仔細瞧瞧。）

【例2】 A: I can't solve this problem.
（我無法解決這個問題。）
B: Let me *check it out.*（讓我看看。）

【例3】 That store looks nice. Let's go *check it out.*（那家店看起來很棒，我們去看看。）

check *sth.* out 這個成語，受詞若較長，則放在 out 的後面，例如：

Please *check out* all the goods in the store.
（請檢查店裡所有的商品。）〔gudz〕*n. pl.* 商品
I want to *check out* the new cars.
（我想去看一看那些新車。）

8. *Let's give it a try.*

try〔 traɪ 〕*n.* 嘗試；努力　　***give it a try*** 試一試

> 　　try 的主要意思是「嘗試」，當動詞。在此 try 當名詞，***Let's give it a try.*** 的意思是「我們試一試吧。」
>
> 　　這句話也可說成：Let's give it a shot. (我們試一試吧。)【shot〔 ʃɑt 〕*n.* 射擊；嘗試】也有美國人說：Let's try it. 凡是到一家新的、沒去過的餐館，就可以說：Let's check it out. Let's give it a try. 這些句子。

　　美國人喜歡說這些話的原因，是由於他們有傳統的開拓精神 (pioneer spirit)，他們很喜歡嘗試新的事物，去沒去過的地方，做沒做過的事等。他們常說：

Try something new. (嘗試新的事物。)

Let's do something new.

　　(我們做一些沒做過的事吧。)

Let's do it in a different way.

　　(我們用不同的方法來做。)

Let's see the unseen. (我們去看沒看過的東西吧。)

Let's do what's never been done before.

　　(我們去做一些過去從來沒做過的事吧。)

Let's explore the unknown world.

　　(我們去探索未知的世界吧。)

explore〔 ɪk'splor 〕*v.* 探索

unknown〔 ʌn'non 〕*adj.* 未知的

【對話練習】

1. A：**Here we are.**

   B：Great.
   I'm excited.
   I'm glad we are here.

   A：我們到了。

   B：太棒了。
   我好興奮。
   真高興我們到了。

2. A：**We are here.**

   B：Yes, we are.
   I can't believe it.
   That took no time at all.
   【take〔tek〕*v.* 花費】

   A：我們到了。

   B：是啊，我們到了。
   我真不敢相信。
   完全不花任何時間。

3. A：**We made it.**

   B：Wonderful.
   That was fast!
   We got here in no time at
   all.【*in no time* 立刻】

   A：我們到了。

   B：太棒了。
   好快喔！
   我們一下子就到了耶。

4. A：**This is it.**

   B：Alright.
   Looks nice.
   Let's go in.

   A：就是這裡。

   B：好啊。【表同意】
   看起來不錯。
   我們進去吧。

5. A : **This is the place.**

  B : Really?
  It looks great.
  I'm very excited.

A：就是這裡。

B：眞的嗎？
  這裡看起來眞棒。
  我非常興奮。

6. A : **It looks good.**

  B : I agree.
  You're right.
  It really looks nice.

A：看起來不錯。

B：我同意。
  你說的對。
  看起來眞的很棒。

7. A : **Let's go in.**

  B : OK.
  I'm ready.
  Let's do it.

A：我們進去吧。

B：好。
  我準備好了。
  我們走吧。

8. A : **Let's check it out.**

  B : I'm with you.
  Let's go for it.
  Let's take a look.
  【 *go for it* = try it = do it 】

A：我們去看看吧。

B：我贊成。
  我們進去看看吧。
  我們去看看。

9. A : **Let's give it a try.**

  B : Good idea!
  I can't wait!
  Let's give it a shot.

A：我們試一試吧。

B：好主意！
  我等不及了！
  我們試一試吧。

BOOK 3

6. Table for two.

Table for two.	我們要兩個位子的桌子。
Nonsmoking section.	我們要非吸煙區的座位。
Can we sit by a window?	我們可不可以坐靠窗的位子？
Two menus, please.	請拿兩份菜單。
We're in a hurry.	我們趕時間。
We're pressed for time.	我們時間緊迫。
What's today's special?	今日特餐是什麼？
What's your best dish?	你們最好的菜是什麼？
What are you famous for?	你們以什麼菜出名？

✼✼ ─────────

nonsmoking〔nɑn'smokɪŋ〕*adj.* 禁煙的
section〔'sɛkʃən〕*n.* 區域
menu〔'mɛnju,'menju〕*n.* 菜單　　hurry〔'hɝɪ〕*n.* 匆忙
in a hurry 匆忙地　　press〔prɛs〕*v.* 壓
be pressed for time 時間緊迫
special〔'spɛʃəl〕*n.* 特餐　　dish〔dɪʃ〕*n.* 菜餚
famous〔'feməs〕*adj.* 有名的
be famous for 以～有名

【背景説明】

　　每個人都有機會請朋友到餐廳吃飯，一進餐廳，就可以對餐廳接待人員，説這九句英文。這一回很容易背，你試試看。

1. *Table for two.*

　　這句話源自 We'd like a table for two.（我們想要兩個位子的桌子。）美國人喜歡簡化，table 前的 a 常常省略。

【比較】　*Table for two.*【常用】
　　　　　A table for two.【正，少用】

　　進餐廳最常用的兩句話，就是 *Table for two.* 或 *We'd like a table for two.*

　　去餐廳吃飯，人多的時候，如果有六個人，就説：We have six.（我們有六個人。）等於 We have a party of six.（我們一共有六個人。）也有人説：There are six of us.（我們有六個人。）【party〔'partɪ〕n. 一行（人）】

2. *Nonsmoking section.*
nonsmoking〔nɑn'smokɪŋ〕*adj.* 禁煙的
section〔'sɛkʃən〕*n.* 區域

　　Nonsmoking section.（非吸煙區。）也可以説成 Nonsmoking area. 也可只説 Nonsmoking.。
　　　　　　　〔'ɛrɪə〕*n.* 區域

　　餐廳有吸煙區（smoking section）和非吸煙區，一般進了餐廳，服務生會問你：*Smoking or nonsmoking?*（要吸煙區或非吸煙區？）

BOOK 3

有些美國人說：Do you have a nonsmoking section?（你們有沒有非吸煙區？）或 Do you have a nonsmoking area? 也有美國人說：Table for two. *In nonsmoking.* 或 Table for two. *In the nonsmoking section.*（我們要兩個位子的桌子。要非吸煙區。）

這些話來自於，在美國有些州禁止吸煙，像紐約州，所有公共場所都禁煙。在中西部及南部各州，像密西西比州和德州等，有些餐廳，專門是給卡車司機或工廠的工人用餐，那裡就沒有非吸煙區。

也有美國人說：We want the nonsmoking section.（我們想要非吸煙區的座位。）或 We prefer the nonsmoking section.（我們比較喜歡非吸煙區的座位。）

3. *Can we sit by a window?*

這句話的意思是「我們可不可以坐在靠窗的位子？」也可以說成：*Can we sit near a window?*

你也可以東張西望地說：Can we sit over there?（我們可不可以坐在那裡？）或是說：Can we sit anywhere?（我們可不可以隨便坐？）或 Can we sit where we like?（我們可不可以找我們喜歡的位子坐？）

如果餐廳在高樓層，你就可以說：We'd like a table with a good view.（我們想要景觀好的桌子。）

4. *Two menus, please*.

menu〔'mɛnju,'menju〕*n.* 菜單【這個字好背，只要記住
men 加上 u 即可】

請餐廳服務生拿菜單來的說法有：

> *Two menus, please*.【最常用】
> （請拿兩份菜單。）

= We'd like *two menus, please*.
（請給我們兩份菜單。）【常用】

menu

= We want *two menus, please*.
（我們要兩份菜單。）

= We need *two menus, please*.
（我們需要兩份菜單。）

= Can you bring us *two menus*?
（可不可以拿兩份菜單給我們？）

= Can you give us *two menus*?
（可不可以給我們兩份菜單？）

5. *We're in a hurry*.（我們趕時間。）

hurry〔'hɝɪ〕*n.* 匆忙　　*in a hurry* 匆忙地

也有美國人説：We're kind of in a hurry.（我們有
點趕時間。）【*kind of* 有一點】

6. *We're pressed for time*.

press〔prɛs〕 *v.* 壓
be pressed for time 時間緊迫

　　press 的主要意思是「壓」，be pressed for time 的字面意思是「因爲時間而受到壓迫」，引申爲「時間緊迫」。表示「時間緊迫；趕時間」的說法很多：

> *We're pressed for time*.（我們時間緊迫。）
> = We're in a hurry.（我們趕時間。）
> = We're in a rush.（我們很急。）
> 　　　　　〔rʌʃ〕 *n.* 匆忙

　　有些美國人喜歡說：We're in a real hurry.（我們真的很趕時間。）也有人說：We're on the run.（我們趕時間。）【*on the run = in a hurry*】

　　在好的餐廳，如果你不先對服務生說：We're pressed for time. 他們的服務，往往會很慢。爲了強迫餐點上得快，你一進門，就可以先跟在門口的服務人員說：

We only have *forty minutes*.
（我們只有四十分鐘。）
We have to be somewhere.
（我們必須到別處去。）
Can we make it?（我們來得及嗎？）

7. *What's today's special?*（今日特餐是什麼？）

special〔'spɛʃəl〕*n.* 特餐；特價品

special 的主要意思是「特別的」，在這裡當名詞，作「特餐」解。

很多餐廳為了促銷，都有每日特餐（today's special），由於大量供應，所以價錢便宜，食物新鮮。

What's today's special?

這句話也可說成：What's your special for today? 或 What's the special of the day?

8. *What's your best dish?*

dish〔dɪʃ〕*n.* 盤子；菜餚

dish 的主要意思是「盤子」，在這裡作「菜餚」解。大的餐廳要生存，就至少要有一道最好的菜。問服務生：「你們最好的菜是什麼？」說法有：

What's your best dish?（你們最好的菜是什麼？）

= What's your most popular dish?
（你們最受歡迎的菜是什麼？）

= What's your number one dish?
（你們最好的菜是什麼？）

= What's your specialty?（你們的招牌菜是什麼？）

【specialty〔'spɛʃəltɪ〕*n.* 拿手好菜；招牌菜】

9. *What are you famous for?*

famous〔'feməs〕*adj.* 有名的

be famous for 以～有名

這句話字面的意思是「你們以什麼有名？」引申爲「你們以什麼菜出名？」也可以説成：What's this place famous for? (這裡什麼菜有名？；這家餐廳以什麼出名？)

也有很多人説：What's your specialty? (你們的招牌菜是什麼？)

【比較】

What are you famous for?【語氣較強】

What's your specialty?【一般語氣】

> What are you famous for?

吃東西可不簡單，吃得好，就長得好 (You are what you eat.) 到有名的餐廳吃飯，就要吃他們最好的菜 (the best dish)，才划得來。

到高級的餐廳吃飯，點最便宜的，最划得來，因爲總不會差到哪裡去。到小餐廳吃飯，就可點他們最貴的菜，「大店小吃，小店大吃」，是吃東西的秘訣。

【對話練習】

【A：Customer (顧客)；B：Hostess (女接待員)】

1. A：Table for two.

   B：Right this way.
   Follow me, please.
   Just one moment.

   A：我們要兩個位子的桌子。

   B：請走這邊。
   請跟我走。
   請等一下。

2. A：Nonsmoking section.

   B：Sure.
   We can do that.
   Please follow me.

   A：請給我們非吸煙區的位子。

   B：當然。
   我們可以這麼做。
   請跟我來。

3. A：Can we sit by a window?

   B：Of course.
   Let me see.
   Yes, we have a table over
   there.

   A：我們可不可以坐靠窗的位子？

   B：當然。
   我看看。
   可以，那裡有位子。

4. A：Two menus, please.

   B：No problem.
   I'll get them.
   I'll be right back.

   A：請給我們兩份菜單。

   B：沒問題。
   我會去拿。
   我馬上回來。

5. A：We're in a hurry.

   B：I understand.
   We will do our best.
   You should make it in
   time.

   A：我們趕時間。

   B：我了解。
   我們會盡力。
   你們應該來得及。

BOOK 3

【A：Customer (顧客)；B：Hostess (女接待員)】

6. A : **We're pressed for time**.
   B : Then order the special.
   They make it fast.
   It'll be here in no time.
   【order〔'ɔrdɚ〕v. 點 (餐)
   in no time 立刻】

A：我們時間緊迫。
B：那麼就點特餐。
　　他們很快就做好了。
　　立刻就可以送來。

7. A : **What's today's special?**
   B : Our special is roast beef.
   That includes side dishes.
   The dessert is cheesecake.
   【roast〔rost〕adj. 烤的
   side dish 配菜
   dessert〔dɪ'zɝt〕n. 甜點】

A：今日特餐是什麼？
B：我們的特餐是烤牛肉。
　　包含配菜。
　　甜點是起士蛋糕。

8. A : **What's your best dish?**
   B : I recommend the lobster.
   In my opinion, it's the best.
   You won't find better seafood
   anywhere else.
   【lobster〔'lɑbstɚ〕n. 龍蝦】

A：你們最好的菜是什麼？
B：我推薦龍蝦。
　　我認為它是最好的。
　　你在別的地方吃不到這麼
　　好的海鮮。

9. A : **What are you famous for?**
   B : Our prime rib is number
   one.
   Everybody likes it.
   You'll like it for sure.
   【prime〔praɪm〕adj. 上等的　　rib〔rɪb〕n. 肋骨】

A：你們以什麼菜出名？
B：我們的上等肋骨牛排是最
　　好的。
　　大家都喜歡。
　　你們一定會喜歡的。

7. *We're ready to order.*

We're ready to order.	我們要點菜了。
We know what we want.	我們決定好了。
Can you take our order now?	你現在可以幫我們點菜嗎？
I'll have the special.	我要點特餐。
She'll try the combo.	她要總匯。
We both want salads with that.	我們倆都要附沙拉。
Ice water for her.	她要冰開水。
Hot water for me.	我要熱開水。
That's it for now.	現在先點這些。

** ———————————————

ready〔'rɛdɪ〕*adj.* 準備好的　order〔'ɔrdɚ〕*v.,n.* 點菜
take one's order 接受某人點菜　have〔hæv〕*v.* 吃
special〔'spɛʃəl〕*n.* 特餐
combo〔'kɑmbo〕*n.* 綜合在一起的人或事物；總匯
salad〔'sæləd〕*n.* 沙拉　*ice water* 冰水
for now 目前；暫時

【背景説明】

　　這回是介紹在餐廳裡點餐，最常用的九句話，有了這九句話做基礎，你用英文點餐，就會充滿信心了。

1. *We're ready to order.*

　　這句話字面意思是「我們準備好要點菜了。」也就是中國人所説的「我們要點菜了。」中文裡的「要」，就相當於英文裡的 be ready（準備好）。在餐廳裡，你只要説 We're ready.，服務生就知道你要點菜了。

　　美國人的習慣是，在高級餐廳裡，並不會招手呼喊服務生，而只是身體移動一下，或用眼神表示他們要點菜了即可，一般美國人在餐廳裡等服務生，都很有耐心。

We're ready to order.

【比較】 ***We're ready to order.***【最常用】
　　　　 We're all set to order. 【常用】

2. *We know what we want.*

　　在餐廳裡，美國人常説這句話，***We know what we want.*** 字面的意思是「我們知道我們要的東西。」引申為「我們決定好了。」（ = *We have decided.*)

　　在有些餐廳，一進去服務生會問你：**"Do you know what you want** or would you like to see a menu?"意思是「你要吃什麼？或是你想要看菜單嗎？」如果你回答 **"We know what we want."**，意思就是「我們已經決定好了，我們要點菜了。」

　　不要看這麼簡單的句子，你沒有背過怎麼會用？這是美國文化，非記住不可。

【例1】　We're regular customers.
　　　　（我們是老主顧了。）
　　　　【regular (ˈrɛgjələ) *adj.* 經常的；定期的】
　　　　We eat here very often. (我們常來這裡吃。)
　　　　You know what we want.
　　　　（你知道我們要吃什麼。）

【例2】　A: Can I get you a menu?
　　　　　　（要不要拿菜單給你看？）
　　　　B: No, thanks. ***I know what I want***.
　　　　　　I'll have Meal No. 1. 【不可說成 *a Meal No. 1*】
　　　　　　（不，謝謝。我決定好了。我要一號餐。）

【例3】　（在商店，像玩具店、鞋店等。）
　　　　店員：　Do you need any help?
　　　　　　　（你需要幫忙嗎？）
　　　　顧客：　No, thank you. ***I know what I want***.
　　　　　　　（不用，謝謝。我知道我要什麼。我可以
　　　　　　　　自己拿。）

3. *Can you take our order now?*

take one's order 接受某人點菜

　　take order 的主要意思是「接受命令」，take one's order 本來意思是「接受某人的命令」(= *take an order from sb.*)，在這裡作「接受某人點菜」解。這句話的意思是「你現在可以幫我們點菜嗎？」。

【比較1】　order 可用複數形，但句意不同。

Can you take our order now?
【表示一個人點所有人的菜】

Can you take our orders now?
(= *Can you take all of our orders now?*)
（你現在可以幫我們每個人點菜嗎？）
【強調給每個人點每個人的菜，這種情況很少。】

【比較2】　**Can you take our order now?**【常用，較客氣】

Can we order now?【常用，客氣】
（我們現在可以點菜嗎？）

We'd like to order now.【常用，一般語氣】
（我們現在想點菜。）

We want to order now.【較不客氣】
（我們現在想點菜。）

BOOK 3

4. *I'll have the special.*

have〔 hæv 〕*v.* 吃   special〔'spɛʃəl 〕*n.* 特餐

　　　句中的 have 作「吃」解，整句話的意思是「我要吃特餐。」也就是中國人説的「我要點特餐。」也可以説成：I'll have the special of the day. 或 I'll have today's special. (我要今日特餐。)

在餐廳裡點菜的説法很多：

I'll have the special.
(我要點特餐。)
= I'll order the special.
= I'll take the special.

= I want the special.
= I'd like the special.
= I'll try the special.

= Give me the special, please.
= The special for me, please.
= The special, please.

I'll have the special.

---

special 和 house special 都是指「特餐」，通常是便宜的，而 specialty 是指「招牌菜」，是該店最有名的菜。

【比較】 **I'll have the special.** (我要吃特餐。)
　　　　〔special = house special 〕
　　　　I'll have the specialty. (我要吃招牌菜。)
　　　　　　　　〔'spɛʃəltɪ 〕*n.* 招牌菜

5. ***She'll try the combo.*** (她要點總匯。)

combo〔ˈkɑmbo〕*n.* 綜合在一起的人或事物；總匯

> combo 這個字在一般英漢字典上都找不到，但在美國餐廳裡常常使用，把各種食物綜合在一起，稱做 combo，這個字源自 combination〔ˌkɑmbəˈneʃən〕*n.* 結合，可能是因為美國人喜歡簡化，於是發明了這個新字 combo，如：seafood combo（海鮮總匯）、Italian combo（義大利總匯）、cheese combo（起士總匯）等，但「綜合水果盤」稱作 fruit platter〔ˈplætɚ〕。
>
> ***She'll try the combo.*** 這句話字面意思是「她要試試總匯。」中國人的文化中只會說「她想要吃總匯。」，美國人因為勇於嘗試新東西，所以常用 ***try*** 這個字。菜單上雖然寫的是 seafood combo，但美國人點菜時，通常只說 the combo。

6. ***We both want salads with that.***
(我們倆都要附沙拉。)

salad〔ˈsæləd〕*n.* 沙拉

　　餐廳裡的特餐，通常都附有沙拉或湯，供顧客選擇，有時兩者皆有，句中的 with 作「附有；附帶」解。

【例1】 I'd like a garden salad with French dressing. (我要庭園沙拉，附法式沙拉醬。)
【dressing〔ˈdrɛsɪŋ〕*n.* 沙拉醬】

【例2】 I'll have tea with a slice of lemon.
(我要茶，附一片檸檬。)【slice〔slaɪs〕*n.* 薄片】

【例3】 I'll have mashed potatoes with gravy.
(我要馬鈴薯泥，淋上肉汁。)
【mashed〔mæʃt〕*adj.* 搗碎的　gravy〔ˈgrevɪ〕*n.* 肉汁】

7. *Ice water for her*.

ice water 冰水

這句話源自：*Please bring ice water for her.*
（請給她冰開水。）

【比較】 *Ice water for her.*【常用】

Please bring her ice water.【正】

Please bring ice water for her.【正，少用】

類似的說法有：

Ice water for her.（她要冰開水。）

= She wants ice water.

= She'll have ice water.

= She'll take ice water.

8. *That's it for now*.

for now 目前；暫時

That's it. 是慣用句，意思是「就這樣；就這些。」，等於 That's all.。點完了菜，你就可以說 That's it. 或 That's all. 加上 for now，意思是「我現在先點這些。」講這句話會讓服務生比較高興，因為你可能還會再點，在美國餐廳裡，你點的東西越多，服務生的小費越多。

That's it for now.（我現在先點這些。）

= That's all for now.

= That'll be good for now.

= That'll be enough for now.

【對話練習】

1. A：We know what we want.

　 B：That's good.
　　　I'm glad.
　　　That makes it easier.

2. A：We're ready to order.

　 B：OK.
　　　Here I come.
　　　I'm ready when you are.

3. A：Can you take our order now?

　 B：I sure can.
　　　Just a second.
　　　I'll be right there.

4. A：I'll have the special.

　 B：Good choice!
　　　It's very popular.
　　　I think you'll like it.

5. A：She'll try the combo.

　 B：One combo it is.
　　　What side dishes do you
　　　want?
　　　Which salad dressing do
　　　you prefer?
　　　【prefer〔prɪˈfɝ〕v. 比較喜歡】

A：我們決定好了。

B：很好。
　　我很高興。
　　這樣容易多了。

A：我們要點菜了。

B：好的。
　　我來了。
　　你們決定好了，我就可以
　　幫你們點。

A：你現在可以幫我們點菜嗎？

B：當然可以。
　　請稍等。
　　我馬上來。

A：我要點特餐。

B：選得好！
　　特餐很受歡迎。
　　我想你會喜歡的。

A：她要總匯。

B：一份總匯。
　　你要什麼配菜？

　　你比較喜歡哪一種沙拉醬？

6. A： **We both want salads with that**.

   B： Caesar or garden salads?
   Small or medium?
   Which salad dressing do
   you prefer?

   【Caesar〔'sizɚ〕*n.* 凱撒
   dressing〔'drɛsɪŋ〕*n.* 調味醬】

   A：我們倆都要附沙拉。

   B：凱撒還是庭園沙拉？
   小的還是中的？
   你們比較喜歡哪一種沙
   拉醬？

7. A： **Ice water for her**.

   B： No problem.
   Sure thing.
   I'll get it right away.

   【*right away* 馬上】

   A：她要冰開水。

   B：沒問題。
   當然。
   我馬上送過來。

8. A： **Hot water for her**.

   B： Hot water it is.
   Anything else to drink?
   Some juice or a soda?

   【soda〔'sodə〕*n.* 汽水】

   A：我要熱開水。

   B：要熱開水。
   要喝點別的嗎？
   要喝點果汁還是一杯汽
   水嗎？

9. A： **That's it for now**.

   B： Are you sure?
   How about dessert?
   Let me know if you change
   your mind.

   【dessert〔dɪ'zɝt〕*n.* 甜點】

   A：現在先點這些。

   B：你確定嗎？
   那甜點呢？
   如果你改變主意，再告
   訴我。

BOOK 3

8. Eat up!

Eat up!	吃啊！
Eat some more!	再多吃一點！
Eat as much as you can.	儘量吃。
Fill up!	儘量吃！
Keep eating.	多吃一點。
You can eat more than that.	你可以再多吃一點。
Don't be polite.	不要客氣。
You can't be full!	你不可能吃飽了！
You can do better than that!	你可以再多吃一點！

** ————————————————

eat up 吃啊

as…as one can 儘可能（*= as…as possible*）

fill up 裝滿；變滿　　polite〔pəˋlaɪt〕*adj.* 客氣的

full〔fʊl〕*adj.* 充滿的；吃飽的

【背景說明】

美國人在餐桌上，常使用這九句話，來勸別人多吃一點，以後你要請客，這九句話就可以派上用場。

1. *Eat up!*

在所有的字典，只找到 eat *sth*. up，都找不到 *Eat up!* 這個慣用句，只有 NTC American Slang Dictionary 中有說明。一般人只知道，Eat it up! 是「吃完吧！」的意思，很少人知道美國人常說的 *Eat up!* （吃啊！）。這句話是用來催促你的朋友吃東西。

Eat up!

【例1】 Come on! *Eat up!* （快來吃啊！）

【例2】 *Eat up!* There's plenty more.
（吃啊！還有很多。）【plenty〔'plɛntɪ〕*adv.* 非常地】

【例3】 Don't be shy. *Eat up!*
（別不好意思。吃啊！）【shy〔ʃaɪ〕*adj.* 害羞的】

【例4】 This tastes great. *Eat up!*
（這很好吃。吃啊！）

【例5】 *Eat up!* Don't leave anything.
（吃啊！別剩下。）

【例6】 *Eat up!* There's more food coming.
（吃啊！還有很多食物要上。）

注意：*eat up* 和 *eat sth. up* 意思完全不同：

【比較】 ***Eat up!***（吃啊！）【催促別人吃東西】

Eat it up!（吃完！）【表示別剩下】

但是，Drink up! 等於 Finish your drink! 意思
只有「喝完！」沒有「喝吧！」的意思。

【比較】 中文：喝完！

英文：***Drink up!***

中文：喝吧！

英文：Have a drink!

Drink up!

2. *Eat some more!*

　　　這句話的意思是「再多吃一點！」也可説成
Eat more!（多吃一點！）

【比較】 ***Eat some more!***

　　　【語氣較強，吃飯中或飯後皆可説】

Eat more!【語氣較弱，在吃飯中説】

3. *Eat as much as you can.*

　as…as one can　儘可能（ = *as…as possible*)

　　　這句話字面意思是「你能吃多少就吃多少。」引
申為「儘量吃。」這句話和中國人的思想相同。

　　　Eat as much as you can.【最常用】

　= Eat as much as possible.【較常用】

　= Eat as much as you possibly can.【常用】

4. *Fill up!*

fill〔fɪl〕*v.* 填滿　　***fill up*** 裝滿；變滿

　　　fill 的主要意思是「填滿」，fill up 主要意思是「把～加滿油」，例如你到加油站，你可以和加油站的員工說：Fill it up.（把油加滿。）人吃飯和汽車加油一樣，也用 fill up。而 fill up 在這裡字面意思是「填滿」，引申為「儘量吃。」有幽默的意味。fill up 在此是及物、不及物兩用的動詞片語，所以也可說成：Fill yourself up. 這兩個成語都很常用。

Fill it up!

【比較】***Fill up!***（儘量吃！）【一般語氣】
　　　　Fill yourself up!（儘量吃吧！）【語氣較強】

Fill up! 這句話美國人常說，我們一定要搞清楚：

【例1】A: ***Fill up!*** There's a lot more.
　　　　　（儘量吃！還有很多。）
　　　　B: I'm working on it.（我正在努力。）
　　　　【***work on it*** 繼續努力】

【例2】A: ***Fill up!*** You can do it!
　　　　　（儘量吃！你吃得下的！）
　　　　B: I'm about to burst.（我的肚子快要撐破了。）
　　　　【burst〔bɝst〕*v.* 爆炸；破裂】

【例3】A: Make yourself at home. ***Fill up!***
　　　　　（別客氣，儘量吃！）
　　　　B: If you say so.（既然你這麼說，我就不客氣了。）

5. *Keep eating*.

這句話中國人不會說，因為它代表了美國文化。美國人在家裡吃飯，大家全部就座後才開動，每盤食物用傳遞的方式，每人各取自己要的份量，通常吃完之後，不好意思再拿，於是就產生了 *Keep eating*. 這句話，叫別人「繼續吃。」就像中國人說的「多吃一點。」

我們在家裡請美國人吃飯，就可以說 "*Keep eating*."，意思和 Eat some more. 相同。唯有背熟了 *Keep eating*. 你才會說出美國人平常習慣說的話。

6. *You can eat more than that*.

這句話字面意思是「你可以吃得比那更多。」表示「你可以再多吃一點。」看到你的客人太客氣了，不好意思吃，你可以說：

You can eat more than that.

Don't stop. (不要停止。)

Eat as much as you can. (儘量吃。)

You can eat more than that.

(你可以再多吃一點。)

7. *Don't be polite.*

polite〔pə'laɪt〕*adj.* 有禮貌的；客氣的

這句話字面意思是「不要有禮貌。」引申為「不要客氣。」也有美國人說：Don't be so polite.（不要那麼客氣。）

在餐桌上，你還可以說：

Don't be afraid to eat up.（儘管吃啊。）

Don't be afraid to eat more.（儘管多吃一點。）

Don't be afraid to eat as much as you can.

（別擔心，吃越多越好。）

【這裡的 afraid 並不是指「害怕」，而是指「擔心」。】

【比較】 *Don't be polite.*【最常用】

Don't be shy.（不要不好意思。）【常用】

8. *You can't be full!*

full〔ful〕*adj.* 充滿的；吃飽的

美國人和中國人一樣，請客時會勸別人多吃一點，full 的主要意思是「充滿的」，在這裡作「吃飽的」解。這句話後面可用驚嘆號或句點。

You can't be full.（你不可能吃飽了。）

= You can't be finished.（你不可能吃完，不吃了。）

= You can't be done already.

（你不可能已經吃完，不吃了。）

【finished 和 done 的用法很重要，詳見 p.10–3，10–4】

9. *You can do better than that!*

這句話字面意思是「你可以做得比那更好！」在此引申為「你可以再多吃一點！」等於 You can eat more than that! 這句話句尾可用驚嘆號或句點。

這句話也可用來責備人，表示「你可以做得更好！」在美國，老師看到學生考不好，就會說這幾句話：

This is below your ability.
（你這次表現失常喔。）

I'm disappointed.
（我很失望。）

You can do better than that!
（你可以做得更好！）

You can do better than that! 也可以簡化成：You can do better! 或加強語氣，說成：You can do a lot better than that!

【例】 Your score was just average. （你的成績平平。）
　　　　〔skor〕*n.* 分數　　〔'ævərɪdʒ〕*adj.* 普通的
　　　You can do better! （你可以表現得更好！）

【比較】 You can do better! 【最常用，語氣輕鬆】
　　　　You can do a lot better! 【常用，語氣較強】
　　　　You can do better than that!
　　　　【最常用，一般語氣】
　　　　You can do a lot better than that!
　　　　【常用，語氣最強】

【對話練習】

1. A：**Eat up!**
　B：OK.
　　I will.
　　I'll do my best.

2. A：**Eat some more!**
　B：I can't.
　　I'm stuffed.
　　I can't eat another bite.
　　【stuffed〔stʌft〕*adj.* 吃得很飽的，
　　　比 full 語氣強烈。】

3. A：**Eat as much as you can**.
　B：No problem.
　　Whatever you say.
　　I'll eat a lot.

4. A：**Fill up!**
　B：You got it!
　　Don't worry.
　　I'm really hungry.

5. A：**Keep eating**.
　B：Relax.
　　I'm taking a break.
　　I'll eat some more in a
　　minute.【*take a break* 休息一下
　　in a minute 立刻】

A：吃啊！
B：好的。
　　我會的。
　　我會盡力。

A：再多吃一點！
B：我不行了。
　　我吃得很飽了。
　　我一口也吃不下了。

A：儘量吃。
B：沒問題。
　　遵命。
　　我會吃很多。

A：儘量吃！
B：沒問題！
　　別擔心。
　　我真的很餓。

A：多吃一點。
B：放輕鬆。
　　我現在休息一下。
　　我馬上會再多吃一點。

BOOK 3

6. A : **You can eat more than that.**　　A：你可以再多吃一點。

　　B : I really can't.　　　　　　　　B：我真的不行了。
　　　 That's it.　　　　　　　　　　　就這麼多了。
　　　 That's all I can eat.　　　　　　我就只能吃這麼多了。

7. A : **Don't be polite.**　　　　　　A：不要客氣。

　　B : I won't be.　　　　　　　　　　B：我不會的。
　　　 I'll help myself.　　　　　　　　我會自己拿。
　　　 Don't worry about me.　　　　　別擔心我。
　　　【*help oneself* 自行取用】

8. A : **You can't be full!**　　　　　A：你不可能吃飽了！

　　B : I'm sorry I am.　　　　　　　　B：很抱歉，我真的飽了。
　　　 I'm really full.　　　　　　　　　我真的好飽。
　　　 I'm totally stuffed.　　　　　　　我吃得好飽、好飽。
　　　【totally (ˈtotl̩ɪ) *adv.* 完全地】

9. A : **You can do better than　　　A：你可以再多吃一點！
　　　 that!**

　　B : I really can't.　　　　　　　　B：我真的沒辦法。
　　　 That's all I can do.　　　　　　　我只能吃這麼多了。
　　　 It was delicious, though.　　　　不過的確很好吃。
　　　【though (ðo) *adv.* 不過；可是】

9. I like this place.

I like this place.	我喜歡這個地方。
It's my kind of place.	這是我喜歡的地方。
It's just perfect for me.	這裡非常適合我。
It's comfortable.	這裡很舒服。
I feel so relaxed.	我覺得非常輕鬆。
I feel right at home.	我覺得非常舒適。
What a nice place!	這地方真好！
I can be myself here.	我在這裡很自在。
I could stay here all day.	但願我能整天都待在這裡。

** ───────────────

kind〔kaɪnd〕*n.* 種類   just〔dʒʌst〕*adv.* 很；非常
perfect〔'pɝfɪkt〕*adj.* 完美的；適合的
comfortable〔'kʌmfətəbl̩〕*adj.* 舒服的
relaxed〔rɪ'lækst〕*adj.* 輕鬆的
feel at home 舒適；感覺輕鬆
be oneself 舒適；自在   stay〔ste〕*v.* 停留

【背景説明】

這一回太棒了，凡是你到了一個好地方，你都可以
用這些話來稱讚。稱讚的話說越多越好，不但稱讚人，
也要稱讚地方。這九句話經過特別安排，很容易背。

1. *I like this place.*

美國人早上見了面，都會說 "I like～"，做爲開
場白。旅行的時候，想和不認識的人說話，也會說 "I
like～"。

I like your hairstyle. (我喜歡你的髮型。)
I like your outfit. (我喜歡你這套衣服。)
I like your watch. (我喜歡你的手錶。)
【outfit〔'aut,fɪt〕*n.* 服裝】

I like your camera. (我喜歡你的相機。)
I like your T-shirt. (我喜歡你的 T 恤。)
I like your backpack. (我喜歡你的背包。)
【backpack〔'bæk,pæk〕*n.* 背包】

watch

I like your bracelet. (我喜歡你的手鐲。)
I like your brooch. (我喜歡你的胸針。)
I like your necklace.
(我喜歡你的項鍊。)
I like your earrings.
(我喜歡你的耳環。)

backpack

necklace   earrings

bracelet〔'breslɪt〕*n.* 手鐲   brooch〔brotʃ〕*n.* 胸針
necklace〔'nɛklɪs〕*n.* 項鍊   earrings〔'ɪr,rɪŋz〕*n. pl.* 耳環

"I like~"的使用太普遍了，甚至可表示「認可」，如：

I like what you said. ***I like*** that.

（我喜歡你說的話。我同意你。）

She is an interesting teacher. ***I like*** that.

（她是個很風趣的老師。我喜歡上她的課。）

美國人喜歡表達自己的感受。他們很喜歡說：

"I like~"。到了好地方，就說：

I like this place. (我喜歡這個地方。)

I like the view. (我喜歡這裡的視野。)

I like the atmosphere. (我喜歡這裡的氣氛。)
('ætməs,fɪr) *n.* 氣氛

I like the design. (我喜歡這裡的設計。)
(dɪ'zaɪn) *n.* 設計

I like the decoration. (我喜歡這裡的裝潢。)
(,dɛkə'reʃən) *n.* 裝飾

I like the lighting. (我喜歡這裡的燈光。)
('laɪtɪŋ) *n.* 照明

2. ***It's my kind of place.***

kind〔kaɪnd〕*n.* 種類

這句話字面的意思是「它是我這種人的地方。」引
申為「我喜歡這個地方。」或「這是我喜歡的地方。」
這句話美國人也常說成：This is my kind of place.
一般 of 表部份關係，在此表同位的關係，像 the city
of Taipei (台北市)，the city 和 Taipei 是同位語。
（詳見「文法寶典」p.588)

　　　"my kind of~" 在字典上找不到，但美國人很常用，凡是自己喜歡的東西，都可以這麼說。

This is delicious. It's *my kind of food*.
（這真好吃。我喜歡這個食物。）

This sounds great. It's *my kind of music*.
（這真好聽。我喜歡這個音樂。）

She's great. She's *my kind of girl*.
（她真棒。我喜歡這個女孩。）

This city has it all. It's *my kind of place*.
（這個城市什麼都有。我喜歡這個地方。）

What an exciting film! That's *my kind of movie*.
（電影好刺激啊！我喜歡那部電影。）

This weather is beautiful. It's *my kind of day*.
（天氣真好。我喜歡這樣的日子。）

3. *It's just perfect for me.*

just〔dʒʌst〕*adv.* 很；非常；完全地
perfect〔ˈpɝfɪkt〕*adj.* 完美的；適合的

perfect 之後要用 for，不可接 to。

【比較1】 *It's just perfect for me*.
（它非常適合我。）【正】
It's just perfect *to me*. 【誤】

【比較2】 This job is perfect for me. 【正】
（這個工作很適合我。）
This job is perfect *to me*. 【誤】

4. *It's comfortable.*

comfortable〔ˋkʌmfətəbl̩〕*adj.* 舒服的；使人舒服的

comfortable 可修飾「人」及「非人」，例如：

I feel *comfortable* here.（我在這裡覺得很舒服。）
This sofa is very *comfortable*.
（這個沙發坐起來很舒服。）

到了一個好地方，你可以説：

This place is *comfortable*.（這個地方很舒服。）
I feel *comfortable* around here.
（我在這裡覺得很舒服。）

當你買了一雙好的鞋子，你就
可以説：

The shoes are comfortable.

The shoes are *comfortable*.
（這雙鞋子穿起來真舒服。）
I feel *comfortable* in these
　　shoes.
（我穿這雙鞋子真舒服。）

5. *I feel so relaxed.*

relax〔rɪˋlæks〕*v.* 使放鬆
relaxed〔rɪˋlækst〕*adj.* 輕鬆的；放鬆的

　　relax 這個字，主要的意思是「使放鬆」，當動詞
用，它的過去分詞 relaxed，已經完全轉化成形容詞，
就和 tired（疲倦的）一樣，relaxed 作「輕鬆的」解。
so 只是加強語氣，作「非常」解，等於 very。

【比較】 *I feel relaxed.*【正】
　　　　 I feel relax.
　　　　　【誤，這個字美國人常拼錯】

I feel relaxed.

美國人喜歡表達自己的感覺，
所以這種說法很多。他們常
說 "*I feel~.*"

> *I feel* relaxed. (我覺得很輕鬆。)
> = *I feel* comfortable. (我覺得很舒服。)
> = *I feel* at home. (我覺得很自在。)
>
> = *I feel* loose. 【loose〔lus〕*adj.* 輕鬆的】
> 　 (我覺得很輕鬆。)【美國年輕人喜歡說】
> = *I feel* at ease. 【*at ease* 輕鬆的】
> 　 (我覺得很輕鬆。)
> = *I feel* mellow. 【mellow〔'mɛlo〕*adj.* 放鬆的】
> 　 (我覺得很放鬆。)

6. *I feel right at home.*

　right〔raɪt〕*adj.* 右邊的；正確的　*adv.* 正好；恰好
　feel at home 舒適；感到輕鬆

　　right 這個字常當副詞用，用於加強語氣，

　　　Please do it *right* now. (請現在立刻去做。)

　　　We have everything we need *right* here.
　　　(我們需要的東西，這裡都有了。)

　　　Come *right* home after school.
　　　(放學後立刻回家。)

I feel *right* at home. 這句話字面意思是「我覺得
就在家裡。」家裡是最輕鬆的地方，所以引申爲
「我感到很輕鬆。」feel at home 因爲使用太頻繁，
在字典上已經成爲成語，作「舒適；感到輕鬆」解。

【比較】　I feel at home.【常用】

　　　　　I feel right at home.【最常用】

　　　　　I feel very much at home.【常用】

　　　　　（我覺得非常自在。）

　　　　　I just feel right at home.【常用】

　　　　　（我眞是覺得很自在。）

　　　　　I feel just right at home.【誤】

7. *What a nice place!*

　　　這句話是 "What a nice place *this is*!" 的省
略，在文法書上，「*What a* + 名詞 + 主詞 + 動詞！」
是感嘆句的公式，但事實上，美國人很喜歡把後面
的「主詞 + 動詞」省略。（詳見「文法寶典」p.646）

　　　What 所形成的感嘆句，美國人天天都說，例
如，他們看到一個美女，就會說 What a girl!（好
漂亮的女孩！）男生看到女生身材很好，就會說
What a body!（身材眞好！）
天氣很好，他們會和朋友說
What a day!（天氣眞好！）
看到好電影，就說 What a
movie!（電影眞棒！）。

What a day!

美國人到了一個好的地方，就會說，

> What a place! (這個地方真好！)
> = ***What a nice place!*** (這個地方真是好！)
> = What a nice spot! (這個地點真好！)
> = What a nice location! (這個位置真好！)

上面的 nice，都可用 good 或 great 取代。

8. *I can be myself here.*

   be *oneself* 行動自然；舒適

這句話字面意思是「在這裡我可以做我自己。」引申為「我在這裡很自在。」或「我在這裡覺得很舒服。」

當你和朋友在一起，感覺很好的時候，你可以說：*I can be myself* when I'm with you. (我和你在一起很舒服。)

如果你的朋友不快樂的時候，你就可以說：*I can't be myself* when you're unhappy. (當你不快樂的時候，我心裡也不舒服。)

當一個人要去面試或約會，你可以勸他說：Be yourself. (自然一點。)

I'm not myself today.

當你身體不舒服，你就可以說：I'm not myself today. (我今天不舒服。)

9. *I could stay here all day.* (這地方太好了。)

這句話是由 I wish I could stay here all day. 簡化而來，字面意思是 「但願我整天都能待在這裡。」引申為「這地方太好了。」用假設法助動詞

> *I could stay here all day.*

could 表示「希望」，並非真的要整天待在這裡，這種用法很普遍，美國人也說：

> *I could stay here forever.*
> (但願我能永遠待在這裡。)
> *I could live here.* (但願我能住在這裡。)
> *I could come here every day.*
> (但願我每天都能來。)

這些句子都表示「我很喜歡這裡，這個地方太好了。」講這些假設法的句子是美國人的習慣，和中國人的思想不同。

【劉毅老師的話】

背過「一口氣背會話」後，要利用機會，不斷地說，效果更佳。像 What a nice place! I can be myself here. I could stay here all day. 就可以天天說。

【對話練習】

【A 和 B 兩人到了一個很好的地方】

1. A：**I like this place.**

   B：Me too.
   It's great.
   It's really nice.

A：我喜歡這個地方。

B：我也是。
這裡很棒。
這裡真好。

2. A：**It's my kind of place.**

   B：I agree.
   I like it, too.
   It's a great place.

A：這是我喜歡的地方。

B：我同意。
我也喜歡。
這個地方很棒。

3. A：**It's just perfect for me.**

   B：I'm with you.
   I totally agree.
   It couldn't be better.

A：這裡非常適合我。

B：我贊成。
我完全同意。
不可能再更好了。

4. A：**It's comfortable.**

   B：It sure is!
   It's so relaxing.
   I feel perfectly at ease.
   【relaxing〔rɪ'læksɪŋ〕*adj.* 令人放鬆的
   perfectly〔'pɝfɪktlɪ〕*adv.* 非常地
   feel at ease 覺得自在】

A：這裡很舒服。

B：的確是！
這裡讓人很放鬆。
我覺得非常自在。

5. A: **I feel so relaxed.**

   B: That makes two of us.
   It's so peaceful here.
   It really calms me down.
   【 peaceful (ˈpisfəl) *adj.* 寧靜的
      calm sb. down 使某人平靜】

A：我覺得非常輕鬆。

B：我也一樣。
　　這裡非常寧靜。
　　這真的能讓我平靜下來。

6. A: **I feel right at home.**

   B: So do I.
   This place is really special.
   It's like a home away from home.

A：我覺得非常舒服。

B：我也是。
　　這個地方真的很特別。
　　它就是另一個家。

7. A: **What a nice place!**

   B: You're right.
   It's awesome.
   This place is fantastic.
   【 awesome (ˈɔsəm) *adj.* 很棒的
      fantastic (fænˈtæstɪk) *adj.* 很棒的】

A：這地方真好！

B：你說得對。
　　這裡真棒。
　　這地方太棒了。

8. A: **I can be myself here.**

   B: I feel the same way.
   It's just like home.
   This is the place for me.

A：我在這裡很自在。

B：我也有同感。
　　這裡就像自己家一樣。
　　這裡很適合我。

9. A: **I could stay here all day.**

   B: So could I.
   It's just perfect.
   I really love this place.

A：但願我能整天待在這裡。

B：我也是。
　　這裡太完美了。
　　我真是喜歡這個地方。

BOOK 3

10. *Check, please.*

We're ready.	我們準備要結帳了。
We're done.	我們吃完了。
Check, please.	請給我們帳單。
We're finished.	我們吃完了。
We're set to go.	我們要走了。
Please bring our bill.	請拿我們的帳單來。
We're all together.	我們一起結帳。
Do you take this card?	你們接不接受這張信用卡？
Do I pay you or the cashier?	我付給你，還是付給櫃台？

BOOK 3

** ────────────────

ready〔'rɛdɪ〕*adj.* 準備好的
done〔dʌn〕*adj.* 完成的；結束的
check〔tʃɛk〕*n.* 支票；帳單
finished〔'fɪnɪʃt〕*adj.* 完成的；結束的（= *done*）
set〔sɛt〕*adj.* 準備好的（= *ready*）
bill〔bɪl〕*n.* 帳單　　take〔tek〕*v.* 接受（= *accept*）
card〔kɑrd〕*n.* 卡；卡片　　pay〔pe〕*v.* 付錢
cashier〔kæ'ʃɪr〕*n.* 會計；櫃台；出納員

【背景説明】

在餐廳吃完飯後，要叫服務生來結帳，該説些什麼話呢？這九句是最佳的選擇。

1. *We're ready.*
   We're done.
   Check, please.

在餐廳吃完飯後，可以向服務生招手，表示要結帳。這三句話美國人最常用。***We're ready.*** 的字面意思是「我們準備好了。」在這裡的意思是「我們吃完了；我們準備要結帳了。」

2. *We're done.*（我們吃完了。）

這句話在這裡源自 ***We're done*** *with the meal.*（我們吃完飯了。）***be done with*** 是一個成語，表示「做完」。done 已經成為純粹的形容詞，作「完成的；結束的」解。

例：***We're done with*** our homework.
（我們功課做完了。）

I'***m done with*** this report.
（我這份報告寫完了。）

Are you ***done with*** everything?
（你是不是全部都做完了？）

> 很多中國人，不敢説 *We're done*. 因爲及物動
> 詞，人做主詞要用主動；非人做主詞，要用被動。
> 他們只敢説：The job is done. 他們不敢説 *We're*
> *done* with the job.
>
> 例： 中文説：「工作做完了。」
>
> 英文就説："The job is done." 或是 "We're
> done with the job." 省略以後，就變成 *We're*
> *done*. 這是美國人喜歡説話説一半的典型例子。

3. *Check, please.* (請給我們帳單。)
   check〔tʃɛk〕*n.* 支票；帳單

   > 美國人也常説：Could I have the check, please?
   > 或 Could I have the bill, please?【句中的 Could，可
   > 用 Can 代替】也有人説：We'd like the bill, please.
   > (請給我們帳單。)最常用的就是 *Check, please*. 在
   > 這裡的意思是「請給我們帳單。」

4. *We're finished.*
   finished〔'fɪnɪʃt〕*adj.* 完成的；結束的(= *done*)

   > 這句話在這裡源自：
   > *We're finished* with the
   > meal. (我們吃完這餐飯了。)
   > *be finished with* 是一個成
   > 語，表「做完；完成」，等
   > 於 *be done with*。

We're finished.

   > *We're finished*. 和 *We're done*. 意思和句子來源
   > 都相同，在這裡都表示「我們吃完了。」

finish 這個字，可當及物和不及物動詞。

中文： 我們做完了。

英文： *We're finished*. 【最常用，這句話是 We're
finished with something. 的省略。】

We've finished. 【常用，finish 在此是不及物動詞。】

We finished it. 【正，少用，finish 在此是及物動詞。】

We finished. 【正，少用，finish 在此是不及物動詞。】

【例1】 A: Have you done your homework?
（你功課做完了嗎？）

B: Yes, *I'm finished* (*with it*).
（是的，我做完了。）

= Yes, *I'm done* (*with it*).

【例2】 A: Have you cleaned your room?
（你房間打掃完了嗎？）

B: Yes, *I'm finished* (*with it*).
（是的，我打掃完了。）

= Yes, *I'm done* (*with it*).

【例3】 A: Have you finished your research?
（你研究做完了嗎？）　〔'rɪsɜtʃ〕*n.* 研究

B: Yes, *I'm finished* (*with it*).
（是的，我做完了。）

= Yes, *I'm done* (*with it*).

　　一般人不會用 *I'm done*. *I'm finished*. 都是因
爲受到文法的影響，不敢用，背了「一口氣背會話」
以後，你講這些話，就有信心了。

BOOK 3

5. *We're set to go.* (我們要走了。)

　　set 〔 sɛt 〕 v. 設立　*adj.* 準備好的 (= *ready*)

　　　　這句話也可說成：We're ready to go. (我們
要走了。) 也可加強語氣說成：We're all set to go.
(我們準備好要走了。) 也可以簡化成：We're set.
意思和 We're ready. 一樣，都表示「我們好了。」

　　　　美國人也常說：*We're all set.* 句中的 set 主要
當動詞用，作「安置」解，*We're all set.* 的字面意
思是「我們全部被安置妥當了。」在此引申為「我們
準備好了。」set 現在已由過去分詞轉化成形容詞，
作「準備好的」解，*all set* 已成為一個成語，也作
「準備好的」解。

【例1】　A: Are you ready? (你好了沒有？)
　　　　　B: I'm *all set*. (我好了。)

【例2】　A: Are you ready for the test?
　　　　　　　(你考試準備好了沒有？)
　　　　　B: I'm *all set*. I studied all night.
　　　　　　　(我準備好了。我唸了整個晚上。)

【例3】　A: Are you *all set* to move?
　　　　　　　(你準備好要搬家了嗎？)
　　　　　B: Yes, I'm packed and ready to go.
　　　　　　　〔 pækt 〕 *adj.* 打包好的
　　　　　　　(是的，我的行李打包好了，可以走了。)
　　　　　【I'm packed. 的用法，詳見 p.448～450】

【比較】　*We're all set.* (我們準備好了。)【最常用】
　　　　　We're set. (我們準備好了。)【正，語氣稍弱】

BOOK 3

6. *Please bring our bill.* (請拿我們的帳單來。)

bill〔bɪl〕*n.* 帳單

這句話也可以説成：
Please bring the bill. 或
Bring our bill, please.
或 Bring the bill, please.

Please bring our bill.

【比較】　*Please bring our bill.*【語氣較正式】
　　　　　Please bring our check.【語氣較輕鬆】

大多數美國人在餐廳多用 check，在美國以外
的英語系國家，多用 bill。在美國，用 bill，語氣
較正式。

7. *We're all together.*

這句話字面的意思是「我們全部在一起。」在
這裡表示「我們一起結帳。」這句話也可以説成：
All together. (一起付。)

也有美國人説：Put it all on one check. 或
簡化爲 All on one check. 或 All on one. 都表示
「一起付。」説這句話並不一定表示要請客，也
許是一起結帳，事後再各付各的。

當很多人一起去吃飯的時候，有些餐廳就會
自動地把百分之十五的小費加在帳單上，因爲他
們怕你不付那麼多小費。很多人不知道，往往會
重覆付。

8. *Do you take this card?*

take〔tek〕*v.* 接受（= *accept*）

card〔kɑrd〕*n.* 卡；卡片　　**credit card** 信用卡
　　　　　　　　　　　　　　〔ˈkrɛdɪt〕

這句話也可以說成：

Do you take this credit
card? 或 Do you take
this?，都表示「你們接不
接受這張信用卡？」句中
的 take 可以用 accept 來
取代。

【比較】***Do you take this card?***【最常用，語氣輕鬆】
　　　　　Do you accept this card?【常用，較正式】

9. *Do I pay you or the cashier?*

cashier〔kæˈʃɪr〕*n.* 會計；櫃台；出納員

　　這句話的意思是「我付給你，還是付給櫃台？」
cashier 這個字不太好唸，所以美國老師教小孩唸
這個字時，說這個字是「現金（cash）加上耳朵
（ear）」，唸快就變成〔kæˈʃɪr〕。

　　美國人也常說：Do I pay here or at the door?
（我在這裡付，還是在門口付？）

　　也可以問服務生：How do I pay?（我如何付？）
或 Where do I pay?（我在哪裡付？）

【對話練習】

【A 是 Customer（顧客）；B 是 Waiter（男服務生）或 Waitress（女服務生）】

1. A：**We're ready**.

   B：OK.
   I'll bring your check.
   I'll be right back.

   A：我們準備要結帳了。

   B：好的。
   我會把你們的帳單拿來。
   我馬上回來。

2. A：**We're done**.

   B：I understand.
   I'll get your check.
   I'll be right with you.

   A：我們吃完了。

   B：我知道。
   我會去拿你們的帳單。
   我馬上來。

3. A：**Check, please**.

   B：Sure thing.
   I'll be right there.
   Just give me a second.

   A：請拿我們的帳單來。

   B：好的。
   我馬上來。
   請等一下。

4. A：**We're finished**.

   B：Are you sure?
   Can I bring you anything
   else?
   We have some great
   desserts.

   【dessert〔dɪˈzɝt〕*n.* 甜點】

   A：我們吃完了。

   B：你們確定嗎？
   要我拿任何其他的東西給
   你們嗎？
   我們有些很棒的甜點。

BOOK 3

5. A：We're set to go.

   B：I'll bring your bill.
     I'll be back in a minute.
     I hope you enjoyed the meal.

A：我們要走了。

B：我會把你們的帳單拿來。
    我馬上回來。
    希望你們用餐愉快。

6. A：Please bring our bill.

   B：Coming right up.
     Are you all together?
     Who gets the check?

A：請給我們帳單。

B：馬上來。
    你們要一起付嗎？
    帳單給誰？

7. A：We're all together.

   B：No problem.
     I'll put it all on one.
     Here you are.

A：我們一起付。

B：沒問題。
    我會把帳算在一起。
    帳單在這裡。

8. A：Do you take this card?

   B：Yes, we do.
     We take all major credit
     cards.
     I'll bring it right back.
     【right〔raɪt〕*adv.* 馬上】

A：你們接不接受這張信用卡？

B：是的，我們接受。
    所有主要的信用卡，我們
    都接受。
    我會馬上把它拿回來。

9. A：Do I pay you or the cashier?

   B：It's up to you.
     Do as you please.
     You can pay here or at the
     door.

A：我付給你，還是付給櫃台？

B：由你決定。
    悉聽尊便。
    你可以在這裡付，或是去
    門口付。

BOOK 3

11. I need to wash up.

Excuse me a moment.	對不起，我離開一下。
I'll be right back.	我很快就回來。
Please wait for me.	請等我。
Nature's calling.	我內急。
I need to wash up.	我需要洗個手。
I need to use the facilities.	我需要上洗手間。
Where's the bathroom?	廁所在哪裡？
Which way should I go?	我該往哪裡走？
Where can I find a restroom?	哪裡有洗手間？

BOOK 3

** ————————————————

excuse〔ɪk'skjuz〕*v.* 原諒
moment〔'momənt〕*n.* 片刻
nature〔'netʃə〕*n.* 自然；生理需求
wash up 洗手洗臉
facilities〔fə'sɪlətɪz〕*n. pl.* 衛生設備
bathroom〔'bæθ,rum〕*n.* 廁所
restroom〔'rɛst,rum〕*n.* 洗手間 (= *rest room*)

【背景說明】

　　很多人學了好幾年的英文，和朋友在一起，要告訴朋友想去洗手間，卻不知道該怎麼說。背了這九句話，你就很會說了。

1. ***Excuse me a moment.***
   excuse〔ɪkˋskjuz〕v. 原諒
   moment〔ˋmomənt〕n. 片刻

Excuse me
a moment.

　　早期英國皇室宴會，中途離席是很不禮貌的，要先道歉，說 "Excuse me."，後來 "Excuse me." 也用在其他地方。"Excuse me." 主要意思是「對不起。」，常用於 ①和別人搭訕，②打斷別人說話，③從別人身邊擠過，④沒聽清楚別人說的話。

　　"Excuse me a moment." 這句話字面意思是「原諒我一會兒。」這裡引申為「對不起，我要離開一下。」

【例1】***Excuse me a moment.*** I have to take a call.
（對不起，我要離開一下。我必須接個電話。）

【例2】***Excuse me a moment.*** I need to use the bathroom.
（對不起，我要離開一下。我必須去上洗手間。）

【比較】 ***Excuse me a moment.*** 【常用，語氣輕鬆】
= Excuse me for a moment. 【最常用，較正式】

Excuse me a minute. 【少用】
= Excuse me for a minute. 【最常用】

Excuse me a second. 【少用】
= Excuse me for a second. 【最常用】
〔ˈsɛkənd〕*n.* 秒

上面最常用的句子，都有 for。

【例】 Excuse me for $\left\{\begin{array}{l}\text{a moment.}\\\text{a minute.}\\\text{a second.}\end{array}\right\}$ I see an

old friend. I'll be right back.

（對不起，我要離開一下。我看到一個老
朋友。我很快就回來。）

這一回選用 ***Excuse me a moment.*** 因為語氣輕鬆。

2. ***I'll be right back.***

中國人說「我很快就回來。」，英文的說法很多：

I'll be right back.
= I'll be back right away. 【***right away*** 立刻】
= I'll be back in a second. 【***in a second*** 立刻】

= I'll be back in a moment. 【***in a moment*** 立刻】
= I'll be back in a flash. 【***in a flash*** 立刻】
〔flæʃ〕*n.* 閃光
= I'll be back as soon as possible.
【***as soon as possible*** 儘快】

I'll be right back. 和 I'll come back soon.，
兩者意義不同。

【比較】*I'll be right back.*

（我很快就回來。）

I'll come back soon.

（我很快會回來。）

【表示允諾】

come back 和 be back 意思不一樣，例如，男朋
友出遠門，可以和女朋友說："I'll call you. I'll
write you. I promise you *I'll come back*."（我會
打電話給妳。我會寫信給妳。我答應妳我會回來。）但
是，如果你去洗手間，你不需要允諾，你就不能說
I'll come back soon. 因爲你一定會回來，你只能說
I'll be right back.（我很快就回來。）

【例1】 Excuse me. I need a drink.
　　　　⎰ *I'll be right back.*【正】
　　　　⎱ *I'll come back soon.*【誤，不需允諾】
　　　　（對不起，我需要喝點飲料。我很快就回來。）

【例2】 Oh, I forgot my hat.
　　　　⎰ *I'll be right back.*【正】
　　　　⎱ *I'll come back soon.*【誤，不需允諾】
　　　　（噢！我忘記我的帽子了。我很快就回來。）

【例3】 Excuse me. I have to make a phone call.
　　　　⎰ *I'll be right back.*【正】
　　　　⎱ *I'll come back soon.*【誤，不需允諾】
　　　　（對不起，我得打個電話。我很快就回來。）

3. *Please wait for me.*

　　　這句話的意思是「請等我。」也有美國人說：
Please wait. 或 Please wait here.。

4. *Nature's calling.*

nature〔'netʃɚ〕 *n.* 自然；生理上的需求
call〔kɔl〕 *v.* 召喚

> 　　　這句話字面的意思是「大自然在召喚。」引申
> 爲「我想上洗手間。」說這句話有點幽默的味道。
> 當男孩和女孩在一起，爲了避免尷尬，美國人說
> "Nature's calling."，大家就知道他要去上廁所了。

【例1】 Please stop the car. *Nature's calling.*
　　　　（請停車。我內急。）

【例2】 Excuse me.　Where's the bathroom?
　　　　Nature's calling.
　　　　（對不起，廁所在哪裡？我想上廁所。）

【例3】 Excuse me.　I drank too much.
　　　　Nature's calling.　I really have to go.
　　　　（對不起，我喝太多了。我想上洗手間。我眞
　　　　的得走了。）

BOOK 3

5. *I need to wash up.*

wash up 洗手洗臉 (= *wash one's hands and face*)

　　這句話的意思是「我需要洗個手、洗把臉。」
也有「我要上洗手間。」的意思。受過高等教育的
美國人，在吃飯的時候，如果說 I need to use
the bathroom. (我需要上廁所。)，怕別人倒胃口，
所以他們就會婉轉地說：*"I need to wash up."*
或 *"I need to wash my hands."*。

沒有指定廁所的時候，美國男生喜歡說的有：

I need to take a leak. 【最常用，較粗魯】
　　　　　〔 lik 〕*n.* 撒尿

I need to take a piss. 【最常用，可在家人面前說】
　　　　　〔 pɪs 〕*n.* 小便

I need to take a whiz. 【常用，較粗魯】
　　　　　〔 hwɪz 〕*n.* 嘶嘶聲；撒尿

美國女生喜歡說的有：

I need to pee. 【常用】
　　　　　〔 pi 〕*v.* 撒尿；小便

I need to go pee. 【常用】

I need to take a pee. 【常用】
　　　　　〔 pi 〕*n.* 小便；尿

I need to go potty. 【小孩和女生常用】
　　　　　〔 'pɑtɪ 〕*n.* 廁所

　　上廁所的說法太多了，可以寫一本書，以後有機
會再說。

BOOK 3

6. *I need to use the facilities.*

facility〔fə'sɪlətɪ〕*n.* 設備
facilities〔fə'sɪlətɪz〕*n. pl.* 衛生設備；廁所

facility 的主要意思是「設備」，句中的 the facilities
是指「衛生設備」，講這句話即是婉轉地告訴對方，
「我需要上洗手間。」也可說成：I want to use the
facilities. 或 I need to go to the facilities.。

7. *Where's the bathroom?*

bathroom〔'bæθ,rum〕*n.* 浴室；廁所

英文中的 toilet〔'tɔɪlɪt〕，可指「廁所」，但也可指
「馬桶」，說起來不好聽，所以一般美國人都不說，
他們習慣用 bathroom（浴室），或其他字來代替。

【比較】 *Where's the bathroom?*（廁所在哪裡？）
　　　 【正常語氣，常用】

Where's the toilet?（馬桶在哪裡？）
【劣，千萬不要說。這句話對美國人來說，很不
　文雅，只有低下階層的人才說，因為 toilet 含
　有「馬桶」的意思。】

Where's the W.C.?（廁所在哪裡？）
【劣，千萬不要說】
【W.C. = water closet，指「抽水馬桶」】
這句話美國人不說，只有英國人說。如果你在美
國說這句話，美國人會認為你是外國人，英文要
練到，讓美國人認為你是本地人才行。

「廁所在哪裡？」的問法很多：

Where's the bathroom?【最常用】

= Where's the restroom?【常用】

= Where's the washroom?【常用】
　　　　　　　　　（'waʃ,rum）*n.* 廁所；洗手間

= Where's the men's room?

= Where's the ladies' room?

= Where are the facilities?【委婉的說法】

= Where's the lavatory?【在學校、飛機上常用】
　　　　　　　　　（'lævə,torɪ）*n.* 洗手間；盥洗室

= Where's the powder room?
　　【*powder room*「女用化妝室」，約有 1%美國上流社會
　　的婦女會這麼說，特別是在高級場合中使用】

= Where's the latrine?【這句話使用於軍隊裡】
　　　　　　　　　（lə'trin）*n.*（軍營的）廁所

　　在美國酒吧或路邊的小餐館裡，男人在一起喜
歡說粗話，他們會說：

Where's the john?【john（dʒɑn）*n.* 男廁所】

Where's the head?【head（hɛd）*n.* 男廁所】

Where's the can?【can（kæn）*n.* 男廁所】

　　為什麼廁所叫 john 呢？因為在 1956 年，有個
英國人叫 Sir John Harington 發明了抽水馬桶
　　　　　　　　　　　　（'hɛrɪŋtn̩）
（flush toilet）。而 head 則是源自船上空間小，
廁所馬桶的形狀像人頭一樣大，所以，在船上的

廁所，多稱爲 "head"，現在已運用到日常生活中。
can 則有「屁股」和「廁所」的意思。到了美國酒
吧或小餐館，說這些話，當地的男人聽到會很爽，
一定會笑。

8. *Which way should I go?*

　　　　這句話的意思是「我該
往哪裡走？」，也有人說成
Which way do I go?。

Which way
should I go?

9. *Where can I find a restroom?*

restroom〔ˈrɛstˌrum〕*n.* 洗手間 (= *rest room*)
【以前 restroom 是兩個字，寫成 rest room，現在愈來
愈多人用一個字 restroom，所以，兩種寫法都可以。】

　　　　這句話的字面意思是「我在哪裡能找到洗手間？」
也就是「哪裡有洗手間？」。

　　"*Where can I find~?*" 是一個很常用的句型。

【例】 *Where can I find* McDonald's?
　　　　（哪裡有麥當勞？）

　　　　Where can I find a place to park?
　　　　（哪裡有停車的地方？）　〔park〕*v.* 停車

　　　　Where can I find a good hotel?
　　　　（哪裡有好的旅館？）

Where can I find an ATM?
（哪裡有提款機？）
【*ATM* 提款機；自動櫃員機（= *automatic teller machine*）】

Where can I find a water fountain?
（哪裡有飲水機？） 〔ˈfaʊntṇ〕*n.* 飲水機

Where can I find a bus stop?
（哪裡有公車站牌？）

Where can I find a bank?（哪裡有銀行？）
Where can I find a post office?（哪裡有郵局？）
Where can I find a bookstore?（哪裡有書店？）

10. 問「廁所在哪裡」，以 bathroom 為例的說法總整理

Where's the *bathroom*?【最常用】
（廁所在哪裡？）

Where is a *bathroom*?【最常用】
（哪裡有廁所？）

Where can I find a *bathroom*?【最常用】
（哪裡有廁所？）

Is there a *bathroom* here?【較常用】
（這裡有廁所嗎？）

Is there a *bathroom* nearby?【較常用】
（附近有廁所嗎？） 〔ˈnɪrˈbaɪ〕*adv.* 在附近

Is there a *bathroom* around here?【常用】
（這附近有廁所嗎？）

Where's your ***bathroom***?【常用】

（你們的廁所在哪裡？）【在屋內、在商店時使用】

Do you have a ***bathroom***?【常用】

（你們有廁所嗎？）

Can you tell me where the ***bathroom*** is?

（你能不能告訴我廁所在哪裡？）【較常用】

Do you know where the ***bathroom*** is?

（你知道廁所在哪裡嗎？）【最常用】

Do you know where I can find a ***bathroom***?

（你知道哪裡有廁所？）【較常用】

I'm looking for a ***bathroom***. Can you help

me out?（我在找廁所。你能幫個忙嗎？）【常用】

bathroom 本來是指家裡面的「浴室」，由於浴室裡都有廁所，這個字原本是在家裡面使用的，由於講習慣了，所以美國人即使到外面公共場所，也把廁所稱為 bathroom。

【劉毅老師的話】

　　「一口氣背會話」每一回中英文一起背，要背到 10 秒鐘之內，很辛苦，但是一旦背完，永遠不忘記，還是很划得來。

【對話練習】

1. A：**Excuse me a moment.**
   B：No problem.
   Don't be polite.
   Do what you have to do.

   A：對不起，我離開一下。
   B：沒問題。
      別客氣。
      做你該做的事。

2. A：**I'll be right back.**
   B：Take your time.
   You don't have to rush.
   I'm not in a hurry.

   A：我很快就回來。
   B：慢慢來。
      不用急。
      我不趕時間。

3. A：**Please wait for me.**
   B：You got it. (= *No problem.*)
   I'll be right here.
   I'm not going anywhere.

   A：請等我一下。
   B：沒問題。
      我就在這裡等。
      我不會走開。

4. A：**Nature's calling.**
   B：I understand.
   Go ahead.
   I'll see you in a little bit.
   【 bit〔bɪt〕*n.* 一會兒
   in a little bit 再過一會兒 】

   A：我想上洗手間。
   B：我了解。
      去吧。
      一會兒見。

5. A：**I need to wash up.**
   B：The restroom is down the hall.
   Don't hurry.
   I'll wait here. 【 hall〔hɔl〕*n.* 走廊 】

   A：我需要洗手間。
   B：廁所就在走廊那邊。
      不用急。
      我會在這裡等。

BOOK 3

6. A : I need to use the facilities.

   B : I want to go, too.
   I'll go after you.
   I'll wait till you get back.

A：我需要上洗手間。

B：我也要去。
等你回來我再去。
我會等你回來。

7. A : Where's the bathroom?

   B : I'm not sure.
   It might be that way.
   You're asking the wrong
   person.

A：廁所在哪裡？

B：我不太確定。
可能在那邊吧。
你問錯人了。

8. A : Which way should I go?

   B : Go straight down this
   hallway.
   Turn right at the corner.
   You'll see it on your left.

   【hallway〔ˈhɔl,we〕*n.* 走廊】

A：我該往哪裡走？

B：沿著這個走廊直走。

在轉角右轉。
你的左手邊就是了。

9. A : Where can I find a restroom?

   B : I'm sorry.
   I don't know.
   Your guess is as good as
   mine.

   【此句是慣用句】

A：哪裡有廁所？

B：抱歉。
我不知道。
我跟你一樣不知道。

BOOK 3

12. *It's about that time*.

It's about that time.	時間差不多了。
It's time to say good-bye.	是該說再見的時候了。
I have to get going.	我必須走了。
I hate to leave.	我真不願意離開。
I don't want to go.	我不想走。
It's been a lot of fun.	和你在一起都很快樂。
You take care.	你保重。
You take it easy.	你好好保重。
Let's get together again real soon.	我們儘快再聚一下吧。

** ——————————————

get going 動身；離開
hate〔het〕*v.* 恨；真不願意；真不喜歡
fun〔fʌn〕*n.* 樂趣　　***take care*** 保重
take it easy 放輕鬆
real〔'riəl〕*adv.* 真正地；非常

【背景説明】

這一回太有用了，天天都可以用得到。只要你
和朋友告別，就可以說這九句話。這些話非常感
人，充滿感情，會讓別人喜歡你。

1. *It's about that time.*

It's about that time.

這句話字面的意思是「大
約是那個時間。」引申為「時
間差不多了。」語氣非常婉轉，
暗示要告別了。

【比較1】　It's time to go. (該走了。)【語氣直接】

　　　　It's about time to go. 【語氣婉轉】

　　　　(差不多該走了。)

　　　　It's about that time. (時間差不多了。)

　　　　【語氣婉轉，about that time 後面不再接其他字詞】

【比較2】　*It's about that time.* You should find

　　　　a job. (時間差不多了。你該找個工作了。)

　　　　【It's about that time. 後面，不可再接子句，

　　　　只能接句子。】

　　　　It's about time you should find a job.

　　　　(是你該找工作的時候了。)

　　　　【It's about time 後接假設法子句，詳見

　　　　「文法寶典」p.370】

2. *It's time to say good-bye.*

這句話的意思是:「是該說再見的時候了。」也可
說成:It's time to go our separate ways. (該是我
們分道揚鑣的時候了。) 或 It's time for me to leave.
(是我該走的時候了。)

3. *I have to get going.*

get going ① 動身;離開 (= *leave ; depart*)
② 開始工作 (= *begin a job*) ③ 趕快 (= *hurry up*)

在不同的字典上,get going 都有不同的解釋,
我們歸納了以上三個主要的意思。***I have to get***
going. 在這裡的意思是「我必須走了。」

告訴別人說:「我必須走了。」說法太多了,下
面是九個常用的句子:

> ***I have to get going.*** 【最常用】 [***get going*** = leave]
> = I have to get moving. 【較常用】 [***get moving*** = leave]
> = I have to go. 【最常用】

> = I have to leave. 【較常用】
> = I have to split. 【常用】 [***split*** = leave quickly]
> = I have to run. 【最常用】 [***run*** = leave in a hurry]

> = I have to take off. 【常用】 [***take off*** = leave]
> = I have to hit the road. 【較常用】
>   [***hit the road*** (上路) = leave]
> = I have to get out of here. 【常用】
>   [***get out of here*** = leave here]

4. *I hate to leave.*

　I don't want to go.

hate〔het〕*v.* 恨；憎恨；真不願意；真不喜歡

　　hate 的主要意思是「恨」，這句話的字面意思是「我很恨離開。」中國人離開的時候，不會有「恨」的這種想法，**美國人用** hate **很普遍，但不表示真的恨。**

　　這句話的意思應該是「我不想離開。」*I hate to leave.* 和 *I don't want to go.* 是兩個同意義的句子，將兩句意義相同的話一起說，有加強語氣的作用。

　　　美國人常說 "*I hate to* + 原形動詞" 就像中文的「我真不願意～；我真不喜歡～。」一樣普遍，在這裡並沒有「恨」的思想在裡面。

　　【例】*I hate to* trouble you.

　　　　(= *I really don't want to trouble you.*)

　　　　(我真不願意麻煩你。)

　　　I hate to eat this. (= *I really dislike eating this.*)

　　　　(我不喜歡吃這個。)

　　　I'd hate to see her again.

　　　　(= *I really prefer not to see her again.*)

　　　　(我不想再見到她。)

　　　上面句子中的 hate，並不表示「憎恨」，而是表示「真不願意 (*really don't want to*；*really prefer not to*)，或真不喜歡 (*really dislike V-ing*)」。

BOOK 3

hate 之後除了接不定詞以外，還可以接名詞或動名詞，多半當「討厭；不喜歡」解，等於 dislike。

　　I *hate* Monday mornings. (我討厭星期一早上。)
　　I *hate* rainy weekends. (我討厭週末下雨。)
　　I *hate* paying taxes. (我討厭繳稅。)
　　I *hate* waiting in line. (我討厭排隊等候。)
　　I *hate* traffic jams. (我討厭塞車。)

【比較】　I hate Monday mornings.【最常用】
　　　　　(我討厭星期一早上。)
　　　　　I dislike Monday mornings.【極少用】
　　　　　(我不喜歡星期一早上。)
　　　　　I really don't like working on
　　　　　　Monday mornings.【常用】
　　　　　(我真不喜歡在星期一早上工作。)

　　美國很老一輩的人說 hate，有時可能真正表示「恨」，但是現在的一般人，由於 *hate* 這個字使用多了，就沒那麼強烈。

當美國人真正恨一個人，他們會說：

　　　　　I really hate her. (我真的恨她。)
　　　　　【須加上 really，才表示中文的「恨」】
　　　　　I can't stand her. (我受不了她。)
　　　　　I think she is awful. (我認為她很糟。)

　　如果老闆把你開除，中國人會說：「我恨他。」美國人會說：*I really hate him*. (我真恨他。) 也有人說：I want to kill him. (我想殺死他。) 當然，不是真正想要把他殺死。

美國前總統夫人希拉蕊（Hillary Clinton），在
她的回憶錄（Living History）中説：I wanted to
wring Bill's neck.（我想勒死他。）
這句話和 I wanted to kill him. 一
樣，都是美國人真正恨一個人時所
説的話。【wring〔rɪŋ〕*v.* 扭；絞】

Hillary Clinton

5. *It's been a lot of fun.*

　fun〔fʌn〕*n.* 樂趣；有趣的事物或人　*adj.* 有趣的

　　　　句中的 fun 是名詞。這句話源自：*It's been a lot
of fun* being with you.（和你在一起，一直很快樂。）

　【比較】It's a lot of fun.（真好玩。）
　　　　　【和朋友在一起時，任何時候都可以説】

　　　　It's been a lot of fun.（和你在一起都很快樂。）
　　　　　【要離別的時候，和朋友説】

　　　It's been a lot of fun. 也可以接動名詞片語做
真正主詞，把句子加長。（詳見「文法寶典」p.444）

　　It's been a lot of fun talking with you.
　　（和你談話真是有趣。）【要結束談話的時候説】

　　It's been a lot of fun working with you.
　　（和你一起工作真是有趣。）
　　【要下班的時候，和同事告別時説】

　　It's been a lot of fun spending time with you.
　　（和你在一起真有趣。）【和朋友道別的時候説】

BOOK 3

【比較1】***It***'s fun ***to talk with you***. 【正】
　　　　虛主詞　　　　　眞正主詞

It's fun ***talking with you***. 【正】
　　　　虛主詞　　　　　眞正主詞

　　It's fun 後面可接不定詞或動名詞，做眞正主詞，表一般觀念或事實。

【比較2】***It***'s been fun ***talking with you***. 【正】
　　　　虛主詞　　　　　眞正主詞

It's been fun ***to talk with you***. 【誤】

　　It's been fun 後面，只能接動名詞做眞正主詞，因爲 It's been fun 是完成式，表示動作已完成，此時就不是觀念或事實的問題，強調的是「動作」，所以，該用動名詞片語，做 It 的眞正主詞，表示已有的經驗，而不能用不定詞，來表示「尚未發生的動作」。

6. *You take care.*
   You take it easy.

You take care.
You take it easy.

　　Take care. 的意思是「保重。」，源自 Take care of yourself. (照顧你自己。) 是再見時常說的話。

　　Take it easy. 主要意思是「放輕鬆點。」一般人剛到美國都不習慣，爲什麼美國人再見的時候都說 ***Take it easy***. 因爲美國人容易緊張，怕發生事情，所以，他們再見的時候，都說 ***Take it easy***. 就和我們中文的「保重」一樣普遍。

　　You take care. *You take it easy*. 命令句中有了You，有加強語氣的作用，這兩句話可翻成：「你保重。你好好保重。」加上*you* 也是美國人再見時常説的話，特別是紐約人。

　　對於學生，他們常接著説：*Don't study too hard*.（不要太用功了。）對於上班族，他們常説：*Don't work too hard*.（工作不要太努力了。）

　　中國人的習慣是，再見時會説：「好好用功。（Study hard.）；好好工作（Work hard.）」這和美國人的文化完全相反。所以，以後看到美國同學，再見的時候，要説：*Don't study too hard*. *Take it easy*. 這都是美國人喜歡説的幽默話。

7. *Let's get together again real soon.*
　real〔'riəl〕*adj.* 眞的
　　　　　　　adv. 眞正地（ = *really* ）；非常（ = *very* ）

　　get together 有很多意思，在這裡是作「聚一聚」解。當你想要和朋友聚一聚的時候，你可以説：

　　Let's get together.（我們聚一下吧。）【隨口説説】
　　Let's get together again.（我們再聚一下吧。）
　　Let's get together again soon.
　　（我們趕快再聚一下吧。）
　　Let's get together again real soon.【最有誠意】
　　（我們儘快再聚一下吧。）

【比較】

Let's get together again
real soon.【正，常用】

Let's get together again
really soon.

【文法對，但無人用】

為什麼美國人不說 *really soon* 呢？因為 really 是兩個音節，soon 是一個音節，兩個音節的 really 修飾一個音節的 soon，唸起來不順；就如同他們會說 I sure can. 不說：*I surely can.*（誤）

如果強調只是我們兩個人，就可說成：

Let's <u>the two of us</u> **get together again real soon**.
　　　　同 位 語
（我們兩個人儘快再聚一下吧。）
【the two of us 是 Let's 中的 us 的同位語】

再見的時候只說聲 Good-bye，不夠熱情，人和人之間相處，見面時要熱情，再見也要說一些好聽的話，「**一口氣背會話**」不只是教你英文，還告訴你在社會上如何與人交往，如何求生存。像這回最後一句，如果你只說 Let's get together.，就不夠真誠，說一句長長的 *Let's get together again real soon*.，讓別人聽了多麼舒服，講好聽的話，你不花多少力氣，卻收穫無窮。

【對話練習】

1. A: **It's about that time.**　　　　A：時間差不多了。

   B: I agree.　　　　　　　　　　B：我同意。
   Our time is almost up.　　　　　我們的時間差不多到了。
   We both have to get going.　　　我們兩個必須要走了。

2. A: **It's time to say good-bye.**　A：是該說再見的時候了。

   B: I know.　　　　　　　　　　B：我知道。
   I have to leave.　　　　　　　我必須離開。
   We must go our separate　　　　我們必須分道揚鑣了。
   ways.
   【separate〔ˋsɛpərɪt〕*adj.* 分開的】

3. A: **I have to get going.**　　　　A：我必須走了。

   B: So do I.　　　　　　　　　　B：我也是。
   It's getting late.　　　　　　　時候不早了。
   I have to hit the road.　　　　　我必須走了。

4. A: **I hate to leave.**　　　　　　A：我真不願意離開。

   B: Me too.　　　　　　　　　　B：我也是。
   I want to stay.　　　　　　　我想留下來。
   I really like it here.　　　　　我真的很喜歡這裡。

BOOK 3

5. A: I don't want to go.

   B: I understand.
      I'd like to stay, too.
      I like this place a lot.

   A：我不想走。

   B：我了解。
      我也想留下來。
      我很喜歡這個地方。

6. A: It's been a lot of fun.

   B: It really has.
      It's been a great time.
      Let's do it again soon.

   A：和你在一起一直很愉快。

   B：的確是。
      一直很愉快。
      我們很快再聚一聚吧。

7. A: You take care.

   B: I will.
      The same to you.
      See you again.

   A：你保重。

   B：我會的。
      你也一樣。
      再見。

8. A: You take it easy.

   B: You, too.
      Don't work too hard.
      I'll see you again soon.

   A：你好好保重。

   B：你也一樣。
      工作不要太努力了。
      我們很快就會再見面的。

9. A: Let's get together again
      real soon.

   B: I'd like that.
      That's a great idea.
      Let's meet again real soon.

   A：我們儘快再聚一下吧。

   B：我喜歡。
      這主意不錯。
      我們儘快再見個面吧。

「一口氣背會話」經 BOOK 3

唸「一口氣英語」要像唸經一樣，每天大聲唸，從起床到睡覺，唸得比看得快，最後不看也會唸，養成習慣後，你會全身舒爽，你試試看，奇妙無比。只背英文，速度快到一分鐘之內唸完，就終生不會忘記。

1. Hey!
   Taxi!
   Over here!

   How're you doing?
   Thanks for stopping.
   Downtown, please.

   I just arrived.
   I want to go downtown.
   I want to see the sights.

2. I'm looking for fun.
   Where is the action?
   Where is a happening place?

   I want some excitement.
   Where should I go?
   Where do people go?

   Please fill me in.
   Please give me the lowdown.
   Can you introduce a good place?

3. *I* need some help.
   I'd like your advice.
   Where's a good place to eat?

   I want good food.
   I want a great meal.
   I want the best food around.

   Where do the locals go?
   Where's a popular place?
   I want to eat where the locals eat.

4. What's the fare?
   How much do I owe you?
   How much should I pay?

   Here you go.
   Here is one hundred.
   Just give me twenty back.

   Keep the rest.
   That's your tip.
   Have a good one.

5. Here we are.
   We are here.
   We made it.

   This is it.
   This is the place.
   It looks good.

   Let's go in.
   Let's check it out.
   Let's give it a try.

6. Table for two.
   Nonsmoking section.
   Can we sit by a window?

   Two menus, please.
   We're in a hurry.
   We're pressed for time.

   What's today's special?
   What's your best dish?
   What are you famous for?

7. We're ready to order.
   We know what we want.
   Can you take our order now?

   I'll have the special.
   She'll try the combo.
   We both want salads with that.

   Ice water for her.
   Hot water for me.
   That's it for now.

8. *Eat* up!
   Eat some more!
   Eat as much as you can.

   Fill up!
   Keep eating.
   You can eat more than that.

   Don't be polite.
   You can't be full!
   You can do better than that!

9. I like this place.
   It's my kind of place.
   It's just perfect for me.

   It's comfortable.
   I feel so relaxed.
   I feel right at home.

   What a nice place!
   I can be myself here.
   I could stay here all day.

10. *We're* ready.
    We're done.
    Check, please.

    We're finished.
    We're set to go.
    Please bring our bill.

    We're all together.
    Do you take this card?
    Do I pay you or the cashier?

11. Excuse me a moment.
    I'll be right back.
    Please wait for me.

    Nature's calling.
    I need to wash up.
    I need to use the facilities.

    Where's the bathroom?
    Which way should I go?
    Where can I find a restroom?

12. *It's* about that time.
    It's time to say good-bye.
    I have to get going.

    I hate to leave.
    I don't want to go.
    It's been a lot of fun.

    You take care.
    You take it easy.
    Let's get together again real soon.

BOOK 4 搭機出國旅遊

▶4-1 打電話向旅行社訂購機票：

> I'm going to New York.
> I'm leaving next Friday.
> I'd like a round-trip ticket.

▶4-2 辦理登機手續時，要求坐好位子：

> I'm checking in.
> Here's my ticket and passport.
> I have two bags and one carry-on.

▶4-3 在飛機上，要求空姐服務：

> Could I have a blanket?
> Could I have an apple juice?
> Could I have a cup of hot water?

▶4-4 到達目的地出境時，與移民官說：

> Here's my passport.
> Here's my immigration form.
> My return ticket is inside.

▶4-5 在機場打電話預訂旅館：

> I'd like to book a room.
> I'd like to make a reservation.
> I need it for tonight.

▶4-6 到了飯店，辦理登記住宿：

> I have a reservation.
> I'm here to check in.
> What do I have to do?

▶4-7　打電話給房務部，要求服務：

Hello, housekeeping.
I'm going out for a while.

▶4-8　搭巴士車去市中心，問司機路：

Does this bus go downtown?
How much does it cost?
How do I pay?

▶4-9　到站後，和司機或新認識的朋友告別：

Nice meeting you.
Nice talking to you.
I enjoyed our chat.

▶4-10　打電話，要求櫃檯晚點退房：

This is room 704.
I'm leaving today.
What time is checkout?

▶4-11　整理行李時，提醒同伴別忘記東西：

Are you all packed?
Are you ready to go?

▶4-12　打電話告訴櫃檯即將退房：

Hello, front desk?
I'm getting ready to check out.
I'll be down in ten minutes.

1. I'd like a round-trip ticket.

I'm going to New York.	我要去紐約。
I'm leaving next Friday.	我下星期五走。
I'd like a round-trip ticket.	我要一張來回票。
I want to go economy.	我要坐經濟艙去。
Do you have special fares?	你們有沒有特別的票價？
Do you have promotional rates?	你們有沒有促銷價？
My departure time is flexible.	我的出發時間很有彈性。
I don't mind a stopover.	我不介意中途停留。
I want an unbeatable price.	我要最棒的價錢。

BOOK 4

**────────────────────

round-trip〔'raʊnd'trɪp〕*adj.* 來回的
economy〔ɪ'kɑnəmɪ〕*adv.* 坐經濟艙   fare〔fɛr〕*n.* 票價
promotional〔prə'moʃənḷ〕*adj.* 促銷的
rate〔ret〕*n.* 價格   departure〔dɪ'pɑrtʃɚ〕*n.* 離開；出發
flexible〔'flɛksəbḷ〕*adj.* 有彈性的   mind〔maɪnd〕*v.* 介意
stopover〔'stɑpˌovɚ〕*n.* 中途停留
unbeatable〔ʌn'bitəbḷ〕*adj.* 最好的；最棒的；無法擊敗的

【背景説明】

買機票還是向旅行社買，最便宜。不論是在電話裡面，或是到旅行社買機票，説這九句話，就可以買到最便宜的機票。

1. ***I'm going to New York.***

現在進行式，除了表示「現在正在」以外，還可以表示「不久的未來」。這句話的意思是「我要去紐約。」美國人也常説：

I'm flying to New York.
（我要搭飛機去紐約。）

I want to go to New York.
（我想要去紐約。）

I'm going to New York.

I'd like to fly to New York.
〔flaɪ〕v. 搭飛機
（我想搭飛機去紐約。）

I'd like a ticket to New York.
（我想要一張到紐約的機票。）

I'd like to book a flight to New York.
（我想預訂到紐約的機票。）
【book〔bʊk〕v. 預訂　　flight〔flaɪt〕n. 班機】

I need a ticket to New York.
（我需要一張到紐約的機票。）

2. ***I'm leaving next Friday.***

這句話的意思是「我下星期五走。」也可以說：

I plan to leave next Friday. (我打算下星期五走。)
I want to leave next Friday. (我想要下星期五走。)
I want to go next Friday. (我想要下星期五走。)

I plan to fly out next Friday.
(我打算下星期五搭飛機走。)【*fly out* 搭機離去】
I plan to go next Friday. (我打算下星期五去。)
I plan to take off next Friday.
(我打算下星期五出發。)【*take off* 離開 (= *leave*)】

如果說「我這星期五走。」英文就是：

I'm leaving Friday.
I'm leaving on Friday.
I'm leaving this Friday.

I'd like a
round-trip ticket.

BOOK 4

3. ***I'd like a round-trip ticket.***
I'd like 我想要 (= *I want*)
round-trip 〔ˈraʊndˈtrɪp〕 *adj.* 來回的
【如果是名詞，就要寫成 round trip。】
round-trip ticket 來回票

這句話的意思是「我要一張來回票。」

【比較】***I'd like a round-trip ticket.*** 【常用】
I'd like to buy a round-trip ticket. 【少用】

如果你要買的是單程票，你就可以說：I'd like a
one-way ticket. (我要一張單程票。)
〔ˈwʌnˈwe〕 *adj.* 單程的

4. *I want to go economy.*

economy〔ɪˈkɑnəmɪ〕① *adv.* 坐經濟艙 (= *economy class*)
　　　　　　　　　　　② *n.* 經濟艙 (= *economy class*)

> 這句話的意思是「我要坐經濟艙去。」句中的 go
> economy，等於 go economy class。

【比較】

> I want economy. 【常用】
> (我要經濟艙。)
> I want economy class.
> (我要經濟艙。)【常用】
> ***I want to go economy.*** 【最常用】
> (我要坐經濟艙去。)
> I want to go economy class. 【常用】
> (我要坐經濟艙去。)

這句話也可以說成：

> I want to travel economy.
> (我要坐經濟艙旅行。)
> I want to take economy. (我要坐經濟艙。)
> I want to fly economy. (我要坐經濟艙。)

可以說 go economy，卻不能說 *go business* 或 *go first*。

> 【比較】***I want to go economy.***
> 　　　　(我要坐經濟艙去。)【可說 go economy class 】
> 　　　　I want to go business class.
> 　　　　(我要坐商務艙去。)【不可說 *go business* 】
> 　　　　I want to go first class.
> 　　　　(我要坐頭等艙去。)【不可說 *go first* 】

BOOK 4

5. ***Do you have special fares?***

fare〔fɛr〕*n.* 車資;(飛機的)票價

這句話的意思是「你們有沒有特別的票價?」這
類的話很多,下面是按照美國人常用的次序排列:

> ***Do you have special fares?***【最常用】
> Do you have any special deals?
> (你們有沒有特別划算的價錢?)
> 【deal 的用法,詳見 p.159】
> Do you have any bargains?
> (你們有沒有便宜的價錢?)
>
> Do you have any special rates?
> (你們有沒有特別的價錢?)
> Do you have any discount prices?
> (你們有沒有打折的價錢?)
> Do you have any bargain prices?
> (你們有沒有便宜的價錢?)
>
> Do you have any reduced prices?
> (你們有沒有打折的價錢?)
> Do you have any reduced rates?【最少用】
> (你們有沒有打折的價錢?)

6. ***Do you have promotional rates?***

promotional〔prə'moʃənl〕*adj.* 促銷的
rate〔ret〕*n.* 費用;價格

這句話的意思是「你們有沒有促銷價?」航空公
司為了宣傳,往往會推出 promotional rates(促銷
價),買票的時候問一問,說不定會撿到便宜。

BOOK 4

7. **My departure time is flexible.**
   departure〔dɪ'partʃə〕n. 離開；出發
   flexible〔'flɛksəbl̩〕adj. 有彈性的

   這句話的意思是「我的
   出發時間很有彈性。」也可
   以說成：

My departure time is flexible.

   I can go anytime.
   （我任何時候去都可以。）
   I can depart anytime.
   （我任何時候離開都可以。）
   I can leave anytime.
   （我任何時候離開都可以。）
   【depart〔dɪ'part〕v. 離開】

   也有美國人說：

   I'm willing to fly anytime.
   （我願意任何時候搭機。）
   【willing〔'wɪlɪŋ〕adj. 願意的】

8. **I don't mind a stopover.**
   mind〔maɪnd〕v. 介意；反對
   stopover〔'stap,ovə〕n.（旅程中的）中途停留

   這句話的意思是「我不介意中途停留。」也可說
   成：I don't mind a layover.
   〔'le,ovə〕n. 中途停留

9. *I want an unbeatable price.*

unbeatable〔ʌn'bitəbḷ〕*adj.* 最好的；最棒的；
無法擊敗的

unbeatable 的字面意思
是「無法擊敗的」，引申為
「最棒的；最好的」。這句話
的意思是「我要最棒的價錢。」

美國人常說 unbeatable，如：

They are an *unbeatable* team.
(= *Their team can't be beat.*)
（他們是最棒的團隊。）

Their prices are *unbeatable*.
(= *Their prices can't be beat.*)
（他們的價錢最好。）

Their service is *unbeatable*.
(= *Their service can't be beat.*)
（他們的服務是最好的。）

【team〔tim〕*n.* 隊　beat〔bit〕*v.* 打敗】

┌─【劉毅老師的話】─────
│　　找出最適合自己的背誦方法，每
│一回大聲快速地唸十分鐘，不要停，
│就可以永遠記下來了。
└─────────────────────

【對話練習】

1. A : **I'm going to New York.**

   B : Good choice.
   It's a great city.
   It's the perfect time to go.
   【perfect〔'pɝfɪkt〕*adj.* 完美的】

   A：我要去紐約。

   B：這個選擇不錯。
   紐約是很棒的都市。
   這個時候去最適合。

2. A : **I'm leaving next Friday.**

   B : Friday is convenient.
   There are more flights on Friday.
   Leave early and beat the afternoon rush.
   【beat〔bit〕*v.* 避開
   rush〔rʌʃ〕*n.* 蜂擁而至】

   A：我下星期五走。

   B：星期五很方便。
   星期五的班機較多。

   早點出發，可以避開下午的人潮。

3. A : **I'd like a round-trip ticket.**

   B : You got it.
   It's no problem at all.
   I'll get you a round-trip ticket.

   A：我要一張來回機票。

   B：沒問題。
   沒問題。
   我會給您一張來回機票。

4. A : **I want to go economy.**

   B : That might be difficult.
   Economy class is usually full.
   You might have to go standby.
   【standby〔'stænd,baɪ〕*adv.* 備用地；待命地】

   A：我要坐經濟艙去。

   B：可能會有困難。
   經濟艙通常會客滿。
   你可能要排候補。

5. A : **Do you have special fares?**　A：你們有沒有特別的票價？

　　B : We have a couple.　　　　　B：我們有幾個。
　　　　They require a longer stay.　　　需要停留較長的時間。
　　　　They require that you stay　　　需要停留一星期。
　　　　one week.

6. A : **Do you have promotional**　A：你們有促銷價嗎？
　　　　rates?

　　B : We have one at the moment.　B：我們目前有一個。
　　　　It's with a new airline.　　　　那是新航線。
　　　　It's buy one, get one free!　　　買一送一！
　　(= *It's buy one and get one free.*)

7. A : **My departure time is flexible.**　A：我的出發時間很有彈性。

　　B : That's a big help.　　　　　B：那會有很大的幫助。
　　　　It gives us more options.　　　這樣讓我們有較多的選擇。
　　　　You'll get a flight for sure.　　你一定會有機位的。

8. A : **I don't mind a stopover.**　A：我不介意中途停留。

　　B : That's good.　　　　　　　B：很好。
　　　　Many of the lower fares　　　很多低價的票都需要中途
　　　　require one.　　　　　　　　停留。
　　　　I'll try to keep it short.　　　我會盡量讓停留時間短一點。

9. A : **I want an unbeatable price.**　A：我要最棒的價錢。

　　B : I'll try.　　　　　　　　　B：我會試試看。
　　　　It depends on what's　　　　要看還有什麼票。
　　　　available.
　　　　But I'll give it my best shot.　　不過我會盡力。

【*depend on* 視～而定　available〔ə'veləbḷ〕*adj.* 可獲得的】

2. *Airport Check-in*

I'm checking in.	我要辦登機手續。
Here's my ticket and passport.	這是我的機票和護照。
I have two bags and one carry-on.	我有兩件行李要託運，還有一件手提行李。
I want an aisle seat.	我要靠走道的座位。
I want to sit in the front.	我要坐前面的座位。
Can you get me a first row seat?	你能不能給我第一排的座位？
How about the emergency row?	緊急出口旁的那排座位怎麼樣？
Please try your best.	請你儘量試試。
I appreciate your effort.	辛苦了，謝謝你。

** ————————————

check in 辦理登機手續   passport〔'pæs‚port〕*n.* 護照
bag〔bæg〕*n.* 行李   carry-on〔'kærɪ‚ɑn〕*n.* 手提行李
aisle〔aɪl〕*n.* 走道   front〔frʌnt〕*n.* 前面
row〔ro〕*n.* 排   emergency〔ɪ'mɝdʒənsɪ〕*adj.* 緊急的
try one's *best* 盡力（= *do* one's *best*）
appreciate〔ə'priʃɪ‚et〕*v.* 感激   effort〔'ɛfɚt〕*n.* 努力

【背景説明】

　　出國搭飛機，到了機場，拿著機票到航空公司櫃台，你就用得到這九句絕佳的英語。説這些話，你可以得到飛機上最好的座位。

1. ***I'm checking in.***
   check in 辦理登機手續

I'm checking in.

　　這句話的字面意思是「我現在正在辦理登機手續。」但是現在進行式也可表示「不久的未來」，所以這句話的意思是「我要辦理登機手續。」也可説成：

　　I want to check in. (我要辦登機手續。)
　　I'd like to check in. (我要辦登機手續。)
　　I'm here to check in. (我來辦登機手續。)

2. ***Here's my ticket and passport.***
   ticket〔ˈtɪkɪt〕*n.* 車票；機票
   passport〔ˈpæsˌport〕*n.* 護照

　　這句話的意思是「這是我的機票和護照。」我們中國人説「飛機票」，美國人只説 ticket，只有在需要區別時，他們才説 air ticket 或 plane ticket。

【例】I have a ***bus ticket*** for you. I couldn't get an ***air ticket***.
　　（我買了客運車票給你。我買不到飛機票。）

一般文法書上都寫著：

$$\left.\begin{array}{l} \text{Here} \\ \text{There} \end{array}\right\} \text{is} + 單數名詞$$

$$\left.\begin{array}{l} \text{Here} \\ \text{There} \end{array}\right\} \text{are} + 複數名詞$$

【比較】 *Here's* my ticket. (這是我的機票。)

　　　　Here are our tickets. (這是我們的機票。)

但是，要注意，Here is/are 或 There is/are 之後，若有兩個以上的主詞，以靠近動詞的主詞單複數為準。(詳見「文法寶典」p.397)

【例】 *Here is* a pen and a pencil. Which do you prefer?

　　　　(這裡有原子筆和鉛筆。你比較喜歡哪一個？)

文法規則是按照人類的語言歸納而成的，你不可能說 Here is a pen，接著說 and a pencil 後，再把前面自己所說的話改成 Here are。學英文最好從實際口語中，來印證文法，如果只是利用所學的有限文法規則來造句，往往會出錯。

到航空公司辦理登機手續的時候，如果你有 e-ticket (= electronic ticket「電子機票」)，你就可以說：Here's my e-ticket. (這是我的電子機票。)

3. ***I have two bags and one carry-on.***
   bag〔bæg〕*n.* 行李
   carry-on〔ˈkærɪˌɑn〕*n.* 手提行李

I have two bags and one carry-on.

　　這句話的意思是：「我有
兩件行李要託運，還有一件手
提行李。」

　　「行李」的説法有很多種：

　　　bag〔bæg〕*n.* 行李
　　　baggage〔ˈbægɪdʒ〕*n.* 行李【物質名詞，不可數】
　　　luggage〔ˈlʌgɪdʒ〕*n.* 行李【物質名詞，不可數】

　　美國人最常用的是 *bag*，機場櫃台人員常問：
How many ***bags*** are you checking in? (你有幾
件行李要託運 ?)。【***check in*** 在此作「託運」解】

【比較】 I have two ***bags*** to check in. 【最常用】
　　　　 I have two pieces to check in. 【常用】
　　　　　　〔ˈpisɪz〕*n. pl.* 件；個
　　　　 I have two pieces of luggage to check in.
　　　　 【正，但美國人幾乎不用】
　　　　 I have two pieces of baggage to check in.
　　　　 【正，但美國人不用】

　　在文法上，luggage 和 baggage 都是不可數名
詞，要用單位名詞表「數」的觀念。但美國人的生
活步調越來越快，語言也因此而簡化，既然有了
bag 這個簡單的字，當然不需要用到 *baggage*，
更不需要説 *two pieces of baggage* 了，同樣地，
two pieces of luggage 也一樣，將慢慢被淘汰，

現在幾乎沒什麼人用。你看，我們從前學那麼多，都學錯了，*baggage* 和 *luggage* 背了半天，結果都不是美國人所說的話，他們多只用 ***bag***。學英文要學從美國人口中說出來的話，才是上策。

---

carry-on〔ˈkærɪˌɑn〕*adj.* 隨身攜帶的 (*small enough to be **carried** aboard and stored **on** an airplane, train or bus by a passenger*)。***carry-on*** 這個字，一般字典還當形容詞用，作「隨身攜帶的」解，事實上，carry-on 也可做名詞用，等於 carry-on bag (隨身手提行李)。現在美國人日常生活中，大都把 carry-on bag 簡化成 ***carry-on*** 或 ***carryon***。

【比較】 I have two ***carry-ons***.【最常用】
(我有兩件手提行李。)

I have two ***carry-on*** bags.【常用】

【例1】 Most airlines allow only one ***carry-on***.
〔ˈɛrˌlaɪnz〕*n. pl.* 航空公司
(大部分航空公司只允許攜帶一件手提行李。)

【例2】 All ***carry-ons*** must be hand-searched.
(所有的手提行李都必須打開檢查。)
【hand-search〔ˈhændˌsɝtʃ〕*v.* 用手檢查，此字是新字，字典上沒有】

---

carry-on 這個字源自於動詞片語 ***carry sth. on*** (帶著某物上去)，例如：Has anyone given you anything to ***carry on***? (有任何人託你帶東西上飛機嗎？)

4. *I want an aisle seat.*

aisle〔aɪl〕*n.* 走道

在櫃台 check in 的時候，他們通常會問：

Would you like an aisle or window seat?

（你要靠走道還是靠窗的
座位？），如果你想要靠
走道的座位，你可以回答：

I want an aisle seat.

（我要靠走道的座位。）【最常用】

I'd like an aisle seat.【最常用】

（我想要靠走道的座位。）

I prefer an aisle seat.【最常用】

（我比較喜歡靠走道的座位。）

Can you get me an aisle seat?【較常用】

（你能不能給我靠走道的座位？）

Can you put me in an aisle seat?【常用】

（你可以安排我坐靠走道的座位嗎？）

Can you put me on the aisle?【常用】

（可以安排我坐靠走道嗎？）

【此句是慣用句，等於 *Can you put me in an aisle seat?*】

Can I have an aisle seat?【較常用】

（我可以坐靠走道的座位嗎？）

Can I sit in an aisle seat?【較常用】

（我可以坐靠走道的座位嗎？）

I need an aisle seat.【較不常用】

（我需要靠走道的座位。）

BOOK 4

如果你飛長途，在天上，靠窗戶什麼也看不
到，外國人高頭大馬，飛機座位小，擠在裡面很
難過。靠走道可以伸伸腿，起來走動也方便，對
身體比較有益。

5. ***I want to sit in the front.*** (我要坐前面的座位。)
front〔frʌnt〕*n.* 前面　*adj.* 前面的
in the front 在前面

　　這句話也可說成：I want to sit near the front.
(我要坐靠近前面的座位。) I want (我要) 可說成
I'd like (我想要) 或 I prefer (我比較喜歡)。

6. ***Can you get me a first row seat?***
get〔gɛt〕*v.* 得到；拿來　　row〔ro〕*n.* 排

　　這句話的意思是「你能不能給我第一排的座
位？」get 這個字的主要意思是「得到」，在這裡
作「拿來」解，英文意思是 give 或 bring。這種
用法使用頻率非常高，尤其是請別人拿東西來：

【例1】***Can you get*** me a cup of hot water?
　　　　(你能不能幫我拿杯熱開水？)

【例2】***Can you get*** me that book?
　　　　(你能不能幫我拿那本書？)

【例3】***Can you get*** me an appointment with
Dr. Smith?
　　　　(你能不能幫我安排請史密斯醫師看診？)

【例4】 ***Can you get*** me to the station in ten minutes?（你能不能十分鐘之內載我到車站？）

【例5】 ***Can you get*** me a better price?
（你能不能給我一個更好的價錢？）

【例6】 ***Can I get*** you something?
（要我拿點東西給你嗎？）

　　Can you get me a first row seat? 也可説成 Can you get me a seat in the first row? 意思都是「你能不能給我一個第一排的座位？」first 可以用 front 取代。

【比較】 Can you get me *a seat in the front row*?
（你能不能給我一個第一排的座位？）
Can you get me *a seat in the front*?
（你能不能給我一個前面的座位？）

這兩句話意義不同，雖然 front 這個字，當形容詞是指「前面的」或「最前面的」，但是 a seat in the front row 卻是指「最前排的一個座位」，即「第一排的一個座位」（a seat in the first row 或 a first row seat）。但是 in the front 是指「在前面的」，不一定是第一排。

　　搭飛機選擇座位，最好的座位是第一排靠走道的位子，空間大又舒服，如果是沒有頭等艙或商務艙的小飛機，第一排的座位通常是留給大人物。搭飛機要求坐在第一排，是最佳的選擇。

BOOK 4

7. *How about the emergency row?*

emergency 〔 ɪˈmɝdʒənsɪ 〕 *n.* 緊急情況　*adj.* 緊急的

　　　　每架飛機都有數個緊急出口（emergency exit），
靠近緊急出口的那一排座位稱作 emergency row，
這排座位空間較大，起飛時，空中小姐就坐在你對

面，坐在 emergency row 的
座位，既舒適，又可和美麗的
空姐聊天，也可以隨時請她們
爲你服務。在櫃台 check in
時，想要求坐 emergency
row 的座位，你可以説：

> ### *How about the emergency row?*
> （緊急出口旁的那排座位怎麼樣？）
>
> Can you try the emergency row?
> （你能不能試試看，給我緊急出口旁的那排座位？）
>
> Can I sit in the emergency row?
> （我可以坐在緊急出口旁的那排座位嗎？）
>
> Are there any emergency row seats open?
> （緊急出口旁的那排座位有空位嗎？）
>
> Any chance I can sit in the emergency row?
> (= *Is there any chance I…?*)
> （我有機會坐在緊急出口旁的那排座位嗎？）
>
> Is it possible to sit in the emergency row?
> （我有可能坐在緊急出口旁的那排座位嗎？）

8. *Please try your best.*

   try one's best 盡力 (= *do one's best*)

   這句話的意思是「請盡力。」這類的説法很多：

   > *Please try your best.* (請盡力。)
   > Please do your best. (請盡力。)
   > Please do the best you can do.
   > (請儘量做你能做的。)
   >
   > See what you can do. (看你能爲我做什麼。)
   > 【後面可加上 for me】
   > Do what you can. (做你所能做的。)
   > No matter what, I appreciate it.
   > (無論結果怎樣，我都感謝你。)
   > 【No matter what 源自 *No matter what happens*
   > (美國人不説)】

9. *I appreciate your effort.*

   appreciate〔ə'priʃɪͺet〕*v.* 感激
   effort〔'ɛfət〕*n.* 努力；辛苦

   在櫃台要求好座位後，立刻就説些感謝的話，讓
   他不得不幫你的忙。這句話的意思是「我非常感謝你
   的努力。」類似中國人習慣説的「辛苦了，謝謝你。」

   感謝別人的説法很多：

   > *I appreciate your effort.* (辛苦了，謝謝你。)
   > Thanks for your help. (謝謝你的幫忙。)
   > Thank you so much for your help.
   > (非常感謝你的幫忙。)

BOOK 4

10. 補充説明

登機手續辦完，可以再問一句：Is this flight
full?（這班飛機客滿了嗎？），如果對方回答：
It's not full.（不滿。），這時你就要最後一個上
飛機，可以自己選擇空位，以便起飛後，能躺在
整排座位上睡覺。如果航空公司櫃台小姐回答：
It's full.（座位滿了。）或 It's almost full.（座
位幾乎滿了。），你就要早點登機，以便把手提行
李順利地放在行李架上，你最後登機，搞不好，
沒有位子放你的行李了，行李被迫放在很遠的地
方，很麻煩。

有經驗的旅行家常説：It's best to be the
first for a buffet and the last to get on a plane.
　　　　〔 bu'fe 〕 *n.* 歐式自助餐
（吃自助餐要第一個進餐廳，坐飛機要最後一個上
飛機。）吃自助餐搶第一，既有最多的選擇，又
乾淨；坐飛機要最後一個登機，可以自由選擇好
位子。

【劉毅老師的話】

背一段時間以後，説不定會有厭
倦的感覺，此時，應該背一篇英語演
講，你會覺得更充實。

【對話練習】

1. A：**I'm checking in**.

   B：Welcome!
   Thank you for choosing our airline.
   May I see your ticket, please?

   A：我要辦登機手續。

   B：歡迎！
   感謝您選擇本航空公司。

   我可以看一下您的機票嗎？

2. A：**Here's my ticket and passport**.

   B：Thank you.
   Let me check everything.
   I'll verify your information.
   【verify (ˈvɛrəˌfaɪ) v. 證實】

   A：這是我的機票和護照。

   B：謝謝。
   讓我檢查一下。
   我要核對您的資料。

3. A：**I have two bags and one carry-on**.

   B：Please tag your bags.
   Let's weigh your bags.
   Please place them on the scale.
   【tag (tæg) v. 附上標籤
   scale (skel) n. 磅秤】

   A：我有兩件行李要託運，還有一件手提行李。

   B：行李請附上標籤。
   我來稱一下行李多重。
   請把它們放在磅秤上。

4. A：**I want an aisle seat**.

   B：I have bad news.
   The aisle seats are all booked.
   How about a window or middle seat?

   A：我要靠走道的座位。

   B：壞消息。
   靠走道的座位全滿了。
   靠窗戶或中間的座位好嗎？

BOOK 4

BOOK 4

5. A : **I want to sit in the front**.

   B : We can do that.
   That won't be a problem.
   We have plenty of seats
   available.
   【available〔əˈveləbḷ〕*adj* 可獲得的】

A : 我要坐前面的座位。

B : 可以。
沒問題。
我們有很多空位。

6. A : **Can you get me a first row**
   seat?

   B : It's your lucky day!
   We have one seat left!
   It's yours.

A : 你能不能給我第一排的
座位？

B : 您今天真幸運！
我們還剩一個位子！
這個位子是您的了。

7. A : **How about the emergency**
   row?

   B : The emergency row is full.
   We have no open seats.
   Those always go fast.
   【go〔go〕*v* 消失】

A : 緊急出口旁的那排座位
怎麼樣？

B : 那一排座位全滿了。
沒有空位了。
那些位子總是很快就沒
了。

8. A : **Please try your best**.

   B : Don't worry, I will.
   I'll do everything I can.
   I know this is important to
   you.

A : 請你儘量試試。

B : 別擔心，我會的。
我會盡力。
我知道這對您很重要。

9. A : **I appreciate your effort**.

   B : It's no trouble at all.
   I'm happy to help you.
   Enjoy your flight.

A : 辛苦了，謝謝你。

B : 一點都不麻煩。
我很樂意協助您。
祝您旅途愉快。

3. *In-flight Service*

Could I have a blanket?	可不可以給我一條毯子？
Could I have an apple juice?	能不能給我一杯蘋果汁？
Could I have a cup of hot water?	能不能給我一杯熱開水？
I'm not in a hurry.	我不急。
It's not an emergency.	這不是緊急情況。
I can wait.	我可以等。
When do we eat?	我們什麼時候吃飯？
When do we arrive?	我們什麼時候到達？
How long till we get there?	我們還要多久才會到？

BOOK 4

** ——————————————

blanket〔ˈblæŋkɪt〕*n.* 毯子   juice〔dʒus〕*n.* 果汁
in a hurry 匆忙
emergency〔ɪˈmɝdʒənsɪ〕*n.* 緊急情況

【背景説明】

在飛機上，座椅旁邊有一個按鈕，你只要按一下，空姐就會過來，問道：Did you press the call button? Can I help you? (你有沒有按叫人服務的按鈕？需要我幫忙嗎？) 你就可以一口氣說這九句話。

1. *Could I have a blanket?*

blanket〔'blæŋkɪt〕*n.* 毯子

【這個字好背，blank (空白) 加上 et】

Can I have a blanket?

【比較】

> *Could I have a blanket?*
> (能不能幫我拿條毯子？)
> 【常用，用假設法助動詞 could，表示自己不該問，因此，這句話比較有禮貌】

> Can I have a blanket?
> (能不能拿條毯子給我？)【常用】

美國人也常說：

> Please give me a blanket.
> (請給我一條毯子。)【常用】

> I'd like a blanket, please.
> (我要一條毯子，可以嗎？)

2. ***Could I have an apple juice?***
apple〔'æpḷ〕*n.* 蘋果
apple juice 蘋果汁
【重讀在 apple】

> *Could I have an apple juice?*

這句話意思是「可不可
以給我一杯蘋果汁？」也可
說成：

> ***Could I have*** some apple juice?
> （可不可以給我一些蘋果汁？）

> ***Could I have*** a carton of apple juice?
> 　　　　　　　〔'kɑrtṇ〕*n.* 紙盒
> （可不可以給我一盒蘋果汁？）

【比較】　***Could I have an apple juice?***【常用】
　　　　　【雖然在文法上，物質名詞須用單位名詞表
　　　　　「數」的觀念，但是 juice 和 water，tea，
　　　　　coffee，milk 一樣，是物質名詞的例外】

Could I have a glass of apple juice?
　　　　【常用，但在飛機上不用，因為飛機上多不用
　　　　glass（玻璃杯）】

旅行在外，多喝蘋果汁，能夠增強免疫力，英
文有句諺語：An apple a day keeps the doctor
away.（一天吃一顆蘋果，就不需要看醫生。）

但是，蘋果汁太甜，如果加上熱開水，是不錯
的選擇。土耳其人就常喝熱蘋果汁，來保持身體
健康。

BOOK 4

3. *Could I have a cup of hot water?*

這句話意思是「可不可以給我一杯熱開水？」也可說成：*Could I have* some hot water?（能不能給我一些熱開水？）

如果你想加檸檬，你可以再說：

Could I have a slice of lemon in that?
（可不可以替我加一片檸檬在裡面？）

如果你在一般餐廳裡要熱開水，服務生可能會偷懶，直接倒水龍頭的熱水給你，事實上，那個水比水龍頭的冷水還不衛生，看情形不對，你就可以強調說：

I want really hot water.（我要真的很熱的開水。）
I want boiled water.（我要煮開的水。）
I don't want warm water.（我不要溫開水。）

在飛機上的冷水是礦泉水，很安全，但在餐廳裡，要喝水最好是滾燙的開水（really hot water），才安全。

在飛機上面，如果你要冰開水時，你可說：

Could I have cold water?（可不可以給我冷開水？）
Could I have an ice water?
（可不可以給我一杯冰開水？）
Could I have some ice water?
（可不可以給我一些冰開水？）
Could I have a water with lots of ice?
（可不可以給我一杯加很多冰塊的水？）

　　原則上，water 是物質名詞，不可數，要用單位名詞表「數」的觀念，如「一杯水」是 a glass of water，「一杯熱開水」是 a cup of hot water，「有把手的杯子」叫做 cup，通常用來裝熱飲。現在，美國人逐漸簡化，「一杯水」可以直接説 *a water*，「兩杯水」説 *two waters*。同樣地，tea 和 coffee 也可説是物質名詞的例外，一杯茶是 *a tea*，兩杯茶是 *two teas*；一杯咖啡是 *a coffee*，兩杯咖啡是 *two coffees*。

【比較 1】 I'd like a water. 【正，常用】

　　　　　 I'd like some water. 【正，常用】

　　　　　 I'd like a glass of water. 【正】

　　　　　 I'd like a cup of water.
　　　　　 【正，少用，因為只有熱開水才用 cup】

【比較 2】 *I'd like a hot water.* 【正，少用】

　　　　　 I'd like a cup of hot water. 【正，常用】

　　　　　 I'd like a glass of hot water.
　　　　　 【很少用，因為玻璃杯會燙手】

在飛機上，如果你要柳橙汁，你就可以説：

　　　Could I have some orange juice?

　　　（可不可以給我一些柳橙汁？）

　　　【orange juice 的重讀在 orange】

Could I have an orange juice?

（可不可以給我一杯柳橙汁？）

Could I have a glass of orange juice?

（可不可以給我一杯柳橙汁？）

如果你想多喝一點，你要一整罐可樂，你可以説：

Could I have a whole can of Coke?

（可不可以給我一整罐可口可樂？）

【can〔kæn〕*n.* 罐　Coke〔kok〕*n.* 可口可樂】

如果你想要加冰塊，你可以説：

Could I have a can of Coke
with a glass of ice?

（可不可以給我一罐可口可樂和一杯冰塊？）

4. *I'm not in a hurry.*
in a hurry 匆忙

這句話意思是「我不急。」也可以説：Take
your time.（慢慢來。）或 I'm not pressed for
time.（我不急。）。【*be pressed for time* 時間緊迫】

5. *It's not an emergency.*
emergency〔ɪˈmɝdʒənsɪ〕*n.* 緊急情況

這句話的意思是「這不是緊急情況。」也可以説
成：It's not urgent.（不急。）也可以更有禮貌地
説：It's not that important.（並沒有那麼重要。）

【urgent〔ˈɝdʒənt〕*adj.* 緊急的】

6. *I can wait.*

這句話的意思是「我可以等。」也可說成：I don't mind waiting.（我不介意等一等。）

在餐廳裡，如果你想待久一點，看看書，你可以和服務生說：

> *I can wait.*（我可以等。）
> I have a lot of time.（我時間很多。）
> I'm not going anywhere.（我哪兒也不去。）
> 【開玩笑語氣】

7. *When do we eat?*

在飛機上，問空服員什麼時候吃飯，預先知道吃飯時間，可以提早上廁所，免得排隊。因為很多乘客，一看到要供餐了，就會搶著上廁所。

下面六句，都常用，不過我們還是按照美國人常用次序排列：

> ***When do we eat?***（我們什麼時候吃飯？）【最常用】
> What time do we eat?（我們什麼時候吃飯？）【最常用】
> What time will we be served?【較常用】
> （我們什麼時候供餐？）
>
> When is the mealtime?（什麼時候吃飯？）【較常用】
> 【mealtime（'mil,taɪm）*n.* 吃飯時間，不可寫成 *meal time*】
> When is our mealtime?（我們什麼時候吃飯？）【常用】
> When will we be served?（我們什麼時候供餐？）【常用】
> （sɝvd）*v.* 上（菜）；供餐

8. *When do we arrive?*

「我們什麼時候到達？」的問法很多：

When do we arrive? (我們什麼時候到達？) 【最常用】
When do we get there? 【較常用】
(我們什麼時候到？)
When will we land? (我們何時降落？) 【常用】
【land〔lænd〕*v.* 降落】

When does the plane get there? 【常用】
(飛機什麼時候到達？)
What's our arrival time? (我們何時到達？) 【最常用】
What's the arrival time? 【較常用】
(抵達時間是什麼時候？) 【arrival〔ə'raɪvl〕*n.* 到達】

9. *How long till we get there?*

這句話源自：*How long do we have to wait till we get there?*

How long till we get there?

這句話的字面意思是「在我們到達以前，還要等多久？」也就是「我們還要多久才會到？」這種說法很多：

How long till we get there? 【最常用】
How long till we arrive? 【最常用】
(我們還要多久才會到？)
How many more hours until we arrive? 【較常用】
(我們還要幾個小時才會到？)

How much more time till we get there?【常用】
（我們還要多久才會到？）
How much time left till we get there?【常用】
（我們還剩多久會到？）
How much time do we have left till we get
  there?（我們還剩多久會到？）【常用】

How much longer till we get there?【較常用】
（我們還要多久才會到？）
How long do we have left till we get there?
（我們還剩多久會到？）【常用】
【以上句子的 till，可改成 until】

在飛機上，下面三句話，美國人也常說：

How much more time to go?
（還要飛多久？）【常用】
【*to go* 剩下】
How much longer do we have?
（我們還要飛多久？）【最常用】
How much time do we have left?
（我們還剩多久時間？）【較常用】

─── 【劉毅老師的話】───

唸的速度要快，背的速度要快，
才能很快變成直覺。

【對話練習】

1. A: **Could I have a blanket?**

   B: Of course you can!
      I'll get you one right away.
      Do you need anything else?

   A：可不可以給我一條毯子？

   B：當然可以！
      我會立刻幫您拿一條。
      您還需要其他東西嗎？

2. A: **Could I have an apple juice?**

   B: I'm out of apple juice.
      Let me get some more.
      I'll be back in a jiffy.
      【jiffy〔ˊdʒɪfɪ〕*n.* 片刻
      in a jiffy 立刻】

   A：可不可以給我一杯蘋果汁？

   B：我沒有蘋果汁了。
      我再去拿。
      我馬上回來。

3. A: **Could I have a cup of hot water?**

   B: Sure thing!
      Coming right up!
      Is that all?

   A：可不可以給我一杯熱開水？

   B：當然可以！
      馬上來！
      就這樣嗎？

4. A: **I'm not in a hurry**.

   B: You're too kind.
      You don't need to say that.
      I can help you right now.

   A：我不急。

   B：您太客氣了。
      您不必這麼說。
      我可以立刻幫您拿。

5. A: **It's not an emergency**.

   B: That's all right.
      I'm happy to do it.
      I'll be back in a moment.
      【***in a moment*** 立刻】

   A：這不是緊急情況。

   B：沒關係。
      我很樂意做這件事。
      我馬上回來。

6. A：**I can wait.**

   B：**How polite!**
   You're thoughtful!
   That's a kind thing to say.
   【thoughtful (ˋθɔtfəl) *adj.* 體貼的】

A：我可以等。

B：您眞客氣！
   您眞體貼！
   您這麼說眞體貼。

7. A：**When do we eat?**

   B：**Dinner is in one hour.**
   And breakfast will be served
   two hours before we land.
   Snacks are also available
   upon request.
   serve (sɜv) *v.* 供應
   land (lænd) *v.* 降落
   snack (snæk) *n.* 點心
   upon request 一經要求】

A：我們什麼時候吃飯？

B：晚餐還有一小時。
   早餐會在降落前兩小時供
   應。
   也可向我們要點心。

8. A：**When do we arrive?**

   B：**We'll arrive at 8:30 a.m.**
   That's local time.
   The captain will remind you
   when it's time to reset your
   watch. 【captain (ˋkæptən) *n.* 機長
   reset (riˋsɛt) *v.* 重新調整】

A：我們什麼時候到達？

B：我們將在上午八點半到達。
   那是當地時間。
   機長會提醒您何時該調
   整您的手錶。

9. A：**How long till we get there?**

   B：**We'll be there soon.**
   The flight is on time.
   We arrive in about two hours.

A：我們還要多久才會到達？

B：我們很快就到了。
   班機很準時。
   我們再過兩個小時就到了。

BOOK 4

4. *Immigration*

Here's my passport.	這是我的護照。
Here's my immigration form.	這是我的入境表。
My return ticket is inside.	我的回程機票在裡面。
I just arrived from Taiwan.	我剛從台灣到這裡。
I'm here on vacation.	我來這裡度假。
I have a tourist visa.	我有觀光簽證。
I'll be in the States for two weeks.	我將在美國待兩週。
I'll be staying at the Holiday Inn.	我將住在假日飯店。
Thank you for helping me.	感謝你幫忙。

** —————————————————————

passport〔'pæs,port〕n. 護照
immigration〔,ımə'greʃən〕n. 入境
form〔fɔrm〕n. 表格　　*return ticket* 回程票
inside〔'ın'saıd〕adv. 在裡面　　*on vacation* 度假中
tourist〔'turıst〕adj. 觀光的　　visa〔'vizə〕n. 簽證
the States 美國　　stay〔ste〕v. 暫住；住宿（旅館）
inn〔ın〕n. 旅館；飯店

【背景説明】

　　到美國入境，先通過移民局，再通過海關和檢疫，背完這九句話，就可順利通過移民局。

1. *Here's my passport.*
   passport〔'pæs,port〕*n.* 護照

　　　　這句話前面也可以加一句：Hi, officer!（嗨！長官！），再接著説：Here's my passport.（這是我的護照。）或説：This is my passport.（這是我的護照。）

2. *Here's my immigration form.*
   immigration〔,ɪmə'greʃən〕*n.* 入境
   emigration〔,ɛmə'greʃən〕*n.* 出境　　form〔fɔrm〕*n.* 表格

　　　　這句話的意思是「這是我的入境表。」也有人説：Here's my immigration card.（這是我的入境卡。）

im + migr + ation	e + migr + ation
in + *move* + *n.*（入境）	*out* + *move* + *n.*（出境）

3. *My return ticket is inside.*
   return ticket 回程票　　inside〔'ɪn'saɪd〕*adv.* 在裡面

　　　　到美國旅行，最好把回程機票夾在護照裡，免得別人向你要。這句話的意思是「我的回程機票在裡面。」如果你把機票和護照放在一起，交給移民局，你就説：Here's my passport and my return ticket. 當然，機票給他看時，也可説：Here's my return ticket.

BOOK 4

4. *I just arrived from Taiwan.*

這句話的意思是「我剛從台灣到這裡。」也可說成：

I just came from Taiwan. (我剛從台灣來。)
I just flew in from Taiwan.
(我剛從台灣搭飛機到這裡。) **{fly in 搭飛機到達}**

移民局的人想知道你從哪裡來，以便他們能推知你來的真正目的。

5. *I'm here on vacation.*
vacation〔ve'keʃən〕*n.* 假期
on vacation 度假中

這句話字面的意思是
「我在這裡是度假中。」
也就是「我來這裡度假。」這種説法很多：

I'm here on vacation.
I'm here for a holiday. (我來這裡度假。)
I'm here to join a tour. (我來這裡參加旅行團。)

I'm here to visit. (我來這裡玩。)
I'm here to travel. (我來這裡旅行。)
I'm here to sightsee. (我來這裡觀光。)
【tour〔tur〕*n.* 觀光旅行　sightsee〔'saɪt,si〕*v.* 觀光】

6. *I have a tourist visa.*
tourist〔'turɪst〕*adj.* 觀光的
visa〔'vizə〕*n.* 簽證 (簽證是外國大使館簽發的入境許可，
通常是蓋在或貼在護照上)

這句話的意思是「我有觀光簽證。」

7. ***I'll be in the States for two weeks.***

state〔stet〕*n.* 州　　***the States*** 美國

　　　state 是「州」的意思，美
國的全名是 the United States
of America（美利堅合衆國）。

「美國」的説法有五種：

> 【比較】　the States【最常用】
> 　　　　　the U.S.【第二常用】
> 　　　　　the U.S.A.【常用，取自全名的縮寫】
> 　　　　　the United States【常用】
> 　　　　　*America*【極少用】
> 　　　　　*the United States of America*【極少用】

　　　美國人説話喜歡簡短扼要，the United States
of America 太長，他們懶得説，就説 the States。
不喜歡説 America 的原因，是因爲美國人強調的重
點是「聯合、團結」，他們寧可説 the United States。
而且 America 還有「美洲」的意思，像北美洲
（North America）、中美洲（Central America）
和南美洲（South America），容易混淆。説 America
還會引起南美洲的人不滿，他們不喜歡美國人説：
"I'm from America." 因爲他們覺得「美洲」又不
全是美國人的。

　　　I'll be in the States for two weeks.（我將在
美國待兩週。）在這裡也可説成：I'll be here for
two weeks.（我將在這裡兩週。）或 I'm staying
here for two weeks.（我將在這裡停留兩週。）

BOOK 4

8. *I'll be staying at the Holiday Inn.*

stay〔ste〕v. 暫住；住宿（旅館）

inn〔ɪn〕n. (鄉下的) 旅館

Holiday Inn (假日飯店)，是一家連鎖飯店，有
的是五星級大飯店，爲什麼用 Inn，不用 Hotel 呢？
inn 本來意思是「小旅館」，應該是木造的鄉下小旅
館，用 inn 讓客人感覺到，在大飯店也可享受到，
小旅館的輕鬆悠閒。這句話也可說成：I'll be at
the Holiday Inn. (我將住在假日飯店。)

【比較1】

　I'll be staying at the Holiday Inn.

　　(我將住在假日飯店。)

　【「未來進行式」可表未來預定的行動，詳見「文法寶典」p.348，
　　在這裡表示已確定要住】

　I'll stay at the Holiday Inn.

　　(我將住在假日飯店。)

　【打算住，但尚未訂房】

【比較2】

　A: Which hotel do you prefer?
　　(你比較喜歡哪個飯店？)

　B: *I'll stay at the Holiday Inn.*
　　(我將住在假日飯店。)【未確定】

　A: How can I reach you?
　　(我要如何和你連絡？)

　B: *I'll be staying at the Holiday Inn.*
　　(我將住在假日飯店。)【已確定】
　　【reach〔ritʃ〕v. 連絡】

BOOK 4

【對話練習】

1. A：**Here's my passport.**
   B：Thank you.
   So, you're from Taiwan?
   What brings you to the United
   States?

   A：這是我的護照。
   B：謝謝。
      嗯，你來自台灣？
      你爲什麼來美國？

2. A：**Here's my immigration form.**
   B：Thanks, I'll take that.
   Let's take a look.
   Everything looks OK.

   A：這是我的入境表。
   B：謝謝，我會拿。
      讓我看看。
      一切看起來都沒問題。

3. A：**My return ticket is inside.**
   B：I see it.
   You're returning in two weeks?
   That's fine.

   A：我的回程機票在裡面。
   B：我看到了。
      你兩週後要回去？
      沒問題。

4. A：**I just arrived from Taiwan.**
   B：Is that right?
   That's a nice place.
   I've heard many good things
   about Taiwan.

   A：我剛從台灣到這裡。
   B：是嗎？
      那是個好地方。
      我聽過很多有關台灣的
      很好的事情。

5. A：**I'm here on vacation.**
   B：Enjoy yourself.
   Have a good time.
   Where are you planning to go?

   A：我來這裡度假。
   B：好好玩。
      玩得愉快。
      你打算去哪裡？

BOOK 4

6. A : **I have a tourist visa**.

   B : Yes, I see that.
   You can only stay two months.
   And you cannot engage in any type of work while you are here.

A：我有觀光簽證。

B：是的，我看到了。
你只能停留兩個月。

而且你在這裡的期間不得從事任何工作。

7. A : **I'll be in the States for two weeks**.

   B : Is that all?
   That's too short.
   You'll just have to come back again.

A：我將在美國待兩週。

B：就這樣啊？
時間太短了。
你一定得再回來。

8. A : **I'll be staying at the Holiday Inn**.

   B : I'll write that down.
   That's your contact address.
   Let us know if you move.
   【contact〔'kɑntækt〕*n.* 聯絡】

A：我將住在假日飯店。

B：我會寫下來。
那是你的聯絡地址。
如果你要離開，請通知我們。

9. A : **Thank you for helping me**.

   B : Don't mention it.
   That's my job.
   You are very welcome.

A：感謝你幫忙。

B：不客氣。
這是我的工作。
不客氣。

5. *I'd like to book a room*.

I'd like to book a room.	我要預訂一個房間。
I'd like to make a reservation.	我要預訂房間。
I need it for tonight.	我今天晚上要住。
I prefer twin beds.	我比較喜歡有兩張床的房間。
I'll settle for a double.	我可以勉強接受一張雙人床。
Do you have any vacancies?	你們有沒有空房間？
What are your rates?	你們的房間價格是多少？
What can you do for me?	你能幫個忙嗎？
Do you have a complimentary breakfast?	你們有免費的早餐嗎？

BOOK 4

** ————————————

book〔buk〕*v.* 預訂　　reservation〔ˌrɛzɚˈveʃən〕*n.* 預訂
make a reservation 預訂　　prefer〔prɪˈfɝ〕*v.* 比較喜歡
twin〔twɪn〕*adj.* 雙胞胎的；成對的
twin beds 兩張一樣的床；有兩張單人床的房間
settle〔ˈsɛtl̩〕*v.* 安頓；安定；安身　　*settle for* 勉強接受
double〔ˈdʌbl̩〕*n.* 雙人房；有一張雙人床的房間
vacancy〔ˈvekənsɪ〕*n.* 空房間　　rate〔ret〕*n.* 價格
complimentary〔ˌkɑmpləˈmɛntərɪ〕*adj.* 免費的

【背景説明】

　　要打電話預訂旅館，該怎麼說呢？背了這九句話，你就可以用英文預訂旅館，而且又可以得到好的價錢。

1. ***I'd like to book a room.***
   （我想要預訂一個房間。）
   book〔buk〕*v.* 預訂
   （= reserve〔rɪ'zɜv〕*v.* 預訂）

I'd like to book a room.

　　這句話也可以説成：I'd like to reserve a room.

2. ***I'd like to make a reservation.***
   I'd like to 我想要（= *I want to*）
   reservation〔ˌrɛzə'veʃən〕*n.* 預訂
   make a reservation 預訂【飯店房間、飛機座位、餐廳座位等】

　　這句話在這裡的意思是「我要預訂房間。」如果打電話到航空公司，就是「我要預訂機位。」；打電話到餐廳，就是「我要預訂座位。」

【比較】

　　I'd like to make a reservation.【最常用】
   = I want to make a reservation.【較常用】
   = I'm calling to make a reservation.【常用】
   【calling〔kɔl〕*v.* 打電話】

3. ***I need it for tonight.***（我今天晚上要住。）

　　　這句話如果說清楚一點，就可說成：I need a room for tonight.（我需要一個房間，今天晚上要住。）

【比較】 I need a room ***for tonight.***【較常用】
　　　　 I need a room tonight.【常用】

tonight 可以改成其他時間。

【例 1】 I need a room ***for tomorrow night.***
　　　　（我需要一個房間，明天晚上要住。）

【例 2】 I need a room ***for next Saturday and Sunday.***
　　　　（我需要一個房間，下星期六、日要住。）

【例 3】 I need a room ***for the weekend of May 10th.***
　　　　（我需要一個房間，五月十號週末要住。）

4. ***I prefer twin beds.***（我比較喜歡有兩張床的房間。）
prefer〔prɪˈfɝ〕v. 比較喜歡
twin〔twɪn〕adj. 雙胞胎的；成對的

　　　　twin 這個字很好記，就是 t 加上 win（贏）。twin 原指兩個雙胞胎其中之一，在這裡作形容詞，是指「兩個一樣的」，twin beds 的意思就是「兩張一樣的床」，即「兩張床」。***I prefer twin beds.*** 也可以說成：I prefer ***a room with twin beds.*** 或 I prefer ***a room with two single beds.***（我比較喜歡有兩張單人床的房間。）

在中國人的思想中，很少說「我比較喜歡」，但美國人常說，因爲講 prefer，語氣比較婉轉，讓聽的人比較舒服。

【例】

I *prefer* a room with a view.
（我比較喜歡有景觀的房間。）

I *prefer* a room at the end of the hall.

（我比較喜歡在走廊盡頭的房間。）

I *prefer* a nonsmoking room.
（我比較喜歡禁煙的房間。）

hall〔hɔl〕*n.* 走廊
nonsmoking〔nɑn'smokɪŋ〕*adj.* 不許抽煙的

5. *I'll settle for a double.*（我可以勉強接受一張雙人床。）
settle〔'sɛtḷ〕*v.* 安頓；安定；安身
settle for （雖不很滿意但還是）勉強接受
（ = *to accept in spite of incomplete satisfaction*）
double〔'dʌbḷ〕*n.*（旅館的）雙人房間
　　　　　　　 adj. 雙人的；供兩人用的

a double 的意思是「兩個人住的房間；房間裡只有一張雙人床」。(a room for two ; a room with a double bed)

這句話字面的意思是「一張雙人床也會使我安定」，引申爲「我也可以勉爲其難地接受一張雙人床。」

I'll settle for a double.

= I'll settle for *a double bed*.

= I'll settle for *a room with a double bed*.

【例】 I have no choice. I'll *settle for* this.

（我沒有選擇。我只能勉強接受這個。）

I had to *settle for* my second choice.

（我只好退而求其次。）

I want the best. I won't *settle for* second best.

（我要最好的。我不會勉強接受第二好的。）

美國一般旅館的房間分類：

1. single room　單人房

2. twin beds（ = *room with two single beds* ）有兩張單人
床的房間

3. double (= *double bed room* = *room with a double bed*)
有一張雙人床的房間

4. room with two double beds　有兩張雙人床的房間

美國學生旅行，爲了節省，往往四個人住一間房間，這
種房間，每張床可睡兩個人，每間房間可住四個人。

6. ***Do you have any vacancies?*** (你們有沒有空房間？)
vacancy〔ˈvekənsɪ〕*n.* 空房間；空位；(職務) 空缺

這句話也可以說成：Do you have any rooms
available? 或 Do you have any rooms?
【available〔əˈveləbḷ〕*adj.* 可獲得的；可用的】

7. *What are your rates?*

rate〔ret〕*n.* 價格；費用；比例；比率

　　這句話源自：What are your room rates?
（你們的房間價格是多少？）

> What are
> your rates?

　　rate 的主要意思是「比
率」，凡是會有波動的價格，
都用 rate，像「電話費」，是
telephone rates；「郵資」
是 postal rates；「淡季價
格」是 off-season rates。

8. *What can you do for me?*

　　這句話字面的意思是「你能為我做什麼？」就
像中文的「你能不能替我想想辦法？」在這裡暗示，
「你能不能給我好價錢？」也可說成：How can
you help me?

【例1】 I want the best price you can give.
　　　　What can you do for me?
　　　　（我要你能給我的最好的價錢。你能不
　　　　　能替我想想辦法？）

【例2】 Help me out. *What can you do for me?*
　　　　Give me your best offer. I can wait.
　　　　（幫我一個忙。你能不能替我想想辦法？
　　　　　給我最好的價錢。我可以等待。）
　　　　【offer〔'ɔfɚ〕*n.* 報價；開價；提供】

去戲院買票，如果票已經賣完了，你可以跟戲院的職員說：

What can you do for me? Is there any
way you can help me?
（你能不能替我想想辦法？有沒有什麼辦法
你可以幫助我？）

**What can you do for
me?** 這句話太有用了，凡
是你有困難，找別人幫忙，
或是討價還價的時候，都
可以用。

What can you
do for me?

9. **Do you have a complimentary breakfast?**
complimentary〔ˌkɑmpləˈmɛntərɪ〕*adj.* 稱讚的；免費的

complimentary 這個字的名詞是 compliment
〔ˈkɑmpləmənt〕*n.* 稱讚，先背 compliment 加上
ary 就容易多了。

complimentary 這個字的主要意思是「稱讚的；
問候的」，後來轉變為「免費的；贈送的；招待的」，
因為 Actions speak louder than words.（行動勝
於言辭。）用送禮物來代替稱讚或問候，所以凡是在
美國旅館中，看到 complimentary 這個字，就表示
是「免費的」。像有些旅館中有 complimentary
drinks（免費飲料）、complimentary fruit（免費水
果）。這句話的意思是「你們有沒有免費的早餐？」

這句話也可以說成：

Do you offer a complimentary breakfast?
（你們有沒有提供免費的早餐？）
Do you provide a complimentary breakfast?
（你們有沒有提供免費的早餐？）
Do you serve a complimentary breakfast?
（你們有沒有供應免費的早餐？）

也有美國人說：

　 Does your rate include breakfast?
= Does your rate include complimentary breakfast?
= Does your rate include free breakfast?
（你們的房價有沒有包含免費的早餐？）

【比較】 *Do you have complimentary breakfast?*
　　　 Do you have *a complimentary breakfast?*

第一句意味著飯店的一種政策，永遠提供早餐。
第二句是問有沒有免費的早餐給我？事實上，
兩句的意義差別不大。

BOOK 4

　　預訂旅館可有學問，如果到風景區去旅行，需要
先預訂好旅館，以免到時候沒房間住。到了目的地以
後，再多方打聽，可以打電話，或親自去旅館比較價
錢，如果價錢便宜，你就可以把預訂的旅館取消，反
正，在美國預訂旅館不要訂金。

　　在城市的大飯店，走進去問的價錢（walk-in
rate）通常是最貴，最好先打電話預訂（make a
reservation），才能得到最好的價錢。

【對話練習】

1. A：**I'd like to book a room.**

   B：I can help you.
      Can you tell me the date?
      Please give me some more
      information.
      【information〔͵ɪnfəˈmeʃən〕 *n.*
      資訊】

   A：我要預訂一個房間。

   B：我可以幫得上忙。
      可以告訴我日期嗎？
      請多告訴我一些資訊。

2. A：**I'd like to make a
      reservation.**

   B：Thank you for calling.
      It's a pleasure to serve you.
      What date would you like
      to reserve?

   A：我要預訂房間。

   B：謝謝您的來電。
      很榮幸能為您服務。
      您想預訂什麼日期？

3. A：**I need it for tonight.**

   B：Give me a second.
      Let me check our list.
      Yes, we can accommodate
      you.

   A：我今天晚上要住。

   B：請等一下。
      我檢查一下我們的名單。
      可以，我們可以安排您住
      宿。

4. A：**I prefer twin beds.**

   B：That might be difficult.
      All our twin-bed rooms are
      booked.
      I could put you on our
      waiting list.

   A：我比較喜歡有兩張床的房間。

   B：可能會有困難。
      我們有兩張床的房間都被預
      訂了。
      我可以幫您排在候補的名單
      上。

5. A : **I'll settle for a double**.

   B : You might have to do that.
   We have a few doubles left.
   Would you like me to
   reserve one for you?

A : 我可以勉強接受一張雙人床。

B : 您可能得這樣了。
   我們還剩幾間雙人房。
   你要我爲您預訂一間嗎？

6. A : **Do you have any vacancies?**

   B : Sorry, we're all booked up.
   We're full right now.
   We don't have anything
   available.

A : 你們有沒有空房間？

B : 抱歉，我們已經被預訂一空了。
   我們現在客滿了。
   我們沒有房間了。

7. A : **What are your rates?**

   B : Our weekday rates start at $69.
   Our weekend rates start at $99.
   For holidays and the high
   season, add twenty dollars.

A : 你們的房間價格是多少？

B : 平日的價格是 69 元起。
   週末的價格是 99 元起。
   假日和旺季，須加 20 元。

8. A : **What can you do for me?**

   B : Let me look into it.
   I'll see what I can do.
   I promise I'll do my best.

A : 你能不能替我想想辦法？

B : 我研究看看。
   我看看能幫上什麼忙。
   我保證會盡力。

9. A : **Do you have a
   complimentary breakfast?**

   B : We sure do!
   We offer a continental
   breakfast.
   It includes your choice of
   pastries, coffee and juice.

A : 你們有免費的早餐嗎？

B : 當然有！
   我們提供歐式早餐。

   包括您可任選的糕餅類食物、
   咖啡和果汁。

BOOK 4

6. *Hotel Check-in*

I have a reservation.	我已經有預訂了。
I'm here to check in.	我來辦理住房手續。
What do I have to do?	我必須做什麼？
How much is the deposit?	押金要多少錢？
Here's my credit card.	這是我的信用卡。
Should I fill out a form?	我該不該填寫表格？
I'd like a quiet room.	我想要一個安靜的房間。
I'd like a room with a view.	我要一個有景觀的房間。
Can I see the room first?	我可不可以先看房間？

BOOK 4

** ————————————————

reservation〔ˌrɛzə'veʃən〕*n.* 預訂
check in 登記住宿
deposit〔dɪ'pɑzɪt〕*n.* 押金
credit〔'krɛdɪt〕*n.* 信用　　card〔kɑrd〕*n.* 卡；卡片
credit card 信用卡　　***fill out*** 填寫
form〔fɔrm〕*n.* 表格　　quiet〔'kwaɪət〕*adj.* 安靜的
view〔vju〕*n.* 風景　　first〔fɝst〕*adv.* 先

【背景説明】

已經預訂好旅館後，一到旅館的櫃檯，就可以
用到這九句話，要求到好的房間。

1. ***I have a reservation.***
   reservation〔͵rɛzə'veʃən〕*n.* 預訂

   這句話也可以説成：I've
   made a reservation.，都表示
   「我已經有預訂了。」

2. ***I'm here to check in.*** (我來辦理住房手續。)
   check in   登記住宿

   凡是需要登記的，都稱作 check in，像在旅館
   辦理住房手續，或在機場辦理登機手續。

   【比較】 ***I'm here to check in.***【年輕人喜歡説】
   I'm here to register.【年紀大的人喜歡説】
   (我來辦理住房手續。)
   【register〔'rɛdʒɪstə〕*v.* 登記】

3. ***What do I have to do?***

   這句話的意思是「我必須做什麼？」
   美國人也常説：
   What should I do? (我應該做什麼？)
   What do I need to do? (我需要做什麼？)
   What do you want me to do? (你要我做什麼？)

4. *How much is the deposit?*

deposit〔dɪˈpɑzɪt〕*n.* 押金

這句話的意思是「押金多少錢？」deposit 主要的意思是「存（款）」，在這裡作「押金」解。到了較小的飯店，你可以問：Do you require a deposit?（你們需不需要押金？）或 Is a deposit required?（需要押金嗎？）【require〔rɪˈkwaɪr〕*v.* 需要；要求】

留押金的目的，是為了怕你把旅館的設備弄壞，因為如果你不結帳就走了，為了一點小錢，他們也無法告你。

5. *Here's my credit card.*（這是我的信用卡。）

credit〔ˈkrɛdɪt〕*n.* 信用　　card〔kɑrd〕*n.* 卡；卡片
credit card 信用卡

到外國住旅館，他們怕你不結帳就離開，通常就會叫你用信用卡先刷卡，不簽名；如果你不結帳就離開，他們也可以向銀行請款。

在美國，沒有信用卡，幾乎無法住旅館或租車，即使是小旅館，如果沒有信用卡，除了要先付住宿費以外，還要付一些押金（deposit〔dɪˈpɑzɪt〕），他們會說：Sir, you have to leave a deposit.（先生，你需要留一點押金。）

6. ***Should I fill out a form?***

　　fill out 填寫　　form〔fɔrm〕*n.* 表格

　　　　這句話的意思是「我該不該填一個表格？」也可
　　說成：Do I have to fill out a form?（我需不需要
　　填表格？）或 Do you want me to fill out a form?
　　（你要不要我填表格？）

　　你也可以説：

　　　　　Is there a form to fill out?【常用】
　　　　　（有沒有什麼表格要填？）
　　　　　Is there something to fill out?【常用】
　　　　　（有什麼要填的沒有？）
　　　　　Do I have to fill anything out?【最常用】
　　　　　（我需要填寫任何東西嗎？）

7. *I'd like a quiet room.*

　　I'd like 我想要（= I want）
　　quiet〔'kwaɪət〕*adj.* 安靜的

> *I'd like a quiet room.*

　　　　這句話的意思是「我想
　　要一個安靜的房間。」也可
　　説成：Can I have a quiet
　　room?（可不可以給我一個
　　安靜的房間？）如果強調，你要最安靜的房間，你就
　　可以説：I'd like the quietest room you have.（我
　　要你們最安靜的房間。）

8. **I'd like a room with a view.**（我要一個有景觀的房間。）

view〔vju〕n. 風景

　　在大城市，有 view 的房間，和沒有 view 的房間，價格差很多。也有很多旅館，他們沒有價格上的差別。如果你不要求，他們就會把沒有 view 的房間先給你，好的房間留著賣給挑剔的客人。

這句話也可説成：

　　I'd like a room *with a good view*.
　= I'd like a room *with a nice view*.
　　（我要一個有好景觀的房間。）
　　I'd like the room *with the best view*.
　　（我要一個景觀最好的房間。）
　　【因為最好的只有一間，所以用 the room】

如果想要看海景，你就可以説：

　　I'd like a room *with an ocean view*.
　　（我要一個可以看到海景的房間。）

如果想要看游泳池的美女，你就可以説：

　　I'd like a room *with a view of the
　　swimming pool*.
　　（我要一個可以看到游泳池的房間。）

9. *Can I see the room first?*

first〔fɜst〕*adv.* 先

Can I see the room first?

這句話的意思是:「我可不可以先看看房間?」

住旅館,要求先看房間,比較安全,可以避免住到有煙味或太吵的房間。即使是五星級的飯店,也可以要求先看房間。如果你 check in 以後,對房間不滿意,才要換,就太麻煩了,因為行李要搬來搬去。

想先看房間,除了說 *Can I see the room first?* 以外,還可以說:

Do you mind if I see the room first?

(你介不介意我先看看房間?)

Is it OK if I see the room first?

(我可以先看看房間嗎?)

Is it possible to see the room first?

(我有可能先看看房間嗎?)

如果你對房間不滿意,你就可以說:

I am sorry.(很抱歉。)

I'm not comfortable with that room.

(我對那間房間不滿意。)

I'd like to see another room.

(我想看看其他房間。)

BOOK 4

看了所有房間，如果還是不滿意，你想換旅館，
你就可以說下面的話，比較不會尷尬：

I am sorry.

（很抱歉。）

I changed my mind.

（我改變主意了。）

也可以更婉轉地說：

I am sorry.（我很抱歉。）

I'd like to think about it.（我要考慮一下。）

I need more time.（我需要一點時間考慮考慮。）

如果還是覺得心裡不安，可再說三句：

I might be back.（我或許會回來。）

I might come back later.〔'letɚ〕*adv.* 稍後；以後

（我以後也許會再回來。）

Thank you for your time.

（謝謝你，佔用你的時間了。）

【劉毅老師的話】

學英文最簡單的方法，就是「背」。「一口氣
背會話全集」共 1,296 個句子，只要中英文一起
背，背熟之後，你講出來的英文，比美國人都好，
因為是背過的句子，說起來最有信心。

【對話練習】

1. A：**I have a reservation**.
　 B：You came to the right place.
　　　Please fill out this form.
　　　I can check you in.

　　　　A：我已經有預訂了。
　　　　B：您來對地方了。
　　　　　　請填寫這張表格。
　　　　　　我可以讓您登記住宿。

2. A：**I'm here to check in**.
　 B：Do you have a reservation?
　　　Do you have your
　　　reservation code?
　　　What's your last name?
　　　【code〔kod〕*v.* 代碼；代號
　　　　　last name 姓 】

　　　　A：我來辦理住房手續。
　　　　B：您有預訂嗎？
　　　　　　您有預訂的代碼嗎？

　　　　　　您貴姓？

3. A：**What do I have to do?**
　 B：First, show me your ID.
　　　Second, sign your name
　　　right here.
　　　Third, you must pay a
　　　deposit.【sign〔saɪn〕*v.* 簽名】

　　　　A：我必須做什麼？
　　　　B：首先，把您的身分證拿給我看。
　　　　　　第二，在這裡簽名。

　　　　　　第三，您必須付押金。

4. A：**How much is the deposit?**
　 B：Twice the daily room rate.
　　　We accept credit cards.
　　　Or you can pay by cash.

　　　　A：押金要多少錢？
　　　　B：每日房價的兩倍。
　　　　　　我們收信用卡。
　　　　　　你也可以付現。

5. A：**Here's my credit card**.
　 B：Thanks, I'll need it.
　　　I have to check it.
　　　I'll bring it right back.

　　　　A：這是我的信用卡。
　　　　B：謝謝，我會需要用到它。
　　　　　　我必須核對一下。
　　　　　　我馬上就會把它還給您。

BOOK 4

6. A : **Should I fill out a form?**

B : Yes, please.
We need your information.
You must complete this form.
【complete〔kəm'plit〕v. 完成;使完整】

A：我該不該填寫表格？

B：是的，麻煩您。
我們需要您的資料。
您必須填寫這張表格。

7. A : **I'd like a quiet room.**

B : That's no problem.
All our rooms are quiet.
I'll put you at the end of the
hall.【hall〔hɔl〕n. 走廊】

A：我想要一個安靜的房間。

B：沒問題。
我們所有房間都很安靜。
我會安排您住在走廊的
盡頭。

8. A : **I'd like a room with a view.**

B : You're in luck.
We have some top floor
vacancies.
I'll put you in one of those
rooms.
【vacancies〔'vekənsɪz〕n.pl. 空房間
top floor 頂樓　*in luck* 運氣好】

A：我要一個有景觀的房間。

B：您運氣真好。
我們的頂樓有一些空房
間。
我會安排您住其中一間。

9. A : **Can I see the room first?**

B : Of course, you can.
Please wait a minute.
I'll arrange for someone to
escort you.
【*arrange for sb. to V.* 安排某人做~
escort〔ɪ'skɔrt〕v. 護送】

A：我能不能先看房間？

B：當然可以。
請等一下。
我會安排一個人陪您去。

BOOK 4

7. *Hello, housekeeping?*

Hello, housekeeping?	喂，房務部嗎？
I'm going out for a while.	我要出去一會兒。
Could I have my room cleaned right now?	能不能馬上幫我打掃房間？
I'd like extra towels.	我要額外的毛巾。
I'd like a toothbrush and razor.	我要一支牙刷和一支刮鬍刀。
Please bring me a pot of hot water.	請拿一壺熱開水給我。
I have dirty laundry.	我有髒衣服要送洗。
I have clothes to be washed.	我有衣服要送洗。
What should I do?	我該怎麼做？

BOOK 4

** ──────────────

hello〔hə'lo, 'hʌlo〕*interj.* 喂
housekeeping〔'haʊs,kipɪŋ〕*n.* 房務部
while〔hwaɪl〕*n.* 一會兒；一段時間
clean〔klin〕*v.* 打掃　***right now*** 現在；立刻
extra〔'ɛkstrə〕*adj.* 額外的　towel〔'taʊəl〕*n.* 毛巾
toothbrush〔'tuθ,brʌʃ〕*n.* 牙刷　razor〔'rezɚ〕*n.* 刮鬍刀
pot〔pɑt〕*n.* 壺　laundry〔'lɔndrɪ〕*n.* 送洗的衣物

【背景説明】

在飯店的房間裡面，可打電話給 housekeeping （房務部），要求一些額外的服務。

1. *Hello*, *housekeeping?*
housekeeping〔'haʊsˌkipɪŋ〕*n.*
房務部

Hello, housekeeping?

這句話的意思是「喂，房務部嗎？」也可以説成：

Housekeeping?（房務部嗎？）
Hi, housekeeping?（嗨，房務部嗎？）
Is this housekeeping?（是房務部嗎？）

如果你不知道 housekeeping 的電話，你可以打給接線生（operator），你可以先説：Hi!（嗨！），或 Hi, operator.（嗨，接線生。）或 Hello, operator.（喂，接線生。）再接著説：

I'd like housekeeping.【最常用】
（我要找房務部。）
Can you get me housekeeping?【最常用】
（你可以幫我接房務部嗎？）
Can you switch me to housekeeping?
（你可以幫我接房務部嗎？）【switch〔swɪtʃ〕*v.* 轉換】

Can you connect me to housekeeping?
（你可以幫我接房務部嗎？）【connect〔kə'nɛkt〕*v.* 接通】
Housekeeping, please.（請接房務部。）
Please get me housekeeping.（請幫我接房務部。）

2. *I'm going out for a while.*

while〔hwaɪl〕*n.* 一段時間；一會兒

這句話的意思是「我要出去一會兒。」也可說成：
I'll be out for a while. 或 I'm leaving for a while.
for 後面，可加固定時間，如：I'm going out for
an hour.（我要出去一個小時。）

3. *Could I have my room cleaned right now?*

clean〔klin〕*v.* 打掃　　*right now* 現在；立刻

這句話的意思是「能不能馬上幫我打掃房間？」
也可說成：I'd like my room cleaned right now.
（我希望你們能立刻打掃我的房間。）或 Please have
someone clean my room right now.（請立刻叫人
打掃我的房間。）

在飯店裡面住，如果不先叫 room service 來
打掃房間，搞不好你下午回來的時候，房間還沒整
理，很不方便。打電話請他們先來打掃，就會方便
很多。

4. *I'd like extra towels.*

would like 想要（= *want*）
extra〔'ɛkstrə〕*adj.* 額外的　　towel〔'tauəl〕*n.* 毛巾

這句話的意思是「我要額外的毛巾。」extra 並沒
有指明多要一條或兩條。也可說成：I'd like more
towels.

如果你要指定大浴巾，你就可以說：Could I have more bath towels? (我可以多要浴巾嗎?) 美國人習慣，通常不說明，就是要兩條。如果你要毛巾，就是 hand towel，小方巾則是 washcloth。

5. ***I'd like a toothbrush and razor.***
toothbrush〔'tuθ,brʌʃ〕*n.* 牙刷
razor〔'rezɚ〕*n.* 刮鬍刀

這句話的意思是「我要一支牙刷和一支刮鬍刀。」英文避免重覆，and 後面 a razor 的 a 可省略。

奇怪，很多五星級飯店，什麼都供給，就是沒有牙刷和刮鬍刀。但是，如果你打電話要，他們就會送來。通常美國人都會付一兩塊美金的小費。

6. ***Please bring me a pot of hot water.***
pot〔pɑt〕*n.* 壺

這句話的意思是「請拿一壺熱開水給我。」hot water 也可說成 boiled water。【boiled〔bɔɪld〕*adj.* 煮沸的】也可以說：

Please give me a pot of hot water.
(請給我一壺熱開水。)
Please bring up a pot of hot water.
(請拿一壺熱開水上來。)
Please bring me some hot water.
(請拿一些熱開水給我。)

　　在飯店裡面，喝水很有學問，喝冰箱裡的礦泉水，或是飲料，說不定已經放了很久，不安全，如果喝他送來的水，不管是冷水或溫開水，都很危險，說不定是從自來水管出來的。喝煮沸的熱開水，是最佳的選擇。

7. *I have dirty laundry.*

　　這句話的意思是「我有髒衣服要送洗。」

　　在飯店裡，只要說 *I have dirty laundry.* 或 I have laundry. 別人就知道，你有衣服要送洗。

　　laundry 這個字很有趣，中國人和美國人都不太會用。凡是要送洗，或剛洗好的衣物，都叫做 laundry〔ˈlɔndrɪ, ˈlɑn-〕*n.* (= *clothes, sheets, etc. that need to be or have just been washed*)。

BOOK 4

　　所有的字典上都沒寫清楚 laundry 的用法，我們特舉九個例子：

【例1】　Is my *laundry* done yet?
　　　　　(= *Have you washed my clothes yet?*)
　　　　　(我的衣服洗好了嗎？)

【例2】　I have to do my *laundry*. (我必須洗衣服。)
　　　　　(= *I have to wash my clothes.*)

【例3】　You should do your *laundry* twice a week.
　　　　　(= *You should wash your clothes*
　　　　　　　twice a week.)
　　　　　(你應該一星期洗兩次衣服。)

【例4】 You should separate the colors when you do your *laundry*.
(= *You should separate the colors when you wash your clothes.*)
(你洗衣服時，應該將不同顏色的衣物分開。)

【例5】 Where is the *laundry*?
(= *Where is the place to wash clothes?*)
(在哪裡洗衣服？)

【例6】 The *laundry room* is in the basement.
(洗衣間在地下室。)
【basement〔'besmənt〕 *n.* 地下室】
【laundry 是名詞，修飾名詞 room，表功用】

【例7】 A: Where do you do your *laundry*?
(你都在哪裡洗衣服？)
B: I go to a laundromat.
(我都去自助洗衣店。)
【laundromat〔'ləndrəmæt〕 *n.* 自助洗衣店】

【例8】 Don't hang out your dirty *laundry* in public.
(= *Don't wash your dirty linen in public.*)
(家醜不可外揚。)

【例9】 I did your *laundry* for you.
(我幫你把衣服洗好了。)
(= *I washed your clothes for you.*)

8. *I have clothes to be washed.*

I have clothes
to be washed.

　　這句話的意思是「我有衣
服要送洗。」也可説成：I have
clothes to be cleaned. 或 I
have clothes to be laundered.
【launder〔ˈlɔndɚ〕*v.* 洗】

　　如果你的衣服很名貴，需要乾洗，你就可以
説：I have clothes to be dry-cleaned.（我有衣
服要乾洗。）

9. *What should I do?*

　　這句話的意思是「我該怎麼做？」也可以説成：
Please tell me what I should do. 或 Please
tell me what to do.（請告訴我該怎麼做。）

　　説完 *What should I do?* 以後，可接著説一
句：Where should I put them?（我應該把它們放
在哪裡？）

　　這一回九句，分成三組，第一組是叫客房服務
部來打掃房間；第二組是要額外的毛巾、牙刷、刮
鬍刀，和熱開水；第三組是要送洗髒衣服。在全世
界，你不管到哪個旅館，這九句話都用得到。

BOOK 4

【對話練習】

1. A : **Hello, housekeeping?**

   B : This is housekeeping.
   Vicky speaking.
   How may I help you?

2. A : **I'm going out for a while.**

   B : Thanks for letting us know.
   We'll clean your room while
   you are out.
   Is there anything else we can do
   for you?

3. A : **Could I have my room cleaned
   right now?**

   B : You sure can.
   We'll get right to it.
   We'll send someone right up.

4. A : **I'd like extra towels.**

   B : No problem at all.
   Extra towels it is!
   Housekeeping will drop them
   off when they clean your room.

5. A : **I'd like a toothbrush and razor.**

   B : I'll send up a toothbrush right
   away.
   I'm sorry, we don't supply razors.
   Our gift shop has razors for sale.

A : 喂，房務部嗎？

B : 這裡是房務部。
   我是維琪。
   需要我幫什麼忙嗎？

A : 我要出去一會兒。

B : 謝謝您讓我們知道。
   我們會在您出去時幫您打
   掃房間。
   還有什麼要我們爲您服務
   的嗎？

A : 能不能馬上幫我整理房
   間？

B : 當然可以。
   我們會立刻處理。
   我們會立刻派人上去。

A : 我想要額外的毛巾。

B : 沒問題。
   要額外的毛巾！
   房務部在打掃房間時會放
   毛巾。

A : 我想要一支牙刷和刮鬍刀。

B : 我會立刻把牙刷送上去。

   很抱歉，我們不提供刮鬍刀。
   我們的禮品店有賣刮鬍刀。

6. A : **Please bring me a pot of hot water**.

　　B : We'll get right on it.
　　　　It will take just a couple of minutes.
　　　　I'll send it up as soon as it's ready. 【*a couple of*　幾個】

A：請拿一壺熱開水給我。

B：我們會立刻處理。
　　只要幾分鐘就好。

　　一準備好，我就會送上去。

7. A : **I have dirty laundry**.

　　B : We'll take care of it.
　　　　We'll be up to get it.
　　　　Our laundry service is available 24 hours.

A：我有髒衣服要送洗。

B：我們會負責。
　　我們會上來拿。
　　我們有二十四小時的送洗服務。

8. A : **I have clothes to be washed**.

　　B : We do laundry here.
　　　　We also dry-clean clothes.
　　　　We even have a coin-operated laundromat.

A：我有衣服要送洗。

B：我們這裡有洗衣服的服務。
　　我們也有乾洗衣服的服務。
　　我們甚至有投幣式的自助洗衣店。

9. A : **What should I do?**

　　B : Please fill out the laundry form.
　　　　We'll be there in a minute to get your clothes.
　　　　You'll have them back first thing tomorrow.

　　　　【*first thing*　首先；立即】

A：我該怎麼做？

B：請填寫送洗表格。

　　我們會立刻過去拿您的衣服。
　　我們明天一早就會把它們送回去給您。

BOOK 4

8. Does this bus go downtown?

Does this bus go downtown?	這部巴士是不是去市中心？
How much does it cost?	需要花費多少錢？
How do I pay?	我該怎麼付錢？
I want the shopping district.	我要去購物區。
How long does it take?	需要多少時間？
How many stops are there?	要坐多少站才到？
Which stop is the best?	哪一站最好？
Please tell me where to get off.	請告訴我在哪裡下車。
Please tell me one stop ahead.	請在前一站告訴我。

** ────────────────

downtown〔'daʊn'taʊn〕*adv.* 到市中心
cost〔kɔst〕*v.* 花費　　pay〔pe〕*v.* 付錢
shopping〔'ʃɑpɪŋ〕*n.* 購物　*adj.* 購物用的
district〔'dɪstrɪkt〕*n.* 區；區域
take〔tek〕*v.* 需要；花費（時間）
stop〔stɑp〕*n.* （公車）車站　*get off* 下車
ahead〔ə'hɛd〕*adv.* 在前面

【背景説明】

　　不管到哪個國家去旅行，搭巴士或公車是一件樂事。看到任何巴士，都可直接在車門口，大聲問司機：*"Does this bus go downtown?"* 要了解當地的文化，到市中心是最好的選擇。

1. *Does this bus go downtown?*
   downtown〔'daʊn'taʊn〕*adv.*
   到市中心

Does this bus go downtown?

　　這句話的意思是「這部巴士是不是去市中心？」你也可以跟司機大聲喊：Are you going downtown? (你是不是要到市中心？) 或 Are you heading downtown? (你是不是要往市中心方向走？)【head〔hɛd〕*v.* 朝…方向前進】

如果看到車子停在那裡不動，你可以問司機：

When are you leaving? (你何時走？)

What time are you leaving? (你什麼時候走？)

How much longer? (還要多久？)

(= *How much longer until this bus gets going?*)

不少美國人說：

When does this bus take off?

(這部巴士什麼時候走？)

When do you take off? (你什麼時候走？)

take off 的意思是「起飛」，在這裡作「離開」解，等於 leave。

BOOK 4

2. *How much does it cost?*

cost〔kɔst〕*v.* 花費

> 　　這句話的意思是「需要花費多少錢？」問車費是
> 多少的説法有很多：
>
> 　　How much? (多少錢？)【常用】
> 　　How much is it? (多少錢？)【最常用】
> 　　***How much does it cost?***【最常用】
> 　　(需要花費多少錢？)
>
> 　　How much should I pay?【常用】
> 　　(我該付多少錢？)
> 　　How much do I pay? (我要付多少錢？)【最常用】
> 　　What's the bus fare? (公車票價是多少？)
> 　　【fare〔fɛr〕*n.* 車費；票價】【較常用】
>
> 　　What's the cost? (費用是多少？)【較常用】
> 　　What's the fare? (車費是多少？)【較常用】
> 　　What's the price? (價格是多少？)【常用】

3. *How do I pay?*

　　這句話的意思是「我該怎麼付錢？」也可説成：

　　　　How do I pay it?【it 是指 fare】
　　　　(我該怎麼付錢？)

　　這句話説完後，可接著説：

　　　　Do I pay now? (我現在付錢嗎？)
　　　　Do I pay later? (我待會再付嗎？)

或問公車司機：

Do I pay now or later?（我是現在還是待會才付錢？）

Do I pay here?（我是不是要在這裡付錢？）

Do I pay you?（我是不是要付錢給你？）

Do I pay someone?（我是不是要付錢給某個人？）

如果公車有投錢的機器，你可以說：

Do I put it in the slot?

（我是不是要把錢投入投幣口中？）

Do you give change?（你們會不會找錢？）

Do I need exact change?（我需要投剛好的零錢嗎？）

【slot〔slɑt〕*n.* 投幣口　exact〔ɪgˈzækt〕*adj.* 確切的】

有的公車司機有賣乘車證，你可說：

Can I buy a pass?（我可不可以向你買乘車證？）

Can I buy a day pass?（我可不可以買一日乘車證？）

【day pass 是「整日都可使用的乘車證」】

Do you sell passes?（你有沒有賣乘車證？）

【pass〔pæs〕*n.* 乘車證；通行證】

如果司機不賣乘車證，你就可以問他：

Where can I buy a bus pass?

（我在哪裡可以買到公車乘車證？）

Where can I get a bus pass?

（我在哪裡才能買到公車乘車證？）

Where do they sell bus passes?

（他們哪裡有賣公車乘車證？）

4. *I want the shopping district.*

district (ˈdɪstrɪkt) *n.* 區；區域

　　　　這句話字面的意思是「我要購物區。」很難和中國人的思想相結合。引申為「我要去購物區。」等於 I want to go to the shopping district. 這種和中國人思想不同的句子，你一定要背下來，才會使用。

有些美國人説：

　　I want to get off at the shopping district.
　　（我要在購物區下車。）
　　I want to get to the shopping district.
　　（我要去購物區。）
　　I'm trying to get to the shopping district.
　　（我想去購物區。）

也有美國人説：

　　I'm hoping to get to the shopping district.
　　（我希望到購物區。）

【比較】 *I want the shopping district.* 【最常用】
　　　　I want to go to the shopping district. 【最常用】
　　　　I'm going to the shopping district. 【常用】

5. *How long does it take?*

take (tek) *v.* 花費（時間）；需要

　　這句話的意思是「需要多少時間？」也可以説：

　　How long does it take to get there?
　　（到那裡要多少時間？）
　　How long does it take from here?
　　（從這裡去要多少時間？）

6. *How many stops are there?*

stop〔stɑp〕*n.*（公共汽車）車站

這句話的字面意思是「有多少站？」引申為「要坐多少站才到？」源自：*How many stops are there till we get there?*（到那裡還有多少站？）【正，少用】

美國人也常說：How many stops till we get there? 和 How many stops is it?（還有多少站？）【這句話的⋯is it 後面省略了 to get there。】

7. *Which stop is the best?*

這句話的意思是「哪一站最好？」也可說成：

Which stop is the closest?（哪一站最近？）
Which stop is the nearest?（哪一站最近？）
Which stop is the most convenient?
（哪一站最方便？）

Which stop is my stop?（我要坐到哪一站？）
Which stop should I get off at?
（我該在哪一站下車？）
What's the name of the stop I should get off at?（我該下車的那一站，站名是什麼？）

8. *Please tell me where to get off.*

get off 下車

這句話的意思是「請告訴我在哪裡下車。」也可說成：
Please tell me when to get off.（請告訴我何時下車。）

BOOK 4

其他的說法有：

Could you tell me where to get off?【較有禮貌】
Can you tell me where to get off?

Could you show me where to get off?【較有禮貌】
Can you show me where to get off?

　　where to get off 可改成 when to get off。而
where to get off 是由名詞子句 where I should get
off 演變而來。

9. ***Please tell me one stop ahead.***
ahead 〔 ə'hɛd 〕 *adv.* 在前面

　　　　這句話的意思是「請在前一站告訴我。」也可以
說成：Please tell me one stop before.

其他說法有：

Could you tell me one stop ahead?
（你可以在前一站告訴我嗎？）
Could you tell me one stop before?
（你可以在前一站告訴我嗎？）
Could you let me know before we get there?
（在我們到達那裡之前，你可以讓我知道？）
上面三句的 Could 可改成 Can，但是用 Could 比較有禮貌。

　　　　也有美國人說：Please tell me ahead of time.
（請提前告訴我。）【*ahead of time* 提前】

【對話練習】

1. A：**Does this bus go downtown?**

B：It sure does!

It goes right downtown.

Climb aboard!〔right〔raɪt〕*adv.*

正好　aboard〔ə'bord〕*adv.* 到車上〕

A：這輛巴士是不是去市中心？

B：當然是！

它正好就是去市中心。

上車吧！

2. A：**How much does it cost?**

B：It costs one dollar.

Do you have exact change?

I'm afraid I can't make change

for me.〔*make change* 找零錢〕

A：需要花費多少錢？

B：要一塊錢。

你有剛好的零錢嗎？

我恐怕不能找錢給你。

3. A：**How do I pay?**

B：Pay when you get on.

Put your money in the slot.

That's right.

〔slot〔slɑt〕*n.* 投幣口〕

A：我該怎麼付錢？

B：上車時付錢。

把錢投入投幣口。

對啦。

4. A：**I want the shopping district.**

B：That's a great area.

That's a good place to see.

This bus goes right by there.

A：我要去購物區。

B：那一區不錯。

那個地方值得一看。

這輛巴士會經過那裡。

5. A：**How long does it take?**

B：It takes about twenty minutes.

In rush hour, it may take longer.

Traffic is pretty bad then.

〔*rush hour* （交通）尖峰時間〕

A：需要多少時間？

B：大約需要二十分鐘。

在尖峰時間，可能要更久。

那時的交通狀況很糟。

BOOK 4

6. A : **How many stops are there?**

B : There are ten stops.
They're marked on route map.
Here's a copy for you.

【mark〔mɑrk〕*v.* 標示
route〔rut〕*n.* 路線
copy〔'kɑpɪ〕*n.* 一份】

A：有多少站才到？

B：有十站。

在路線圖上有標示。

這裡有一張可以給你。

7. A : **Which stop is the best?**

B : If you're going shopping,
City Square is best.
There are a lot of shops
around there.
You won't have to walk too
far. 【square〔skwɛr〕*n.* 廣場】

A：哪一站最好？

B：如果你要去購物，市府
廣場站最好。

那附近有很多商店。

你不需要走太遠。

8. A : **Please tell me where to get
off**.

B : I'll tell you right now.
I'll also tell you when we get
there.
You want the City Square
stop.

A：請告訴我在哪裡下車。

B：我現在就告訴你。

到那裡時，我也會告訴
你。

你要到市府廣場站。

9. A : **Please tell me one stop ahead**.

B : OK.
Can do.
I'm glad I can help you out.

A：請在前一站告訴我。

B：好的。

可以。

我很高興能幫你的忙。

9. Nice meeting you.

Nice meeting you.	很高興認識你。
Nice talking to you.	和你談話很愉快。
I enjoyed our chat.	和你聊天很開心。
Here's my number.	這是我的電話號碼。
Let's keep in touch.	讓我們保持聯絡。
Call me if you'd like.	如果你願意，打電話給我。
Good luck.	祝你好運。
Have a great one.	再見。
I hope we can meet again.	希望我們可以再見面。

BOOK 4

** ────────────────

meet〔 mit 〕*v.* 認識；見面
enjoy〔 ɪn'dʒɔɪ 〕*v.* 喜歡；享受
chat〔 tʃæt 〕*n.* 聊天
number〔 'nʌmbɚ 〕*n.* 號碼；電話號碼
keep in touch 保持聯絡　　***good luck*** 祝你好運
great〔 gret 〕*adj.* 很棒的

【背景説明】

　　　　在巴士車上，遇到一個陌生人，聊完天之後，
要告別時，該説什麼話呢？有了這九句話，就不會
尷尬了。

1. *Nice meeting you*.

meet〔 mit 〕*v.* 見面；認識

Nice meeting you.

　　　meet 的主要意思是「見
面」，在這裡作「認識」解。
這句話的意思是「很高興認
識你。」是 It was nice
meeting you. 的省略。

　　原則上，初次見面時説：Nice to meet you. 或
It's nice to meet you. 意思是「很高興認識你。」道
別時説：*Nice meeting you*. 或 It was nice meeting
you. 但現在已經沒有嚴格的區分了。再見的時候，我
們可説：

　　Nice meeting you. (很高興認識你。)【最常用】
　　It's nice meeting you.【誤】
　　【因爲已經認識，須用過去式動詞 was】
　　It was nice meeting you.【較常用】
　　It's been nice meeting you.【常用】

　　Nice to meet you.【最常用】
　　It was nice to meet you.【較常用】
　　It's been nice to meet you.【常用】

2. *Nice talking to you*.

　　這句話源自 It's been nice talking to you.，意思是「和你談話很愉快。」也可說成：Nice talking with you.（和你談話很愉快。）或 Nice chatting with you.（和你聊天很愉快。）【chat〔tʃæt〕v. 聊天】

【比較】　*Nice talking to you*.【正，最常用】
　　　　　Nice talking with you.【正，常用】
　　　　　Nice chatting with you.【正，有些人說】
　　　　　Nice chatting to you.【誤】

3. *I enjoyed our chat*.
enjoy〔ɪn'dʒɔɪ〕v. 喜歡；享受
chat〔tʃæt〕n. ,v. 聊天

　　這句話的意思是「和你聊天很開心。」這類的話很多：

　　I enjoyed our talk.（和你談話很愉快。）【最常用】
　　I enjoyed our chat.【最常用】
　　I enjoyed talking to you.【較常用】
　　（和你談話很愉快。）

　　I enjoyed talking with you.【較常用】
　　（和你談話很愉快。）
　　I enjoyed our conversation.【常用】
　　（和你談話很愉快。）
　　I enjoyed chatting with you.【常用】
　　（和你談話很愉快。）

BOOK 4

4. *Here's my number*.

美國人常説這句話，來代替 Here's my phone number.（這是我的電話號碼。）

【比較】 ***Here's my number.***【最常用】

　　　　Here's my phone number.【常用】

　　　　Here's my telephone number.【正，較少用】

一般説來，在巴士車上認識的人，美國人通常只跟對方説：***Here's my number.*** 或 Here's my address.（這是我的地址。），或 Here's my e-mail address.（這是我的 e-mail 地址。）

address〔əˋdrɛs〕*n.* 地址

e-mail〔ˋiˏmel〕*n.* 電子郵件（= *electronic mail*）

在正式場合，經過別人介紹，交換名片時，你就可説：Here's my card.（這是我的名片。）

【比較】　Here's my card.【最常用】

　　　　Here's my business card.【常用】

　　　　Here's my name card.【少用】

　　　　【business card 和 name card 都是「名片」】

Here's my card.

5. *Let's keep in touch.*

   keep in touch 保持聯絡

   (= *stay in touch*)

Let's keep in touch.

　　　這句話的意思是「讓我
們保持聯絡。」也可說成：
Let's stay in touch.

【比較】***Let's keep in touch.***
　　　　　　【講這句話，讓聽者比較輕鬆】
　　　　Keep in touch. (要保持連絡。)
　　　　　　【讓聽者稍有壓力，對初次認識者有一點點不適合】

6. *Call me if you'd like.*

　　　這句話源自 Call me if you'd like to. ，意思是
「如果你願意的話，打電話給我。」

請別人打電話給你的說法很多：

　　　Call me if you'd like. 【最常用】
　　　Call me if you'd like to. 【最常用】
　　　(如果你願意的話，打電話給我。)
　　　Call me if you want to. 【常用】
　　　(如果你想要的話，打電話給我。)

　　　Call me sometime. 【常用】
　　　(找個時間打電話給我。)
　　　Call me anytime. 【常用】
　　　(任何時候都可以打電話給我。)

BOOK 4

Give me a call. (打個電話給我。)【常用】
Give me a call sometime. 【較常用】
(找個時間打電話給我。)
Give me a call anytime. 【較常用】
(任何時候都可以打電話給我。)
【*give sb. a call* 打電話給某人】

Feel free to call. 【最常用】
(別客氣，打電話給我。)
Feel free to call me. 【最常用】
(別客氣，打電話給我。)
Feel free to keep in touch. 【常用】
(別客氣，和我保持連絡。)
【*feel free to V.* 請自由地…】

7. *Good luck.*

> 這句話源自 I wish you good luck.，意思是
> 「祝你好運。」也可加強語氣說成：Good luck to
> you.。對女孩可以說 Good luck, girl.，對男生就可
> 以說 Good luck, man.，對公車司機或在酒吧裡喝酒
> 的人，都可說這句話。對兩個人以上，不管男女，都
> 可以說：Good luck, you guys. (祝你們好運。)
> 【guys〔gaɪz〕*n. pl.* 人】

8. *Have a great one.*

> 這句話的意思是「再見。」，和 Have a good
> one. 意思相同，one 等於 day，源自 I hope you
> have a great day. 【詳見 p.268】。

9. *I hope we can meet again.*

　　這句話的意思是「我希望我們能再見。」meet
可當及物和不及物動詞，這句話也可說成 I hope
I can meet you again.（我希望我能再見到你。）

希望再見面的說法很多：

I hope we can meet again.

I hope we meet again.

　（我希望我們再見面。）

I hope to meet you again.

　（我希望再見到你。）

I hope I can see you again.

　（我希望能再看到你。）

I hope we see each other again.

　（我希望彼此能再見面。）

I hope we run into each other again.

　（我希望我們能再碰見。）【*run into* 碰見】

　　編者的一位美國朋友，他就靠這一回的九句話，
認識很多女朋友，他的說法是，把自己的電話號碼
給她，The ball is in her court.（選擇權在她。）
他坐在家裡，就有女孩子會打電話給他。如果和女
孩子要電話號碼，有兩次被拒絕的危險，第一，她
可能不給你電話，第二，打電話給她，可能會被她
拒絕。

BOOK 4

【對話練習】

1. A: **Nice meeting you**.　　　　　　A: 很高興認識你。

　　B: Nice meeting you, too.　　　　B: 我也是。
　　　I enjoyed talking with you.　　　和你談話我很高興。
　　　I enjoyed meeting you.　　　　　我很高興認識你。

2. A: **Nice talking to you**.　　　　　A: 和你談話很愉快。

　　B: Nice talking to you, too.　　　B: 和你談話我也很愉快。
　　　I enjoyed it.　　　　　　　　　　我很愉快。
　　　It was a real pleasure.　　　　　和你談話真是一大樂事。

　　　【pleasure〔ˈplɛʒɚ〕 *n.* 樂事；樂趣】

3. A: **I enjoyed our chat**.　　　　　A: 和你聊天很開心。

　　B: So did I!　　　　　　　　　　B: 我也很開心！
　　　It was very nice.　　　　　　　　感覺很好。
　　　Let's do it again soon.　　　　　我們儘快再找時間聊。

4. A: **Here's my number**.　　　　　A: 這是我的電話號碼。

　　B: Thanks.　　　　　　　　　　　B: 謝謝。
　　　Let me give you mine.　　　　　　我也把我的給你吧。
　　　Do you have a pen?　　　　　　　你有筆嗎？

5. A: **Let's keep in touch**.　　　　　A: 讓我們保持聯絡。

　　B: Great idea.　　　　　　　　　B: 好主意。
　　　I'd like that a lot.　　　　　　　我很喜歡。
　　　I'd like to keep in touch　　　　我會和你保持聯絡。
　　　with you.

6. A：**Call me if you'd like**.

　　B：OK, I will.
　　　 I will for sure.
　　　 I promise to give you a
　　　 call.

A：如果你願意，打電話給我。

B：好，我會的。
　 我一定會的。
　 我保證一定會打電話給
　 你。

7. A：**Good luck**.

　　B：Same to you.
　　　 I hope everything works
　　　 out for you.
　　　 I'm sure it will.
　　　 【*work out*　順利進行】

A：祝你好運。

B：你也一樣。
　 我希望你一切順利。

　 我相信一定會的。

8. A：**Have a great one**.

　　B：Thank you, I will.
　　　 I'm sure it'll be a good
　　　 day.
　　　 You have a nice day, too.

A：祝你有個美好的一天。

B：謝謝你，我會的。
　 我相信今天會是美好的
　 一天。
　 也祝你有美好的一天。

9. A：**I hope we can meet again**.

　　B：Me too.
　　　 Let's meet for sure.
　　　 I'd really like to get
　　　 together again.

A：我希望我們能夠再見面。

B：我也希望。
　 我們一定會再見的。
　 我真的很希望能再聚一
　 聚。

BOOK 4

10. *Can I check out late?*

This is room 704.	這是 704 號房。
I'm leaving today.	我今天要離開。
What time is checkout?	退房時間是什麼時候？
Can I check out late?	我能不能晚一點退房？
Can I stay another two hours?	我可不可以多待兩個小時？
It would really help me out.	這真的會幫了我的忙。
That would be great.	那會很棒。
That would be a big help.	那會幫我很大的忙。
I'd really be grateful.	我會非常感激。

**

checkout〔'tʃɛk,aut〕*n.* 結帳退房
late〔let〕*adv.* 晚　　stay〔ste〕*v.* 停留
help sb. out 幫忙某人　　great〔gret〕*adj.* 很棒的
grateful〔'gretfəl〕*adj.* 感激的

【背景説明】

　　一般飯店是上午十一點鐘之前，必須結帳退房
（check out）。如果你想待久一點，你可以打電話
向櫃台要求，通常對方都會通融一、兩個小時。

1. *This is room 704.*

　　　這句話的意思是「這是 704 號房。」

> *This is room 704.* 中的 704，要唸成：seven-
> oh-four，即 seven-o-four，不可唸成 *seven-zero-*
> 〔o〕　　　　　　　　〔o〕
> *four*（誤）或 *seven hundred and four*（誤）。如果房
> 間號碼是 5525，就有兩種唸法：① five-five-two-
> five ② fifty-five-twenty-five。

　　　This is room 704. 也可說
成：I'm in room 704. 或 This
is 704. 如果只說 *Room 704.*
就比較不禮貌了。

> This is
> room 704.

2. *I'm leaving today.*

　　　這句話字面的意思是「我今天要離開。」也就
是「我今天要走。」現在進行式可以表示「不久的
未來」。中國人最常說的是「我今天要走。」美國
人卻最常用 *I'm leaving today.*

【比較】*I'm leaving today.*【最常用】

I'm going today. (我今天要走。)【較少用】

I'm checking out today.【最常用】

(我今天要退房。)

所以，說英文不可把中文直接翻成英文，句子即使對，卻往往不符合美國人說話的習慣。

3. *What time is checkout?*

checkout〔'tʃɛk,aʊt〕 *n.* 結帳退房

這句話也可以說成：When is checkout? (退房時間是什麼時候？)

4. *Can I check out late?*

late〔let〕 *adv.* 晚

這句話的意思是：「我能不能晚一點退房？」也可以說：Can I check out two hours late?

(我能不能晚兩個小時退房？)

5. *Can I stay another two hours?*

這句話的意思是「我可不可以多待兩個小時？」也可以說：Can I stay until one? (我可不可以待到下午一點？) 或 Can I overstay two hours? (我可不可以多待兩個小時？)【overstay〔'ovɚ'ste〕 *v.* 待得超過～時間】

【比較】Can I stay until one?【最常用】

Can I stay until one o'clock?【正，少用】

Can I stay until one p.m.?【正，美國人不用】

6. *It would really help me out.*

help sb. out 幫忙某人

這句話的意思是「這會真正幫了我的忙。」用假設法助動詞 would，表示你尚未幫助我。

help sb. out「幫某人的忙」(詳見 p.158) It would …
為什麼用 would (詳見 p.160)。

7. *That would be great.*

這句話的意思是「那會很棒。」用假設法助動詞 would 表示尚未幫助，暗示如果幫助了，那將會很棒。

【比較 1】 That's great. 和 *That would be great.*
用法不同。

　　A: I got a scholarship. (我得到了獎學金。)
　　B: That's great. (很棒。)【正】
　　　That would be great. 【誤，因動作已發生】

【比較 2】 A: I want to go with you. (我想跟你去。)
　　B: *That would be great.* (那會很棒。)【正】
　　　That's great. (很棒。)【正】

BOOK 4

I want to go with you.

That would be great.

8. *That would be a big help*.

這句話的意思是：「那會是一個大的幫助。」引申為「那會幫我很大的忙。」等於 That would be a big favor.【favor〔'fevɚ〕*n.* 恩惠】

9. *I'd really be grateful*.

grateful〔'gretfəl〕*adj.* 感激的

這句話的意思是「我會非常感激。」等於 I'd be so grateful. 也可說成：I'd really appreciate it.
【appreciate〔ə'priʃɪ,et〕*v.* 感激】

I'd really be greatful.

感激的話說愈多愈好，不要怕不好意思，禮多人不怪。

BOOK 4

【劉毅老師的話】

The English revolution is now!
（英文的改革就是現在！）

One Breath English is your weapon.
（「一口氣背會話」是你的武器。）

Pick it up and fire!（拿起武器開槍！）

【對話練習】

1. A：**This is room 704.**

   B：Good morning.
      What can I do for you?
      How can I be of service?
      【service（'sɜvɪs）*n.* 幫助】

   A：這是 704 號房。

   B：早安。
      我能為您效勞嗎？
      我能幫您什麼忙嗎？

2. A：**I'm leaving today.**

   B：I understand.
      I'll total up your bill.
      I'll get everything ready.
      【*total up* 合計】

   A：我今天要離開。

   B：我明白了。
      我會幫您合計帳單。
      我會把一切準備好。

3. A：**What time is checkout?**

   B：Checkout time is 11 a.m.
      You can come to the front desk
      anytime before then.
      I'll have your bill ready.
      【*front desk* 櫃台
         bill（bɪl）*n.* 帳單】

   A：退房時間是什麼時候？

   B：退房時間是上午 11 點。
      您可以在那之前隨時到
      櫃台。
      我會將您的帳單準備好。

4. A：**Can I check out late?**

   B：I can't answer that.
      Please hold the line.
      I'll connect you with my
      supervisor.
      【connect（kə'nɛkt）*v.* 替（某人）接
         supervisor（ˌsjupɚ'vaɪzɚ）*n.* 主管   *hold the line* 電話不掛斷】

   A：我可以晚一點退房嗎？

   B：我無法回答您。
      請稍等。
      我幫您接給我的主管。

BOOK 4

5. A : **Can I stay another two hours?**　　A：我可不可以多待兩個小時？
   B : That sounds OK.　　　　　　　　　B：聽起來沒問題。
      We can allow that.　　　　　　　　　　我們可以讓您那樣做。
      Let me notify housekeeping.　　　　　　我會通知客房服務部。
      【housekeeping (ˈhaʊsˌkipɪŋ) *n.*
      客房服務部】

6. A : **It would really help me out.**　　　A：這真的會幫了我的忙。
   B : I'm glad to help.　　　　　　　　　B：我很樂意幫忙。
      We're happy to serve you.　　　　　　　我們很高興為您服務。
      We try to satisfy.　　　　　　　　　　我們會盡力讓您滿意。
      【satisfy (ˈsætɪsˌfaɪ) *v.* 令人滿意】

7. A : **That would be great.**　　　　　　A：那會很棒。
   B : It's no problem at all.　　　　　　　B：不用客氣。
      We're glad we can help.　　　　　　　　我們很高興能幫得上忙。
      We aim to please.　　　　　　　　　　我們就是想要讓您滿意。
      【aim (em) *v.* 打算；企圖】

8. A : **That would be a big help.**　　　　A：那會幫我很大的忙。
   B : I'm happy to help.　　　　　　　　B：我很樂意幫忙。
      Let me know if there's　　　　　　　　如果有其他事情可以為您
      anything else I can do for you.　　　　效勞，一定要讓我知道。
      We're here to serve you.　　　　　　　我們在這裡就是要為您服
      　　　　　　　　　　　　　　　　　　務。

9. A : **I'd really be grateful.**　　　　　A：我會非常感激。
   B : I'll take care of it.　　　　　　　　B：我會處理。
      You're a loyal customer.　　　　　　　您是我們忠實的顧客。
      We look forward to seeing　　　　　　我們期待能再次看到您。
      you again.
      【loyal (ˈlɔɪəl) *adj.* 忠實的　　***look forward to V-ing*** 期待】

11. Are you all packed?

Are you all packed?	你全都打包好了嗎？
Are you ready to go?	你好了沒有？
Make sure you have everything.	確定你東西都帶齊了。
Don't forget anything.	不要忘掉任何東西。
Don't leave anything behind.	不要忘記帶走任何東西。
Take a second look around.	再到處看看。
Check again.	再檢查。
Check one more time.	再檢查一次。
Better safe than sorry.	安全總比後悔好。

BOOK 4

**────────────────

pack〔pæk〕*v.* 打包　　ready〔'rɛdɪ〕*adj.* 準備好的
make sure 確定　　*leave~behind* 忘記帶走～
take a look 看一看　　around〔ə'raʊnd〕*adv.* 到處
one more time 再一次　　safe〔sef〕*adj.* 安全的
sorry〔'sɔrɪ〕*adj.* 遺憾的；後悔的

【背景説明】

　　當你要走的時候，你和同住在一起的同伴説些什麼話呢？這九句話是最好的選擇。

1. *Are you all packed?*
   pack〔pæk〕*v.* 打包

> 　　這句話字面意思是「你是不是全部被打包了？」實在很難引申爲「你全都打包好了嗎？」一般説來，及物動詞人當主詞，要用主動，非人當主詞，才能用被動，在這裡，可看成是一個例外。
>
> 　　美國人常説的 *Are you packed?* 應該是由 Have you packed? 演變而來。
>
> 【比較1】 *Are you packed?*【正，最常用】
> 　　　　 Have you packed?【正，較正式】
>
> 【比較2】 中文： 你全打包好了沒有？
> 　　　　 英文： *Are you all packed?*【正】
> 　　　　　　　 *Have you all packed?*【誤】
> 　　　　【第二句話的意思應該是「你們全體都打包好了沒有？」】
>
> *Are you all packed?* 有兩個意思：
> ① 你全打包好了沒有？Are you / all pácked?
> ② 你們全體都打包好了沒有？Are you all / pácked?
>
> 　　由於這個句子短，語調和停頓上，沒有什麼大的區別，也可以不強調，也可以不停頓。

Are you packed? 和 Are you done?（你做完了沒有？）及 Are you finished?（你做完了沒有？）的用法一樣，在文法上很難解釋，編者查遍所有字典，也請教過不少美國的語言學者，都沒辦法解釋清楚，他們最多只能將 packed 解釋成形容詞。編者認為，以後，在新的字典上，應該這樣註明：packed〔pækt〕*adj.* ①打包好了的 ②擠滿的。

看看下面的例子：

【例1】 ***Are you packed*** for the trip?
（你要去旅行的行李打包好了嗎？）

【例2】 ***Are you packed*** for the flight?
（你要搭飛機的行李打包好了嗎？）
【flight〔flaɪt〕*n.* 班機；搭飛機旅行】

【例3】 ***Are you all packed*** for your move to the new house?
（你要搬新家的行李全打包好了嗎？）
【move〔muv〕*n.* 搬家】

問別人行李打包好了沒有，說法很多：

Are you packed?【最常用】
（你打包好了嗎？）

Are your bags packed?【常用】
【美國人最常稱「行李」為 bag】
（你的行李打包好了嗎？）

Are your bags ready?【常用】
（你的行李準備好了沒有？）

Have you packed? (你打包好了嗎？)【常用】

Have you packed your bags yet?

(你的行李已經打包好了嗎？)【yet〔jɛt〕adv. 已經】

Have you packed your things yet?

(你的東西已經打包好了嗎？)

Are you packed? 或 ***Are you all packed?***，

在文法上，應該要把 packed 當形容詞用，這句話

很常用，我們非要背下來不可。

2. ***Are you ready to go?***

ready〔ˈrɛdɪ〕adj. 準備好的

這句話字面的意思是「你準備好要走了沒有？」

引申爲「你好了沒有？」這句話也可以說成：

Are you ready to leave?

(你準備好要走了沒有？)

Are you ready? (你好了沒有？)

Are you all set? (你好了沒有？)【***all set*** = ready】

3. ***Make sure you have everything.***

這句話字面的意思是「確定你什麼都有。」引申

爲「確定你東西都帶齊了。」這句話也可以說成：

Be sure you have everything.

Be sure to take everything with you.

Do you have everything you need?

美國人也常說：Got everything you need?

(需要的東西都帶了吧？)

4. *Don't forget anything.*

　　這句話的意思是「不要忘掉任何東西。」前面可以加一句 Think carefully. (仔細想想。)

5. *Don't leave anything behind.*
leave ~ behind 遺留；忘記帶走

> *Don't leave anything behind.*

　　這句話字面的意思是「不要留下任何東西在後面。」，引申為「不要忘記帶走任何東西。」也可以只說：Don't leave anything. (不要留下任何東西。)

6. *Take a second look around.*
take a look 看一看　　second〔'sɛkənd〕*adj.* 第二次的
around〔ə'raʊnd〕*adv.* 到處

　　這句話字面的意思是「再第二次到處看一看。」引申為「再到處看看。」這種說法很多：

Take a second look around. (再到處看看。)【最常用】
Take another look around. (再到處看看。)【最常用】
Take one more look around. (再到處看一看。)【常用】

Look around again. (再到處看一看。)【最常用】
Look around one more time. (再到處看一看。)【常用】
Look around another time. (再到處看看。)【常用】

　　如果叫你的朋友趕快到處看一看，你就可以說：
Take a quick look around.

BOOK 4

7. **Check again.**

check〔 tʃɛk 〕 v. 檢查

這句話的意思是「再檢查。」，也可說成：

Check it again. (再檢查。)
Check everything again. (再檢查每樣東西。)
Double check. (再檢查。)
【Double〔 'dʌbl̩ 〕 adv. 雙重地】

8. **Check one more time.**

one more time 再一次

這句話意思是「再檢查一次。」也可說成：
Check everything one more time. (每樣東西再檢
查一次。) check 是及物和不及物兩用動詞。

你可以和你的同伴說很多句：

Check your bags. (檢查你的行李。)
Check your wallet. Make sure everything
    is there. (檢查你的皮夾。確定東西都在裡面。)
Check the bathroom.

(檢查浴室。)
【wallet〔 'walɪt 〕 n. 皮夾】

Check under the bed.
(床底下看一看。)
Check around. (到處看看。)
Check everywhere. (四處看看。)

BOOK 4

9. ***Better safe than sorry.***

safe〔sef〕*adj.* 安全的

sorry〔'sɔrɪ〕*adj.* 遺憾的；後悔的

　　這句話是一句諺語，源自 It's better to be safe than sorry.，意思是「安全總比後悔好。」

【例1】　A: Should I take an umbrella?
　　　　　　　（我應該帶傘嗎？）
　　　　　B: ***Better safe than sorry.***
　　　　　　　（安全總比後悔好。）
　　　　　　【umbrella〔ʌm'brɛlə〕*n.* 雨傘】

【例2】　A: Should I go see the doctor?
　　　　　　　（我應該去看醫生嗎？）
　　　　　B: ***Better safe than sorry.***
　　　　　　　（安全總比後悔好。）

【例3】　A: Do you think I should make a reservation for dinner?
　　　　　　　（你認為我晚餐應該先訂位嗎？）
　　　　　B: ***Better safe than sorry.***
　　　　　　　（安全總比後悔好。）
　　　　　　【reservation〔ˏrɛzə'veʃən〕*n.* 預訂】

　　這一回的九句話，除了第一句外，還可以用在坐公車、火車、計程車，要下車時和同行的人說，提醒他不要忘了帶東西。

BOOK 4

【對話練習】

1. A：**Are you all packed?**

   B：Yes, I am.
   I packed an hour ago.
   I'm all set.
   【set〔sɛt〕*adj.* 準備好的】

   A：你全都打包好了沒？

   B：是的，我好了。
   我一小時前就打包好了。
   我都準備好了。

2. A：**Are you ready to go?**

   B：You bet I am!
   I'm really ready to go.
   I'm just waiting for you.
   【*You bet.* 當然。(=*Of course.*)】

   A：你好了沒有？

   B：我當然好了！
   我真的好了。
   我只是在等你。

3. A：**Make sure you have everything.**

   B：That's good advice.
   Let me look one more time.
   I don't want to lose anything.
   【advice〔əd'vaɪs〕*n.* 勸告】

   A：確定你東西都帶齊了。

   B：那是很好的建議。
   我再看一次。
   我不想弄丟任何東西。

4. A：**Don't forget anything.**

   B：Don't worry.
   I checked carefully.
   I haven't forgotten a thing.

   A：不要忘掉任何東西。

   B：別擔心。
   我仔細檢查過了。
   我沒忘掉任何東西。

5. A：**Don't leave anything behind**.　　A：不要忘記帶走任何東西。

　　B：I never do.　　　　　　　　　　　B：我從沒忘記。
　　　　I'm very careful.　　　　　　　　　　我會很小心。
　　　　I always double-check.　　　　　　　我一向會再檢查一次。
　　　　【double-check〔'dʌbḷ'tʃɛk〕v.
　　　　　再檢查】

6. A：**Take a second look around**.　　A：再到處看看。

　　B：I already have.　　　　　　　　　B：我已經看過了。
　　　　I've got everything.　　　　　　　　　我所有的東西都拿了。
　　　　Relax, everything is OK.　　　　　　放輕鬆，一切都沒問題。
　　　　【relax〔rɪ'læks〕v. 放鬆】

7. A：**Check again**.　　　　　　　　A：再檢查一次。

　　B：OK, I will.　　　　　　　　　　B：好，我會的。
　　　　I'll check one more time,　　　　　　我會再檢查一次，確定
　　　　just to be sure.　　　　　　　　　　一下。
　　　　It'll put my mind at ease.　　　　　　這樣會讓我覺得安心。
　　　　【*at ease* 輕鬆的】

8. A：**Check one more time**.　　　　A：再檢查一次。

　　B：OK, I'll make a last check.　　　B：好的，我會做最後的檢查。
　　　　I'll check the bathroom.　　　　　　我會檢查浴室。
　　　　I'll look under the bed.　　　　　　我會看看床底下。

9. A：**Better safe than sorry**.　　　A：安全總比後悔好。

　　B：I totally agree.　　　　　　　　B：我完全同意。
　　　　I always say that, too.　　　　　　我也常說這句話。
　　　　You can never be too careful.　　　　再怎麼小心也不為過。
　　　【totally〔'totḷɪ〕adv. 完全地　　*cannot be too~* 再怎麼~也不為過】

BOOK 4

12. *I'm getting ready to check out*.

Hello, front desk?	喂，櫃台嗎？
I'm getting ready to check out.	我快要準備退房了。
I'll be down in ten minutes.	我再過十分鐘就下來。
Please send someone up.	請派個人上來。
Please check my room.	請檢查我的房間。
I haven't used the fridge.	我沒有用過冰箱。
I need to get to the airport.	我必須到機場去。
Do you have a shuttle bus?	你們有短程往返的公車嗎？
Do you have any suggestions?	你有沒有什麼建議？

** ———————————————

hello〔hə'lo, 'hʌlo〕*interj.* 喂
front〔frʌnt〕*adj.* 前面的　　***front desk*** 櫃台
check out 結帳退房　　send〔sɛnd〕*v.* 派遣
fridge〔frɪdʒ〕*n.* 冰箱 (= refrigerator〔rɪ'frɪdʒə,retə〕)
get to 到達　　airport〔'ɛr,port〕*n.* 機場
shuttle〔'ʃʌtl̩〕*adj.* 短程往返的
shuttle bus 短程往返的公車
suggestion〔sə'dʒɛstʃən〕*n.* 建議

BOOK 4

【背景説明】

在飯店裡，先打電話告訴櫃台你要退房，可以
節省你在櫃台等待的時間，免得櫃台人員，到你來
的時候，才打電話請人檢查你房間的冰箱等。

1. *Hello, front desk?* (喂，櫃台嗎？)
hello〔həˋlo,ˋhʌlo〕*interj.* 喂 (電話中的招呼語)
front desk　(旅館的) 櫃台

> 在「KK 音標發音字典」上，hello 的發音有四
> 種：〔hɛˋlo;həˋlo;ˋhɛlo;ˋhʌlo〕，但美國人最常用
> 的是〔həˋlo〕或〔ˋhʌlo〕。hello 是美國人常用的打
> 招呼用語，也可以用 hi〔haɪ〕*interj.* 嗨 取代。

front desk 是指「旅館的櫃台」，現在已經可指
「櫃台人員」了，也就是 front desk staff。
【staff〔stæf〕*n.* 工作人員】

2. *I'm getting ready to check out.*
ready〔ˋrɛdɪ〕*adj.* 準備好的　　*check out* 結帳退房

> I'm ready. 的現在進行式是 I'm getting
> ready. 現在進行式除了表示「現在正在」以外，還
> 有其他用法，在這裡表示「不久的未來」。這句話的
> 意思是「我快要準備退房了。」也可說成：I'm about
> to check out. (我就要退房了。)

BOOK 4

美國人常說 I'm getting ready. 之類的話。

【例1】 **Are you getting ready** for your final exam?
（你的期末考快準備好了吧？）
【final〔ˈfaɪn̩〕adj. 最後的】

【例2】 **Are you getting ready** to find a job?
（你是不是快準備好找工作了？）

【例3】 **Are you getting ready** for your trip
next month?
（你下個月的旅行快要準備好了吧？）

【比較】 ***I'm getting ready to check out.***
（我快要準備好退房了。）【表示快要準備好】
I'm ready to check out.【表示已準備好】
（我已經準備好要退房了。）

「快要準備好要退房」，常用的說法：

I'm about to check out.
（我即將要退房。）【*be about to* 即將】
I'm about to leave. （我即將要離開。）
I'm checking out soon. （我很快就要退房了。）

「已經準備好要退房」，常用的說法有：

I'm ready to check out. （我準備好要退房了。）
I need to check out. （我需要退房。）
I'm checking out. （我就要退房了。）

美國人喜歡說 I'm ready. 之類的話，因為他們凡事
都會預先準備，這和中國文化不同。

3. *I'll be down in ten minutes.*

down〔daʊn〕*adv.* 由上而下；（由北）向南；向那邊；
在那邊；從這裡

in 表「再過～」。

　　這句話的意思是「我再過十分鐘就下來。」down
這個字，在這裡是副詞當形容詞用，做主詞補語。
（詳見「文法寶典」p.228）

【比較】*I'll be down in ten minutes.*【正，常用】
　　　　I'll come down in ten minutes.【正，少用】

　　飯店也許是高樓，也許只有一層樓，都可以說這
句話。I'll be down. 不一定指「從上到下」，也可以
指「由北向南」、「向那邊」、「在那邊」。

【例】 The water fountain is down the hallway.
　　　（飲水機就在走廊那邊。）
　　　fountain〔'faʊntn̩〕*n.* 飲水機
　　　hallway〔'hɔl,we〕*n.* 走廊

There is a post office down on the corner.
　　（在轉角那邊有一間郵局。）【corner〔'kɔrnɚ〕*n.* 轉角】

I'm leaving in a minute. I'll be right down.
　　（我就要走了。我馬上下來。）【right〔raɪt〕*adv.* 立刻】

【比較】in，after，within 的意義不同：

　　in ten minutes 是表示「再過十分鐘」，in an hour
表示「再過一小時」，in a minute「再過一分鐘」，表示
「再過一會兒」，in a moment「再過片刻」即表示「不
久」，in a second「再過一秒鐘」，即表示「不久」。

BOOK 4

字面上説來，*I'll be down in ten minutes.* 主要的意思是「再過十分鐘整，我就下來。」事實上有其他含意。

I'll be down in ten minutes.

① I'll be down ten minutes from now.
（再過十分鐘我就下來。）

② I'll be down within ten minutes.
（我會在十分鐘之內下來。）

這句話如果説成：I'll be down *after* ten minutes. 意義就不同了。

I'll be down *after* ten minutes.
= I won't be down within ten minutes.

這句話的含意是，我現在有事，我十分鐘之內不會下來，也許二十分鐘、三十分鐘之後，反正我十分鐘之內，不會下來，這句話應翻成「我在十分鐘之內不會下來。」

如果説成：I'll be down *within* ten minutes. 意思就是「我會在十分鐘之內下來。」

在這裡 in、within 和 after 的區別是：in 大於或等於 within，in 小於或等於 after。【within ≤ **in** ≤ after】

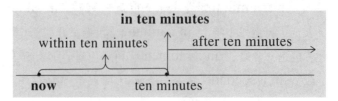

4. ***Please send someone up.***

send〔sɛnd〕*v.* 派遣

這句話的意思是「請派個人上來。」如果飯店只有一層樓，你可以說：Please send someone to my room. (請派個人到我房間。)

5. ***Please check my room.***

check〔tʃɛk〕*v.* 檢查

這句話的意思是「請檢查我的房間。」在飯店裡面，你結帳的時候，他們會馬上派人到你的房間，檢查冰箱、房間的設備，看看有沒有減少或損壞。

6. ***I haven't used the fridge.***

fridge〔frɪdʒ〕*n.* 電冰箱 (= refrigerator〔rɪˈfrɪdʒəˌretə〕)

真是奇怪，我們在課本上學的「電冰箱」，是 refrigerator，但是美國人不論說和寫，都用 fridge，幾乎不用 refrigerator。

這句話的意思是「我沒有用過冰箱。」也可說成：I didn't use the fridge. (我沒有使用冰箱。) 有些飯店將小冰箱稱作 minibar。所以，也可說成：I haven't used the minibar. (我沒有用過小冰箱。) 或 I didn't use the minibar. (我沒有使用小冰箱。)【minibar〔ˈmɪnɪˌbar〕*n.* 小冰箱】

7. **I need to get to the airport.**

　　get to 到達　　airport〔'ɛr,port〕*n.* 機場

　　這句話的意思是「我必須到機場去。」

　　【比較】**I need to get to the airport.**【較常說】

　　　　　　I need to go to the airport.【較少說】

8. **Do you have a shuttle bus?**

　　shuttle〔'ʃʌtḷ〕*adj.* 定時往返的；短程往返的

　　　　n. 往返的班車

　　　　【背這個字，先背 shut 再加上 tle，就行了。】

　　shuttle bus 短程往返的公車

　　　　凡是來回穿梭的，都叫 shuttle，如 space
　　shuttle（太空梭）。這裡的 a shuttle bus 是指 an
　　airport shuttle bus（到
　　機場的來回班車）。也有
　　downtown shuttle bus
　　（到市中心的來回班車）。

　　　　a shuttle bus 也可以簡稱 a shuttle，因為
　　shuttle 這個字也可以當名詞，作「往返的班
　　車」解。

　　【比較】Do you have a **shuttle**?

　　　　　　（你們有往返的班車嗎？）【最常用】

　　　　　　Do you have a shuttle bus?

　　　　　　（你們有往返的公車嗎？）【常用】

Do you have an ***airport shuttle***?
（你們有往返機場的班車嗎？）【常用】
Do you have an ***airport shuttle bus***?
（你們有往返機場的班車嗎？）【少用】

也可以問飯店人員：Do you have a shuttle
service?（你們有沒有接送服務？）

9. ***Do you have any suggestions?***
suggestion〔 səˈdʒɛstʃən 〕*n.* 建議

這句話的意思是「你有
沒有什麼建議？」也可說成：
What do you suggest?
（你有什麼建議？）

Do you have any
suggestions?

你也可以問：

What's the best way?
（什麼方式最好？）
What should I do?（我該怎麼做？）
How should I go?（我該如何去？）

BOOK 4

┌─ 【劉毅老師的話】 ─

背完「一口氣背會話」後，為什麼英文
會講得比美國人好呢？因為你所說的每一句
話，都是優美的、正確的、體貼的。

【對話練習】

1. A：**Hello, front desk?**

   B：Yes, this is the front desk.
   Good morning.
   How can I help you?

   A：喂。櫃台嗎？

   B：是的，這裡是櫃台。
   早安。
   要我為您效勞嗎？

2. A：**I'm getting ready to check out.**

   B：Thank you for calling.
   We'll prepare your bill.
   We'll be ready to check you out.

   A：我快要準備退房了。

   B：謝謝您打電話來。
   我們會準備好您的帳單。
   我們會準備好讓您退房。

3. A：**I'll be down in ten minutes.**

   B：We'll be waiting.
   Thank you for notifying us.
   It will only take a minute to
   check you out.

   A：我再過十分鐘就下來。

   B：我們會等您。
   謝謝您通知我們。
   馬上就能幫您結帳退房。

4. A：**Please send someone up.**

   B：I'll do that right away.
   I'll send someone to get your
   bags.
   He should be there in five
   minutes.

   A：請派個人上來。

   B：我立刻派人上去。
   我會派人去拿您的行李。

   他應該五分鐘後就到。

5. A：**Please check my room.**

   B：We'll be right there.
   Please wait a moment.
   Housekeeping will be there in
   a minute.

   A：請檢查我的房間。

   B：我們馬上到。
   請等一下。
   房務部人員會馬上到達。

   【housekeeping (ˈhaʊsˌkipɪŋ) *v.* 房務部】

6. A : **I haven't used the fridge.**

　B : That's fine.

　　　I'll tell the checkout person.

　　　There will be no charge for

　　　the mini-bar.

　　　【charge〔tʃɑrdʒ〕*n.* 費用

　　　mini-bar〔'mɪnɪ'bɑr〕*n.*（客房

　　　內的）小冰箱】

A : 我沒有用過冰箱。

B : 好的。

　　我會告訴負責退房的人。

　　將不會收取小冰箱的費用。

7. A : **I need to get to the airport.**

　B : There's an airport bus.

　　　It runs every hour.

　　　You can catch it on the

　　　corner up the street.

　　　【run〔rʌn〕*v.* 行駛

　　　catch〔kætʃ〕*v.* 趕上

　　　up the street 街道那邊】

A : 我必須到機場去。

B : 有機場巴士。

　　每個小時一班。

　　你可以在街道那邊的轉角搭

　　乘。

8. A : **Do you have a shuttle bus?**

　B : Sorry, we don't have a

　　　shuttle.

　　　We do have a limo.

　　　Or I could call you a taxi.

A : 你們有短程往返的公車嗎？

B : 抱歉，我們沒有短程往返的

　　班車。

　　我們有豪華轎車。

　　或者我可以幫你叫一部計程車。

9. A : **Do you have any**

　　　suggestions?

　B : I suggest you take a cab.

　　　A taxi is the best way.

　　　A shuttle takes twice as

　　　long!

A : 你有沒有什麼建議？

B : 我建議你搭計程車。

　　搭計程車是最好的方式。

　　短程往返的班車會花兩倍長的

　　時間！

BOOK 4

語言應該回歸自然

　　很多人英文學不好，都說沒有英語環境、沒有外國老師，其實，很多到美國的移民，一生苦學英文，到死以前，還是沒能學好英文，他們說出來的話，被美國人戲稱是 Chinglish（洋涇濱英語）。雖然在美國長期居住，今天東學一句，明天西學一句，學的都是模模糊糊的，學得模糊，說得也模糊，天天說英文，卻不知道自己說得對不對，說起英語來，當然沒有信心。

　　「一口氣背會話」把美國口語的精華，一句一句、一回一回、一册一册地烙印在讀者的腦海中，你講的每一句話，都是經過研究，精心編排過的，背得滾瓜爛熟以後，說出來的話，當然有信心。編者研究一輩子的英文文法，現在發現，學生實在不應該先學文法，語言應該回歸自然，只要背美國人平常所說的話，就行了。

　　美國人平常所說的話，和他們所寫出來的不一樣，他們寫得正式嚴謹，講得幽默輕鬆，那些寫會話書的美國人，都是學了不少文法，他們往往不敢將他們平常講的話，付諸於文字，例如，美國人常說：*I'm done.*（我做完了。）*I'm finished.*（我做完了。）會話書中，卻避而不寫。編者年輕的時候，到美國讀書，聽到美國同學問："*Are you all packed?*"（你的行李是不是都打包好了？）這句話在書上，美國人只敢寫出 "Have you packed?"（你的行李打包好了嗎？）當你聽到很多的話，和你學的不一樣，你講起話來，就沒有信心了。

　　有了「一口氣背會話」，學好英語，不再是少數人的專利，什麼都不要管，只要背就行了，人人都能夠背，人人都能夠學好英文。

劉毅

「一口氣背會話」經 BOOK 4

唸英文要像唸經一樣，每天大聲唸，從起床到睡覺，唸得比看得快，最後不看也會唸，養成習慣後，你會全身舒爽，你試試看，奇妙無比。

1. *I'm* going to New York.
I'm leaving next Friday.
I'd like a round-trip ticket.

I want to go economy.
Do you have special fares?
Do you have promotional rates?

My departure time is flexible.
I don't mind a stopover.
I want an unbeatable price.

2. I'm checking in.
Here's my ticket and passport.
I have two bags and one carry-on.

I want an aisle seat.
I want to sit in the front.
Can you get me a first row seat?

How about the emergency row?
Please try your best.
I appreciate your effort.

3. *Could I have* a blanket?
Could I have an apple juice?
Could I have a cup of hot water?

I'm not in a hurry.
It's not an emergency.
I can wait.

When do we eat?
When do we arrive?
How long till we get there?

4. *Here's my* passport.
Here's my immigration form.
My return ticket is inside.

I just arrived from Taiwan.
I'm here on vacation.
I have a tourist visa.

I'll be in the States for two weeks.
I'll be staying at the Holiday Inn.
Thank you for helping me.

5. *I'd like to* book a room.
I'd like to make a reservation.
I need it for tonight.

I prefer twin beds.
I'll settle for a double.
Do you have any vacancies?

What are your rates?
What can you do for me?
Do you have a complimentary breakfast?

6. *I* have a reservation.
I'm here to check in.
What do I have to do?

How much is the deposit?
Here's my credit card.
Should I fill out a form?

I'd like a quiet room.
I'd like a room with a view.
Can I see the room first?

7. Hello, housekeeping.
I'm going out for a while.
Could I have my room cleaned right
now?

I'd like extra towels.
I'd like a toothbrush and razor.
Please bring me a pot of hot water.

I have dirty laundry.
I have clothes to be washed.
What should I do?

8. Does this bus go downtown?
How much does it cost?
How do I pay?

I want the shopping district.
How long does it take?
How many stops are there?

Which stop is the best?
Please tell me where to get off.
Please tell me one stop ahead.

9. *Nice* meeting you.
Nice talking to you.
I enjoyed our chat.

Here's my number.
Let's keep in touch.
Call me if you'd like.

Good luck.
Have a great one.
I hope we can meet again.

10. This is room 704.
I'm leaving today.
What time is checkout?

Can I check out late?
Can I stay another two hours?
It would really help me out.

That would be great.
That would be a big help.
I'd really be grateful.

11. *Are you* all packed?
Are you ready to go?
Make sure you have everything.

Don't forget anything.
Don't leave anything behind.
Take a second look around.

Check again.
Check one more time.
Better safe than sorry.

12. Hello, front desk?
I'm getting ready to check out.
I'll be down in ten minutes.

Please send someone up.
Please check my room.
I haven't used the fridge.

I need to get to the airport.
Do you have a shuttle bus?
Do you have any suggestions?

BOOK 5 和老外看電影

▶5-1 介紹兩位朋友彼此認識：：

> Do you know Andy?
> Have you met Andy?
> Let me introduce you.

▶5-2 向新認識的朋友介紹自己：

> My name is Pat.
> It's nice to meet you.
> How do you do?

▶5-3 打電話約朋友出來玩：

> When are you free?
> What's a good time?
> When do you want to get together?

▶5-4 向朋友建議去看電影：

> I got a great idea.
> Let's go out tonight.
> Let's go see a movie.

▶5-5 和朋友討論看哪一部電影：

> What's playing?
> What's showing?
> Anything really good?

▶5-6 到了電影院，排隊買票：

> Pick a movie.
> What looks good?
> What are we going to see?

▶5-7 告訴朋友自己堅持要請客：

It's my treat.
It's on me.
Let me pay.

▶5-8 進了電影院裡面，和朋友挑選座位：

Where do you want to sit?
Sit wherever you want.
Sit anywhere you like.

▶5-9 請旁邊的人小聲一點：

Please be quiet.
Please keep it down.
Could you lower your voice?

▶5-10 向別人道歉：

I'm sorry.
I apologize.
It's my fault.

▶5-11 和朋友討論剛看過的電影：

How was the movie?
What did you think?
Did you like it?

▶5-12 對朋友表達感謝：

What a great night!
I had a wonderful time.
I enjoyed myself a lot.

1. Let me introduce you.

Do you know *Andy*?	你認不認識安迪？
Have you met *Andy*?	你有沒有見過安迪？
Let me introduce you.	讓我替你介紹。
Andy, this is Pat.	安迪，這是派特。
Pat, this is Andy.	派特，這是安迪。
I'm glad you two could meet.	我很高興你們兩個能夠認識。
Andy is an old friend.	安迪是我的老朋友。
He is a great guy.	他是個好人。
You two have a lot in common.	你們兩個有很多共同點。

BOOK 5

** ———————————————————

know〔no〕*v.* 知道；認識　　Andy〔'ændɪ〕*n.* 安迪 (男子名)

meet〔mit〕*v.* 會面；認識

introduce〔͵ɪntrə'djus〕*v.* 介紹

Pat〔pæt〕*n.* 派特 (男子名或女子名皆可)

glad〔glæd〕*adj.* 高興的　　great〔gret〕*adj.* 很棒的

guy〔gaɪ〕*n.* 人　　***have a lot in common*** 有很多共同點

【背景説明】

　　　　一般美國人的習慣，是先把男士介紹給女士；
把年輕的介紹給年長的，把地位低的介紹給地位高
的。背了這九句話後，你就很會用英文介紹朋友了。

1. ***Do you know Andy?*** (你認不認識安迪？)
Have you met Andy? (你有沒有見過安迪？)
know〔no〕*v.* 知道；認識
Andy〔'ændɪ〕*n.* 安迪 (男子名)【這個字好記，and 加上 y 即可】
meet〔mit〕*v.* 會面；認識

　　　　這二句話你唸唸看，很順，一下子就背下來
了。Have you met Andy? 字面的意思是「你有
沒有見過安迪？」引申爲「你認不認識安迪？」這
句話也可以説成：Have you met Andy before?
字面的意思是「你以前有沒有見過安迪？」也就是
「你認不認識安迪？」所以，know 和 meet 都有
「認識」的意思。

Let me introduce you.

2. ***Let me introduce you.***
introduce〔ˌɪntrə'djus〕*v.* 介紹

　　　這句話在這裡源自：

　　　Let me introduce you *to Andy.*
　　　(讓我把你介紹給安迪。)
　　　Let me introduce you *to each other.*
　　　(讓我介紹你們彼此認識。)

> 美國人說話喜歡簡化，有時說話說一半，Let me introduce you. 就是典型的例子。因為前兩句已經提到過 Andy，就不需要再重覆了。

> ***Let me introduce you.*** 【最常用】
> （讓我替你介紹。）
> Let me introduce you to Andy. 【最常用】
> Let me introduce you to each other. 【常用】
> （讓我介紹你們彼此認識。）
> Let me introduce you two. 【常用】
> （讓我介紹你們兩位認識。）
> Let me introduce you guys. 【常用】
> （讓我介紹你們兩個人認識。）

3. ***Andy, this is Pat.*** （安迪，這是派特。）
   ***Pat**, this is Andy.* （派特，這是安迪。）
   Pat〔pæt〕*n.* 派特（男子名或女子名皆可）

   這兩句話，也可以簡化成：

   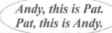

   Andy, Pat.
   Pat, Andy.

4. ***I'm glad you two could meet.***
   glad〔glæd〕*adj.* 高興的

   這句話的意思是：「我很高興你們兩個能夠認識。」
   美國人也常說：It's a pleasure to introduce you two.
   （很高興介紹你們兩位。）

【比較】 下面兩句話意思相同，都很常用：

   I'm glad you two could meet.【語氣較客氣】

   I'm glad you two *can meet.*【一般語氣】

5. *Andy is an old friend.*

>   中國人說「安迪是我的老朋友。」美國人常只說 Andy is an old friend. *源自* Andy is an old friend *of mine.* 也有美國人說：Andy is a good friend.（安迪是我的好朋友。），這兩句話都是美國人喜歡說話說一半的例子。
>
> 【比較1】 *Andy is an old friend.*【常用】
>   Andy is an old friend *of mine.*【正，較少用】
>
> 【比較2】 Andy is a good friend.【常用】
>   Andy is a good friend *of mine.*【正，較少用】

  背了「一口氣背會話」，就不會說出一些文法正確，但美國人聽起來怪怪的句子。

6. *He is a great guy.*

great〔gret〕*adj.* 很好的；很棒的

guy〔gaɪ〕*n.* 人；傢伙

  這句話的意思是「他是個好人。」這種說法還有很多：

   He is a nice guy.（他是個好人。）

   He is a good guy.（他是個好人。）

   He is a wonderful guy.（他是個很好的人。）

He is a happy guy. (他是個開朗的人。)

He is an interesting guy. (他是個風趣的人。)

He is a funny guy. (他是個風趣的人。)
　　　〔'fʌnɪ 〕*adj.* 風趣的

He is a special guy. (他是個特別的人。)

He is a remarkable guy. (他是個了不起的人。)
　　　〔 rɪ'mɑrkəbḷ 〕*adj.* 了不起的

He is an awesome guy. (他是個很棒的人。)
　　　〔'ɔsəm 〕*adj.* 很棒的

　　上面十句話中，***He is a great guy.*** He is a nice guy.　He is a good guy. 最常用。

7. ***You two have a lot in common.***

common〔'kɑmən 〕*adj.* 共同的

in common　共有的；共同的

have a lot in common　有很多共同點

　　(= *have much in common*)

　　　common 的主要意思是作「共同的」解，此時 common 是形容詞，in common 是一個成語，意思是「共有的；共同的」，有些成語是由「介詞 + 形容詞」所形成，詳見 p.3–5。這句話的意思是「你們兩個有很多共同點。」

　　　You two have a lot in common.【最常用】

　= You two are a lot alike.【較常用】

　　(你們兩個很像。)【alike〔ə'laɪk 〕*adj.* 相像的 】

　= You two are very similar.【常用】

　　(你們兩個非常相似。)

　【similar〔'sɪmələ 〕*adj.* 相似的 】

BOOK 5

【對話練習】

1. A：**Do you know Andy?**
   B：No, I don't.
   I don't know Andy.
   We've never met.

   A：你認不認識安迪？
   B：不，我不認識。
   我不認識安迪。
   我們從未見過面。

2. A：**Have you met Andy?**
   B：No, I haven't.
   I've never met Andy.
   Sorry to say, we've never met.

   A：你認識安迪嗎？
   B：不，不認識。
   我不認識安迪。
   很遺憾，我們從未見過面。

3. A：**Let me introduce you.**
   B：That would be great.
   I'd really like that.
   I'd really like to meet Andy.

   A：讓我替你們介紹。
   B：太好了。
   我真的很想認識他。
   我真的很想認識安迪。

4. A：**Andy, this is Pat.**
   B：Hello.
   How are you?
   It's nice to meet you.

   A：安迪，這是派特。
   B：哈囉。
   你好嗎？
   很高興認識你。

5. A：**Pat, this is Andy.**
   B：How do you do?
   I'm glad to meet you.
   I've heard a lot about you.

   A：派特，這是安迪。
   B：你好。
   很高興認識你。
   久仰，久仰。

6. A: **I'm glad you two could meet**.

   B: So am I.
I love meeting new people.
You can never have too many friends.

  A：我很高興你們兩個能夠認識。

   B：我也是。
我喜歡認識新朋友。
朋友永遠不嫌多。

7. A: **Andy is an old friend**.

   B: That's nice.
Old friends are the best!
How long have you been friends?

  A：安迪是我的老朋友。

   B：太好了。
老朋友是最好的！
你們是多久的朋友了？

8. A: **He's a great guy**.

   B: So I've heard.
It's a pleasure to meet you, Andy.
I'm sure we're going to get along fine.

  A：他是個好人。

   B：我聽說了。
很高興認識你，安迪。

    我相信我們能處得很好。

9. A: **You two have a lot in common**.

   B: Really, do you mean it?
I'm glad you think so.
We'll have a lot to talk about.

  A：你們兩個有很多共同點。

   B：真的，你是說真的嗎？
我很高興你這麼認為。
我們會有很多話題可聊。

BOOK 5

2. How do you do?

My name is Pat.	我的名字是派特。
It's nice to meet you.	很高興認識你。
How do you do?	你好。
I'm from Taiwan.	我是台灣人。
I'm a student.	我是個學生。
How about you?	你呢？
Where are you from?	你是哪裡人？
What do you do?	你從事什麼行業？
Been here long?	你在這裡很久了嗎？

BOOK 5

** ——————————————————————

meet〔mit〕*v.* 認識

【背景説明】

　　見到外國朋友，該如何自我介紹？有了這一單元，你就有話可説了。

1. *My name is Pat.*

　　這句話的意思是「我的名字是派特。」也可以説成：I'm Pat. (我是派特。)

2. *It's nice to meet you.*
   meet〔mit〕*v.* 認識

　　這句話的意思是「很高興認識你。」也可説成：Good to meet you. 或 Glad to meet you.

　　原則上，初次見面時説：It's nice to meet you. 或 Nice to meet you.

　　再見時説：Nice meeting you. 或 It was nice meeting you.

　　事實上，現在美國人，初次見面的時候，也常説 Nice meeting you.【詳見 p.432】

　　介紹認識時，比較正式的説法有：
How nice to meet you! (真高興認識你！)
How very nice to meet you! (非常高興認識你！)
I'm pleased to make your acquaintance.
(我很高興認識你。)　　〔əˈkwɛntəns〕*n.* 認識
【*make sb's acquaintance* 認識某人】

BOOK 5

3. *How do you do?*

這句話的意思是「你
好。」不是問句，而是初
次見面的問候語，對方也
用 How do you do? 回答。

現在也有美國人初次見面時用 How are you?
（你好嗎？）來問候。

【比較】 *How do you do?*【只有一個意思，等於 Hello.】
How are you?
【有兩個意思：①你好。(= Hello.) ②你好嗎？】

4. *I'm from Taiwan.*

這句話的意思是「我是台灣人。」

【比較】 *I'm from Taiwan.*（我是台灣人。）【常用】
I come from Taiwan.（我是台灣人。）【少用】
I came from Taiwan.【與上面二句意思不同】
（我從台灣來的。）

這句話可以加長，囉哩囉嗦說一大堆：

I'm from Taiwan.（我是台灣人。）
I was born there.（我在那裡出生。）
That's my home.（台灣是我的家鄉。）

My home is Taiwan.（我的家在台灣。）
My family lives there.（我的家人住在那裡。）
【family 指「全體家人」，表一個集合體，所以用單數】
It's really a great place.（它真的是個很棒的地方。）

Come visit. (來玩吧。)

You're welcome anytime. (隨時歡迎你來。)

I'd love to show you around.

(我會很樂意帶你到處參觀。)

【*show sb. around* 帶某人到處參觀】

5. *I'm a student.*

這句話的意思是「我是個學生。」如果你是來這裡讀書的，就可以說：I'm a student here. 如果你是來旅行的，就可以說：

I'm traveling here. (我來這裡旅行。)

I'm visiting here. (我來這裡遊覽。)

【visit 在此作「遊覽」解】

如果你是在這裡工作，你就可以說：

I'm working here. (我來這裡工作。)

My company is here. (我的公司在這裡。)

I'm here on business. (我來這裡出差。)

6. *Where are you from?*

這句話的意思是「你是哪裡人？」如果要客氣一點的話，就可說：*May I ask,* "Where are you from?" (請問你是哪裡人？)

【比較】 *May I ask,* "Where are you from?" 【常用】

May I ask where you are from?

【文法對，極少人用】

BOOK 5

7. *What do you do?*

這句話的意思是「你從事什麼行業？」這句話說快以後，發音就有改變：

【比較】 ***What do you do?***【慢速發音】
〔hwɑt〕〔du〕〔ju〕〔du〕

Whadaya do?【快速發音】
〔hwɑdəjə〕　〔du〕

8. *Been here long?*

這句話源自：Have you been here long?（你在這裡很久了嗎？）其實是在問「你來這裡多久了？」（= *How long have you been here?*）通常不用 Yes 或 No 回答，而是直接講時間。

類似的說法還有：

How long have you been living here?
（你住在這裡多久了？）
How long have you been in Taiwan?
（你來台灣多久了？）
How long have you been working here?
（你在這裡工作多久了？）
How long have you been studying here?
（你在這裡唸書多久了？）

【對話練習】

1. A : **My name is Pat.**

 B : Nice to meet you, Pat.
 I like your name.
 It's easy to remember.

A：我的名字是派特。

B：很高興認識你，派特。
 我喜歡你的名字。
 很容易記。

2. A : **It's nice to meet you.**

 B : It's nice to meet you, too.
 Have we met before?
 May I ask your name?

A：很高興認識你。

B：我也很高興認識你。
 我們以前見過嗎？
 請問你叫什麼名字？

3. A : **How do you do?**

 B : Hello.
 How do you do?
 Nice to meet you.

A：你好。

B：哈囉。
 你好嗎？
 很高興認識你。

4. A : **I'm from Taiwan.**

 B : Really, how interesting!
 I've heard a lot about
 Taiwan.
 I want to visit there
 someday.

A：我是台灣人。

B：真的，好有趣！
 我聽說過很多有關台灣
 的事。
 我將來有一天想去那裡
 遊覽。

5. A : **I'm a student.**

 B : Good for you.
 What do you study?
 What is your major?
 【major（ˋmedʒɚ）*n.* 主修科目】

A：我是個學生。

B：太好了。
 你唸什麼？
 你主修什麼？

BOOK 5

6. A：**How about you?**

   B：I'm a graduate student.
      I'm a research assistant.
      I also teach part-time.

    【graduate (ˈgrædʒʊɪt) *adj.* 研究所的
     assistant (əˈsɪstənt) *n.* 助理
     part-time (ˈpɑrtˈtaɪm) *adv.* 兼差地】

A：你呢？

B：我是研究所學生。
  我是研究助理。
  我有時也兼課。

7. A：**Where are you from?**

   B：I'm from New York State.
      I'm not from the city.
      I grew up in a nice small
      town.

    【nice〔naɪs〕*adj.* 好的；可愛的】

A：你是哪裡人？

B：我是紐約州的人。
  我不是都市人。
  我是在一個可愛的小
  鎮長大。

8. A：**What do you do?**

   B：I'm a student now.
      I'll be a professor soon.
      I plan to teach English
      literature.

    【professor〔prəˈfɛsɚ〕*n.* 教授
     literature (ˈlɪtərətʃɚ) *n.* 文學】

A：你從事什麼行業？

B：我現在是學生。
  我很快就要當教授了。
  我打算教英國文學。

9. A：**Been here long?**

   B：I've been here six years.
      It's hard to believe it.
      The time has really flown by.

    【*fly by*（時光）飛逝】

A：你在這裡很久了嗎？

B：我在這裡六年了。
  很難相信。
  時間真的過得很快。

BOOK 5

3. When are you free?

When are you free?	你什麼時候有空？
What's a good time?	什麼時候好呢？
When do you want to get together?	你要什麼時候碰面呢？
Anytime is OK.	任何時間都可以。
Just let me know.	只要告訴我就好了。
I'll be there for sure.	我一定會到。
Where shall we meet?	我們在哪裡見面好呢？
Where's a good place?	什麼地方好呢？
I don't want to miss you.	我不想遇不到你。

BOOK 5

** ―――――――――――――――――

free〔fri〕*adj.* 有空的　　*get together* 聚會
let sb. know 告訴某人　　*for sure* 一定
miss〔mɪs〕*v.* 錯過；沒找到；沒遇到

【背景説明】

　　想邀請朋友見面,該怎麼説才是最體貼的呢?
説得好、説得誠懇,就不會被拒絕。

1. **When are you free?**

　　這句話的意思是「你什麼時候有空?」,這種説法
很多:

When are you free?
When are you available? (你什麼時候有空?)
　　　　　　〔ə'veləbḷ〕 *adj.* 有空的
When are you off? (你什麼時候有空?)
　　　　　　〔ɔf〕 *adj.* 空閒的

When can you get out? (你什麼時候可以外出?)
When can you get away?
(你什麼時候可以離開?)
When do you have free time?
(你什麼時候有空?)

2. **What's a good time?**

　　這句話是 What's a good time for us? 的省略,
意思是「什麼時候好呢?」,也可説成:What's a
good time to meet? (什麼時候見面好呢?),或
What's a good time to get together? (什麼時候
見面好呢?),或 What's a convenient time?
(什麼時間方便呢?)。

3. *When do you want to get together?*

　　這句話的口語寫法是：When do you wanna
get together? 要注意，want to 要快速唸成
wanna〔ˈwɑnə〕。

【比較】　When shall we meet?【語氣較正式】
　　　　（我們什麼時候見面好呢？）
　　　When do you want to get together?
　　　　（你要什麼時候見面呢？）【語氣較輕鬆】

4. *Anytime is OK.*

　　這句話的意思是「任何時間都可以。」，也可加
強語氣說成：Anytime is OK with me.（我任何
時間都可以。）OK = O.K.（兩種寫法都可以）

　　Anytime is OK.
　= Anytime is O.K.
　　【O.K. 後面如果是句點，就不須再點一點了。】

5. *Just let me know.*
let sb. know　通知某人；告訴某人

　　這句話的意思是「只要告訴我就好了。」也可
說成：Just tell me. 或 Just tell me when. 或 Just
tell me when you want to meet.

BOOK 5

6. *I'll be there for sure.*

sure〔ʃʊr〕*adj.* 確定的　　*for sure* 一定；確實地

> 　　這句話意思是「我一定會在那裡。」。有些特殊的成語，是由「介詞＋形容詞」所組成的，像：
> at large（逍遙法外），in general（一般說來），
> in short（簡言之），in particular（特別地），
> for good（永遠地），of late（最近），in vain
> （徒勞無功），before long（不久）等。
>
> 　　在成語字典上，for sure 等於 for certain，
> 但是，美國人很少用 for certain，可能是因為
> for sure 比較簡單，美國人的語言崇尚簡單。

I'll be there for sure.

= I'm sure I'll be there.

（我確定我會在那裡。）

= I'll be there no matter what.

（無論如何我會在那裡。）

【比較】 *I'll be there for sure.*【最常用】
I'm sure I'll be there.【常用】
I'm certain I'll be there.【少用】
I'll be there for certain.【很少用】

7. *Where shall we meet?*

　　這句話的意思是「我們在哪裡見面好呢？」，shall 用
於第一人稱和第三人稱疑問句，表示詢問對方的意見，
通常作「好不好；要不要；好呢」解。（詳見「文法寶典」p.310）

【比較1】 ***Where shall we meet?***【常用，徵求對方的意見】
Where ***will*** we meet? (我們將在哪裡見面？)
【這句話表單純未來，如旅行團團員問導遊，
或學生問老師「我們要在哪裡集合？」。】

【比較2】 See you tomorrow. When ***shall*** we
meet?【徵求對方意見】
(明天見。我們什麼時候見面好呢？)
When ***will*** we have the class trip?
(我們什麼時候將辦全班旅行呢？)【表單純未來】

【比較3】 Where ***shall*** we put our bags?【徵求對方意見】
(我們的行李放在哪裡好呢？)
When ***will*** we receive our uniforms?
(我們什麼時候可以收到我們的制服呢？)
【表單純未來】【uniform〔ˈjunəˌfɔrm〕*n.* 制服】

 * will 在代名詞做主詞的疑問句中，可表示單純未
來或意志未來，要看上下文而定。shall 用於徵求
對方的意見，所以聽起來比較客氣。

BOOK 5

8. ***Where's a good place?***

這句話的意思是「什麼地方好？」也可加強語氣說
成：Where's a good place ***to meet***? (在哪裡見面好？)

9. ***I don't want to miss you.***
miss〔mɪs〕*v.* 錯過；想念；沒找到；沒遇到

這句話是雙關語，在這裡作「我不想遇不到你」解。
另外一個意思是「我不想去想念你。」

【對話練習】

1. A：**When are you free?**
   B：I'm free on Saturday.
   　 I have nothing planned.
   　 My schedule is open all day.

A：你什麼時候有空？
B：我星期六有空。
　 我沒有計畫。
　 我整天都有空。

2. A：**What's a good time?**
   B：After lunch is best.
   　 The afternoon is more
   　 convenient.
   　 Two o'clock is a good time
   　 for me.

A：什麼時候好呢？
B：午餐後最好。
　 下午比較方便。

　 我覺得兩點鐘可以。

3. A：**When do you want to get
   together?**
   B：Let's get together tonight.
   　 Can you make it tonight?
   　 Can we get together tonight
   　 at seven?

A：你要什麼時候碰面呢？

B：我們今晚碰面好了。
　 你今晚可以嗎？
　 我們今晚七點碰面好嗎？

4. A：**Anytime is OK.**
   B：That's great!
   　 That makes it easy.
   　 Thanks for being so flexible.

A：任何時間都可以。
B：太好了！
　 那樣就簡單了。
　 謝謝你時間這麼彈性。

5. A：**Just let me know**.

　　B：I know right now.

　　　　I can tell you this minute.

　　　　We'll meet at seven

　　　　tomorrow.

A：只要告訴我就好了。

B：我現在就想到了。

　　我立刻就可以告訴你。

　　我們明天七點見面。

6. A：**I'll be there for sure**.

　　B：I have no doubt.

　　　　I know you'll be there.

　　　　I can always count on you.

A：我一定會到。

B：我毫不懷疑。

　　我知道你會到。

　　我總是能夠信任你。

7. A：**Where shall we meet?**

　　B：Let's meet at the restaurant.

　　　　That will be easier for both

　　　　of us.

　　　　I'll wait for you there.

A：我們在哪裡見面好呢？

B：我們在餐廳碰面吧。

　　那對我們兩個來說會比較方

　　便。

　　我會在那裡等你。

8. A：**Where's a good place?**

　　B：Let's meet out front.

　　　　Let's meet at the entrance.

　　　　I'll be waiting right next to

　　　　the door.

A：什麼地方好呢？

B：我們在大門口見。

　　我們在入口見。

　　我就在大門口旁邊等你。

9. A：**I don't want to miss you**.

　　B：Don't worry, you won't.

　　　　I know where to meet.

　　　　I don't want to miss you,

　　　　either.

A：我不想遇不到你。

B：別擔心，不會的。

　　我知道在哪兒見面。

　　我也不想遇不到你。

BOOK 5

4. *Let's go see a movie.*

I got a great idea.	我有一個很棒的點子。
Let's go out tonight.	我們今晚出去吧。
Let's go see a movie.	我們去看電影吧。
It's been a long time.	已經好久了。
We need to relax.	我們需要放鬆一下。
We need to do something new.	我們需要做一些新的事情。
What do you say?	你覺得怎麼樣？
How do you feel?	你覺得怎麼樣？
How does a movie sound?	看電影怎麼樣？

BOOK 5

** ————————————

I got 我有　　great〔gret〕*adj.* 很棒的

idea〔aɪˈdiə〕*n.* 主意；點子

relax〔rɪˈlæks〕*v.* 放鬆　　sound〔saʊnd〕*v.* 聽起來

【背景説明】

　　　想要邀請朋友去看電影，英文該怎麼説才好？
背完這九句話之後，你就很會説了。

1. ***I got a great idea.***
　　great〔gret〕*adj.* 很棒的
　　idea〔aɪ'diə,-'dɪə〕*n.* 主意；點子；想法；意見

> 　　這句話非正式的寫法是：***I gotta great idea.***
> got 和 a 連音，唸成 gotta〔'gɑtə〕。一般人只會
> 説，I *have* a great idea. 但是如果你會説：***I got***
> a great idea. 你説的話就更像美國人了。

　　　這句話的意思是「我有一個很棒的點子。」也可
説成：I've got a great idea.

　　【比較】　***I got a great idea.*** 【常用，語氣輕鬆】
　　　　　　　I've got a great idea. 【常用，一般語氣】
　　　　　　　I *have* a great idea. 【常用，較正式】

I got a great idea. 中的 a great，可改成其他的字：

　　I got ***a great*** idea.（我有一個很棒的點子。）
　　I got ***a good*** idea.（我有一個好點子。）
　　I got ***a fun*** idea.（我有一個有趣的點子。）

　　I got ***a wonderful*** idea.（我有一個很棒的點子。）
　　I got ***an exciting*** idea.（我有一個好玩的點子。）
　　I got ***an interesting*** idea.（我有一個有趣的點子。）

2. ***Let's go out tonight.***

　　　這句話的意思是「我們今晚出去吧。」也有美國人說：Let's go out and have some fun.（我們出去玩吧。）凡是你要邀請別人出去的時候，你都可以說這兩句話。

3. ***Let's go see a movie.***
（我們去看電影吧。）

　　去看電影的說法太多了。

【比較1】

Let's go see a movie. 【常用】
Let's see a movie. 【常用】
Let's go to the movies.
　　【常用，movies 是「電影院」，因為電影院多集中在一起，所以用複數。】

【比較2】

Let's go see a movie. 【最常用】
Let's go and see a movie. 【正，常用】
Let's go to see a movie. 【正，常用】
　　【這種用法和 Let's go eat. 不同。詳見 p.51】

4. ***It's been a long time.***

　　　這句話的意思是「已經好久了。」源自：***It's been a long time*** *since we've done something.* 也可說成：We haven't done anything for a long time.
（我們很久沒在一起做什麼事了。）

【例1】　A: I haven't seen you in months.

（我好幾個月沒見到你了。）

B: You're right. *It's been a long time*.

（沒錯。已經好久了。）

【例2】　A: *It's been a long time*. Where have
you been?（已經很久了。你到哪裡去了？）

B: I've been busy with a new job.

（我一直忙著新工作。）

5. *We need to relax.*

relax〔rɪˈlæks〕*v.* 放鬆

We need to relax.

這句話的意思是「我們
需要放鬆一下。」等於 We
need to take it easy.（我
們需要放輕鬆一下。）

【詳見 p.89】

6. *We need to do something new*.

這句話的意思是「我們需要做一些新的事情。」等
於 We need a change.（我們需要改變。）也可說成：
We need to do something different.（我們需要做一
些不同的事情。）也有美國人說：We need to do
something exciting.（我們需要做一些好玩的事。）

美國人的文化，是喜歡創新，他們喜歡新東西、
新事物，他們常說：Let's try new things.（我們嘗
試一點新鮮的事情吧。）

7. ***What do you say?***

say〔se〕v. 說；表達意見

　　這句話字面的意思是「你說什麼？」引申為「你覺得怎麼樣？」你也可以連問三句：

　　　What do you say? (你覺得怎麼樣？)
　　　What do you think? (你認為怎麼樣？)
　　　What's your opinion? (你的意見如何？)

8. ***How do you feel?***

　　這句話的意思是「你覺得怎麼樣？」也可說成：
How do you feel about that? 或 How about that?
that 是指 that idea (那個點子) 或 that suggestion
(那個建議)。

9. ***How does a movie sound?***

sound〔saʊnd〕v. 聽起來

　　這句話的字面意思是「電影聽起來如何？」引申為「看電影怎麼樣？」這句話也可以加強語氣說成：
How does a movie sound to you? (你覺得看電影怎麼樣？) 源自 ***How does** the idea of seeing **a movie sound** to you?* (看電影這個點子你覺得如何？)

sound 作「聽起來」解，常用於徵詢對方意見。

　　【例】　How does a walk to the park sound?
　　　　　　(散步到公園如何？)

【對話練習】

1. A：**I got a great idea**.
   B：Please tell me.
   　　What's your idea?
   　　I would really like to know.

A：我有一個很棒的點子。
B：請告訴我。
　　你有什麼點子？
　　我真的很想知道。

2. A：**Let's go out tonight**.
   B：I'd love to go out.
   　　Thank you for asking me.
   　　I accept your invitation.

A：我們今晚出去吧。
B：我想出去。
　　謝謝你邀請我。
　　我接受你的邀請。

3. A：**Let's go see a movie**.
   B：That's a wonderful idea.
   　　That sounds perfect.
   　　I really love to see movies.

A：我們去看電影吧。
B：這個點子真棒。
　　聽起來太完美了。
　　我真的很想看電影。

4. A：**It's been a long time**.
   B：It really has been a long time.
   　　It's been many months.
   　　I haven't seen a movie in
   　　ages. 【*in ages* 很久】

A：已經好久了。
B：真的很久了。
　　已經好幾個月了。
　　我很久沒看電影了。

5. A：**We need to relax**.
   B：You're so right.
   　　I totally agree.
   　　I couldn't agree with you more.

A：我們需要放鬆一下。
B：你說得很對。
　　我完全同意。
　　我非常同意。

　　【此句是慣用句，字面的意思是「我沒辦法更同意你了。」】

6. A：**We need to do something new**.

　B：We sure do.
　　We need to do new things.
　　I don't want to be bored.

A：我們需要做一些新的事情。

B：我們當然需要。
　我們需要做新的事情。
　我不想覺得無聊。

7. A：**What do you say?**

　B：I say "Let's go!"
　　Let's hit the movies.
　　Let's go see a show.

　　【*hit the movies* 去看電影】

A：你覺得怎麼樣？

B：我說「走吧！」
　我們去看電影吧。
　我們去看電影吧。

8. A：**How do you feel?**

　B：I think it's a great idea.
　　I'm excited.
　　I think it'll be fun.

A：你覺得怎麼樣？

B：我覺得這個主意很棒。
　我很興奮。
　我想一定很好玩。

9. A：**How does a movie sound?**

　B：A movie sounds great
　　to me.
　　It's a wonderful idea.
　　I'm so glad you thought
　　of it.

A：看電影怎麼樣？

B：看電影聽起來不錯。

　這個點子真棒。
　我很高興你想到這個點子。

5. What's playing?

What's playing?	在上演什麼電影？
What's showing?	在上演什麼電影？
Anything really good?	有什麼真的好看的電影？
What choices do we have?	我們有什麼可以選？
What do you want to see?	你想看什麼電影？
What times are the shows?	電影什麼時候開演？
You choose the movie.	你來選擇電影。
I'll let you decide.	我讓你決定。
I'm game for anything.	我什麼都願意。

BOOK 5

** ————————————

play〔ple〕*v.*（戲、電影等）上演；上映

show〔ʃo〕*v.*（電影）上映；（戲劇）演出　*n.* 戲；電影

choice〔tʃɔɪs〕*n.* 選擇　　time〔taɪm〕*n.* 時刻

choose〔tʃuz〕*v.* 選擇　　decide〔dɪ'saɪd〕*v.* 決定

game〔gem〕*adj.* 願意的

【背景說明】

　　　看電影是大多數人的娛樂。和朋友商量看什麼電影，該說些什麼呢？背了這一回以後，你就有話可說了。

1. ***What's playing?***
   play〔ple〕v. (戲、電影等) 上演；上映

> 　　這句話源自：What's playing at the theater? 字面的意思是「電影院正在上演什麼？」就像我們中文所說的「在上演什麼電影？」
> 【theater〔'θiətə〕n. 戲院；電影院】

What's playing?

這種說法還有很多：

　　What shows are playing?【較常用】
　　　（在上演什麼戲；在上演什麼電影？）
　　What movies are playing?【常用】
　　　（上演什麼電影？）
　　What's on? (在上演什麼電影？)【最常用】
　　【源自 *What's on the screen?* (這句話美國人不說)】
　　【show〔ʃo〕n. 戲；電影　screen〔skrin〕n. 銀幕】

　【比較】　What's on?【最常用】
　　　　　　= What's on at the movies?【較常用】
　　　　　　= What's on at the cinema?【常用】

2. ***What's showing?***

　　show〔ʃo〕*v.*（電影）上映；（戲劇）演出

　　　　這句話源自 What's showing at the theater?

　　字面的意思有兩個：①電影院正在上演什麼電影？

　　②戲院正在演什麼戲？在

　　這一回裡的意思是「上演

　　什麼電影？」

　　其他的說法有：

　　　　What's showing at the cinema?【常用】
　　　　　　　　　　　〔'sɪnəmə〕*n.* 電影院

　　= What's showing tonight at the movies?【最常用】

　　= What movies are showing at the theater?

　　（電影院在上演什麼電影？）【較常用】

　　【cinema = movies = theater = movie theater】

3. ***Anything really good?***

　　　　這句話源自：Is there ***anything really good?***

　　字面的意思是：「有什麼真的好的東西？」在這裡的

　　意思是：「有什麼真的好看的電影？」

【舉一反三】

　　中文：有什麼真的好吃的？

　　英文：Anything really good ***to eat?***

　　中文：有什麼真的好看的？

　　英文：Anything really good ***to see?***

　　中文：有什麼真的好的事情可以做的？

　　可以說：Anything really good ***to do?***

4. ***What choices do we have?***
choice〔tʃɔɪs〕*n.* 選擇

　　這句話字面的意思是「我們有什麼選擇？」引申
爲「我們有什麼可以選？」這是美國人的思想，因爲
他們喜歡自由、喜歡選擇，這和中國人的文化不同，
不背就不會説。

　　這句話源自：What choices do we have to
select from?（我們有什麼可以選？）也可説成：
What options do we have?（我們有什麼選擇？）
【select〔sə'lɛkt〕*v.* 選擇　options〔'ɑpʃənz〕*n.pl.* 選擇】

其他説法有：

What are the choices?（我們有什麼選擇？）
(= *What are our choices?*)
What are the options?（我們有什麼選擇？）
(= *What are our options?*)

5. ***What do you want to see?***

　　這句話的字面的意思是「你想要看什麼？」在
這裡的意思是「你想看什麼電影？」美國人也常説：

What looks good?（哪部電影看起來好？）【最常用】
(= *What movie looks good?*)
What kind of movies do you like?【常用】
（你喜歡看哪一類的電影？）
What do you feel like watching?【較常用】
（你想看什麼電影？）

6. *What times are the shows?*

　　time〔taɪm〕*n.* 時間；時刻（表）

　　show〔ʃo〕*n.* 戲；電影

　　　　這句話源自：What times are the shows at?
意思是「各個電影的上演時間是什麼？」也就是「電影什麼時候上演？」

　　　　times 用複數，是表示各個電影的上映時刻。
What times are the shows? 也可說成 When are the shows?

　　【比較】　*What times are the shows?*【最常用】
　　　　　　What times are the shows at?【常用】
　　　　　　At what times are the shows?【少用】
　　　　　　【「介系詞＋時間名詞」所形成的副詞片語，
　　　　　　介系詞常省略。（詳見「文法寶典」p.546）】

7. *You choose the movie.*

　　choose〔tʃuz〕*v.* 選擇

　　　　這句話的意思是「你來選擇電影。」也可以只
說：You choose.（你選擇。）或 You decide.（你決定。）美國人也常說：

　　　　You pick the show.（你來選擇電影。）
　　　　You decide on the movie.
　　　　（你來選擇電影。）【*decide on* 選擇（＝*choose*）】
　　　　You select the movie.（你來選擇電影。）

BOOK 5

8. *I'll let you decide*.

這句話的意思是「我讓你決定。」這是很體貼的
話。這種說法很多：

I'll let you decide. (我讓你決定。)【最常用】
I'll let you choose. (我讓你選擇。)【最常用】
I'll let you select. (我讓你選擇。)【常用】
【select〔sə'lɛkt〕v. 選擇】

I'll let you pick. (我讓你挑選。)【最常用】
I'll let you make the decision. 【常用】
(我讓你做決定。)【pick〔pɪk〕v. 挑選】

9. *I'm game for anything*. (我什麼都願意。)
game〔gem〕n. 遊戲；比賽 v. 賭博
adj. 願意的 (= *willing*)；勇敢的 (= *brave*)

game 的主要意思是「遊戲；比賽」，比賽往往是
一種賭博，所以，game 當動詞用的時候，有「賭博」
的意思。要賭博，就要「有勇氣」、要「勇敢」，要
「願意」，所以 game 當形容詞的時候，有「願意的」、
「心甘情願的」、「勇敢的」等意思。

【例1】 She is *game* for any risk.
(她敢冒任何風險。)

【例2】 I'm *game* to do anything no matter
how dangerous it is.
(我願意做任何事，不管有多危險。)

BOOK 5

　　由於 game 的主要意思是「遊戲」，所以也會有輕鬆、幽默的語氣。

【例1】

　　Is anybody *game* for pizza?

　　(= *Is anybody willing to eat pizza?*)

　　（有沒有人願意吃披薩？）

【例2】

　　I'm *game* to give it a try.

　　（我願意試一試。）

【例3】

　　A: Let's ask those girls to dance.

　　　　（我們去邀請那些女孩跳舞吧。）

　　B: I'm *game* if you are.

　　　　（如果你願意，我也願意。）

【例4】

　　A: How about a game of chess?

　　　　（下盤棋如何？）

　　　　【chess〔tʃɛs〕*n.* 西洋棋】

　　B: I'm *game* anytime, anyplace.

　　　　（任何時間、地點我都行。）

BOOK 5

【對話練習】

1. A：**What's playing?**

   B：There's a lot playing.
   They have a lot of choices.
   They have seven movies
   showing.

   A：在上演什麼電影？

   B：有很多電影在上演。
   他們提供很多選擇。
   他們有七部電影在上演。

2. A：**What's showing?**

   B：There are three action movies.
   There is one horror movie.
   There is also a martial arts
   movie.【horror (ˈhɑrə) n. 恐怖
   martial arts 武術】

   A：上演什麼電影？

   B：有三部動作片。
   一部恐怖片。
   還有一部武俠片。

3. A：**Anything really good?**

   B：There is one great movie.
   It stars Jackie Chan.
   He plays a policeman in
   America.【stars (stɑrz) v. 由～主演】

   A：有什麼真的好看的電影？

   B：有一部很棒的電影。
   是由成龍主演的。
   他演一位美國的警察。

4. A：**What choices do we have?**

   B：We have lots of choices.
   They have a good variety of
   movies.
   The theater has seven different
   shows.
   　【variety (vəˈraɪətɪ) n. 多樣性】

   A：我們有什麼可以選？

   B：我們有很多選擇。
   他們有各種電影。

   那家戲院有七部不同的
   電影。

5. A : **What do you want to see?**

　B : I like serious movies.

　　 I want to see something deep.

　　 I want to be moved and inspired.

　　【serious〔'sɪrɪəs〕*adj.* 嚴肅的

　　　 move〔muv〕*v.* 使感動

　　　 inspire〔ɪn'spaɪr〕*v.* 激勵】

　A：你想看什麼電影？

　B：我喜歡主題嚴肅的電影。

　　　我想看有深度的電影。

　　　我想要被感動，並得到

　　　啓發。

6. A : **What time are the shows?**

　B : There are shows all day.

　　 We should go to a matinee.

　　 It's usually cheaper.

　　【matinee〔,mætn̩'e〕*n.* 白天公演】

　A：電影什麼時候開演？

　B：整天都有。

　　　我們可以去看白天場。

　　　通常會比較便宜。

7. A : **You choose the movie.**

　B : Thanks for the chance.

　　 I appreciate the opportunity.

　　 That makes me feel special.

　A：你來選擇電影。

　B：謝謝你給我這個機會。

　　　我很感激有這個機會。

　　　那讓我覺得很特別。

8. A : **I'll let you decide.**

　B : That's nice of you.

　　 I appreciate the offer.

　　 Let's pick a movie together.

　A：我讓你決定。

　B：你人真好。

　　　謝謝你的提議。

　　　我們一起選一部電影吧。

9. A : **I'm game for anything.**

　B : I feel the same way.

　　 I can watch anything.

　　 I'm game for anything, too.

　A：我什麼都願意。

　B：我有同感。

　　　我看什麼都可以。

　　　我也是什麼都願意。

BOOK 5

6. *Pick a movie.*

Pick a movie.	挑一部電影。
What looks good?	哪部電影看起來好呢？
What are we going to see?	我們要看什麼電影？
I'll wait in line.	我去排隊。
I'll get the tickets.	我去買票。
Why don't you go take a look around?	你何不到處去看看？
See what's going on.	去隨便看看。
See what they have.	看看他們有什麼。
Check out the food court.	看看美食廣場有什麼好吃的。

BOOK 5

**

pick〔pɪk〕v. 挑選　　*wait in line* 排隊
get〔gɛt〕v. 買　　*take a look* 看一看
around〔ə'raʊnd〕adv. 四處
be going on 進行；發生　　*check out* 看看
court〔kort〕n. 庭院

【背景説明】

　　當你和你的朋友，到了電影院門口，在買票前，你和你的朋友要説些什麼話呢？這一回內容相當精彩。

1. *Pick a movie.*
   pick〔 pɪk 〕*v.* 挑選

　　pick 有很多意思，主要意思是「撿（起）」，這句話字面的意思是「撿一部電影。」引申為「挑選一部電影。」這句話有幽默、輕鬆的語氣。

「選一部電影」的説法還有：

　　Select a movie. (選一部電影。)
　　〔 sə'lɛkt 〕*v.* 挑選
　　Choose a movie. (選擇一部電影。)
　　Decide on a movie. (選一部電影。)
　　【*decide on* 決定；選定】

2. *What looks good?*

　　這句話字面的意思是「什麼看起來好？」在這裡引申為「哪部電影看起來好呢？」，等於 What movie looks good?，這句話也可加強語氣説成：What looks good to you? (你覺得哪部電影看起來好呢？)

BOOK 5

美國人也常説：

What do you like?（你喜歡什麼？）
What movie do you like?（你喜歡什麼電影？）

Which one looks good?（哪部電影看起來好呢？）
Which movie looks good?（哪部電影看起來好呢？）
Which movie looks the best?
（哪部電影看起來最好？）

3. ***What are we going to see?***

這句話的意思是「我們要看什麼？」也可説成：
What movie are we going to see?（我們要看什麼電影？）

你也可以問身旁的人：

What do you want to see?（你想看什麼？）
What movie do you want to see?
（你想看什麼電影？）

4. ***I'll wait in line.***
in line 排成一排
wait in line 排隊

中國人説：「我去排隊。」排隊的「排」有「等待」的意味，所以英文説成：***I'll wait in line.*** 美國人也常説：I'll wait.（我去排隊。），Let me wait.（讓我去排隊。）或 I'll wait for the tickets.（我去排隊買票。）這些話中的 wait，都是由 wait in line 簡化而來，這又是一個美國人説話説一半的例子。

當你在排隊時，如果有人插隊，你就可以說：

Don't cut. (不要插隊。) (= *Don't cut in line.*)

Please wait in line. (請排隊。)

Excuse me, the line is here.

這句話字面意思是「對不起，隊伍在這裡。」，引申爲「對不起，請你排隊。」

事實上，美國人非常守規矩，不管在什麼地方都會排隊，你想排隊的時候，你可以說：*Are you waiting in line?* (你在排隊嗎？)

5. *I'll get the tickets*.

get ﹝ gɛt ﹞ *v.* 買

get 主要意思是「得到」，這裡當「購買」解，這句話意思是「我來買票。」也可說成：Let me get the tickets. (讓我來買票。)

【比較】 *I'll get the tickets*. 【最常用】

I'll buy the tickets. 【常用】

(我去買票。)

I got the tickets. 【常用，語氣較堅定】

(我去買票。)

6. *Why don't you go take a look around?*

take a look 看一看　　around ﹝ ə'raʊnd ﹞ *adv.* 到處；四處

這句話的意思是「你何不到處去看看？」就像我們中國人所說的「你到處去看看吧。」

BOOK 5

「Why don't you + 原形動詞？」表「建議」。這和中國人的思想不同。

【例1】 ***Why don't you*** sit down for a while?

> *Why don't you sit down for a while?*

美國人思想：你為什麼不坐一下？
中國人思想：你坐一下吧！

【例2】 ***Why don't you*** join us for lunch?

美國人思想：你為什麼不跟我們一起吃午餐？
中國人思想：跟我們一起吃午餐吧！

【例3】 ***Why don't you*** give her a call?

美國人思想：你為什麼不打個電話給她？
中國人思想：打個電話給她吧！

所以，以後，凡是建議別人做什麼，就應該用 **"*Why don't you~?*"**，說話才像美國人。

【比較1】

Why don't you go take a look around? 【最常用】
Why don't you go and take a look around? 【常用】
Why don't you go to take a look around? 【較少用】

【比較2】

Why don't you go take a look around?
（你去四處看看吧。）【表建議，較客氣】
You go take a look around.
（你去四處看看。）【表命令，較不客氣】

BOOK 5

【比較 3 】

Why don't you go take a look around?

（你去四處看看吧。）

【用 go take a look around 強調「離開我去四處看看」。】

Why don't you take a look around?

（你四處看看吧。）

7. *See what's going on.*

這句話字面的意思是「看看發生什麼事。」含有「去看看有沒有什麼好玩的東西、有趣的事情」等意思，相當於中文所説的「去隨便看看。」

See what's going on.（去隨便看看。）
= See what's happening.
= See what's up.

What's up? What's happening? What's going on? 是美國人打招呼的口頭禪，詳見 p.6。

8. *See what they have.*

這句話的意思是「看看他們有什麼。」源自 See what they have *to eat*.（看看他們有什麼東西可以吃的。）或 See what they have *to buy*.（看他們有什麼東西可以買的。）

美國人説話喜歡簡單，就把 See what they have 後面的 to eat，to buy，to drink，to offer 等要説的話，放在心裡不説。

【文法分析】

See what they have.

= See what they have to buy.

= See anything that they have to buy.

中文也是一樣啊！我們可以説：「看看他們有什麼。」，也可以説：「看他們有什麼可以買的。」等。

9. **Check out the food court.**

court〔kort〕*n.* 庭院

這句話的意思是「看看美食廣場有什麼好吃的。」，在美國的 mall（購物中心）裡面，往往都有一兩層全部賣吃的，稱做 food court，就像我們百貨公司裡的「美食廣場」，food court 字面意思是「食物的庭院」，中國人和外國人，都會爲「餐飲區」取那麼好聽的名字。

在 mall 裡面的電影院，才有 food court，一般電影院附設有小吃店（snack bar）或販賣部（concession）。進了電影院，尚未入場，要請朋友去買爆米花，就可説：

Please get me a popcorn at the concession.
　　　　　　　　　〔'pɑp,kɔrn〕*n.*　　〔kən'sɛʃən〕*n.*
　　　　　　　　　爆米花　　　　　　　販賣部

（請幫我到販賣部買一份爆米花。）

【對話練習】

1. A：**Pick a movie**.

   B：Thanks for the choice.
   Let's choose together.
   That's the best way to
   decide.

2. A：**What looks good?**

   B：The new sci-fi picture
   looks good.
   Or maybe the Jackie Chan
   movie.
   Anything is fine with me.

   【sci-fi (ˈsaɪˈfaɪ) *n.* 科幻小說】

3. A：**What are we going to see?**

   B：Let's watch Titanic.
   The actors are excellent.
   I heard it's a great movie.

   【Titanic (taɪˈtænɪk) *n.* 鐵達尼號】

4. A：**I'll wait in line**.

   B：Let's wait together.
   I'll wait with you.
   I can keep you company.

   【*keep sb. company* 陪伴某人】

A：挑一部電影。

B：謝謝你讓我選。
我們一起選吧。
那是決定看哪部片最好
的方法。

A：哪部電影看起來好呢？

B：那部新的科幻片看起來
不錯。
也許可以看看成龍的電
影。
我什麼電影都可以。

A：我們要看什麼電影呢？

B：我們看「鐵達尼號」吧。
演員很棒。
聽說是一部很棒的電影。

A：我去排隊。

B：我們一起排吧。
我和你一起排。
我可以陪你。

BOOK 5

5. A：**I'll get the tickets.**

　　B：Let's both get the tickets.
　　　I want to pay my share.
　　　I don't want you to pay.
　　　【share〔ʃɛr〕n.（費用的）分攤；部份】

A：我去買票。

B：我們倆一起去買票。
　　我的部份我要自己付。
　　我不想要你出錢。

6. A：**Why don't you go take a look around?**

　　B：I can't leave you.
　　　We came together.
　　　We can look around together.

A：你何不到處去看看？

B：我不能離開你。
　　我們一起來的。
　　我們可以一起到處去看看。

7. A：**See what's going on.**

　　B：Everything looks good.
　　　I love to look around.
　　　It all looks great to me.

A：去隨便看看。

B：每樣東西看起來都很好。
　　我喜歡到處看看。
　　我覺得一切看起來都很棒。

8. A：**See what they have.**

　　B：It looks like there are lots of
　　　shops.
　　　They sell all kinds of things
　　　here.
　　　There's also a good food court.

A：看看他們有什麼。

B：看起來好像有很多商店。

　　他們這裡什麼東西都賣。

　　也有一個不錯的美食廣場。

9. A：**Check out the food court.**

　　B：That's a great idea.
　　　Let's do it together.
　　　Let's get a bite after we buy
　　　the tickets.
　　　【bite〔baɪt〕n. 食物；小吃】

A：看看美食廣場有什麼好吃的。

B：好主意。
　　我們一起去看看吧。
　　我們買完票去吃點東西吧。

7. *It's my treat.*

It's my treat.	我請客。
It's on me.	我請客。
Let me pay.	讓我付錢。
Be my guest.	我請客。
I'm paying.	我來付錢。
I got it.	我買單。
Don't say a word.	不要爭。
It's my pleasure.	這是我的榮幸。
Next time you can pay.	下次你可以付。

BOOK 5

** ─────────────

treat〔trit〕*n.* 招待;請客

pay〔pe〕*v.* 付錢　　guest〔gɛst〕*n.* 客人

Be my guest. 我請客。

word〔wɜd〕*n.* 話　　pleasure〔'plɛʒə〕*n.* 榮幸

next time 下一次

【背景説明】

　　　請客雖然損失一點錢，卻是一項好的投資。投資錢在人的身上，利息最高。你要請別人吃飯，這九句話就可以用得到。

1. *It's my treat.*

It's my treat.

　　treat〔 trit 〕 *n., v.* 招待；請客

　　　　treat 主要意思是「招待」，這句話字面的意思是「它是我的招待。」引申為「我請客。」，也可簡化成 My treat.（我請客。）

　　　　treat 也可當動詞用，表示「請客」，是及物和不及物兩用動詞：

【比較1】 I'm treating.（我請客。）【treat 做不及物動詞】
　　　　　I'm treating you.（我請你。）
　　　　　　【treat 做及物動詞，語氣稍強】

【比較2】 Let me treat.（讓我請客。）
　　　　　Let me treat you.（讓我請你。）

【比較3】 I want to treat.（我想要請客。）
　　　　　I want to treat you.（我想要請你。）

2. *It's on me.*

　　　　這句話的意思是「我請客。」，it 指「帳單」（= bill；check），如果你看到帳單，你就可以説：The bill is on me. 或 The check is on me.（我來付帳。）on 有很多意思，在這裡作「由～付錢」解。

【例1】　Have another coffee *on me*.
　　　　　（再來一杯咖啡，我請客。）

【例2】　Let's take a cab. *It's on me*.
　　　　　（我們坐計程車吧。我出錢。）

【例3】　Let's get a drink. *It's on me*.
　　　　　（我們去喝點東西。我請客。）
　　　　　【cab〔kæb〕*n.* 計程車　　drink〔drɪŋk〕*n.* 飲料】

3. *Let me pay*.

pay〔pe〕*v.* 付錢

Let me pay.

　　　這句話的意思是「讓我付
錢。」也可說成：Let me pay
the bill. (讓我付帳。)，或
Let me foot the bill. (讓我
付帳。)。bill 可用 check 或 tab 取代，這三個字都可
當「帳單」解。【foot〔fʊt〕*v.* 付(帳)　　tab〔tæb〕*n.* 帳單】

4. *Be my guest*.

guest〔gɛst〕*n.* 客人

　　　這句話的字面意思是「做我的客人。」在這裡引
申為「我請客。」**Be my guest**. 可引申出三個意思：

①　我請客。(= *It's my treat*.)
　　Don't argue with me. *Be my guest*.
　　（別和我爭。我請客。）【argue〔'ɑrgju〕*v.* 爭論】
　　Let's have dinner. *Be my guest*.
　　（我們去吃晚餐。我請客。）
　　Let's see a movie. *Be my guest*.
　　（我們去看電影。我出錢。）

BOOK 5

② 請便。(= *Go ahead*.)

A: Can I use your cell phone?
（我可以借用你的手機嗎？）【*cell phone* 手機】

B: ***Be my guest***. (請便。)

③ 請不要客氣。(= *Make yourself at home*.)

My home is your home. ***Be my guest***.
（我家就是你家。請不要客氣。）

5. *I'm paying*.

這句話字面意思是「我正要付錢。」由於現在進行式可表示「不久的未來」，所以在這裡的意思是「我來付錢。」pay 也可當及物動詞用，所以美國人也常說：I'm paying the bill. (我來付帳。)。也有人說：

I'm paying for it. (我來支付費用。)
【句中的 paying，後面省略了 money (錢)，it 是指費用，pay for~ 在這裡指「支付~的錢」。】

I'm paying. 也可加強語氣說成：

I'm paying for us. (我們的帳我來付。)
I'm paying for you. (你的帳我來付。)

6. *I got it*.

這句話字面的意思是「我拿到了。」可以引申出很多意思，參照 p.40。

在這裡引申為「我買單。」，句中的 it 是指「帳單」。

【比較】 ***I got it***. (我買單。)【用過去式表示已經拿到了，語氣堅定，一定要付，事實上並不一定拿到帳單。】

I'll get it. 【語氣較弱，只是表示願意付錢。】

7. *Don't say a word.*

word〔wɜd〕*n.* 話

這句話美國人常說,但在所有字典上都沒有。
當你想要請客,不想讓對方付錢時,你就可以說:
Don't say a word. 此時的意思是「不要爭。」,
相當於 Don't argue with me.(不要和我爭。)
Don't say a word. 在不同的句中,有不同的意
思,主要意思是「不要說了。」

【例1】　A: Let's all go Dutch.(我們各付各的。)
　　　　B: *Don't say a word.* I'm paying.
　　　　　　(不要爭。我付錢。)【*go Dutch* 各付各的】

【例2】　A: It's dangerous. Don't do it.
　　　　　　(那很危險,別去做。)
　　　　B: *Don't say a word.* I can do it.
　　　　　　(別說了,我做得到。)

8. *It's my pleasure.*

pleasure〔'plɛʒɚ〕*n.* 快樂;榮幸

這句話的意思是「這是我的榮幸。」也可說成:
It's a pleasure. 如果更謙虛一點,就可以說:
It's an honor. 或 It's an honor for me.
　　　〔'ɑnɚ〕*n.* 榮幸;光榮

9. *Next time you can pay.*

next time 下一次

這句話的意思是「下次你可以付。」也可說成:
Next time I'll let you pay.(下一次我會讓你付錢。)

BOOK 5

【對話練習】

1. A : **It's my treat**.

   B : You're too generous!
   You're very kind!
   I won't argue with you!
   【generous〔'dʒɛnərəs〕*adj.* 慷慨的】

   A：我請客。

   B：你太慷慨了！
   你太客氣了！
   我不會和你爭！

2. A : **It's on me**.

   B : Thanks for the offer.
   I can't let you pay.
   I'm treating you this time.
   【offer〔'ɔfɚ〕*n.* 提議】

   A：我請客。

   B：謝謝你的提議。
   我不能讓你付錢。
   這次我請你。

3. A : **Let me pay**.

   B : Sorry, I won't let you
   pay.
   It's not fair.
   Let's just go Dutch.
   【fair〔fɛr〕*adj.* 公平的】

   A：讓我付錢。

   B：對不起，我不會讓你付
   的。
   那樣不公平。
   讓我們各付各的。

4. A : **Be my guest**.

   B : That's very generous of you.
   But I can't let you do that.
   Let's just split the cost.
   【split〔splɪt〕*v.* 分攤】

   A：我請客。

   B：你真慷慨。
   但是我不能讓你請。
   我們分攤費用吧。

5. A：**I'm paying**.

   B：I can't allow that.

   　　Let's both pay.

   　　Let's share the cost.

   　　【share〔ʃɛr〕*v.* 分攤】

A：我來付錢。

B：我不能讓你那樣做。

　　我們兩個一起付吧。

　　我們一起分攤費用吧。

6. A：**I got it**.

   B：No, I got the check.

   　　This time it's mine.

   　　Next time I'll let you pay.

A：我買單。

B：不，我買單。

　　這次我付帳。

　　下次我會讓你付。

7. A：**Don't say a word**.

   B：I can't keep quiet.

   　　You're a good friend.

   　　Good friends share everything.

   　　【quiet〔'kwaɪət〕*adj.* 安靜的

   　　　share〔ʃɛr〕*v.* 分享；分擔】

A：不要爭。

B：我不能不跟你爭著付錢。

　　你是我的好朋友。

　　好朋友要分擔一切。

8. A：**It's my pleasure**.

   B：I know you mean it.

   　　You're a true friend.

   　　I just can't let you pay.

A：這是我的榮幸。

B：我知道你是認真的。

　　你真是我的好朋友。

　　我就是不能讓你付。

9. A：**Next time you can pay**.

   B：No, let me pay today.

   　　Next time you can get it.

   　　Don't argue with me.

A：下次你可以付。

B：不，今天讓我付。

　　下次你買單。

　　別和我爭了。

BOOK 5

8. *Where do you want to sit?*

Where do you want to sit?	你想坐在哪裡？
Sit wherever you want.	坐任何你想要坐的地方。
Sit anywhere you like.	坐任何你喜歡坐的地方。
I'm not picky.	我不挑剔。
You call the shots.	由你決定。
Any place is fine with me.	我任何地方都可以。
There's a nice spot.	有一個好地方。
No one will bother us.	沒有人會打擾我們。
We can stay away from the crowd.	我們可以避開人多的地方。

BOOK 5

** ────────────────

picky〔'pɪkɪ〕*adj.* 挑剔的　　shot〔ʃɑt〕*n.* 發射
call the shots 發號施令；做決定
spot〔spɑt〕*n.* 地點；場所；地方
bother〔'bɑðə〕*v.* 打擾　　***stay away from*** 遠離
crowd〔kraʊd〕*n.* 人群

【背景説明】

　　在美國看電影，並沒有對號入座，你和你朋友在一起，該説些什麼話，來選擇位子呢？這九句話可用在很多方面，像餐廳、車站，都可以用。

1. *Where do you want to sit?*

　　這句話的意思是「你想坐在哪裡？」也有美國人説：

　　Where do you feel like sitting?（你想坐在哪裡？）
　　Where shall we sit?（我們該坐在哪裡？）
　　Where should we sit?（我們應該坐在哪裡？）

　　Where is a good place to sit?（坐哪裡好？）
　　Where's a good place to sit?（坐哪裡好？）
　　Where is a nice spot to sit?（坐哪個地方好？）
　　　　　　　　　　　　　　〔 spɑt 〕*n.* 地點；地方

2. *Sit wherever you want.*

　　這句話的意思是「坐任何你想要坐的地方。」也可以説成：Sit wherever you want to.（坐任何你想要坐的地方。）或 Sit wherever you like.（坐任何你喜歡坐的地方。）wherever 可以改成 where。像 Sit where you want.（坐你想坐的地方。）

　　【比較】　Sit wherever.（隨便你坐哪裡。）【常用】
　　　　　　　Sit wherever you want.【最常用】
　　　　　　　Sit wherever you want to.【較常用】

3. *Sit anywhere you like.*
anywhere〔'ɛnɪ,hwɛr〕*adv.* 任何地方

這句話的意思是「坐任何你喜歡坐的地方。」
anywhere 是一個字,不能分成兩個字。

【比較1】 ***Sit anywhere you like.***【正】
Sit *any where* you like.【誤】

【比較2】 anywhere 等於 in any place,或 anyplace。
Sit in any place you like.【正】
Sit *anyplace* you like.【正,較常用】
Sit any place you like.【誤】
　【anyplace 作連接詞,是一個字,不能寫成
　any place,在 The American Heritage
　Dictionary 中有此字。】

4. *I'm not picky.*
picky〔'pɪkɪ〕*adj.* 挑剔的

這句話的意思是「我不挑剔。」picky 這個字,
美國人常説。你看到一個人很挑剔,東挑西揀,你
就可以説:"Don't be so picky." (不要那麼挑剔。)

當別人問你要吃什麼東西的時候,你可以説:

I'm not picky. (我不挑剔。)
I'm easy to please. (我很容易取悦。)
I'm easy to satisfy. (我很容易滿足。)
please〔pliz〕*v.* 取悦
satisfy〔'sætɪs,faɪ〕*v.* 滿意;滿足

5. *You call the shots.*

shot〔ʃɑt〕*n.* 發射

call the shots 發號施令（= *give orders*）；做決定
（= *make the decision*）

> ***You call the shots.*** 源自古時候有錢人，開槍
> 對空打獵，僕人會對主人說：***You call the shots.***
> （你發號施令。）現在常引申為「由你決定。」（= *You*
> *make the decision.*）要注意，shots 一定是複數形。

6. *Any place is fine with me.*

這句話字面的意思是「任何地方對我都可以。」
引申為「我任何地方都可以。」可簡化為：Any place
is fine.（任何地方都可以。）其他説法有：

Any place is OK with me.（任何地方我都可以。）
Any seat is OK with me.（任何位子我都可以。）
Anywhere is fine with me.（任何地方我都可以。）

上面三句的 with me 都可以省略。

7. *There's a nice spot.*

spot〔spɑt〕*n.* 地點；場所；地方

這句話的意思是「有一
個好地方。」也可以加強語
氣説成：There's a nice
spot over there.（那裡有一
個好地方。）也可以説成：

There's a
nice spot.

There's a nice place.（有一個好地方。）
There's a nice area.（有一個好地方。）
There's a nice seat.（有一個好位子。）

BOOK 5

8. *No one will bother us.*

bother〔'bɑðɚ〕 *v.* 打擾

這句話的意思是「沒有人會打擾我們。」也可以加強語氣說成：No one will bother us there.（在那裡沒有人會打擾我們。）

【比較】 ***No one will bother us.***【最常用】
（沒有人會打擾我們。）
No one will disturb us.【較常用】
（沒有人會打擾我們。）
No one will trouble us.【常用】
（沒有人會打擾我們。）
disturb〔dɪ'stɝb〕 *v.* 打擾
trouble〔'trʌbl̩〕 *v.* 麻煩；擾亂

9. *We can stay away from the crowd.*

stay away from 遠離　　crowd〔kraʊd〕 *n.* 人群

這句話的字面意思是「我們可以遠離人群。」也就是「我們可以避開人多的地方。」等於 We can avoid the crowd.【avoid〔ə'vɔɪd〕 *v.* 避開】

【比較】 Let's stay away from the crowd.【最常用】
Let's sit away from the crowd.【較常用】
（我們坐離人多的地方遠一點。）
Let's keep away from the crowd.【常用】
（我們離開人多的地方。）

【對話練習】

1. A：**Where do you want to sit?**
   B：Let's sit over there.
   　　Let's sit in the middle.
   　　It looks like a good spot.

　　A：你想坐在哪裡？
　　B：我們去坐那裡吧。
　　　　我們去坐在中間吧。
　　　　那個位置看起來不錯。

2. A：**Sit wherever you want**.
   B：I'll do that.
   　　I see a good place.
   　　Please follow me.

　　A：坐你想要坐的地方。
　　B：我會的。
　　　　我看到一個好地方。
　　　　請跟我來。

3. A：**Sit anywhere you like**.
   B：Anywhere is OK.
   　　It's all the same to me.
   　　I really don't care where I sit.

　　A：坐任何你喜歡坐的地方。
　　B：任何地方都可以。
　　　　對我而言都一樣。
　　　　我真的不在乎坐哪裡。

4. A：**I'm not picky**.
   B：I know you're not picky.
   　　You're easy to please.
   　　You're an easy-going person.

　　A：我不挑剔。
　　B：我知道你不挑剔。
　　　　你很容易取悅。
　　　　你是個隨和的人。

5. A：**You call the shots**.
   B：I'd rather not.
   　　I'd rather you decide.
   　　Better yet, let's decide
   　　together. 【yet〔jɛt〕*adv.* 甚至】

　　A：由你決定。
　　B：我寧願不要。
　　　　我寧願讓你決定。
　　　　要不，我們一起決定吧。

BOOK 5

6. A : **Any place is fine with me.**　　　A：任何地方我都可以。

　　B : That's how I feel.　　　　　　B：我就是這麼覺得。
　　　　Any seat is fine.　　　　　　　任何位子都可以。
　　　　One place is as good as　　　　每個地方都一樣。
　　　　another.

7. A : **There's a nice spot.**　　　　　A：有一個好地方。

　　B : You're right!　　　　　　　　B：你說得對！
　　　　That's a great spot!　　　　　　那是個好地方！
　　　　Hurry, let's get it!　　　　　　趕快，我們去坐吧！

8. A : **No one will bother us.**　　　　A：沒有人會打擾我們。

　　B : I hope you are right.　　　　　B：我希望你是對的。
　　　　I hope we won't be　　　　　　我希望我們不會被打擾。
　　　　disturbed.
　　　　I like to have it quiet.　　　　　我喜歡安靜一點。

9. A : **We can stay away from**　　　A：我們可以避開人多的地
　　　　the crowd.　　　　　　　　　方。

　　B : Good idea.　　　　　　　　　B：好主意。
　　　　It'll be quieter here.　　　　　　這裡會比較安靜。
　　　　We'll hear the movie　　　　　我們會更清楚地聽到電
　　　　better.　　　　　　　　　　　影的聲音。

BOOK 5

9. Please be quiet.

Please be quiet.	請安靜一點。
Please keep it down.	說話請小聲一點。
Could you lower your voice?	你能不能把聲音降低一點？
You're too loud.	你太大聲了。
You're too noisy.	你太吵了。
You're disturbing everybody.	你打擾到大家了。
Sorry to say that.	很抱歉我那麼說。
I hope you don't mind.	我希望你不要介意。
Please don't take offense.	請不要生氣。

BOOK 5

** ——————————————

quiet〔ˈkwaɪət〕*adj.* 安靜的   lower〔ˈloɚ〕*v.* 降低
voice〔vɔɪs〕*n.* 聲音   loud〔laʊd〕*adj.* 大聲的
noisy〔ˈnɔɪzɪ〕*adj.* 吵鬧的
disturb〔dɪˈstɝb〕*v.* 打擾   mind〔maɪnd〕*v.* 介意
offense〔əˈfɛns〕*n.* 冒犯   *take offense* 生氣

【背景説明】

　　無論在戲院、餐廳、教室，或任何公共場所，看到有人在大聲説話，都可以説這九句美妙的英語，來勸告他們，但語氣一定要柔和，態度一定要謙卑，以免激怒對方。

　　你也可以用這九句話，來提醒身旁的人，説話聲音小一點。

1. *Please be quiet.*
   quiet〔'kwaɪət〕*adj.* 安靜的

Please be quiet.

　　這句話的意思是「請安靜一點。」可簡化成 Quiet, please. (請安靜。)

【比較】 ***Please be quiet***. (請安靜一點。)【最常用】
　　　　Please keep quiet.
　　　　(請保持安靜。)【有人用】
　　　　Please keep it quiet. (請保持安靜。)
　　　　【常用，it 指吵鬧聲 (noise)，或任何其他聲音。 】

2. *Please keep it down.*

　　在這裡的 it 指聲音，這句話字面意思是「請把聲音放低。」，也就是「說話請小聲一點。」和 Please be quiet. 句意相同。

3. *Could you lower your voice?*

lower〔'loɚ〕*v.* 降低　　voice〔vɔɪs〕*n.* 聲音

　　這句話的意思是「你能不能把聲音降低一點？」，
lower 主要是形容詞 low（低的）的比較級，在這裡
是動詞，作「降低」解。

【比較】　Please lower your voice.【最客氣】
　　　　　Could you lower your voice?【很客氣】
　　　　　Can you lower your voice?【客氣】

4. *You're too loud.*

loud〔laʊd〕*adj.* 大聲的

> You're too loud.
> You're too noisy.

　　　這句話的意思是「你太
大聲了。」文法上很難解釋，
人怎麼會「大聲」呢？這句
話是慣用句，也可說成：

Your voice is too loud.（你的聲音太大了。）
You're talking too loud.（你說話太大聲了。）
That's too loud.（太大聲了。）【loud 也可以當副詞用】

5. *You're too noisy.*

noisy〔'nɔɪzɪ〕*adj.* 吵鬧的

　　這句話的意思是「你太吵了。」美國人也常說：
You're making too much noise.（你太吵了。），或
That's too noisy.（太吵了。）【*make noise* 製造噪音】

【比較】　*You're too noisy.*【正，常用】
　　　　　Your voice is too noisy.【誤】
　　　　　Your talking is too noisy.【誤】

BOOK 5

6. *You're disturbing everybody.*
   disturb〔dɪ'stɝb〕v. 打擾

   這句話的意思是「你打擾到大家。」也可説成：
   You're disturbing us. (你打擾到我們。)

   【比較】 *You're disturbing everybody.*【常用】
   　　　　You're bothering everybody.【最常用】
   　　　　【美國人一般最常用 bother〔'baðɚ〕v. 打擾，
   　　　　但用 disturb，顯示説話者受過高等教育】

7. *Sorry to say that.*

   這句話是 I'm sorry to say that. 的省略，意
   思是「很抱歉我那麼說。」凡是責備人以後，立刻
   説：*Sorry to say that.*，有補救作用。

8. *I hope you don't mind.*
   mind〔maɪnd〕v. 介意

   這句話的意思是「我希望你不要介意。」也可
   説成： I hope you don't feel bad.
   　　　　（我希望你不要難過。）
   　　　　I hope I haven't upset you.
   　　　　　　　　　　　〔ʌp'sɛt〕v. 使生氣
   　　　　（我希望我沒有惹你生氣。）
   　　　　I hope I haven't hurt your feelings.
   　　　　（我希望我沒有使你難過。）
   　　　　【*hurt sb's feelings* 傷害某人的感情】

9. ***Please don't take offense.***

offense〔əˋfɛns〕*n.* 攻擊;冒犯
take offense 生氣

Please don't take offense.

　　offense 主要意思是「攻擊;冒犯」,take offense 字面的意思是「接受攻擊或冒犯」,引申爲「生氣」,這句話意思是「請不要生氣。」
叫別人不要生氣的說法還有:

> Don't be mad. (不要生氣。)
> = Don't get mad.
>
> = Don't be angry.
> = Don't get angry.
>
> = Don't be upset.
> = Don't get upset.
> 　　　　　〔ʌpˋsɛt〕*adj.* 生氣的

10. 補充說明

> 　　凡是看到你的朋友,因爲你說的話,而不高興時,就可以立刻說:Sorry to say that. I hope you don't mind. Please don't take offense.
> 記住,凡是你說錯話,或說了不好聽的話,就要說這三句話,及時補救。

BOOK 5

【對話練習】

1. A：**Please be quiet**.

  B：Sorry to disturb you.
  Sorry about the noise.
  I promise to be quiet.

2. A：**Please keep it down**.

  B：Sure.
  Sorry I disturbed you.
  It won't happen again.

3. A：**Could you lower your voice?**

  B：Of course I can.
  I didn't realize I was so loud.
  My apologies.

4. A：**You're too loud**.

  B：Please forgive me.
  I have a loud voice.
  I sometimes forget.

5. A：**You're too noisy**.

  B：It's not me!
  You have the wrong person!
  I'm not making any noise!

A：請安靜一點。

B：抱歉打擾到你。
  我太大聲了，很抱歉。
  我保證會安靜一點。

A：說話請小聲一點。

B：當然好。
  很抱歉打擾到你。
  這種情形不會再發生了。

A：你能不能把聲音降低一點？

B：當然可以。
  我不知道自己這麼大聲。
  我道歉。

A：你太大聲了。

B：請原諒我。
  我的聲音很大。
  我有時候會忘記。

A：你太吵了。

B：不是我！
  你找錯人了！
  我沒有製造任何噪音啊！

6. A：**You're disturbing everybody**.

A：你打擾到大家了。

B：Don't complain to me.
I'm not the only one.
Everyone else is making
noise, too.

B：別跟我抱怨。
又不是只有我一個。
大家也都在製造噪音
啊。

7. A：**Sorry to say that**.

A：很抱歉那麼說。

B：Don't be sorry.
I should thank you.
Thanks for reminding me.

B：不用感到抱歉。
我應該謝謝你的。
謝謝你提醒我。

【remind〔rɪ'maɪnd〕*v.* 提醒】

8. A：**I hope you don't mind**.

A：我希望你不會介意。

B：I don't mind at all.
I'm grateful to you.
You are nice to let me
know.

B：我一點都不介意。
我很感激你。
你人真好，願意告訴
我。

9. A：**Please don't take offense**.

A：請不要生氣。

B：I'm not offended.
I'm not angry at all.
It doesn't upset me one bit.

B：我沒有生氣。
我一點也不生氣。
這完全不會使我生氣。

【offend〔ə'fɛnd〕*v.* 冒犯；使生氣
not…one bit 一點也不
(= *not…a bit* = *not…at all*)】

BOOK 5

10. *I'm sorry.*

I'm sorry.	我很抱歉。
I apologize.	我道歉。
It's my fault.	是我的錯。
I was wrong.	我當時錯了。
You are right.	你是對的。
Please forgive me.	請原諒我。
I didn't mean it.	我不是有意的。
It wasn't on purpose.	那不是故意的。
It won't happen again.	這種事不會再發生了。

BOOK 5

** ——————————

apologize 〔ə'palə‚dʒaɪz〕 v. 道歉

fault 〔fɔlt〕 n. 過錯　　forgive 〔fə'gɪv〕 v. 原諒

mean 〔min〕 v. 有…的意思；本意是

purpose 〔'pɝpəs〕 n. 目的

on purpose 故意地　　happen 〔'hæpən〕 v. 發生

【背景説明】

學會道歉，太重要了。每個人都會説錯話、做
錯事，道歉不花費一毛錢，卻有很大的效果。

1. *I'm sorry.*（我很抱歉。）

I'm sorry.

I'm sorry. 也可只説 Sorry.
（抱歉。）類似的説法很多：

> *I'm sorry.*（我很抱歉。）
>
> I'm so sorry.（我很抱歉。）
>
> I'm very sorry.（我非常抱歉。）
>
> I'm really sorry.（我眞的很抱歉。）
>
> I'm extremely sorry.（我非常抱歉。）
> 〔ɪk'strimlɪ〕*adv.* 極度地；非常
>
> I'm terribly sorry.（我非常抱歉。）
> 〔'tɛrəblɪ〕*adv.* 非常
>
> I'm sorry about that.（那件事我很抱歉。）
>
> I'm sorry about what I did.
> （我對我所做的事，覺得很抱歉。）
>
> I'm sorry about what I said.
> （我對我所說的話，覺得很抱歉。）

BOOK 5

> I'm sorry about everything.
>
> （我對這一切覺得很抱歉。）
>
> I'm sorry about it all.
>
> （我對這一切覺得很抱歉。）
>
> You can't believe how sorry I am.
>
> （你不會相信我有多抱歉。）

上面十二個句子中的 I'm，都可以改成 I feel，也很常用。

如：
> I feel sorry. （我覺得很抱歉。）
>
> I feel so sorry. （我覺得很抱歉。）
>
> I feel very sorry. （我覺得非常抱歉。）

2. *I apologize*.

apologize〔ə'pɑlə،dʒaɪz〕v. 道歉

這句話的意思是「我道歉。」比 I'm sorry. 正式。apologize 的名詞是 apology〔ə'pɑlədʒɪ〕n. 道歉。

【比較】 *I apologize*. （我道歉。）【最常用】

I owe you an apology. 【好的句子】

（我應該向你道歉。）

Please accept my apology. 【常用】

（請接受我的道歉。）

Please accept my apologies. 【少用】

（請接受我的道歉。）

3. *It's my fault.* (是我的錯。)

fault〔 fɔlt 〕 *n.* 過錯

【比較】 My fault. (我的錯。)【輕鬆語氣】

It's my fault. (是我的錯。)【一般語氣】

It's all my fault. (都是我的錯。)【加強語氣】

【例 1】

A: Who made this mistake?

(誰犯了這個錯？)

B: *My fault.* (是我的錯。)

【例 2】

A: Who broke the remote control?

(誰弄壞了遙控器？)

B: *It's my fault.* I dropped it.

(是我的錯。我讓它掉到地上。)

break〔 brek 〕 *v.* 弄壞

remote control〔 rɪ'mot kən'trol 〕 *n.* 遙控器

drop〔 drɑp 〕 *v.* 使掉落

【例 3】

What a mess!
Who did this?

A: What a mess!

Who did this?

(這麼亂！誰弄的？)

B: *It's all my fault.* I'm to blame.

(都是我的錯。我該受責備。)

【mess〔 mɛs 〕 *n.* 亂七八糟   blame〔 blem 〕 *v.* 責備】

4. *I was wrong.*
   You're right.

這兩句話太重要了，可以解決所有的紛爭。意思
是「我當時錯了。你是對的。」，強調我過去是錯的，
你現在所說的話是對的。

如果爭論的是一般的事實時，就可以都用「現在式」：

【例】 I'm a loud talker. (我說話很大聲。)

You always ask me to lower my voice.

(你總是要求我小聲一點。)

I am wrong. (我是錯的。)

You are right. (你是對的。)

【lower〔'loɚ〕*v.* 降低　　voice〔vɔɪs〕*n.* 聲音】

對於過去的事情，就要用「過去式」，例如：

【例1】 You tried to help me. (你想幫助我。)

I lost my temper. (我卻發了脾氣。)

I was wrong. (我錯了。)

You were right. (你是對的。)

【*lose one's temper* 發脾氣】

【例2】 Your advice was correct.

(你的建議是正確的。)

I should have listened. (我早該聽你的。)

I was wrong. (我錯了。)

You were right. (你是對的。)

【advice〔əd'vaɪs〕*n.* 勸告；建議】

5. *Please forgive me.*

forgive〔 fɚˈgɪv 〕 *v.* 原諒

> 這句話的意思是「請原諒我。」中國人講這句話，心理狀態很沈重，好像犯了什麼大錯，美國人說這句話的語氣比較輕鬆，沒那麼嚴重。

> 例如，當你在機場排隊通關，你急著要趕飛機，想插隊，你就可以說：
>
> *Please forgive me.*
> （請原諒我。）
> I'm in a hurry.（我很急。）
> Can I go ahead of you?
> （我可不可以排在你前面？）

> 當美國人向你借東西，他們往往會先拿了，再說：
> *Please forgive me.*（請原諒我。）
> I used your pen.（我用了你的筆。）
> I borrowed it without asking.
> （我沒有先問過你就借去用了。）

Please forgive me. 的其他說法有：

> *Forgive me.*（原諒我。）
> *Can you forgive me?*（你能原諒我嗎？）
> *I hope you can forgive me.*
> （我希望你能原諒我。）

BOOK 5

6. *I didn't mean it.*

mean〔min〕*v.* 表示…的意思；本意是

　　　這句話字面的意思是「我不是有意的。」也就是「我不是故意的。」可以加強語氣說成：I didn't mean to do it. (我不是故意這樣做的。)

【比較】

I didn't mean it.
【最常用】

I didn't mean to do it.
【常用】

I didn't mean it.

7. *It wasn't on purpose.*

purpose〔ˈpɝpəs〕*n.* 目的
on purpose 故意地

　　　這句話的意思是「那不是故意的。」美國人也常說：I didn't do it on purpose. (我不是故意這麼做的。)

8. *It won't happen again.*

happen〔ˈhæpən〕*v.* 發生

　　　這句話的意思是「這種事不會再發生了。」也可說成：It will never happen again. (這種事絕不會再發生了。) 或 I won't do it again. (我不會再做這樣的事了。)

【對話練習】

1. A：**I'm sorry**.
　 B：That's OK.
　　 I understand.
　　 Apology accepted.

2. A：**I apologize**.
　 B：I accept your apology.
　　 We all make mistakes.
　　 Let's forget about it.

3. A：**It's my fault**.
　 B：Don't say that.
　　 It's nobody's fault.
　　 You didn't do anything wrong.

4. A：**I was wrong**.
　 B：I'm glad you realize it.
　　 It's a chance to improve.
　　 Please be more careful.

5. A：**You're right**.
　 B：Now you know it.
　　 You shouldn't doubt me.
　　 I'd never mislead you.
　　【mislead〔mɪs'lid〕*v.* 誤導】

A：我很抱歉。
B：沒關係。
　 我了解。
　 我接受你的道歉。

A：我道歉。
B：我接受你的道歉。
　 我們都會犯錯。
　 我們把它忘了吧。

A：是我的錯。
B：別那麼說。
　 不是任何人的錯。
　 你沒做錯任何事。

A：我當時錯了。
B：我很高興你能了解。
　 這是個改進的機會。
　 請你更小心一點。

A：你是對的。
B：現在你知道了。
　 你不該懷疑我的。
　 我絕不會誤導你的。

BOOK 5

6. A: **Please forgive me.**

   B: I forgive you.
   Nobody is perfect.
   Let's just forget about it.

A：請原諒我。

B：我原諒你。
沒有人是完美的。
我們就算了吧。

7. A: **I didn't mean it.**

   B: I believe you.
   I know you didn't mean it.
   You're not that kind of
   person.

A：我不是有意的。

B：我相信你。
我知道你不是有意的。
你不是那種人。

8. A: **It wasn't on purpose.**

   B: We all know that!
   It was an honest mistake.
   It could have happened to
   anyone.
   【*honest mistake* 無心之過】

A：那不是故意的。

B：我們大家都知道！
那是無心之過。
那可能會發生在每個
人的身上。

9. A: **It won't happen again.**

   B: That's the right attitude!
   That's what I like to hear.
   We should learn from our
   mistakes.

A：這種事不會再發生了。

B：那才是正確的心態！
那就是我想聽到的。
我們應該從錯誤中學習。

BOOK 5

11. How was the movie?

How was the movie?	電影怎麼樣？
What did you think?	你認為怎麼樣？
Did you like it?	你喜歡嗎？
I thought it was terrific.	我認為很棒。
I really enjoyed it.	我真的很喜歡。
I highly recommend it.	我非常推薦它。
It was worth it.	它是值得的。
It was very entertaining.	它非常有趣。
I give it two thumbs up.	我給它最高的評價。

BOOK 5

** ————————————————————

terrific〔təˊrɪfɪk〕*adj.* 很棒的

enjoy〔ɪnˊdʒɔɪ〕*v.* 喜歡

highly〔ˊhaɪlɪ〕*adv.* 非常；高度（地）

recommend〔͵rɛkəˊmɛnd〕*v.* 推薦

worth〔wɝθ〕*adj.* 值得的   thumb〔θʌm〕*n.* 大拇指

【背景説明】

看完電影以後，走出電影院，總會和朋友聊聊天，表達你對電影的看法。

1. *How was the movie?*

這句話的意思是「電影怎麼樣？」也可以説成：How was it? (怎麼樣啊？) 或 How did you like it? (你覺得怎麼樣？)。

2. *What did you think?*

這句話的意思是「你認爲怎麼樣？」用過去式的原因，是因爲電影已經看過了。如果你有任何建議，要問別人的看法時，你就要用：What do you think? (你認爲怎麼樣？)。

3. *Did you like it?*

這句話的意思是「你喜歡嗎？」也可以説成：Did you enjoy it? (你喜歡嗎？) 或 Did you think it was good? (你覺得好看嗎？)

How was the movie?
What did you think?
Did you like it?

4. ***I thought it was terrific.***

terrific〔tə'rɪfɪk〕*adj.* 很棒的；極好的

　　這句話的意思是「我認為很棒。」terrific 的同義字
很多，我們按照美國人看完電影後，最常用的次序排列：

> 【比較】 I thought it was ***great***.【最常用】
>
> I thought it was ***wonderful***.【最常用】
>
> I thought it was ***excellent***.【最常用】
> 　　　　　　　　　　　　〔'ɛksḷənt〕*adj.* 優秀的
>
> I thought it was ***outstanding***.【最常用】
> （我認為很傑出。）〔aut'stændɪŋ〕*adj.* 傑出的
>
> ***I thought it was terrific.***【最常用】
>
> I thought it was ***fantastic***.【常用】
> 　　　　　　　　　　　　〔fæn'tæstɪk〕*adj.* 很棒的
>
> I thought it was ***super***.【常用】
> 　　　　　　　　　　　〔'supɚ〕*adj.* 很棒的
>
> I thought it was ***awesome***.【常用，年輕人喜歡用】
> 　　　　　　　　　　　　〔'ɔsəm〕*adj.* 很棒的
>
> I thought it was ***marvelous***.【常用】
> 　　　　　　　　　　　　〔'mɑrvḷəs〕*adj.* 很棒的

　　「一口氣背會話」中，所用的句子，以最恰當為
第一優先，以常用為第二優先。

5. ***I really enjoyed it.***

enjoy〔ɪn'dʒɔɪ〕*v.* 喜歡；享受

　　這句話的意思是「我真的很喜歡。」也可以說成：
I like it a lot.（我非常喜歡。）

6. *I highly recommend it.*

highly〔'haɪlɪ〕*adv.* 非常；高度（地）
recommend〔,rɛkə'mɛnd〕*v.* 推薦；稱讚

> 　　highly 和 high 不一樣，highly 是表示「非常」，
> 意義上等於 very 或 very much。這句話的意思是
> 「我非常推薦它。」含有「它很棒」的意思，在此的
> 「推薦」，是指「稱讚」。
>
> 【比較】
>
> 　*I highly recommend it.*
> 　　（我非常推薦它。）【最常用】
> 　I strongly recommend it.
> 　　（我強力推薦它。）【最常用】
> 　*I very recommend it.*【誤】
> 　I recommend it very much.【正】
> 　　（我非常推薦它。）
> 　【very 可修飾形容詞或副詞，修飾動詞應該用 very much。】
>
> I highly recommend it.
>
> 　　美國人也常說：I'd recommend it to anyone.
> （我會向大家推薦它。）這句話是美國人的文化，
> 美國人喜歡把好的東西，介紹給別人，中國人不
> 習慣表達這種思想。

7. *It was worth it.*

worth〔wɝθ〕*adj.* 值得的

> 　　worth 這個字，是特殊形容詞，因為它可以接受詞，
> 這句話的意思是「它是值得的。」
>
> 　　到電影院看電影，等於是一個小賭博，因為你不知
> 道電影值不值得看。安全的做法是，問剛看完電影的人：

How was the show?（電影怎麼樣？）

Did you like it?（你喜不喜歡？）

Was it worth it?（值不值得？）

如果他們回答是：*"Yes, **it was worth it.**"*（是的，它是值得的。）你再去看這部電影，就比較保險了，不會吃虧、浪費時間。

> ***It was worth it.*** 也可説成：
>
> It was worth watching.（它值得看。）
>
> It was worth seeing.（它值得看。）
>
> It was worth the price.（它值回票價。）

8. ***It was very entertaining.***

entertaining〔͵ɛntɚˈtenɪŋ〕*adj.* 令人愉快的；有趣的

這句話的意思是「它非常有趣。」也有人説：

It's fun to watch.（它看起來很有趣。）

It's very enjoyable.（它非常有趣。）
　　　　　　〔ɪnˈdʒɔɪəbḷ〕*adj.* 有趣的

It's a must-see.（它是部非看不可的電影。）
　　　　　〔ˈmʌstˈsi〕*n.* 應該看的東西

9. ***I give it two thumbs up.***

thumb〔θʌm〕*n.* 大拇指

這句話字面的意思是「我給他翹起兩個大拇指。」引申爲「我給它最高的評價。」

這句話也可以説成：I give it the thumbs up.
（我向它翹拇指表示讚賞。）

【也可以寫成 thumbs-up〔ˈθʌmzͺʌp〕*n.* 翹拇指】

【對話練習】

1. A：**How was the movie?**　　　　　A：電影怎麼樣？
   B：The movie was super.　　　　　B：那部電影很棒。
   　　It was great.　　　　　　　　　　它真的很棒。
   　　I'm so glad we saw it.　　　　　很高興我們來看了。

2. A：**What did you think?**　　　　　A：你認為怎麼樣？
   B：I loved the movie.　　　　　　　B：我很喜歡那部電影。
   　　I thought it was outstanding.　　我覺得很棒。
   　　It was really worth the price.　　真是值回票價。

3. A：**Did you like it?**　　　　　　　A：你喜歡嗎？
   B：No, I didn't like it.　　　　　　B：不，我不喜歡。
   　　It was too violent.　　　　　　　太暴力了。
   　　I don't like to see lots of　　　　我不喜歡看太多血腥
   　　blood.　　　　　　　　　　　　　場面。

4. A：**I thought it was terrific.**　　　A：我認為很棒。
   B：It was a great movie.　　　　　　B：它是一部很棒的電影。
   　　It was excellent.　　　　　　　　的確很棒。
   　　I might see it again.　　　　　　我可能會再來看一次。

5. A：**I really enjoyed it.**　　　　　　A：我非常喜歡它。
   B：I'm glad to hear that.　　　　　B：聽你這麼說我很高興。
   　　I did, too.　　　　　　　　　　　我也是。
   　　We made a good choice.　　　　我們做了很好的選擇。

BOOK 5

6. A：**I highly recommend it**.

　B：So do I.

　　I'm going to tell all my
　　friends about it.

　　I'm going to spread the word.

　　【*spread the word*　散播消息】

A：我非常推薦它。

B：我也是。

　　我要去跟我所有的朋友
　　說。

　　我會去散播消息。

7. A：**It was worth it**.

　B：I think so, too.

　　I'm glad it was worth the
　　money.

　　I hate to waste time or
　　money.

A：它是值得的。

B：我也這麼覺得。

　　我很高興它值回票價。

　　我討厭浪費時間或金
　　錢。

8. A：**It was very entertaining**.

　B：It certainly was.

　　I laughed out loud.

　　What was your favorite part?

　　【*out loud*　出聲地】

A：它非常有趣。

B：的確是。

　　我笑得很大聲。

　　你最喜歡哪個部份？

9. A：**I give it two thumbs up**.

　B：That's high praise.

　　It deserves it.

　　It's the best movie I've seen
　　all year.

　　【*deserve*〔dɪˈzɝv〕*v.* 應得】

A：我給它最高的評價。

B：那真是很高的讚美。

　　這是它應得的。

　　它是我一整年看過最好
　　的電影。

BOOK 5

12. *What a great night!*

What a great night!	多麼美好的一個晚上！
I had a wonderful time.	我玩得好愉快。
I enjoyed myself a lot.	我玩得很愉快。
You're good company.	和你在一起很快樂。
You're fun to be with.	和你在一起很愉快。
I like hanging out with you.	我喜歡和你在一起。
Thanks for tonight.	感謝你今天晚上的一切。
Let's do it again.	我們下次再約。
I'm lucky to have a friend	我真幸運，有像你這樣的
like you.	朋友。

** ——————————

great〔gret〕*adj.* 很棒的
wonderful〔'wʌndəfəl〕*adj.* 很棒的
enjoy oneself 玩得愉快
company〔'kʌmpənɪ〕*n.* 同伴　　fun〔fʌn〕*adj.* 有趣的
hang out with 和～在一起　　lucky〔'lʌkɪ〕*adj.* 幸運的

BOOK 5

【背景說明】

　　和朋友聚會後，就可說這九句話，表達你的
快樂和感謝，使別人高興的話，說愈多愈好。

1. *What a great night!* （多麼美好的一個晚上！）
   great〔gret〕*adj.* 很棒的

　　這個感嘆句是由 What a
great night *it is*! 省略而來。
現在美國人已經習慣只說：
What a great night! 如果現
在說過去，還有人用：What
a great night it was!

What a great night!

　【比較 1】 *What a great night!* 【最常用】
　　　　　　（多麼美好的一個晚上！）
　　　　　　What a great night it is! 【文法對，無人用】
　　　　　　（那是多麼美好的一個晚上！）

現在談到過去的時候：

　【比較 2】 What a great night *it was*! 【少用】
　　　　　　（多麼美好的一個晚上！）
　　　　　　What a great night *I had*! 【少用】
　　　　　　（我渡過了一個多麼美好的夜晚！）
　　　　　　I had a great night. 【常用】
　　　　　　（我渡過了一個很棒的夜晚。）
　　　　　　It was a great night. 【常用】
　　　　　　（那是一個很棒的夜晚。）

BOOK 5

> **"What + a(n) + 名詞！"** 形成感嘆句。
>
> 【例】 What a nice night! (多麼美好的一個夜晚！)
>
> What a special night! (多麼特別的一個夜晚！)
>
> What a nice evening! (多麼美好的一個晚上！)
>
> What a surprise! (真令人驚訝！)
>
> What a super gift! (多麼棒的禮物！)
> 〔ˈsupɚ〕*adj.* 很棒的
>
> What an awful day! (今天真是糟透了！)
> 〔ˈɔfl〕*adj.* 糟糕的

2. *I had a wonderful time.*

wonderful 〔ˈwʌndɚfəl〕*adj.* 很棒的

這句話字面的意思是「我有很棒的時光。」引申為「我玩得好愉快。」

wonderful 有很多同義字可取代：

【比較】 下面是經過研究，按照美國人的常用次序排列，第 1 至 4 句，使用頻率非常接近：

① I had a good time. (我玩得很愉快。)【第一常用】

② I had a really good time.【第二常用】
(我真的玩得很愉快。)

③ I had a great time. (我玩得很愉快。)【第三常用】

④ *I had a wonderful time.* (我玩得好愉快。)

⑤ I had a nice time. (我玩得很愉快。)

⑥ I had a really nice time. (我真的玩得很愉快。)

⑦ I had a terrific time. (我玩得很愉快。)
　　〔 təˋrɪfɪk 〕adj. 很棒的

⑧ I had a marvelous time. (我玩得很愉快。)
　　〔ˋmɑrvḷəs 〕adj. 很棒的

⑨ I had a fantastic time. (我玩得很愉快。)
　　〔 fænˋtæstɪk 〕adj. 很棒的

　　除了上面九句以外，有些年輕人喜歡說：I had
an awesome time. (我玩得很愉快。) 可列為第 10 個。
　　〔ˋɔsəm 〕adj. 很棒的

3. *I enjoyed myself a lot.*
　enjoy oneself 玩得愉快 (= *have a good time* = *have fun*)
　a lot 非常 (= *very much*)

　　這句話的意思是「我玩
得很愉快。」美國人喜歡說
enjoy，天天說 *I enjoy*，
才會讓別人喜歡。

> *I enjoyed myself a lot.*

> *I enjoyed* myself tonight.
> (我今天晚上玩得很愉快。)
> *I enjoyed* tonight. (我今天晚上很愉快。)
> *I enjoyed* the whole night.
> (我整個晚上都很愉快。)
>
> *I enjoyed* everything. (這一切都令我很愉快。)
> *I enjoyed* being with you. (我喜歡和你在一起。)
> *I enjoyed* your company. (和你在一起很愉快。)
> 　　〔ˋkʌmpənɪ 〕n. 陪伴

4. *You're good company.*

company〔'kʌmpənɪ〕 *n.* 同伴；公司

　　從前的「公司」都是由幾個「同伴」組成，所以，company 的主要意思是「公司」和「同伴」，作「同伴」解時，是不可數名詞。companion〔kəm'pænjən〕 *n.* 同伴，則是可數名詞，兩者意義不完全相同。

【比較】 *You're good company.*【不用 a】
　　　　（和你在一起很愉快。）
　　　　You're a good companion.【有 a】
　　　　（你是一個好夥伴。）

　　You're good company. 的字面意思是「你是好的同伴。」由於 company 是偏重暫時性的，所以，這句話應該翻成「和你在一起很愉快。」

【比較】 *You're good company.*【最常用】
　　　　（和你在一起很愉快。）
　　　　You're nice company.【常用】
　　　　（和你在一起很愉快。）
　　　　You're excellent company.【常用】
　　　　　　　　　　〔'ɛkslənt〕 *adj.* 優秀的
　　　　（和你在一起很愉快。）

　　當你和美國人一起去旅行，有時候 He is good company.（和他在一起很愉快。）有時候 He is bad company.（和他在一起不愉快。）當他表現不錯，你就可以說：*"You're good company."* （和你在一起很愉快。）

BOOK 5

如果你和他在一起不愉快，你就可以說：You're not very good company today. What's the matter? (今天和你在一起覺得怪怪的。怎麼了？)

companion 是偏重長期的夥伴。像：A dog is a very good companion. (狗是很好的同伴。) 旅行的時候，當你和同伴在一起，你如果說：You're a good companion. 是指「你是一個好的同伴。」並不表示現在和你在一起很愉快 (*You're good company*.)。

You're good company.

5. *You're fun to be with*.

fun 〔 fʌn 〕 *adj.* 有趣的

這句話的意思是「和你在一起很愉快。」to be with 是不定詞片語當副詞用，修飾 fun。為什麼 with 後面不接受詞呢？因為當不定詞有了意義上的受詞時，就不能再有文法上的受詞。(詳見「文法寶典」p.411)

【比較】 *You're fun* { *to be with*. (正)
                            to be with you. (誤)

You're fun to be with. 句中已有 you 為意義上的受詞，就不需要再重覆受詞 you 了，英文總是會避免重覆。

BOOK 5

【比較】 下面六個句子，按照使用頻率排列，前
三個較接近：

You're fun to be with. 【最常用】

（和你在一起很愉快。）

You're a lot of fun.

（你非常風趣。）【最常用】

You're a fun person.

（你很風趣。）【最常用】

You're fun. 【常用】

（你很風趣。）

You're fun to be around.

（和你在一起很愉快。）【常用】

You're fun to go out with. 【常用】

（和你一起出去很愉快。）

*You're fun to be with.
I like hanging out
with you.*

6. *I like hanging out with you.*

hang〔hæŋ〕*v.* 懸掛　*hang out* 閒散地打發時間

hang out with 和～在一起

> 　　hang 的主要意思是「懸掛」，hang out 的字面意
> 思是「掛在外面」，美國在五、六十年代，年輕人喜
> 歡在公園、在牆角，或在一排賣汽水的販賣機旁，坐
> 著不動，就像把衣服或帽子掛在外面不動一樣。直到
> 現在，我們還常常看到一群美國人，坐在那裡不動，
> 也不講話。所以 hang out with 字面的意思是「和～
> 一起掛在外面（不動）」，現在引申為「和～在一起」
> (= *spend time with*)。

很多字典上 hang out 的翻譯都不對，其用法看看下面的例子就知道了：

【例1】 Let's ***hang out*** this afternoon.

　　　　(= *Let's spend some time together this afternoon.*)

　　　　(我們今天下午聚一聚。)

【例2】 Let's ***hang out*** at the mall this weekend.
　　　　〔mɔl〕 *n.* 購物中心

　　　　(= *Let's spend some time together at the mall this weekend.*)

　　　　(我們這個週末一起去購物中心吧。)

【例3】 Are you free tonight?

　　　　Do you want to ***hang out with*** us?

　　　　(= *Do you want to spend time with us?*)

　　　　(你今天晚上有空嗎？你想和我們聚一聚嗎？)

　　你見到美國人，你就可以說："I like hanging out with you." 他通常會回答："Me too."

　　I like hanging out with you.

　　　　(我喜歡和你在一起。)

= I like going out with you.

　　　　(我喜歡和你一起出去。)

= I like spending time with you.

　　　　(我喜歡和你在一起。)

BOOK 5

7. *Thanks for tonight.*

這句話的意思是「感謝你今天晚上的一切。」源自 *Thank you for everything that you did for me tonight.*

【比較1】 ***Thanks for tonight.***【語氣輕鬆】
Thank you for tonight.【一般語氣】

【比較2】 ***Thanks for tonight.***【常用】
Thanks for everything.【常用】
Thanks for everything tonight.【少用】

8. *Let's do it again.*

這句話字面的意思是「我們再做它。」引申為「我們下次再約。」或「我們下次再出去。」(= *Let's go out again.*)。

要常說 ***Let's do it again.*** 之類的句子：

Let's do it again soon. (我們快點再約。)
Let's do it again real soon. (我們趕快再約。)
Let's do it again as soon as possible.
(我們儘快再約。)

Let's do it again sometime. (我們找時間再約。)
Let's do it again at your convenience.
(你方便的時候,我們再約。)
Let's do it again whenever you're free.
(你有空的時候,我們再約。)
【***at one's convenience*** 在某人方便的時候】

9. *I'm lucky to have a friend like you.*

lucky〔ˈlʌkɪ〕*adj.* 幸運的

這句話的意思是「我真幸運，有像你這樣的朋友。」也可以加強語氣說成：I'm so lucky to have a friend like you.（我非常幸運，有像你這樣的朋友。）

so lucky 也可用 very lucky（非常幸運）或 really lucky（真是幸運）來代替。

如果你是男生的話，你可以說：

I'm a lucky guy to have a friend like you.
〔gaɪ〕*n.* 人
（我很幸運，有像你這樣的朋友。）

如果你是女生的話，你可以說：

I'm a lucky girl to have a friend like you.
（我真是個幸運的女孩，有像你這樣的朋友。）

I'm a lucky girl to have a friend like you.

這一回的九句非常感人，和朋友玩了一天，告別的時候，你如果說了這九句話，他會高興死了，你要別人對你好，你就得先對別人好。養成會說感謝的話，你將是最大的贏家。

【對話練習】

1. A : **What a great night!**
   B : I totally agree.
      It was perfect.
      Everything was fantastic.

   A：多麼美好的一個晚上！
   B：我完全同意。
      真是太完美了。
      一切都很棒。

2. A : **I had a wonderful time.**
   B : I had a great time, too.
      I enjoyed every minute.
      I hate to see it end.

   A：我玩得好愉快。
   B：我也玩得很愉快。
      我一直玩得很愉快。
      我真不願意看到它結束。

3. A : **I enjoyed myself a lot.**
   B : So did I.
      It was a blast.
      I'm so glad you came out tonight.
      【blast〔blæst〕*n.* 狂歡的聚會；歡樂】

   A：我玩得很愉快。
   B：我也是。
      真的很愉快。
      很高興你今晚能出來。

4. A : **You're good company.**
   B : Thanks for the compliment!
      What a nice thing to say!
      I like being with you, too.
      【compliment〔'kɑmpləmənt〕*n.* 稱讚】

   A：和你在一起很快樂。
   B：謝謝你的讚美！
      你能這麼說真好！
      我也喜歡和你在一起。

5. A : **You're fun to be with.**
   B : You're a fun person, too!
      And you're very interesting!
      I always have fun with you.

   A：和你在一起很愉快。
   B：你也很風趣！
      而且你很有趣！
      我和你在一起，總是覺
      得很愉快。

6. A：**I like hanging out with you.**

　B：I feel the same way.
　　 Spending time with you is
　　 great.
　　 I love going out with you.

7. A：**Thanks for tonight.**

　B：Don't thank me!
　　 I should thank you!
　　 You deserve all the thanks.
　　 【deserve〔dɪˈzɝv〕*v.* 應得】

8. A：**Let's do it again.**

　B：We must do it again!
　　 It was such a good time!
　　 I'll be disappointed if we
　　 don't!
　　 【disappointed〔͵dɪsəˈpɔɪntɪd〕*adj.*
　　 失望的】

9. A：**I'm lucky to have a friend
　　 like you.**

　B：I feel the same way about
　　 you.
　　 You're a super friend.
　　 Let's always be good friends.

A：我喜歡和你在一起。

B：我有同感。
　 和你在一起眞棒。

　 我喜歡和你一起出去。

A：感謝你今天晚上的一切。

B：別謝我！
　 我該謝謝你！
　 該被感謝的人是你。

A：我們下次再約。

B：我們一定要再約一次！
　 眞的玩得很愉快！
　 如果沒再約一次，我會
　 很失望！

A：我眞幸運，有像你這樣
　 的朋友。

B：我對你也有同樣的感覺。

　 你這個朋友眞棒。
　 我們永遠當好朋友吧。

BOOK 5

一口氣背會話，一背上癮！！

　　一部好的電影，可以歷久不衰，成為經典；一本好書，可以流傳千古。只有好的、精緻的東西，才能經得起時間的考驗。萬里長城上，沒有倒過的牆，永遠是那麼壯觀；歷年來修復過的部份，看起來就是不一樣，修補的部份，總是會不斷地倒塌。

　　「一口氣背會話」的製作過程相當艱辛，因為我們必須從語言的海洋中，抽出最精華、最有用的句子，還要特殊編排，才能琅琅上口。每一回都經過編者實際背過，改了又改，務必使「一口氣背會話」編寫得像經文一樣，讓讀者容易背下來，並且背完之後，全身舒服為止。

　　多少人為英文瘋狂？多少人熱愛英文？又有多少人最後放棄？為什麼？因為沒有目標，東學一點、西學一點，辛辛苦苦學了又忘記，不會開口說英文，是終生的遺憾。

　　「一口氣背會話」，沒有年齡、時間、地點的限制，隨時隨地都可以背。一定要將每一回九句，中英文一起背熟到十秒鐘之內，變成直覺，不需要思考，能夠脫口而出為止。這些句子會像烙印一樣，牢牢地銘刻在你的腦海裡。背這些好的句子，不僅能使你忘卻煩惱，身體變好，更能讓你變成一個很體貼、有愛心的人，讓你成為人人喜歡的人，You will become a better person.

劉　毅

「一口氣背會話」經 BOOK 5

唸英文要像唸經一樣，每天大聲唸，從起床到睡覺，唸得比看得快，最後不看也會唸，養成習慣後，你會全身舒爽，你試試看，奇妙無比。

1. Do you know *Andy*?
   Have you met *Andy*?
   Let me introduce you.

   Andy, this is Pat.
   Pat, this is Andy.
   I'm glad you two could meet.

   Andy is an old friend.
   He is a great guy.
   You two have a lot in common.

2. My name is Pat.
   It's nice to meet you.
   How do you do?

   I'm from Taiwan.
   I'm a student.
   How about you?

   Where are you from?
   What do you do?
   Been here long?

3. When are you free?
   What's a good time?
   When do you want to get together?

   Anytime is OK.
   Just let me know.
   I'll be there for sure.

   Where shall we meet?
   Where's a good place?
   I don't want to miss you.

4. I got a great idea.
   Let's go out tonight.
   Let's go see a movie.

   It's been a long time.
   We need to relax.
   We need to do something new.

   What do you say?
   How do you feel?
   How does a movie sound?

5. *What's* playing?
   What's showing?
   Anything really good?

   What choices do we have?
   What do you want to see?
   What times are the shows?

   You choose the movie.
   I'll let you decide.
   I'm game for anything.

6. Pick a movie.
   What looks good?
   What are we going to see?

   I'll wait in line.
   I'll get the tickets.
   Why don't you go take a look around?

   See what's going on.
   See what they have.
   Check out the food court.

7. *It's* my treat.
   It's on me.
   Let me pay.

   Be my guest.
   I'm paying.
   I got it.

   Don't say a word.
   It's my pleasure.
   Next time you can pay.

8. Where do you want to sit?
   Sit wherever you want.
   Sit anywhere you like.

   I'm not picky.
   You call the shots.
   Any place is fine with me.

   There's a nice spot.
   No one will bother us.
   We can stay away from the crowd.

9. *Please* be quiet.
   Please keep it down.
   Could you lower your voice?

   You're too loud.
   You're too noisy.
   You're disturbing everybody.

   Sorry to say that.
   I hope you don't mind.
   Please don't take offense.

10. *I*'m sorry.
    I apologize.
    It's my fault.

    I was wrong.
    You are right.
    Please forgive me.

    I didn't mean it.
    It wasn't on purpose.
    It won't happen again.

11. How was the movie?
    What did you think?
    Did you like it?

    I thought it was terrific.
    I really enjoyed it.
    I highly recommend it.

    It was worth it.
    It was very entertaining.
    I give it two thumbs up.

12. What a great night!
    I had a wonderful time.
    I enjoyed myself a lot.

    You're good company.
    You're fun to be with.
    I like hanging out with you.

    Thanks for tonight.
    Let's do it again.
    I'm lucky to have a friend like you.

BOOK 6 帶老外去郊遊

▶ 6-1 到了禮拜五的時候，就可以跟朋友說：

Thank God it's Friday.
The weekend is here.
We made it through the week.

▶ 6-2 另一位朋友，就可以回答說：

I agree.
I'm with you.
You're absolutely right.

▶ 6-3 你可以接著跟朋友說：

What can we do?
Where should we go?
Where's a great place?

▶ 6-4 你可以提議說：

Let's go hiking.
Let's head for the hills.
Let's leave the city behind.

▶ 6-5 你可以再跟朋友說：

Let's get ready.
Let's make a plan.
It's better to be prepared.

▶ 6-6 你可以邀請朋友上你的車：

Please get in.
Sit up front.

►6-7　在車子裡面，看到油表顯示汽油不夠，你就對朋友說：

We need gas.
We're on empty.
We're running out of gas.

►6-8　在加油站和服務人員說：

Hi!
Twenty bucks, please.
Make it regular.

►6-9　兩個人在爬山，你叫你的朋友趕快跟你走：

Hurry up!
Move faster.
Pick it up.

►6-10　你可以鼓勵走不動的人說：

You can do it.
You have what it takes.
I believe in you.

►6-11　在山上看到很好的風景，就說：

Wow!
What a view!
It's really awesome!

►6-12　晚上你的朋友要下車了，你就跟他說：

Good night.
Sleep well.
Sweet dreams.

1. Thank God it's Friday.

Thank God it's Friday.	謝天謝地，今天是星期五。
The weekend is here.	週末到了。
We made it through the week.	我們熬過了這個禮拜。
I'm psyched.	我很興奮。
I'm very excited.	我非常興奮。
I'm all fired up.	我非常興奮。
Let's get away.	我們去玩吧。
Let's do something special.	我們做一些特別的事吧。
You only live once.	人只能活一次。

** ————————————————

God〔gɑd〕*n.* 上帝　　weekend〔'wik'ɛnd〕*n.* 週末
make it 成功；辦到　　*through the week* 整個禮拜
psyched〔saɪkt〕*adj.* 興奮的；已做好心理準備的
excited〔ɪk'saɪtɪd〕*adj.* 興奮的
fired up 興奮的；熱心的　　*get away* 逃脫；去旅行

【背景説明】

　　美國人一到了星期五，就很高興，因爲星期六、星期天可以休息。到了星期五下班的時候，你就可以説這九句話。

1. **Thank God it's Friday.**

　　God〔gɑd〕n. 上帝

> 　　這句話字面的意思是「謝謝上帝，是星期五。」引申爲「謝天謝地，今天是星期五。」
>
> 　　美國有名的「星期五餐廳」，就叫 T.G.I. Friday's，它的全名就是來自 Thank God it's Friday. 每到星期五，美國人就喜歡説這句話。
>
> 　　當美國人做完一項艱苦的工作，感到很輕鬆的時候，就會説："Thank God!" 就像中文的「謝天謝地！」一樣，信教、不信教的人，都可以説。
>
> 　　Thank God it's Friday. 源自 Thank God that it's Friday. 原則上，that 常省略，Thank God 直接接子句。
>
> 【例】**Thank God** we didn't have an accident.
> 　　（感謝上帝，我們沒發生意外。）
> **Thank God** we passed the exam.
> 　　（謝天謝地，我們通過了考試。）
> **Thank God** we made it home safely.
> 　　（感謝上蒼，我們平安到家了。）

Thank God it's payday. (謝天謝地，今天發薪水。)

〔'pe͵de 〕 *n.* 發薪日

Thank God it's quitting-time.〔'kwɪtɪŋ͵taɪm 〕 *n.* 下班時間

(感謝老天爺，下班了。)【也有美國人寫成 quitting time 】

Thank God it's time to go home.

(謝天謝地，可以回家了。)【放學或下班時説 】

Thank God we're done. (謝天謝地，我們做完了。)

Thank God we're finished.

(謝天謝地，我們做完了。)

【We're done. 和 We're finished.，參照第三冊 p.10-3、10-4 】

Thank God we made it.

(感謝上帝，我們做到了。)

【比較 1 】　*Thank God* it's Friday. 【正】

Thank God that it's Friday. 【正，極少用 】

Thank God! It's Friday. 【誤，美國人不説 】

【理論上好像可以變成兩句話，事實上美國人不説。因為
這句話美國人説得太多了，分成兩句慢慢説，太奇怪了。】

【比較 2 】　句子長的時候，Thank God 後面就要接逗點，
或感嘆號，或接 that 子句。

Thank God, my brother got a full scholarship.

(謝天謝地，我哥哥得到全額的獎學金。)【正，最常用 】

Thank God! My brother got a full scholarship.

【正，較常用 】〔scholarship 〔'skɑlɚ͵ʃɪp 〕 *n.* 獎學金 】

Thank God that my brother got a full
scholarship. 【正，常用 】

Thank God my brother got a full scholarship. 【誤 】

BOOK 6

【比較3】 如果是短句，但卻是美國人不常說的話，此時
　　　　　Thank God 之後，可接逗點。

Thank God you're safe.【正，最常用】

Thank God, you're safe.【正，常用】

Thank God *that* you're safe.【正，少用】

Thank God! You're safe.【劣】

【文法正確，但美國人不說，因為句子短，當說
　Thank God 時，很興奮，會不停頓，直接就
　繼續說。】

2. ***The weekend is here.***

weekend〔'wik'ɛnd〕*n.* 週末

　　這句話字面的意思是「週末在這裡。」引申為
「週末到了。」

【比較】 中文：週末到了。

　　　　 英文：The weekend is here.【正】

　　　　　　　 The weekend has arrived.

　　　　　　　【正，美國人極少用】

凡是「…到了」，都可用 "is here" 表示。

【例】 Summer vacation *is here*.（暑假到了。）

　　　 The rainy season *is here*.（雨季到了。）

　　　 Your taxi *is here*.（你的計程車到了。）

　　　 Christmas *is here*.（聖誕節到了。）

　　　 The doctor *is here*.（醫生來了。）

　　　 The newspaper *is here*.（報紙來了。）

3. *We made it through the week.*

make it 成功;辦到;做到

through〔θru〕*prep.*(表示時間)自始至終;從頭到尾

through the week 是指「整個禮拜」。

　　這句話字面的意思是「我們成功地渡過整個禮拜。」引申為「我們熬過了這個禮拜。」

　　說這句話的語氣非常幽默,因為美國人工作時非常敬業,在這裡暗示一個禮拜的辛苦工作,終於過去。

　　也有人說:We made it to Friday.(我們熬到星期五了。)

類似的説法有:

The soldier *made it* through basic training.

(這個士兵撐過了基本訓練。)

We *made it* to graduation day.

(我們終於熬到畢業了。)

The old man *made it* to retirement.

(那位老人終於等到退休了。)

【retirement〔rɪ'taɪrmənt〕*n.* 退休】

We *made it* through high school.

(我們終於唸完高中了。)

We *made it* to the end of the month.

(我們撐到月底了。)

We *made it* through the airport.

(我們通過機場的檢查了。)

4. *I'm psyched.*

psych〔saɪk〕*v.* 使興奮；使做好心理準備

psyched〔saɪkt〕*adj.* 興奮的（= *excited*）；已做好
心理準備的（= *completely mentally ready*）

【注意發音，一般字典沒有】

psych 這個字的發音很特別，ps 的 p 不發
音，如 psychology〔saɪˈkɑlədʒɪ〕*n.* 心理學，
psych 中的 ch 唸 /k/ 的音，h 不發音。psych
是情感動詞，用法和 excite、interest、surprise
一樣，人當主詞時，用過去分詞 psyched，很多
美國字典，已經把這類的字，當作形容詞用。

I'm psyched. 的意思有兩個：

① 我很興奮。（= *I'm excited.*）

② 我已做好心理準備。（= *I'm ready.*）

【比較1】psyched 的後面，可加 up，加強語氣。

I'm psyched.【一般語氣】

（我很興奮。）

I'm psyched up.【加強語氣】

（我非常興奮。）

【比較2】現在比較年輕的人，喜歡使用 psyched。

I'm psyched.【四、五十歲以下的人喜歡說】

I'm excited.【通俗，一般人常說】

　　psyched 這個字，由於是新字，一般書上沒有，你要常説，它有兩個意思，要看前後句意判斷，有的時候，兩個意思都有，在此比較著重於 excited。

【例】 That's great! I'm really *psyched*.
　　　（真棒！我真高興。）【psyched = excited】
　　　I'm really *psyched* for this test.
　　　（這場考試，我已經有心理準備。）
　　　【psyched = mentally ready】
　　　I'm *psyched* to go home.
　　　（我很高興要回家了；我準備要回家了。）
　　　【psyched 等於 excited 和 mentally ready，此時的
　　　　psyched，表示「既高興，又準備好了」。】

　　　I'm *psyched* to hear that.
　　　（我很高興聽到那件事情。）【psyched = excited】
　　　I'm *psyched* to see you.
　　　（我很高興見到你。）【psyched = excited】
　　　I'm *psyched* about the party tonight.
　　　（對於今天晚上的宴會，我很興奮。）
　　　【psyched = excited】

　　　I'm *psyched* about the game.
　　　（對於這場比賽，我很興奮。）
　　　I'm *psyched* about the winter vacation.
　　　（想到寒假，我就很興奮。）
　　　I'm *psyched* we're going to Japan next week.
　　　（我真高興，我們下星期要去日本。）

BOOK 6

5. **I'm very excited.**

excited〔ɪk'saɪtɪd〕*adj.* 興奮的

這句話的意思是「我非常興奮。」

【比較1】 中文：我非常興奮。

英文：I'm very excited.【正】

I'm very exciting.

【誤，情感動詞，人做主詞，應用被動。】

I'm very exciting. 的意思是「我非常令人興奮。」

【例】 Hire me for the show. I'm very exciting. I'm not boring.

(請我表演吧。我會令人興奮，我不會讓大家覺得無聊。)

【比較2】 下面是按照使用頻率排列：

① I'm excited. (我很興奮。)【第一常用】

② I'm **very** excited. (我非常興奮。)【第二常用】

③ I'm **so** excited. (我非常興奮。)【第三常用】

④ I'm **really** excited. (我真是興奮。)

⑤ I'm **truly** excited. (我真是興奮。)

⑥ I'm **awfully** excited. (我興奮得不得了。)
〔'ɔflɪ〕*adv.* 非常；不得了

BOOK 6

6. *I'm all fired up.*

fired up 興奮的；熱心的（= *excited*；*enthusiastic*）

> fire up 源自「發動引擎」(start an engine)，或是「給爐灶添燃料」。
>
> *fire sb. up* 或 *fire up sb.* 的字面意思是「給某人點火」，引申為「激勵某人」(= *motivate sb.*)。

【例】 See if you can *fire* John *up*. He is so depressed.

> （看你可不可以激勵一下約翰。他很沮喪。）

> *fire sb. up* 的被動是 *sb. be fired up*，因此，*I'm all fired up.* 的字面意思是「我全身都被點燃了。」引申為「我現在全身有精神了。」或「我非常興奮。」或「我已經準備好要接受挑戰。」(= *I'm ready for anything.*)

> I'm all fired up. 到底該怎麼翻譯呢？要看實際情況或前後句意來決定。所有的意思都是由字面的意思「我全部被點燃了。」引申而來。

> 當你很高興的時候，例如你要去旅行、找到新工作，或當你準備好要做任何事的時候，你都可以說：

> I'm fired up. (我真興奮。)
> I'm all fired up. (我非常興奮。)
> I'm all fired up about it.
> (我已經完全準備好要接受挑戰了。)

BOOK 6

I'm all fired up. 也可説成 I'm really fired up. 意思都是「我非常興奮。」really 和 all 一樣，也可作「很；非常」解。

在比賽的時候，中國人常喊「加油！加油！」美國不説 *Add gas!* (誤) 常喊：Let's get fired up! Let's get fired up! 常常幾百個人，愈喊愈大聲、愈喊愈瘋狂。

中外文化不同，中國人所説的「加油！」是叫參賽者努力，美國人説的是 Let's get fired up! (讓我們振作起精神吧！)

在教室裡、運動場上，或是軍隊裡，都可説這句話來激勵大家。就像我們中文所説的「加油！」一樣普遍。爲什麼美國人説 "Let's get fired up!" 呢？字面的意思是「我們被點燃吧！」也就是「振作起來吧！」(= *Let's get motivated!*)

7. *Let's get away.*

get away 這個成語的字面意思是「離開」，通常引申爲：①逃脫 (= *escape*) ②去旅行 (= *take a trip*)。

Let's get away. 在這裡的意思是「我們去玩吧。」可能是去旅行，也可能去哪裡走動走動，也可以説成：Let's go away.

美國人看到有人工作很辛苦，會常說：You should get away. (你應該休息一下。) (= *You should take a break*.) 幾個美國人在一起，他們常喜歡說：We should get away. 或 We need to get away. 意思是「我們應該離開此地去渡假。」

【比較1】 ***Let's get away.*** (我們去玩吧。)
Let's get away from here.
(= *Let's get out of here*.)
(我們離開這裡吧。)

【比較2】 ***Let's get away.*** (我們去玩吧。)
Let's get out. (我們到外面去吧。)
(= *Let's get outside*.)

【比較3】 ***Let's get away.*** (我們去玩吧。)
Let's go. (走吧。)

這兩句話不一樣，Let's get away. 等於 Let's go somewhere. 有強調離開此地去他處渡假或玩的意思。

Let's get away. 或 ***Let's go away.*** 可能源自於罪犯要逃跑的時候說的。所以說這句話的時候，有點幽默的語氣，表示要脫離困境，到別處去輕鬆輕鬆，例如，囚犯跑了，就是 The prisoner got away. (那個犯人跑了。)

【例】 We need a break. ***Let's get away***.

（我們需要休息一下。我們去玩吧。）

Let's get away this weekend.

（我們這個週末去渡假吧。）

We have a three-day weekend.

Let's get away.

（我們有三天的週末假期。我們去渡假吧。）

美國人有節慶的時候，通常會把假期挪到禮拜五
或禮拜一，成為 three-day weekend，又稱為
long weekend。

8. *Let's do something special.*

這句話的意思是「我們做一些特別的事吧。」

下面是按照美國人使用的頻率排列：

① ***Let's do something special.*** 【第一常用】

（我們做一些特別的事吧。）

② Let's do something *different.* 【第二常用】

（我們做一些不同的事吧。）

③ Let's do something *exciting.* 【第三常用】

（我們做一些令人興奮的事吧。）

④ Let's do something *we haven't done before.*

（我們做一些我們過去沒做過的事吧。）

⑤ Let's do something *fun.*

（我們做一些好玩的事吧。）

⑥ Let's do something *interesting.*

（我們做一些有趣的事吧。）

⑦ Let's do something *crazy*.

（我們做一些瘋狂的事吧。）

⑧ Let's do something *wild*.

（我們做一些瘋狂的事吧。）

⑨ Let's do something *worthwhile*.

（我們做一些值得做的事吧。）

wild〔waɪld〕*adj.* 瘋狂的
worthwhile〔ˈwɜθˈhwaɪl〕*adj.* 值得做的

⑩ Let's do something *unique*.

（我們做一些和別人完全不一樣的事吧。）

⑪ Let's do something *unusual*.

（我們做一些不尋常的事吧。）

⑫ Let's do something *inexpensive*.

（我們做一些不花什麼錢的事情吧。）

unique〔juˈnik〕*adj.* 獨一無二的
unusual〔ʌnˈjuʒʊəl〕*adj.* 不尋常的
inexpensive〔ˌɪnɪkˈspɛnsɪv〕*adj.* 便宜的

【這句話是美國人的文化，他們常喜歡說節省錢之類的話，事實上，他們很浪費。】

背「一口氣背會話」，見到人就會脫口說出 Let's do something special. 如果這句話說膩了，就可以用上面的其他句子來代替。

BOOK 6

9. *You only live once.*

　　這句話是固定用法，You 泛指「一般人」。這句話的意思是「人只能活一次。」含有「在人的一生當中，只活一次，不要浪費時間。」英文解釋是：You only have one chance in life. Don't waste a minute. No time to waste.

【比較1】 *You only live once.*【正】【You 代表所有的人】
We only live once.
【劣，極少用，因為 We 只是表「我們」，意思較狹猛】

【比較2】 *You only live once.*【正】
You can only live once.【劣】
【這句話是中式英文，美國人不說，除非你特別加強語氣。】

【比較3】 *You only live once.*【較常用，已成固定用法】
You live only once.【劣，較少用】

【比較4】 *You only live once.*【正】
We can only live once.【劣】

上面各個註明【劣】的句子並沒有錯，你說這些話，美國人聽得懂，但是並不是他們平常習慣說的話。*You only live once.* 是慣用句。

下面是美國人常說的，按照使用頻率排列：

① *You only live once.*【第一常用】

② You only have one life to live.【第二常用】
（人只能活一次。）

③ You only go around once.（人生只能走一回。）

④ You only have one life.（人只能活一次。）

⑤ You only get one chance in life.
（人生只有一次機會。）

　　You only have one shot.（人只有一次機會。）
　　　　　　　　　　〔ʃɑt〕*n.* 射擊；機會

你可以常跟別人說：

> *You only live once.*（人只能活一次。）
> Just do it.（想做就做。）
> Don't waste time.（不要浪費時間。）

> *You only live once.*（人只能活一次。）
> Give it your best shot.（儘量努力。）
> Don't let opportunities pass you by.
> （不要錯過機會。）【*pass sb. by* 走過某人的旁邊】
> 【這句話的字面意思是「不要讓機會從你旁邊走過。」
> 　引申為「不要錯過機會。」】

【對話練習】

1. A：**Thank God it's Friday.**　　　A：謝天謝地，今天是星期五。

　　B：You got that right.　　　　　B：你說對了。

　　　Fridays are the best.　　　　　　星期五最棒。

　　　Everybody loves Friday night.　　大家都喜歡星期五的晚上。

　　　【*get ~ right* 把~弄對；徹底理解~】

2. A：**The weekend is here.**　　　　A：週末到了。

　　B：What a relief!　　　　　　　B：真是令人鬆一口氣！

　　　We made it to the weekend.　　　我們熬到週末了。

　　　Happy days are here again!　　　快樂的日子又到了！

　　　【relief〔rɪ'lif〕*n.* 放心；鬆了一口氣】

3. A：**We made it through the week.**　A：我們撐過了這個禮拜。

　　B：Praise the Lord!　　　　　　B：讚美上帝！

　　　We should celebrate!　　　　　　我們應該慶祝！

　　　We survived another week!　　　　我們又安然渡過了一個星

　　　【Lord〔lɔrd〕*n.* 上帝　　　　　期！

　　　　survive〔sə'vaɪv〕*v.* 自~中生還】

4. A：**I'm psyched.**　　　　　　A：我很興奮。

　　B：You look psyched.　　　　　B：你看起來很興奮。

　　　You look excited.　　　　　　　你看起來很興奮。

　　　What's the special occasion?　　是什麼特別的日子嗎？

　　　【occasion〔ə'keʒən〕*n.* 場合；

　　　　特殊的節日】

5. A : **I'm very excited**.

　B : I'm excited, too.
　　　I know how you feel.
　　　The excitement is driving me
　　　crazy. 【excitement〔ɪk'saɪtmənt〕*n*.
　　　興奮；令人興奮的事
　　　drive sb. crazy 使某人瘋狂】

6. A : **I'm all fired up**.

　B : I can see that.
　　　You're climbing the walls!
　　　It's written all over your face!
　　　【*climbing the walls* 激動
　　　write on one's face「臉上明白地表現
　　　出」，有了 all over 時，on 就必須省略。】

7. A : **Let's get away**.

　B : That's a fantastic idea.
　　　We need some adventure.
　　　We deserve to have some fun.
　　　【fantastic〔fæn'tæstɪk〕*adj*. 很棒的】

8. A : **Let's do something special**.

　B : I totally agree.
　　　I feel the same way.
　　　Let's do something we'll
　　　remember forever.

9. A : **You only live once**.

　B : Well, that's what they say.
　　　You have to take a chance.
　　　You'll never know until you try.
　　　【*take a chance* 冒險；碰運氣】

A：我非常興奮。

B：我也很興奮。
　　我知道你的感覺。
　　這件令人興奮的事讓我
　　瘋狂。

A：我非常興奮。

B：我可以看得出來。
　　你很激動！
　　從你的臉上看得很清楚！

A：我們去玩吧。

B：那是很棒的主意。
　　我們需要一些冒險。
　　我們應該要開心一下。

A：我們做些特別的事情吧。

B：我完全同意。
　　我有同感。
　　我們去做一些可以永遠
　　記得的事情吧。

A：人只能活一次。

B：嗯，大家都這麼說。
　　你必須冒險一試。
　　要試過才知道。

BOOK 6

2. I agree.

I agree.	我同意。
I'm with you.	我支持你。
You're absolutely right.	你說得完全對。
That's for sure.	那是確定的。
That's the truth.	那是事實。
That's how I feel.	我也有同樣的感覺。
I feel the same way.	我有同感。
I couldn't agree more.	我完全同意。
You're right on the money.	你說得非常正確。

** ————————————————

be with 同意；和…一致；支持
absolutely〔'æbsə,lutlɪ〕*adv.* 完全地；絕對地
for sure 毫無疑問的；確定的
truth〔truθ〕*n.* 事實；眞理
can't agree more 非常同意；完全同意
on the money 恰到好處；非常正確

【背景説明】

　　這一回太重要了，用的機會太多了，不論別人
講什麼，只要你同意，你就可以説這些話。同意別
人，你可以説一句，也可以説很多句，説得愈多，
會使別人愈高興。

1. *I agree.*

　　這句話的意思是「我同意。」美國人也常説：
I agree. I agree. I agree. 連續説三句，表示強烈
同意。

【比較】　*I agree.*【一般語氣】
I agree with you.（我同意你。）【語氣稍強】
I totally agree.（我完全同意。）【加強語氣】
I agree with you 100%.【語氣最強】
（我百分之百同意你。）

2. *I'm with you.*

be with 同意；和…一致；支持

　　這句話的意思是「我同意你；我和你意見一致；
我支持你。」

【比較】　*I'm with you.*【一般語氣】
I'm with you for sure.【語氣較強】
（我毫無疑問地支持你。）【*for sure* 毫無疑問】
I'm with you all the way.【語氣最強】
（我完全支持你。）
【*all the way* 完全地；無保留地；自始至終】

BOOK 6

【例】 That's a great idea. *I'm with you*.

（那是個好主意。我同意你。）

I'm on your side. *I'm with you*.

（我站在你這一邊。我支持你。）

Whatever you decide to do, *I'm with you*.

（不管你決定做什麼，我都支持你。）

3. *You're absolutely right*.

absolutely〔'æbsə,lutlɪ〕*adv.* 完全地；絕對地

這句話的意思是「你說得完全對。」

【比較】 You're right.（你說得對。）【一般語氣】

You're so right.【語氣較強】

（你說得很對。）

You're absolutely right.【語氣最強】

（你說得完全對。）

4. *That's for sure*.

for sure 毫無疑問的；確定的；肯定的

這句話的意思是「那是確定的。」重視文法
的人，這句話可能就不敢說了，一般成語字典中，
for sure 是副詞片語，事實上，for sure 也可以
放在 be 動詞後面，當形容詞片語，做主詞補語。
不管別人說什麼，你只要同意，你就可以說：
That's for sure.

【例1】　A: The weekend always passes too
　　　　　 quickly. (週末總是過得太快了。)
　　　　 B: *That's for sure.* (那是肯定的。)

【例2】　A: Edward is a fun guy. (愛德華很風趣。)
　　　　 B: *That's for sure.* (那是確定的。)

【例3】　A: She's never satisfied. (她永遠不滿足。)
　　　　 B: *That's for sure.* (那是毫無疑問的。)

> 　　*That's for sure.* 這句話，美國人很常說，一定
> 要記下來。無論你説完什麼話以後，都可以加上
> *That's for sure.* 由於使用太多了，*That's for sure.*
> 已經可以放在句中，成爲插入語。所謂「插入語」，
> 就是不影響整句話的文法結構，這種句子在「東華
> 英漢大辭典」p.3493 可以找到。

如：　She will come, *that's for sure.*
　　　（她會來，那是毫無疑問的。）
　　　【that's for sure 是插入語】
　　　Time flies, *that's for sure.*
　　　（時間過得很快，那是一定的。）
　　　Beauty is only skin-deep, *that's for sure.*
　　　（美麗是膚淺的，那是毫無疑問的。）

　　上面句中的 *that's for sure* 也都可改爲 that's for
certain，意義相同。當然也可以寫成兩句話，像：All
good things must come to an end. *That's for sure.*
（天下沒有不散的筵席。那是一定的。）

5. *That's the truth.*

truth〔truθ〕*n.* 事實;眞理

　　truth 的主要意思是「事實」,在此作「眞理」
解,這句話字面的意思是「那是眞理。」引申爲
「你說得對。」

【例1】　A: She is a beauty. (她是個美女。)
　　　　　B: *That's the truth.* (你說得對。)
　　　　　【beauty〔'bjutɪ〕*n.* 美女】

【例2】　A: He's always late.　He's never on time.
　　　　　　　(他老是遲到。他從不準時。)
　　　　　B: *That's the truth.* (你說得對。)
　　　　　【*on time* 準時】

【例3】　A: He works like hell. (他拼命工作。)
　　　　　B: *That's the truth.* (你說得對。)
　　　　　【*like hell* 拼命地】

　　That's the truth. 非常常用,是很多美國人
的口頭禪,反正不管對方說什麼,只要你同意,
你都可說:*That's the truth.*

　　也有美國人說:

That's true. (你說得對。)
That's so true. (你說得很對。)
That's really true. (你說得眞對。)

6. *That's how I feel*.

　　這句話源自 *That's the way how I feel.*（誤，
文法對，美國人不説）但美國人説：That's the way
I feel. 或 That's how I feel. 這兩句話字面的意思
是「那是我的感覺。」引申為「我也有同樣的感覺。」

> ***That's how I feel.***
> = I feel the same.
> = I feel the same way.

【比較1】　***That's how I feel.***【較常用】
　　　　　That's the way I feel.【常用】
　　　　　（我有同樣的感覺。）

【比較2】　***That's how I feel.***【一般語氣】
　　　　　That's how I feel about it, too.【加強語氣】
　　　　　（我也有同樣的感覺。）

7. *I feel the same way*.

　　這句話的意思是「我也有同樣的感覺。」也可説
成：I feel the same way as you.（我的感覺和你一
樣。）或 I feel that way, too.（我也那麼覺得。）
相反的就是：I don't feel the same way.（我不這
麼覺得。）

BOOK 6

8. *I couldn't agree more.*

　　這句話字面的意思是「我沒辦法更同意了。」
引申為「我完全同意。」這句話美國人常說，各種
考試中，也常出現。

【比較】 ***I couldn't agree more.*** 【正，常用】
I couldn't agree more with you. 【正，少用】
I couldn't agree with you more. 【正】

9. *You're right on the money.*

on the money 恰到好處；
非常正確　這個成語源自美
國輪盤賭博，你剛好把籌碼
放在贏的數字上。

　　on the money 通常放在 You're right 之後，用
來加強語氣。

　　這句話的意思是「你說得非常正確。」

【比較】 You're right. (你說得對。)【一般語氣】
You're right on. (你說得很對。)【語氣稍強】
You're right on the money. 【語氣最強】
(你說得非常正確。)

　　　　You're right on. 這句話源自 You're right
on the money. 證明美國人常喜歡說話說一半。
現在 right on 已經變成一個成語，表示「完全對；
完全正確；非常正確」。

【對話練習】

1. A：**I agree**.

　B：And there's no time like the present.

　　Let's take our chances.

　　Let's give it a shot.

　　【*give it a shot* 嘗試】

　A：我同意。

　B：現在正是時候。

　　我們冒險吧。

　　我們試試看吧。

2. A：**I'm with you**.

　B：Good choice.

　　You made the right decision.

　　You can't go wrong with me.

　A：我支持你。

　B：這是明智的選擇。

　　你做了正確的決定。

　　跟著我絕不會錯。

3. A：**You're absolutely right**.

　B：I'm glad you think so.

　　I was hoping you would say that.

　　Now we see eye to eye.

　　【*see eye to eye* 抱持相同意見】

　A：你說得完全對。

　B：你這麼認為，我很高興。

　　我正希望你會那麼說。

　　現在我們的看法一致了。

4. A：**That's for sure**.

　B：I disagree.

　　I'm not sure about that.

　　That is still up in the air.

　　【disagree〔͵dɪsə'gri〕*v.* 不同意
　　up in the air 未決定的】

　A：那是確定的。

　B：我不同意。

　　那一點我不確定。

　　那還不確定。

BOOK 6

5. A：**That's the truth.**

　　B：That's what I thought.
　　　Thanks for telling me.
　　　Thanks for being honest.

A：你說得對。

B：那正是我的想法。
　謝謝你告訴我。
　謝謝你這麼誠實。

6. A：**That's how I feel.**

　　B：I know how you feel.
　　　I respect your feelings.
　　　I used to feel that way, too.

　　　【respect〔rɪ'spɛkt〕v. 尊重
　　　***used to V*.** 以前】

A：我也有同樣的感覺。

B：我知道你的感覺。
　我尊重你的感覺。
　我以前也那麼覺得。

7. A：**I feel the same way.**

　　B：I'm glad you told me.
　　　That's a relief.
　　　I was hoping you'd feel
　　　that way.

　　　【relief〔rɪ'lif〕n. 放心；鬆了一口氣】

A：我也有同樣的感覺。

B：我很高興你告訴我。
　眞是令我鬆了一口氣。
　我正希望你也那麼覺得。

8. A：**I couldn't agree more.**

　　B：What a relief.
　　　I'm glad you agree.
　　　I'm glad I have your support.

　　　【support〔sə'port〕n. 支持】

A：我完全同意。

B：眞是令我鬆了一口氣。
　我很高興你同意。
　有你的支持，我很高興。

9. A：**You're right on the money.**

　　B：I hope I'm right.
　　　This is very important.
　　　This means a lot to me.

A：你完全對。

B：我希望我是對的。
　這一點很重要。
　這對我而言意義重大。

3.　*What can we do?*

What can we do?	我們能做什麼？
Where should we go?	我們該去哪裡？
Where's a great place?	哪個地方好？
Any ideas?	有沒有什麼點子？
Any suggestions?	有什麼建議嗎？
Anywhere is fine with me.	我去什麼地方都可以。
Let's go to the ocean.	我們去海邊。
Let's hit the beach.	我們去海灘吧。
I haven't been there in ages.	我很久沒去那裡了。

** ————————————————————

great〔gret〕*adj.* 很棒的
idea〔aɪ'diə〕*n.* 主意；想法；點子
suggestion〔sə'dʒɛstʃən〕*n.* 建議
ocean〔'oʃən〕*n.* 海洋
hit〔hɪt〕*v.* 打擊；到達；達到　　*in ages* 很久

BOOK 6

【背景説明】

當你要和朋友出去玩，你可以用這九句話，來徵求對方的意見。

1. *What can we do?*

這句話的意思是「我們能做什麼？」也可以説成：Can you think of anything we can do?
（你可不可以想想有什麼事我們可以做？）

> *What can we do?* 後面可以加上單字或片語。
>
> What can we do *for fun*?
> （我們能做什麼好玩的事？）
>
> What can we do *for excitement*?
> 〔ɪkˋsaɪtmənt〕*n.* 興奮；刺激
> （我們能做什麼好玩的事？）
>
> What can we do *this weekend*?
> （我們這個週末能做什麼？）
>
> What can we do *to improve*?
> （我們要怎麼做才能改進？）
>
> What can we do *for his birthday*?
> （我們要怎麼慶祝他的生日？）
>
> What can we do *to learn English*?
> （我們要如何學英文？）

2. *Where should we go?*

　　　　這句話的意思是「我們該去哪裡？」也可以說
成：Where do you think we should go?（你認
為我們該去哪裡？）或 Where do you want to
go?（你想去哪裡？）

3. *Where's a great place?*
　　great〔gret〕*adj.* 極好的；很棒的

　　　　這句話的意思是「哪個地方好？」也可以說成：
Can you think of a great place?（你可以想個好
地方嗎？）place 後面，可加 to go 或 to go to。

　　　　下面都是美國人常說的話，我們按照使用頻率
排列：

① *Where's a great place?*（哪個地方好？）【第一常用】
② Where's a great place to go?【第二常用】
　　（去哪個地方好？）
③ Where's a great place to go to?【第三常用】
　　（去哪個地方好？）

④ Where's a good place?（哪個地方好？）
⑤ Where's a good place to go?（去哪個地方好？）
⑥ Where's a good place to go to?（去哪個地方好？）

⑦ Where's the best place?（哪個地方最好？）
⑧ Where's the best place to go?（去哪個地方最好？）
⑨ Where's the best place to go to?
　　（去哪個地方最好？）

BOOK 6

除了 a great place, a good place 或 the best place 以外，下面也是美國人常說的話：

Where's an exciting place?【第一常用】
　　　　(ɪkˋsaɪtɪŋ) adj. 好玩的
（哪個地方好玩？）

Where's an interesting place to go?【第二常用】
（去哪個地方最有趣？）

Where's a cool place to go to?【第七常用】
　　　　(kul) adj. 酷的；涼爽的
（去哪個地方最酷？）

Where's a super place? (哪個地方最好？)【第八常用】
　　　　(ˋsupɚ) adj. 極好的
Where's a wonderful place to visit?【第四常用】
（去哪個地方最棒？）

Where's an excellent place to go to?【第五常用】
（去哪個地方最好？）

Where's a worthwhile place?【第六常用】
　　　　(ˋwɝθˋhwaɪl) adj. 值得的
（哪個地方值得去？）

Where's a wild place? (哪個地方最瘋狂？)【第九常用】
　　　　(waɪld) adj. 瘋狂的；野生的
Where is the number one place to go?【第三常用】
（去什麼地方是第一個選擇？）

除了上面所講的以外，還有：Where's a happening place? (哪裡有熱鬧的地方？)【詳見 p.247】和 Where's a popular place? (大家喜歡去哪裡？)【詳見 p.258】

4. *Any ideas?*

idea〔aɪˈdiə〕*n.* 主意；想法；點子

這句話源自：Do you have any ideas? (你有沒有什麼點子？) 如果你問別人 Any ideas? 就是指「有沒有什麼點子？」

【比較】 Any ideas?【正，較常用】
　　　　 Any idea?【正，常用】

美國人也常在 ideas 前面，加上形容詞。

　　Any good ideas?【最常用】
　　(有沒有什麼好點子？)
　　Any exciting ideas?【常用】
　　(有沒有什麼好玩的點子？)
　　Any crazy ideas?【年輕人常說】
　　(有沒有什麼瘋狂的點子？)

5. *Any suggestions?*

這句話的意思是「有什麼建議嗎？」源自：Do you have any suggestions? (你有什麼建議嗎？)

Any 後雖然可接單、複數名詞，但是美國人極少使用 *Any suggestion?* (劣) 如果指一項建議，他們說：Do you have a suggestion? (你有沒有一個提議？) 或 Give me a suggestion. (給我一個建議吧。)

美國人也常用 suggest，來徵求對方的意見，下面三句話，美國人常說：

Can you suggest anything?
（你有沒有什麼能夠建議的？）
Can you suggest something?
（你能夠給些建議嗎？）
What do you suggest?（你有什麼建議？）

徵求別人的意見，是一件好事，你說得愈多，愈受人歡迎。

6. *Anywhere is fine with me.*

這句話的意思是「我去什麼地方都可以。」下面是美國人常說的話，像是一個公式：

Anywhere is fine.【最常用】
Anywhere is fine to me.【較不常用】
Anywhere is fine for me.【常用】
Anywhere is fine with me.【較常用】

上面四句話中的 Anywhere 可用 Any place 取代；fine 可用 OK 取代。下面三句話使用頻率非常接近：

Anywhere is OK.（任何地方都可以。）
Any place is OK.（任何地方都可以。）
Any place is OK with me.（我哪裡都可以去。）

美國人也常說：

I can go anywhere. (我哪裡都可以去。)

I am willing to go any place.

(我願意去任何地方。)

Anywhere sounds great to me.

(去哪裡我都覺得很好。)

7. ***Let's go to the ocean.***

ocean〔ˊoʃən〕*n.* 海洋

這句話字面的意思是「我們去海洋。」在中國人的思想中，是不可思議的，我們怎麼可能到海洋去，又不是去自殺！在這句話中，the ocean 是 the oceanfront 的省略。

oceanfront〔ˊoʃən͵frʌnt〕*n.* 海岸邊
(= *land bordering an ocean*)

美國人在海岸邊，往往有很多的餐廳及商店，那個地方，就叫做 oceanfront。那裡也許有 beach（海灘），也許沒有 beach。

當我們說：Let's go to the ocean. 意思是「讓我們到海邊去玩。」也許是去海邊逛那些商店、餐廳，也許是去海灘玩。在字典上，目前還找不到 ocean 是「海岸邊」的意思，但是，編者深信，將來早晚會有。

BOOK 6

【比較1】 Let's go to the ocean.【正，最常用】

Let's go to the oceanfront.

【正，少用，因為美國人說話喜歡簡短】

Let's go to the waterfront.【正，常用】

〔'wɔtə‚frʌnt)〕 *n.* 海岸；河岸；湖岸

【比較2】 Let's go to the ocean.【正】

Let's go to the sea.【誤】

因為美國東西岸濱臨大西洋（the Atlantic
Ocean）或太平洋（the Pacific Ocean），
因為兩邊都有 ocean，所以美國人只要想去
海邊，就會說 Let's go to the ocean.

【比較3】 Let's go to the ocean.（我們去海岸邊。）

Let's go to the beach.（我們去海灘吧。）

〔 bitʃ 〕 *n.* 海灘

the ocean 大於 the beach，因為 beach 專門指
「海灘」，而 the ocean 是指 the oceanfront，
包含海灘，或在海岸上的商店、餐廳等。

　　在美國紐約，人們喜歡說：Let's go to the
shore. 或 Let's go to the coast. 他們通常開車
〔 ʃor 〕 *n.* 海岸；岸邊　　　　〔 kost 〕 *n.* 海岸
到那裡逛逛，那裡通常只是岩石峭壁，沒有沙灘
（beach）或是有熱鬧商店的海邊（oceanfront）。

　　美國人除了說 Let's go to the ocean. 之外，
還常說：

How about the ocean? (去海邊逛逛好嗎？)

How about going to the ocean?

(去海邊逛逛好嗎？)

How does the ocean sound to you?

(你想不想去海邊？)

Let's go see the ocean. (去海邊吧。)

Let's visit the ocean. (去海邊玩吧。)

Let's check out the ocean. (去海邊看看吧。)

ocean　　　　　　　　　　　oceanfront

8. ***Let's hit the beach***.

hit〔hɪt〕*v.* 打擊；到達；達到

　　　hit 的主要意思是「打擊」，像美國小孩常說：
Don't hit me. (不要打我。) He hit me. (他打我。)
但是，在這句話中，hit 卻是表示「去～；到～」
(= *go to*)。

　　　Let's hit the beach. 字面的意思是「讓我們打
擊海灘。」引申為「我們去海灘吧。」說這句話有
幽默的語氣。

BOOK 6

美國人説話，常喜歡用 hit 來代替 go to
或 visit。例：

Let's hit the mall.（我們去購物中心吧。）
(= Let's go to the mall.)

Let's hit the Burger King.（我們去漢堡王吧。）
(= Let's visit the Burger King.)

Let's hit a convenience store.
(= Let's go to a convenience store.)
（我們去便利商店吧。）

I need to **hit** the bathroom.（我需要上廁所。）
〔'bæθ,rum 〕*n.* 廁所

I need to **hit** a 7-11.（我需要去 7-11 便利商店。）

I need to **hit** the road.（我需要上路了。）

9. *I haven't been there in ages.*

age 的主要意思是「年齡」或「時代」，美國
人常説的 in ages，在目前所有的字典中，都查
不到，字典上只有 for ages，事實上，*in ages*
比 for ages 要常用，兩者意義相同，都表示 for
a long time（很久）。

【例】 I haven't done that *in ages*.
（我很久沒做那件事情。）
I haven't seen you *in ages*.
（我很久沒見到你了。）
She hasn't gone swimming *in ages*.
（她很久沒去游泳了。）

【比較 1】

> I haven't been there *in ages*.【較常説，適合寫】
> = I haven't been there *for ages*.【較少説，適合寫】
> = I haven't been there *in a long time*.【較常説】
> = I haven't been there *for a long time*.【常用】
> （我很久沒去那裡了。）

【比較 2】

I haven't been there *in ages*.【最常用】
（我很久沒去那裡了。）
I haven't been there *in years*.【常用】
（我好多年沒去那裡了。）【*in years* = *in many years*】
I haven't been there *in months*.【常用】
（我好幾個月沒去那裡了。）
【*in months* = *in many months*】
I haven't been there *in days*.【常用】
（我好幾天沒去那裡了。）【*in days* = *in many days*】

也可以明確地説成：

I haven't been there *in five years*.
= I haven't been there for five years.
（我已經五年沒去那裡了。）
【in 在此表示「在…（期間）」，也常表示「再過（多久）」。】

BOOK 6

【對話練習】

1. A：**What can we do?**

   B：I'm not sure.

   　　I don't know.

   　　Let me think about it.

2. A：**Where should we go?**

   B：Let's go downtown.

   　　Let's go to the mall.

   　　Let's go to a coffee shop.

   　　【mall〔mɔl〕*n.* 購物中心】

3. A：**Where's a great place?**

   B：The beach is a good place.

   　　The park is not bad.

   　　The university campus is

   　　a nice place to walk.

   　　【university〔ˌjunə'vɝsətɪ〕*n.* 大學

   　　campus〔'kæmpəs〕*n.* 校園】

4. A：**Any ideas?**

   B：I'm sorry.

   　　I'm all out of ideas.

   　　I can't think of anything.

   　　【*be out of* 缺乏；沒有】

A：我們能做什麼？

B：我不確定。

　　我不知道。

　　讓我想想看。

A：我們該去哪裡？

B：我們去市中心吧。

　　我們去購物中心吧。

　　我們去咖啡店吧。

A：哪個地方好？

B：海灘是個不錯的地方。

　　公園不錯。

　　大學校園是散步的好地

　　方。

A：有沒有什麼點子？

B：很抱歉。

　　我完全沒有點子。

　　我想不到任何點子。

BOOK 6

5. A：**Any suggestions?**

　B：Yes, I have one.

　　I have a suggestion.

　　I suggest we get out of here.

　　　A：有什麼建議嗎？

　　　B：是的，我有一個。

　　　　我有一個建議。

　　　　我建議我們離開這裡。

6. A：**Anywhere is fine with me.**

　B：You're easy to please.

　　You're very polite.

　　I like that about you.

　　　【please〔pliz〕*v.* 取悅

　　　　polite〔pə'laɪt〕*adj.* 有禮貌的】

　　　A：我去什麼地方都可以。

　　　B：你真是容易取悅。

　　　　你真是客氣。

　　　　我喜歡你這一點。

7. A：**Let's go to the ocean.**

　B：Good idea.

　　I love the ocean.

　　That's a super place to go.

　　　【super〔'supɚ〕*adj.* 極好的】

　　　A：我們去海邊吧。

　　　B：好主意。

　　　　我喜歡海邊。

　　　　能去那裡真是太棒了。

8. A：**Let's hit the beach.**

　B：That's OK with me.

　　I'm game for anything.

　　That's an offer I can't refuse.

　　　【*be game for* 願意

　　　　offer〔'ɔfɚ〕*n.* 提議

　　　　refuse〔rɪ'fjuz〕*v.* 拒絕】

　　　A：我們去海灘吧。

　　　B：我都可以。

　　　　我願意做任何事。

　　　　那是我無法拒絕的提議。

9. A：**I haven't been there in ages.**

　B：Well, not much has changed.

　　It's still the same old place.

　　It's like time has stood still.

　　　【*stand still* 停止；停頓】

　　　A：我很久沒去那裡了。

　　　B：嗯，沒什麼改變。

　　　　仍然是老樣子。

　　　　好像時間靜止了一樣。

BOOK 6

4. *Let's go hiking*.

Let's go hiking.	我們去郊遊吧。
Let's head for the hills.	我們去爬山吧。
Let's leave the city behind.	讓我們遠離城市的喧囂。
I can't wait to go.	我迫不及待要去。
I can smell the fresh air already.	我已經可以聞到新鮮的空氣。
There's nothing like Mother Nature.	沒有什麼能比得上大自然。
Rain or shine, we're going.	不管天氣如何，我們都要去。
Nothing can stop us.	沒有什麼可以阻止我們。
Maybe we won't come back.	也許我們不會回來了。

**

hike〔haɪk〕*v.* 健行；郊遊　　***head for*** 朝…前進
hill〔hɪl〕*n.* 山丘　　***leave~behind*** 遺留~；留下~
smell〔smɛl〕*v.* 聞到　　fresh〔frɛʃ〕*adj.* 新鮮的
air〔ɛr〕*n.* 空氣　　***nothing like*** 沒有什麼能比得上
Mother Nature （孕育萬物的）大自然
rain or shine 無論晴雨；無論情況如何
stop〔stɑp〕*v.* 阻止　　maybe〔'mebɪ〕*adv.* 也許

【背景説明】

美國人和中國人一樣，喜歡戶外活動，他們喜歡去爬山（go hiking），或到公園去（go to the park）。

1. ***Let's go hiking***.
   hike〔haɪk〕*v.,n.* 遠足；健行；徒步旅行

> 【比較】***Let's go hiking***.
> （我們去爬山吧。）【通常是能夠走上去的山】
> Let's go mountain climbing.
> （我們去登山吧。）
>
> 中文説：「我們去爬山。」可能是走上去，也可能是攀登上去。美國人的説法不同，走上去，就是 go hiking；爬著上去，就是 go mountain climbing，通常要帶很多繩子。【詳見「演講式英語」p.223】

下面九句話的意思都是「我們去爬山吧。」我們按照方便記憶的順序排列，三句爲一組：

> Let's hike. 【第一常用】
> ***Let's go hiking***. 【第二常用】
> Let's take a hike. 【第三常用】
>
> Let's go take a hike. 【第六常用】
> 【此句是雙關語，含有「滾開。」的意思，等於 Get lost.】
> Let's go for a hike. 【第四常用】
> Let's go on a hike. 【第五常用】

Let's go out for a hike.【第七常用】

Let's do some hiking.【第八常用】

Let's go do some hiking.【第九常用】

　【*go + V-ing* 去～（V-ing 大部份是指運動或遊戲）】

美國人常邀請朋友說：

　Let's go hiking.（我們去爬山吧。）

Let's go swimming.（我們去游泳吧。）

Let's go shopping.（我們去買東西吧。）

Let's go camping.（我們去露營吧。）

Let's go backpacking.

　（我們背著背包去健行吧。）

Let's go fishing.（我們去釣魚吧。）

　【camp〔kæmp〕*v.* 露營
　　backpack〔ˈbæk͵pæk〕*v.* 背背包健行
　　fish〔fɪʃ〕*v.* 釣魚】

　　Let's go hiking. 可以說成：Let's do some hiking. 同樣地，Let's go shopping. 也可以說成：Let's do some shopping. 但是，Let's go swimming. 卻不能說成：*Let's do some swimming*.（誤）可以說成：Let's go for a swim. 美國人不說 *Let's go walking*.（誤）而說 Let's go for a walk.（我們去散步吧。）

　【比較】*Let's go hiking*.（我們去郊遊吧。）
　　　　　Let's go for a walk.（我們去散步吧。）

Let's go hiking. 不一定是去爬山，通常去較遠的地方，去享受大自然，有樹木、有森林，或是有溪流的地方。hike 的英文解釋是 go on a walk out in nature for pleasure or exercise，所以，Let's go hiking. 最好的意思是「我們去郊遊吧。」或「我們去爬山吧。」要看實際情況而定。

2. *Let's head for the hills.*

head for 朝…前進 (= *proceed or go in a certain direction*)

hill〔hɪl〕*n.* 山丘

這句話的意思是「我們朝著山丘方向走吧。」引申為「我們去爬山吧。」在中國人的思想中，很少把山分成大山或小山，美國人通常把七百五十公尺以下的小山，稱作 hill。中國人很少說「山丘」，只說「山」。

【比較】 *Let's head for the hills.*

【正，常用，有引申的涵義】

Let's head for the mountains.

(我們朝山的方向前進吧。)

【正，字面意思】

head for the hills 因為使用太頻繁，已經變成固定用法，還有一個涵義是「逃走」(= *escape*)。源自美國人看到印地安人來了，他們常說：Head for the hills. The Indians are coming. (快逃。印地安人來了。)

因為 Let's head for the hills. 已經成為慣用句，是固定用法，只要是去爬山，不管大山、小山，都說這句話。而 Let's head for the mountains. 表示「我們朝著山的方向走吧。」

【比較】 Let's head for the *hills*. 【正】
　　　　Let's head for the *hill*. 【誤】

在字典上 hill 可用單複數，但在這裡，美國人已經習慣用複數，因為山丘多半是好幾個在一起。

Let's head for the hills. 的類似說法有：

Let's go to the mountains. (我們去爬山。)
Let's travel to the mountains. (我們到山上去玩。)
　　　　〔ˈtrævl〕*v.* 行進
Let's go toward the mountains. (我們去山上。)
　　　　(tord,təˈwɔrd) *prep.* 朝著…方向

上面三句的 mountains，美國人不習慣改成 hills。因為 go to the mountains 和 head for the hills 已經說習慣了，變成固定用法。

【比較】 中文：我們去爬山吧。
　　　　英文：Let's go to the mountains. 【正】
　　　　　　　Let's go to the hills. 【誤】
　　　　　　　Let's head for the hills. 【正】

下面六句美國人常說：

Let's *head for* the hills. (我們去爬山吧。)

Let's *head for* home. (我們回家吧。)【for 可省略】

Let's *head for* the beach. (我們去海邊吧。)
〔 bitʃ 〕*n.* 海邊

Let's *head for* the mall. (我們去購物中心吧。)
〔 mɔl 〕*n.* 購物中心

Let's *head for* downtown. (我們去市中心吧。)
〔'daʊn'taʊn 〕*n.* 市中心

Let's *head for* the park. (我們去公園吧。)

3. *Let's leave the city behind.*

leave ~ behind 遺留；留下；忘記帶走

這句話字面的意思是「我們把這個城市留在後面吧。」引申為「我們遠離城市的喧囂。」(= *Let's get away from this city.*) 也可以說成：We'll leave the city behind. (我們要離開這個城市。)

美國人常說 *leave ~ behind*，如：

Don't *leave* anything *behind*.
(不要忘記任何東西。)【參照 p.451 】

Let's *leave* all our worries *behind*.
〔'wɝɪz 〕*n. pl.* 煩惱
(我們把所有的煩惱都忘掉吧。)

Don't *leave* me *behind*. I want to go, too.
(不要丟下我。我也要去。)

BOOK 6

4. *I can't wait to go.*

這句話的字面意思是「我沒辦法等待要去。」
引申為「我迫不及待要去。」也可以加強語氣說
成：I just can't wait to go. 或只說：I just
can't wait.

美國人喜歡說 *I can't wait.* 之類的話，例如：

> *I can't wait* to graduate.
> 〔'grædʒʊ͵et〕v. 畢業
> （我迫不及待要畢業。）
> *I can't wait* to see you.【在電話中常說】
> （我迫不及待要見你。）
> *I can't wait* to see that movie.
> （我迫不及待要看那部電影。）
>
> *I can't wait* to travel to the States.
> （我迫不及待要去美國旅行。）
> *I can't wait* to get married.
> （我迫不及待要結婚了。）
> *I can't wait* for payday. 〔'pe͵de〕n. 發薪日
> （我希望發薪水那天趕快來到。）
>
> *I can't wait* to go swimming.
> （我很想去游泳。）
> *I can't wait* to get out of the rain.
> （我迫不及待要去躲雨。）
> *I can't wait* to eat. （我很想吃東西。）

5. ***I can smell the fresh air already.***

smell〔smɛl〕*v.* 聞到　　fresh〔frɛʃ〕*adj.* 新鮮的
air〔ɛr〕*n.* 空氣

　　這句話的意思是「我已經可以聞到新鮮的空氣。」源自：Even though I'm not there yet, ***I can smell the fresh air.***（雖然我還沒去那裡，我已經可以聞到新鮮的空氣。）這是美國人的習慣說法，表示對未來的預期。這句話也可以說成：I can almost smell the fresh air now.（我現在幾乎已經可以聞到新鮮的空氣了。）

6. ***There's nothing like Mother Nature.***

nothing like 沒有什麼能比得上
Mother Nature （孕育萬物的）大自然

　　這句話的字面意思是「沒有什麼東西像大自然那樣。」引申為「沒有什麼能比得上大自然。」（= *Nothing can compare to Mother Nature.*）
【compare〔kəm'pɛr〕*v.* 比較　　***compare to*** 比得上】

美國人常說：

　　There's nothing like home-cooked food.
　　（沒有什麼東西能比得上家裡煮的食物。）
　　There's nothing like falling in love.
　　（沒有什麼能比得上談戀愛的感覺。）【***fall in love*** 戀愛】
　　There's nothing like spending time with you.
　　（沒有什麼能比得上和你在一起，更令人愉快。）

BOOK 6

7. ***Rain or shine, we're going.***

rain or shine 無論晴雨；無論情況如何

這句話的意思是「無論晴雨，我們都要去。」
也就是「不管天氣如何，我們都要去。」

rain or shine 源自 no matter whether it rains or shines，是固定用法，不可說成 *shine or rain* (誤)。

Rain or shine, we're going.
= Whether it rains or shines, we're going.
= No matter whether it rains or shines, we're going.
= No matter what, we're going.

rain or shine 雖然主要是指天氣，也會有「無論情況如何」的意思。例：I know I can depend on you, rain or shine. (我知道在任何情況下，我都可以依靠你。)

美國人常說：

Don't worry. I'll be there, ***rain or shine***.
(別擔心。無論晴雨，我一定會去。)
Rain or shine, we're leaving on Sunday.
(無論晴雨，我們星期天都會離開。)
We're having the picnic, ***rain or shine***.
(無論晴雨，我們都要舉行野餐。)

8. *Nothing can stop us.*

stop〔stɑp〕*v.* 阻止

這句話的意思是「沒有什麼可以阻止我們。」

在這裡也可以加強語氣說成：

Nothing can stop us from going.【最常用】

（沒有什麼可以阻止我們去。）

Nothing can prevent us from going.【常用】
〔prɪˈvɛnt〕*v.* 阻止

（沒有什麼事可以阻止我們去。）

Nothing can keep us from going.【較常用】

（沒有什麼可以阻止我們去。）

【prevent, stop, keep 接受詞後，都有 from，
表「阻止某人做某事」。】

9. *Maybe we won't come back.*

maybe〔ˈmebɪ〕*adv.* 也許

這句話的意思是「也許我們不會回來了。」這
是美國人的幽默，和中國人的思想完全不同，中
國人甚至忌諱說這類不吉利的話。

這句話的涵義是 Maybe we'll like it so
much we won't come back.（也許我們會很喜
歡那裡，而不想回來。）

美國人也常說：

We might not come back.【第一常用】
（我們也許不會回來了。）

We might stay there forever.【第五常用】
（我們也許永遠待在那裡。）

We may never come back.【第四常用】
（我們可能永遠都不回來了。）

We might not make it back.【第三常用】
（我們也許回不來了。）
【*make it back* 回來（= *come back*）】

We might decide to stay.【第二常用】
（我們也許會決定留在那裡。）

We may never return.【第六常用】
（我們可能永遠都不回來了。）

【劉毅老師的話】

　　「一口氣背會話」背的時候，一定要
連中文一起背，也可以先背英文，再背中
文，如此印象深刻。

【對話練習】

1. A：**Let's go hiking.**

　B：Sounds good to me.
　　 I need some exercise.
　　 I love to get outdoors.
　　 【outdoors (ˈaʊtˈdorz) *adv.* 到戶外】

A：我們去爬山吧。

B：聽起來不錯。
　 我需要一些運動。
　 我喜歡去戶外。

2. A：**Let's head for the hills.**

　B：That's a nice idea.
　　 It's cooler there.
　　 The air is fresh and clean.

A：我們去爬山吧。

B：好主意。
　 那裡比較涼快。
　 空氣既新鮮又乾淨。

3. A：**Let's leave the city behind.**

　B：I'm with you.
　　 Let's hit the road.
　　 Let's leave this place behind.
　　 【*hit the road* 上路】

A：讓我們遠離城市的喧囂。

B：我贊成。
　 我們走吧。
　 我們離開這個地方吧。

4. A：**I can't wait to go.**

　B：Neither can I.
　　 I'm tired of this place.
　　 I need to get away.
　　 【*be tired of* 對～厭倦】

A：我迫不及待要去。

B：我也是。
　 我厭倦了這個地方。
　 我需要離開。

BOOK 6

5. A : **I can smell the fresh air already**.

   B : I know what you mean.
I feel the same way.
I can't wait to get there.

6. A : **There's nothing like Mother Nature**.

   B : I totally agree.
The outdoors is great.
I love camping and hiking.
【totally〔'totḷɪ〕*adv.* 完全地
   the outdoors 戶外 (視為單數)】

7. A : **Rain or shine, we're going**.

   B : That's the spirit.
We're going for sure.
We're going no matter what.
【spirit〔'spɪrɪt〕*n.* 精神
   for sure 確定】

8. A : **Nothing can stop us**.

   B : That's right.
Nothing will stop us.
Nothing can stand in our way.
【***stand in*** *one's* ***way*** 阻礙某人】

9. A : **Maybe we won't come back**.

   B : That's not a problem.
We can stay as long as we like.
We can come and go as we please.
【please〔pliz〕*v.* 喜歡;想做】

A：我已經可以聞到新鮮的空氣。

B：我知道你的意思。
我也有相同的感覺。
我迫不及待要去那裡。

A：沒有什麼可以比得上大自然。

B：我完全同意。
戶外真棒。
我喜歡露營和爬山。

A：不管天氣如何,我們都要去。

B：就是要有那種精神。
我們確定要去。
無論如何,我們都要去。

A：沒有什麼可以阻止我們。

B：沒錯。
沒有什麼可以阻止我們。
沒有什麼可以阻礙我們。

A：也許我們不會回來了。

B：那不是問題。
我們想要待多久都可以。
我們可以隨意來來去去。

5. Let's get ready.

Let's get ready.	我們要做好準備。
Let's make a plan.	我們做個計劃吧。
It's better to be prepared.	最好要預先準備好。
We need supplies.	我們需要一些東西。
We need some stuff.	我們需要買一些東西。
Let's go grocery shopping.	我們去買東西吧。
Just keep it simple.	只要簡單就好。
Just stick to the basics.	要一切從簡。
Don't buy anything fancy.	不要買華而不實的東西。

** ———————————————————

ready〔ˋrɛdɪ〕*adj.* 準備好的   prepare〔prɪˋpɛr〕*v.* 準備
supplies〔səˋplaɪz〕*n. pl.* 用品；必需品；補給品
stuff〔stʌf〕*n.* 東西   grocery〔ˋgrosərɪ〕*n.* 雜貨
simple〔ˋsɪmpḷ〕*adj.* 簡單的   *stick to* 堅持
basics〔ˋbesɪks〕*n. pl.* 基本原理；基本原則
fancy〔ˋfænsɪ〕*adj.* 精美的；昂貴的

BOOK 6

【背景説明】

　　要去郊遊前，可説這九句話，建議朋友和你一起去買一些東西。這一回的資料，往往也可用在其他的場合。

1. ***Let's get ready.***

　　ready〔ˈrɛdɪ〕*adj.* 準備好的

　　這句話的意思是「我們要做好準備。」美國人常説 ***Let's get ready.*** 之類的話：

　　　　Let's ***get ready.***【第一常用】
　　　　（我們要做好準備。）
　　　　Let's ***get ready***, OK?【第二常用】
　　　　（我們準備準備，好嗎？）
　　　　We should ***get ready.***【第三常用】
　　　　（我們應該做好準備。）

　　　　I think we should ***get ready.***【第六常用】
　　　　（我認爲我們應該要做好準備。）
　　　　Would you like to ***get ready?***【第七常用】
　　　　（你要不要準備準備？）
　　　　Do you want to ***get ready?***【第八常用】
　　　　（你要不要準備準備？）

It's time to *get ready*.【第四常用】

（是該準備的時候了。）

It's about time to *get ready*.【第五常用】

（大概是該準備準備的時候了。）

It's time we *got ready*.【第九常用】

（該是我們準備的時候了。）

【It's time 後面用假設法，詳見「文法寶典」p.374】

Let's get ready 後面可接 for 加上名詞，表示「為～準備」。

Let's *get ready for* our trip.

（為我們的旅行準備準備吧。）

Let's *get ready for* the meeting.

（我們要為開會做準備。）

Let's *get ready for* the party.

（我們要為宴會做準備。）

Let's *get ready for* the test.

（我們要準備好考試。）

Let's *get ready for* their arrival.

（我們要為他們的到來做好準備。）

Let's *get ready for* anything.

（我們要準備好一切。）

> **Let's get ready** 也常接不定詞：
>
> Let's **get ready** to go. (我們準備準備走吧。)
> Let's **get ready** to go home.
> (我們準備準備回家吧。)
> Let's **get ready** to go out.
> (我們準備準備出門吧。)
>
> Let's **get ready** to do it.
> (我們準備準備去做這件事吧。)
> Let's **get ready** to work.
> (我們準備開始工作吧。)
> 【老師常說這句話，表示「我們準備上課吧。」】
> Let's **get ready** to eat.
> (我們要準備準備吃東西了。)

【比較1】 下面兩句話意義相同：

Let's get ready. 【常用，通俗】
Let's be ready. 【少用，有點像書本英文】

【比較2】 **Let's get ready**. 【較常用】
= Let's prepare. 【常用】

2. **Let's make a plan**.

這句話的意思是「我們做個計劃吧。」也有美國人
說：Let's make some plans. (我們做一些計劃吧。)

【比較】 **Let's make a plan**. 【較常用】
= Let's get a plan. 【常用】
= Let's have a plan. 【常用】

3. *It's better to be prepared.*

prepare〔prɪ'pɛr〕*v.* 準備

有些動詞，主動語態與被動語態的意義相同，
像 prepare、determine（決定）、graduate（畢業）、
marry（結婚）等【詳見「文法寶典」p.388】。所以：

> *It's better to be prepared.*【常用】
> = It's better to prepare.【常用】
> （最好要預先準備好。）

It's better to be prepared. 源自 It's better
to be prepared *in advance.* 或 It's better to be
prepared *ahead of time.*【*in advance* 預先
（= *ahead of time*）】

It's better 是一項有禮貌的提議，例如：

> *It's better* that way.（那樣子比較好。）
> 　　　　　〔we〕*n.* 樣子
> *It's better* if we go together.
> （如果我們一起走，會比較好。）
> *It's better* to wait.（等一等比較好。）

> *It's better* to leave early.（最好早點走。）
> *It's better* not to be late.（最好不要遲到。）
> *It's better* if we take the train.
> （如果我們坐火車，會比較好。）

4. ***We need supplies.***

supplies〔 sə'plaɪz 〕*n. pl.* 用品；必需品；補給品

> supply 這個字，可當動詞和名詞，作「供應」解，它的複數形式，是指「必需品」、「補給品」、「用品」，像 household supplies（家庭用品）、military supplies（軍隊的補給品）、office supplies（辦公用品）、medical supplies（醫藥用品）、school supplies（學校用品）。
>
> *supplies* 這個字，也可以指「東西」(things；stuff)。***We need supplies.*** 的字面意思是「我們需要一些東西。」引申為 We have to buy supplies.（我們需要買一些東西。）或 We need to get supplies.（我們需要弄一點東西來。）

這類的説法有：

> ***We need supplies.***（我們需要一些東西。）【第一常用】
> We need some supplies.【第四常用】
> （我們需要一些東西。）
>
> We need to buy supplies.【第二常用】
> （我們需要買一些東西。）
>
> We need to buy some supplies.【第五常用】
> （我們需要買一些東西。）
> We need to get supplies.【第三常用】
> （我們需要弄一點東西來。）
>
> We need to get some supplies.【第六常用】
> （我們需要弄一些東西來。）
> 【need to 可用 have to 代替，使用頻率相同】

5. *We need some stuff*.

stuff〔stʌf〕*n.* 東西

> 　　stuff 這個字，當動詞時，主要意思是「填塞」，當名詞時，主要意思是「原料；材料」，是不可數名詞。
>
> 　　在日常生活當中，美國年輕人很喜歡用 stuff 這個字，作「東西；物品」解。例如，他們找不到東西，他們會說：Where is my stuff?（我的東西在哪裡？）送朋友走的時候，美國人常說：Don't forget your stuff.（不要忘了你的東西。）吃到好東西時，他們會說：This stuff tastes good.（這個東西嚐起來很香。）
>
> 　　*We need some stuff*. 字面的意思是「我們需要一些東西。」引申為「我們需要買一些東西。」（= *We need to buy some stuff*.）或「我們需要弄一些東西來。」（= *We need to get some stuff*.）

【比較】　*We need some stuff*.

　　　　　　【常用，和家人、朋友在一起時常說】

　　　　= We need some things.【常用】

　　　　　　【要注意，stuff 用單數，因為它不可數，things 要用複數，這兩句話都很常用，使用頻率相同。】

美國人常説的有：

We need stuff. 【第四常用】
（我們需要一些東西。）
We need some stuff. 【第一常用】
（我們需要一些東西。）

We need to buy stuff. 【第六常用】
（我們需要買一些東西。）
We need to buy some stuff. 【第三常用】
（我們需要買一些東西。）

We need to get stuff. 【第五常用】
（我們需要弄一點東西。）
We need to get some stuff. 【第二常用】
（我們需要弄一些東西來。）
【need to 可用 have to 代替，使用頻率相同】

6. ***Let's go grocery shopping.***
grocery〔ˈɡrosərɪ〕 *n.* 雜貨

　　在英漢字典上，大部份都把 grocery 翻成「食品雜貨」，這和我們中國人所説的話格格不入，因爲中國人的語言中，沒有「食品雜貨」。從前美國人説的grocery，大部份指食品，像咖啡、糖、麵粉、罐頭、水果等，現在人們不只需要食物了，所以 grocery還包含肥皂、火柴、香煙、報紙、雜誌等家庭用品，所以，grocery 最好的翻譯，應該是「雜貨」。***Let's go grocery shopping.*** 就是「我們去買雜貨吧。」也就是「我們去買東西吧。」。

BOOK 6

【比較】*Let's go grocery shopping.*

（我們去買東西吧。）

【「東西」是指「以食品爲主的雜貨」，不包含衣服等】

Let's go window-shopping.

（我們去逛街吧。）

【不購買東西，只是逛街瀏覽櫥窗】

Let's go shopping.（我們去買東西吧。）

【在這裡「東西」是泛指「一切東西」，包含衣服】

下面的話美國人常說：

Let's go food shopping.

（我們去買一些食物吧。）

Let's go clothes shopping.（我們去買衣服吧。）

Let's go Christmas shopping.

（我們去買點聖誕節需要的東西吧。）

【在美國，聖誕節有送禮物的習俗，他們通常會大肆採購。】

7. *Just keep it simple.*

simple〔'sɪmpḷ〕*adj.* 簡單的

這句話的字面意思是「只要保持簡單。」引申爲「只要簡單就好。」

例如美國人帶你出去玩，你可以說：Don't spend too much money. *Just keep it simple.*（不要花太多錢。只要簡單就好。）你到別人家裡作客，你可以說：Please don't prepare a big meal for me. *Just keep it simple.*（請不要爲我準備大餐。只要簡單就好。）

BOOK 6

在這一回中，Just keep it simple. 意思是 Whatever you buy, just keep it simple. (無論你買什麼，簡單就好。) 暗示「不要買太多、不要買貴的東西。」(*Don't buy too much.* *Don't buy expensive products.*)

下面九句話，我們按照使用頻率排列：

① Keep it simple. 【第一常用】
（以簡單爲原則。）

② ***Just keep it simple.*** 【第二常用】
（只要簡單就好。）

③ Please keep it simple. 【第三常用】
（請以簡單爲原則。）

④ I want you to keep it simple.
（我希望你以簡單爲原則。）

⑤ I'd like you to keep it simple.
（我希望你以簡單爲原則。）

⑥ I hope you can keep it simple.
（我希望你能夠以簡單爲原則。）

⑦ Always keep it simple.
（總是要以簡單爲原則。）

⑧ Remember to keep it simple.
（記住要以簡單爲原則。）

⑨ Keep it simple and you can't go wrong.
（簡單就不會錯。）

8. *Just stick to the basics*.

stick〔stɪk〕*n.* 棍子   *v.* 黏住（常和 to 或 with 連用）

stick to   堅持

basics〔'besɪks〕*n. pl.* 基本原理；基本原則

> stick 當名詞時，主要意思是「棍子」，像
> 「筷子」，是 chopsticks，當動詞時，主要意思
> 是「黏住；貼著」，例如「把郵票貼在信上。」就
> 是 Stick the stamp on the letter. 在這裡，*stick
> to* 引申為「堅持」。
>
> basic 通常當形容詞，作「基本的」解，等
> 於 fundamental。當名詞時，一定要用複數形。
> *basics* 的主要意思是「基本原則；基本原理；基
> 本因素；基本規律等」。
>
> *Just stick to the basics*. 意思是「只要堅持基
> 本原則就好。」在這裡暗示「只要買我們所需要的
> 東西就好了。」(*Just buy what we need*.) 或「只
> 要買我們所需要的基本食物。」(*Just buy the basic
> foods we need*.) 在這裡，中文最好的翻譯是「要
> 一切從簡。」
>
> *Stick to the basics*. 英文解釋是 Follow the
> regular, fundamental way of doing something.
> （按照一般基本的方式做某事。）或 Stick to the
> basic principles. （堅持基本原則。）
> 〔'prɪnsəpl̩z〕*n. pl.* 原則

下面六句話，我們按照使用頻率排列：

① Stick to the basics. 【第一常用】
（堅持基本原則。）

② *Just stick to the basics.* 【第二常用】
（只要堅持基本原則就好。）
【在這一回中，引申為「只要一切從簡。」】

③ Please stick to the basics. （請堅持基本原則。）

④ I'd like you to stick to the basics.
（我希望你堅持基本原則。）

⑤ I want you to stick to the basics.
（我希望你堅持基本原則。）

⑥ I want to remind you to stick to the basics.
（我要提醒你，要堅持基本原則。）
【remind〔rɪ'maɪnd〕v. 提醒】

在中國人的思想中，沒有 Stick to the basics. 這句話，我們一定要習慣使用。特別注意，要用複數形的 *basics*。

Stick to the basics. Don't overdo it.
〔'ovɚ'du〕v. 做得過份
（要堅持基本原則。不要做得過份。）

Stick to the basics. Don't buy too much.
（要一切從簡。不要買太多。）

Stick to the basics. Don't get off track.
（要堅持基本原則。不要離開目標。）
【*get off track* 離題；離開目標】

> *Stick to the basics*, and you'll succeed.
>
> （堅持基本原則，你就會成功。）
>
> *Stick to the basics*, and you can't go wrong.
>
> （堅持基本原則，你就不會出錯。）
>
> *Stick to the basics* and never give up.
>
> （堅持基本原則，永遠不要放棄。）【*give up* 放棄】

9. *Don't buy anything fancy.*

fancy〔'fænsɪ〕*adj.* 精美的；別緻的；（價格）過高的；昂貴的

這句話的意思是「不要買任何華而不實的東西。」

fancy 當動詞時，主要意思是「想像」，當形容詞時，意思是「想像出來的」、「高級的；高檔的；漂亮的；昂貴的」，通常是好到讓人覺得有點奢侈（extravagant）或炫耀（showy）的味道。
〔ɪk'strævəgənt〕　　　〔'ʃoɪ〕

例如，你看到一個人戴著一頂很漂亮、花俏的帽子，你就可以說：What a fancy hat! It looks very nice.（好漂亮的帽子！看起來很棒。）看到一個女孩子，穿著漂亮的衣服，你就可以說：That's a very fancy outfit. It looks pretty on you.
〔'aʊt,fɪt〕*n.* 服裝

（那件衣服很漂亮。妳穿起來很漂亮）

【fancy 這個字，可表示稱讚，作「漂亮的」解，也可批評，作「華而不實的」解，要看實際情況而定。】

BOOK 6

【對話練習】

1. A：**Let's get ready**.
   B：OK.
   I agree.
   That's a good idea.

   A：我們要做好準備。
   B：好的。
   我同意。
   那是個好主意。

2. A：**Let's make a plan**.
   B：We should.
   We should make a plan.
   It's time to make a plan.

   A：我們做個計劃吧。
   B：我們應該要。
   我們應該要做個計劃。
   是該做個計劃的時候了。

3. A：**It's better to be prepared**.
   B：That's the truth.
   You are so right.
   Always be prepared.

   A：最好要預先準備好。
   B：你說得對。
   你說得很對。
   一定要做好準備。

4. A：**We need supplies**.
   B：Yes, we do.
   We're running low.
   We're low on supplies.
   【*run low* 缺乏
   be low on ～快用完了】

   A：我們需要一些東西。
   B：是的，我們需要。
   我們的東西快沒了。
   我們的東西快用完了。

5. A : **We need some stuff**.

   B : We sure do.
   We don't have a thing.
   We need to buy a lot.

A：我們需要買一些東西。

B：我們的確需要。
我們沒有東西了。
我們需要買很多。

6. A : **Let's go grocery shopping**.

   B : I'll make a list.
   I know just what we need.
   It won't take long.

A：我們去買東西吧。

B：我會列一張清單。
我知道我們需要什麼。
不會很久。

7. A : **Just keep it simple**.

   B : That's good advice.
   That's sound advice.
   I won't argue with that.
   【advice〔əd'vaɪs〕 *n.* 忠告；建議
   sound〔saʊnd〕 *adj.* 明智的；正確的
   argue〔'ɑrgjʊ〕 *v.* 爭論】

A：只要簡單就好。

B：那是個好建議。
那是個好的建議。
我對那一點沒有爭議。

8. A : **Just stick to the basics**.

   B : You're right.
   That's the way.
   Always stick to the basics.

A：只要一切從簡。

B：你說得對。
就是應該那樣。
總是要一切從簡。

9. A : Don't buy anything fancy.

   B : **Don't worry about me**.
   I'm very frugal.
   I won't waste a cent.
   【frugal〔'frugl̩〕 *adj.* 節儉的】

A：不要買任何華而不實的
東西。

B：不要擔心我。
我非常節儉。
我不會浪費一分錢。

BOOK 6

6. Please get in.

Please get in.	請上車。
Sit up front.	坐到前面來。
Feel free to adjust the seat.	你可以調整座位。
Buckle up.	把安全帶扣上。
Fasten your seat belt.	扣好你的安全帶。
We don't want a ticket!	我們不想要罰單！
You can relax.	你可以放心。
I'm a safe driver.	我開車很安全。
I'll get you there in one piece.	我會平安地載你到那裡。

** ——————————————————

get in 進入；上車　　up〔ʌp〕*adv.* 向
front〔frʌnt〕*adv.* 向前面　　*up front* 向前面；在前面
feel free to V. 自由地～　　adjust〔ə'dʒʌst〕*v.* 調整
buckle〔'bʌkl̩〕*v.* 扣上　　*buckle up* 扣上安全帶
fasten〔'fæsn̩〕*v.* 繫上；扣上　　*seat belt* 安全帶
ticket〔'tɪkɪt〕*n.* 罰單　　relax〔rɪ'læks〕*v.* 放鬆
get〔gɛt〕*v.* 使到達　　*in one piece* （人）平安無事地

【背景説明】

　　當你邀請朋友上你的車子，你想請他坐在前面，就可以説這九句話。

1. ***Please get in.***

　　get in 進入；上車

　　　　get in 的基本意思是「進入」，這句話的意思是「請上車。」也可以説成：Please get in the car. 在美語中，上小車用 get in，上大車用 get on，像 Let's get on the bus. (我們上公車吧。)

　　　　美國人邀請別人上車的説法有很多：

　　Get in. (上車。)【第八常用】【只有親密的朋友才用】
　　Get in the car. (上車。)【第十一常用】
　　Get in, please. (請上車。)【第二常用】

　　Please get in. (請上車。)【第一常用】
　　Please get in the car. (請上車。)【第三常用】
　　Get in the car, please. (請上車。)【第四常用】

　　Come on, get in. (趕快，上車吧。)【第五常用】
　　Let's get in. (我們上車吧。)【第六常用】
　　Let's get in the car. (我們上車吧。)【第七常用】

BOOK 6

Hop in. (上車。)【第九常用】

Jump in. (上車。)【第十常用】

Let's get in and go. 【第十二常用】

(我們上車出發吧。)

【hop〔hɑp〕v. 跳（= jump）　**hop in** 上車（= jump in）】

get in 還有一個意思是「進來」。像 Please get in. (請進來。) Let's get in the house.

(我們到屋子裡面去吧。)

2. *Sit up front.*

up〔ʌp〕adv. 向　　front〔frʌnt〕adv. 向前面

up front 向前面；在前面

　　　這句話的意思是「坐到前面來。」也可以禮貌地說：Please sit up front. (請坐到前面來。) up front 是個成語，在這裡表示「向前面；在前面」，一般字典上不容易找到，但是美國人常用。

【比較】　Sit *up front*. 【正】

　　　　　Sit front. 【誤】

　　　　up front 是個成語，不能分開，雖然 up 是副詞，front 也是副詞，但 Sit up. 的意思是「坐直。」而「坐到前面。」可以說 Sit in the front. 也可以說成 Sit up in the front. 就是不能說 *Sit front*.

從下面例句可知，up front 是個副詞片語。

Get *up front*. (到前面來。)
Come *up front*. (到前面來。)
Stand *up front*. (站到前面來。)

Recite *up front*. (到前面來背書。)
〔rɪˈsaɪt 〕*v.* 背誦
Go *up front*. (到前面去。)
I want you *up front*. (我要你到前面來。)
【這句話是 I want you to come up front. 的省略】

叫別人「坐到前面來」的説法有：

Sit up front. (坐到前面來。)【第一常用】
Sit up in the front. (坐到前面來。)【第六常用】
Sit in the front. (坐在前面。)【第五常用】

Sit in the front seat. (坐前面的位子。)【第二常用】
You can sit up front. (你可以坐到前面來。)【第三常用】
Sit up front, please. (請坐到前面來。)【第四常用】

Sit up front with me.【第七常用】
(到前面來和我一起坐。)
Sit up front next to me.【第八常用】
(到前面來坐在我的旁邊。)
Sit up front in the passenger seat.【第九常用】
(坐到前面駕駛座旁的座位。)
【*passenger seat* 駕駛座旁的座位】

BOOK 6

如果邀請朋友坐在後面，就説：Sit in the back.
（坐在後面。）或 Get in the back.（到後面坐。）
不能説成：*Sit down back.*（誤）或 *Sit up back.*（誤）
因爲 **Sit up front.**（坐在前面。）是慣用句。

3. *Feel free to adjust the seat.*
   feel free to V. 自由地～
   adjust〔əˈdʒʌst〕v. 調整

   這句話字面的意思是「覺得自由地去調整座位。」
   引申爲「你可以調整座位。」(= *You can adjust the
   seat.*)

   「Feel free to + 原形動詞」的句型，美國人
   常説，如美國人到你家作客，你可以跟他説：

   Make yourself at home. Feel free
   to do whatever you like.
   （請不要客氣。你可以做任何你喜歡做的事。）

   你請美國人到餐廳裡吃飯，你可以跟他説：

   Feel free to order some more. It's
   on me.（你可以再多點一些。我請客。）
   【order〔ˈɔrdɚ〕v. 點（菜） **be on sb.** 某人請客】

   你和外國人一起看電視，你可以跟他説：

   Feel free to change the channel.
   （你可以轉台。）〔ˈtʃænl̩〕n. 頻道

   所以，Feel free to V. 可翻成「你可以～」。

4. *Buckle up*.

buckle〔ˈbʌklʲ〕*v.* 扣上；扣住；扣緊 *n.* 皮帶頭
buckle up 扣上安全帶

　　在字典上，buckle 當名詞，作「鈕環」解，事實上，「皮帶頭」就叫做 buckle，當動詞時，就是「扣上」。「把皮帶扣上。」就是 Buckle your belt. 看到別人皮帶沒有扣上，就說：Your belt is unbuckled.

　　Buckle up. 的意思是「把安全帶扣上。」是專門用在汽車或飛機上的慣用句。在 "The American Heritage Dictionary" 中的英文解釋是 use a safety belt, especially in an automobile。

　　在美國的高速公路，往往會有個標示，上面寫著 "Buckle up for safety." 意思就是「為了安全，要扣上安全帶。」

　　下面的說法都很常用，我們按照使用頻率排列：

① ***Buckle up***. (把安全帶扣上。)【第一常用】
② Please buckle up. (請把安全帶扣上。)【第二常用】
③ Don't forget to buckle up.
　　(不要忘了把安全帶扣上。)

④ Buckle up, please. (請把安全帶扣上。)
⑤ Buckle your seat belt. (把你的安全帶扣上。)
　　【美國人不說 *Buckle up your seat belt.* (誤)】
⑥ You must buckle up. (你必須把安全帶扣上。)

5. *Fasten your seat belt.*

fasten〔'fæsn〕*v.* 繫上；扣上
seat belt 安全帶（= *seatbelt*）

　　fasten 這個字，是由 fast 加上 en 組成，但是發音的時候，卻把 t 省略，唸成〔'fæsn〕，意思是「繫上；扣上」或「綁在一起」。這句話的意思是「扣好你的安全帶。」在這句話中的 fasten 等於 buckle。

「把安全帶扣好。」的說法，常用的有六個：

　　　　Buckle up.【第一常用】
　　= Buckle your seat belt.【第六常用】
　　= *Fasten your seat belt.*【第五常用】

　　= Put your seat belt on.【第三常用】
　　= Get your seat belt on.【第四常用】
　　= Wear your seat belt.【第二常用】
　　【*put~on* 穿上；戴上（= *get~on* = *wear*）】

請朋友把安全帶扣好的說法有：

Fasten your seat belt.【第一常用】
Please fasten your seat belt.【第二常用】
Could you fasten your seat belt?【第五常用】

You should fasten your seat belt.【第七常用】
You must fasten your seat belt.【第八常用】
You have to fasten your seat belt.【第九常用】

Don't forget to fasten your seat belt.【第六常用】

I'd like you to fasten your seat belt.【第四常用】

I want you to fasten your seat belt.【第三常用】

【第七、第八、第九常用的句子，使用頻率非常接近】

6. *We don't want a ticket!*

ticket〔'tɪkɪt〕*n.* 罰單；票

　　　ticket 的主要意思是指「票」，公車票叫做 bus ticket，火車票叫做 train ticket，機票叫做 plane ticket，美國人習慣簡化，在能夠表明什麼票的情況下，他們只說 ticket。

　　　「交通罰單」叫做 traffic ticket，美國人簡化成 ticket。We don't want a ticket! 意思是「我們不想要罰單！」源自 We don't want to get a ticket!

　　　下面是美國人常說的話，我們按照使用頻率排列：

　　① *We don't want a ticket!*【第一常用】
　　　（我們不想要罰單！）

　　② We don't want to get a ticket!【第二常用】
　　　（我們不想要接到罰單！）

　　③ We don't want to pay for a ticket!【第三常用】
　　　（我們不想要付罰單！）

BOOK 6

④ We don't want a fine!
（我們不想要被罰款！）

⑤ We don't want to get fined!
（我們不想要被罰款！）

⑥ We don't want to pay a fine!
（我們不想要付罰款！）

【fine〔faɪn〕n. 罰款　v. 處以罰款】

⑦ Let's not get a ticket!（我們不要罰單！）

⑧ Let's not get a fine!（我們不要被罰款！）

⑨ Let's not get stopped by the cops!
（我們不要被警察攔下來！）

【stop〔stɑp〕v. 攔下　cop〔kɑp〕n. 警察】

7. *You can relax.*

relax〔rɪˈlæks〕v. 放鬆

　　這句話字面的意思是「你可以放輕鬆。」在這裡引申爲「你可以放心。」雖然中國人不習慣説 You can relax. 因爲 relax 有點像是大人對小孩講話，但是美國人常用，並沒有那麼嚴肅。

　　這句話也可以只説成：Relax.（放心。）或 You just relax.（你儘管放心。）也有美國人説成：You can take it easy. 美國人的想法，就是「你放輕鬆點。」等於中國人的想法「你放心。」要記住，無論你説 *You can relax.* 或 Take it easy. 這些話都是非常自然，沒有不禮貌的語氣。

You can relax. 的其他説法有：

I want you to relax. (我希望你放心。)

I want you to feel relaxed.

(我希望你放輕鬆。)

I want you to feel totally relaxed.

(我希望你完全放心。)

relaxed〔rɪˈlækst〕*adj.* 放鬆的
totally〔ˈtotl̩ɪ〕*adv.* 完全地

也可以加強語氣説成：

Don't be nervous. (不要緊張。)

Don't worry. (不要擔心。)

Don't be afraid. (不要害怕。)

【nervous〔ˈnɜvəs〕*adj.* 緊張的】

上面三句話，中國人認爲很嚴重，美國人的
思想中卻是較自然。

8. *I'm a safe driver.*

這句話字面的意思是「我是一個安全的駕駛。」
在中國人的思想中，就是「我開車很安全。」或「我
開車很小心。」

【比較 1】 注意中英文思想的差別：

中文： 我開車很安全。

英文： *I drive safely.* 【誤，文法對，但美國人不説】

I'm a safe driver. 【正】

BOOK 6

【比較 2】

中文：	我開車很小心。
英文：	I drive carefully.【正，少用】
	I'm a careful driver.【正，常用】

【比較 3】 下面的句子意思接近，我們按照使用
的頻率排列：

① *I'm a safe driver.*【第一常用】
（我開車很安全。）

② I'm a careful driver.【第二常用】
（我開車很小心。）

③ I'm a good driver. （我開車技術很好。）

④ I'm a defensive driver.
（我開車可以隨時應付突發情況。）

⑤ I'm a cautious driver.
（我開車很謹慎。）

⑥ I'm an alert driver.
（我開車會很有警覺。）

cautious〔'kɔʃəs〕*adj.* 謹慎的；小心的
defensive〔dɪ'fɛnsɪv〕*adj.* 防禦的
alert〔ə'lɜt〕*adj.* 留心的；警覺的

9. *I'll get you there in one piece.*

get〔gɛt〕*v.* 使到達

in one piece （人）平安無事地；（東西）未受損的

　　這句話的意思是「我會平安地載你到那裡。」

我們中國人說：「我要載你到那裡。」英文是：

　　　I'll get you there.

　＝ I'll take you there.

　＝ I'll drive you there.

　　【drive〔draɪv〕*v.* 開車載（某人）】

　　但是，不能說 *I'll bring you there.*（誤），

　　這句話文法對，但是美國人不說。

---

　　in one piece 這個成語很幽默，你說的時候，
美國人都會笑。

【例】 You came home so late. I'm glad
　　 you're still *in one piece.*

　　（你那麼晚回家。我很高興你還平安。）

　　 We're lucky to get back *in one piece.*

　　（我們真幸運，能夠平安回來。）

　　 Congratulations! You came back
　　 in one piece.（恭喜你！你平安回來了。）

　　美國人說 *in one piece* 這類的話，並非一定
表示經歷過危險，只是美國人喜歡表現幽默而已。

I'll get you there in one piece. 也可以加強語氣說成：

I promise *I'll get you there in one piece*.
（我保證，我會平安地載你到那裡。）

Don't worry. *I'll get you there in one piece*.
（不要擔心。我會平安地載你到那裡。）

Just relax. *I'll get you there in one piece*.
（儘管放心。我會平安地載你到那裡。）

下面三句話，意思相同：

> *I'll get you there in one piece.* 【常用】
> = I'll get you there safe and sound. 【常用】
> = I'll get you there safely. 【常用】
> （我會平安地載你到那裡。）
> 【*safe and sound* 安然無恙地】

【對話練習】

1. A：**Please get in**.

   B：You first.
   You go first.
   You get in first.

   A：請上車。

   B：你先請。
   你先請。
   你先上車。

2. A：**Sit up front**.

   B：How thoughtful of you.
   Thanks so much.
   I appreciate it.
   【thoughtful (ˈθɔtfəl) *adj.* 體貼的
   appreciate (əˈpriʃɪ͵et) *v.* 感激】

   A：坐到前面來。

   B：你真體貼。
   非常謝謝你。
   非常感謝。

3. A：**Feel free to adjust the seat**.

   B：How?
   How do I do it?
   I don't know how.

   A：你可以調整座位。

   B：怎麼做？
   我要怎麼做？
   我不知道要怎麼做。

4. A：**Buckle up**.

   B：I was just about to do it.
   I always do it.
   I always play it safe.
   【*be about to* 正要
   play it safe 求安全；不冒險】

   A：把安全帶扣上。

   B：我正要扣上它。
   我總是會扣上它。
   我總是注重安全。

5. A : **Fasten your seat belt**.

   B : I will for sure.
   I didn't forget.
   I know that's the law.
   【law〔lɔ〕*n.* 法律；規定】

A：扣好你的安全帶。

B：我一定會扣上。
我沒忘記。
我知道那是規定。

6. A : **We don't want a ticket!**

   B : No, we don't.
   We can't afford it.
   Traffic tickets are expensive.
   【afford〔ə'fɔrd〕*v.* 負擔得起】

A：我們不想要罰單！

B：是啊，我們都不想要。
我們負擔不起。
交通違規的罰單是很貴
的。

7. A : **You can relax**.

   B : I am relaxed.
   I'm already relaxed.
   I'm not nervous at all.
   【nervous〔'nɝvəs〕*adj.* 緊張的】

A：你可以放心。

B：我很放心。
我已經很放心了。
我一點也不緊張。

8. A : **I'm a safe driver**.

   B : I know you are.
   I know you're safe.
   I trust you with my life.
   【*trust sb. with sth.* 把某物託付
   給某人】

A：我開車很安全。

B：我知道你是。
我知道你開車很安全。
我把生命都託付給你了。

9. A : **I'll get you there in one piece**.

   B : That's good to know.
   With you, I feel safe.
   I can relax and enjoy the
   ride.

A：我會平安地載你到那裡。

B：知道會這樣眞好。
有你載我，我覺得很安全。
我可以放鬆心情好好搭
車。

BOOK 6

7. *We need gas*.

We need gas.	我們需要加油。
We're on empty.	我們快沒油了。
We're running out of gas.	我們的汽油快用完了。
It's time to fill up.	該是加滿油的時候了。
It's now or never.	現在不加油就完了。
We can't get stuck here.	我們不能被困在這裡。
There's a station up ahead.	前方有個加油站。
They have both full and self-service.	他們有全面服務，也有自助。
Do you want to pump the gas?	你要不要加油？

** ——————————————

gas〔gæs〕*n.* 汽油（= *gasoline*〔'gæsḷ,in,,gæsḷ'in 〕）
empty〔'ɛmptɪ〕*adj.* 空的　*n.* 空箱；空瓶；空桶
run out of 用完　***fill up*** 裝滿；在汽車油箱內裝滿油
stick〔stɪk〕*v.* 困住；使動彈不得；使進退兩難
station〔'steʃən〕*n.* 站（在此指 gas station 加油站）
full service 全面服務　***self-service*** 自助
pump〔pʌmp〕*v.* 抽（水）　　***pump the gas*** 加油

【背景説明】

當你和朋友一起開車，車子需要加油時，你
該怎麼説呢？這一回九句就可派上用場了。

1. ***We need gas.***
   gas〔gæs〕*n.* 汽油
   = gasoline〔'gæsḷ,in,ˌgæsḷ'in〕

> gas 的主要意思是「氣體」或「瓦斯」，gasoline
> 才是「汽油」，但是，現在的美國人已經習慣把「汽
> 油」稱作 gas。
>
> We need gas. 的意思是「我們需要汽油。」引
> 申爲「我們需要加油。」源自 We need to get gas.

美國人常説的有：

We need gas.（我們需要加油。）【第一常用】
We need to get gas.（我們需要加油。）【第三常用】
We need to buy gas.（我們需要加油。）【第五常用】
【本句和中國人思想不同，中國人通常不説「買油」。】

We need some gas.【第二常用】
（我們需要一些汽油。）
We need to get some gas.【第四常用】
（我們需要加一些汽油。）
We need to buy some gas.【第六常用】
（我們需要加一些汽油。）

We need to add gas. (我們需要加油。)【第七常用】

We need to gas up. (我們需要加油。)【第八常用】

We need to go get some gas right away.

(我們需要立刻加些汽油。)【第九常用】

【add〔æd〕v. 加　　***gas up***　(給汽車) 加汽油

right away　立刻 】

2. ***We're on empty.***

empty〔ˈɛmptɪ〕adj. 空的　　n. 空的容器

　　empty 主要意思是「空的」，當形容詞用，empty 當名詞用時，是指「空箱；空瓶；空桶；空盒」等空的容器。empty 在這裡是指 an empty gas tank (空的油箱)。

　　〔tæŋk〕n. 油箱

　　We're on empty. 字面的意思是「我們在空的油箱上。」引申為「我們快沒油了。」這句話源自油錶的指針指到 "E"，所以：

　　We're on empty. (我們快沒油了。)

= The needle's on empty.

= The needle's on E.

【needle〔ˈnidl̩〕n. 針；指針 】

下面都是美國人常說的話，句意大致相同：

We're on empty. (我們快沒油了。)【第二常用】

We're riding on empty. (我們快沒油了。)【第四常用】

We're riding on E. (我們快沒油了。)【第三常用】

We're on E. (我們快沒油了。)【第一常用】

We're riding on an empty tank.

(我們的油箱快沒油了。)【第五常用】

The needle is on empty.【第六常用】

(我們快沒油了。)

We're almost on empty.【第八常用】

(我們快沒油了。)

We're just about on empty.【第九常用】

(我們快沒油了。)

We're close to empty.【第七常用】

(我們快沒油了。)

【*just about*　差不多；幾乎 (= *about* = *almost*)

　be close to　接近】

We're on empty. 和 *We're on E*. 等，都是
美國人常說的話，所有的字典上都找不到，我們
一定要背下來，説起話來，才像美國人。*We're
on empty*. 可能源自騎摩托車的人所説的話，因
為他們騎在空的油箱上。

3. *We're running out of gas*.

　run out of　用完

　　　這句話的意思是「我們汽油快用完了。」這裡
　用「現在進行式」表示「不久的未來」。(詳見「文
　法寶典」p.341)

美國人常説 running out of：

> **We're running out of gas.**
> （我們汽油快用完了。）
> We're running out of money.
> （我們快沒錢了。）
> We're running out of time.
> （我們快沒時間了。）

下面是美國人常説的話，我們按照使用頻率排列：

① **We're running out of gas.** 【第一常用】
　　（我們汽油快用完了。）

② We're almost out of gas. 【第二常用】
　　（我們幾乎沒油了。）

③ We're just about out of gas.
　　（我們汽油就快用完了。）
　　【*be out of* 用完　just 修飾 about，加強語氣。】

④ We'll be out of gas soon.
　　（我們汽油要用完了。）

⑤ Our gas is almost gone.
　　（我們汽油幾乎用光了。）

⑥ Our gas will be gone soon.
　　（我們汽油快要用光了。）
　　【gone〔gɔn〕*adj.* 用光了的】

BOOK 6

4. *It's time to fill up.*

fill up 裝滿；在汽車油箱內裝滿油

　　fill up 是及物和不及物兩用動詞片語，這句話的意思是「該是加滿油的時候了。」源自 It's time for us to fill up the gas tank.（該是我們加滿油的時候了。）

　　下面都是美國人常說的話，我們按照使用頻率排列：

① We need to fill up.【第一常用】
　　（我們需要加滿油。）

② We have to fill up.【第二常用】
　　（我們必須加滿油。）

③ We should fill up.（我們應該加滿油。）

④ *It's time to fill up.*
　　（該是加滿油的時候了。）

⑤ It's time to fill up the tank.
　　（該是將油箱加滿油的時候了。）

⑥ It's time to find a station and fill up.
　　（該是找加油站加滿油的時候了。）
　　【station〔ˈsteʃən〕n. 站，在此是 gas station 的簡稱】

5. *It's now or never.*

　　這句話在這裡的意思是「現在不加油就沒機會了。」源自 Either we do it now, or we'll never do it. (我們現在不做,就永遠沒辦法做。)

　　now or never 有很多意思,要看前後句意決定。在字典上的意思是「機會難得;勿失良機」。

【例】 This is your only chance. *It's now or never.* (這是你唯一的機會。勿失良機。)

6. *We can't get stuck here.*

stick〔stɪk〕*v.* 困住;使動彈不得;使進退兩難

　　stick 的主要意思,前面說過是「棍子」,當動詞用時,除了當「黏住;堅持」外,還有一個主要意思是「刺」(pierce),當一個人被刺到了,就是被困住了。塞車的時候,美國人常說:We're stuck here. We can't move. (我們被困在這裡。我們動彈不得。)

　　We can't get stuck here. 的意思是「我們不能被困在這裡。」這句話美國人也常說成:We don't want to get stuck here. (我們不想被困在這裡。)

7. ***There's a station up ahead.***

station 的主要意思是「站」或「車站」，美國
人喜歡簡化，就把 gas station（加油站），或
filling station（加油站），簡稱爲 station。也有
美國人把「加油站」稱爲 service station，唯一不
同的是，service station 還可以幫你修汽車。

up 是「向」，ahead 是指「在前面」，在這裡
是副詞 up 修飾副詞 ahead，用以加強 ahead 的
語氣。

There's a station ***ahead***.【一般語氣】
（前面有個加油站。）
= There's a station ***up ahead***.【語氣稍強】
（前面方向有個加油站。）
= There's a station ***right up ahead***.【語氣最強】
（就在前面方向有個加油站。）
【right 加強 up ahead 的語氣。】

下面三句話，美國人也常説：

There's a gas station.
（那裡有個加油站。）
There's a gas station ahead.
（前面有個加油站。）
There's a gas station up ahead.
（前面方向有個加油站。）

8. ***They have both full and self-service.***

full-service   *adj.* 提供全面服務的
full service   *n.* 全面服務
self-service   *n.* 自助   *adj.* 自助的

　　美國的加油站有兩種，一種是 *self-service*（自助），自己刷信用卡、自己加油；另外一種是叫別人替你加油，稱作 ***full service***（全面服務）。有的加油站兩者都有，full service 的油價比較貴一點。

　　在字典上，full-service 當形容詞，self-service 可當形容詞和名詞。而 full-service 這個形容詞，變成複合名詞，應寫成 ***full service***。像 They have full service.（他們提供全面服務。）

　　They have both full and self-service. 的意思是「他們有全面服務，也有自助。」源自 They have both full service and self-service. 注意，***full service*** 沒有連字號。也可說成：They offer both full and self-service.（他們提供全面服務和自助。）

【比較】 They have both full and self-service. 【正】
　　　　 They have both full- and self-service. 【誤】
　　　　【因爲 full-service 只能當形容詞用】

9. *Do you want to pump the gas?*

pump〔pʌmp〕*v.* 抽（水）　　*pump the gas* 加油

> 　　pump 的主要意思是「抽水機」，當動詞的時候，是「抽（水）」，由於「加油」是把油抽出來，加到油箱，所以 *pump the gas*，就是「加油」。這句話的意思是「你要不要加油？」可能暗示：

① 你要自己加油或叫別人加油？

Do you want to pump our gas or have them do it?

② 你要加油還是讓我加油？

Do you want to pump or shall I do it?

下面是常用的有關「加油」的説法：

Do you want to *pump the gas*?【第一常用】
（你要不要加油？）

Do you want to *fill the tank*?【第四常用】
（你要不要加油？）【tank〔tæŋk〕*n.* 油箱】

Do you want to *take care of the gas*?【第三常用】
（你要不要負責加油？）【*take care of* 負責】

Do you want to *pump it*?【第二常用】
（你要不要加油？）

Do you want to *fill her up*?【第六常用】
（你要不要把車加滿油？）

【*fill…up* 加滿　her 是指汽車，fill her up 也可以説成 fill it up。】

Do you want to *put in the gas*?【第五常用】
（你想加油嗎？）【*put in* 放入　*put in the gas* 加油】

　　問別人要不要去做什麼事，都可以說：Do you want to do it? 或 Do you want to get it? 意思是「你要不要做這件事？」【get it 有很多意思，在此等於 do it】所以，在這裡也可以指「你要不要加油？」

Do you want to pump the gas? 也可說成：

Would you like to pump the gas?

（你要不要加油？）【第二有禮貌，第五常用】

Could you pump the gas?

（你可以加油嗎？）【第三有禮貌，第一常用】

Can you pump the gas?

（你可以加油嗎？）【第四有禮貌，第二常用】

Will you pump the gas?

（你要不要去加油？）【第五有禮貌，第三常用】

Could I ask you to pump the gas?

（我可以請你加油嗎？）【第一有禮貌，第四常用】

Do you know how to pump the gas?

（你知不知道如何加油？）【第六有禮貌，第六常用】

　　這句話字面的意思是「你知不知道如何加油？」但是往往暗示「可不可以請你去加油？」美國人想叫別人煮點咖啡，往往會說：Do you know how to make the coffee?（你知不知道如何煮咖啡？）往往暗示「你可不可以去煮咖啡？」。你看，美國人有多虛偽。

BOOK 6

【對話練習】

1. A：**We need gas**.

   B：You're right.
   We're low on gas.
   We need some gas.

2. A：**We're on empty**.

   B：Oh, my God!
   We're on E.
   We're in trouble now!

3. A：**We're running out of gas**.

   B：I know that.
   I'm looking for a station.
   We need to find one fast.

4. A：**It's time to fill up**.

   B：Not yet.
   We still have gas.
   We have half a tank.
   【*not yet* 尚未】

A：我們需要加油。

B：你說的沒錯。
   我們的汽油不夠。
   我們需要一些汽油。

A：我們快沒油了。

B：噢，我的天啊！
   我們快沒油了。
   我們現在有麻煩了！

A：我們的汽油快用完了。

B：我知道。
   我正在找加油站。
   我們需要趕快找到一家。

A：該是加滿油的時候了。

B：還不用。
   我們還有汽油。
   我們還有半箱。

5. A：**It's now or never**.

　B：I agree.

　　　We have to act now.

　　　We must do something now.

　　　【act〔 ækt〕*v.* 行動】

A：現在不加油就沒機會了。

B：我同意。

　　我們現在必須採取行動。

　　我們現在必須想想辦法。

6. A：**We can't get stuck here**.

　B：Absolutely not.

　　　That would be awful.

　　　That would really be bad.

　　　【absolutely〔'æbsə,lutlı〕*adv.* 絕對地
　　　awful〔'ɔfl̩〕*adj.* 可怕的】

A：我們不能被困在這裡。

B：當然不行。

　　那會很可怕。

　　那會很糟糕。

7. A：**There's a station up ahead**.

　B：Thank God.

　　　We need one so bad.

　　　We need a gas station now.

　　　【bad〔 bæd〕*adv.* 很；非常】

A：前面有個加油站。

B：謝天謝地。

　　我們非常需要加油站。

　　我們現在需要找個加油
　　站。

8. A：**They have both full and
　　　self-service**.

　B：That's great.

　　　We have a choice.

　　　Which one do you prefer?

A：他們有全面服務，也有
　　自助。。

B：太棒了。

　　我們可以選擇。

　　你比較喜歡哪一種？

9. A：**Do you want to pump the gas?**

　B：I'd really rather not.

　　　I don't know how it works.

　　　I've never owned a car.

A：你要不要加油？

B：我真的寧願不要。

　　我不知道怎麼加。

　　我不曾擁有過汽車。

BOOK 6

8. Gas Station

Hi!	嗨！
Twenty bucks, please.	請加二十元的油。
Make it regular.	加普通汽油。
Check the tires.	檢查輪胎，看有沒有氣。
Check the engine.	檢查引擎。
I think I'm low on oil.	我覺得我的機油不夠。
How does it look?	看起來怎樣？
What's the total?	總共多少錢？
Thanks for your great service.	謝謝你良好的服務。

**　——————————

hi〔haɪ〕*interj.* 嗨　　buck〔bʌk〕*n.* 元
regular〔'rɛgjələ〕*adj.* 普通的　*n.* 普通汽油
check〔tʃɛk〕*v.* 檢查　　tire〔taɪr〕*n.* 輪胎
engine〔'ɛndʒən〕*n.* 引擎　　total〔'totḷ〕*n.* 總額
great〔gret〕*adj.* 很棒的
service〔'sɝvɪs〕*n.* 服務

【背景説明】

　　當汽車開到加油站，想要請加油站人員替你
加油，你就可以説這九句話。

1. *Hi!*

hi〔haɪ〕*interj.* 嗨

　　在美國碰到不管認不認識的人，都可以説 *"Hi!"*
（嗨！）或 "Hello!"（哈囉！）其他所有打招呼用語，
在「演講式英語」的「英會話總整理」p.303 中，有詳
細的説明。

2. *Twenty bucks, please.*

buck〔bʌk〕*n.* 元（= *dollar*）

　　這句話的意思是「請加二十元的油。」等於
I'd like twenty dollars' worth of gas.（我要二
十元的油。）
　　　　　　　　　　　〔wɝθ〕*n.* 值～的份量

　　如果要加滿，就説：Fill up.（加滿。）或 Fill
it up. 或 Fill her up. 在上一回中有説明。

　　下面都是美國人常説的話：

　　Twenty.（加二十元的油。）【第十常用，稍不禮貌】

　　Twenty, please.【第三常用】

　　（請加二十元的油。）

　　Give me twenty, please.【第四常用】

　　（請幫我加二十元的油。）

BOOK 6

Twenty bucks, *please*.【第一常用】
（請加二十元的油。）
Twenty dollars, please.【第二常用】
（請加二十元的油。）

I'd like twenty dollars, please.【第八常用】
（我想請你幫我加二十元的油。）
I'd like twenty bucks, please.【第九常用】
（我想請你幫我加二十元的油。）

Could I have twenty?【第五常用】
（我可以加二十元的油嗎？）
Could I have twenty, please?【第六常用】
（我可以加二十元的油嗎？）
Could I have twenty bucks, please?【第七常用】
（我可以加二十元的油嗎？）
【上面三句話中的 Could，也可以說成 Can。】

3. *Make it regular*.

regular 〔'rɛgjələ 〕 *n.* 普通汽油

　　這句話的意思是「我要加普通汽油。」Make it～.
的用法，詳見 p.69。

　　regular 的主要意思是「一般的」，在加油站，
當名詞用，指「普通汽油」。super 〔'supə 〕是指「高
級汽油」，premium 〔'primɪəm 〕是「最高級汽油」。
regular，super，premium 原則上都是形容詞，只有
在加油站，才當名詞用，因為美國人喜歡簡化，已經

把後面的 gas 省略掉了，美國人不說 *regular gas* (誤)。
到美國加油站，只要說 Regular. 他們就知道，你要加
的是「普通汽油。」

　　下面都是美國人常說的話：

Regular. (普通汽油。)【第八常用】
Regular, please. (請加普通汽油。)【第一常用】
I'd like regular, please.【第四常用】
(我要普通汽油，好嗎？)

Make it regular.【第二常用】
(我要加普通汽油。)
Could you make it regular?【第十常用】
(可以幫我加普通汽油嗎？)

Give me regular. (給我普通汽油。)【第七常用】
Could you give me regular?【第九常用】
(你可以給我普通汽油嗎？)

I'll take regular.【第六常用】
(我要普通汽油。)
I'd like regular.【第三常用】
(我要普通汽油。)
I'll have regular.【第五常用】
(我要普通汽油。)

4. *Check the tires.*

check〔tʃɛk〕v. 檢查　　tire〔taɪr〕n. 輪胎

　　這句話的意思是「檢查輪胎。」在加油站，就是「檢查輪胎的氣壓；檢查輪胎，看有沒有氣。」（= *Check the air pressure of the tires.*）在修車廠，就是「檢查輪胎是不是有問題。」

　　下面都是美國人常在加油站說的話，我們按照使用頻率排列：

① ***Check the tires.***【第一常用】
　　（檢查輪胎，看有沒有氣。）

② Please check the tires.【第二常用】
　　（請檢查輪胎，看氣夠不夠。）

③ Could you please check my tires?【第三常用】
　　（能不能請你幫我檢查輪胎，看氣夠不夠？）

④ Could you please check the tires?
　　（能不能請你檢查輪胎，看有沒有氣？）

⑤ Could you check the tires?
　　（你能不能檢查一下輪胎，看有沒有氣？）

⑥ Could you check my tires?
　　（你能不能幫我檢查一下輪胎，看有沒有氣？）

⑦ Are my tires OK?（我的輪胎行不行啊？）

⑧ How do my tires look?（我的輪胎看起來如何？）

⑨ I'd like you to check the tires.
　　（我希望你幫我檢查輪胎，看有沒有氣。）

⑩ I'd like you to check my tires.

（我希望你替我檢查輪胎，看有沒有氣。）

⑪ Could you tell me if my tires are OK?

（你能不能告訴我，我的輪胎行不行？）

⑫ Can you check my tire pressure?

（你能不能替我檢查一下輪胎的氣壓？）

【pressure〔'prɛʃə 〕*n.* 壓力（在此指「氣壓」）】

5. *Check the engine.*

engine〔'ɛndʒən 〕*n.* 引擎

這句話的意思是「檢查引擎。」在美國有 full
service 的加油站，也提供這項服務。加油的人員
會幫你把引擎蓋打開，檢查機油（check the oil）、
檢查水箱，看水夠不夠、檢查電池等。如果你要
他們全部檢查，你可以說：Check everything.
（全部檢查一下。）

　　下面都是美國人在加油站常說的話：

Check the engine.【第六常用】

（檢查引擎。）

Please check the engine.【第四常用】

（請檢查引擎。）

Could you please check the engine?【第五常用】

（請檢查引擎，好嗎？）

BOOK 6

Check under the hood.（檢查引擎。）【第三常用】

〔 hʊd 〕 *n.* (引擎上的) 車蓋

Please check under the hood.【第一常用】

（請檢查引擎。）

Could you please check under the hood?

（請檢查引擎，好嗎？）【第二常用】

　　上面各句的 check，都可說成 check out，但是沒有 check 來得常用。

【比較】　***Check the engine.***【較常用】

　　　　　Check out the engine.【常用】

6. ***I think I'm low on oil.***

low〔 lo 〕 *adj.* 不足的 < on >

be low on ～不足；～快用完了

oil〔 ɔɪl 〕 *n.* 油；石油；機油 (= *engine oil*)

　　這句話的意思是「我覺得我的機油不夠。」通常汽車機油不會不夠，但由於舊車會漏油，就會變得不夠。be low on 這個成語，字典上找不到，但美國人常說：

I'm really *low on* cash right now.

（我現在真的缺現金。）

The car *is low on* gas.（汽車快沒油了。）

　　在所有字典上找不到 oil 是「機油」的意思，因為美國人說話時，已經習慣把 engine oil（機油）簡化成 oil。

下面四句，使用頻率相同，都很常用：

I think I'm low on oil.

（我覺得我的機油不夠。）

I might be low on oil.

（我的機油也許不夠。）

I could be low on oil.（我的機油可能不夠。）

I'm afraid I'm low on oil.

（我恐怕機油不夠。）

7. *How does it look?*

這句話的意思是「看起來怎樣？」也可以加強
語氣說成：How does it look to you?（你覺得看
起來怎樣？）

下面是美國人常說的話：

How does it look?（看起來怎樣？）【第一常用】

How does the engine look?【第一常用】

（引擎看起來怎樣？）

How does everything look?【第一常用】

（一切看起來怎樣？）

What does it look like?（看起來怎樣？）【第四常用】

What's the situation?（情況如何？）【第九常用】

Tell me how it looks.【第八常用】

（告訴我看起來怎樣。）

【situation〔ˌsɪtʃʊˈeʃən〕*n.* 狀況】

Is the engine looking OK? 【第六常用】

（引擎看起來還好吧？）

Is everything OK?（一切都還好吧？）【第二常用】

Is everything under the hood OK?【第五常用】

（引擎還好吧？）

Am I in good shape?（我的車子還好吧？）【第三常用】

Do I need anything?（我需要任何東西嗎？）【第七常用】

Tell me: how does it look?【第八常用】

（告訴我它看起來怎樣？）

【*in good shape* 狀況良好】

8. *What's the total?*

total〔'totl〕 *n.* 總額　　*adj.* 全部的

這句話的意思是「總共多少錢？」

下面各句意義相同：

What's the total?（總共多少錢？）【第一常用】

What's the total cost?（總共多少錢？）【第三常用】

What's the total price?（總共多少錢？）【第三常用】

【cost〔kɔst〕 *n.* 費用　　price〔prais〕 *n.* 價格】

What's my total?（我總共多少錢？）【第二常用】

What's the damage?（要付多少錢？）【第四常用】

What's the bill?（帳單多少錢？）【第五常用】

【damage〔'dæmɪdʒ〕 *n.* 損害　　*the damage* 費用

bill〔bɪl〕 *n.* 帳單】

9. ***Thanks for the great service.***

  great〔gret〕*adj.* 很棒的　　service〔'sɝvɪs〕*n.* 服務

　　　加油站人員替你服務以後，你就可以說這句話
表示感謝。這句話的意思是「謝謝你的良好服務。」

下面的話，你都可以說：

  You did a great job. (你做得很好。)【第三常用】
  I really appreciate it. (我真的很感激。)【第六常用】
  I really want to thank you. 【第八常用】
  (我真的要謝謝你。)
  【appreciate〔ə'priʃɪ,et〕*v.* 感激】

  Thanks for the service. (謝謝你的服務。)【第十常用】
  Thanks for your service. (謝謝你的服務。)【第七常用】
  Thanks for everything. 【第一常用】
  (感謝你所做的一切。)

  Thanks for the great service. 【第四常用】
  (謝謝你的良好服務。)
  Thanks for the quality service. 【第九常用】
  (謝謝你高品質的服務。)
  Thanks for the excellent service. 【第五常用】
  (謝謝你的最佳服務。)
  【quality〔'kwɑlətɪ〕*adj.* 品質好的】

  Thanks for the good job. 【第十一常用】
  (你做得很好，謝謝你。)
  Thanks for your help. (謝謝你的幫助。)【第二常用】
  Thanks for your nice service on my car. 【第十二常用】
  (謝謝你為我的車子提供好的服務。)

BOOK 6

下面各句也常用：

Thank you for the great service. 【第三常用】
（謝謝你的良好服務。）

I really appreciate the great service. 【第五常用】
（我真的感謝你的良好服務。）

I appreciate your help. 【第二常用】
（我感謝你的幫助。）

Thank you for your help. 【第一常用】
（謝謝你的幫助。）

I'm thankful for your help.
（我感謝你的幫助。）【第六常用】

I appreciate everything you've done. 【第四常用】
（我感謝你所做的一切。）

　　表示感謝的說法很多，在「演講式英語」的「英語會話總整理」中，有完整的歸納。

【對話練習】

1. A：**Hi!**

　B：Hello.

　　How's it going?

　　How are you today?

A：嗨！

B：哈囉。

　你好嗎？

　你今天好嗎？

2. A：**Twenty bucks, please**.

　B：OK.

　　Sure thing.

　　You got it.

　　【*sure thing*　當然好；可以】

A：請加二十元的油。

B：好的。

　當然可以。

　沒問題。

3. A：**Make it regular**.

　B：Sounds good.

　　Just stay where you are.

　　It will only take a minute.

　　【*a minute*　一會兒（時間）】

A：加普通汽油。

B：好的。

　你只要留在原位。

　只要一下子就好了。

4. A：**Check the tires**.

　B：My pleasure.

　　I'll do it now.

　　I'll check them right now.

A：檢查輪胎，看有沒有氣。

B：這是我的榮幸。

　我現在就檢查。

　我現在就檢查它們。。

5. A : **Check the engine**.

B : I can't.
It's locked.
Please unlock the hood.
【lock〔lɑk〕*v.* 鎖住
unlock〔ʌn'lɑk〕*v.* 開～的鎖】

A：檢查引擎。

B：我沒辦法。
它被鎖住了。
請打開引擎蓋。

6. A : **I think I'm low on oil**.

B : Let me check it.
You might be right.
You could be low on oil.

A：我覺得我的機油不夠。

B：讓我檢查一下。
你也許是對的。
你的機油可能不夠。

7. A : **How does it look?**

B : It looks low.
It's very low.
You need oil badly.
【badly〔'bædlɪ〕*adv.* 很；非常】

A：看起來怎樣？

B：它看起來不夠。
它非常少。
你非常需要機油。

8. A : **What's the total?**

B : The gas is twenty.
The oil is two ninety nine.
That's twenty three fifty
with tax.
【tax〔tæks〕*n.* 稅】

A：總共多少錢？

B：汽油二十元。
機油二塊九毛九。
含稅總共二十三塊五
毛。

9. A : **Thanks for the great service**.

B : You're more than welcome.
It's been a pleasure.
It's a pleasure serving you.
【*more than* 非常
pleasure〔'plɛʒɚ〕*n.* 榮幸】

A：謝謝你良好的服務。

B：不客氣。
這是我的榮幸。
為您服務是我的榮幸。

9. Hurry up!

Hurry up!	趕快！
Move faster.	走快一點。
Pick it up.	快一點。
Keep up.	要跟上。
Don't slow down.	不要慢下來。
Don't fall behind.	不要落後。
Keep pace with me.	跟著我的腳步一起走。
We can walk and talk.	我們可以一面走路，一面聊天。
I enjoy walking with you.	我喜歡和你一起走路。

** ───────────────

hurry〔'hɝɪ〕*v.* 趕快　　***hurry up*** 趕快

move〔muv〕*v.* 移動；走動　　***pick it up*** 趕快

keep up 跟上　　***slow down*** 減慢速度；慢下來

fall behind 落後　　pace〔pes〕*n.* 步調；速度

keep pace with 和…齊步前進；和…並駕齊驅

enjoy〔ɪn'dʒɔɪ〕*v.* 喜歡

【背景説明】

　　不管是爬山，還是散步，當你的同伴落在後面時，你就可以説這一回九句。

1. ***Hurry up!***

hurry〔'hɝɪ〕*v.* 趕快　　***hurry up*** 趕快

　　Hurry up! 和 Hurry! 意思相同，都表示「趕快！」但是，Hurry up! 可説成 Hurry it up!。

【比較1】 Hurry up!【正，常用】
　　　　　= Hurry!【正，常用】

【比較2】 Hurry it up!【正，常用，it 可以指任何事】
　　　　　（趕快！）
　　　　　Hurry it!【誤，文法對，但美國人不説】

　　下面是美國人常説的話：

　　　Hurry!（趕快！）【第二常用】
　　　Hurry up!（趕快！）【第一常用】
　　　Hurry it up!（趕快！）【第三常用】

　　　Please hurry up.（請趕快。）【第五常用】
　　　Can you hurry up?【第九常用】
　　　（你可不可以快一點？）
　　　You got to hurry up.【第六常用】
　　　（你必須趕快。）【***got to*** 必須】

We have to hurry up.【第八常用】

（我們必須趕快。）

We're in a hurry.【第七常用】

（我們在趕時間。）【*in a hurry*　匆忙】

Come on, hurry up!【第四常用】

（好啦，趕快！）

　　最禮貌的說法是：Could you hurry up, please?（可不可以請你快一點？）當你在等自動提款機（ATM）或公共電話的時候，就可以跟陌生人說這句話。

　　我們中國人催促別人，像「趕快」、「快一點」，找不出幾句，但是在美語中，卻太多了，我們把美國人常用的，歸納如下，使用頻率都很接近，只能分成最常用、較常用、常用三類：

　　 Hurry!【最常用】

= *Hurry up!*【最常用】

= Hurry it up!【最常用】

= Get moving!【較常用】

= Get going!【較常用】

= Get the lead out!【常用】
　　　〔lɛd〕*n.* 鉛
【字面意思是「把鉛拿掉！」引申為「趕快！」。】

= **Get a move on!**【較常用，move〔muv〕*n.* 移動】

= **Shake a leg!**【常用，字面意思是「搖腿！」，引申
爲「趕快！」，有幽默的意味。】

= **Snap to it!**【較常用，詳見「教師一口氣英語」p.8-7】

= **Look alive!**【較常用，在此表示「趕快！」，詳見
「教師一口氣英語」p.8-6】

= **Step on it!**【較常用，源自腳踏到油門。】

= **Make it quick!**【常用】

= **Double time!**【常用，Double time. 源自
Double speed, half time.（兩倍的速度，一半
的時間。）簡化以後，變成 Double time.】

= **On the double!**【較常用，源自兩步併作一步】

= **Get it in gear!**【常用，gear〔gɪr〕*n.* 排檔
Get it in gear!（把它放在排檔中！），即表示
「要趕快走了！」】

2. ***Move faster.***

move〔muv〕*v.* 移動；走動；搬家

　　move 最主要的意思是「移動」，Move faster.
的字面意思是「移動快一點。」可引申為「走快一
點。」（= *Go faster.*）或「做快一點。」（= *Do it
faster.*）在這一回中，作「走快一點。」解。

下面說法都常用：

> ***Move faster.***（走快一點。）【第一常用】
> Move faster, please.（請走快一點。）【第二常用】
> Please move faster.（請走快一點。）【第三常用】
>
> We need to move faster.【第六常用】
> （我們需要走快一點。）
> We have to move faster.【第七常用】
> （我們必須走快一點。）
> You've got to move faster.【第八常用】
> （你必須走快一點。）
>
> Get going.　Move faster.【第九常用】
> （趕快。走快一點。）
> Come on, move faster.【第五常用】
> （好啦，走快一點。）
> Please try to move faster.【第四常用】
> （請儘量走快一點。）

3. ***Pick it up.***

pick〔pɪk〕*v.* 挑選（= *select*）　　***pick up*** 增加（速度）

> pick up 在成語字典中，有十六個意思，最主要的意思是「拾起；舉起；拿起」，在這裡作「增加（速度）」講。Pick it up. 的字面意思是「把它撿起來。」通常東西掉到地上，父母都會說「快點撿起來。」所以，Pick it up. 在這裡引申為「快一點。」

下面都是美國人常說的話：

Pick it up!（快一點！）【第一常用】

Come on, **pick it up!**【第四常用】
（拜託，走快一點！）

Pick up the pace.（加快腳步。）【第三常用】

You need to **pick it up**.【第五常用】
（你必須快一點。）

Pick it up a little.（快一點。）【第二常用】

We really should pick up the pace.【第六常用】
（我們真的需要加快腳步。）

4. **Keep up**.

keep up 這個成語有四個主要意思：①堅持
（= *persevere*）②維持良好狀況（= *maintain in good condition*）③跟上；不落後（= *not to fall behind*）④忍受；忍耐（= *endure under strain*）。

這句話在這裡的意思是「不要落後。」或
「要跟上。」

美國人常說的有：

Keep up.（要跟上。）【第一常用】

Please **keep up**.（請你要跟上。）【第四常用】

Keep up, OK?（要跟上，好嗎？）【第三常用】

Try to *keep up*. (要儘量跟上。)【第二常用】

Do your best to *keep up*.【第五常用】
(儘你的力量跟上。)

I hope you can *keep up*.【第六常用】
(我希望你能跟上。)

Keep up with me. (要跟上我。)【第七常用】

Keep up if you can.【第九常用】
(如果你能夠，就跟上吧。)

Keep up with everybody.【第八常用】
(要跟上大家。)

5. *Don't slow down.*

slow down 減慢速度；慢下來 (= *decrease speed*)

這句話的意思是「不要慢下來。」

下面是美國人常説的話：

Don't slow down. (不要慢下來。)【第一常用】

Please don't slow down.【第二常用】
(請不要慢下來。)

Try not to slow down.【第五常用】
(儘量不要慢下來。)

Don't start to slow down.【第四常用】
(不要開始慢下來。)

Don't slow down, OK?【第六常用】
(不要慢下來，好嗎？)

Try not to slow down if you can.【第九常用】
(如果你能夠的話，就儘量不要慢下來。)

I hope you don't slow down.【第七常用】
（我希望你不要慢下來。）

I don't want you to slow down.【第八常用】
（我不希望你慢下來。）

Don't let yourself slow down.【第三常用】
（不要讓你自己慢下來。）【*slow down* 減速】

6. ***Don't fall behind.***

fall behind 落後（*= lag in pace or progress*）

　　這句話的意思是「不要落後。」Don't fall
behind. 可能指「速度上不要落後。」或「功課、
進度不要落後。」

　　下面是美國人常說的話：

Don't fall behind.【第一常用】

Don't fall behind everybody.【第三常用】
（不要落後他人。）

【這句話是 Don't fall behind everybody else. 的簡化。】

Please don't fall behind.【第二常用】
（請不要落後。）

You can't fall behind.【第五常用】
（你不能落後。）

Don't let yourself fall behind.【第四常用】
（不要讓自己落後。）

I hope you don't fall behind.【第六常用】
（我希望你不要落後。）

7. *Keep pace with me.*

pace〔pes〕*n.* 步調；速度

keep pace with 和…齊步前進；和…並駕齊驅

　　這句話的字面意思是「要保持和我的步調一致。」引申為「跟上我的速度。」(= *Walk at the same speed as me.*) 這句話也可說成：Keep up with me. (跟上我。)

　　下面都是美國人常說的話，我們按照使用頻率排列：

① ***Keep pace with me.***【第一常用】
　　(跟上我的速度。)

② Keep up the pace.【第二常用】
　　(跟上我的速度。)

③ Please keep up the pace.
　　(請跟上我的速度。)

④ Try to keep pace. (儘量跟上我的速度。)

⑤ Try to keep up the pace.
　　(儘量跟上我的速度。)

⑥ Please try to keep up the pace.
　　(請儘量跟上我的速度。)

⑦ Keep pace. (跟上我的速度。)
　　【省略 with me】

⑧ Keep the pace. (跟上我的速度。)

⑨ Keep the pace, OK?
　　(跟著我的腳步一起走，好嗎？)

BOOK 6

8. *We can walk and talk.*

這句話的意思是「我們可以一面走路，一面聊天。」源自 We can walk and talk at the same time.（我們可以同時一面走，一面聊天。）或 We can walk and talk as we go.（當我們走路的時候，我們可以一面走，一面聊天。）

這句話也可以說成：

We can talk while we walk.
= We can talk as we walk.
= We can talk while we're walking.
（我們可以一面走路，一面聊天。）

9. *I enjoy walking with you.*
enjoy〔ɪn'dʒɔɪ〕v. 喜歡

這句話的意思是「我喜歡和你一起走路。」

當你和朋友一起走路的時候，下面的話講越多越好：

I really like walking with you.【第七常用】
（我真的喜歡和你一起走路。）
It's a pleasure walking with you.【第一常用】
（和你一起走路真愉快。）
It's fun walking with you.【第五常用】
（和你一起走路真有趣。）
【pleasure〔'plɛʒɚ〕n. 樂趣　fun〔fʌn〕adj. 有趣的】

You're good company.【第二常用】

（有你陪伴真好。）

You're fun to walk with.【第三常用】

（和你一起走路真有趣。）

You're a good walking companion.【第九常用】

（你是一個散步的好伙伴。）

company〔'kʌmpənɪ〕*n.* 公司；同伴（不可數名詞）

companion〔kəm'pænjən〕*n.* 同伴（可數名詞）

【詳見「一口氣英語⑤」p.12–6】

I like walking with you.【第四常用】

（我喜歡和你一起走路。）

I like walking with you very much.【第八常用】

（我很喜歡和你一起走路。）

It's nice to walk with you.【第六常用】

（和你一起走路真好。）

It's fun to walk with you.【第六常用】

（和你一起走路很有趣。）

It's nice to walk with you.【第六常用】

（和你一起走路真好。）

It's nice walking with you.【第六常用】

（和你一起走路真好。）

【對話練習】

1. A：**Hurry up!**

 B：I'm trying.

 　I'm trying to hurry.

 　I'm doing my best.

2. A：**Move faster.**

 B：Take it easy.

 　Relax a little.

 　What's the rush?

 　【rush〔rʌʃ〕*n.* 匆忙】

3. A：**Pick it up.**

 B：Slow down.

 　We're not in a hurry.

 　We have lots of time.

4. A：**Keep up.**

 B：I'm doing OK.

 　I'm right behind you.

 　I'm keeping up.

 　【right〔raɪt〕*adv.* 恰好；就】

A：趕快！

B：我正在努力。

　我正在努力要快一點。

　我正在盡力。

A：趕快。

B：放輕鬆。

　放輕鬆一點。

　急什麼？

A：快一點。

B：慢一點。

　我們又不急。

　我們有很多時間。

A：要跟上。

B：我沒問題。

　我就在你後面。

　我快跟上了。

5. A : **Don't slow down**.　　　　A : 不要慢下來。

　　B : I won't.　　　　　　　　B : 我不會

　　　I promise.　　　　　　　　　我保證。

　　　I'll keep up the pace.　　　　我會跟上你的腳步。

6. A : **Don't fall behind**.　　　　A : 不要落後。

　　B : I'm sorry.　　　　　　　　B : 我很抱歉。

　　　I can't help it.　　　　　　　我沒辦法。

　　　I'm going as fast as I can.　　我正在儘量快了。

　　　【*can't help it* 不得不；忍不住】

7. A : **Keep pace with me**.　　　A : 跟上我的速度。

　　B : That's not easy.　　　　　B : 那不容易。

　　　You're in good shape.　　　　你很健康。

　　　I'll try to keep up.　　　　　我會努力跟上你。

　　　【*in good shape* 健康狀況良好】

8. A : **We can walk and talk**.　　A : 我們可以一面走路，一面聊天。

　　B : I like that idea.　　　　　B : 我喜歡那個主意。

　　　I hope we do it.　　　　　　我希望我們可以這樣。

　　　Slow down and talk with　　　你放慢腳步，跟我說說話。

　　　me.

9. A : **I enjoy walking with you**.　A : 我喜歡和你一起走路。

　　B : The feeling is mutual.　　　B : 我也有同感。

　　　We move at the same pace.　　我們走路的步調相同。

　　　Our steps are in sync.　　　　我們的步調一致。

　　　【 mutual (ˈmjutʃuəl) *adj.* 互相的

　　　　pace (pes) *n.* 步調

　　　　sync (sɪŋk) *n.* 同步調

　　　　in sync 步調一致】

10. You can do it.

You can do it.	你可以做到。
You have what it takes.	你有能力。
I believe in you.	我相信你。
Hang tough.	堅持下去。
Hang in there.	要堅持下去。
Just keep trying.	只要繼續努力。
Go all the way.	要走完全程。
Go for the gold.	爭取第一。
Go as far as you can.	儘量發揮你的潛力。

**　＊＊**

take〔tek〕v. 需要　　hang〔hæŋ〕v. 懸掛
tough〔tʌf〕adj. 堅硬的；不屈不撓的
hang tough 堅持下去；不洩氣
just〔dʒʌst〕adv. 只要　　try〔traɪ〕v. 嘗試；努力
all the way 自始至終；一直
gold〔gold〕n. 黃金　　*go far* 走遠；成功

【背景説明】

　　每當你遇到缺乏信心的人時，就可以用這九句話來鼓勵他們。

1. ***You can do it.***

> 這句話的意思是「你可以做到。」
>
> ***You can do it.*** 【第一常用】
> = You can make it. (你可以做到。)【第二常用】
> 　【***make it*** 成功；辦到】
> = You have the ability. (你有能力。)【第三常用】
>
> = You're smart enough. (你夠聰明。)【第五常用】
> = You're good enough. (你夠棒。)【第六常用】
> = You're able to do it. (你能夠做到。)【第四常用】
> 　【ability (ə'bɪlətɪ) *n.* 能力　smart (smɑrt) *adj.* 聰明的】

　　下面都是美國人常説的話：

> ***You can do it.*** 【第一常用】
> You can do it if you try. 【第九常用】
> (如果你努力的話，就可以做到。)
> You can do it if you work hard. 【第十常用】
> (如果你努力的話，就可以做到。)
>
> I know you can do it. 【第二常用】
> (我知道你可以做到。)
> I feel you can do it. 【第五常用】
> (我覺得你可以做到。)
> I believe you can do it. 【第六常用】
> (我相信你可以做到。)

I'm confident you can do it. 【第八常用】
（我確信你可以做到。）
I'm positive you can do it. 【第七常用】
（我肯定你可以做到。）

confident〔'kɑnfədənt〕adj. 有信心的；確信的
positive〔'pɑzətɪv〕adj. 肯定的

You can do it for sure. 【第三常用】
（你一定可以做到。）【*for sure* 必定】
You can do it no problem. 【第四常用】
（你可以做到，沒問題的。）

2. *You have what it takes.*
take〔tek〕v. 需要

這句話源自：

You have *the ability that* it takes to do this.
‖
what

字面的意思是「你有做這件事情所需要的能力。」
引申為「你有能力。」

You have what it takes.（你有能力。）
= You have the ability.（你有能力。）
= You have the right stuff.（你有能力。）
【stuff 字面意思是「東西」，引申為「特質」。
the right stuff 必要的能力（= *the necessary ability*）】

下面是美國人常説的話：

You have what it takes.【第一常用】

（你有能力。）

You have what it takes to succeed.【第五常用】

（你有成功的能力。）

You have what it takes to do the job.【第六常用】

（你有能力做這件工作。）

I know you have what it takes.【第二常用】

（我知道你有能力。）

I'm sure you have what it takes.【第三常用】

（我確定你有能力。）

I'm confident you have what it takes.【第四常用】

（我確信你有能力。）

3. *I believe in you*.

一般字典都沒有把 believe 和 believe in 的區別弄清楚。believe *sb*. 是「相信某人的話」，believe in 就有很多意思，要看實際情況或前後句意決定，通常作「相信；信任；信仰」解，而不是作「相信某人的話」解。

【比較1】 **I believe you**.（我相信你的話。）

= I know you're telling me the truth.

I believe in you.（我信任你。）

= I have confidence in you.

【比較2】*I believe God.*

　　【誤，因為你不可能相信上帝的話，而且上帝
　　又不可能說話。】

I believe in God.（我相信上帝。）

　　【此時 believe in 作「相信…的存在」解。】

　　下面三句話你可以常和朋友說，語氣都比 I
believe in you. 要強：

　　I totally believe in you.【語氣較強】
　　（我完全相信你。）
　　I know that I believe in you.【一般語氣】
　　（我知道我相信你。）
　　I want you to know that I believe in you.
　　（我要你知道我相信你。）【語氣最強】

4. ***Hang tough.***

hang〔hæŋ〕*v.* 懸掛
tough〔tʌf〕*adj.* 堅硬的；不屈不撓的
hang tough 堅持下去；不洩氣

　　這句話字面的意思是「堅強地吊掛在那裡，不
鬆手。」就像是一個堅強的人掛在懸崖上一樣，所
以，*Hang tough.* 引申為「堅持下去。」在文法上，
這句話中的 hang（懸掛），和 stand（站）、sit（坐）、
lie（躺），都可以接形容詞，做主詞補語。

【例】 He hangs <u>tough</u>. (他個性堅忍不拔。)
　　　　　　　　形容詞

He stands <u>tall</u>. (他抬頭挺胸。)
　　　　　　形容詞

She sat <u>silent</u> in her room.
　　　　　形容詞

(她在房間裡靜靜地坐著不說話。)

She lay <u>quiet</u>. (她靜靜地躺在那裡。)
　　　　　形容詞

> ***Hang tough***. (堅持下去。)
> = Stay tough.
> = Stay strong.

> = Persist.
> = Persevere.
> = Be persistent.

persist〔pə'zɪst, pə'sɪst〕v. 堅持
persevere〔͵pɜsə'vɪr〕v. 堅忍
persistent〔pə'sɪstənt〕adj. 堅持的

> = Hang in there.
> = Don't quit.
> = Don't give up.

【quit〔kwɪt〕v. 停止　　***give up*** 放棄】

下面三句話美國人也常說：

You got to ***hang tough***. (你必須堅持下去。)

Hang tough to succeed.

(為了成功，要堅持下去。)

Hang tough, and you'll make it.

(堅持下去，你就會成功。)

【***make it*** 成功；辦到】

BOOK 6

5. *Hang in there*.

hang〔hæŋ〕*v.* 懸掛；吊著

這句話可能源自拳擊賽，選手要堅持待在拳擊
台裡面。美國人待在哪裡，喜歡用 hang，所以，
Hang in there. 原指要待在拳擊台裡面，引申為
「要堅持下去；不要洩氣。」

> ***Hang in there***.（堅持下去。）
> = Stick with it.（堅持下去。）
> = Stick to it.（堅持下去。）

> = Don't quit.（不要放棄。）
> = Don't give up.（不要放棄。）
> = Don't give in.（不要屈服。）
> = Don't stop.（不要停止。）

【quit〔kwɪt〕*v.* 放棄　***stick with*** 堅持（= *stick to*）】

下面是美國人常說的話：

> ***Hang in***.（堅持下去。）【第一常用】
> ***Hang in there***.（堅持下去。）【第二常用】
> Just ***hang in***.（只要堅持下去。）【第三常用】
>
> I hope you ***hang in***.【第四常用】
> （我希望你堅持下去。）
> I hope you can ***hang in***.【第五常用】
> （我希望你能堅持下去。）
> I hope you can ***hang in there***.【第六常用】
> （我希望你能堅持下去。）

You have to *hang in there*.【第九常用】

（你必須堅持下去。）

You must *hang in there*.【第十常用】

（你必須堅持下去。）

You should *hang in there*.【第十一常用】

（你應該堅持下去。）

I know you can *hang in there*.【第十三常用】

（我知道你能堅持下去。）

I expect you to *hang in there*.【第十四常用】

（我希望你能堅持下去。）【expect〔ɪk'spɛkt〕v. 希望】

I advise you to *hang in there*.【第十五常用】

（我勸你堅持下去。）【advise〔əd'vaɪz〕v. 勸告】

Hang in there, OK?【第七常用】

（堅持下去，好嗎？）

Hang in there for me.【第八常用】

（為我堅持下去。）

I'm counting on you to *hang in there*.【第十二常用】

（我要靠你堅持下去。）【*count on* 依靠】

6. ***Just keep trying***.

just〔dʒʌst〕*adv.* 只要（= *simply*）
keep + V-ing 表「繼續～」。
try〔traɪ〕*v.* 嘗試；努力

　　這句話的意思是「只要繼續努力。」***Just keep
trying***. 也可以說成：Just keep going.（只要繼續
進行。）或 Just keep at it.（只要繼續做。）【見「教
師一口氣英語」p.4-12】美國人喜歡在動詞前面用 just，
表示「你所要做的只是…」，這句話等於 All you
have to do is keep trying.

【比較】***Just keep trying***.（只要繼續努力。）
　　　　Just keep on trying.
　　　　（只要繼續努力，不要停。）

　　雖然 keep + V-ing 表示「繼續」，keep
on + V-ing 表示「(有間斷地)繼續」，在這裡，
兩句話意思很接近。

7. ***Go all the way***.

all the way 自始至終；完全地；一直；無保留地

　　這句話的意思是「要走完全程；要做完。」等
於 Do it from start to finish. 也可以說成：Go
the whole way. 說這句話要小心，***Go all the
way***. 還有一個意思是「有性關係」（= *have sexual
relations*）。例：If you go all the way, you stand
a chance of getting pregnant.（如果你有性關係，
你就有機會懷孕。）

下面是美國人常說的話，都表示「要走完全程。」
或「要做完。」

Go all the way.（要走完全程；要做完。）

Go the whole way.（要走完全程；要做完。）

Go the whole distance.（要走完全程；要做完。）

【whole〔hol〕*adj.* 全部的　distance〔'dɪstəns〕*n.* 距離】

Go till the end.（要走到最後；要做完。）

Go until it's over.（要走到結束為止；要做完。）

Go until you can't go any more.

（要走到無法再走為止；要做完。）

【end〔ɛnd〕*n.* 結束；最後　***not…any more*** 不再…】

8. ***Go for the gold.***

gold〔gold〕*n.* 黃金　　***go for*** 去拿；爭取（= *try for*）

這句話美國人常說，尤其是運動員，但所有的
中外字典都查不到。字面的意思是「去拿金子。」或
「去拿金牌。」此時 gold 是指 gold medal（金牌）。
所以，***Go for the gold.*** 的引申意思是「爭取第一。」

Go for the gold.（爭取第一。）

= Try to be the best.

= Try to be number one.

【比較 1】 Go for it.（試一試，不要怕。）

Go for the gold.（爭取第一。）

【比較 2】 Go for broke.（全力以赴；孤注一擲。）

【詳見「劉毅演講式英語①」p.1~24】

Go for the gold.（爭取第一。）

BOOK 6

9. *Go as far as you can.*

　go far　走遠；成功

　　這句話字面的意思是「能走多遠，你就走多遠。」
引申爲「儘量發揮你的潛力。」

　　下面都是美國人常説的話，我們按照使用頻率
排列：

　① Go far. (要成功。)【第一常用】
　② *Go as far as you can.*【第二常用】
　　（儘量發揮你的潛力。）
　③ Go as far as you can go.
　　（儘量發揮你的潛力。）

　④ Go as far as possible.
　　（儘量發揮你的潛力。）
　⑤ Go as far as you possibly can.
　　（儘量發揮你的潛力。）
　⑥ Go as far as you can possibly go.
　　（儘量發揮你的潛力。）

【對話練習】

1. A：**You can do it**.

   B：I hope I can.
   　　I really want to do it.
   　　I'll keep trying till I
   　　do it.

2. A：**You have what it takes**.

   B：I hope I do.
   　　I'm willing to try.
   　　I'm willing to work very hard.
   　　【willing〔'wɪlɪŋ〕*adj.* 願意的】

3. A：**I believe in you**.

   B：Thank you for your support.
   　　You are a loyal friend.
   　　You help me out a lot.
   　　【loyal〔'lɔɪəl〕*adj.* 忠實的
   　　help sb. out 幫助某人脫離困境】

4. A：**Hang tough**.

   B：I'll try.
   　　I'll hang in there.
   　　I promise not to quit.

A：你可以做到。

B：我希望我可以。
　　我眞的想要做。
　　我會繼續努力，直到我
　　能做到爲止。

A：你有能力。

B：我希望我有。
　　我願意嘗試。
　　我願意非常努力地工作。

A：我相信你。

B：謝謝你的支持。
　　你是個忠實的朋友。
　　你幫了我很多。

A：堅持下去。

B：我會努力。
　　我會堅持下去。
　　我保證不會放棄。

BOOK 6

5. A：**Hang in there**.
　 B：You, too.
　　 Don't quit.
　　 Stick it out.
　　【*stick it out* 堅持到底】

6. A：**Just keep trying**.
　 B：I will.
　　 I always do.
　　 I don't give up easily.

7. A：**Go all the way**.
　 B：I plan to.
　　 I'll keep going till the
　　 end.
　　 I'll go all the way.

8. A：**Go for the gold**.
　 B：I will.
　　 That's what I want.
　　 I'm giving 100 percent.
　　【*give 100 percent* 盡全力】

9. A：**Go as far as you can**.
　 B：You know that I will.
　　 I'm going for broke on this one.
　　 Nothing can stop me now.
　　【*go for broke* 全力以赴】

A：要堅持下去。
B：你也是。
　 不要放棄。
　 要堅持到底。

A：只要繼續努力。
B：我會的。
　 我一直不斷在努力。
　 我不會輕易放棄。

A：要走完全程；要做完。
B：我打算這麼做。
　 我會持續走到最後；
　 我會做完。
　 我會走完；我會做完。

A：爭取第一。
B：我會的。
　 那正是我想要的。
　 我會盡全力。

A：儘量發揮你的潛力。
B：你知道我會的。
　 這一次我會全力以赴。
　 現在沒有什麼可以
　 阻止我。

11. Wow! What a view!

Wow!	哇啊！
What a view!	這景色眞棒！
It's really awesome!	眞棒！
I'm inspired.	我受到了鼓舞。
I'm glad I'm here.	我很高興能來到這裡。
I'll remember this forever.	我會永遠記得。
What an amazing sight!	多麼令人嘆爲觀止的景觀！
What a special moment!	多麼特別的時刻！
It's like a dream come true.	它就像是夢想成眞。

**

wow〔waʊ〕*interj.* 哇啊   view〔vju〕*n.* 景色
awesome〔'ɔsəm〕*adj.* 可怕的；令人敬畏的；很棒的
inspire〔ɪn'spaɪr〕*v.* 激勵；鼓舞；使感動；給予靈感
glad〔glæd〕*adj.* 高興的   forever〔fə'ɛvə〕*adv.* 永遠
amazing〔ə'mezɪŋ〕*adj.* 驚人的   sight〔saɪt〕*n.* 景觀
moment〔'momənt〕*n.* 片刻；時刻
a dream come true 夢想成眞

BOOK 6

【背景説明】

當你看到一個很好的景色，你就可以説這九句話，表示自己很高興。

1. **Wow! What a view!**
   wow〔waʊ〕*interj.* 哦；啊；哇啊【表驚訝、喜悦、痛苦等】
   view〔vju〕*n.* 景色

   美國人凡是看到好的東西，通常會説 "**Wow!**"（哇啊！）

   What a view! 的意思是「這景色眞棒！」在文法上，「What＋a＋名詞＋主詞＋動詞」，形成感嘆句，但是在這裡，美國人少説 What a view it is!（誤）it is 必須省略，其他地方有時可保留，但都少用。

   下面各句都包含美國人常説的感嘆詞：

   > **Wow!** What a view!【第一常用】
   > （哇啊！這景色眞棒！）
   > **God!** What a view!【第三常用】
   > （天啊！這景色眞棒！）
   > **My God!** What a view!【第六常用】
   > （我的天啊！這景色眞棒！）

Boy! What a view!【第二常用】

（哇！這景色真棒！）

Oh, boy! What a view!【第八常用】

（噢，哇！這景色真棒！）

Man! What a view!【第五常用】

（啊！這景色真棒！）

【boy〔bɔɪ〕*interj.* 咦；哇

man〔mæn〕*interj.* 哦；啊】

Oh, man! What a view!【第九常用】

（噢，哇！這景色真棒！）

Oh! What a view!【第四常用】

（噢！這景色真棒！）

Ooh! What a view!【第十常用】

（喔！這景色真棒！）

【ooh〔u〕*interj.* 喔】

Aah! What a view!【第十一常用】

（啊！這景色真棒！）

Cool! What a view!【第十二常用】

（太酷了！這景色真棒！）

My goodness! What a view!【第七常用】

（天啊！這景色真棒！）

aah〔ɑ〕*interj.* 哦；啊（= *ah*〔ɑ〕）

cool〔kul〕*adj.* 酷的；了不起的

goodness〔'ɡʊdnɪs〕*interj.* 天啊（= *God*）

BOOK 6

下面是美國人常說的話：

> ***What a view!*** （這景色眞棒！）【第一常用】
> ***Wow! What a view!*** 【第二常用】
> （哇啊！這景色眞棒！）
> What a really nice view! 【第三常用】
> （這景色眞好！）

What a nice view this is! 【第七常用】
（這景色眞好！）
What a nice view from here! 【第八常用】
（從這裡看出去的景色眞好！）
This is a really great view. 【第六常用】
（這景色眞棒。）

This view is great! （這景色眞棒！）【第五常用】
This view is amazing! 【第四常用】
（這景色眞是令人嘆爲觀止！）
What a spectacular sight! 【第九常用】
（這景色眞是壯觀！）
This view is out of this world. 【第十常用】
（這景色眞是太棒了！）

amazing〔əˋmezɪŋ〕*adj.* 驚人的
spectacular〔spɛkˋtækjələ〕*adj.* 壯觀的
out of this world 極好的

看到好的景色，有很多種說法：

What a view! (這景色真棒！)【第一常用】
What a beautiful view! (這景色真漂亮！)【第三常用】
What a wonderful view! (這景色真棒！)【第二常用】

What a fantastic view! (這景色真棒！)【第六常用】
What a terrific view! (這景色真棒！)【第八常用】
What a remarkable view! (這景色真棒！)【第十常用】

    fantastic〔fæn'tæstɪk〕*adj.* 很棒的
    terrific〔tə'rɪfɪk〕*adj.* 很棒的
    remarkable〔rɪ'mɑrkəbḷ〕*adj.* 了不起的；傑出的

What a tremendous view! (這景色真棒！)【第十常用】
What a breathtaking view!【第七常用】
(這景色真是壯麗！)
What a magnificent view!【第九常用】
(這景色真是壯麗！)

    tremendous〔trɪ'mɛndəs〕*adj.* 極好的
    breathtaking〔'brɛθ,tekɪŋ〕*adj.* 令人興奮的；壯麗的
    magnificent〔mæg'nɪfəsṇt〕*adj.* 壯麗的

What an awesome view! (這景色真棒！)【第五常用】
What an incredible view!【第四常用】
(這景色真是美得令人無法相信！)
What an unforgettable view!【第十常用】
(這景色真是令人難忘！)

    awesome〔'ɔsəm〕*adj.* 很棒的
    incredible〔ɪn'krɛdəbḷ〕*adj.* 令人無法相信的
    unforgettable〔ʌnfɚ'gɛtəbḷ〕*adj.* 令人難忘的

【比較】 ***What a view!***
What a scenery! (誤)

我們中國人說「風景眞美。」英文是 The scenery is beautiful. 但是不能説 *What a scenery!* (誤) 因爲 scenery 不可數。可以説：What a view! 或 What a sight! 或 What a scene!

sight〔saɪt〕*n.* 景觀；風景　　scene〔sin〕*n.* 風景
scene 是「一場；一幕」，表示「特定的景色」；scenery 是指「全部景色」，在這裡，y 是集合名詞字尾，像 army（陸軍）、family（家庭）等。

2. *It's really awesome!*

awesome〔ˈɔsəm〕*adj.* 可怕的；令人敬畏的；很棒的
【一般字典上都沒有作「很棒的」解，但美國人常用】

這句話的意思是「眞棒！」

Awesome! 也可以單獨使用，相當於 Great! 或 Excellent! 意思是「棒極了！」或「好極了！」。

美國人常説 awesome：

It's *awesome!*（眞棒！）【第一常用】
It's so *awesome!*（眞棒！）【第五常用】
It's just *awesome!*（眞棒！）【第六常用】

It's really awesome!（眞棒！）【第二常用】
It's totally *awesome!*（眞棒！）【第三常用】
　　　　〔ˈtotl̩ɪ〕*adv.* 完全地
It's an *awesome* view!【第八常用】
（這景色眞棒！）

This is *awesome!*（眞棒！）【第四常用】

This view is *awesome!*【第七常用】

（這景色眞棒！）

This view is really *awesome!*【第九常用】

（這景色眞棒！）

3. *I'm inspired.*

inspire〔ɪnˋspaɪr〕*v.* 激勵；鼓舞；使感動；給予靈感

這句話的意思是「我受到了鼓舞。」inspire 是情感動詞，和 interest（使有興趣）、surprise（使驚訝）一樣，人做主詞要用「被動」，非人做主詞要用「主動」或是現在分詞。(詳見「文法寶典」p.390)

下面三句話可以説明情感動詞的用法：

It inspires me.（它鼓舞了我。）【正，較少用】

= *I'm inspired.*（我受到了鼓舞。）【正，常用】

= It's inspiring.（它眞是令人振奮。）【正，常用】

中國人看到了美好的風景，不會説「我受到鼓舞」或是「它給我靈感」之類的話，但是美國人常説，這是中外文化的不同，這句話在這裡的意思，相當於中國人所説的「我有精神了。」

BOOK 6

下面都是美國人常說的話：

It inspires me.【第一常用】

（我受到了鼓舞；我有精神了。）

I'm so inspired.【第九常用】

（我受到了很大的鼓舞；我很有精神了。）

I feel so inspired.【第三常用】

（我覺得十分振奮；我覺得很有精神了。）

It's inspiring.【第四常用】

（這真是令人振奮。）

It's an inspiration.【第五常用】

（這真是令人振奮。）

It's very inspirational.【第六常用】

（這非常令人振奮。）

inspiration〔͵ɪnspəˈreʃən〕*n.* 鼓舞；激勵；靈感
inspirational〔͵ɪnspəˈreʃənḷ〕*adj.* 鼓舞的；給予靈感的

This is very inspiring.【第七常用】

（這非常令人振奮。）

This is so inspiring.【第八常用】

（這非常令人振奮。）

This is inspiring.【第二常用】

（這真是令人振奮。）

I'm inspired. 有三個主要意思：①我受到了鼓舞。②我很感動。(= *I'm moved*.) ③我有靈感了。

4. *I'm glad I'm here*.

glad〔glæd〕*adj.* 高興的

這句話的字面意思是「我很高興在這裡。」就像我們中文所說的「來到這裡真好。」也有美國人加強語氣說成：I'm so glad I'm here. 意思是「我很高興能來到這裡。」下面都是美國人常說的話：

I'm glad I'm here.【第一常用】
（我很高興能來到這裡。）

I'm glad I'm here today.【第三常用】
（我很高興今天能來到這裡。）

I'm glad I'm here with you.【第十一常用】
（我很高興能和你一起在這裡。）

I'm glad I'm here to see this.【第十二常用】
（我很高興能來這裡看到這個。）

I'm lucky I'm here.【第四常用】
（我很幸運能來這裡。）

I thank God I'm here.【第九常用】
（感謝上帝，我能來這裡。）

I'm happy I'm here.【第二常用】
（我很高興能來這裡。）

I'm delighted I'm here.【第五常用】
（我很高興能來這裡。）

I'm thrilled I'm here.【第六常用】
（能來這裡我覺得很興奮。）

　delighted〔dɪˈlaɪtɪd〕*adj.* 高興的
　thrilled〔θrɪld〕*adj.* 激動的；興奮的

BOOK 6

I'm grateful I'm here. 【第七常用】
(我很感激能來這裡。)

I'm thankful I'm here. 【第八常用】
(我很感激能來這裡。)

I'm pleased I'm here. 【第十常用】
(我很高興能來這裡。)

grateful ('gretfəl) *adj.* 感激的
thankful ('θæŋkfəl) *adj.* 感激的
pleased (plizd) *adj.* 高興的

【比較】 下面兩句話意思相同，使用頻率也相同：

I'm glad *I'm here*. 【常用】
I'm glad *to be here*. 【常用】

下面也是美國人常說的話，我們按照使用頻率排列：

① I'm glad to be here. 【第一常用】
(我很高興能來到這裡。)

② I'm happy to be here. 【第二常用】
(我很高興能來到這裡。)

③ I'm thrilled to be here. 【第三常用】
(能來到這裡，我很興奮。)

④ I'm delighted to be here.
(我很高興能來到這裡。)

⑤ I'm pleased to be here.
(我很高興能來這裡。)

⑥ I'm fortunate to be here.
(我很幸運能來這裡。)

【fortunate ('fɔrtʃənɪt) *adj.* 幸運的 】

5. ***I'll remember this forever.***

remember〔rɪ'mɛmbɚ〕*v.* 記得

forever〔fɚ'ɛvɚ〕*adv.* 永遠

這句話的意思是「我將永遠記得。」句中的
forever 也可寫成 for ever，但是這是英式用法，
美國人較少使用。

下面是美國人常說的話：

I'll remember this forever.【第一常用】
（我將永遠記得。）

I'll remember this for as long as I live.
（我將一輩子記得。）【第十常用】

I'll remember this till the day I die.
（我到死之前都會記得。）【第十一常用】

I'll always remember this.【第三常用】
（我會永遠記得。）

I'll remember this for sure.【第五常用】
（我一定會記得。）

I'm sure I'll remember this.【第六常用】
（我確信我一定會記得。）

【*for sure* 必定】

I won't forget this.（我不會忘記。）【第四常用】

I'll never forget this.【第二常用】
（我永遠都不會忘記。）

I could never forget this.【第八常用】
（我永遠都不會忘記。）

This is unforgettable.【第七常用】

（這是令人難忘的。）

This will always be on my mind.【第九常用】

（這將永遠在我心裡。）

It will be impossible for me to forget this.

（我不可能會忘記。）【第十二常用】

【*on one's mind* 惦記；記在心上】

6. *What an amazing sight!*

amazing〔ə'mezɪŋ〕*adj.* 驚人的

sight〔saɪt〕*n.* 景象；景觀；景色

一般說來，sight 是指可看到的景象（ = *a view of something seen*）。如果你站在旅館裡，向外看到遠處美麗的風景，像高山等，你可以說：*What an amazing view!*（多麼令人嘆爲觀止的風景！）

如果你站在旅館窗口，看到的是一個高樓大廈，你可以說：*What an amazing sight!*（多麼令人嘆爲觀止的景觀！）

看到任何特別的東西，像萬里長城（Great Wall）、大峽谷（Grand Canyon）之類的東西，都可說：*What an amazing sight!*。

7. ***What a special moment!***

moment〔ˈmomənt〕*n.* 片刻;時刻

這句話的意思是「多麼特別的時刻!」也可以
說成:This is a special moment. (這是一個特
別的時刻。) 或 I feel this is a very special
moment. (我覺得這是一個非常特別的時刻。)

8. *It's like a dream come true.*

這句話的意思是「它就像夢想成眞。」*a dream
come true* 是一個成語,是固定用法,是一個名詞
片語,意思是「夢想成眞」(= *a dream that has
come true*)。這句話也有美國人說成:It's just
like a dream come true. (就像夢想成眞。) 或
It feels like a dream come true. (它使人覺得像
是夢想成眞。)

美國人常說 *a dream come true* :

【例】 When I was admitted to the university,
it was *a dream come true*.
(當我獲得那所大學的入學許可時,眞是夢
想成眞。)

If I can go to Paris, it will be *a dream
come true*.
(如果我能到巴黎去,就是夢想成眞。)

BOOK 6

【對話練習】

1. A：**Wow!**

   B：Are you OK?
     What's the matter?
     What's going on?

A：哇啊！

B：你還好嗎？
   怎麼了？
   發生什麼事了？

2. A：**What a view!**

   B：I totally agree.
     This view is remarkable.
     It's out of this world.

A：這景色真棒！

B：我完全同意。
   這景色真棒。
   這景色非常的棒。

3. A：**It's really awesome!**

   B：It's more than that.
     It's one of a kind.
     It's special in every way.
     【*one of a kind* 獨一無二的
     way〔we〕*n.* 方面】

A：真棒！

B：不只是那樣。
   它是獨一無二的。
   它在每一方面都很特別。

4. A：**I'm inspired.**

   B：I'm glad to hear that.
     That's why we're here.
     I'm inspired, too.

A：我受到了鼓舞。

B：我很高興聽到這件事。
   這就是為什麼我們會在這裡。
   我也受到鼓舞了。

5. A：**I'm so glad I'm here.**

   B：Me, too.

      We are blessed.

      This is a wonderful experience.

      【blessed〔'blɛsɪd〕*adj.* 幸福的】

A：我很高興能來到這裡。

B：我也是。

   我們真幸福。

   這是個很棒的經驗。

6. A：**I'll remember this forever.**

   B：I'm with you.

      I'll never forget this.

      This will stay with me forever.

A：我會永遠記得。

B：我同意。

   我絕不會忘記的。

   我永遠會記得這件事。

7. A：**What an amazing sight!**

   B：It sure is.

      It's so beautiful.

      I want to take some pictures.

      【*take a picture* 拍照】

A：多麼令人嘆爲觀止的景觀！

B：它的確是。

   它真是優美。

   我想要照一些相片。

8. A：**What a special moment!**

   B：It really is.

      I'm truly grateful.

      I'm thankful I can experience this.

      【experience〔ɪk'spɪrɪəns〕*v.* 經歷】

A：多麼特別的時刻！

B：它的確是。

   我真的很感激。

   我很感激能有這樣的經驗。

9. A：**It's like a dream come true.**

   B：I can't believe my eyes.

      Pinch me so I know it's real.

      We have truly found paradise! 【pinch〔pɪntʃ〕*v.* 捏】

A：它就像是夢想成真。

B：我無法相信我的眼睛。

   捏我一下，讓我知道這是真的。

   我們真的找到樂園了！

BOOK 6

12. Good night.

Good night.	晚安。
Sleep well.	好好睡。
Sweet dreams.	祝你有甜美的夢。
Get some rest.	好好休息休息。
Have a good sleep.	睡個好覺。
Have a peaceful night.	希望你晚上睡得好。
See you in the morning.	明天早上見。
See you bright and early.	明天一大早見。
Tomorrow is a big day.	明天很重要。

** ────────────────────────

sweet〔swit〕*adj.* 甜蜜的；甜美的
dream〔drim〕*n.* 夢
rest〔rɛst〕*n.* 休息；睡眠　　sleep〔slip〕*n.* 睡；睡眠
peaceful〔'pisfəl〕*adj.* 寧靜的；平靜的
bright〔braɪt〕*adj.* 明亮的；發亮的；陽光燦爛的
bright and early 一大早（= *very early*）
big〔bɪg〕*adj.* 大的；重要的

【背景説明】

一般人晚上和朋友再見，只會説 Good night.
背了這九句以後，你就變成一個熱情的人了，你每
天晚上和朋友告別的時候，就有很多話説了。

1. ***Good night***.

美國人晚上再見時，習慣説：***Good night***.
這句話是由 Have a good night. 演變而來。我
們中國人説「晚安。」美國人説「有一個好的晚
上。」意思很接近。

下面都是美國人常説的話：

Good night. (晚安。)【第一常用】
Have a good night. (晚安。)【第二常用】
I hope you have a good night. 【第四常用】
(我希望你有一個美好的夜晚。)

Have a good evening. (晚安。)【第三常用】
Have a peaceful evening. (晚安。)【第五常用】
Have a restful evening. (晚安。)【第六常用】
peaceful〔ˈpisfəl〕*adj.* 平靜的；寧靜的
restful〔ˈrɛstfəl〕*adj.* 寧靜的

一般會話試題中，晚上見面的時候，説 Good
evening. 再見的時候説 Good night. 事實上，在
高級場合，也有美國人説 Good evening. 或 Have
a good evening. 作爲再見用語，在 NTC's
Dictionary 中，也有説明。

BOOK 6

2. *Sleep well.*

這句話的意思是「好好睡。」源自 I hope
you sleep well. (我希望你好好睡。)

下面是美國人常說的話，我們按照使用頻率排列：

① *Sleep well.* (好好睡。)【第一常用】
② Sleep tight. (睡個好覺。)【第二常用】
③ Sleep peacefully. (睡個好覺。)

tight〔taɪt〕*adv.* 充份地；好好地
peacefully〔'pisfəlɪ〕*adv.* 安穩地

④ I hope you sleep well tonight.
(我希望你今晚睡個好覺。)
⑤ I hope you sleep deeply tonight.
(我希望你今晚睡得很熟。)
⑥ I hope you sleep soundly tonight.
(我希望你今晚睡得很熟。)

deeply〔'diplɪ〕*adv.* 深深地；深沈地
soundly〔'saʊndlɪ〕*adv.* 熟睡地

美國父母喜歡和小孩說：

Sleep well. (睡個好覺。)
Sleep tight. (好好睡。)
Don't let the bedbugs bite.
(睡覺不要被打擾。)

bedbug〔'bɛd,bʌg〕*n.* 臭蟲，這句話的字面
意思是「不要讓臭蟲咬。」，不可說成：*Don't
let the bedbugs bite you.* (誤)

3. *Sweet dreams.*

sweet〔swit〕*adj.* 甜蜜的；甜美的

dream〔drim〕*n.* 夢　*v.* 做（夢）

　　　這句話的意思是「祝你有甜美的夢。」源自：

　　　　I <u>wish</u> <u>you</u> <u>sweet dreams</u>.
　　　　　授與動詞　間接受詞　　直接受詞

　　　　（我祝你有甜美的夢。）

　　或 I hope you have sweet dreams.

　　　　（我希望你有甜美的夢。）

　類似 Sweet dreams. 的說法有：

　　　　Pleasant dreams.（祝你好夢連連。）

　　　　Dream sweet dreams.

　　　　（祝你多做幾個好夢。）

　　　　Dream pleasant dreams.

　　　　（祝你多做幾個好夢。）

　　　　【pleasant〔'plɛznt〕*adj.* 令人愉快的】

【比較 1】 *Sweet dreams.*【正，一般語氣】

　　　　　Have sweet dreams.【正，語氣較強】

　　　　　I hope you have sweet dreams.【正，語氣最強】

【比較 2】 道晚安時，祝福別人好夢連連時，通常
　　　　　用複數的 dreams。

　　　　　Sweet dreams.【正】

　　　　　A sweet dream.【誤】

　　　　　Have a sweet dream.【正，較少用】

BOOK 6

下面是美國人常說的話，我們按照使用頻率
排列：

① ***Sweet dreams.*** 【第一常用】
（祝你有甜美的夢。）

② Pleasant dreams. 【第二常用】
（祝你好夢連連。）

③ Sweet dreams tonight. 【第三常用】
（祝你今晚有甜美的夢。）

④ Pleasant dreams tonight.
（祝你今晚好夢連連。）

⑤ I hope you have sweet dreams.
（我希望你有甜美的夢。）

⑥ I hope you have pleasant dreams.
（我希望你好夢連連。）

⑦ I wish you sweet dreams.
（我祝你有甜美的夢。）

⑧ I wish you pleasant dreams.
（我祝你好夢連連。）

⑨ I hope all your dreams are happy.
（我希望你所有的夢都愉快。）

⑩ I hope all your dreams are good ones.
（我希望你所有的夢都是好夢。）

BOOK 6

4. *Get some rest.*

rest〔rɛst〕*n.* 休息；睡眠

這句話的意思是「好好休息休息。」

【比較1】　*Get some rest.*【正】

　　　　　Get a rest.【誤】

【比較2】　下面兩句話意思不同：

　　　　　Get some rest.（好好休息休息。）

　　　　　Take a rest.（休息一會兒。）

Get some rest. 是指較長的休息，如回家睡覺、回家休息等。而 Take a rest. 是指短時間的休息，等於 Have a rest.（休息一下。）

5. *Have a good sleep.*

sleep〔slip〕*n.* 睡；睡眠

這句話的意思是「睡個好覺。」也有人說：

Get a good sleep.

下面都是美國人常說的話，我們按照使用頻率排列：

① *Have a good sleep.*（睡個好覺。）【第一常用】

② Get a good night's sleep.【第二常用】

　　（晚上睡個好覺。）

③ I hope you get a good night's sleep.

　　（我希望你晚上睡個好覺。）

BOOK 6

④ Have a good sleep tonight.

（祝你今晚睡得好。）

⑤ Have a good night's sleep.

（祝你晚上睡個好覺。）

⑥ Get a good sleep tonight.

（祝你今晚睡個好覺。）

⑦ You need a good night's sleep.

（你晚上需要睡個好覺。）

⑧ You need to get a good night's sleep.

（你晚上需要睡個好覺。）

⑨ You should get a good night's sleep.

（你應該晚上睡個好覺。）

6. *Have a peaceful night*.

peaceful（'pisfəl）*adj.* 寧靜的；平靜的

這句話字面的意思是「希望你有個寧靜的夜晚。」引申為「希望你晚上睡得好。」用 peaceful 這個字，暗示你晚上睡得好，沒有人打擾。

下面是美國人常說的話：

Have a peaceful night.【第一常用】

（希望你有個寧靜的夜晚；希望你晚上睡得好。）

Have a peaceful sleep.【第二常用】

（希望你睡得好。）

I hope you have a peaceful night.【第四常用】

（我希望你有個寧靜的夜晚。）

Have a peaceful evening.【第三常用】

（希望你有個寧靜的夜晚。）

Have a peaceful night and sleep well.

（希望你晚上睡得好。）【第五常用】

【and sleep well 也可說成 ,sleep well，句中的
and 可用逗點來代替。】

Have a peaceful night and good sleep.

（希望你晚上睡得好。）【第六常用】

7. *See you in the morning.*

這句話的字面意思是「早上見到你。」引申爲
「明天早上見。」

下面都是美國人常說的話，都表示「明天早
上見。」

See you in the morning.【第一常用】

See you tomorrow morning.【第二常用】

Catch you in the morning.【第四常用】

【catch〔kætʃ〕v. 抓住　這句話字面的意思是「明天早
上抓你。」引申爲「明天早上見。」是幽默的說法。】

Catch you tomorrow morning.【第五常用】

I'll catch you in the morning.【第六常用】

I'll see you in the morning.【第三常用】

I'll meet you in the morning.【第七常用】

I'll see you for sure in the morning.【第九常用】

I'll contact you in the morning.【第八常用】

【*for sure* 必定　contact〔kən'tækt,'kɑntækt〕v. 與⋯接觸】

BOOK 6

8. *See you bright and early.*

bright〔braɪt〕*adj.* 明亮的；發亮的；陽光燦爛的
bright and early 一大早（= *very early*）

> 這句話的意思是「明天一大早見。」*bright and early* 字面的意思是「又亮又早」，可能是指像在太陽剛出來時那麼早，所以引申為「一大早」。*bright and early* 不可說成 *early and bright*（誤）。
>
> 下面是美國人常說的話：
>
> **See you bright and early.**【第一常用】
> = Catch you bright and early.【第三常用】
> = I'll see you bright and early.【第二常用】
>
> = I'll catch you bright and early.【第四常用】
> = I'll see you early tomorrow.【第五常用】
> = I'll see you early tomorrow morning.【第六常用】

9. *Tomorrow is a big day.*

big〔bɪg〕*adj.* 大的；重要的

> 這句話的字面意思是「明天是個大日子。」引申為「明天很重要。」或「明天會很忙。」依上下文而定。由於「明天」一定會來到，是不變的事實，所以可用現在式代替未來式。（詳見「文法寶典」p.326）當然也可以說成：Tomorrow will be a big day.

下面都是美國人常說的話，經過調查，使用頻
率大致相同：

> ***Tomorrow is a big day.*** （明天很重要。）
> Tomorrow is a new day.
> （明天又是新的一天。）
> Tomorrow is another day.
> （明天又是另一天。）
>
> Tomorrow is a brand-new day.
> （明天是全新的一天。）
> Tomorrow is a busy day.
> （明天是忙碌的日子。）
> Tomorrow is an important day.
> （明天是重要的日子。）
> 【brand-new〔'brænd'nju〕*adj.* 全新的】

下面三句話意思相同：

> ***Tomorrow is a big day.*** 【最常用】
> Tomorrow is going to be a big day. 【較常用】
> Tomorrow will be a big day. 【常用】
> 【going to 唸成 gonna〔'gɔnə〕】

【對話練習】

1. A：**Good night.**
   B：You, too.
   　　You have a good night.
   　　I hope you sleep well.

2. A：**Sleep well.**
   B：I will, thanks.
   　　I'm exhausted.
   　　I'll sleep like a baby.
   　　【exhausted〔ɪgˈzɔstɪd〕*adj.* 筋疲
   　　力盡的】

3. A：**Sweet dreams.**
   B：The same to you.
   　　I wish you sweet dreams.
   　　Have a wonderful sleep.

4. A：**Get some rest.**
   B：Thank you, I will.
   　　I'm dead tired.
   　　I'll be asleep very soon.
   　　【dead〔dɛd〕*adv.* 非常地
   　　asleep〔əˈslip〕*adj.* 睡著的】

A：晚安。
B：你也是。
　　晚安。
　　我希望你睡個好覺。

A：好好睡。
B：我會的，謝謝。
　　我累壞了。
　　我會睡得像嬰兒一樣。

A：祝你有甜美的夢。
B：你也是。
　　我希望你也有甜美的夢。
　　祝你睡個好覺。

A：好好休息休息。
B：謝謝你，我會的。
　　我真的很累。
　　我會很快就睡著。

5. A：**Have a good sleep.**　　　　　A：睡個好覺。
　 B：You sleep well, too.　　　　　B：你也睡個好覺。
　　　Have a great night.　　　　　　晚安。
　　　I'll see you in the morning.　　明天早上見。

6. A：**Have a peaceful night.**　　　A：希望你晚上睡得好。
　 B：Thanks.　　　　　　　　　　　B：謝謝。
　　　You too.　　　　　　　　　　　你也一樣。
　　　I'll see you in the morning.　　明天早上見。

7. A：**Tomorrow is a big day.**　　　A：明天很重要。
　 B：You are right.　　　　　　　　B：你說得對。
　　　Tomorrow is very important.　　明天非常重要。
　　　Tomorrow is a busy day.　　　　明天會很忙。

8. A：**See you in the morning.**　　A：明天早上見。
　 B：I hope so.　　　　　　　　　　B：我也希望。
　　　I'll be looking for you.　　　　我會去找你。
　　　Let's get together for sure.　　我們一定要碰到面。
　　　【*get together* 聚在一起
　　　　for sure 必定】

9. A：**See you bright and early.**　A：明天一大早見。
　 B：Yeah, I'll see you.　　　　　　B：好的，明天見。
　　　The earlier, the better.　　　　越早越好。
　　　Early morning is the best time.　一大早是最好的時刻。
　　　【「the + 比較級…the + 比較級」表「愈…就愈～」。】

BOOK 6

「一口氣背會話」經 BOOK 6

唸英文要像唸經一樣，每天大聲唸，從起床到睡覺，唸得比看得快，最後不看也會唸，養成習慣後，你會全身舒爽，你試試看，奇妙無比。

1. Thank God it's Friday.
   The weekend is here.
   We made it through the week.

   I'm psyched.
   I'm very excited.
   I'm all fired up.

   Let's get away.
   Let's do something special.
   You only live once.

2. *I* agree.
   I'm with you.
   You're absolutely right.

   That's for sure.
   That's the truth.
   That's how I feel.

   I feel the same way.
   I couldn't agree more.
   You're right on the money.

3. What can we do?
   Where should we go?
   Where's a great place?

   Any ideas?
   Any suggestions?
   Anywhere is fine with me.

   Let's go to the ocean.
   Let's hit the beach.
   I haven't been there in ages.

4. *Let's* go hiking.
   Let's head for the hills.
   Let's leave the city behind.

   I can't wait to go.
   I can smell the fresh air already.
   There's nothing like Mother Nature.

   Rain or shine, we're going.
   Nothing can stop us.
   Maybe we won't come back.

5. *Let's* get ready.
   Let's make a plan.
   It's better to be prepared.

   We need supplies.
   We need some stuff.
   Let's go grocery shopping.

   Just keep it simple.
   Just stick to the basics.
   Don't buy anything fancy.

6. Please get in.
   Sit up front.
   Feel free to adjust the seat.

   Buckle up.
   Fasten your seat belt.
   We don't want a ticket!

   You can relax.
   I'm a safe driver.
   I'll get you there in one piece.

7. We need gas.
We're on empty.
We're running out of gas.

It's time to fill up.
It's now or never.
We can't get stuck here.

There's a station up ahead.
They have both full and
    self-service.
Do you want to pump the gas?

8. Hi!
Twenty bucks, please.
Make it regular.

Check the tires.
Check the engine.
I think I'm low on oil.

How does it look?
What's the total?
Thanks for your great service.

9. Hurry up!
Move faster.
Pick it up.

Keep up.
Don't slow down.
Don't fall behind.

Keep pace with me.
We can walk and talk.
I enjoy walking with you.

10. *You* can do it.
You have what it takes.
I believe in you.

Hang tough.
Hang in there.
Just keep trying.

Go all the way.
Go for the gold.
Go as far as you can.

11. Wow!
What a view!
It's really awesome!

I'm inspired.
I'm glad I'm here.
I'll remember this forever.

What an amazing sight!
What a special moment!
It's like a dream come true.

12. Good night.
*S*leep well.
*S*weet dreams.

Get some rest.
Have a good sleep.
Have a peaceful night.

See you in the morning.
See you bright and early.
Tomorrow is a big day.

本書由「一口氣英語①～⑥」合訂而成。
強調中英文一起背,改書名爲「一口氣背
會話上集①～ ⑥」。

一口氣背會話上集①～⑥

主　　　編 / 劉　毅
發　行　所 / 學習出版有限公司　　　☎ (02) 2704-5525
郵 撥 帳 號 / 05127272 學習出版社帳戶
登　記　證 / 局版台業 2179 號
印　刷　所 / 裕強彩色印刷有限公司
台 北 門 市 / 台北市許昌街 10 號 2F　☎ (02) 2331-4060
台灣總經銷 / 紅螞蟻圖書有限公司　　☎ (02) 2795-3656
本公司網址　www.learnbook.com.tw
電 子 郵 件　learnbook@learnbook.com.tw

書＋CD 一片售價:新台幣五百八十元正

2017 年 9 月 1 日新修訂

本書改編自「一口氣英語①～⑥」

因為有您，劉毅老師
心存感激，領路教育

　　「領路教育」是2009年成立的一家以英語培訓為主的教育機構，迄今已經發展成為遍佈全國的教育集團。這篇文章講述的是「領路教育」與臺灣教育專家劉毅老師的故事。作為「一口氣英語」的創始人，劉毅老師一直是「領路教育」老師敬仰的楷模。我們希望透過這篇文章，告訴所有教培業同仁，選擇這樣一位導師，選擇「一口氣英語」，會讓你終生受益。

劉毅老師與「領路教育」劉耿董事長合影

一、濟南年會，領路教育派七位老師參加培訓

　　2014年4月，劉毅老師在濟南組織了「第一屆一口氣英語師訓」，這是「一口氣英語」第一次在大陸公開亮相。「領路教育」派出7位老師趕往濟南參加，因為團隊表現優異，榮獲了最優秀團隊獎，Windy老師還獲得了師訓第一名。劉毅老師親自為大家頒發了證書，並且獎勵了Windy老師往返臺灣的機票費用。他希望更多的優秀老師，能夠更快地學到這個方法，造福更多學生。這一期對大陸老師的培訓，推動了兩岸英語教育的交流，也給大陸英語培訓，注入了全新的方式和動力。

二、效果驚人，「領路教育」開辦「一口氣英語班」

　　培訓結束後，「領路教育」很快組織並開設了「暑假一口氣英語演講班」。14天密集上課，孩子們取得的成效令人驚訝！孩子獲得了前所未有的自信！苦練的英文最美，背出的正確英文最自信。孩子們回到學校，走上講臺，脫口而出英文自我介紹時，留給整個課堂的是一片驚訝，和雷鳴般的掌聲！這也讓我們對劉毅「一口氣英語」的教學效果更加信服。

三、Windy老師成為劉毅一口氣英語培訓講師

　　自此，我們開始著手開了更多的「一口氣英語」班級，越來越多的區域出現了非常多優秀的「一口氣英語」老師。「領路教育」逐漸發明了一套「一口氣英語」班級的激勵系統，特色的操練方式和展示的配套動作。由於在「領路教育」有了成功的教學實踐，Windy老師收到劉毅老師的邀請，作為特邀講師，協助「一口氣英語」在各地的師訓工作。

四、連續三場千人講座，助推劉毅一口氣英語的全國傳播

　　2016年10月18日，在「領路人商學院週年慶典暨千人峰會」的同時，「領路教育」順利組織了劉毅「一口氣英語」在長沙的首屆師訓，劉毅老師親臨現場授課，並且接連在長沙、太原、武漢三地開展「劉毅一口氣英語千人講座」，向學生、家長展示「一口氣英語」學習效果，場場爆滿，反應熱烈！